Small-Town BRIDES

ROMANCE COLLECTION

9 Romaces Develop Under the Watchful Eyes of Neighbors

Small-Town
BRIDES
ROMANCE COLLECTION

Kelly Eileen Hake, Kathleen Y'Barbo
Janet Lee Barton, Susan Downs,
Darlene Franklin, Pamela Griffin,
Debby Mayne, Donita Kathleen Paul, Marjorie Vawter

BARBOUR BOOKS
An Imprint of Barbour Publishing, Inc.

Run of the Mill © 2002 by Susan Downs
A Second Glance © 2002 by Donita Kathleen Paul
The Caretaker © 2002 by Kelly Eileen Hake
Leap of Faith © 2003 by Pamela Griffin
A Blessing for Beau © 2013 by Darlene Franklin
American Pie © 2002 by Debby Mayne
Victorious © 2003 by Kathleen Y'Barbo
Language of Love © 2006 by Janet Lee Barton
A Shelter from the Storm © 2013 by Marjorie Vawter

Print ISBN 978-1-63409-671-3

eBook Editions:
Adobe Digital Edition (.epub) 978-1-63409-842-7
Kindle and MobiPocket Edition (.prc) 978-1-63409-843-4

All scripture quotations are taken from the King James Version of the Bible.

This book is a work of fiction. Names, characters, places, and incidents are either products of the author's imagination or used fictitiously. Any similarity to actual people, organizations, and/or events is purely coincidental.

Published by Barbour Books, an imprint of Barbour Publishing, Inc., P.O. Box 719, Uhrichsville, OH 44683, www.barbourbooks.com

Our mission is to publish and distribute inspirational products offering exceptional value and biblical encouragement to the masses.

 Member of the
Evangelical Christian
Publishers Association

Printed in Canada.

Contents

Run of the Mill

by Susan Downs

Dedication

To my daughters-in-law, Jara and Sarah.
God blessed me when He blessed my sons
with brides as wonderful as you.
No one will ever accuse either of you
of being *Run of the Mill!*

Chapter 1

Is everything all right here?" Kathleen McKenna stood on the front porch of the Steadman mansion and craned her neck to see past the young servant girl who had answered the door. "I debated all the way over whether or not I should still come. When I saw the Steadman pew empty in church today, I worried the family might have taken ill."

Before the girl could respond, the familiar voice of Kathleen's best friend, Isabel Steadman, wafted from the dark interior. "We are all fine, Kathleen. Just unexpectedly detained this morning." Isabel stepped out of the shadows and, dismissing the girl with a smile and a nod, she swung the door open wide. "Come in. Come in. When I passed through the kitchen a few moments ago, Cook said she could serve up dinner as soon as you arrived."

Kathleen glanced down at the brown spatters on her Sunday-best dress. "My boots are a muddy mess after traveling the footpath from church. Perhaps I should leave them here on the porch." She scraped her feet back and forth across the doormat in an attempt to dislodge the worst of the caked-on mud.

Isabel grabbed the carpetbag Kathleen clutched under her arm and pulled both her guest and the bag over the threshold. "Come on in and don't you worry about a little mud. I doubt the condition of your shoes could be any worse than those." Isabel nodded to the foyer's marble-tiled floor where someone had left the most enormous pair of men's work boots Kathleen had ever seen. And the filthiest.

Just past the shoes, in the middle of the usually immaculate entryway, a higgledy-piggledy tower of wooden crates, bandboxes, and trunks reached almost to the crystal chandelier.

"If he had not come bearing gifts, we women of the house might have been furious," Isabel said with a soft chuckle. "Then again, I have never seen Mother Steadman angry with anyone."

"Oh, Isabel, you have a houseguest!" Kathleen took a step back. "I mustn't intrude. I will take my dinner at the boardinghouse with the other mill girls today."

"Nonsense." While she spoke, Isabel removed Kathleen's shawl from her shoulders and draped it over a peg on the coat tree, then she set the carpetbag on the floor. "I look forward all week to seeing you on Sunday, and your place is already set at the table. Who else would fill me in on all the mill news? Surely you don't expect Carter to provide an accurate report. He might own the place, but he doesn't know beans about the latest goings-on with the girls. Besides, Carter's cousin isn't a guest at all.

Though he's not been home since Carter and I wed, Maxwell occupies the third floor of this house when he isn't traveling."

A shiver of discomfort washed over Kathleen at the prospect of dining with Carter's cousin, Maxwell Steadman. She had only seen him from afar on the infrequent occasions when he visited the mill. Still, his size, his demeanor, his commanding presence, his nomadic existence—in short, everything about him intimidated her. And as everyone she worked with at the mill knew, she was not one to be easily daunted by a man.

She didn't imagine today's noon meal at Steadman Manor would be the pleasant event she had come to expect every Sunday. However, when Isabel looped arms with Kathleen and coaxed her toward the dining room, she pasted on a smile and tried to share Isabel's enthusiasm as her friend prattled on.

"You will never guess what those crates hold—"

Kathleen looked back over her shoulder at the mountain of wooden boxes. All she could see were bits of straw poking through the slats.

Isabel couldn't wait for an answer. "Lemons!" she exclaimed.

"Lemons?" Kathleen echoed. The very utterance of the word made her mouth water, and she was suddenly able to pinpoint the source of the faint citrus smell she had detected when she entered the foyer.

"They hold *lemons,*" Isabel repeated, squeezing Kathleen's arm. "Fresh from Florida. Maxwell gives them to his sailors to prevent scurvy, but he bought more on this trip than they can possibly eat before the fruit goes bad, so he gave us these crates to sell or use as we see fit. Carter says we can deliver them to the girls at Kindred Hearts this afternoon."

"Won't they be thrilled?" Kathleen had never seen her friend so excited. Her jubilance proved contagious.

"They will think Christmas has come all over again when we present them with flannel nighties and with lemons, too." Isabel's eyes sparkled with glee as she eyed the carpetbag. "You did bring the nightgowns, didn't you?"

Kathleen nodded in answer to the question. "Yes, dear friend. You needn't worry. Pegeen, Grace, and I finished the trim work on the last gown Thursday."

At the pronouncement, Isabel gave Kathleen's arm another squeeze.

"Your husband's misfortune at having to shut down the mill because of all this rain proved to be our gain," Kathleen confided to her friend. "I've been able to complete a number of personal projects this week. Although, come payday, I am sure to miss my usual piece rate bonus."

"Miss Kathleen, knowing the miracles you work on that loom, I have no doubt you will make up the yardage in a matter of hours," Carter Steadman said as he entered the dining room by way of the adjoining parlor. "Wouldn't you agree with me, Dear?" He bowed to Kathleen in greeting while Isabel released her hold on Kathleen's arm and moved to stand by her husband's side.

"I think I deserve a little credit for Kathleen's success," Isabel said with a mischievous grin. "Everything she knows about weaving, she learned from me." The three shared a laugh before a serious look supplanted Carter's jovial expression.

"All joking aside, Miss Kathleen, I made careful note of the fact that, despite the shutdown, you took it upon yourself to spend a good many hours cleaning the looms in your weave room. Such dedication to your responsibilities won't go unrewarded." As his litany of praise continued, Kathleen dropped her gaze and studied the intricate pattern of the dining room's Persian rug.

Her cheeks burning with the heat of embarrassment, she looked up to protest her employer's compliments, but he had turned back toward the parlor. "Maxwell, I'll have you know that, due to the efforts of my head weaver here, no time will be wasted when the rainwaters recede from the tailrace and wheelpit in sufficient measure to restart our machinery." Carter motioned for his cousin to join them in the dining room. "In light of the news you just shared with me, this could prove invaluable."

The massive frame of the man whom most of Eastead covertly referred to as "the Shipping Steadman" filled the doorway. Kathleen had to tip her head back in order to look him in the eye. She moistened her lips and schooled her features in hopes of masking her alarm. The face-to-face reality of Maxwell Steadman loomed even larger and more intimidating than her distant memory of him.

"Cousin, let me introduce you to one of my most prized employees, Miss Kathleen McKenna. It's been nearly two years now since she signed on to work for us in the mill. Her father thought our 'land of steady habits' was becoming a bit too congested for his taste, so sold their Connecticut farmland and loaded the rest of the family in a Conestoga headed for Indiana's wide-open spaces. Miss Kathleen stayed behind to earn a bit of income for the family until the others could get sufficiently settled."

Carter then turned toward her. "Miss Kathleen, I would like you to meet Maxwell Steadman, president and principal shareholder of Steadman Shipping Company."

While Maxwell Steadman shared the same chisel-cut, square jaw and slightly cleft chin as his cousin, the family resemblance ended there. He towered a good three inches over Carter, and his tanned, weather-beaten skin testified to years of exposure to the elements. One glance at his mariner's muscular bulk convinced Kathleen that he had single-handedly hoisted many a sail. She suspected the two cousins might have also inherited the same hair color, but years in the sun had streaked the Shipping Steadman's cinnamon brown mane with shimmering strands of gold.

"Pleased to make your acquaintance, Miss McKenna." Acting every bit the part of a perfect gentleman, he reached out and took her by the hand, then dipped over it in a polite bow. When he straightened to his full height, she found herself tensing under his scrutiny. His eyes reminded her of thick molasses, yet she wondered if any sweetness lay hidden in their depths. He was, after all, a seaman and merchant by trade.

"Considering the high regard with which my cousin holds certain weavers previously in his employ," he continued, "Carter's compliment must, indeed, be well deserved."

Kathleen did not know quite how to take his remarks. His granite expression refused to reveal whether he intended to pay her a compliment—or send a subtle, barbed statement of disapproval at his upper-class cousin's choice of a working-class bride. He shot a fleeting glance toward the newlyweds, and Kathleen traced his movements. She could tell by the look on Isabel's face that her dear friend shared her bewilderment.

To throw her even more off-kilter, when Kathleen glimpsed his way again, Maxwell Steadman flashed her a slow, disarming smile. Her attempts to return his friendly overture with a smile of her own brought an unbidden and unwelcome flash of excitement fluttering through her chest and set off a ringing in her ears.

Mercifully, Vivian Steadman, Carter's mother and Maxwell's aunt, chose this precise moment to make her entrance into the dining room, thus saving Kathleen from having to formulate an intelligent response. Though the saintly matriarch never would complain, she approached them in short, wooden strides, and at once, Kathleen recognized the damp weather's ill effect on Mrs. Steadman's rheumatism.

"Children, shall we take our seats? Cook tells me dinner is getting cold."

◆　◆　◆

"Well, Nephew, I see you've met Miss Kathleen." Aunt Vivian's feigned whisper carried across the room for all to hear as, in slow, measured steps, Maxwell escorted her to her seat at the head of the dining table. By the time Maxwell managed to slide his aunt's chair up to the table, Carter had already assisted both of the younger women into their places and was taking a seat next to his wife.

Aunt Vivian dropped all pretense of speaking only to Maxwell when he moved to take the one remaining empty seat—sandwiched between his aunt and their fair young dinner guest. "We count our lovely Miss Kathleen among the chiefest of the many blessings Carter's new bride brought into our lives," she said.

Maxwell could see through his aunt's innocent remarks. He had fallen prey to her matchmaking wiles before. Indeed, he had noted the loveliness of Miss Kathleen McKenna. He could not refrain from staring at the petite and comely young woman with her dark chestnut hair, pale, fair skin, and eyes the same soft green as the costly celadon he'd purchased on his last voyage to the Orient. However, as much as he admired her beauty, he considered it foolish to entertain any romantic notions concerning a subordinate member of the working class, and he saw no blessing or benefit in Carter's stooping to wed someone like Isabel, no matter how pretty or beguiling she might be.

When Maxwell took his seat directly across from Carter, he caught an interchange of affectionate glances between the newlyweds. The two appeared thoroughly intoxicated by the very presence of the other, but Maxwell shook off the prick of jealousy that needled him as he watched the lovebirds.

During his last visit, Maxwell had been taken aback by Carter's obvious infatuation with one of the mill girls in his employ. During the course of his most recent journey, he'd fully expected his cousin to come to his senses. Instead, Carter's obsession with Isabel appeared to have intensified. The realization startled and perplexed

Maxwell. After all, Carter might have chosen any of Eastead's eligible debutantes as his bride—one with something to bring to a marriage besides the clothes on her back and a pretty smile.

If Aunt Vivian's enthusiastic and vocal support of Isabel were any indication, the Steadman family's intolerant position on such mismatched unions had certainly softened over the short course of one generation. According to whispered family folklore, in addition to Maxwell's and Carter's fathers, a third son had once stood in line to inherit the Steadman fortunes. However, when the fabled Esau Steadman chose a life mate considerably below his family's means and social standing, Grandfather Steadman had promptly disowned him and forbidden anyone to speak his son's name in his presence again. Grandfather Steadman would never have allowed a mill girl to dine at his table.

Maxwell cast a sideways glance at Kathleen McKenna, then shook his head to dismiss these domestic matters from his thoughts. A host of far more pressing business items vied for his attention. He didn't have time to concern himself with Byronic musings. Such affairs played little significance in his life, after all. He prided himself on his confirmed bachelorhood. He loved his carefree, vagabond ways. He never intended to marry—neither for love nor money.

Aunt Vivian called on Carter to ask the blessing, after which a uniformed maid bearing a soup tureen promptly appeared from the kitchen. Once all had been served, Maxwell waited for his aunt to commence eating before he spooned a large bite of clam chowder into his mouth.

"Maxwell, you don't mind if I share with our present company the matters we were just discussing in the parlor, do you?"

Carter's request so caught Maxwell off guard, a clam tidbit lodged in his throat and he fought to swallow without choking. He managed a raspy, "Certainly," before reaching for his water glass. He dared not argue the point here and now, but for Carter to bring up matters of trade and commerce as topics of dinner conversation seemed, at the least, somewhat ill-mannered. Far beyond that, for him to disclose such professional concerns with these members of the fairer sex struck Maxwell as downright unconventional. Preposterous.

He drained the water from his glass, yet a lingering urge to cough tickled at his throat.

Miss Kathleen leaned in toward him as she passed the bread basket. "Are you all right, Mr. Steadman?" she murmured, concern shadowing her features.

"Fine," he rasped and nodded toward his bowl of chowder. "I have been so long deprived of Cook's good food, I got caught making a glutton of myself is all."

"Perhaps you are simply trying to smother your sorrows in the soup, my boy." Carter jabbed at the air toward Maxwell with his empty spoon and chuckled. "Forgive me. I did not intend to make light of your hapless circumstances, but I have to believe the Lord has a reason for allowing this delay of your voyage to England."

Maxwell offered Carter a thin-lipped smile but kept his comments to himself. Although God might have played a part in the tempest that destroyed his clipper's sails, he highly doubted the scoundrel of an overseer, Jedidiah Drake, had consulted the Almighty before leaving Steadman Shipping high and dry.

"Ladies," Carter began, "when Maxwell landed in Eastead this morning, a messenger presented him with a packet containing two rather dire reports." He paused to give all three women sufficient time to cluck and "my-my" their condolences to Maxwell. "While none of us takes any pleasure in Maxwell's misfortune, you might find it interesting to learn that our former agent at Steadman Textiles, Harlan Jefford, convinced Jedidiah Drake, the overseer of Steadman Shipping, to enter into a new business venture with him. The two set off for California on Friday—without the courtesy of Drake serving a day's notice to poor Maxwell here."

From the little bit of information Carter had told him earlier in the day about Jefford, Maxwell well understood why Isabel, in particular, might be pleased to know she wouldn't be running into the former mill agent on the streets of Eastead anytime soon. However, his overseer's desertion to join Jefford's camp left Maxwell with no one he could trust to manage his business while he traveled abroad. Good men were hard to come by. Carter had been forced to manage the entire mill operation personally since he'd dismissed Jefford back in December and had only hired a new mill agent from Boston within the past month. Maxwell was at a decided disadvantage since his own travels kept him from making the acquaintance of any prospective candidates who might already live in the region.

"What a pity," his aunt exclaimed. "You were no doubt hoping to set sail right away, what with warm weather coming on." She shifted in her seat to look at Carter. "Son, isn't there any way you can help?"

Maxwell leaned to one side to allow the servant to trade his empty soup bowl for a plate heaped with a generous portion of his favorite fare—Yankee pot roast and all the trimmings. Yet while the meal looked and smelled delicious, he found he no longer had much of an appetite.

"I appreciate your concern, Aunt Vivian, but according to the other report I received this morning, even if I found a new overseer tomorrow, I couldn't lift anchor until I'd outfitted the *Steadfast* with a full complement of fresh sails." Maxwell sighed and absentmindedly jabbed at a parsnip with his fork. "She's my only clipper in port right now, and she limped into harbor last week with her sails in shreds after encountering an intense gale a few miles offshore." He glanced at Carter, who was rubbing his chin in contemplation. They studied one another for a long moment before Carter abruptly turned his attention to Miss McKenna.

"Miss Kathleen, I'll run this by Agent Woolery first thing tomorrow morning, but frankly, at this point, both you and I have a better working knowledge of the mill and the weave rooms than he does. If this freshet has, indeed, blown out to sea, I can't think of any reason why we couldn't shift our production schedule tomorrow and set our spindles and looms to do a rush order of sailcloth for my cousin here. Can you?"

While Carter spoke, Maxwell rested his fork against his plate and pushed back from the table just far enough to easily observe Miss McKenna's response. He was already growing somewhat accustomed to his cousin's unorthodox business practices and odd way of dealing with subordinates—women in particular. He did not, however, expect the reaction of the young lady at his side.

The hitherto demure and soft-spoken dinner guest pushed her plate away and, with her back ramrod straight, clasped her folded hands in her lap and leaned toward her employer. She began to shake her head from side to side in calculating slowness. She paused and twisted in her chair to look at Maxwell.

"Mr. Steadman, may I ask how many yards of sailcloth a clipper requires?"

The assertive tone in her voice so took him aback, Maxwell needed a moment to register the fact that she meant the question for him. "Let me think on it for a minute." He tapped his lips with his index finger and rushed through the calculations. He could give her a close estimate immediately, but he thought in this instance he ought to provide a rather accurate figure.

Main-topmast. . . .topgallant. . .mizzen. . . He mentally ticked off the various dimensions of the *Steadfast*'s masts and yards. As he did his figuring, Carter and the two younger women discussed in hushed undertones the modifications the mill would need to make to the spindles and looms in order to put this spur-of-the-moment work order into motion, while his forever-patient aunt Vivian observed their proceedings in silence. Her quiet tolerance bore testimony to the many such meals-turned-business-meetings she had sat through in her day.

When Maxwell felt confident of his total, he cleared his throat and lightly nudged Miss McKenna's elbow to gain her attention again.

"Twelve thousand five hundred yards—thirteen thousand should be more than sufficient."

He half-expected her to cower at the daunting figure. Instead, Maxwell watched her expression brighten. Her celadon green eyes sparkled with fiery excitement and darted to and fro beneath her spiked eyebrows as though she were ciphering a complex mathematical equation without the aid of pencil and paper.

"Oh, that's nothing," she said with a swish of her hand. "We've three hundred looms each producing fifty yards a day, so we could weave that amount of yardage in a day or two without a bit of trouble. The delay comes, of course, in the preparatory setup and finish work." She spoke to him as a teacher would a thickheaded pupil. "The cotton duck you need for sail sheeting requires a denser thread than what our spindles are producing for the shirting we are weaving now, and the looms would need to be adjusted to provide a tighter, sturdier weave. In addition, the mill may find it necessary to temporarily employ seamstresses skilled in the art of sail-making to do the finish work."

She looked first at Carter, then back to him, before settling her gaze on Carter again. "With all due respect to both Mr. Steadmans, it appears to be neither a prudent use of the shipping company's finances nor of the mill's labor force to fill such a small order. Perhaps you could convince the Shipping Steadman to consider multiplying his order, say, tenfold?"

Maxwell bit his lip to keep from laughing aloud at her reference to him. *The*

Shipping Steadman, indeed. Plainly, there were too many Mr. Steadmans in the room. He could see he would need to come up with a different form of address if he kept company with his cousin in the presence of Miss McKenna for any length of time. Judging from the way Carter seemed to value her opinion, the prospect could be a definite possibility, and the more Maxwell thought about it, the more he warmed to the idea.

Maxwell had never known a beautiful woman like Kathleen McKenna could also be so sharp-witted and quick with figures. She obviously had a good head for business, a thought that struck Maxwell as altogether unnatural. He could never ask anyone because his curiosity would certainly be misconstrued; however, he wondered why a beauty like Miss McKenna had not yet married. She was well into her marriageable years. He guessed her to be at least nineteen or twenty. Perhaps the reason had something to do with her having to postpone her assumption of the preferred vocation of most women—homemaking and child rearing—in order to enter into millwork as a means of supporting her family.

He generally held to the opinion that wives were better left in the dark in matters of commerce, lest they be construed as meddling in affairs they had no business concerning themselves with. The man who had to live with a woman as assertive and sure of herself in economic issues as Kathleen McKenna appeared to be would undoubtedly face many challenges. Even so, Maxwell suspected that the man fortunate enough to take Miss McKenna for his bride might be wise to consult her before making any major business decisions.

"Miss Kathleen has a point," Carter said, rousing Maxwell from his reverie. "Your other clippers are bound to need new suits of sails before long if they don't now, and you could have a sufficient supply of sheeting to dress your entire fleet. If that prospect doesn't appeal to you, no doubt you could find a buyer, either here or abroad, for such sturdy fabrics. You supply Steadman Textiles with our raw cotton, and I'm certain you can vouch for the quality of our finished product. What do you say, Maxwell?"

"I say I am amenable to the idea, provided we give first priority to getting the *Steadfast* seaworthy. I must admit, I am rather embarrassed that I didn't come up with this concept myself long ago. We may have just stumbled upon a profitable venture for the both of us, thanks to your Miss McKenna." Maxwell tipped his head to acknowledge the young lady's contributions, and she flushed a delightful shade of crimson.

Music filled the air as the mantel clock in the parlor chimed the hour.

"Oh, my, Kathleen, the time!"

Both Maxwell and their dinner guest jumped at Isabel's exclamation.

"We must get to Kindred Hearts right away, before Miss Amy puts the little ones down for their naps and we miss giving them their gifts."

Chapter 2

While Carter drove the wagon down Croner Hill and over the few short blocks to the Kindred Hearts Orphanage, Maxwell rode in the back amid the lemon crates and Aunt Vivian's last-minute donation of a fifty-pound sack of Georgia cane sugar. All the way, he silently groused about agreeing to accompany Carter as he escorted the two ladies on their little mission of charity. If the mysterious Miss McKenna, with her enchanting eyes, had not been standing behind his cousin when Carter had asked him to come, Maxwell felt certain he would have declined the invitation; but he had not wanted her to presume him a cad.

He had no business tagging along. He couldn't take credit for the gift of citrus they were delivering. If Carter or Isabel had asked his opinion, he would have told them it made much more sense to sell the scarce commodity for top dollar and then make a small cash donation to the orphans from the proceeds. Even if he had thrown his full support behind this idea, he never saw himself as much of a public do-gooder. His younger brother, Lucas, possessed enough sanctimonious piety for the both of them. Unlike Lucas, Maxwell wasn't one to seek recognition for any of his benevolent deeds. He should have pleaded exhaustion from his journey home and headed straight for his rooms on the third floor.

When they pulled up in front of the establishment—the epitome of residential repose—the knot in Maxwell's stomach cinched even tighter. He deplored the prospect of spending his Sunday afternoon perched on the edge of some delicate parlor chair. Beads of sweat dampened the back of his neck at the very thought of making conversation with the house matron, Amy Ross, while surrounded and mauled by a host of giggly little girls.

Amy, a couple of years younger than Maxwell, had grown up in Eastead and married Jason Ross, one of his school chums. She was left a widow when Jason died some four years earlier, although Maxwell couldn't recall the circumstances surrounding his death. During one of Aunt Vivian's previous matchmaking campaigns, she had tried to get Maxwell to call on Amy after the young widow had gone through a reasonable mourning period. In the back of his mind, he questioned whether today's charitable presentation played a part in a surreptitious conspiracy to throw him and Amy together.

Maxwell had long suspected his aunt Vivian worked hard to surround him with eligible bridal candidates whenever he breezed through town. He cast a suspicious glance toward Kathleen McKenna, who sat beside Isabel on the wagon bench.

Then and there, he vowed to hold Carter's wife to her promise.

Isabel had announced, upon catching a look at the cloudless blue sky and inhaling deep gulps of the rain-swept spring air, that when she and Kathleen were finished, she would see her friend to her boardinghouse and then walk home alone the remaining short distance. "If you so choose," she'd said, "you men are free to leave as soon as you carry the goods inside and allow a moment for proper introductions and salutations to be made." At the time, Maxwell had riled at the idea of her presuming to tell him what he could and could not do, but now he felt more than willing to accept Isabel's offer.

He scrambled off the flatbed and hoisted a crate onto his shoulder while Carter helped the women from the wagon and retrieved Miss McKenna's carpetbag from under the seat. Maxwell nodded for the others to go ahead of him, but Miss McKenna paused at his side, her anticipation palpable.

"I am so glad you agreed to come along." She flashed him a wide smile. "I think you'll find your heart warmed to see the gratitude of the girls when they receive our gifts."

Maxwell stopped and looked at Isabel's friend. He couldn't yet decide whether she was another innocent victim ensnared in one of Aunt Viv's schemes, or if she was a conniving partner in a plot to tame him. Regardless, he marveled at her complexity. If all women behaved like this Kathleen McKenna, he felt certain he would never understand a one. At first meeting, he'd thought the young lady tranquil and sedate. Then, in matters of business, she'd assumed an authoritative and resolute air. Now, she appeared as eager and excited as a six year old surprised with a party on her birthday.

He looked toward the white clapboard residence. "I am not much good with children," he said, swallowing hard. "I've never spent any length of time around little girls."

"You needn't worry. Most won't bite, although little Ruthie may chatter your leg off." She laughed, but if she meant to mock him, her words held no sting.

Miss Kathleen pointed toward the house, her teasing forgotten. "Look, someone is coming. Perhaps one of the girls saw us arrive."

The front door opened wide, and Maxwell expected to see a slip of a young thing, or two or three, racing out to greet them. Instead, the familiar figures of Parson Hull and his wife stepped onto the porch. Each carried a child. Amy Ross followed them outside. She handed the parson a small suitcase before pulling the door closed behind her. At the sight of the foursome coming up the walk, she brightened and waved.

"What perfect timing!" the young widow called out, dabbing at the corner of her eyes with a lace handkerchief. "You all can be the first of our church folk to offer hearty congratulations to the Hull family." She paused, then added, "Maxwell, it is especially nice to see you again after such a long absence."

"Likewise, Amy," he offered in exchange of the greeting, then nodded his hello to the others. "Parson and Mrs. Hull."

"I pray this means what I think it does," Miss McKenna said softly as she clutched her skirts and skittered up ahead of Maxwell so she could address Isabel. "Aren't little Betty and her baby sister the perfect match for the Hulls?" Her question met with a quick hug from Isabel.

Although Maxwell didn't have a clue what the women were talking about, he smiled to himself at the two friends' feminine exchange. While his companions made their way to the stoop, he lagged behind on the walkway, lowering the lemon crate from his shoulder to the ground. He watched while the others clambered up to the porch. The women surrounded Mrs. Hull and the babe in her arms, and Carter moved in next to Parson Hull.

Maxwell paid particular note of the protective way in which Amy Ross squeezed in between Parson and Mrs. Hull and began to pat the blanketed bundle Mrs. Hull held. "Two of my sweet girls are going to have new parents. . . ," Amy managed to say before a catch in her voice rendered her speechless. She kneaded at her lower lip as though desperately trying to keep her emotions at bay.

A slow-in-coming comprehension dawned on Maxwell. The parson and his wife were assuming the raising of these two orphans—and one a cripple, judging by the slightly twisted and misshapen form of the older child's right leg. He felt sorry for the clergy couple, despite the fact that these dear folks showed nary a sign of disappointment at the prospect of rearing someone else's offspring. No two souls could be any more humble and kind and Christian than they. He didn't understand why God had not granted the Hulls' prayers for children of their own.

"These children are truly blessed by your taking them under your wing, Parson, Mrs. Hull," Maxwell said, drawing closer to the group. "As always, you model a higher standard of Christian charity for all of us to emulate." He meant his remarks as a compliment, but a puzzled expression swept across the minister's face.

"The blessing is all ours, not theirs," Parson Hull replied. "God has showered us with more joy than we could ever deserve by bringing these children into our lives to love. We've always wanted to be parents, and now the Lord has answered our prayers."

"Reverend, you will make a wonderful father," Carter said, tousling the chestnut curls of the toddler in the minister's arms. The wee one giggled and squealed, "My papa!" Then she coyly buried her face in the crook of her new father's neck.

Isabel peeked under the covers at the infant Mrs. Hull cradled to her bosom. "Carter's right. No child could ask for better parents than the two of you. And if you ask me, this one looks just like her new mama."

"Do you think so? Really?" Mrs. Hull beamed at Isabel's remark. "Miss Amy said the same thing." The new mother stroked the sleeping baby's cheek, then tipped her head toward the toddler in her husband's arms. "With her big sister Betty's approval, we've decided to name her Dorothy. It means 'a gift from God.' "

While the cluster of adults murmured their endorsement of the name, Amy cleared her throat. "Please forgive me. I do hate to leave this happy celebration, but I left Ginger inside alone to try and console little Ruthie. The poor dear is rather upset over her best friend leaving Kindred Hearts. I'd best be getting back inside." She patted Mrs. Hull's sleeve. "And you'd best be getting these new daughters of yours out of this cool spring air. You wouldn't want them sick your first days together. I'll stop by tomorrow afternoon to see how you four are getting along."

"I am sure, with the Lord's help, we will manage just fine. However, we welcome a visit from you any time," Parson Hull answered. "And if you would, please tell Betty's friend that she'll come back to visit often." He smiled at his wife and moved to take his leave. "Shall we go home, Mama?"

Isabel pulled back and let Mrs. Hull ease past her and down the porch steps. The parson, with Betty still clinging to him, followed close behind his wife. "With your permission, we'll follow you inside," Isabel said to Amy. "We brought along some surprises that might serve to ease the sadness of saying good-bye."

Amy eyed the crate on the ground at Maxwell's feet. "How delightful—and another example of God's perfect timing. Although I suspect we shall have to suspend our weekly sewing circle this afternoon. Our emotions are in such a tizzy, I don't believe any of us could sew a straight seam."

Maxwell heaved the crate back onto his shoulder and had climbed one step when Miss McKenna exclaimed, "Wait. We have to catch the parson's family before they leave. Isabel, we forgot to give Betty and Baby Dorothy their new nighties."

Isabel grabbed the carpetbag from her husband, then the two friends breezed by Maxwell on their way to catch the Hulls. "We'll be right back. You men just wait here," Isabel called over her shoulder. Miss McKenna was already shouting for the parson to stop.

"I will see to the girls and try to corral them into the parlor," Amy said, excusing herself at the door. "You all come right on in when you're ready. Don't bother to knock."

Carter and Maxwell unloaded the wagon and deposited the crates on the porch while they awaited the women's return. Maxwell offered to retrieve the final load and left Carter sitting on the porch step to catch his breath. He had just slung the sack of sugar onto his back when the ladies returned, and he fell into step behind them as they made their way up the walk. The two friends were so engrossed in their conversation, they didn't bother to acknowledge him.

"You know, if Carter and I are unable to have children, I believe I would like to adopt a baby," Isabel announced. She and Miss McKenna had each taken a handle of the carpetbag, and they toted it between them.

"I've decided," Miss McKenna returned, "that if I ever get a husband, I'm going to adopt one of the Kindred Hearts' girls, even *if* we start to build our family the typical way. Of course, I'm thrilled for the Hulls, but all along I secretly harbored a plan in my heart to adopt Betty and her baby sister after the right man came my way." As she spoke, she skipped a step to match her gait to that of her friend. "From here on out, that's one of my requirements for a prospective suitor. He must share my love for the orphans."

"Poor girl," Maxwell muttered under his breath. Even one as pretty as Miss McKenna would be hard-pressed to find a husband who lived up to such expectations. He feared that with her stringent stipulations, his cousin's head weaver might be setting herself up for a life of spinsterhood. Could she really pity the orphans that much? Would her pity last when the child she adopted ran into mischief? Surely she didn't think she could love an orphan like she could love a child born to her.

◆ ◆ ◆

The clatter and high-pitched voices of children filtered from the parlor as Kathleen led the way inside. She and Isabel had emptied the carpetbag of the remaining flannel nighties by the door, and now she balanced her half of the soft, ribboned parcels under her chin. The Steadman cousins trailed behind, one toting the sack of sugar and the other carrying a crate of lemons.

Unable to see over the top of her stack of flannel gowns, Kathleen fumbled for the handle on the parlor's etched-glass sliding doors; but before she could manage the task, someone on the other side swooshed them wide open. She felt a pair of arms tackle her about the knees, and she teetered before regaining her solid footing.

"Miss Kaf-ween!" Even without seeing her, Kathleen instantly recognized the sweet, childish lisp of three-year-old Ruthie. "They took'd our Betty away—and her widdle baby sistah, too." A gentle sob punctuated the girl's declaration of despair. Kathleen crouched and, sliding the stack of gowns onto the parlor's rug, she scooped Ruthie into her embrace.

"Aye," called Ginger, "'tis me you should blame for Ruthie's assault." The copper-topped Irish lass came slowly toward Kathleen from across the room. "Aunt Amy set a pot o' tea to boilin' and left me in charge, but Ruthie wiggled off me lap and escaped before I could ensnare her again." The oldest girl under Amy Ross's care, Ginger was of an age when she could be on her own. However, her poor eyesight prevented her from making her way in the world, so she worked to assist Amy in any way she could.

"Ruthie is fine." Kathleen struggled to stand with the youngster who had locked her legs around Kathleen's waist. "Leave her with me. I want to have a word with her."

As the other girls flocked to Isabel and the two men, Kathleen carried little Ruthie over to the parlor's settee and nestled her onto her lap. Kathleen stroked the child's cheek and tried to explain. "I know you will miss Betty, but we must think of our poor, lonely Parson and Mrs. Hull." Ruthie kept her head down, twisting and untwisting the hem of her apron. "They had no little girls to love in their house, no children at all. Yet here at Kindred Hearts, there are more than you have yet learned to count. Besides, Betty's new home is just down the street, and I am quite certain she'll be coming to play with you from time to time."

"Aunt Amy says so, too." Little Ruthie, her dark eyes round as buttons, gazed up at Kathleen. Unspent tears pooled along the child's bottom eyelids, and her nose needed a good wiping. Kathleen pulled out the handkerchief she kept tucked up her sleeve and performed the tasks in a couple of quick swipes.

"No more tears now. I have someone I want you to meet, and we brought you surprises."

Ruthie squirmed to get down. "I like surpri—" She stopped midsentence at the sight of an unfamiliar giant of a man filling the parlor doorway. Her mouth dropped open. As fast as she had freed herself of Kathleen's embrace, she scurried back up into her lap. "He's not coming to 'dopt me, is he, Miss Kaf-ween?" But for the fear sparkling in Ruthie's wide eyes, Kathleen might have laughed.

"Dear me, no." Kathleen gave the little one a squeeze. "That man is Mr. Steadman's cousin. His name is Mr. Steadman as well—Mr. Maxwell Steadman—but unlike Miss Isabel's husband, this Mr. Steadman has no wife. He travels to faraway places like Georgia and Florida, and a part of our surprise came all the way from there."

Kathleen glanced at the Shipping Steadman. His pained expression telegraphed his discomfort.

Beside him, the older girls made a grand production of sniffing the handfuls of lemons they had drawn from Carter's opened crate. One had ventured to bite into a lemon's rind, and the others burst into gales of laughter at her resulting sour face.

Isabel had doled out her supply of the gowns, and several of the younger girls held them over the bodices of their pinafores, twirling and pirouetting in circles. In the midst of this cheerful chaos, Maxwell Steadman stood stock-still, his arms folded across his chest like a turtle withdrawing into its shell. Kathleen hardly recognized the bulk of a man who had possessed the power to intimidate her a few hours earlier. Shirking behind Isabel, he no longer cowed Kathleen with his suave mystique. Instead, he presented a living, breathing illustration of such words as *apprehensive. . .uncomfortable. . .vexed. . .helpless. . .distressed.* This mammoth man who sailed the high seas and perhaps had even stood face-to-face with pirates appeared wholly unsettled by a roomful of little girls.

A sly smile tugged at the corners of Kathleen's mouth as she coaxed Ruthie back to her feet. "You see the soft, new nighties Miss Isabel gave to the other girls? Well, I made one especially for you. While I find yours, why don't you go and introduce yourself to the other Mr. Steadman? Tell him I suggested you request that he read a Bible story to you and the other girls."

She knew Ruthie loved being read to more than anything, and whatever hesitation the youngster felt about approaching the stranger would fly away at the prospect of a story. "I wouldn't wonder, if you asked him real nice and polite, but that he'd let you sit on his lap while he reads. He spends all his time around gruff and grouchy men, and I feel certain he would enjoy getting to know a sweet little girl like you."

Ruthie's ringlets bounced like springs as she agreed. She darted in and out among the other girls and planted herself at Maxwell Steadman's side, craning her neck to look up at him. Kathleen couldn't hear with all the other commotion in the room, but she positioned herself to watch Ruthie. After four vigorous yanks at his coattail, Mr. Maxwell glanced Ruthie's way, and the toddler pumped her pudgy finger to indicate for him to lean down. Thin-lipped, he hunched to her level while Ruthie stretched on her tiptoes and cupped her hand to speak into his ear.

As he straightened and Ruthie began to tug him toward the red velvet settee, he shot a steely-eyed stare Kathleen's way. The scene invoked visions of a great bear caught in a honeyed trap, and for an instant she almost felt sorry for the man. She almost regretted preying on his one exposed weakness. She almost rose to rescue him. Almost.

Chapter 3

Kathleen jarred from her sleep, her heart pounding. Perspiration soaked her pillow's casing. The acrid taste of smoke burned her parched throat and dried out her sinuses. She instinctively felt her face to ascertain whether or not she had singed off her lashes and eyebrows.

At the feathery brush of her lashes against her fingertips, she crossed that lissome line from half-awake to fully alert, and she released a sigh of relief as she realized she'd been dreaming.

Staring into the murky blackness of the boardinghouse bedroom Kathleen shared with two roommates, she recognized the slow and heavy breathing of Grace as she slept, accompanied by Pegeen's soft snore. Kathleen punched her pillow and sank back into its goose-down softness.

The more she thought about her dream—no, nightmare—the more absurd it seemed. One of Maxwell Steadman's clipper ships had broken free of its moorings and floated from Boston upriver to Eastead. With Mr. Maxwell standing at the bow and the ship's sails flapping in shreds like strips of burial shroud, the vessel plowed into the side of the textile mill, landing the man right in front of Kathleen's looms. Before he could offer a word of explanation, one of the weave room's whale oil lamps set afire a tattered remnant of sailcloth, which, in turn, touched off an inferno in the wooden building filled with combustible dry goods. While the circle of flame and heat pressed in upon Kathleen, Mr. Maxwell reached out from the ship, coaxing, pleading for her to take his hand and let him draw her to safety. Still, she hesitated. Despite the ever-encroaching danger, she wondered—should she entrust her rescue to the man from whose hand all this chaos sprang? She awoke before deciding.

Kathleen didn't really understand the wellspring of the dream. Maxwell Steadman may have disrupted her life for a short time, but she didn't really think of his rush order for sailcloth as a crisis of life-and-death proportions. Even so, her mind had raced most of the night with the details of what needed to be done in the morning to prepare her weave room for the work at hand. And regardless of how hard she fought the tendency, pleasant recollections of yesterday afternoon with the handsome merchant danced and played in her thoughts.

Rising on one elbow, Kathleen flipped her pillow over and thumped it again, then buried her face. She owned neither a watch nor clock, so she had no way of knowing the time. She measured her hours by the chimes that rang from the mill tower. The carillons signaled the workers' early morning wake-up call, noon meal, and the workday's beginning and end. But for sleepless nights like this one, she had little need for a timepiece.

She kicked her tangled nine-patch quilt away from her feet and rolled onto her side. Then her back. Then to her other side.

Kathleen's mind refused to rest.

She suspected she had Carter to thank that another roommate had not yet been assigned to assume the vacant spot left by Isabel when she married the mill's owner. Having an entire bed of her own rated as pure luxury, but she was especially grateful at a time such as this. She wouldn't have wanted to inflict a night full of her fidgeting on another poor soul.

After an insufferable length of time, the faint clatter of pots and pans filtered up through the floorboards from the first-floor kitchen, and she knew the boarding-house matron, Mrs. Cox, had begun breakfast preparations. This meant the time must be around four-thirty. Kathleen threw off her covers and slid out of bed. She felt her way in the dark to the straight-backed bedside chair where she'd laid out her everyday calico and apron before retiring the night before. Trying her best to keep quiet, she began to dress by feel alone.

"Aye! I fear to ask ye." Pegeen's sleepy voice sludged through the darkness. "Did I again slumber through the rise-and-shine call?" In the former days when their workday started at five o'clock, Pegeen had been given to sleeping through the four-forty-five wake-up bell. Grace and Kathleen had been forced to employ all means of torture to roust her from her bed, lest she be put on report and her pay docked. However, since Carter Steadman's decision to institute a ten-hour workday in place of their fourteen-hour schedule, Pegeen had yet to oversleep. Now, they not only slept an hour later, but they also enjoyed a hearty breakfast at the boardinghouse before going to the mill. It was a pleasant change from the old routine of taking a thirty-minute breakfast break two hours into their workday.

"No, no. Go back to sleep," Kathleen urged in a half-whisper. "I am sorry if I wakened you. I thought I would go into work early. You have another hour before the bell rings." Pegeen needed no further coaxing to fall silent, and before Kathleen had tiptoed from the room with her boots in hand, Pegeen's soft snore again rent the air.

The steps creaked with Kathleen's every footfall. When she reached the bottom of the staircase, she paused long enough to don her shoes, then she passed into the kitchen. After she splashed cold water on her face and smoothed her hair into place with her damp hands, she swigged a cup of milk and absconded with a thick slice of sourdough bread to eat on the run. All the while, Mrs. Cox chittered laments about Kathleen not watching after her health. . .and not getting her rest. . .and not eating a proper breakfast.

With Mrs. Cox still tsk-tsking her disapproval, Kathleen grabbed her cape off the row of coat pegs hanging by the door. Then, still wolfing down her bread break-fast, she hastened outside, and by the light of a full moon, she crossed the muddy road to the mill. She made a hurried visit to the outhouse before tramping up the rickety outer stairwell as far as the second-floor weave room, where she spent a major portion of her waking hours.

No hint of daylight yet shone through the floor-to-ceiling windows, which spanned the depth of the room on both sides. Even in broad daylight, however, years' worth of an accumulated mixture of cotton fibers, potato starch, and whale-oil soot coated the windows with an opaque film.

She opened the window nearest the door to allow a bit of fresh air into the stuffy room. Then Kathleen moved down one side of the long, narrow hall and back up the other, raising the flame on the whale-oil lamps and illuminating Weave Room Number One. She paused to survey the one hundred silent looms.

Soon, when the six o'clock bell signaled the call to work and the mill girls all stood at their stations, Agent Woolery would throw the lever to set the pulleys and belts in motion and send power to the machinery. The looms' shuttles would start their clacking. A deafening roar would supplant the stillness, and she would have to strain in order to understand the loudest shout yelled inches from her ear. Still, she found the familiar clamor and its accompanying routine comforting.

As she did every morning, she prayed and asked God not only to watch over the workers and keep them safe, but also to bless the fruits of their labor and use what they produced to meet a special need in the life of its recipient. The thought of Maxwell Steadman being that recipient in the coming days sent a smile playing across Kathleen's lips as she breathed an "amen."

Kathleen moved to the corner of the weave room closest to the door, where the baskets of full bobbins were stored. She knelt down to scrutinize the supply of thread remaining in their reserves, then gauged the time required for her girls to weave it into shirting. By her estimate, the spinners should be able to start supplying them with the heavier thread for sailcloth about the same time the weavers exhausted their current stock of the lighter-weight thread.

Her attention was torn away from her calculations when she heard a man's voice filtering up from the street and through the window she had opened for ventilation just moments before. At first, she attached the voice to the short and squat figure of Agent Woolery, but as soon as she heard her name mentioned, she recognized the distinct speech of Maxwell Steadman. Her pulse raced as she listened to her employer's handsome, seafaring cousin speak of her; and though she knew she should not be privy to Mr. Maxwell's private conversation, the shock of his words kept her frozen where she knelt.

"I'm surprised a maverick like you didn't just give Miss McKenna full run of the mill instead of hiring a new agent. If half of what you tell me about her is true, I don't believe you could find a more capable employee—male or female."

"Quite frankly, the thought did cross my mind," returned the voice of Carter Steadman. "She certainly has the intellect and aptitude for the position, but I figured if I were to promote her from among the ranks of her peers into a position of authority over them, well, as the Scriptures say, 'A prophet is without honor in his own country.' I feared she wouldn't receive the respect and authority that would be due a person of such position. Besides, one with her excellent skills at the loom may very well prove harder to replace than an agent. She has quick hands as well as a quick mind."

Kathleen drew a deep breath. She longed to savor these sweet words of honor from her employer, but his voice trailed off, and she realized they were walking away from the open window and up the stairwell. If she didn't make haste, in a matter of moments, the Steadman cousins would discover she had been eavesdropping.

As noiselessly as she could, she scrambled down the aisle toward her assigned workstation. When the two men stepped into the room, she appeared to be intently examining a shuttle.

"Ah, Miss Kathleen," Carter Steadman exclaimed as he led his cousin through the labyrinth of looms toward the two looms that comprised her workstation. "I should have known we would find you here. We were on our way to my office and noticed the light shining from this weave room. I figured our new man had come in early to get a jump on the day." He ran his hand lightly across the warp threads of one of her looms as though he were playing a harp. "I am glad to have a chance to speak with you, however."

Mr. Maxwell nodded to Kathleen. "Morning," he offered in abbreviated greeting before flashing her a wide smile.

"Good morning, Mr. Steadman." The inside of Kathleen's mouth felt like it had been stuffed with cotton as she returned his smile. She recalled the haste in which she had dressed, and she knew she must surely look a fright. Thankfully, both of the Steadmans seemed preoccupied with business rather than with her appearance. Having completed the customary pleasantries, her employer launched into the topic at hand.

"On our way over, Maxwell and I were discussing his plans to secure fresh crewmen from among the Irish when he travels to Europe. Due to the famine and insufferable conditions in Ireland of late, my good cousin shall provide stateside passage for the families of the sailors as well, in exchange for their commitment to extended years of service." As Carter Steadman spoke, Kathleen caught a glimpse of his cousin. Deep creases furrowed his brow, and he stood with his arms crossed, rocking his head slowly up and down in agreement.

"He tells me he already has an emissary recruiting men in and around Bray," Carter continued.

Kathleen jerked her focus back to her employer. Her roommate, Pegeen, hailed from a small fishing village near Bray. For all these many months, the Irish girl had been slaving to save enough money to pay for her sister, Francine's, passage from there to the States, but she still needed to set so much more aside. Even though she did not share Kathleen's faith, Pegeen had asked her roommate to pray for God's help in allowing her sister to join her soon.

Even now, Kathleen winged a prayer heavenward. *Precious Savior, if only there were some way Maxwell could be convinced to bring Francine back with him, perhaps such a miracle would nudge Pegeen to a personal relationship with You!* Carter Steadman presented a possible answer to her prayer before she could say a word.

"Maxwell set me to thinking," he said, rubbing his fingers along the watch fob that dangled from his waistcoat. "Our workforce is already somewhat depleted, and with summer coming on, we are sure to lose a few more of our mill girls to marriage and the like. Steadman Textiles could provide jobs for at least a dozen or two of these destitute and starving souls, and Maxwell says he could make room aboard the *Steadfast* for their passage. The way I see it, we all stand to benefit from such a plan."

Tingles raced down Kathleen's spine and gooseflesh erupted on her arms. "Sir, you would be doing me a tremendous personal favor by considering a Miss Francine O'Malley, the sister of my roommate Pegeen, as one of the potential candidates for this program. She still lives at what's left of their family homestead near Bray, and I know Pegeen is anxious to be reunited with her kin. In fact, just last week Pegeen's bunkmate, Grace, announced her decision to return home come summer, so Francine could move right into our room."

She caught Maxwell Steadman studying her as she spoke. A look of bewilderment crinkled his features. "You have an Irish roommate?" he asked. "I thought our local Irish confined themselves to the other side of Old Presser Bridge."

"Most do," Kathleen replied. "But the boardinghouses for the Irish lasses were full when Pegeen arrived in Eastead. Isabel and I first offered to take Pegeen into our room as an act of Christian charity, but I am certain Isabel would agree—Pegeen has blessed our lives much more than we've been a blessing to her. She is a sweet and loyal friend." She lowered her voice almost to a whisper, even though no one but the three of them were in the room. "She certainly helps to temper Grace's sour disposition."

"And I can vouch for her hard work ethic," Carter Steadman interjected. "I've found the vast majority of the Irish to be excellent employees."

Kathleen watched as Maxwell cocked his head to one side and stroked his clean-shaven chin. She could tell the idea of their so freely accepting the Irish as equals puzzled him. Yet, while she still had a good deal to learn about him, she knew one thing for certain. If he possessed even an ounce of the Steadman blood that flowed through Carter Steadman's veins, he would be incapable of taking unscrupulous advantage of the current famine in Ireland by hiring that country's citizens as cheap labor and forcing them into jobs that amounted to slavery.

Maxwell Steadman's intense gaze traveled, first to her, then to Carter. "Do you support Miss McKenna's idea?" His eyebrows spiked in question.

"I do. Wholeheartedly," Carter replied.

At Carter's commendation, Maxwell drew what looked like a small ledger book from the pocket of his topcoat along with a nub of a graphite pencil and began to scribble something down. "When I write my man in Bray about screening mill employee candidates, I'll ask him to get in touch with your friend's sister straight away." He looked up from his writing and glanced at Kathleen.

She drummed her fingers across her lips while she thought about how she might obtain the information Mr. Maxwell needed without letting on to Pegeen about their plans. "I want to keep things a secret until we can surprise Pegeen with her sister's arrival. That way, she won't be disappointed if things don't work out for whatever reason." Kathleen looked toward Maxwell, and his gaze met hers. Suddenly, she knew what to do.

"I have a plan that just might work," she said, squaring her shoulders. "You see, Pegeen only learned to read and write this past year, and she still struggles with some of the bigger words, so I stand ready to assist her. But she needs my aid less and less with each passing day." She didn't try to keep the hint of pride from lacing her words, for after the countless evenings she and Pegeen had worked together by lamplight, Kathleen found great satisfaction in her pupil's success.

"If she follows true to form, during today's noon break, rather than go back to the boardinghouse for dinner, Pegeen will carry her letter to the mill store for posting. Perhaps I can tell her I need to pick something up from the store and offer to mail her letter for her when I go. If I mention the fact that Mrs. Cox is serving shepherd's pie—Pegeen's favorite—I am almost certain to pull off the ruse. Then I shall simply copy down her sister's address from the letter before I post it and deliver the information to Mr. Carter Steadman's office before the bells chime the call to return to work."

Maxwell chuckled. "You seem quite adept at deceptive schemes, Miss Kathleen. However, it would be most helpful if you would drop off the information to my shipping office instead of taking it to Carter. You needn't go much out of your way, and you would save me from having to make another trip to the mill before dispatching a carrier to Boston."

"Yes, sir. As you wish." She sensed Maxwell's enthusiasm for their newly-hatched scheme was growing with each passing moment.

Mill girls trickled through the weave room door in a steady stream, indicating the fast-approaching hour for the workday to begin. The two Steadmans took their leave and jostled their way toward the exit against the incoming sea of women.

"Top o' the mornin'," Pegeen said in greeting to Kathleen when she took her place at the pair of looms next to Kathleen's. "Although, considerin' me vague recollection as to the wee hour of the morning when ye arose, ye must be thinkin' the day be half-done by now."

"No, quite the contrary. I look forward to seeing what glorious blessings the Lord may bestow on us today." Kathleen picked off a strand of thread that had clung to her sleeve and rolled it between her fingers. "Say, Pegeen, I need to pick up a couple things at the mill store during the noon break. . . ." She struggled to maintain an air of nonchalance in her voice. Dropping her gaze, Kathleen looked at the balled fiber she held before flicking it to the floor. "If you'd like, I could post your letter to your sister when I go."

"Now, such a dear friend you are." Pegeen pulled the sealed packet from her apron pocket and held it out to Kathleen. "When I learned Matron Cox would be serving up the shepherd's pie for the noon meal, I'd nearly decided to wait till tomorrow for the postin'."

Kathleen tried to take the envelope from Pegeen, but rather than releasing her hold, Pegeen yanked it back. "Oh, but 'tis famished ye'll be—missin' both breakfast and dinner besides."

With a gentle tug, Kathleen wrested the letter from Pegeen and buried it into the depths of her pocket before the other girl could change her mind. "I will pick a few crackers from the barrel and buy a wedge of cheese. You needn't worry about me." She took a step back, quite pleased with herself for achieving success in this first part of the plot to reunite Pegeen and Francine. "Pegeen, I have a feeling deep in my bones that we are soon to witness some monumental changes in our lives."

Kathleen inwardly winced at her own words, fearing she might have let her guard down too soon and expressed too much exuberance. Just then, peals rang out from the mill bell tower, proclaiming the start of another workday. She breathed a sigh of relief, knowing that in a matter of seconds the racket of the machinery would render impossible any further discussion.

"This bone-deep feelin' might not be tied to the comely frame of Maxwell Steadman, what passed by me on his way out the door, would it?"

The belts and pulleys overhead rumbled and rattled into earsplitting action. Kathleen answered Pegeen with a smile and a noncommittal shrug before turning away. She jerked the levers on her two looms to set them into motion, and though she could feel Pegeen staring at her, she refused to make eye contact with her friend.

Pegeen's speculation of a second budding Steadman/mill girl romance was wholly absurd. Pure folly. Still, Kathleen knew her friend well enough to know that, with just a shrug, she had turned Pegeen's thoughts to romantic musings—and away from any other suspicions.

◆　◆　◆

Throughout the morning, Kathleen struggled with tasks that, any other day, she performed as naturally as breathing. Time and again, she caught herself staring at the beater bar on one of her looms as it slammed its threads into place, while at her other loom, a shuttle's untended empty quill ruined several inches of cloth. She forgot to move the temple hooks that kept her web snug and found herself tying more weaver's knots than she usually did in the course of a week. Had Carter Steadman happened by and observed her blunderings, he would have withdrawn the glowing recommendation of her that he'd given Mr. Maxwell earlier.

When Agent Woolery passed through the weave room to announce they would be resetting their looms and starting on the sailcloth after the noon break, he had to repeat his request that Kathleen oversee the transition. She had been scratching at a spot on the bodice of her mustard-yellow gingham and wondering if she had time to change into her other work dress before presenting

Maxwell Steadman with Francine's address.

Not since her first day at the mill had Kathleen felt so inept. Too many competing thoughts vied for her attention. Her stomach had been growling since ten o'clock. She found it increasingly more difficult to stifle her yawns. She couldn't wait to leave the murky air of the weave room and let the spring breezes clear her head.

At the first clang of the noon bell, Kathleen shut down her looms and rushed to beat the mass exodus toward the door. "Enjoy your meal," she called over her shoulder to Pegeen. "I'll see you back here at half past the hour."

Chapter 4

Sorry, Mr. Steadman, but Drake never had me doing anything but accounting and book work. He took care of all the merchant and customer dealings himself." Vern Witherspoon, the droopy-eyed bookkeeper, sat facing Maxwell on the other side of the desk. He held a jumbled stack of invoices and receipts in his broad lap.

Even though the two men had spent the greater part of the morning sifting through the pile of papers, the bundle Witherspoon clutched amounted to a pittance compared to what remained on the desk. Purchase orders, warehouse inventory lists, and yellowed correspondence rose into a mound so thick and deep and wide, not a trace of the wood surface appeared.

Maxwell pushed back in his chair and rose. He raked his fingers through his hair, then began to massage his aching temples.

"You are free to go on back to your books now. I'm not expecting you to fix all the mess left by that rascal Drake. I'll try to get caught up on the backlog in the coming weeks before I sail for Europe, but I need to warn you, Witherspoon. If I can't find a new overseer before then, you may have to help out as best you can in my absence, and my chances of finding a qualified prospect on such short notice are mighty slim."

"Yes, Sir. I'll do whatever I can to help you out, Mr. Steadman." The accountant gathered up his armload of documents. His chair scraped across the wood floor as he stood, and Maxwell watched as his slouching accountant shuffled out of the room.

Maxwell shuddered to think of the business Steadman Shipping might lose if he didn't find a new overseer—and fast. When he and Witherspoon started their work session, he'd held out some hope that he might be able to train the fellow to take over the post vacated by Jedidiah Drake. However, it quickly became apparent that, while the bursar's dull and plodding disposition suited him for a job that required him to keep his nose buried in ledgers day after day, he lacked any aptitude for dealing with people.

Maxwell's head throbbed, and he couldn't yet bring himself to return to the monumental task at hand. He turned to look out the window. A barge bearing the Steadman Shipping insignia and laden with cotton bails floated downriver in the direction of the mill's warehouses. Usually such a sight filled him with a sense of pride and accomplishment. Today, he felt only dread as he realized that the ship's cargo would produce a batch of paperwork that would soon hit his desk.

Cast all your cares upon Him, for He careth for you. The scriptural exhortation, oft recited by his aunt Vivian, popped into his thoughts. In the past, he had always tried to handle his problems on his own. Although he saw himself as a Christian, he wasn't one to spout long and flowery prayers like his brother, Lucas. He didn't want to bother God with his little problems when the Almighty had so many bigger issues needing His attention. Yet Maxwell could no longer stave off this growing feeling of being overwhelmed.

Right where he stood, he closed his eyes and whispered, "Please, God. You know I'm not much of one to ask for help, but I could use some divine wisdom. Point me to the right man for this overseer's job."

Looking up, he scanned the river's far bank. Shanties dotted the hillside. Maxwell grimaced to think that many of the men in his employ lived in such squalor. No one could lay the blame on him. He paid a fair wage to all his workers. Yet many chose to drink their salaries away instead of providing a decent home for their families.

A growing number of Irish immigrants crowded into hovels, claiming the eastern quadrant of the ghetto. They had more honorable reasons for living on the poor side of Eastead. They saved every spare cent they earned to pay the way for family members still in Ireland to cross over to America—Pegeen and Francine's story replayed time and again.

The image of Pegeen's Good Samaritan with celadon green eyes flashed through his mind. His personal observations, albeit brief, added to Carter's praise of his head weaver's good head for business, convinced Maxwell that Miss McKenna would make a tremendous overseer. If only she were a man instead of a lowly mill girl.

He pulled his watch from his vest pocket and checked the time. His heartbeat quickened at the thought that she would enter his office within the hour.

◆　◆　◆

Although tempted to amble by the crocuses and savor the warm spring breeze and brilliant blue sky, Kathleen traversed the short distance to the mill store in record time. Even so, a man she recognized as one of the mill's mule spinners had somehow managed to arrive ahead of her.

While the storekeeper waited on him, she availed herself of the pen and inkwell at the end of the long counter. She copied the address, written in Pegeen's amateur cursive, onto a scrap of paper. Just in case anything happened to the paper before she could deliver it to Mr. Maxwell, she tried to set the information to memory. Then she tucked the valuable data in the deepest recesses of her apron pocket and went to help herself to several crackers from the cracker barrel.

By the time she'd sliced a wedge from the grocer's giant cheese wheel, the mule spinner had finished his business, and the storekeeper was waiting to serve her. "How do, Miss," Mr. Mathers greeted her in his slow, backwoods drawl, his beard and mustache further muffling his words.

"I need to post this letter for my friend Pegeen and pay for my food," she said, stretching out both her hands and offering him the items so he could total her bill.

"If you will, please add the total to my account."

He thumped Pegeen's letter against his palm. "I seem to recall I'm holding a letter addressed to you as well. I figured to send it home with Mrs. Cox if you didn't come 'round in a day or two." He turned his back to her to search the various cubby-holes of his desk. "Yup. Here 'tis."

He shoved the well-traveled envelope across the counter toward her. She picked it up and inspected the handwriting. Her mother's unmistakable penmanship revealed the letter's author.

Kathleen couldn't afford to dally more than a minute, two at the most, if she hoped to give Francine's address to Mr. Maxwell and make it back to the mill on time, but she was anxious to learn the latest news of the family. Months had passed since she'd last heard from her folks. Besides, she had to appease her hunger pangs before she headed down River Row toward the Steadman Shipping offices.

She shoved the letter into her apron pocket and gathered up her crackers and cheese. Excusing herself from Mr. Mathers's prying glances, Kathleen went outside and perched on the edge of one of the wooden rockers that lined the store's porch.

A shower of crumbs rained onto her lap when she bit into a cheese-topped biscuit. Between bites, and using her one free hand, Kathleen pulled her mail from out of her pocket and broke the wax seal. When she gave the page a quick shake to open its folds, a silvery daguerreotype fell out.

The photograph bore the images of a stern-faced man and three impish-looking boys—all strangers to Kathleen. The man, who sported mutton-chop whiskers, appeared to be about the age of her father. She guessed the age range of the boys to be between ten and fourteen, the same as her own younger brother and two sisters. Her curiosity piqued, she turned to her mother's letter and began to read:

Dearest Kathleen,

I hope this letter finds you in good health and still enjoying your mill work. We all be fine here in Indiana, but the farm keeps us all too busy to sit down and write. Not much news to report anyway. Our days are pretty much taken up with the same old routines and the usual chores of farming life.

No doubt you wonder why I am sending a stranger's photograph with my letter, so I shall explain forthwith. I think I may have mentioned this man, Amos Grundy, when I wrote you about our last summer's barn-raising. Mr. Grundy is a widower, left to raise his three boys on his own. His wife died soon after we took up homesteading on the property adjacent to his. Well, your pa has been discussing you with Mr. Grundy. He told him of our plan to bring you out here as soon as the crops bear ample harvest to provide for the family without your mill income.

Last time they talked, your pa mentioned that we are setting our sights on bringing you out in the fall. (I had hopes of keeping this a surprise till summer, but considering the circumstances, I thought I'd best let you in on our secret now.) Upon hearing this news, Mr. Grundy asked your pa if he thought you might be agreeable to the idea of allowing him to court you whenever you were settled. He is anxious to find another wife and a mother for his boys. As you can see by the photograph, the gentleman is a good deal older than you. Even so, he is well established and seems like a mighty dependable and hard-working man. Knowing how you love children, I figured you might cotton to the idea of a ready-made family. . . .

Kathleen clenched her fists, crumpling the letter as she lowered it to her lap. She could bear to read no further. A jumble of conflicting thoughts and emotions assailed her. When her folks first moved out west and she went to work for the mill, she had cried herself to sleep, she missed them so. She'd constantly longed for the day when she would receive word that she could join them. However, she had now grown accustomed to living on her own. She liked the independence she had found away from her father's domination, and the thought of being under the authority of the solemn Amos Grundy appealed to her even less.

Kathleen stared back at the four pairs of steely eyes that glared up at her from the daguerreotype. *Dear Father,* she silently prayed, *if this is what You want for my life, please take away this sadness and give me Your peace.* She feared nothing short of a miracle would bring her prayer request to pass.

As much as she loved children, she didn't trust the glint of malice she saw sparking from these boys' eyes. She suspected the trio would seek to make her life miserable with their mischief. Moreover, when the time came for her to marry, she didn't want to wed as the replacement for an old farmer's wife. All her life, she had imagined her husband would be someone closer to her age. Someone with a kind smile, a sharp mind, a gentle strength, and an adventuresome spirit. Someone like. . .

Maxwell Steadman!

Kathleen leaped from her seat, tucking her mother's letter and the Grundy family daguerreotype securely in her apron pocket. She fingered the rest of the pocket's contents to make sure she still carried Francine's address as she hurried down the steps in the direction of Steadman Shipping Company. Her heart pounded harder, faster with each step.

When she entered the outer office, a roly-poly gentleman looked up from his work long enough to point her toward an open door. Before Mr. Maxwell noticed her, she took in the room's disheveled condition and noted his frazzled state. She felt a pang of pity for him at the sight of the chaos he'd come home to face. *The poor man really looks like he could use some help,* she thought. Just then, he glanced up and saw her standing in the doorway. His troubled expression relaxed into a smile.

"Come in and have a seat, Miss McKenna. It won't take me but a moment to shove these papers out of the way." Mr. Maxwell stood as he spoke. He reached for a batch of papers and began tapping them on the desk to square them into a neat bundle.

"Thank you, but I really can't stay or I will be late returning to work." Kathleen felt around in her pocket for the note she'd come to deliver. She tried to ignore the sinking feeling that tugged at her spirit as her hand touched the stiff outline of her mother's letter and its enclosure.

"Here is the name and address of Pegeen's sister." She held it out for him to take. "I want you to know, Sir, how much I appreciate your willingness to go to all this trouble for my friend. Surely such kindness won't go unnoticed or unrewarded by the Lord."

Mr. Maxwell reached out and took the slip of paper from Kathleen's hand. When he did, his fingers brushed lightly against hers, and a warm ripple traveled up her arm.

"I've found reward enough in your appreciation," he replied. "I've always been one to enjoy the planning of a good surprise."

◆　◆　◆

That evening when she returned to the boardinghouse after work, Kathleen read over her mother's letter in its entirety before shoving it in a hatbox under her bed. In a postscript, her mother had suggested Kathleen write a letter of personal introduction to Mr. Grundy, returning to him the valuable daguerreotype he had so graciously sent for her to see. Though she knew she should, Kathleen never quite found the time to pen a reply to her mother nor compose a letter to her unwelcome suitor.

With eye-blinking swiftness, the weeks passed by and the production of the Shipping Steadman's rush order drew near completion. Over the course of the thirty workdays during those five weeks, Mr. Maxwell wandered through the weave room each afternoon to check on the progress of his sailcloth production. Kathleen always knew when he had entered the room. She would look up from her loom in hopes of stealing a quick glimpse of him, and every time, she caught him studying her. Only after they had exchanged surreptitious nods and smiles would he leave the mill; and always after he had gone, Kathleen required several minutes to still her racing heart and dry her perspiring hands.

Each of the five Sundays throughout Mr. Maxwell's stay in town, he squeezed onto the end of the Steadman family pew next to Carter. From her prescribed seat four rows behind the Steadmans, Kathleen inclined her ear toward Maxwell during the singing of the hymns and recitation of the responsive readings. She let herself fall silent and strained to pick out his thundering bass voice among all the other worshippers, a pleasant warmth washing over her.

During one such time, Pegeen jabbed her in the side. "This is the third Sunday you've done this," she rasped. "Turn to hymn number fifty-one." When Kathleen tried to show her that she'd found the right page, Pegeen just shook her head. "I'm thinkin' your mind is on a certain man, rather than on God."

After Parson Hull pronounced the benediction and the congregation filed out the door past the minister and his family, Kathleen found Vivian Steadman waiting for her on the church steps. Mr. Maxwell stood behind her, sneaking a peppermint to little Betty Hull, and Kathleen spied him giving the toddler an exaggerated wink. Mrs. Steadman looped her arm through her nephew's and insisted upon Kathleen walking with them, claiming she'd sent Carter and Isabel on ahead.

It was on that very Sunday, as they turned onto the lane leading up Croner Hill, that Mrs. Steadman stopped in the middle of the road and exclaimed, "Enough of this stodgy 'Mr. Steadman' and 'Miss McKenna' nonsense. There's no reason why you can't refer to one another by your given names whenever you are away from the confines of work." In order to keep peace with the dear woman, both Kathleen and Maxwell complied.

The following Sunday afternoon, Maxwell offered to escort Kathleen and Isabel to Kindred Hearts for their sewing circle. He stayed just long enough to slip a little green something into Miss Amy's hand and to give Ruthie a quick piggyback ride around the parlor. Still, Kathleen marveled at the difference between the awkwardness he displayed during his first Sunday visit to Kindred Hearts and the ease with which he now joined the girls in outright tomfoolery.

The more comfortable Kathleen grew in Maxwell's presence and the stronger their friendship grew, the greater her dread of that fast-approaching day when the *Steadfast*, replete with a suit of new sails, would carry him off to sea and out of her life.

Maxwell had no way of giving a specific date when he would return. He often discussed the host of reasons why he wanted to cut his trip short, but he had no way of predicting bad weather while at sea or foreseeing the myriad problems that might arise in the process of transporting the Irish immigrants.

Kathleen worried she might never see him again. If she could not convince her parents to let her remain in Eastead instead of joining them in Indiana, she might very well be gone before Maxwell returned.

During one of her many sleepless nights, as she lay groping for any possible solution to her dilemma concerning Amos Grundy and her parents' reunion plans, a crazy notion took seed. *If only Maxwell were to ask for permission to court me, I would have good reason for Ma and Pa to let me stay in Eastead and decline Mr. Grundy's advances.*

The idea no sooner sprouted than she valiantly endeavored to tamp it down with logic and reason. *Just because Maxwell seems to enjoy my company does not mean he has any romantic ideas in mind. He's never made any overtures along such lines.*

Yet when she almost had herself convinced of her fantasy's impossibility, her internal debate roared on. *If a Steadman could fall in love with a mill girl once, why couldn't it happen again?* And so, like the spring blossoms throughout the village, this bud of hope flowered and grew.

The day before Maxwell was slated to sail for Europe, Kathleen set out for Sunday service under weepy gray skies. An occasional raindrop trickled down the brim of her cornette and splattered onto her shawl while she slogged alone through the village streets.

She had dawdled through her morning constitution until all the other boarders had gone. Pegeen must have sensed her dark mood and her need for solitude. She hadn't pressed when Kathleen had urged her to go on ahead with Grace, promising to join them at the church.

As much as Kathleen wanted to savor each remaining moment in Maxwell's presence, she could not shake the feeling of impending heartbreak. Any hope of Maxwell asking to court her had all but withered away. She wondered if things would have been different had she found the courage to confide in him about Amos Grundy. Until the last few days, she'd felt it sufficient to inform Maxwell that, unless some pressing business kept her in Eastead, she would be joining her family in Indiana come fall. Whenever she talked of such things, he would stare at her and nod with a pensive look in his eye. She'd thought for certain he was on the verge of voicing the words she longed to hear, but those words never came.

While he had remained friendly all along, he had made no advances toward pursuing anything other than an amiable relationship. She realized now the full extent of her foolishness in thinking such a fairy tale might come true. Within a day, she would likely say a final fare-thee-well to the one man in her life with whom she never wanted to part company.

Throughout the worship service, Kathleen found her gaze ever wandering to the slumped form of Maxwell in the pew four rows ahead. Normally, he towered above everyone else, with his shoulders squared and his back erect; but on this Sunday, he bent his head low and seemed as deflated and somber as she. For the first time in more than a month, she had not been able to pick out his voice during the hymns. From her vantage point behind him, he didn't appear to be singing at all. She reasoned that his mind was probably racing with the details and preparations for his upcoming voyage.

Kathleen struggled to join in during Pastor Hull's lengthy prayer. She knew in her heart of hearts that God had not turned a deaf ear to her pleas. Even so, she fought an immature urge to pout when He was apparently answering no.

A patch of blue sky peeked through the clouds as Kathleen walked outside after the service. She ambled toward the cemetery to wait for the Steadman clan to exit the church. The girls from Kindred Hearts dashed by her on their way to Sunday dinner, a chorus of "see you laters" trailing after them.

Vivian Steadman was the first of her family to appear. Waving her lace-tatted handkerchief in the air, she trotted in short, wooden steps toward Kathleen.

"I hope you don't mind, Dear—" As she reached Kathleen's side, Vivian had to stop for breath before she could continue. She patted her chest and fanned her face with her hanky. "Carter and Isabel and I have just a very short call to make on Widow Pike. She's laid up in bed after taking a nasty spill, and we rode the buggy over this morning so we could drop her off a few groceries."

From the corner of her eye, Kathleen saw Maxwell leaning against a maple tree in the churchyard, and without warning, she felt a welling of hot tears threatening to spill over their banks. Kathleen hurriedly whisked them away as Vivian motioned for her nephew to join them.

"I know you aren't acquainted with the widow. Maxwell isn't, either. So I didn't think you would object to letting him escort you on to our house. We'll hurry home, full chisel, quick as the delivery's made."

During the past five weeks, Kathleen had never found herself alone in the company of Maxwell. The prospect left her trembling. A trap had been laid, set, and snapped by Vivian Steadman, and Kathleen had been ensnared before she could say a word.

Maxwell stepped in beside Kathleen as Mrs. Steadman excused herself and headed for the waiting buggy. Cupping his hand under Kathleen's elbow, he guided her in the direction of Croner Hill. "Please don't be upset over Aunt Vivian's blatant matchmaking." Maxwell looked toward the horizon as he spoke. "Actually, this is the one time I solicited her chicanery. You see—"

He stopped alongside the road, and Kathleen followed suit. She watched as he shoved his hands in his trouser pockets and began kicking at a half-buried stone in the soft earth. "Before I leave town, there's a matter I want to discuss with you in private. I have a request I want to make." He looked up at the sky, then back down to his shoes. With a final tap of his boot toe, he sent the stone skittering into the grass.

"I know this may come as quite a surprise to you, so I ask that you hear me out fully before you respond." He darted a glance toward her, and she indicated her agreement with a dip of her head.

"Since Carter has charted the path toward progressive thinking here in Eastead, I talked things over with him, and he assures me he thinks this is a great idea if you are open to it."

He gazed down at Kathleen, and his nervous smile sent fiery meteors blazing through her chest. Her heart began to pound with resurrected hope. She held her breath, afraid even the slightest movement would spoil the moment.

Once he spoke the words, she would breathe again.

Once he spoke the words, she would promise to wait for his return.

Once he spoke the words, she would write her folks with word of her postponed Indiana travel plans. When next she saw her family, she expected to be Maxwell Steadman's bride. Amos Grundy would have to find himself someone else to serve as his replacement wife and mother to his sons.

Maxwell looked left, then right, before taking a half-step to shorten the distance between them. Kathleen couldn't keep from shivering when he leaned toward her ever so slightly.

"I've pondered the possibilities for several weeks now. . . ." He seemed to delight in her growing tension. The weathered laugh lines around his molasses-brown eyes crinkled in merriment.

"Frankly, Kathleen, I've grown more and more certain of my decision with each passing day. Please excuse my choice of words—but you are the perfect man for the job."

She shot him a puzzled glare and silently mouthed, *What?*

"I want to hire you. You'll be the best overseer Steadman Shipping has ever had!"

Chapter 5

Weeks later, Maxwell stood on the *Steadfast's* deck at midship and looked out over the choppy waters of the Atlantic. At their present clip, they were on course for making this his fastest journey ever to Europe and back. Even so, it seemed to him that the days since he'd left home had dragged on without end.

The suspense of not knowing Kathleen's decision about her future tormented Maxwell's thoughts night and day. Even if they made the voyage in record time, he had no way of learning before they reached shore whether she'd still be in Eastead or would have already gone to join her family in Indiana as she had been contemplating.

He'd never thought he would tire of the salt air and surf breezes, but at present he would give it all up for the chance to spend time with Kathleen McKenna. Maxwell's vision blurred as he stared down at the swells, which rocked the ship gently from side to side.

The same sea that used to carry him to grand adventures and distant lands now seemed like a watery prison cell, placing him in solitary confinement away from the one person on earth he wanted to see. The very ocean he once thought he could spend his lifetime sailing upon taunted him by sparkling with the same shimmering green hue he'd seen dancing in Kathleen's eyes.

He recalled that when he'd presented his case for hiring her as overseer, he'd seen those green eyes of hers glisten with tears. He'd wondered from then until now if they were tears of joy or distress.

He had hoped she would accept the position on the spot. Instead, with a controlled voice and staid expression, she had said, "I'll give your proposition due consideration over the course of your absence. You'll have my response when you return."

If Kathleen had decided to reject his offer and had instead continued with her plans to leave in the fall, he simply had to return before she departed to try to change her mind. If she did agree to become Steadman Shipping's overseer, he had already determined to stay in town for as long as it took to see her situated and comfortable in her new post.

Ever since his frustrating encounter with Kathleen on the eve of his departure, Maxwell had been chastising himself for not discussing the job possibility with her earlier. But he had needed until that last day to convince himself he wasn't making a huge mistake. No matter how sharp Kathleen's business acumen, the idea of offering a woman the highest position in his company, second only to him, was not something he had readily come to accept.

Only after carefully weighing the benefits against the liabilities had he decided that hiring Kathleen would be worth the risk. Thanks to Carter, the area merchants with whom Kathleen would have dealings would simply chalk up her hiring as another Steadman idiosyncrasy. After all, if Carter could see his way clear to take a mill girl for a wife, then Maxwell could chance hiring one.

When Carter chose to make Isabel his wife rather than his employee, he made the far better choice. Perhaps you should have done the same. The thought circled round in his mind like a ship caught in a maelstrom. Maxwell tightened his grip on the railing to steady himself. He felt dizzy from imagining what Kathleen's answer might have been had his proposal been one of marriage instead of employment.

"Here now! It's help we're needin'. And fast!"

Maxwell turned to seek out the frantic cry and saw one of the Irish mill girl hirelings coming up the central hatchway from top steerage. When her gaunt form reached the deck and rushed over to him, he recognized her as Pegeen's sister, Francine.

"Oh, Mr. Steadman, Sir, beggin' your pardon, but we've urgent need of a doctor below." Despite her obvious desperation, the lass curtsied before him. "Can you point me to his quarters?"

"Cook Jaggers serves as surgeon in cases of emergency. I'll fetch him straightaway." Maxwell started for the ladder leading down to the galley but stopped and turned back to Francine. "May I tell him the nature of the distress?"

Color flooded the teenager's cheeks. "'Tis Molly, Sir. She's havin' a dreadful time with her birthing. Mrs. Hart's tried to do the midwivin' herself, but there's difficulties beyond her skills, so she sent me to fetch help. The bairn's having an awful struggle trying to enter the world, and Molly appears to be slipping away. We'd best hurry."

"Shall I send down some boiled water and rags?" Maxwell had never witnessed a delivery before, but he vaguely recalled having heard of these items being necessities.

"We're beyond that, Mr. Steadman. A doctor and a miracle are what she's needing now."

The gravity of the situation began to sink in. Maxwell called over his shoulder to the girl on his way down the hatchway leading to the galley. "I'll be back with Jaggers as quick as I can. Tell Mrs. Hart help is on the way."

◆ ◆ ◆

Three young women, one of them Francine, clustered in the narrow steerage passageway at the base of the steps. "Mrs. Hart says ye both should go on in," Francine said, pointing to a cabin door at the opposite end of the passageway.

Maxwell didn't see how his presence would be much help, but he kept his protests to himself. Staying close on the cook's heels, he squeezed past the ladies and followed Jaggers into the cramped quarters. As soon as Maxwell crossed over the threshold, the stench in the room made his stomach lurch.

A still form lay in the bottom berth along the port side, shrouded with a rag of a blanket. The wife of one of the ship's newly hired sailors stood at the bedside, her apron and skirts stained with blood. She held a small bundle in her arms.

"'Tis grateful I am of your making such haste, but our dear Molly is beyond helping now, God rest her soul." At the midwife's words, a tiny bleat of a cry rose from the bundle in her arms. "I did me best to save the new momma. I'm promising you, I did."

"I've no doubt," Maxwell offered. "You're to be commended for your efforts, Mrs. Hart." Tendrils of hair clung to the woman's perspiring forehead. Distress lined her face.

Cook Jaggers knelt beside the berth and touched the foot of the lifeless figure. "You did better than I could have done, Ma'am. I've never helped with a birthing before, so I doubt I'd have been much aid."

Maxwell stared at the moving blanket the midwife clutched. A feeling of utter despair and helplessness overwhelmed him at the scene he beheld. He thought of his brother, Lucas. Always before, he had ridiculed Lucas for throwing away a promising and lucrative business career to enter medical school. Rather than planning on being a physician to the wealthy, Lucas was determined to care for the poor. Suddenly Maxwell held a newfound appreciation for his younger brother. He finally understood why Lucas had chosen such a calling.

"The child." Maxwell's gaze was transfixed on the tiny bundle. "Will it live?"

"Aye. I'm thinking so. She's whole and hearty, and I'll see to her nursin' myself as my own Erin is nearly weaned."

"What of the woman's husband? Is he not onboard?" Maxwell didn't recall one of the new sailors having a wife named Molly, but he was still trying to learn all the men's names, much less those of their families.

Mrs. Hart shook her head. "No. Miz Molly said he died of the typhus back in Febr'ary. Said on his deathbed he'd made her promise to get out of Ireland 'fore the fever took her, too. When Miz Molly signed on as a mill girl back in Bray, she kept secret her being with child. None of us knew. She figured she wouldn't be allowed to immigrate if anyone found out, and she was desperate to provide her wee bairn a chance for a decent life." She gazed at the infant in her arms. "Poor thing doesn't stand much hope of that now, bein' orphaned and all. Whatever will become of the dear? I'd be takin' her in, but with five young'uns, Mr. Hart and me have more stomachs to feed than we can fill now."

Immediately, Maxwell thought of Amy Ross and the Kindred Hearts Orphanage. "I know someone in Eastead who'll give her a home. I'll make the arrangements once we reach shore."

"We've more pressing matters to tend at present." Jaggers rose and stepped back. "Miz Molly's body needs preparing before we can send her to her final resting place in the sea. Mrs. Hart, will you honor the deceased by sewing her final hammock about her?"

"Certainly."

"I'll fetch an extra from the forecastle." Jaggers had one foot over the threshold.

"Have you a needle and thread?"

"Aye. A short while afore, during the birthin', I had them right here at my feet. I fear in all of the panic, they got kicked under the berth." She cast her gaze about the room.

"I'll be fetching the hammock then while you search." The crusty old salt tipped the brim of his hat. "Mr. Steadman, no need for us both to be going." With that he was gone.

"Be a dear—" Before Maxwell knew what had happened, Mrs. Hart thrust the baby in his arms. Ignoring his blubbering protests, she dropped to her knees in search of the missing items.

"What am I to do with you?" Maxwell asked the teeny babe, frowning. "I've never held a baby before." Just then, the infant flung her miniature arms wildly about and managed to grab hold of Maxwell's shirt at the spot just over his heart. He broke out into a wide grin. Now he knew the meaning of the phrase "tugging at one's heartstrings." He marveled at the intricacy of God's handiwork as he studied the baby girl's delicate features and diminutive fingers. If she hadn't been too tightly wrapped, he would have counted her toes.

"Has she a name, Mrs. Hart?" Although Maxwell couldn't bear to take his eyes off the infant to see if the woman had found what she was looking for, he could still hear her rousting about on the floor.

"Alas, no," came a muffled response. "Before we could ask, her momma's soul had departed."

"What would you think of naming her 'Molly' then—in memory of the deceased?"

"I think ye have a fine idea, Sir." Mrs. Hart rose from the floor and shook the dust from her skirts. "Look-a here, but what the wee bairn hasn't taken to you!" the midwife exclaimed, stroking the fuzz of chestnut brown hair on the baby's crown. "Seeing as how she's sleeping snug in your arms, would you mind holdin' her awhile longer as I tend to her mother's final needs?"

◆　◆　◆

When the ship's bell signaled the first dogwatch, the off-duty crew and passengers gathered on deck for a brief committal service before releasing the body of Molly O'Fallon into the sea. The ship's captain, Gable Putney, read Scripture and said a few words before turning to Maxwell to pray. Though no one on board had known the deceased particularly well, all the women wept aloud. Maxwell, too, fought to keep tears at bay.

As the assembly disbursed, Maxwell saw Mrs. Hart and her children waiting for their turn to descend through the hatch leading to steerage. In her arms, she held the infant Molly.

"Might I have a word with you, Ma'am?" Maxwell called out to Mrs. Hart after excusing himself momentarily from his conversation with the captain. She sent her young crew of five down below and crossed the deck to stand before Maxwell and the ship's captain.

"I've been discussing with Captain Putney, here, the issue of the orphan's care. We both appreciate what you're prepared to do in looking after her. However, I feel we owe it to her departed mother not to expose the newborn to the unsanitary conditions of steerage until she's gained some strength." Maxwell wanted to catch a glimpse of little Molly, but Mrs. Hart held her close to her bosom and bundled up against the cool sea breeze.

"I offered the captain to give you my cabin, but he insists on being the one to move off the quarterdeck. We argued about this matter until he pulled rank and ordered me to comply with his command." Maxwell clicked his heels and jerked his right hand away from his brow in mock salute. "Cap'n Putney's bunking with his first mate so you can use his quarters until we reach America. He said he'd never be able to sleep with a crying babe in the cabin next to his anyway."

◆　◆　◆

With ever-increasing frequency, Maxwell found himself offering to look after little Molly so Mrs. Hart could tend to her own family's needs. He had plenty of time on his hands aboard ship, and he saw this as good experience. He planned to amaze everyone with his child-tending skills when he'd go to visit Molly at Kindred Hearts. He could just imagine Kathleen's shocked expression.

Often Maxwell carried the sleeping newborn from the captain's cabin next door to his own and tucked her into an open chest he'd converted into a makeshift crib. He spent his days caressing her delicate skin and memorizing Molly's tiny features, laughing when she puckered her rosebud lips. He marveled that the soft down of her hair matched the chestnut brown shade of Kathleen's. He swore they shared the same celadon green eyes as well, but Mrs. Hart assured him a baby's eye color would change.

By the time they sailed into Boston Harbor three weeks later, Maxwell had taken full charge of Molly's care. He relinquished his ward to Mrs. Hart only at feeding times and during the night's midwatch between midnight and four o'clock. He even mastered the art of nappy changing, though occasionally the odor made him gag. Still, he didn't mind suffering through the unpleasantries for the chance to watch this living, breathing miracle.

When the awe of holding the tiny infant overwhelmed him, he remembered back to the day he met Kathleen. Her words echoed in his heart and mind. He couldn't fathom then how she might ever think it possible to love a child born to another with the same devotion a parent had for a child of his own flesh and blood.

He had thought it most peculiar to consider the caring for an orphan anything other than an act of Christian charity. Now he was beginning to understand what Parson Hull had meant when he'd said he had received a greater joy and blessing from his newly adopted daughters than he could ever hope to give.

This tiny human being held the power to make Maxwell smile even while she slept. And each time Molly latched onto his index finger with the strength of a Lilliputian Goliath, he could feel his heartstrings cinch another notch tighter.

He hated to think of this special time coming to an end. Only his hope of seeing

Kathleen spurred him toward home.

◆　◆　◆

When the bell tolled the end of another workweek at the mill, Kathleen, in symphony with the other weavers, yanked the metal levers to the right of her loom. With a collective shudder, the machines ground to a halt. A deafening stillness ensued.

Kathleen came alongside Pegeen, and together they joined in the push for the door. Although they stepped into the full sun of a late summer day, the air felt cooler to Kathleen after leaving the stifling heat of the steam-powered mill.

"Grace ought to have arrived back home in Vermont 'bout now, given her stage met no delays," Pegeen said as they crossed the dirt road and headed for their boardinghouse.

"I expect you're right," Kathleen agreed. "And I also expect the next time we hear from her, she will have the title 'Mrs.' in front of her name." The fragrance of roses scented the air as they dashed up the stoop and passed Mrs. Cox's prized bushes on their way through the front door.

"I wonder who might take her place in our room." Pegeen climbed three stairs, then paused in midstride and looked back at Kathleen. She lowered her voice to a whisper. "I know I be awful for e'er even thinkin' such things, but I hope whoever joins us possesses a mite sweeter disposition."

Kathleen kneaded her bottom lip to keep from breaking into a wide smile. Her whisper matched Pegeen's. "I have to admit, I've wished for the same myself." So far, she had managed to keep from leaking even the slightest hint of the surprise she hoped would greet Pegeen one day soon. However, with Grace now gone and Pegeen's speculations growing, Kathleen feared that the secret would be increasingly hard to keep.

Abruptly Pegeen stopped moving when she opened their bedroom door, and Kathleen plowed into the Irish girl's back. A squeal split the air. Kathleen worried she'd injured her friend, but before she could express her concern, Pegeen screamed out, "Francine!"

A teenaged version of Kathleen's roommate, dressed in a threadbare gown, leaped up from the edge of the bed and ran toward Pegeen. The two sisters shared hugs and kisses, tears and laughter. Then they stood back, looked at each other, and started the celebration all over again. Kathleen tried to observe the reunion from the hallway but could hardly see for her own happy tears.

"Ooch! Ye have to be tellin' me now." Pegeen pinched Francine's cheek playfully, followed by a gentle love pat. "Who? I mean, what? How can it be that you're here?" In her sister's presence, Pegeen's brogue was thicker than Kathleen had ever remembered hearing before.

"From what I'm understandin', your roommate played more than a wee part in the idea." Francine tipped her head in greeting toward Kathleen, while Pegeen just stared with her mouth agape. "Might'n you be the fair Kathleen I've been hearing so much about? If so, I'll be forever beholden for your kindness."

Kathleen tried to dismiss the embarrassing accolades with a wave. "I did nothing but suggest your name to the two Mr. Steadmans when I heard of their plans to hire new workers from Bray."

"Mercy! Your mention of the Steadman name is remindin' me, I made Mr. Steadman a promise to give ye this note first thing upon our meeting." Francine reached into her pocket and withdrew an embossed note card bearing the Steadman Shipping crest on its wax seal.

As Kathleen accepted the note, heat flooded her cheeks. She felt her knees starting to give way, so she moved to sit down on her bed.

"I'll be going to introduce Francine around to the other girls and giving you a private moment to read." Pegeen offered Kathleen an understanding smile as she tugged her sister toward the door.

Maxwell is home. The realization brought an instant smile.

During the first month after Maxwell's departure, Kathleen had been so heart-broken and embarrassed by her misinterpretation of his feelings for her, she'd set her mind to heading for Indiana before he returned. She had even penned a letter to her parents in which she said she would be willing to consider the courtship of Mr. Grundy when she arrived. Yet, that letter—like all the others—never got mailed.

The longer Maxwell's absence dragged on, the more Kathleen's heart yearned to see him again, until her longing to be in his presence eventually overcame her embarrassment. She determined to accept the overseer's position after all. She must be near him, even if it meant as one in his employ rather than as the one he loved.

She had sealed her decision by finally posting a response to the letter she'd received from her mother more than two months earlier. Kathleen wrote her parents of the rare opportunity she'd been given to serve as the Steadman Shipping overseer. She begged for their understanding of her being unable to join them in Indiana in the fall. Then she asked that they express to Mr. Grundy the honor she felt at his asking to court her—and to please pass along her sincere apologies at having to decline. With one last look at the daguerreotype, she had slipped it in the envelope and breathed a sigh of relief when she handed it over to Mr. Mathers at the mill store to be mailed.

Now, she was ready for a new chapter of her life to begin.

Kathleen traced over the wax imprint on Maxwell's note before breaking the seal. A quiver raced through her as she began to read the bold script written by Maxwell's hand.

> *Dear Miss Kathleen:*
>
> *If you find it convenient, I should like to meet with you this evening prior to the supper hour. Aunt Vivian and Isabel asked me to mention that they will have a place set for you at the table. They hope you can stay and dine with the family after we conclude our business.*
>
> *Best Regards,*
> *Maxwell Steadman*

She knew he had only business in mind. No doubt he wanted to learn her response to his offer of the overseer's job. Still, the thought of seeing Maxwell again after all this time left her trembling.

Kathleen quickly changed into the mint-julep green gown she'd sewn from her new allotment of material. Then she made her excuses to Mrs. Cox as to why she'd be missing supper and headed out the door. Above the chatter of the other boarders, Kathleen could hear the laughter of Pegeen and Francine floating through the sitting room's open window as she passed by.

Kathleen expected a servant to answer when a short while later she pounded the brass knocker on the door of the Steadman mansion. Instead, the appearance of Maxwell sent her pulse racing and left her mouth dry. She had forgotten just how small she felt when standing this close to him.

"Welcome home, Mr. Steadman," she said. After the tension of their last meeting and their lengthy separation, Kathleen no longer felt comfortable calling him by his first name. Suddenly she couldn't think of what else to say. In the looming presence of Maxwell, Kathleen found herself unable to think at all.

"Thank you. I'm happy to be back in Eastead." Maxwell motioned for her to come inside and pushed the door shut behind her. "I'm glad to see you. It was so good of you to come on such short notice."

They stood alone in the expansive marble foyer, although Kathleen could hear noises coming from the library. She thought sure she must be imagining it, but Maxwell seemed as nervous as she. He kept glancing toward the library, then down the hall. He ran his finger around the inside of his collar and tugged.

He cleared his throat before he spoke again. "When last we talked, we left some business unfinished."

Finally, he let his gaze rest on Kathleen, and her insides withered under his scrutiny. Determined not to let her tumultuous emotions show, she put on her most serious expression and gave him a quick nod.

"Let's step into the parlor, shall we?" Maxwell motioned for her to lead the way.

Kathleen poised herself on the edge of the divan, while Maxwell began to pace back and forth on the marble hearth of the cold fireplace. He paused and drew a deep breath.

"I would like to re-address the matter of the position at Steadman Shipping, which we discussed prior to my departure."

As he spoke, Kathleen thought through her response. Her mouth felt so dry, she only hoped her voice wouldn't crack when she accepted the job. She wanted him to think she could be the epitome of professionalism.

"A situation has arisen."

Kathleen jerked her full attention to Maxwell. He was staring at her with a strange look in his eye.

"I have reconsidered my previous offer."

What is he saying? Would he dare deny me the overseer position now? She felt her jaw clinch as a flash of anger shot through her, followed by a heart-piercing pain.

She dropped her gaze to her lap so he wouldn't notice her welling tears.

"I have another proposal. . . . What I believe to be a more suitable arrangement for us both. . ."

He lifted an armless chair and positioned it opposite her, then took his seat and scooted forward so close, his face was within inches of hers. His intent stare forced her to meet his gaze. She felt certain he could hear her heart pounding. Or was she hearing his?

"For weeks I thought about asking you to be my wife when I returned. I had decided if you said yes, I would curtail my travels as much as possible and stay right here in Eastead so I might be near you—and eventually a house full of children. . . ." Maxwell's voice trailed off, and he gave her a slight smile.

"I thought you needed to know these were my thoughts before a sweet Irish lass named Molly came into my life."

At Maxwell's mention of another woman, Kathleen felt the color drain from her face. To her horror, he didn't stop there.

"Please wait here for a moment. There's someone I want you to meet." Maxwell stood abruptly and walked out of the room.

A crushing heaviness filled her being. She feared she might faint. She could not imagine how any man could be so cruel. First, to tell her he'd considered speaking the very words she so longed to hear, only to crush her hopes and shatter her heart—and then to insist on introducing her to the woman who had won his affections away from her. She longed to run before he returned, but her absolute shock kept her frozen in place.

Only a few moments had passed when Kathleen heard Maxwell's heavy footfall on the foyer's marble tile outside the parlor door. *This Molly must have been waiting in the library,* she thought, *eager to swoop in and gloat over her conquest of Maxwell.* The vengeful thought no sooner flashed through Kathleen's consciousness than a pang of guilt ensued.

"God, grant me the ability to be gracious, though I feel anything but," she whispered in prayer. "In my hurt, don't let me lash out at this innocent woman—or Maxwell, either, for that matter."

Determined not to let her emotional state add to her humiliation, she squared her shoulders, drew a deep breath, then rose to meet the woman Maxwell loved.

◆　◆　◆

Maxwell hurried across the foyer and into the library, where Isabel stood waiting for him to take Molly from her arms. He grimaced to think how badly he had bungled his attempt to explain things to Kathleen.

He'd thought it necessary to express what his intentions had been before Molly entered his life because he never wanted Kathleen to think he proposed marriage to her just to give his Molly a mother. Still, he knew he'd left her totally befuddled in the parlor just now. He only hoped she'd forgive him once she fully understood.

"Miss McKenna, I would like to introduce you to Miss Molly O'Fallon—soon to be Molly Steadman, if I have my way."

Kathleen appeared to be studying her hands. At his words, she slowly lifted her gaze to look at him. Her composed demeanor gave way to a look of shock.

"Why, it's a baby!"

"Yes. Didn't I make that clear? During our ocean crossing, little Molly here was orphaned minutes after her birth." Maxwell made shushing sounds to soothe the baby's mewings as he moved to close the distance between Kathleen and him.

Reaching to pull the blanket away from Molly's face, Kathleen leaned in to get a closer look. "But my, she is beautiful. Poor, sweet dear. What's to become of her? Will you turn her over to the care of Miss Amy at Kindred Hearts?"

"Perhaps you didn't understand me a moment ago. I plan to make Molly my daughter and spoil her royally." Maxwell laughed, and the baby started in reaction to the sound, then stilled. "You'll hear all the details in due time. I've decided to reopen my parents' old place on the east side of Croner Hill and make a home for us there. Arrangements have already been made with the woman who served as the baby's nursemaid aboard ship to continue in that capacity." The serious gaze Molly transfixed on him reminded him so much of Kathleen, he laughed again.

He offered the precious bundle for Kathleen to receive. With tendermost care, she took the baby from his arms.

"Kathleen, about that job we discussed—" Maxwell paused, and Kathleen looked up from Molly to gaze into his eyes. He swallowed hard against the lump forming in his throat. Here, right in front of him, were the two most cherished ladies in his life.

"About the job?" Kathleen urged him on with a lift of her eyebrows and a nod.

"Right. About the overseer's position." He took a deep breath and began again. "I've decided there must be a man somewhere out there who can fill that vacancy. But, Kathleen, I could never find another person on earth who can fill the role I'm proposing to you now."

Maxwell stroked Molly's chestnut hair. As he did, his hand brushed against Kathleen's. "From the first day I met you, I admired your good business sense. I've always appreciated your intelligence. Yet as much as I value those qualities in you, I've come to realize in these past months away from you, my feelings go much, much deeper than that."

A tear trickled down each of Kathleen's cheeks, but Maxwell knew by her radiant countenance, they were tears of joy.

"You are a woman of immense heart, Kathleen, always giving yourself freely to everyone you meet." He brushed her tears away with his thumb.

"I've seen how you care for those in need. Just by watching you, I've learned what a genuine Christian should be. You've taught me the true meaning of love."

He patted the blanket around Molly's chest. "You are the one who planted the idea in my mind that a man can love an adopted child with the genuine love of a father. If I hadn't met you, I am quite certain I never would have ventured to let this little girl twist my heart into knots."

The baby chose that moment to let out a squeak, but Maxwell kept his gaze fixed on Kathleen.

"I love you, Kathleen. I can't imagine living my life without you by my side. Please, would you marry me? Be my wife and the mother to whatever children God brings into our lives." He searched her celadon green eyes and found his answer before she spoke the word.

"Yes," she whispered. "It's the only Steadman position I ever really wanted to hold."

Maxwell tenderly encompassed Kathleen and Molly in his arms. "Good, because you are the only woman I ever want to hold." He leaned over the sleeping infant and brushed Kathleen's lips with a kiss.

SUSAN DOWNS

As the wife of a minister, Susan Downs has lived in towns, big and small, all around the world—from her childhood village in Oklahoma to such eclectic states as Indiana, Missouri, Massachusetts, New York, Ohio, and Texas, and even in faraway lands like South Korea. And yet, no matter what her address, wherever her husband of forty-three years is, that's where she calls HOME. Currently, Susan resides in Texas and she is employed as a fiction editor for Guideposts Publications.

A Second Glance

by Donita Kathleen Paul

Dedication

To Case Tompkins and Evangeline Denmark.
Your encouragement reminds me
who is our Lord and King.

Chapter 1

Ginger Finnegan ignored the noise she heard coming from behind the chicken coop. She tilted her head and a lock of straight hair fell out of the bun at her nape. It draped over her cheek like a copper curtain against the afternoon sun. With her fingers she felt the damp material in her hands, systematically exploring the folds and seams until she came to the collar. Satisfied, she snapped the wet nightgown in front of her and reached up to grasp the laundry line. She secured the garment with wooden peg pins and felt inside the basket to pull out another piece.

Just before she shoved the half-filled laundry basket, she heard the noise again, this time from behind the shed. Her foot nudged the basket across the trampled grass. She followed the line with her hand and hung the next gown.

Those rascals are getting closer, Lord. What mischief be in their conniving little hearts? Well now, perhaps me an' Your sweet Holy Spirit can convince them of the error of their ways. For it is sure I am, they're up to no good.

As she hung the next wee nightgown on the line, Ginger first hummed and then began to sing an Irish blessing song she'd learned at her granny's knee:

> *Ah Father, Your goodness to me*
> *   exceeds all that could be*
> *expected to come to some*
> *   who bow to Your majesty.*
>
> *I thank Ye for home and hearth,*
> *   for family and friends*
> *who add to the warmth*
> *   of living me life for Thee.*

Ginger had a fair idea of who would be most likely to plot a prank against her. She cheerfully entered the little girls' names into her song:

> *For Patty and Opal, me dears,*
> *   who lighten me day*
> *with joy and a cheerful way,*
> *   I ask more blessings*

from Your giving heart
  to strengthen them while they play.

And Aunt Amy, Lord, Your kind servant,
  sharing Your love so rare,
may I never cause this good lady
  a minute of shame or despair.

Having planted the seeds she intended, Ginger trilled over the notes of a chorus and went on to the other verses with words her granny had actually sung. At the end of the laundry line, Ginger carefully took a step back and reached up to find the second line.

"You knew we were here, didn't you, Ginger?" Patty called from behind the shed.

"Yes, I did." Ginger repositioned the basket so she could scoot it ahead of her in the opposite direction as she continued hanging the clothes.

A coppery-red head popped out from behind the shed. Although Ginger only saw an outline, she imagined the tight curls glistening in the sunlight and the disgruntled look on her eight-year-old sister's face. Another form emerged beside her sister.

"How do you do that?" asked Opal. Dark hair, dark eyes, skin tanned by the sun, she always shadowed Patty wherever she went each day. Ginger grinned as she saw with her limited vision that Opal at this distance literally appeared as her sister's shadow. At seven years of age, Opal followed Patty as the older girl's willing slave and accomplice.

"Oh, the Lord's been generous with me hearing because me eyesight's so poor."

"We were extra awfully quiet," said Patty with a sigh.

"And do I dare ask what dire deed ye were going to do once ye'd snuck up on me?" Ginger hung another gown.

The two little girls giggled.

"I have a snake," said Patty. "Wanna see?" Ginger suppressed a shudder and nodded. She left the laundry and moved to the back porch steps. Sunshine drenched the area, and Ginger could see the gray mass before she reached out a hand in a habitual gesture of affirmation. She hated to appear awkward just as much as she hated to appear squeamish.

The girls followed her to the stoop. As soon as Ginger sat with her hands held out, Patty placed their captive in her palms. Patty and Opal plopped down on the step to watch her.

Ginger slid her fingers along the warm, dry scales of the foot-long snake.

"Ye've had him awhile, have ye not? He's too dry to be good for him."

"We caught him after breakfast," said Patty.

"And where did ye have him during our midday meal?"

Both girls giggled.

"Well then, maybe ye better not tell me."

The girls giggled even harder.

Ginger held the snake close to her face and turned him in the light.

"Can you see the stripes, Ginger?" asked Patty. "He's got thin yellow stripes. One on his back and two on his sides. I named him Homer."

"Mostly I see the black," said Ginger. "But up close I can see his stripes. I'm thinking he's a ribbon snake, and one we will call a dead snake if ye don't put him back where he belongs."

"How do you know he's a boy snake, Ginger?" asked Opal.

"You're the one who said 'he' when you gave him to me."

Patty sat up straighter, ready to impart her superior knowledge. "All snakes are boys."

Ginger raised her eyebrows and turned her face to her little sister. "How is it that God made only boy snakes, Patty?"

Patty sighed her exasperation. "He wouldn't make anything that ugly and make it a girl. He just wouldn't. God is very nice."

"But God is nice to everyone, Patty, no matter what they look like. It wouldn't be nice for all the boy snakes if God hadn't made them girl snakes for company."

"How come you don't keep company, Ginger?" asked Opal. "Mary's younger than you, and Jeff Miller comes over to sit in the parlor and keep her company. How come nobody keeps you company? Is it 'cause you're blind?"

"Not blind," interrupted Patty, indignantly. "Just near-blind. And no, men don't want wives that are near-blind 'cause of all the things they can't do. Ginger's the only old girl not working in the factory. That shows you she's not gonna be able to keep a house and raise kids. She and me are going to live with Auntie Amy forever and take care of orphans forever and ever."

"I'm perfectly happy to take care of orphans forever and ever, Patty," said Ginger, giving her sister's shoulders a hug with one arm while roughing up her curly red locks with the other. The snake lay in a coil on her apron. "But I'm thinking some handsome young man will charm ye into becoming his wife someday."

"Nope," said Patty with confidence. "If I don't stay and take care of orphans, I'm gonna go out west and see that Mississippi River."

A skittering racket came from above and behind them.

"What's that noise?" Ginger stood abruptly and turned to peer up at the house. The girls bounced to attention beside her.

"Uh-oh," said Opal.

"Alys, you climb right back in that window!" ordered Patty.

"Alys," called Ginger, unable to see more than a dark shape against the white of the clapboards. "What are you doing?"

"She's climbing down the porch roof, Ginger," said Patty, used to being her sister's eyes. "She's gonna break her fool neck."

"Laura and Rissy barred the door so I couldn't get out," called Alys, her angry voice cracked with emotion. "They said they was gonna starve me 'til I let 'em play with my Pennydoll."

"Alys, go back," urged Ginger. "We'll come up and unbar the door."

"She's got Pennydoll under her arm, Ginger. She can't hold on good," announced Patty.

"Oh dear! I'm gonna go get Auntie Amy," cried Opal, and she bolted into the house.

Ginger squinted, trying to see if the little girl was going back to the window. The dark upright form suddenly fell flat against the slanted roof of the porch.

"She's sliding!" screamed Patty.

Ginger quickly sidestepped until she stood directly below the falling girl. With a clatter and whoosh, Alys flew off the edge of the roof and landed on Ginger, knocking her down.

◆   ◆   ◆

Ginger remembered raising her arms in a dual effort to catch little Alys and protect her face. Apparently she had not been successful at either endeavor. With her head swimming and a cacophony of voices clamoring about her, she tried to sit up.

"No, stay down," ordered the familiar voice of Aunt Amy.

Ginger gratefully leaned back on the grass. She tasted blood and felt nauseated.

"Hold this under her nose, but don't smother her," Aunt Amy said.

Immediately a cloth covered Ginger's mouth and nose. She instinctively knocked the arm away that held it.

"Ginger, you're bleeding all over," complained Patty. "I gotta hold this under your nose."

Shadows shifted above Ginger, and a competent hand reapplied the cloth. "Like this, Patty."

"What happened, Auntie Amy?" Ginger reverted to calling the woman the name the little girls called their guardian.

"Alys has broken her arm and your nose. Jess ran to get the doctor."

Ginger groaned. "Not Dr. Morris," she muttered, but Amy Ross had left her side, presumably to attend the younger victim of the accident.

"I'll protect you, Ginger," whispered Patty. "He's a grubby old man, and I hate him!"

"Ye shouldn't hate, Patty. Granny taught us better. Aunt Amy's taught us better. And Jesus, Himself, tells us to love our enemies."

"I'm still gonna sit right with you and not leave even for a minute. Even if Dr. Morris tells me the house is afire, I'm gonna sit right there with you."

Patty's free hand clutched Ginger's sleeve. Ginger lightly clasped the tight fist. "Ye know the man would never do me harm, Patty. He's just a gruff soul with no feeling left in his heart. May the Lord bless him and give him kindness."

"He made you cry." Patty sobbed and laid her head on her big sister's shoulder.

Ginger put an arm around her thin frame and squeezed gently. "'Twas me own stubborn heart that caused the grief, Little Patty. I refused the grace God had given me for the moment and stormed against His will."

"Dr. Morris said you weren't worth his time to look at your eyes."

"That was his ignorance speaking, me girl. If I weren't worth much, God's own

Son wouldn't have bothered to die for me sins, now would He?"

Ginger heard Aunt Amy's approach. Her skirts rustled and a smell of lavender water announced her presence.

"Can you stand, Ginger?" she asked, placing her hand soothingly on the girl's shoulder. "We've taken Alys inside to wait for the doctor. You'll be more comfortable in the parlor, too."

Ginger sat up with the help of both Aunt Amy and Patty.

"I know the blood is alarming," Aunt Amy acknowledged to the younger girl, "but your sister's going to be all right. She isn't fatally injured."

"She tried to catch Alys, Auntie Amy."

Aunt Amy took the blood-soaked cloth as she helped Ginger to her feet.

"I know, and Alys might have broken more than her arm if your sister hadn't broken her fall."

"Auntie Amy, Dr. Morris is mean." Patty's voice trembled. "You won't let him hurt Ginger, will you?"

"Patty," protested Ginger, but dizziness and a wave of nausea prevented her from saying more.

Patty persisted, "You won't let him touch her eyes, will you?"

"He'll examine her, Patty. Ginger looks like she's going to have two black eyes. Why ever are you so upset?"

"Last time he hurt her. He poked and pulled her eyelids and told her she was blind as a bat and should have been drowned when she was born."

The horrified gasp from her guardian roused Ginger to respond. She hugged the form gone rigid beside her.

"It's all right, Aunt Amy. It was a long time ago."

"It most certainly is not all right," said her mentor, returning the hug. "He shall not be allowed to say such outrageous, hurtful things during this visit."

The back door swung open and Rissy's strident voice rent the air. "Hurry, Auntie Amy. The doc's coming in the front door with Jess."

Chapter 2

Aunt Amy guided Ginger to the sofa by the window, ordering her to lie down with her feet up.

"Patty, run and get your sister a fresh cloth." Aunt Amy walked across the room and greeted someone at the door. Ginger listened for the taciturn doctor's nasal tones.

"I'm Dr. Steadman."

The pleasant voice surprised Ginger. A new doctor? She longed to see what he looked like, but moving her head made her nose throb. She closed her eyes. As soon as Patty returned, she'd ask for a description.

Meanwhile, Ginger breathed a sigh of relief. She always tried to alleviate Patty's worries and hide her reaction to the old doctor, but in truth, her stomach turned to stone just at the mention of his name.

"Dr. Morris said he wouldn't come, Aunt Amy," Jess explained. "I passed Mrs. Miller in the lane, and she said this Dr. Steadman had set up shop by the apothecary. And he come right away."

"Came right away," Amy corrected. "I see he did, and we're grateful." She turned to the girls hovering inside the doorway. "Shoo, now. You can wait in the hall or on the porch. We'll tell you as soon as we can how Ginger and Alys are faring. Don't worry now. The good Lord is caring for them."

"I brought Alys her Pennydoll," said Laura. "She dropped her in the hall."

"Thank you, Dear," said Aunt Amy.

All but Patty reluctantly left. Aunt Amy nodded her approval. "You can stay with your sister."

Ginger lay still, listening intently to the doctor's every word. In between the soothing flow of Amy's comforting patter, the doctor interjected a bare minimum of instructions and comments. He uttered each sober phrase with the same lack of warmth. Alys whimpered and then cried out as the doctor straightened the arm. Amy's voice droned on, distracting the young patient with nonsense about her special doll and the dessert Auntie Amy planned for the evening meal. But the doctor offered no sympathy.

Ginger set her jaw. This man's voice sounded younger than old Dr. Morris. And his steps across the room had been firm and steady, unlike the old doctor's shuffle. But his heart beat without the compassion of the Divine Healer.

Ginger imagined Jesus, the Great Physician, taking Alys into his arms, holding

her on his lap, and cuddling away the fear and pain.

Pulling Patty closer, Ginger asked, "What does he look like?"

"He's young, and he looks like Maxwell Steadman, only shorter. He looks strong and he doesn't smile at all. Do you suppose he thinks Alys is gonna die?"

"Surely not! She hasn't had time to sicken. Perhaps he is a man who never smiles a'tall."

"He's too young to be so gloomy," objected Patty.

"Well, he hasn't said anything mean like old Dr. Morris." Ginger would give him that.

"That may be because our auntie Amy's standing right beside him."

"And it may be because he says hardly a word a'tall."

"Sh!" warned Patty. "I think he's done."

"This is to help the child sleep." His voice had a pleasant timbre even if the words were spoken with no enthusiasm. "Drink it all," he instructed.

"It's nasty," complained Alys.

"You've had a nasty fall, so you have to drink the nasty medicine."

Was that supposed to be encouraging? Ginger sighed loudly. *Oh, merciful Father, send Your comforting Spirit to this man, and put a tad of compassion in his voice when dealing with Your precious little ones.*

She saw Dr. Steadman and Aunt Amy walk away from the patient.

Patty patted Ginger's arm. "I'll be right back." She moved over to the other sofa where her friend Alys lay quietly.

"Pennydoll's going to like staying in bed for awhile." Patty kneeled on the hard wooden floor. "She doesn't like adventure very much."

Alys sniffed. "We can do spelling words. Pennydoll's good at spelling."

Patty nodded. "And Auntie Amy will let me bring tea up to you tomorrow when you feel better. We can have a tea party in your room."

"Patty, you aren't mad at me, are you?"

"No, Alys. Why would I be mad at you?"

The voices faded into secretive whispers.

In a minute, the doctor carried Alys up to her bedroom, with Aunt Amy showing the way.

Well, that would be a point in his favor over Doc Morris, thought Ginger. *The old doc wouldna' have gone out of his way to help our aunt Amy.* A new idea occurred to her. *Oh now, Lord, that would be an interesting thing. Suppose the young doctor took notice of our charming widow. Perhaps he would court her. 'Tisn't right that someone so kind and generous not have a man to love and cherish her.* Ginger sighed and pushed aside the ugly loneliness that swelled in her breast. *None of that, Ginger Finnegan. 'Tis your lot to love the children, and 'tis a good life the Lord has provided.*

Patty came back to her big sister.

"Why did Alys think you would be mad at her?" asked Ginger as soon as they were alone.

"She thought she near killed you 'cause you been so still." Patty shoved Ginger

with her hip to gain more room as she sat on the edge of the sofa. "She says she nearly cried when she heard you make a noise 'cause before that she thought you were laid out like her mama was when she died."

"Poor thing. Maybe I can help Aunt Amy bake her a berry tart for your tea party tomorrow."

"One for me, too?"

Ginger could hear the grin in her sister's voice.

"Sure, and I'll be making one very wee tart for me own sister when I make one for her friend."

"How wee?" asked Patty.

"So wee, I'll be cutting a blackberry in two in order to fit it in the crust."

Patty giggled and then became very quiet as the heavy footsteps of a lone man descended the stairs. The sisters reached to hold hands as they faced the doctor without Aunt Amy's fortifying presence.

He entered the room without a word and went to gather his things into his bag at the other sofa. As he straightened, the sunlight from the window behind him outlined his form plainly for Ginger. Dark hair topped a short and stocky build. Without being able to see clearly, Ginger knew the bulk of him was muscle, not flab, for he moved gracefully for a man. He walked over and set his bag on the floor beside Ginger.

"You'll have to move." He addressed Patty and turned to move a straight-backed chair to sit in while he examined his next patient.

Patty's hand tightened around Ginger's.

The chair dropped with a thud beside the sofa.

"Move aside." His deep voice held no patience.

"No," said Patty.

"What's this?" The doctor's voice dropped into a heavy growl.

"I won't let you hurt my sister."

"I'm not here to hurt your sister. I'm in the business of healing." He sat in the chair.

"No, you can't touch her until Auntie Amy comes. I'll defend her to the death. I'll bite you and scratch you and kick you."

"Patty!" Ginger tried to sit up, but Patty lay across her midsection and had successfully wedged Ginger into the crack between the seat cushion and the back of the settee. Ginger floundered briefly and gave up. With the pain in her face and her awkward position, sitting up to reprimand her sister was out of the question.

Patty sobbed. "She's my sister and all I have left in the world. We're nothing but lowly orphans, but we have each other."

"Cease this melodramatic drivel this minute," the doctor ordered. "Who's filled your head with such nonsense?"

"I read extensively to my children, Dr. Steadman. Patty particularly likes the poets." Amy entered the room and came to place her hand on Patty's back. "It's all right to allow Dr. Steadman to examine Ginger now, Patty. Your loyalty does you

credit. Your dramatics do not. Please compose yourself."

Patty slipped off the couch and stood beside her guardian. Auntie Amy put an arm around her.

"Well, then." The doctor cleared his throat. He reached for the cloth and removed the shield Ginger had unconsciously held tighter to her face.

"Here's the bowl of warm water you requested," said Mary. She'd entered the room with the smooth, quiet glide that characterized her. Dr. Steadman took the bowl from the older girl, and Ginger saw his nod without seeing his expression.

Can the man not utter a simple thank-you?

He turned back to his patient, and Ginger had to acknowledge his soothing touch did much to offset his reserved manner. He carefully wiped the dried blood from around her nose and cheeks and set the soiled cloth aside. Gentle fingers probed the swollen flesh below her eyes.

The doctor came into focus as he leaned close. Just inches from her face, his hazel eyes peered into her own. Ginger held still, wondering at the intensity of his gaze. Rarely did she have the opportunity to behold a stranger's countenance.

His warm breath against her cheek smelled of peppermint. She could see the tawny brown of his eyebrows and lashes and the darker stubble on his chin. Mesmerized by his nearness, Ginger studied the clean, strong lines of his face.

Then he spoke. "I see no damage to her eyes. There will be swelling, of course, and bruising. There's a heel print along this cheekbone. I think the girl's boot actually missed her nose."

His callous clinical tone stirred coals of anger in Ginger's breast. *He's got the chance to do Your good, Lord, and he's wrapped it up so tight it can't come out.*

"And are ye thinking I'm deaf as well as blind, Doctor?" she sputtered. "Ye talk as if I'm not lying here listening to every word. 'Her eyes, this cheekbone, her nose!' Well, it be me eyes, me cheekbone, and me nose. There be a person lying beneath the face ye be looking at, and the person would like the courtesy of being addressed in a polite manner, regardless of me being a meek and humble, poor, blind orphan."

Dr. Steadman recoiled against the verbal blast. "If you're meek and humble, I'd fear meeting your aggressive kinsmen," he said. A note of amusement lightened his tone for the first time. "And poor? None of you fortunate young ladies taken into Kindred Hearts are truly poor. I became a doctor to help the families of seafaring fathers and those who work in the mills. You're not blind, so the only veracity in your diatribe is that you're an orphan. I assume you told the truth there."

"Doctor," Amy interrupted. "Both Patty and Ginger are well acquainted with poverty. They were the first to come to me almost four years ago. Their father died in an accident, loading textile goods on a shipping dock. Their mother worked in the mills and wore her strong body down to a frail piece of humanity. A simple congestion carried her away. The little girls managed a living with their grandmother until that dear lady's passing." Amy paused to take a deep breath. "And as for being blind, Dr. Morris informed me the disease in Ginger's eyes was beyond anything medical science could treat."

"Bah!" said the young doctor as he snapped his bag shut. "Bring her to my office next week after the swelling has gone down, and I'll have a good look into her eyes. I suspect that she will benefit from strong lenses in otherwise ordinary spectacles."

Ginger held her breath. Could it be true? Surely not, not for someone like her.

She squinted, waiting for her guardian's response, straining to see the expression on Aunt Amy's face. She saw the rigid posture and wondered at the lady's outrage. She raised a hand to touch her mentor.

Aunt Amy let out a horrified gasp. "Be still, Ginger." Her voice quavered. "Don't move an inch. Doctor, take care."

"What is it, Mrs. Ross?" The doctor lost his arrogant tone as puzzlement invaded his speech.

"There's something moving in Ginger's pocket, the pocket of her apron. There! It moved again."

Ginger stiffened.

"What is it?" she hissed in a terrified whisper.

Patty giggled. She reached into the deep pocket and pulled out the ribbon snake. "It's Homer, Ginger. You had him on your lap when Alys came out the window."

Ginger relaxed, but Auntie Amy stepped back.

"Kindly return. . .Homer to his home, Patty. And I don't mean a drawer in your room. Take him outside where you found him."

"Yes'm." Patty scooted to the door.

"Homer?" The doctor sounded incredulous.

"I believe I mentioned that I read to the children."

"Yes, you did, Mrs. Ross. But I hardly thought *The Odyssey* would be one of your choices."

"My girls may come from unfortunate circumstances, but they each possess a fine mind."

The doctor rose. "I'm sure they do, Mrs. Ross. Now if you'll excuse me."

"Yes, of course, Dr. Steadman. I'll see you to the door."

Ginger grinned to herself as she watched the dark-suited form of the doctor follow Aunt Amy in her mauve day dress out of the room.

"Now, Lord, they be a wee bit prickly with one another, but they are of about the same age, and both easy on the eye." Ginger paused in her prayer to remember the doctor's fine hazel eyes and his stubborn chin. No doubt a'tall. To Ginger's way of thinking, he was a fine-looking man. "Aunt Amy could help him see the joy of Ye, Lord, and he could lighten her load, share the responsibilities, don't Ye know. Iffen it be Your will, Lord, a wee bit of romance wouldna' do them no harm."

Chapter 3

Sprinkles of rain dotted the dusty road in front of Dr. Lucas Steadman as he made his way up the lane toward the apothecary. In a few minutes he'd be in his office. He'd been fortunate to find rooms on a busy street, one where his shingle attracted attention. Nonetheless, it wasn't likely any patient would be waiting for him.

Eastead residents didn't necessarily respect old Dr. Morris, but they went to him out of habit. And perhaps they didn't trust a Steadman to be concerned for their welfare.

Lucas had too much time between patients. But with an office on a main street, his accessibility was beginning to be noticed. Most often business came to him second-hand. When old Doc wasn't available, the injured or sick came to him.

Lucas looked up at the clouds swelling in the sky. The invisible hand of the wind pushed them into banks of gray. For a moment he wondered if his prime location had been good fortune or the manipulation of family patriarch Maxwell.

Ah well, my goal is to help the people of Eastead. Does it really matter if Big Brother puts his oar in? If more of the poor people receive aid, that should be uppermost in my mind.

Lucas stopped beside the road, hunching his shoulders against the quickening rain. *But it isn't, is it, Lord? Your Scriptures say that we all sin and fall short of the glory of God. And I'm proving it. I certainly don't have Your forgiving nature. I don't like having my formerly wayward brother showering me with kindness.*

Just like the older brother in the parable of the prodigal son, I resent Maxwell. I see it, Lord. I know it's wrong, and instead of repenting, I grind my teeth over his generosity.

"Lucas! Lucas Steadman."

The sound of the friendly voice halted him at the corner of North Elm and Congress. He looked over his shoulder and lifted a hand to wave at his old schoolteacher, Mrs. Keller.

"You going to the square?" she asked as she hurried to catch up to him. Her black umbrella bobbed over her head, keeping time with her lively step.

"Yes, Mrs. Keller, and I'm hoping you'll walk with me." Lucas shifted his black bag to his other hand and offered to hold the umbrella for her.

She nodded, smiled with genuine friendship, and resumed her quick trot down the street. Caught off guard, Lucas snapped into motion to fall in beside her.

"Going back to your office?" she asked.

Lucas nodded, wiping the few raindrops off his face.

"I saw that fancy shingle." She turned her head stiffly and gave him a quick wink before focusing again on the street before them. "I always said you'd reach the goals you aimed for.

"Now your brother, Maxwell, I have to admit, has surprised me. You were the brother with all the sense. He was the brother with all the high spirits. Each of you had too much of a good thing. He needed some sense. You needed some humor. Now he's settled down and is showing some responsibility. What about you, Dr. Lucas Steadman? Have you discovered a smile or two in your heart?"

Lucas set his jaw. Getting into a conversation with a woman who'd known him since the first day he walked into the schoolroom had been a mistake. "Mrs. Keller, you know I never did see Maxwell's 'high spirits' as a good thing. He caused my parents grief. He caused the township grief. His pranks were destructive. I was embarrassed to be his brother."

"Ah, so you haven't changed."

Lucas didn't answer. Anything he said would spur Mrs. Keller on to make another unwelcome comment. Yet he couldn't be rude to her, either. This woman had listened for hours when in first grade he had grand schemes to travel the world. The next year, before and after school, he'd yammered on and on about being a journalist for the Boston paper. He'd report all the things he would see and share with people through the printed word. Third grade had toppled his ivory tower. In third grade Timothy O'Rourke stopped coming to school and started working to help support his family.

One afternoon, Lucas went looking for his friend Tim. He crossed the river for the first time. The wooden boards of Old Presser Bridge clapped like the footsteps of the Billy Goats Gruff. He hung over the rail and peered at the dark swirling waters. Throwing sticks into the current, he chuckled as he wondered what troll lived underneath, waiting to eat those passing over.

On the return trip he knew who the troll was. His father was the troll. Or maybe it was just the Steadman Shipping Line and not really his father who hammered hope out of the poor people in the shacks across the river. Surely his father didn't know the miserable conditions the families lived in.

In the middle of the dilapidated bridge, so different from the whitewashed bridge uptown, Lucas dropped his clean linen handkerchief in the water.

He did it on purpose.

His mother always made him carry the crisp white square of linen.

It floated for only a second on the turbulent river. First it took on the dingy brown color of the water around it. Then the current twisted it, tugged it under, and swept it away. Lucas couldn't have rescued it even if he'd tried. One puny scrap of cloth had no chance against the river. And Lucas was just a child watching.

Lucas thought about the tattered clothing, the ragged children in the houses behind him. He'd found Tim's home, but Tim was not there. His mother held a sick baby in her arms. Although the cloth wrapping the baby had been clean, the stains of years marked poverty as Lucas had never seen it before.

"I'm Tim's friend," he told the sad woman.

"Are you?" The words must have been hard to say. They sounded strangled.

"I miss him at school."

"Do you?"

Lucas looked at the limp child.

"Is that Maggie?"

"It is."

"Tim told me about her when she was born in the spring."

"He did?"

"Is she sick?"

"She's dying."

The breath stopped in his throat. He swallowed and breathed again.

"I'll get help."

She gave a lethargic nod and closed the door.

Lucas did try to get help. He went to the next shack and listened to an old woman's diatribe: no money for doctors, no medicine for sick children, no help for the needy. He didn't believe the crone's cynical words and ran to the next home. This man, with rheumy eyes and a toothless snarl, brought curses down on the Steadman name. He ranted at the unknown lad on his doorstep.

"Them two brothers are the devil's own. Misers! They got money for big, fancy houses, but look where we're living. We's the ones who break our backs."

Lucas hurried away, never saying he was the son of this horrible monster everyone hated. He kept pounding on doors and found no one to help.

"Go home to wherever you belong," said the last woman, not unkindly. "We know Lydia's Maggie will die tonight. She asked to be left to rock her child until her babe passes over. We won't disturb her as she says good-bye to little Maggie. Tomorrow we'll stand beside her in her sorrow."

Lucas made one last protest. "But she's alone."

"No, Lad, that she's not. The Lord is with her as she walks through the valley of the shadow of death." She gave his shoulder a gentle shove. "Go on home, now. Back where you belong. This is no place for the likes of you."

On the bridge Lucas watched the waters that carried away the handkerchief. A tangled clump of brush bumped against the bridge supports in the water. The dense, dark mass reminded Lucas of a troll. He watched it float downstream.

The troll was make-believe. His father was not a troll. His father didn't know, couldn't know, about Tim's mother and sister.

Lucas ran to tell him. He ran with all his might, even up Croner Hill. He ran all the way.

He burst in the front door and heard his mother's voice. Her friends laughed in the parlor. He ran past the open door, across the parquet floor, and up the polished stairs.

Lucas barreled into the library without knocking. His father sat at his desk.

Before he opened his mouth with a ready reprimand, Lucas poured out the story of his search for his friend, the dying sister, the sad mother, the angry neighbors—no doctor, no medicine, rags and tattered clothes, no heat, little food.

"And they say it is all your fault, Father. That you and Uncle keep all the money and don't give them any."

His father's face grew red. "You will not associate with such riffraff, Lucas. What was this boy doing at a school on our side of the river?"

"Father, Tim's my friend. Mrs. Keller likes him. He's smart as me."

"Nonsense."

Lucas didn't understand. Just what was nonsense? His friendship with Tim? Or was it that his teacher liked the poor boy? Maybe his father didn't believe that Timothy O'Rourke could be as smart as a Steadman. But the baffling "nonsense" word didn't drive his purpose from Lucas's mind.

"Father, you have to help. Send the doctor."

"Now calm down, Lucas, and listen to me. They wouldn't appreciate my interfering with their ways. Those people are different from us, Son. They have their own medicines—plants and roots and things." Father gestured vaguely with his hand. A fierce frown chased away the uneasy look on his face. "See here. They earn their wages, and I give them what's due without fail. This is preposterous—expecting me to give my money to them. I earn my money and have the right to spend it or save it or invest it as I see fit. They earn their money and spend it however they choose. No doubt much of it is spent on whiskey and dice."

His disapproving glare fell on his young son. "Go now, Lucas, and prepare yourself for supper. I don't want to hear another word of this. And you are forbidden to cross the river again until you are much older and have a realistic grasp of these things. Close the door with more decorum as you leave than you used opening it."

Grasp of what things? Lucas asked himself as he pulled the door shut.

He couldn't ask his mother. Soft laughter still rose from the first-floor parlor. He found his older brother.

Twelve-year-old Maxwell stopped what he was doing and actually sat down to explain the situation. "You've got it wrong, Lucas. They're the lucky ones. Oh, I don't mean not having any money. I wouldn't like that. But they don't have to wear ties and tight jackets and sit without squirming in the front pew of church. They don't have to go to school all day, every day, and they aren't expected to bring honor to their family name. Their mothers don't cringe when they belch. They don't have to be polite to a herd of old ladies. You just got a bad look at things. Don't worry."

"The people said the children die all the time, Maxwell. Lots of children."

"Well, I suppose they were exaggerating some. You know, embellishing a tale to make it more impressive."

Lucas nodded his head. Maxwell certainly got into trouble often enough for "embellishing" a tale.

Lucas left Maxwell and went to his own room. He tried to talk to his mother about it after supper, but she focused on how annoyed she'd been when he clattered into the house.

"I had company, Dear, and you entered just like a ruffian. You didn't acknowledge our guests, and you barged through the house. I know you wouldn't disgrace Mother on purpose. You must be more mindful of your manners."

"Tim's little sister was dying, Mother."

"I'm sure Tim's mother has lots of children, Lucas. She will find comfort in all the others. I don't see how you came to know this Tim. They have so many children, dozens. He shouldn't have been at our school. She may even feel relief that the poor girl is in heaven and she has one less to look after. I don't see why they want so many. I'll have to speak to Mrs. Keller about that boy. She'll know why he came over the river to school. It is most irregular. Of course that was last year, you say, and this year he is gone. Perhaps I won't pursue it. After all, if he is already not attending, it is neither here nor there."

Lucas couldn't press the real issue. His father came in, having smoked his evening cigar as he strolled through the gardens. He took his place in front of the fireplace, an elbow on the mantel, his foot on the andiron. He told an amusing anecdote from his day, and Lucas's mother and brother laughed. The evening progressed in a normal pattern.

To Lucas the stark difference between his comfortable, warm parlor and the desolate shanties across the river etched a line in his heart between right and wrong. His cheerful, unconcerned family stood on the wrong side of that line.

Chapter 4

L ucas smiled as he secured the bandage around Mrs. Miller's arm. She was the third patient he'd seen that day, and he'd just heard the front door open and close again.

"Change the dressing daily, Mrs. Miller. Use this salve." He handed her a squat brown glass jar containing a mixture he'd had the apothecary, Mr. Kranz, mix up to his specifications. Lucas felt good about showing him something new, and he was gratified that the older man had welcomed new ideas fresh from the University of Pennsylvania School of Medicine.

Lucas almost patted his patient on the shoulder but remembered his greatest hurdle establishing a medical practice in his hometown was familiarity. Too many of his prospective patients had watched him run through the streets chasing a hoop, or slide down the snowy hills, or limp home after falling into the canal.

Stiffly courteous, he put his hand under old Mrs. Miller's elbow and helped her to stand. "If you see any sign of infection, come back to me immediately."

"Oh, Mr. Lucas, I mean Dr. Lucas, it feels so much better." She opened her cloth reticule, extracted a large coin, and placed it in his hand. "I'm so glad you've come back to us."

Lucas tucked the half dollar into his vest pocket. His last payment he'd put in the shed behind the building. What was he going to do with two laying hens? Impatient to see who awaited him in the outer office, he edged Mrs. Miller out of the examining room.

At the end of a short hall a curtain of dark calico covered the doorway into the sitting room. Lucas pushed the cloth aside, allowing his patient to move through. Side by side on two straight-backed chairs sat the redheaded sisters from Kindred Hearts Orphanage.

He heard the little one whisper, "Mrs. Miller." The older nodded and stood to face his departing patient.

Lucas needed to straighten his only examining room before the Irish sisters came back. "I'll be with you in just one moment," he said.

The older girl's eyes shifted to him. He noticed their startling green color, much brighter than his own hazel eyes. Her unfocused gaze disturbed him. He should be able to do something about that, and the thought made him glad. Letting the curtain drop, he started back down the hall. He grinned as he heard Mrs. Miller's shrill voice.

"Oh, I burned myself, Dearie, rendering lard and just plain careless. You'd think at my age I'd know not to take my eyes off what I'm doing."

A murmured response didn't make it through the curtain. Lucas strained to hear the words as he gathered up the linen scraps he'd used to clean Mrs. Miller's wound.

Mrs. Miller's voice came clear into the back room. She evidently knew the girls from somewhere. In no hurry to leave, she continued in her usual friendly manner. "You know I used to work some at the big house when I was younger. Came in as an extra maid when Mrs. Steadman, the doctor's mother, had parties or houseguests. Oh my, she gave some mighty fine parties. It was a pleasure just to go and look at the fine clothes and pretty rooms. And to think her son chose to do something like doctoring."

Lucas carried the bowl of water to the window and hurled its contents out into the backyard. He rushed, wanting to get to his next patients before Mrs. Miller told them his entire personal history.

"And he's a good doctor, too. Not like old Arnold Morris."

Now that's good to hear.

"But it's odd, isn't it? A son of a wealthy family choosing to leave his family's business and mingle with the townspeople rather than stay in his own circles. His mother certainly had a busy social life. But he always was different. He was neat as a pin. His parents and brother, careless with their things. He always looked serious. His mother and brother, delighted with life, and his father looked angry."

Yes, that's true, but I've really got to interrupt this. He grabbed a rag and wiped away a smear of ointment from the examining table. *Everyone in this town knows too much about my background, and nobody understands why being their doctor is important to me.*

"All those years I tidied up after them, I never thought I'd be paying a Steadman for services rendered. Makes me feel odd."

Oh, no! Another reason why the townspeople find me hard to accept as a doctor.

"Now his dear mother doted on him even as serious as he was and her being such an important hostess and a little flighty, if you know what I mean. People came from all over the East Coast to her parties, you know."

One of the girls spoke in a low murmur. A pause followed, and Lucas stopped what he was doing, hoping to hear the front door open and shut. Relieved that Mrs. Miller might finally be done spilling his family secrets, Lucas opened a cabinet and stored the last remaining bottles cluttering the countertop. His hand patted the wood above the drawer containing his collection of spectacles with lenses of various strengths.

Lord, I pray that it be Your will to give this young woman the gift of sight. Last summer, I thought I had been a fool to buy Barker's entire stock of spectacles. Now I see Your hand in my friend Barker's decision to dash off to Georgia mere months after he opened his shop in Philadelphia. I trust we have the right pair for the Irish orphan. Won't she be surprised?

"Some of the entertaining I'm sure had to do with business." Mrs. Miller's strident voice broke into his thoughts, and his sense of peace evaporated.

"The Steadman Shipping Line is very important," she continued. "But some of those people were political, straight from Washington, D.C.

"She was a debutante from New York City before she was Mrs. Steadman and had money from her family. And they say when she passed, she gave it all to her second-born son, Lucas, now our doctor. It was in her will. Imagine a woman having enough to call her own to do something like write out a will."

Lucas juggled the wet rag in his hand, frantically looking in the corners of the room for the basket he used to hold laundry. "Where is it?" he muttered.

"I remember when Lucas Steadman wrote to the Boston newspaper, addressed the letter right to the editor. Imagine a boy doing a thing like that! He offered to write articles about the happenings in Eastead—as though anyone would want to read about our little town."

Lucas flung the wet rag out the open window and hurried down the short hallway to the waiting room. He stopped short of the curtain, took a deep breath, and calmly pushed the fabric aside to enter the outer room.

"I'm ready for you, Miss," he said. He didn't like the grin on the older girl's face. Had she heard him rushing? Did she know how anxious he was to cut off Mrs. Miller?

"Good day, Doctor," said the irrepressible gossip.

"Good day, Madame." He turned to the two Irish girls. "If you'll come this way."

Ginger followed with her hand planted firmly on Patty's thin shoulder. She could almost sympathize with the young doctor. Mrs. Miller knew too much about every family in town. She'd been a maid in each of the big houses. And she worked from time to time, helping out in the more modest homes, usually when there was a birth or an illness or houseguests. Besides being a hard worker, she was a good listener, whether she was part of the conversation or eavesdropping. Next to her love of listening came her love of chattering. Pastor Hull's admonishments against gossip went right over the woman's head. Ginger doubted Mrs. Miller knew her passing on this little bit of knowledge and that little bit of history qualified as gossip.

Patty stopped and effectively blocked her sister's way in the narrow passage. She reached up and took hold of Ginger's hand. The doctor's footsteps continued down the hallway.

Patty pulled her sister down and spoke in her ear. "I think we ought to come back when Auntie Amy can come, too. That doctor's not likely to be in a good mood after hearing Mrs. Miller talk about him."

Ginger stooped down even farther to whisper back, "If we aren't feeling brave, Patty me girl, then we'll just have to pretend."

"You're scared, too, aren't you, Ginger?"

Ginger puzzled over the question a moment. The doctor's vulnerability under the good-natured attack of Mrs. Miller's gossip had changed Ginger's perception of him. The sounds of his frantic haste from behind the curtain triggered a response.

Often one of the girls alerted Aunt Amy that Mother Ross was coming down the street.

That cantankerous woman interfered at every opportunity. As Amy Ross's mother-in-law, she held the title to the house they lived in. Periodically, she surprised the orphanage with a visit and scowled at all she met there. Her inspections caused havoc. Amy Ross dealt with it well, but her devoted girls tried to protect their beloved guardian.

When the elder Mrs. Ross came charging down the street, the orphans scrambled to straighten the house before the tyrant's shadow touched the front door.

Ginger's mind dwelt on the mystery of young Dr. Steadman. Perhaps the doctor's curt utterances reflected something other than callousness. Perhaps he was insecure in his new position. And didn't she, herself, often speak with more bravado than she possessed to hide her own insecurity? If she was guilty of such prevarication, perhaps the young doctor was as well.

Ginger smiled at her sister and answered the question.

"Only a wee bit nervous. I'm thinking the doctor has a human heart after all."

Patty squeezed Ginger's hand, and the two hurried to catch up.

"Sit here," said Dr. Steadman, who continued talking while Patty guided Ginger to the chair he indicated.

Ginger chafed under the blunt order. *Well, Lord, only a second ago I thought I could like this man, and now I'm wishing I were home. I take back me suggestion that Ye push our aunt Amy and this man together. It wouldna' do. Give me patience. That's what I be needing, or I'll be telling this oaf to sweeten his words with a please and a thank-you just like he was one of the younger girls.*

Dr. Steadman surveyed her face, touching the bruises gently. As he leaned closer, Ginger again smelled peppermint on his breath. She could see the frown in his expression and wondered if he saw something in her injuries to concern him.

"You're healing well," he said.

Ginger let out a sigh with the breath she had been unconsciously holding.

He leaned back so she could no longer see his features. His voice continued in his coldly professional manner.

"Has your sight always been limited?"

"Aye."

"Any injuries or illnesses as a child which further impaired your vision?"

"Nary a one."

"Do you have any trouble distinguishing colors?"

"No, Doctor, I know me colors." *What? He thinks because I'm weak-sighted, I'm weak-minded as well?*

He came closer, placed his fingertips gently below each eye, and pulled down.

"Look up," he ordered.

Ginger did.

"Down."

She followed his instructions but felt a rage growing within. Was he wasting

73

her time? Did he enjoy these arbitrary commands. What good was it to look up and down with eyes that barely saw?

"To the right, slowly, and then, in one steady movement, all the way to the left."

Once she had complied, he crossed his arms over his chest.

"Certain structural defects can result in blurring of vision. These, we know, are errors of refraction. Your extraocular muscles are performing well. We know that the inside of the eye can be damaged or hold irregularities that affect sight, but it is difficult to see."

Now he be lecturing me. Ginger leaned forward and squinted, trying to get a better look at the instrument he'd picked up off the table. *Lord, Ye wouldna' let this doctor stick part of that thing in me eye? In addition to the patience, I'll be asking Ye for courage.*

Dr. Steadman lit two lanterns and put his hands on Ginger's shoulders to push her back into the position he required. Ginger felt her body tense. What was he going to do?

"At this point in medical advancement, I can only examine the front of the eye, the cornea, and the general condition of the conjunctiva."

"What have ye got in yer hand, Doctor?" Ginger interrupted the flow of unneeded information to get to the thing that troubled her.

"This?"

Ginger saw him hold up a blurred round shape and nodded.

"Just a magnifying glass," he said.

Ginger clenched her hands into fists by her side. She'd tried to avoid this visit to the doctor, but Aunt Amy had gently insisted.

My nerves are twisting, Lord, all over me body. Me lungs don't work. I can't breathe. Me stomach don't work. I'm afraid I'm going to be sick. This doctor's going to poke and prod and find nothing whatever to do for me. So why did Ye have me come here?

Ginger looked straight ahead when Dr. Steadman told her to, and she tried not to think of anything at all. She tried to relax her hands and shifted them to lie in her lap. Aunt Amy had said that assuming a pose of gentility aided a woman's composure.

"Aha, just as I thought. I see no evidence of disease. No injury or scarring to the cornea, no clouding, no pigmented cells on the white surface. Miss. . .uh?" The doctor lowered the magnifying glass.

And why did I think he knew me name? "Finnegan, Ginger Finnegan."

"Miss Finnegan, I have spectacles that will aid you." He crossed the room, pulled a shallow drawer completely out, and strode back to her side.

Ginger's stomach cramped, and again she squeezed together the hands clasped in her lap. *Oh, Lord, could it be?* She closed her eyes and continued to pray, barely aware of the voices and movements around her.

Patty gasped. "Oh, Ginger, there are dozens and dozens of spectacles just like Mrs. Keller wears. Dr. Steadman, where'd you get them all?"

"I trained at the University of Pennsylvania. I grew very interested in the study of ophthalmology. Our School of Medicine has the most progressive programs in the United States. We are to our continent what the University of Edinburgh is to Europe. Many of our faculty trained in Scotland. John McAllister of Philadelphia is famous for his manufacturing of spectacles. Let's try one of these stronger lenses for you, Miss Finnegan."

He placed the drawer on a table. Gently he perched spectacles on the bridge of her nose and guided the wire temple frames under her hair and over her ears. He stepped back.

"Miss Finnegan, you must open your eyes. Only you can tell me if the lenses improve your sight."

Chapter 5

The Finnegan sisters walked hand in hand down the street toward Kindred Hearts.

"Look, Patty, there be leaves on the ground."

Patty giggled. "Of course there are. It's fall."

"No, I mean there be individual leaves, not all blurred together." Ginger took a deep breath as if she could pull the wonder of this day right into her lungs and keep it. She sighed. "Ah, such beauty."

"I don't get it. You could always see color. Why are you so happy?"

Ginger stopped and stared at the ground where the wind had pushed oak and maple leaves against a white picket fence. Autumn had splashed vibrant red, orange, and gold hues along the dirt path. "I can't tell you what it's like, Patty. Everything has sharp edges. The colors are richer. I want to just look and look and look. . .at everything." She quickly raised her face to the trees in the yard.

"Ooo." Swaying, Ginger dropped Patty's hand and put her palms on her cheeks.

"What's wrong?" Patty grabbed her sister's arm.

"The world tilted there for a moment. Dr. Steadman did say it would take awhile to get used to me spectacles." She slowly opened her eyes, then shut them again. "I think the excitement is getting to me, Patty. Me stomach has gone wobbly."

"You're sick?"

"Dizzy, Patty, like you wound me up on the swing hanging from the backyard tree and then let me spin."

"Maybe you should take those spectacles off."

"No!" She opened her eyes and looked straight ahead. A kitten sat on the porch of the house behind the fence. Ginger watched it slowly lick its paw, then methodically stroke its head in a feline bathing ritual.

"There's so much to be seeing," Ginger whispered. With a stronger voice and a smile, she added, "Besides, Patty me dear, how could me stomach be connected to me eyes? I was more nervous, I'm figuring, than I wanted to admit. That's what's set me stomach to whirling about inside me."

"You almost fell off the step of the doctor's office," Patty pointed out.

"Well now, that's what Dr. Steadman was talking about when he said it would take awhile to get used to seeing." Ginger grinned at the view before her. She thanked God for pouring blessings into her with so many lovely sights.

"It's a good thing, being a doctor, helping people," she said. "Did you notice how

Dr. Steadman fairly hummed with joy when he found the right spectacles for me eyes?"

"He grinned," said Patty, taking her sister's hand and giving it a pull. "Let's go. I want all the girls to see you. Won't they be flabbergasted? Aunt Amy will be pleased beyond measure."

"Aye, she will be." With careful steps, Ginger walked beside her sister. "He grinned, all right. Had you ever seen the doctor smile before?"

"Dr. Steadman?"

"Now were we talking about old Doc Morris who smells of camphor and sweat, or young Dr. Steadman who just placed a miracle upon me nose and gave ye a peppermint as we left?"

Patty giggled. "Dr. Steadman."

"So did ye ever see him smile before?"

"I seen him make a tight little sorry smile that didn't mean he was happy. Just something polite to put on his face when he was saying good day to Aunt Amy."

"I'm thinking he has a grand smile. One that makes you feel special."

Patty stopped. "Ginger?"

Ginger looked down quickly and felt again the strange tilting and loss of balance. She grabbed Patty to keep from falling.

"Ginger!" Patty screeched.

"Oh, just a minute. Be still, Patty. The world is moving under me feet, and me stomach is flitting about."

"Should I run to the house? Should I get Aunt Amy? We're almost home, Ginger. Are you going to make it?"

"Aye, just give me a minute. Just a minute."

"You should take off those spectacles, Ginger."

"No! Never. I'm going to wear 'em 'til I go to bed. It can't be the spectacles, don't ye know, Patty? The spectacles are a miracle, a gift from God, Himself. I can see every freckle on yer face, every lash upon yer eyelid, every wrinkle in yer frown. Quit frettin'. I'll be fine."

As the day went on, Ginger began to doubt that she would be fine. If she remained still and focused on one thing, her stomach didn't lurch. Sudden movements, however, made her surroundings pitch and reel. She reached for things and knocked them over, misjudging their positions. Nausea plagued her, and by the time she prepared supper that night, her head ached. As she peeled a carrot, tears streamed down her cheeks. How could her miracle be ruined by this illness?

Aunt Amy bustled into the kitchen and, seeing Ginger's distress, quickly enveloped the young woman in a warm embrace. "Ginger, what's wrong?"

Ginger dropped her knife and carrot on the table and turned to bury her head on her mentor's shoulder. She sobbed, feeling too miserable to try to explain. Her joy had been sabotaged by an awful sickness.

"I'm putting you to bed." Aunt Amy guided her toward the stairs.

"The supper," Ginger objected.

"There are plenty of girls to make our meal. Hush now, and let me take care of you. You've always been a godsend to me, Ginger—helping with the little ones, singing them to sleep, knitting their mittens and scarves, rocking them when they're sick. You always coddle the other children. This time, we will take care of you."

They reached the stairs and started up.

"I'm never sick, Aunt Amy, never." Ginger held her eyes closed against the constant shifting of the world around her. She feared she'd never make it to the second floor.

She heard an anxious voice from above. "Something's wrong with Ginger."

Many hard shoes tapped out an urgent scramble in the hall. As she and Aunt Amy came to the top step, small hands reached to support Ginger. The little girls surrounded her, and with hugs that encumbered her movements, they assisted her to the bedroom she shared with Patty, Susannah, and Alys.

"Mary, Amanda," said Aunt Amy, "will you go down and finish supper? Jess, please fetch Dr. Steadman."

"Oh, no," said Ginger through her weeping, "I don't need the doctor."

"I'll be the judge of that," answered Aunt Amy. "Go, Jess. Patty, turn down the cover on your bed. Ginger, sit down. Susannah, fetch her nightgown."

Within minutes, Ginger lay cocooned in a colorful quilt, her head resting on her feather pillow and her eyes closed tight against the confusion of the room around her.

"Girls, I think Ginger needs some privacy now. I know you all want to help her, but what she needs most is quiet. So let's leave her in peace. Go finish your chores before we eat. If a worry crosses your mind, girls, turn it into a prayer. Patty and Alys, you may stay here."

"Yes, Auntie Amy," said Opal. "Get better, Ginger."

"Get better," echoed Marissa.

"I'll help in the kitchen," said Melody.

A shuffling of feet told Ginger that most of girls had left the room.

"I could read her a story," offered Alys.

"That's a good idea, Alys," said Aunt Amy, "but why don't you wait until after Dr. Steadman has looked at her?"

Ginger felt a small hand on her shoulder. "Do you want to hold Pennydoll? She's good to whisper to."

Ginger felt tears sting her eyes. Alys rarely let Pennydoll out of her arms. Afraid to open her eyes and again feel the room rock and undulate around her, Ginger held out a hand and received the treasured doll into her keeping.

"Rest, Ginger," said Aunt Amy. "Patty and Alys, I trust you to look after her. Call me if you need anything."

With a soft swish of woolen skirts, Aunt Amy left the room, softly closing the door behind her.

Chapter 6

The door creaked open. Ginger stirred from her light doze and listened. A step sounded upon the bare floor, and she knew it wasn't one of the girls nor Aunt Amy.

"Dr. Steadman?"

"Yes, how are you feeling?"

"I think I've been asleep."

A damp cloth rested across her eyes. She peeled it off and tried to sit.

"No, stay still."

"I feel better."

"Stay still."

She heard the scrape of the wooden chair across the floor. He sat next to her and reached out to put his hand on her forehead.

"Where are Patty and Alys?" she asked as his hand withdrew.

"Eating their supper."

"Where are my spectacles?"

He looked around, then reached to the dresser.

"Here."

"Thank you." Ginger fitted them onto her face, tucking the wire loops around each ear.

She watched Lucas Steadman bend to pick up something from the floor. His eyes looked forlorn, but he gave her a feeble smile. Holding up Pennydoll, he asked, "Yours?"

Ginger started to shake her head but remembered the nausea that overwhelmed her when she moved. "No," she whispered.

"I believe the last time I was here, the little girl who fell off the roof clutched this doll in a desperate grip."

"Ye remember?"

"I pay close attention to my patients, Miss Finnegan. It's important to me that I do everything within my power to make them well, and if I can't make them well, to help them be comfortable."

"Ye pay close attention?" Ginger gave an unladylike snort. "Ye didn't even know me name after ye tended me bruises. And ye don't know the name of the little girl who loves that poor doll."

Dr. Steadman's mouth twitched in annoyance. "A patient's name has nothing to do with the treatment of illness."

He rested his elbows on his knees. Holding the doll in both hands, he gently moved it back and forth as he stared at the cloth face.

"Ye seem sad," said Ginger.

"Ira Blake died this afternoon."

"Ah, I see. But he was old, Dr. Steadman, and he's been ailing a long time."

Dr. Steadman nodded.

"Ye not be blaming yerself?"

"No. . .and yes, Miss Finnegan. I did all I could, but the human body is still very much a mystery. It's true we know more than we did a hundred years ago, but so little compared to all we should know. Patients die every day because their doctors just don't know enough." He sighed. "And Miss Finnegan, it is probably due to my ignorance that you have been sick half the day."

"Why is it ye be takin' the blame?" Ginger's hand tightened on the counterpane, her fingers digging into the colored swatches. "Ye haven't even looked at me. I coulda' eaten something bad at breakfast. I might be low with an illness that'll take itself off in a day or two. Ye're makin' judgments too fast, I'm thinking, on very little evidence."

He shook his head, still watching the doll in his hands. "I've talked with Patty and Mrs. Ross. The timing's not right for ingestion of tainted food, and you have no fever. Plus, you ate what the others ate, and no one else is ill.

"No, I think I should have been more cautious in giving you the spectacles. I should have given you some guidelines—wear them only for a few minutes at a time; gradually increase the length of time; avoid excessive motion until you become accustomed to viewing the world with new vision."

Ginger giggled.

"What's funny? I've caused you a great deal of pain today."

"I'm laughing because me sister, Patty, had the good sense to tell me to take off the spectacles. And do you think I listened? Oh no, Ginger Finnegan had her mind made up to see the whole world all at once and all in one day. I was too stubborn to heed her wee, wise voice."

"But if I had—"

"Aye, but ye did, don't ye know? Ye told me that it would be an adjustment, and I was too greedy to mind yer words."

"You're very generous, Miss Finnegan. . .and very forgiving."

"And yer generous and unforgiving, aren't ye, Doctor?"

He shifted his gaze to rest upon her face for the first time. "What do you mean?"

"Ye're generous with yer time and yer talent. And with the things ye possess like yer learning from that fancy School of Medicine in Philadelphia."

"I told you the Steadman Mill—my cousin Carter—takes care of the medical expenses for Kindred Hearts."

"Ye woulda given me the spectacles on yer own, Dr. Steadman. Ye don't fool me. When ye put them onto me face, I could feel the zest of ye rising up and spilling over."

"Zest?"

"Me granny called it the zest of a person, the thing that stirs the blood. For some it's singing a song, or rocking a baby, or watching a planted field pop up with seedlings. Everyone has something that causes that zing. Granny said it happens when ye put yer hand to the right plow."

"I'm sorry, I don't follow your meaning, or rather, your granny's meaning."

Ginger reached out and touched his hand that still cradled Pennydoll. "Everyone has a job to do that God designed just for him or her. When ye're in the midst of doing that job, ye're as close to God as standing by His side. Ye're in partnership with the Almighty. And the satisfaction that rushes through ye is as good as hearing Him say, 'Well done, thou good and faithful servant.' It's yer zest in life."

He sat quietly for a moment, then shrugged. Pulling his hand away from her touch, he pushed the doll into her grasp. Tapping his fingertips on his knees, he looked away.

"You said I was unforgiving."

"Aye, that shows in the way ye talk to people and the stiffness of yer neck and spine. Yer whole body's rigid. Even yer voice is cold and hard. Ye don't give of yerself, and that can only be because ye lack trust. Ye don't trust those around ye. And the reason a person has no trust is because that person has not forgiven someone who betrayed a trust."

"And you are what? Nineteen, twenty years old?"

"Twenty, but I'm quoting me granny who was sixty-nine when she died. And she pulled her wisdom from the Bible, a book from God, who is beyond the counting of years."

He stood.

"You'll wear the spectacles with moderation tomorrow."

"Yes, Dr. Steadman."

"You'll wear them when sitting until you feel comfortable, then try standing and walking."

"Yes."

"You'll take the spectacles off and rest your eyes."

"Yes."

He walked to the door and opened it. Just before leaving, he turned and looked directly into her eyes.

"Miss Finnegan, I can't forgive someone who never recognized he did wrong, who died without giving me the opportunity to make peace with him. It's too late."

The door closed firmly.

"No," whispered Ginger. "I don't know the answer to yer pain, Dr. Lucas Steadman, but I do know it's not too late."

Chapter 7

Lucas shifted the weight of the basket under his arm, and two hens inside cackled their protest once more.

"I'm taking you to a good home, not a stewpot, so just be quiet," he told them.

As he approached the orphanage, he heard laughter from the backyard. Carrying his burden around the side of the house, he came across a half dozen little girls doing a very disorderly raking job. Their piles of autumn leaves varied in size from mountainous to minuscule. Ginger sat on the stoop, bundled up against the cold, her spectacles in her mittened hands.

Two of the girls abandoned their rakes when they saw Dr. Steadman and his basket. Lucas looked down into identical faces and knew he'd never met these two before.

"What have you got?" asked one.

The other squealed. "The basket is moving. Is it a puppy? We need a puppy."

"Chickens," said Lucas. He almost laughed as their eager expressions fell to total disgust in a second. They turned as one and ran to Ginger.

"The doctor has chickens in a basket," said the first to reach her.

"Live chickens," said the other. She didn't quite make her stop in time and fell into Ginger's lap.

A moment of confusion followed as Ginger tried to move the girl off her lap without damaging her spectacles. As soon as possible, she put them on and stood to greet the doctor.

The twins ran back to their game in the piles of leaves, and Lucas came to stand in front of Ginger.

"Chickens?" she asked, tilting her head as she looked up at him.

He nodded. Auburn tendrils escaped her knitted hat, and the wind played with them, making them dance across her cheek. The heavy lenses magnified her green eyes, and he marveled not only at the lovely verdant color but the essence of wonder in them.

"Doctor?"

He realized he was staring as a smile broke across her face. Her joy dazzled him, and he took in a quick breath. He must say something.

"Laying hens. I don't cook. There's no kitchen." He stopped blathering and deliberately breathed, slow and steady, in and out. She was just a woman, an obstreperous lass with an undeniable natural beauty, but nonetheless outspoken and irrepressible. "Yesterday, when I was here, I saw you have a chicken coop."

"The hens are for us?"

"Yes."

She smiled again, and Lucas looked quickly away.

"Faith," she called. "Dr. Steadman brought us two more hens. Will ye please me by putting them in the coop?"

A girl came running to take the basket. She wore too many layers of clothing for him to determine if he'd seen her before. She said a hasty thank-you before darting off to the coop's door.

"Have a seat," said Ginger, moving to one side of the step.

Lucas glanced down and saw her invitation to sit beside her. Panic rose up inside him. He again averted his gaze, watching intently as the eager girls dragged their rakes with little effect through the crisp leaves.

This is ridiculous. What is happening? When have women ever interfered with my plans? His thoughts only had a moment's pause before the answer came tumbling through his well-ordered mind.

This is the first time in my life I haven't had my all-encompassing goal in front of me. I've finished school. I've set up my practice. Patients are beginning to knock on my door. I've relaxed. And now a pretty girl with a winsome smile has turned my head.

Oh, Lord, what is my goal now that my seventeen-year ambition has been attained?

He looked at Ginger's charming face and decided he was too confused to deal with the issue. He cleared his throat, knowing it was a nervous habit and that he gave away his unsettled state of mind each time he did it.

"I think," he said, "I'll help the girls with their chore."

"Aye now, that would be a good thing. They're supposed to be putting those leaves on the garden. Mostly, they're just stirring 'em round the yard like a big batch of porridge. Aunt Amy said I could only supervise today after my illness yesterday. And how do ye tell a child how to rake? Ye have to show 'em, or it's no good a'tall."

Charging into the girls' activity, Lucas confiscated a rake from a more-than-willing child. Enthusiastic cheers and peels of laughter met his action. With long, strong sweeps he began to move the smaller piles past the chicken coop. He raked vigorously, trying to rid his system of an unsettling frustration. The children danced around him, sometimes even managing to help.

Overhead, sullen clouds glowered in the sky. Cold breezes picked up momentum and swished at the leaves, trying to swirl them into the air and scatter them back across the yard. The air smelled of the tart fragrance of crunching leaves. Down the street, a faint trail of smoke from leaves being burned made its way toward the orphanage, adding a whiff of another pleasant odor.

With a suggestion here and a command there, Lucas eventually had his crew organized and the project nearing completion. Every time he looked to the house, he saw Ginger still sitting on the cold step, watching their progress. He ignored the distraction she presented.

Once he yelled, "You should go in out of the cold."

She just waved and flashed him a beguiling smile.

He returned to the work at hand, glaring at the area before him still strewn with festive oak leaves.

"Hot tea!" called Aunt Amy as she put a tray down next to Ginger, then quickly retreated from the cold wind.

The girls sent up a whoop and threw down their rakes. Lucas followed them to the back porch and accepted a mug of strong brew. Honey and milk softened the bitter tea, and he gratefully sipped until he caught Ginger watching him. The warmth stealing through his veins had nothing to do with his drink.

"Tea on the porch?" he asked Ginger as she poured another mug and handed it to Opal.

"Aunt Amy's heart is too big to be leaving the girls out here in the cold for long without giving them something to warm their insides. However, the time it takes to unbundle them, allow them to drink a cup of something warmin', and then bundle them up again and scoot them out the door. . . Well now, ye can see that they wouldna' be getting much work done a'tall. And then there's the sweeping up of leaves and mud the wee girls track in on their shoes." She smiled up at him. "Will ye sit with me now?"

He nodded but had to wait for six little girls to shuffle around on the step before he had a space of his own.

"Thank ye for helping us," Ginger said.

A chorus of thank-yous followed from the girls.

"My pleasure."

A ruckus emanated from the chicken coop.

Ginger chuckled. "It sounds like the old lady hens have decided their wee house has no room for two more biddies."

At the next series of thumps and loud chicken screeches, the girls on the steps rose to their feet and stared anxiously at the shuddering building.

"Will they hurt each other?" asked Opal.

Before either adult could answer, the door banged open and nine irate hens poured out. They scattered across the yard, with one poor fowl harassed by two dominant hens. The others lost interest and slowed to a stop, picking a spot to scratch and peck the ground.

The rooster strutted out of the coop last, conveying a sense of overwhelming dignity. It was clear the fiasco was none of his doing. With a final cacophony of squawks, the two belligerent hens turned their backs on their victim and took up the occupation of the others, a thorough investigation of the newly swept yard.

"I'm thinking we'll be leaving 'em out for a bit," said Ginger. "Maybe without being elbow to elbow in the coop, they can get to know each other."

"Do chickens have elbows?" asked Opal.

"Well now, I know they have toes, and I'm thinking they have knees and elbows, too. What think ye, Dr. Steadman?"

Lucas felt a bubble of mirth rising to his throat. He managed to choke out,

"Chicken anatomy was not part of my course of instruction, Miss Finnegan," before collapsing into undignified guffaws.

The children joined him, and when the hilarity settled, one of the twins challenged him to a game of tag. Of course the girls nominated him "it," but his longer legs gave him an advantage. Ginger watched, and then, defying Aunt Amy's instructions to stay quiet, she pushed her spectacles deep into her pocket and joined the game.

The children loved playing with her. When she was "it," a new set of rules came into play, obviously developed to accommodate her poor vision. Instead of running, they hid. She walked slowly around the yard. Often, just as she passed a hidden child, she'd turn and reach into a bush and grab the player. When Lucas was "it" again, he noticed the girls tried to run interference and keep him from tagging Ginger.

In the end he got her. Grasping her hands, he dragged her back to the "jail."

"Snow! First snow!" yelled the children.

"It's snowing?" asked Ginger. "Let me go. I need to see."

Lucas released her. She dug into her pocket and jerked out the spectacles.

"Here, look," said Lucas, almost as excited as Ginger.

He held out the dark sleeve of his coat. The wool material caught the floating flakes.

"Oh!" She clasped his arm with two hands and brought it close to her eyes. "Oh, dear Lord, another miracle."

She looked up at Lucas. Her face glowed with awe, and he thought what a blessing it would be to share her joy each day of the year. The feeling clutched at his heart, and he struggled to banish it. He must not become involved with this woman before he had time to think logically about his future and establish new goals.

"We'd better put the hens back in the coop," he said.

She nodded, apparently unfazed that he did not share her exultation over a snowflake. She moved slowly to gather the children and tell them to shoo the chickens back in their shelter.

"And this time, me dears, be sure the latch is put on tight."

"Dr. Steadman?"

Lucas turned to see Amy Ross standing in the open kitchen doorway.

"We're about to have supper. Would you join us?"

"Thank you, Mrs. Ross, but I've made arrangements for supper."

"You'll be going up Croner Hill to eat with Mr. and Mrs. Steadman," said Ginger.

Lucas jumped. He hadn't heard her return to his side. The light of day was fading rapidly. He could no longer make out the freckles on her pert nose. He could still see her smile, and that smile made him nervous. He cleared his throat before speaking.

"No, I eat at Mrs. Stanberry's Boardinghouse."

"Ginger," said Aunt Amy, "see that he stays." She turned and went back into the house, closing the door behind her.

"You're telling me you eat at a boardinghouse when you have family who would welcome you to their table?" Ginger's eyes grew large, brimming with disapproval.

"We've never been close," he explained.

"I'm thinking the ones ye need to forgive are not all dead, Dr. Steadman. I'm thinking yer excuse for the way ye be won't matter much when ye stand before God Almighty."

"And I'm thinking, Miss Finnegan, that it's none of your business with whom I eat my meals."

A twitch at the corner of Ginger's mouth grew into a smile, clearing the stormy scowl on her face like the sun breaking through after a rain.

She chuckled. "Aye, yer right, of course. I shouldna' be nattering on about the speck in yer eye when there's a plank in me own."

Lucas crossed his arms over his chest and gave her a nod. He didn't want to venture a statement lest she somehow find a way to continue badgering him.

A twinkle in her eye forewarned him.

"So," she said in a voice that was almost a purr. "That clench in yer jaw and that miserly nod is yer way of admitting ye do have a speck, is it?" She laughed at him when he refused to answer.

"Well," she continued, "we'll send one of the girls down to Mrs. Stanberry's to say ye'll be dining with us. Aunt Amy particularly told me to keep ye, and I'll be in trouble if ye don't stay. Ye wouldna' want me to be in trouble, now would ye?"

The trouble is, thought Lucas as he rigidly kept the smile from stealing onto his face, *I don't want Ginger Finnegan to have any more trouble in her life. Now why should I care, Lord, and what do You want me to do about it?*

The back door creaked open, shedding a ribbon of light across the small porch.

"Coming, Dr. Steadman?" asked Amy Ross.

Lucas kept his eyes on the smiling pixie face before him.

"Yes, Mrs. Ross. I believe I am."

Chapter 8

How did you learn to flirt?" asked Susannah. She set the pan of scrubbed potatoes on the table in front of Ginger.

Startled, Ginger looked up from dicing an onion for the evening stew.

"I can't tell ye how, 'cause I don't know. I've never flirted, not once, in all me days. How could I know how to learn such a thing?"

"Mary says you do. With Dr. Steadman. All the time. He comes here almost every day. For all sorts of reasons, she says, but mostly to see you."

Ginger dropped the onion pieces into a kettle of water and said nothing.

"Are you mad because Mary said that?" asked Susannah.

"No," said Ginger. "I'm thinking about what she said."

She reached for a potato to peel.

"Don't be mad." Susannah sat down and picked up another paring knife. "Mary thinks it's grand. So do I. So do all the girls. We like Dr. Steadman. He's handsome when he smiles."

"Well, there it is, Susannah. I like teasing a smile out of him. I never thought of it as flirting."

"He's been coming here every day for weeks. He's been coming since first snow in September, and now it's December. That's a long time, Ginger."

"No, me girl, ye can't be saying it's every day."

"Almost. He comes to see you, so he must be feeling something for you. What would you say if he asked you to marry him?"

"Susannah!" Ginger stopped what she was doing long enough to glare at her young helper. "He comes to bring us the things he can't use, things traded to him for doctoring. Then he stays to eat with us because. . .well, because he likes our food."

"Mrs. Stanberry is one of the best cooks in the county. She wins ribbons every summer at the fair. They have dessert every night at the boardinghouse. He doesn't stay because our food is better."

"Well, I'm not a candidate for a doctor's wife."

"Why not?" asked Susannah. "Before you had your spectacles, Mary said no man wanted a blind wife to tend his garden, cook his meals, raise his children. But now you can see almost as good as anybody. Why can't you be a doctor's wife?"

"Lucas Steadman would be wanting a wife with more than me pitiful schooling."

"He likes you."

"But think of how some people feel about the Irish."

"Dr. Steadman has more sense than to hold the opinion that all Irish are bad."

"Well, maybe so, but I'm thinking the man wouldna' look twice at the likes of me."

"Ginger! You're not very observant. He's already given you more than a second glance."

Ginger shook her head. "He'd also be needing a fine lady. Remember, he comes from the houses on the hill."

"Isabel and Kathleen Steadman don't come from grand houses, and you read plenty good. And you always help the little girls with their schoolwork, especially their sums. You'd make a good doctor's wife. You're always the one who takes care of any of us when we're sick."

"Aunt Amy takes care of ye."

"You help. Lots."

"This is a foolish discussion we're having. There's no sense nattering on about me and the doctor. Ye're seeing things that cannot be and wasting the time of day doing it. Tell me how ye're doing with memorizing yer poem for Christmas Eve."

"My hands are busy while we talk, Ginger, so I'm not wasting the time of day. You know I get stuck in the last stanza, and you're just trying to change the subject." A knock sounded at the door. Susannah sprang up from her chair to answer.

Ginger turned at the sound of delighted laughter. Susannah threw an impudent grin over her shoulder and stepped back. Dr. Steadman stamped snow off his boots before entering.

Susannah giggled as she took his coat and hat to hang on a hook beside the stove. She giggled more as she poured hot tea in a mug and placed it before him where he sat at the table with Ginger. She giggled every time Ginger sent her a glare.

"Miss Susannah," said Dr. Steadman. "Excessive giggling is a sign of a nervous disorder. Should I prescribe a tonic?"

That set the poor girl off again, and Ginger ordered her from the kitchen.

Dr. Steadman watched her go with his eyebrows raised, then he turned to Ginger. "You're flushed. Are you feeling all right?"

"I'm fine, Doctor. It's the heat from the stove, perhaps."

He narrowed his eyes and studied her a moment.

"Perhaps," he finally agreed.

Ginger sighed her relief when he didn't inquire further into the cause of Susannah's giggles or her own blushes.

"I've brought you something," he said, pushing a book across the table.

Ginger wiped her hands on her apron and picked it up.

"*A Christmas Carol* by Charles Dickens," she read. "Did someone barter this? It's not like yer usual payments. It doesna' cluck nor squeal. Ye canna' eat it, nor wear it, nor use it in some practical manner."

"I got it from Maxwell."

Ginger gasped. "Ye've been to the house?"

He nodded. "After all your nagging to reconcile with my family, I went up there last night."

"Nagging? Me nagging? I never, Dr. Steadman. It's bad of ye to say such a thing."

He laughed. "So you don't nag me, Miss Finnegan? You just mention every time Isabel Steadman or Kathleen Steadman happens to stop by Kindred Hearts. You point out Carter's charitable project with the children in the church. You draw my attention to Maxwell's offer to host the church Christmas party. You just remind me you're praying for my heart to soften. No, you never nag, Miss Finnegan."

Ginger clamped her lips down against an answering smile. "Ye've just described me granny's method of making us see her way of doing things. At times, I wanted to run from her constant nattering."

"But at all times you knew she loved you."

"Aye, that's right, to the point I'd wish she didn't love me quite so much."

"Well, your nattering at me has convinced me you are the best friend I've ever had."

The statement surprised Ginger. She looked directly into his eyes and tried not to be too thrilled by the affectionate warmth she saw there. *So, it's a friend I am. I'm glad to be a friend. . . . I am! Ah, but because of Susannah's silly chatter, for a wee little bit, I let meself hope for more.*

"Tell me how Mr. Maxwell came to give ye this book."

"They, Kathleen and Maxwell, were surprised to see me. I hadn't warned them I was coming."

"Ye don't warn yer family," objected Ginger.

"Well, you might if you've been a curmudgeon forever and barely spoken a civil word to them."

"Aye."

"But as I was saying, they didn't expect me and were in the middle of unpacking crates that had come in on one of Maxwell's ships."

"Why are they Maxwell's ships and not yer ships, too?"

"Father left the business to Maxwell. He said I was too soft. Mother left me all her money, which I used to go to school and set up my practice."

"Was she agreeing for ye to be a doctor?"

"No, she just didn't want her son to starve or wear shabby clothing."

"She loved ye."

He grunted. "To be fair, I know she did. But she didn't understand me. And it distressed her that I associated with lower classes."

"I'm thinking she feared for ye."

"Feared for me?"

"Sure and don't ye know, she'd been tole all her life these people ye befriended were dirty and rough. She probably thought ye'd come home with some strange disease or be killed in a brawl. Her mother's heart couldna' stand the thought of losing ye."

He studied his hands folded on the table.

Ginger sighed. "Am I nagging ye again?"

He nodded and looked up at Ginger. A slow smile moved his lips and spread to his eyes.

"You want me to forgive her."

"Aye, Doctor, and yer father, too."

"All right, Miss Finnegan, you've won. Actually, as I walked home last night under the starry sky, I couldn't help but hear God's voice in my heart. And oddly, He was saying much the same things you've been saying. . .only without the Irish brogue."

"Oh, I'm that glad, Doctor." Ginger picked up her paring knife and another potato. "Now, would ye mind explaining to me just why ye have the same bitterness toward yer brother, Maxwell, and yer cousin Carter?"

"Pride."

"Well, I'm not denying I'm a brilliant person, but one word is not going to clear me confusion on the matter."

"For years, Miss Finnegan, I was the 'Christian' in the family. We all went to church, but I was the one who believed and acted upon that belief."

Ginger tried not to look appalled at the smugness of his words. Apparently she did not succeed.

"You're right," said the doctor. "I was a self-righteous snob. I had this great plan to become a doctor and serve the poor and thus make amends to society for my family's sins. It was an immature attitude that I latched onto as a child, and unfortunately as I grew up, I never relinquished it."

"But why hold yer grudge against the two young Mr. Steadmans?"

"You're going to laugh at me, Ginger. And I don't blame you. I think God must have laughed at my foolishness when He wasn't thoroughly exasperated by my stubbornness."

It took her a minute to answer. He'd called her by her first name. Feelings she knew she had no right to encourage tingled in her chest. *Oh, Susannah and yer foolish talk, what have ye done to me heart?*

"I won't laugh."

"When I came back from medical school and found my brother and cousin reconciled with God, doing good works, and married to godly women, I was disgusted. They'd stolen the march on me. They were doing the generous, kind acts out of the purest of motives. That had been my destiny since I'd started plotting my future when I was eight years old. I was as mad as a hornet that I wasn't the one and only grand benefactor Steadman."

He stopped his tirade and looked at her. "You're smiling."

"But I'm not laughing."

"Your eyes are laughing."

"Well, so is me heart, but ye'll have to be satisfied I'm not rolling on the floor and holding me sides. Will ye let me tell ye why I'm so filled with joy?"

"All right."

"The doctor I first met when Alys slid off the roof and kicked me in the face was stiff and stodgy. God wanted to work through ye to help the people of this town, but ye clogged up yer vessel with yer own self. Now yer letting all that go, and God's going to work mightily through ye, Dr. Steadman. I know He is."

Aunt Amy entered the kitchen. "Susannah said you were here, Doctor. Will you be able to stay for supper?"

"Yes, Mrs. Ross, and I have a book I'd like to read to the girls afterward while they work on their sewing projects." He held up the Dickens novel. "This came in a shipment of books from England. Kathleen thought you and the girls would enjoy it."

A Christmas Carol. I've heard it's good. Pastor Hull recommended it. We'd be delighted for you to join us in the parlor after supper. Wouldn't we, Ginger?"

"Aye, that we would." Ginger smiled at the doctor, and this time she knew she was flirting. But would it do her any good? Now that was the question.

Chapter 9

A lantern dimly lit the space just inside the front door of the orphanage. Already wearing a heavy coat and boots, Ginger pulled on a knitted cap, wrapped a scarf around her neck, and reached for mittens.

Aunt Amy draped a woolen shawl over her charge's shoulders. She patted Ginger's arms and tucked a stray lock of coppery hair under the rim of her cap.

"I should not send you, but I truly fear for Patty, Ruthie, and Opal." Her raspy voice held the lingering effects of a powerful infection in the lungs.

"I'll be all right," assured Ginger.

A chorus of coughing from the bedrooms upstairs echoed down the wood staircase. Ginger and Amy both turned anxious faces upward.

Fear clutched Ginger's heart. It seemed that each girl who became ill had a worse case than the child before. Starting the day after Christmas, the children had taken colds, one after the other. Even Aunt Amy fell to the epidemic, but her convalescence had been cut short by the need to get up and see to the small children. Ginger alone had not succumbed, but days of tending the others showed in circles under her eyes and sagging shoulders.

There must be a turn for the better soon, Lord.

Ginger gathered what strength she had left and squared her shoulders. "Well, I be doing no good with me feet planted here."

"Wait," said Aunt Amy. "Let me pray first."

She put her arms around Ginger and murmured a blessing. Ginger stood mutely, too tired to do much more than soak in the comforting words.

Dr. Steadman had said to send for him if matters got worse. At two in the morning, the condition of three little girls had gone beyond what Amy and Ginger could handle. For hours that night they had watched the girls' breathing become more labored. A hollow, deep cough shook their little frames, and their fevers climbed no matter how many times the women wiped away the perspiration with cold rags. Aunt Amy and Ginger prayed with every breath, then decided to send for the doctor.

"The moon is shining brightly," observed Ginger as Aunt Amy released her. "I'll not lose me way."

Just five months ago, she would never have dared to walk through town by herself. But with the urgency of the girls' illness prodding her, she fought irritation at Aunt Amy's concern. "Now ye go back upstairs to the wee ones, and I'll be back with the doctor as soon as can be."

Once out in the piercing night cold, Ginger bent her head against the biting wind and trudged through a foot of recent snow. Her breath puffed out before her in clouds. Without the gravity of her mission weighing on her, she would have been tempted to stop and marvel at the sparkling scene in the moonlight.

She soon turned off the side street onto a more traveled road in the center of town. There she found wagon-wheel ruts of hard-packed snow. The snow squeaked under her boots. Icy patches threatened to fell her. She carefully chose where to place each step.

Dear Lord, let the doctor be at home, not out with someone else who be ailing. I know many people, in town and around, have been sick with this awful coughing, but we need him, Lord.

Aye, now, I'm not forgetting we need Ye as well. Please send comfort to Aunt Amy, ease the little girls' breathing, Lord, so it isn't so hard for them. Protect them all.

Ginger caught a sob before it rose in her throat. By batting her eyes, she fought tears.

"They'd only freeze on me face, Lord," she muttered. The cold air drawn in when she spoke aloud hurt her lungs.

Straightaway, her mind turned back from her own discomfort to the distress of those at home. *Please, Lord, place yer healing hand on me Patty. I love the little girl, and it would be a blight on me very existence to have to go on without her.*

She broke into a run when she rounded the corner of North Elm and spotted the apothecary with Dr. Steadman's sign hanging just beyond. In order to wake him, she ducked down the alley to the back entrance. He'd said on several occasions patients had roused him by banging on the door closer to the little room in which he slept.

She knocked loudly. Then, too impatient to wait for a response, she began to pound with the side of her closed fist.

"I'm coming! I'm coming!" The doctor opened the door and blinked at her. "Ginger!"

"They're worse," she cried. "Patty and Opal and Ruthie. Ye must come, Doctor."

"I will. Step in out of the cold while I get dressed." He took hold of her arm and pulled her into the dark examining room. The door closed, and she heard him scratching around. Soon a flame leaped up from the end of a matchstick, and he lit a lantern. In the haze of light she saw her cold spectacles had fogged over in the warm air. She stood numbly, looking at the blur.

"Oh," Dr. Steadman exclaimed. He quickly removed her spectacles, blowing on the lenses, then polishing them with the material of his robe.

"Here." He put them back on her face and then placed the lantern in her mittened hand. "Take this through to the sitting room. I'll be ready in just a minute."

Ginger collapsed in the same chair she had sat on when she first came to Dr. Steadman's office. *Thank Ye, Lord, that he's here. Please give him wisdom. Use him to heal our little ones. Give us all the strength to do Yer will. Help the wee ones.*

Her head nodded until her chin rested on the thick knitted scarf around her neck. It had been such a long, hard week. Now Dr. Steadman and the Lord could take over. She dozed.

"Come on, Ginger. I'm ready."

She stood and started toward his voice even before she fully awoke.

"No, we're going out the front."

She ran right into him. His arms came around her to keep them from falling. A moment passed before his hand under her chin forced her to look up. He examined her face.

"Are you all right?" he asked. "When was the last time you slept more than a snatch of a nap?"

She shook her head, unable to answer.

He gently guided her head back down to his shoulder. Pulling a deep breath, he rested his cheek on the top of her knitted cap. His arms tightened, and she enjoyed the warmth of his embrace.

"My dear Ginger, we can't let you get sick as well."

Suddenly he released her, and with hands on her shoulders, turned her around. "Let's go take care of those girls."

She opened the door while he blew out the lantern. As soon as he locked the door behind him, he put his arm around her waist. He left it there, steadying her balance on the icy patches, lending her strength and warmth as they trudged back to the orphanage.

It feels good, thought Ginger. *Oh, Lord, what a privilege 'twould be to have this man by me side forever and a day. I'm asking for miracles tonight. And I know Ye give abundantly. So when Ye've finished healing our wee girls, Ye might touch this man with a love for me whether I deserve it or not. Aye, Lord, I wouldna' mind that miracle a'tall.*

Chapter 10

January twelfth. Three weeks of coughing and fever. Five days since the doctor had come in the middle of the night. He'd practically lived at the orphanage, sitting beside the girls' beds during the night watch, supporting one sick child after another while Ginger or Aunt Amy spooned broth into their little mouths. He also insisted the women get some rest.

During the day he made his rounds and saw a few patients in his office. Every evening he came back to help with the worst cases at the orphanage.

In spite of the dire circumstances, Ginger had stolen some precious memories. One night she knelt beside Opal's bed, holding the sick girl's hand. Dr. Steadman prayed in soothing tones while the tonic he'd given the child took effect. Opal's breathing became less ragged, more steady. Ginger pulled off her spectacles, rested her head on the mattress, and closed her eyes, reveling in the peaceful moment. Dr. Steadman's prayer ended. The hush over the room was too blessed to disturb, so Ginger allowed herself the luxury of not moving, just resting. Then came the miracle she'd asked for.

The doctor bent forward from the chair he sat upon. That sweet smell of peppermint reached her nose, and then she felt the soft touch of his lips brush her forehead.

She opened her eyes and looked at his face. It was close enough that she didn't need her spectacles to see the embarrassment register as he realized she was awake.

"Stealing kisses?" she asked.

He smiled.

"There's no need to steal what would be freely given." The boldness of her words shocked her. Out they'd come with no thought of propriety. She felt her face burn with shame and turned away in confusion.

"No, you don't," said Dr. Steadman. "I like what you just said. I shouldn't have stolen the kiss, Ginger, but there are times when you seem to be the only answer to my loneliness. I'm feeling more comfortable with my family. And bless them, they've taken me back without a word of reproach." He reached to take her two hands in his. "Remember you accused me of being stiff and stodgy."

"Aye, I do."

"I'm better now."

"Aye, much."

"I've quit worrying so much about whether or not I have an image—like 're-spected doctor' or 'benefactor.' I just do my job. I actually enjoy people now. I'm so grateful for your pointing me in the right direction." He squeezed her hands. "I need you. When I feel my muscles getting tight, tense, stiff, I remind myself of your laughing eyes."

His thumb slid gently across the back of one hand. "Be my friend, always?"

"Aye, I will."

Ruthie in the next bed began to cough. She cried as the spasms wracked the sore muscles in her chest.

As the doctor moved to take care of his patient, Ginger gave up resisting falling in love. She treasured each moment she worked by his side. Still, she wasn't sure he loved her the way she did him. With so much to do to make the girls comfortable and with the weariness of working long hours with little sleep, she had little time for romancing.

Sometimes she felt surely Dr. Steadman loved her, too. Then she'd think of how unworthy she was to be his wife and tell herself she was spinning fairy tales. She sought wisdom from the Lord.

Here I am again, Lord, lying in me bed with me bones so tired, I canna' turn over. But am I asleep? No, I am not! And why is that? Because me heart is troubled, full of joy, full of woe.

Does he love me? Why is it Ye're not answering me? Sometimes I think the answer is yes and Ye're showing me he cares. He strokes me cheek so tenderly. He holds me hand while we pray.

Why can't the tiresome man just say, "Ginger, me love, I canna' live a day without ye?" Are the words too big?

Aye, I know I'm whining, Lord, when I should be praising Ye for the returning health of the girls.

Aye, I know I'm an impatient one with no respect for Yer timing of things.

Ye know I love praying with him when he's finished his doctoring and the results of his efforts are in Ye hands. But if he ends one more time with, "And thank You, Lord, for Ginger. Amen," I'm going to kick his shin.

All right, so I won't resort to violence.

Is it because I'm so tired, Lord, that me feelings just won't settle down? Is all this turmoil because I'm not trusting Ye the way I should? Why can't Ye just put it in that aggravating man's head to either kiss me proper or tell me to go soak me head?

Am I grumbling again? Well, I beg Yer forgiveness and ask humbly that Ye remove the source of me griping. Amen.

◆　◆　◆

Even after the girls were allowed out of bed, some still labored for each breath. It had been a hard illness on many of the people in Massachusetts and the surrounding states. Dr. Steadman brought in a newspaper that reported many had died of the congestion, but officials said the epidemic was easing off.

Each day brought hope as one after another of the girls threw off the illness and began to regain strength. Only the littlest tyke in the orphanage still gave them grave concern. Dr. Steadman sat vigil over her bed, or rather he dozed.

Ginger came into the sickroom at first light. She crossed to the window and pushed the curtains aside, hoping to see pink clouds reflecting the promise of a new day. Ice covered most of the inside of the glass pane. Outside a stiff north wind jerked the black bare limbs of the oak in an endless motion that had lasted all night. Pulling the heavy material back across the window, Ginger blocked out the dismal winter scene. She heard the doctor stir behind her and turned.

"How's little Ruthie, Doctor?" she asked.

He heaved a sigh and rose from the chair he'd been in all night. Stretching his arms way above his head, he smiled at his capable nurse.

"At last she's taken her upward turn. She's going to make it, Ginger."

He took Ginger's hands in his as he'd done a dozen times in the past few days. She bowed her head and listened once again as he prayed, this time thanking God for Ruthie's broken fever and restful sleep.

He closed the prayer with, "And thank You, Lord, for Ginger. Amen."

A twitch of annoyance pulled down the corners of Ginger's mouth. *Oh, Lord, another pound of patience, please,* she prayed before she looked up into the doctor's face.

How could she scold, even in her heart, one who had given so much to the children? He looked tired. Lines of weariness across his brow only made him dearer to her. At this moment her fairy tale seemed real. She had to break the spell or perhaps say some foolish thing.

"I'll be getting the well ones up now. Why don't you lay down for a wee bit on the cot in the next room?"

"Yes, I could use a little bit of sleep."

Ginger left him and quietly roused the healthier sleepyheads. In an hour, only three girls remained in bed. She started down the hall with an apron in her hand. Mary and Amanda had gone off to the mill. Jessica would be helping Aunt Amy serve breakfast to the younger children. Ginger searched her tired brain for ways to keep the children happily occupied. Still too weak to go back to school, they became easily bored and crotchety.

"Are you going down to eat?" asked Dr. Steadman behind her.

She turned and smiled. Carrying his jacket over a bent arm, he buttoned his vest as he walked toward her. His normally neat hair needed a combing, and his eyes still looked sleepy.

"Aye."

"I smell Mrs. Ross's pancakes. Mind if I join you?"

"Not a'tall."

The wind rattled the windows, the front door banged open, causing a commotion. A child's light footsteps raced through the house to the foyer. The door slammed shut.

Ginger and Dr. Steadman continued down the stairs. He worked a cufflink into his sleeve. She tied the apron behind her back as she walked.

"It's true, then." The outraged voice came from the elder Mrs. Ross. She stood rigid in the foyer, her expression as glacial as the cold morning outside the door. The harshness of the winter's day had swept right into the house with the disagreeable old woman. She cast a withering glare at the couple descending the stairs.

"Mother Ross," Amy said as she came into the small entranceway from the kitchen. "What's wrong?"

The older woman's head swiveled to pin the young widow with her accusing gaze. "You and your orphans haven't been to church in two weeks. That's one thing wrong. Don't think I didn't notice.

"Then I hear rumors that this man is living in your home. I, of course, did not believe such a vile thing of my son's widow. But here is the proof, seen with my own eyes." She nodded toward the stairs where Lucas and Ginger stood frozen in place. "Can you deny he's been here all night? He's coming down from your bedrooms, and he isn't even fully dressed yet."

"You know this is the doctor, Mother Ross," Amy explained. "He's been here for the girls. I think we would have lost Patty and Ruthie without his skill."

"Excuses! Lies! I will not have you turn my house into a brothel. I will not have this immoral woman living under this roof."

Ginger heard a growl from Dr. Steadman. He left her on the steps and stood before the elder Mrs. Ross. His profile showed his anger, hard and cold. Ginger watched the muscle in his jaw work before he spoke.

"Mrs. Ross, you are speaking out of ignorance. Nothing has gone on here that would cause shame to come upon anyone. That is until you walked through that door with your unfounded and ugly suspicions."

He turned and spoke to Ginger.

"Ginger, pack your belongings and Patty's as well."

"Where are we going?" she croaked.

"To my brother's house. I'll go borrow a closed carriage from him. I don't want Patty out in the cold."

Ginger retreated up the stairs at full speed.

He then addressed Amy. "I'll hire Mrs. Miller to come help you until the other children are fully recovered. I thank you now for the good care you've taken of Ginger and Patty, but with your permission, I'll take over their charge."

"Don't you say yes to that," ordered Mother Ross. "It's indecent."

Lucas turned back to her. She recoiled, taking a step away from his righteous wrath.

"There's nothing indecent about it, Mrs. Ross. Ginger will be my bride. She'll be married out of my brother's house instead of this one."

"I'll say what your mother, God rest her soul, would say, young man. A Steadman does not pick his wife from the Irish rabble. I don't know how your parents could stand the heartache. It is a blessing they have already departed this earth. First your cousin and brother marry mill workers, and now you choose an Irish wench."

"The Irish lady has a pure heart with the glory of our Lord lifting her above the rabble of this earth." Lucas allowed his accusing glare to rest on the well-dressed matron before him. He wanted to be sure she understood that he considered her behavior reprehensible. At the moment he found it hard to believe God loved Mrs. Ross. With difficulty, he restrained his tongue. "I want to marry Ginger Finnegan, and the Irish in her makes her dearer than you could possibly understand."

Behind him something clattered and banged as it bumped down the stairs. They all turned to see a basket at the bottom of the steps with clothing strewn behind it. At the top of the staircase stood Ginger with her palms pressed to either side of her face.

"Dr. Steadman!" she said in a horrified whisper.

He grinned at her. "What?"

For a moment she didn't answer. Then she lowered her hands to her sides and walked down, stopping just two steps from the bottom.

She smiled at him, and a twinkle lightened her eyes. "I love ye," she said.

He stepped forward and put his hands around her waist.

"Well, now," he said in a heavy imitation of her Irish brogue. "I'm thinking that be the best news of the morning. And if ye be willing, I wouldna' mind a kiss a'tall."

She leaned into his embrace and he kissed her.

"Well, I never!" The words were followed by the opening of the front door, a draft of sweet cold air, and the resounding clap of wood against wood as the elder Mrs. Ross departed, slamming the door.

◆　　◆　　◆

Maxwell had not only sent a closed carriage, but a man to drive it. Inside, Patty marveled at the rich leather upholstered seats and the pockets lining the walls on either side of the door.

Ginger curled up under a carriage rug with her Dr. Steadman, contentedly snuggled against his side. "Ye never told me ye love me," she said with a mock pout.

"Sure I did."

"Ye did, now? And when was this? I know the last few weeks have been a strain, but I'm thinking a girl would remember when the man she loves tells her those special words."

"It was the night I asked you to marry me."

"Ye asked me to marry?"

"Sure."

"When?"

"When Opal passed her crisis." He cleared his throat, and Ginger knew he was nervous.

"I don't remember a thing about marriage and love," she told him. "I remember something about friends and needing."

"I said forever," he explained.

"Ah, Lucas me love, ye do need me."

"I do, Ginger, forever. I love you. Will you marry me?"

Patty turned from her examination of a bolster built into the seatback. The armrest moved up to be hidden in the upright cushioned back or extended down for use.

She interrupted her scrutiny to frown at her sister. "I thought that was all settled," she said.

"Shh!" said Ginger.

"I thought that's why we're going to the big house," insisted Patty.

"Shh!" said Lucas. "I'm waiting for the answer."

"Aye, Lucas, I will marry you and be your friend forever."

DONITA KATHLEEN PAUL

Donita has given up on retiring. Each time she retires, she finds a new career. This time she married an author from New Mexico and is resurrecting skills as a wife and homemaker. She's delved into romance, fantasy, history, and is toying with time travel. Writing will always be a part of her life. "The more I take time off to allow my body to relax, the more active my brain gets. I'm have way too much fun to stop."

The Caretaker

by Kelly Eileen Hake

Dedication

To the two unstoppable forces in my life:
God and my mother!

Chapter 1

Amy Ross hurried out to the water pump for what must have been the fifth time that morning. She didn't have long to get the little ones washed for church, or they'd be late again. Last week Pastor Hull told her that although he didn't mind seeing her girls scamper down the aisle just before prayer, some of his other parishioners were not as understanding about the disturbance.

Lost in her musings, Amy didn't notice the goose slipping through the fence and making a beeline for her until it was too late. At the impact, Amy shrieked and clutched the cold water pump handle. That move only compounded the problem when the handle broke and the pump doused her with water. Struggling to free her skirts from the determined goose, she slipped in the slick mud and landed with a dismaying splat. Amy glared at the creature now settling contentedly in her lap. Then she heard it: a deep-throated chuckle from the other side of the fence.

"I believe the culprit belongs to me." The caretaker next door didn't bother to hide his entertainment over the spectacle.

She turned the full force of her glare upon him, picked herself up off the ground, and stalked over to the fence. She tried to ignore the squish of mud in her half-boots.

"I wish you joy of her," she gritted from behind clenched teeth, then thrust the noisy, menacing bird into his arms.

He was about to respond when all sixteen of her girls poured from the house and pushed their way around her. Their cacophony was deafening.

"Auntie Amy! Auntie Amy!"

"What happened? You're all wet!"

"Ducky, Ducky!" three-year-old Ruthie crowed with glee, stretching out to stroke the goose.

"Oh, your best church dress—are we late again?"

"It's not a duck, it's a swan!" Alys caught hold of Ruthie's pudgy hand before it reached the bird.

Amy's anger evaporated as she surveyed her troops, then glanced at their new neighbor. He looked amused and a bit puzzled—not that she could blame him. Her foster family was a bit much to take in all at once. She felt the corners of her mouth quirk upward. Ducky, indeed.

"Children! It's a goose, and we can't be late. Everybody back inside, and make sure you don't leave anything behind!"

As the girls rushed off, Amy turned to face her neighbor. . . or rather, her neighbor's goose, she corrected. Since she came nose-to-bill with the misbehaving bird, Amy realized that its owner must be at least a foot taller than she. She opened her mouth to speak but thought better of it when Jessica began calling from within their small home. "Aunt Aaaammmyyy! We've only got five more minutes 'til we have to go!"

"I'll be by later to fix your pump since it's Gussie's fault it's broken." The assertive baritone voice commanded her attention. "After church."

"Thank you." Amy noticed his rough cambric workman's shirt and broadcloth pants with relief. He must be the new caretaker, so at least she hadn't made a fool of herself before the owner. Still, his offer to fix the pump was a kind one. She favored him with a smile and turned to go back to the house, dragging her sodden skirts with as much dignity as she could muster. She might be coated with mud, but she was still a lady.

Once inside, she hurried up the stairs toward her room. The last caretaker of the adjoining property had been completely irascible. That one frequently voiced his unwelcome opinions: Not only should children be seen and not heard, they really shouldn't be seen! Especially not on his property.

Amy grimaced. How glad she'd been to discover he was only the caretaker! Gladder still when he'd moved away. She prayed this one would be an improvement. He hadn't introduced himself, but he was responsible enough to fix the pump. He looked younger, too, with his broad shoulders and laughing green eyes.

She hastily changed clothes, then tucked one last pin into her wet brown hair. There. That should hold it. Her second-best cotton gray dress would have to do for today. Hearing Jessica call again, she snatched her chip-straw bonnet off the peg near the door and headed out.

The girls milled around outside, skirting mud puddles. As Amy reached the road, all sixteen fell into step around her, whispering and giggling until they reached the church and settled into their usual places. There was even enough time to hug Ginger and whisper last-minute congratulations on her recent marriage. Amy sat in the front row with Mary and the youngest girls, while Susannah and Amanda sat behind, monitoring the older ones. Seventeen people made for a tight fit, but the townspeople generously paid for these two pews.

Accounting columns and lesson plans meandered through Amy's mind while they waited for Pastor Hull to begin. She lifted her hand in greeting to Isabel, Kathleen, and their husbands when they waved from the row across. Kathleen bounced little Molly on her knee as the child began to fuss.

Finally, Parson Hull walked to the pulpit and gave the opening prayer. Afterward, Amy smiled as he nodded at her in approval. The pastor always had a soft spot for them, even more so since he'd adopted Betty and her baby sister. Amy and her girls had made it on time today—water pump fiasco notwithstanding.

After the hymns, about halfway through the sermon, Amy became aware that some of the women in the congregation kept sneaking horrified glances her way.

Considering her rather sizeable entourage, being stared at was nothing new, but this seemed different.

What was everyone gawking at? Afraid everyone was noticing the state of her hair, Amy cautiously raised one hand to check, then frowned. Surely her new bonnet concealed her wet hair. She fingered the delicate mauve ribbons tied jauntily beneath her chin. Jason gave the bonnet to her during their betrothal. The girls "borrowed" it for her birthday and refurbished it using bits from the ragbag. They'd used her favorite color, and several ladies in the congregation complimented her about the charming result.

She lowered her hand into her lap and thought over the past few years. Some people wondered why she gathered orphans instead of getting remarried after Jason's death. Most folks just didn't understand that she knew true love with her husband and could never settle for anything less.

Precious gifts from God, the girls filled her days with purpose and her heart with joy. They were her family now.

Amy rose and blended her voice with those of the other parishioners in the benediction. As she placed a hand upon Ruthie's back to guide her into the aisle, Amy noticed a stain covered her much-mended glove. It was almost the exact shade of mauve she favored.

Recognition hit, and Amy gasped as she touched her face. She drew her fingers away to find a fresh smearing of mauve dye. The water in her hair had made her ribbons run. No wonder all the womenfolk had been staring! And still were. Several women shook their heads, and a few actually pointed at her, as though she were the one lacking in decorum.

Only one option presented itself. Seizing a girl with each hand, she hurried toward the door and tried to ignore the whispers that followed her. As she purposefully strode up the aisle, someone snagged her elbow.

Amy turned to face the disapproving scrutiny of her late husband's mother. She pasted a smile on her mauve-stained face. "Mother Ross, what can I do for you?"

"I'll be over tomorrow to check up on the girls and discuss your wont of conduct," the woman hissed. "Your behavior is scandalous." With that parting shot, she grandly sailed toward the door, leaving Amy and the now wide-eyed girls in her wake.

A small hand tugged on Amy's sleeve. "Do we have to see her again?" a pleading voice whispered. "We just saw her on Wednesday." Several heads bobbed in solemn agreement.

Amy closed her eyes. She wasn't the only one who dreaded Mother Ross's visits.

Since she and Jason married young, he had not thought to draw up a will. It was typical of Jason, who loved life and reveled in each day, to not think of tomorrow. He'd made each day of their single year of marriage a joy.

As a wedding gift, Jason's parents gave them the charming little two-story residence, but Jason never received the deed. Upon his death, Amy's mother-in-law claimed ownership, blaming Amy for the untimely demise of their beloved only child. Although she allowed Amy to use the home as an orphanage, Hortense Ross ensured that the entire town knew of her "generosity" and, although they never parted with money for its upkeep, used it as leverage to "keep an eye on the dear girls" and monitor Amy's behavior. A visit from Mother Ross inevitably meant a thorough inspection of the premises, a stern lecture on decorum, and a large basket of mending to complete before the week was out.

Sighing, Amy pulled herself, mauve stains and all, back to the present. "Yes, I suppose we will see her tomorrow, ladies, so we must make sure the house is neat." She led them home amid protestations that working on the Sabbath was wrong.

"Even Jesus worked on the Sabbath by healing the unfortunate. We just have to make sure we give Mother Ross no reason for disapproval. The Lord understands that we're serving the greater good."

When they reached the house, Amy faced her charges. "Now, girls, I'll hear no more complaining." She ushered them through the mud patch her front yard had become and into the house. "Let's get going."

Amy took off her hat and caught sight of herself in the small hall mirror. "I really am quite a sight," she admitted aloud. The dye from the ribbons stained her light brown hair and left streaks on her cheeks and chin.

"Miss Amy," Susannah asked. "The little ones are changing now, but how are we supposed to clean this morning's dishes without any water?"

Noting Susannah's appalled look, Amy wondered how she could possibly clean her face. She walked out to the yard, praying for a miracle. It was answered. The caretaker came through the gate, holding a bucket of water.

"Hello. I saw you in church and thought you might be needing this." Her gaze slipped from green eyes framed by shining black hair, to trace the line of his broad shoulders and strong arms, and then to the bucket he hefted with one hand.

Amy quickly stifled her embarrassment. "Thank you. We have a lot to do today." She noticed his face cloud over as he stiffened.

"I'll just fix your pump, then I'll be on my way."

"Again, thank you. I've told most of the girls to keep out of the yard because I don't want them to slip in the mud, so they won't bother you." She accepted the pail and lugged it toward the house. The pump would be fixed, and they had water for the day to wash up and clean the house. It seemed all her troubles were solved. *So,* Amy puzzled, *why am I wondering whether I will ever face this man while looking presentable?*

Chapter 2

Tyler Samuels watched his neighbor as she walked away. This one seemed all right—she'd even smiled at the "ducky" misinterpretation—but appearances could be deceiving. He'd thought she'd want the water to wash her face, but she seemed more interested in making the children work—even on Sunday, just like another headmistress he'd known—and she wouldn't let the girls out because she didn't want them to dirty their clothes.

He knew how it could be with orphanages. He'd stick around for a few months to make sure she treated the girls kindly and cared for them properly. His resolution strengthened at the memory of his sister, Emma. She'd been so weak toward the end. . . . His hands curled into fists at the image of another orphanage—another woman entrusted with the care of children. Only that woman hadn't cared for her charges, instead stealing from the orphanage while the children suffered. . .his sister included. He wouldn't let it happen again. No, with the Lord's help, he'd see to it that this was not the case at Kindred Hearts.

"Whatcha doin'?" A small voice piped up behind him, startling Tyler.

He looked over his shoulder to find a small blond girl regarding him with curious hazel eyes—eyes like Emma's. He forced himself to smile. "I'm fixing the water pump."

"Was it your ducky, uh, goose that broke it?"

This time his smile was genuine. "Yes, Gussie's mine." The girl must be about eight years old.

"Can I see it?"

"Anytime. Just climb through that hole over there with some of your friends, and you can see her whenever you want."

"Really?" She visibly brightened.

"What's your name?"

"Prudence." She grimaced. "But don't call me that. Everyone calls me Prudie."

"All right, Prudie it is. I'm Tyler Samuels, but you may call me Mr. Sam."

"Oh. Auntie Amy says you're the new caretaker. I'm glad, 'cuz I didn't like the old one. He was mean when I asked him what he took care of."

The caretaker? In an odd sort of way, he was. He'd really only bought the large house so he could look after the orphanage. He felt protective of the children, and this engaging little minx proved no exception.

"I take care of the house, the plants. . .and even you, if you ever need something."

She backed away. "No. Auntie Amy takes care of me." With all the wisdom of a child, she added, "You can take care of your goose. Oops, I gotta go now."

Tyler watched as she scampered toward the house where Amy stood in the doorway, waiting. He didn't know what to make of this woman. At times she seemed unduly strict, meting out a load of chores on a hot day and not allowing the girls a bit of time for fun, presumably because she didn't want more dirty clothes. Still, tiny Prudie appeared alarmed at the thought of being separated from her.

That didn't matter. If anything, the two aspects of Amy's conduct alarmed him that much more. Many years ago, Mistress Lowland charmed the townsfolk while abusing her charges.

Shrugging his shoulders, Tyler set to work again, ignoring the hot sun as he repaired the water pump. The work went slowly since the parts were so old and badly worn. He smiled. He'd gladly repair half a dozen water pumps to watch Amy's losing battle with a goose.

A shadow fell across him as he labored, and he looked up. No stray cloud overhead blocked the sun as he'd expected. Instead, a shapely figure in gray calico leaned above him, holding out a glass of lemonade. Suddenly realizing how thirsty his work left him, he licked his lips.

"Mr. Sam?" Amy's voice sounded hesitant.

He straightened from his work. "Samuels, Tyler Samuels, Ma'am. The kids may call me Mr. Sam."

"Would you like some lemonade, Mr. Samuels? Maxwell Steadman was kind enough to bring several lemons back for us from his last trip."

"Thank you, Amy." He gratefully accepted the glass.

"The kids call me Auntie Amy." Her voice stopped him before he took a sip. "You, Mr. Samuels," she stressed the syllables of his name, "may call me Mrs. Ross."

She was married? No. He hadn't seen a husband around the house or at church. He eyed her speculatively, recalling he'd only seen her wear gray or mauve—the colors a woman wore after heavy mourning. On the other hand, the colors suited her light honey-brown hair and clear gray eyes. "I'm sorry for your loss." His words rang with undeniable sincerity.

"Thank you."

Anticipating cold refreshment, he raised the glass to his parched lips. Her desperate, "Wait!" didn't register until too late. Tyler took a large sip and promptly began spluttering. The woman was trying to kill him!

"Oh dear." She sighed. "I tried to warn you; the appeal of Prudie's lemonade comes more from her generous heart than the taste of the brew. She asked me to give it to you so she could finish her chores."

A likely story. She probably wouldn't let the child stop working long enough to bring it to him. That—or she merely wanted to see him sample the vile concoction. Did he see a smile hovering on her lips?

"And Prudie. . .found, er, happened upon this while she visited with you." She pulled his pocket watch from her apron pocket.

"That must have fallen out while I worked, but it escaped my notice." He cleared his throat. "I appreciate your returning it. You called her away rather quickly, so she must have forgotten to give it back. Thank her for me, and tell Prudie I'll have a little reward for her the next time I see her."

Amy gasped. "That's not necessary!"

Did she enjoy being so heartless she wouldn't let him give the child a small token of his gratitude? "Neither was the lemonade she so thoughtfully made for me. Sometimes we do things because they are kind, not because they are necessary. Many children would take this for themselves rather than return it." He curled his fingers around the treasured watch. She looked as if she were about to choke but quickly collected herself.

"However, like the lemonade, sometimes the sentiment doesn't quite carry through with the action." She straightened at the look on his face. "All right then. I'm sure she'll be very surprised by your unexpected generosity." Her strangled voice died off as she surveyed the mess around him. "I brought out an empty glass. It looked as though you were almost finished." She held it out, and he traded away the horrid lemonade.

An odd need to justify his continued presence in her yard surfaced. "Almost. These repairs are only temporary. I'll have to purchase some new parts tomorrow." He waited to catch her reaction. She looked uncomfortable, but determined.

"No. Once you've repaired the pump, you've finished your part."

"As near as I can tell, this pump worked just fine for several years and probably would have lasted a long while yet if my goose hadn't come along." Tyler issued a quick prayer for forgiveness for that little exaggeration. He intended to make sure the girls had water, regardless of this opinionated woman's stiff-necked pride.

He noted the play of emotions across her flushed face with interest. Apparently she had some sense because practicality defeated pride and she answered, "Then I have no choice but to again thank you for your generosity, Mr. Samuels."

He nodded and resumed working but watched out of the corner of his eye as she glanced surreptitiously toward the window and hastily poured out the lemonade before going inside.

He still didn't know what to make of Mrs. Ross. She seemed excessively prim for one so young. Lovely to look at, too, he admitted to himself. She was more than presentable when dry and free of mauve dye. Still, he wouldn't let a pretty woman turn his head. There were danger signs.

Mrs. Ross. He couldn't believe he'd called her Amy—it just suited her so much better. Oh, well. It was too late to erase the social gaffe.

After he finished this water pump, he would do his level best to avoid her. Tyler continued working until a stray thought struck him. If she'd been married, could one of those little girls actually be her own daughter?

Chapter 3

Amy straightened the kitchen after breakfast the next day while Jessica and Susannah did the dishes. Mary and Veronica already reported to the mill for their day's work, and the little ones were cleaning their rooms when Mr. Samuels knocked on the kitchen door.

"Hello, Mrs. Ross. I've brought the parts for the water pump. I wanted to let you know so you could get a few bucketfuls of water while it's available."

"Certainly, Mr. Samuels." She spoke quietly, uncertain how to express her gratitude to this enigmatic man filling her doorway. "I hope you didn't go through too much trouble for us. It's working just fine."

"It's no trouble at all. I need to replace a few parts, or it won't work much longer. I saw one of your girls gathering eggs, so I figured you were all done with your breakfast. . .and I wanted to give this to Prudie." Amy followed his gaze to the blue leather-bound book in one of his large, capable-looking hands.

The memory of his flashing green eyes and the determined set of his jaw when she'd tried to talk him out of this course of action the day before made her cautious. "I wish you'd take my word for it, Mr. Samuels. You really don't need to reward her."

His jaw tightened. "As I told you before, Mrs. Ross, I think I should."

Stubborn man! Still, he didn't know Prudie was a reformed—make that reforming—pickpocket. A recent arrival, she'd resorted to thievery to survive and hadn't quite broken the bad habit. If Amy had her way, he would never know. She sighed and sent Jessica to fetch Prudie.

"Hello, Mr. Sam!" Prudie smiled when she saw him.

"Hello, Prudie. I've brought you something as a thank-you for finding my pocket watch."

Amy gave Prudie a meaningful look, and Prudie flushed. The child's words came in a rush. "Thank you, Mr. Sam, but it was really nothing. I mean, you fixed our water pump and all."

He smiled and bent down to be at eye level with her. "Nonsense. This is my reward to you." He held the book out to her. "I got it at the mercantile when I went shopping this morning. My sister had one like it, and I thought you might enjoy one, too."

Prudie looked pleadingly at Amy. Amy gave up and nodded her assent. Prudie accepted the beautiful little book of fairy tales with a wide smile. "Oh, thank you. It's so pretty!"

He grinned, apparently pleased. "Mrs. Ross, my apple trees are full of apples. Why don't you send the girls over to pick some? I'll fill extra buckets with water and finish the pump."

Amy smiled. "How nice. Apples would be welcome." She shut the door as he left and looked down at Prudie, who clutched her book, staring at it with something akin to awe.

"Prudie, look at me." She captured the girl's attention with her firmest tone. "This must never happen again. Promise this is the last time."

Prudie's lower lip quivered, and she looked down. "I know, Auntie Amy, but sometimes I just do it without thinking. I'll try harder—honest I will."

"See that you do." Amy smiled and gave her a hug. "Now go ask Jessica to take you and the others to pick apples." She'd barely finished speaking before Prudie set off, clasping the book to her chest. "Wait a minute. Leave the book with me. We'll read it together after Bible study tonight."

When Prudie skipped off, Amy took a moment to study the book. A truly lovely volume, its delightful illustrations filled nearly every page. She carefully set the book on the hall table, then slipped off to her room to tidy herself. After tucking a few wayward tendrils back into her simple bun, Amy turned her thoughts toward a less pleasant subject. Mother Ross planned to visit again today. The very notion set Amy to pacing about her room. Even this room had become a source of disagreement between them.

Mother Ross had been less than pleased when Amy retained the master bedroom. Although she tried to pass off her bitterness as concern that the children should occupy the largest room by urging Amy to use the small attic as her sanctuary, Amy knew the woman only wanted to make her pay for Jason's death. Still, Amy held firm. A woman needed something to call her own, and she found comfort in the memories this room held.

Amy stopped pacing. She'd lost so much. First, her beloved husband, then their son. His son. . . *And it's all my fault.* Amy shook her head, refusing to indulge in tears. She wouldn't think of it today. She simply had too much to do. She shoved the painful thoughts aside and left the room.

As Amy walked through the hall, she reassured herself all was in readiness for Mother Ross's visit, although the woman would undoubtedly find something out of place. Amy peeked into all the rooms, thanking the Lord once again that the house met their needs.

When she and Jason first moved in, she thought the house perfect for the family they planned. Now her girls filled the two guest rooms and the nursery, and she'd converted the study into yet another bedroom. Each room held one of the older girls and three of the younger. The oldest girls were "in charge" of their own girls, and this small, family-like system proved most effective.

Someone knocked on the door just as Amy reached the bottom of the stairs.

"Isabel! Kathleen! Come in. I'm so glad you're here!" As she took them into the parlor, she whispered under her breath, "Mother Ross is coming today."

The two women exchanged a telling glance and asked in unison, "What can we do?"

Amy bit her lip and stared at the baskets of fabric they held. "I'm thankful for the quilting scraps, but where can I put them?"

"Right here," Kathleen exclaimed as she set her basket in a clearly visible place by the doorway, "and let her see it. When I think of all the hardship that dour old woman has caused you. . ."

Amy grabbed Isabel's basket, chiding her friend for carrying heavy burdens in her delicate condition. Isabel had other ideas.

"Piffle. I'm not even starting to show yet. It's when I can't carry things that you should worry about me. What time do you expect Hortense to arrive?"

Just then the front door whooshed open. Mother Ross never bothered to knock.

Amy took a deep breath and retraced her steps to the front hall. "Good day, Mother Ross, I—"

"What is this?" Her mother-in-law's outraged voice cut short the greeting. "What is this heathenish novel doing in my house?" She swiped the fairy-tale book from the side table and thrust it under Amy's nose.

"It's mine!" Prudie piped up as she took the book.

Mother Ross made an attempt to snatch it back. "I won't allow nonsense penned by the devil himself to remain in my house!"

"I'm sure Parson Hull would be appalled to hear you say so, Mrs. Ross. He gave Betty one exactly like it." Isabel's calming voice halted the woman's tirade as she stepped into the entryway.

Mother Ross's lips stretched painfully into some semblance of a smile. "Really? Well then, the child may keep the book."

At first, the unprecedented capitulation surprised Amy, but she quickly realized her mother-in-law would never offend one of the richest women in Eastead. She cleared her throat.

"Why don't we all go to the parlor, and I'll have one of the girls fix us some tea." Her relief at her friends' presence escalated. Perhaps she would be spared the coming lecture, after all.

"Yes, that will be satisfactory, but first I'd like a word with you, Amy. In private." Steel lay beneath the sugared tone.

Perhaps not. Amy suppressed a sigh. Susannah would be in the kitchen, Isabel and Kathleen waited in the parlor, and she'd set the other girls to stripping beds before they went to pick apples. As much as it rankled, she would be forced to take her mother-in-law to her bedroom, her sanctuary.

They passed every other room in the house, and nothing escaped Mother Ross's attention. She stopped in every doorway and peered into each room as Amy led her down the hallway. When they reached the modest room decorated in shades of blue and cream, Mother Ross picked up the small portrait of Jason from where it sat on Amy's bedside table. She gazed at it longingly, momentarily clasped it to her breast, and reluctantly set it down.

Amy's heart ached right along with the older woman's, and she wished for the ten thousandth time she'd never sent Jason out into that storm. For a moment, the two women silently grieved for him. When Mother Ross lifted her chin, Amy took a deep breath in preparation for the imminent scolding. It wasn't long in coming.

"I know I told you I planned to visit today. Did you really think to avoid my displeasure by inviting the Steadmans' new wives? Really, I am surprised they continue to visit you at all, considering their recently elevated position in society, but then blood will always tell, won't it?"

Anger rose within Amy's heart, but she firmly tamped it down. "I'm blessed in my wonderful friends."

"Indeed, but even their support cannot save your reputation if you continue to comport yourself in such a harum-scarum manner. Few church members will countenance a connection to such a poorly bred woman and her ragtag group of hoydens if you indulge in such unseemly displays. Your actions have been suspect from the moment you engaged the affections of my son. . . ." Her voice wavered, then strengthened with resolve. "Again you justified all of my suspicions by sullying the family name with your latest antics. And in church! Need I remind you of your dependence upon my good graces?"

Amy knew she must choose her words with care, but she would not allow Mother Ross to walk all over her. She whispered a quick prayer before responding. "You've made that abundantly clear, Mother Ross. However, this scandal was caused by nothing more than a broken water pump and could be silenced by a few judiciously chosen words. I trust that your place in society will allow you several avenues to dispel such vicious gossip."

The woman appeared slightly mollified. "I will do what I can, of course."

"You have my appreciation for all you do. Now, I am sure the tea is ready, and my guests are waiting." With that, Amy walked out the door and headed for the stairs, certain Mother Ross wouldn't miss the opportunity to chat with some of Eastead's most influential hostesses.

After they had taken tea and visited a short while, Amy's guests rose to leave. As she walked toward the parlor door, Mother Ross spotted the baskets of material and stopped. "Another quilt? I do hope you intend to donate it to the upcoming bazaar." She added pointedly, "Positively everyone is giving something to help the less fortunate."

Isabel spared Amy when she spoke up. "Yes, it's a little project we're working on, but the quilts we make are intended for the girls, as, I hope, are some of the proceeds from the bazaar. I do, however, admire your efforts to give the girls some employment."

Evangeline hesitantly stepped into the room and tugged on Amy's skirts, wanting to know where they should put the apples.

Mother Ross looked confused. "Of course, but I'm not really sure what you mean."

Isabel smiled. "Why, I'm referring to your wonderful idea of hiring the girls to do your mending." She indicated the basket Mother Ross had brought with her.

Evangeline, probably remembering pricked fingers and crooked stitches, piped up, "Oh, we don't get paid."

Mother Ross flushed. "I hold the conviction that the girls should be industrious." She turned to address Amy, trying to change the subject. "But surely you plan to give something appropriate to the bazaar?"

Kathleen stepped in, picked up the basket of mending, and handed it to Mother Ross. "Why, that's a wonderful idea. Since you understand the girls will be occupied making something for the church bazaar, I'm sure your servants are anxious to resume their duties. Oh, look at the time. We really must be going now."

Taking Kathleen's suggestion, Mother Ross hurried toward the door. Isabel and Kathleen winked conspiratorially at Amy as they followed.

Chapter 4

Tyler glared at the woman who huffed across the lawn, carrying what looked to be a basket of shirts. He and a gaggle of girls had come to the front door to ask Amy where she wanted the apples just in time to overhear the last bit of that exchange. Since the pump sat beneath an open window, he also hadn't missed the dressing-down Amy had withstood from her mother-in-law. Her skillful handling of the situation impressed him.

Mrs. Ross, the elder, displayed all the charm and manners of a shrew. The woman, he decided unequivocally, was a menace; the kind from whom he hoped to shield the girls. She reminded him forcibly of Mistress Lowland. No one deserved the kind of treatment those two women seemed determined to mete out to those less fortunate. He shook his head.

"Mother Ross is always like that," Marissa informed him gravely.

He nodded and looked up to find Amy, as well as two other women, doing the same. "That's right, 'Rissa," Amy exclaimed, scooping the child into her arms. "Mother Ross is difficult, but we each handle grief differently."

The child wriggled to be let down, and Amy hastened to make introductions. "Isabel, Kathleen, this is Mr. Samuels, the caretaker next door who's been kind enough to fix our water pump. Mr. Samuels, these are Mrs. Carter Steadman and Mrs. Maxwell Steadman."

After the requisite social exchange, Tyler was relieved to see the women leave. Their speculative glances did more to make him uncomfortable than the heavy bushel of apples he held. These women had just married his cousins. Were they noticing some vague resemblance between him and their new husbands? He wasn't ready for that yet.

He cleared his throat and turned his attention to the matter at hand. "Have you decided where you want these, Ma'am?"

Amy started. "How foolish of me. I'd like you to take them to the kitchen, if you don't mind. My, those are fine apples. Perhaps there'll be enough so we can make applesauce for the church bazaar."

Tyler opened his mouth to protest that the apples were for the girls but never got the chance.

"Oh, Auntie Amy, there's plenty of apples."

"He gots rows of trees!"

"He has rows of trees," Amy automatically corrected.

Tyler chuckled. "We've gathered seven full bushels besides this one."

"Seven more?" she echoed incredulously as they reached the kitchen and he put the bushel basket down.

"I'm sure you'll be able to use them all." He looked around the crowded room. "The branches were so full they were bending, and the apples shouldn't go to waste."

Her luminous eyes sparkled. "Of course we can put them to good use."

"Applesauce!" Marissa and Evangeline sang out.

"Applesauce?" Scorn filled Alys's tone. "No. Apple-Brown-Betty!"

"Aunt Amy," Jessica pled, "let's make apple pie!"

"Oh, please, can't it be apple butter? You know Rebecca bakes the best bread in the whole world!"

"Cider!" the twins cried in unison.

Tyler interrupted them all. "I have a press. I'd be happy to make juice with the apples you girls missed. In fact," he winked, "I'd gladly trade for an apple cobbler. It's my favorite. I'll bring over some straw and extra barrels so you can pack apples for winter storage. I've plenty of extra for you to use."

Amy nodded happily. "Certainly, Mr. Samuels, and why don't you come over for lunch tomorrow? We're having a simple picnic, but it's the least we can do to thank you for your generosity."

He smiled. "I've finished the pump, so you can get all the water you want. I'll bring over the rest of the apples."

After she'd agreed to this plan, he found himself wondering what he could give them for the church bazaar. He'd continue to let them think of him as the caretaker. It allowed him to watch the girls without having Amy fawn all over him when she learned of his wealth.

For he was rich. Even though Uncle Steadman refused to acknowledge him and his sister after their father died, Tyler managed to make something of himself. Of course, all that came too late to save his sister. After Emma died, he'd been adopted by a family who owned a large, prosperous mercantile. Because the owner was getting on in years and didn't have a son, he wanted someone he could train to take over the business. Tyler grew to love his new family; but when he turned seventeen, the man whose name he'd taken passed away. His foster mother followed her husband to the Lord's waiting arms only two years later.

They'd left the mercantile to Tyler, and he'd become a wealthy man. Still, he'd roamed restlessly, having nothing to tie him down but business. He sold the mercantile and bought a controlling number of shares in an international trading company. He traveled for many years. On his last journey, he'd met a Christian sailor who'd reaffirmed the faith Tyler's adoptive parents once shared with him. He rediscovered the Lord, and although God filled his spiritual void, Tyler still lacked something.

Eventually, Tyler felt drawn back to Eastead, where Uncle Ebenezer had refused to acknowledge his own kin, consigning Tyler and Emma to the orphanage where Emma died. Although it was the hardest decision he'd ever made, Tyler knew he needed to forgive his uncle and acknowledge his own Steadman blood before he could close that chapter of his life.

While wandering through town after learning his uncle had died, Tyler spotted Kindred Hearts. Chafing from his inability to confront his uncle and plagued by the memory of how cruel Mistress Lowland killed Emma through years of neglect, he'd realized something: The Lord was giving him what he so desperately sought—a purpose. He sold his shares in the trading company and spent a small fraction of the amount to buy the huge house next door, where he could easily watch over the children.

For now, everyone thought him a kindhearted caretaker. He grinned at the irony. It provided the perfect cover. Since no one knew his true identity and he tended to resemble his mother, this would give him the perfect opportunity to get to know his cousins without the stigma of past differences.

Thinking back over his years in trading had inspired Tyler, and he suddenly knew just what to get the girls for the church bazaar. He could have it by tomorrow if he hurried, and he'd get to see their excited faces during their picnic.

◆　◆　◆

After the day's end, Amy tucked the girls in with nighttime devotions. Her prayer carried an extra note of gratitude: The visit from Mother Ross had gone by more smoothly than she'd dared hope, and the apples were an unexpected boon. The moment she slipped into bed, she fell fast asleep.

Amy awoke the next morning feeling completely refreshed. Today she and the girls would take care of the apples. They'd dry, preserve, and bake them this week. Mr. Samuels was so kind to the children. In fact, he'd done more for the orphanage in three days than most people did all year. She'd make sure they served apple cobbler as dessert for dinner and bake an extra one for him to take home.

After breakfast, Amy and the younger girls washed the dishes. Jessica and Susannah got busy taking in the rest of the laundry since they hadn't managed to complete it all the day before. As soon as they finished, they'd come in and work with the apples would begin.

First, Amy needed to decide what to do with the apples. Since Mr. Samuels promised to make the cider, they hadn't put any apples aside for juice or jelly. Of the eight bushels, she decided to use two for drying, two for packing in straw and keeping, and three more for applesauce. The remaining bushel would be for snacks and today's apple cobblers.

With the youngest girls thinking of sweet treats and the older ones thinking of winter provisions, everyone set to work with a cheerful heart and busy hands. First, they carried the chosen apples to the cold room and packed them in barrels with straw. Back in the kitchen, the littlest girls squeezed lemon juice and readied the drying pegs while the bigger girls peeled, cored, and sliced the apples. Amy supervised everything and started making cobbler for their picnic lunch.

"Many hands make light work, and soon it will be time for our picnic." Amy cheered her girls on.

Soon they'd finished packing the two bushels of apples for winter storage and were well into drying the others. Noting the old grandfather clock in the parlor had already struck eleven o'clock, Amy called to the children, "Alys, Mary, why don't you make some egg salad? Ruthie, bring me some blankets to take out back for our picnic. And, Evangeline, would you please make the lemonade?"

"I'll make the lemonade, Auntie Amy!"

An emphatic "NO!" from everyone present met Prudie's offer. Striving to lighten the rejection, Amy told her, "Let Evangeline make it today, Prudie. I need you and Carolyn to slice the bread and cheese for lunch."

"Yes, Auntie Amy."

Mr. Samuels would be there soon. As Amy took an armful of blankets to spread on the grass, a knock sounded. She reached and opened the door expectantly. No one stood there.

Amy looked down and found baskets full of lace and fine Irish linen with a note lying on top. "For the girls and church bazaar, from a secret friend in the Lord." That was odd. Kathleen and Isabel never left mysterious notes with their gifts, but Amy couldn't think of anyone else who possessed the wherewithal for such a costly donation. There was enough lace and material to make a fine lace collar for each of the girls' Sunday best, with plenty left over.

Thrilled at this unexpected bounty from the Lord, Amy joyfully carried the baskets into the parlor. First the apples, now this. But who could have sent it?

Chapter 5

Concealed behind the chicken coop where he'd sprinted after placing his basket on the steps, Tyler heard exclamations as Amy carried it into the house. He smiled, pleased beyond all reason by their excitement. He'd thought the note an inspired touch, considering how she'd misconstrued his intentions for the bucket of water and the apples on other occasions. This time, he'd specified the gift was for the girls.

Tyler glanced around, making sure no one would see him emerge from behind the chicken coop. Intrigues were fun, but he still needed to prepare for the inevitable questions his gift would bring if it became known he was their benefactor. He'd visited church for the first time the day before yesterday and met most of the community. The way his cousins and their wives didn't snicker when Amy's ribbons ran impressed him. He still felt a bit guilty about that little scene.

He strode quickly to the door and knocked. A very flushed Amy opened it. He smiled at the sparkle in her eyes—it made her look younger.

"Hello, Mr. Samuels. We were just getting ready to set up our picnic when we received an unexpected bounty." She gestured to the parlor, where several girls examined the linen and lace.

He pretended surprise. "Really? I didn't see anyone when I came over. Sure looks like some nice material, though."

A small frown furrowed her delicate brows. "I'm afraid our benefactor wishes to remain anonymous, Mr. Samuels, but it is an answer to our prayers, in any case."

"Oh?" He waited to hear how she planned to use the lace and Irish linen he'd purchased that morning.

"Indeed, yes. It would appear unseemly if we didn't donate something to the upcoming church bazaar, but now we can fashion lace collars for the charity." Her satisfied pronouncement held no mention of the girls benefitting from the gift.

"Is it so very important that the less fortunate give to charity? I mean, shouldn't the girls be able to use at least some of it for themselves?"

A look of reproach met his pointed inquiry. "Of course it is. No matter how hard life may seem, there are always others in greater need. Anyway, the girls needn't deny themselves. There is plenty for the girls to make a collar each and still contribute to the community."

Pleased to hear her say so, and a bit shamed by the look she'd given him, Tyler ventured, "Just so, Ma'am. Is there anything I can do to help with the picnic?"

Her stiff posture relaxed as she inclined her head. "If you could help me lay out these old blankets while the girls bring out the food, we could begin."

He quickly grabbed some of the blankets and followed her to a large shady patch on the lawn. They laid them out in silence, appreciating the fine weather.

When the girls started placing various platters on two large tree stumps nearby, Tyler suddenly became aware that he'd skipped breakfast. "Sure looks good."

Prudie skipped up next to him with a pitcher of what looked suspiciously like lemonade. "Yep. Egg salad sandwiches and lemonade are my favorite," she confided. She held up the pitcher. "Want some?"

Probably seeing the wariness on his face, Amy took pity on him. "Of course he wants some of Evangeline's wonderful lemonade. Why don't you pour him a glass?" She winked conspiratorially at him as he let out a relieved breath and accepted the glass.

He cautiously sampled the brew. Proclaiming it to be just the thing for a hot day, he turned to his hostess. "I've already met most of the girls, but I'll probably need to hear their names a few more times before I can get them all straight, A—Mrs. Ross." That was a close one.

She summoned the girls, and they all obliged him by saying their names and ages. He by no means could remember all the names and faces, but it was a start. He thought of how Mistress Lowland and her husband always called him "Taylor" instead of "Tyler." Apparently, such mistakes did not happen at Kindred Hearts. Amy readily named any of the girls when she called to them. She could even tell the twins apart!

A clear voice interrupted his thoughts. "Who wants to pray today?"

He was a bit surprised when thirty-four eyes all seemed to gaze in his general direction. "I'd be honored to thank the Lord for the fine company I find myself in today and for the bounty we're about to receive, Mrs. Ross."

Why Amy's approving nod pleased him so, he couldn't say, but she seemed fresh and alive, handling the girls with tender skill and organizing their little feast quite capably. She made quite a fetching picture, with a smile on her lips and the sun warming the golden highlights in her hair as she reached for the hands of the two girls closest to her. The other girls followed suit until they all connected in a large circle.

Tyler bowed his head and wholeheartedly gave thanks to God for everything he could think of—the girls, the food, the sunshine, and the promise of more beautiful days to come. Then they all served themselves from the piles of sandwiches.

"This is excellent," he praised, savoring the flavor of the sandwich made from fresh-baked bread. "Who made lunch today?" He looked around expectantly. Everyone seemed to answer all at once.

"I gathered the eggs," young Evangeline volunteered.

"Susannah baked the bread, but I helped!"

Alys and Mary chimed in, "We made the egg salad."

"I sliced the cheese," Prudie proudly informed him.

"Laura made the sandwiches."

The twins finished, "And Auntie Amy made the cobbler!"

Tyler perked up and turned to Amy. "Cobbler?" He knew he probably sounded like a three year old begging for a favorite treat, but it had been so long since he ate hot-out-of-the-oven apple cobbler.

Amy smiled. "Well, the cat's out of the bag, isn't it? We started work on the apples this morning, and we made the cobbler you requested." She pretended to glare at the girls. "It was supposed to be a surprise."

"We didn't tell him about the other one," Evangeline protested defensively.

"The other one?" Tyler echoed hopefully. He watched as she shrugged in mock defeat.

"You might as well finish telling him, girls."

"Auntie Amy made an extra so you could take it home, Mr. Sam."

"It sure is your lucky day!" Prudie added.

He was inclined to agree with her on that point.

"Can we have some now, Auntie Amy?" the twins chorused, voicing his thoughts. They all turned pleading faces toward her.

"Why don't we let lunch settle for a bit, first?" Her suggestion met with groans. "The sooner we eat it, the sooner our picnic is over, ladies. Then we have to finish work with the apples." The mood suddenly shifted. He bit back his surprise that she actually wanted to give the girls more free time.

"Can we play a game?" one of the more adventurous youngsters questioned.

Soon they began tossing around ideas. After rejecting jackstraws, hide-and-seek, and a few others, they settled on a rousing session of blind man's bluff.

"You're goin' to play with us, too, aren't you, Auntie Amy and Mr. Sam?" Prudie's question was quickly seconded by all the girls.

Tyler raised his eyebrows at his hostess. He was willing to bet she wouldn't do it, but he issued the challenge anyway. "I'll play if you will."

She proved him wrong as she nodded, held up a towel, and gamely answered, "So long as you're 'It' first!" Her smile made her look five years younger, and he couldn't help grinning back as she advanced with the makeshift blindfold.

A short time later, after an exasperated Evangeline gave up trying to catch somebody, everyone collapsed back onto the quilts to catch their breath.

Amy'd forgotten just how much fun the game could be. She looked over her girls, some sipping cool lemonade and others fanning themselves in the heat. The only exceptions were Mr. Sam, Prudie, and the other little ones who waited their turn for a piggyback ride. She couldn't believe how gentle and patient the large man managed to be with her girls. He definitely deserved a reward.

"So," she called out, "who wants to help me clean up and get the apple cobbler?" She bit her bottom lip to keep from laughing as Mr. Sam stopped suddenly, turned around, and galloped over, much to the delight of his tiny rider. The rest of the children eagerly followed.

The dishes and leftovers were cleared away in record time. Soon the warm cinnamon fragrance of dessert wafted over the yard, and everyone was enjoying a piece of the much-anticipated apple cobbler. They all seemed to enjoy it, and Mr. Sam solemnly assured them it was the best thing he'd ever tasted.

He seemed so different today—smiling, laughing, playing with the children. He'd smelled of summer and strength when she'd blindfolded him. The sun glinted off his black hair as he lifted the smaller girls onto his strong back and broad shoulders. He seemed more like a gentle giant than their next-door neighbor.

She watched as he picked up Ruthie and walked toward her, his long stride quickly covering the small distance. The toddler struggled to keep her eyes open. It was no wonder—Ruthie's naptime had usually come and gone by now.

He nodded toward his little bundle, his deep green eyes silently asking for instruction. Amy got up, whispered to Susannah to have the girls pick up and get washed, then gestured for him to follow. Ruthie fell asleep in his arms, and the tender way he held her tugged at Amy's heart.

When they reached the right room, he laid the toddler on her bed and silently backed out. For such a large man, he moved soundlessly. Back in the hall, Amy invited him into the kitchen.

"Here's that apple cobbler we promised you."

He held it up to his nose and inhaled deeply. "Smells as wonderful as the one we just finished. Thank you. You know, the offer for apple juice still stands. Why don't you and the girls come over tomorrow afternoon and we'll get it done?"

Amy told herself she accepted because it was best for the girls—not because she wanted to see him again.

Chapter 6

The girls spent the next few Sundays diligently working with the tatted lace, fashioning delicate collars. Ginger, Isabel, and Kathleen had been invaluable in organizing the girls and containing their excitement about the bazaar. Accompanied by their husbands, the three friends arrived bright and early on Saturday to help get everything packed up for the bazaar.

Amy surveyed her troops rushing back and forth from Maxwell Steadman's wagon, loading the lace collars, old picnic quilts, and the apple cobblers they'd made for the church potluck. Ginger and Lucas joined them, too, and the girls looked forward to the special treat of riding in the wagons designated for the nighttime hay rides. Everyone had bathed on Friday, a night earlier than usual, to prepare for the special event. Amy hoped they would expend some of their energy before Tyl—Mr. Samuels came.

His help since he'd fixed the water pump couldn't be measured. The apples and subsequent picnic made him an unabashed favorite of the girls, and they'd all enjoyed the day spent on his property making apple cider. Even his goose, who'd once again rushed at Amy the second she stepped over the fence to help with the apples, was a hit. Tyler was kind to all her girls, and although she suspected he had a soft spot for her little pickpocket, he never let it show.

At first she worried about how quickly the children became attached to their first male role model. He was, after all, a caretaker. Who knew how long he intended to stay? But it wasn't until he knocked on the door, surrounded by most of her girls, and showed her their new picnic tables and benches that she realized the level of his commitment to her precious charges. He'd even involved Isabel and Kathleen by commissioning them to work with the girls to make new tablecloths.

Tyler Samuels had earned a place in their hearts—and at their new tables. He ate with them more than a few times but always brought something to alleviate the burden of feeding an extra mouth. His understanding surprised Amy almost as much as the astonishing way the girls obeyed him without question.

A knock on the door interrupted her thoughts. She watched as the subject of her musings strode into the house and shook hands with everyone in reach.

"Since some of the girls are to ride in my wagon, and yours isn't quite full, why don't we put the barrels of apple cider in yours?" he asked Carter.

"Great idea. I'll lend a hand."

The women watched as the men exited purposefully. Isabel grinned. "Mr. Samuels is a fine man, Amy, and he gets along so well with everyone in town."

"We're lucky he takes such an interest in the girls," she replied. "He's been a godsend."

"I don't think the girls are the only thing he's interested in," Kathleen stated knowingly.

Ginger nodded. "His smile lights his face when he talks to you or the girls."

"Nonsense, there—"

"What's that?" one of the men asked as they reentered the house.

Kathleen smoothly took over. "We were just discussing the seating arrangements for the wagons. Ours is obviously full to bursting, and Isabel's. . ."

Isabel swiftly caught on. "We'll be carrying Ginger and Lucas and most of the older girls, so we thought you could take up Amy and the smaller girls, Mr. Samuels."

They maneuvered so shamelessly their husbands exchanged knowing grins, but Tyler didn't notice anything amiss. "Sounds good to me." He looked around. "Are all the girls accounted for?"

Amy took a swift head count. "Yes. Susannah, Evangeline, Ruthie, Prudie, Alys, Mary, and the twins will ride with us; everyone else will go with Isabel and Carter." The girls divided into two camps and prepared to walk out to the wagons.

"Wait just a minute, there." Tyler's voice halted their progress. He pulled a small bag from his pocket. "As the Bible says, 'The laborer is worthy of his hire,' and I believe all of you helped to pick and juice my apples a little while ago. Am I right?"

The girls nodded, glad to have their help appreciated and remembered but curious as to what was in the bag. They soon found out as Tyler loosened the drawstrings and ordered, "Hold out your hands and close your eyes." He began depositing a bright, shiny nickel in the hands of every single girl. When he finished, he allowed, "You may open your eyes now."

Obviously trying to sound stern and failing miserably, he clarified, "These are for each of you to spend on whatever you want, but it must be used today. It's my way of thanking you for your help and hospitality." He glanced at Amy as he said this.

Amid startled exclamations and a great many hugs, Amy didn't have the heart to object to this unexpected extravagance. Eighty cents equaled two days of a mill worker's wages, and she knew to an ounce how much sugar and flour that money could buy. His generosity overwhelmed her.

After the girls finished their chorus of thank-yous and trekked out the door to pile into the wagons, Amy turned to Tyler. "You didn't need to do that, but I'm glad you did. Thank you."

He nodded, offered her his arm, and they set out for the annual Founder's Day Church Bazaar and Potluck. Feeling the strength of his arm through his blue cambric shirt, Amy felt a sudden spurt of gratitude for her friends' not-so-subtle plot to seat her beside him. She preferred not to ask herself why.

A few minutes later as the wagons pulled away from the orphanage, Tyler glanced at the woman next to him. Her diminutive stature and worn dress might have made a lesser woman seem plain, but her warmth and generosity were all the adornment she needed. "Beauty should not come from outward adornment. . . . Instead, it should be that of your inner self, the unfading beauty of a gentle and quiet spirit, which is of great worth in the sight of God." His foster mother showed such virtue, and his father often quoted that verse from the first epistle of Peter.

Tyler came to this town to forgive his uncle and lay the past to rest by confronting his kin. Exposing this orphanage headmistress to be as conniving, hard-hearted, and selfish as Mistress Lowland was to give him closure and the assurance that a horrendous wrong wouldn't be repeated. He'd been so locked up in his memories, it had taken him far too long to recognize Amy bore no resemblance to his old nemesis. Now that he realized it, however, he'd make amends.

Coming back to the present, he smiled at his riders' excitement. The wagon pulled into the large grass field next to the church, where tables and booths were already being set up.

Carter and Isabel pulled up alongside them. "Everybody ready to go?" He nodded toward the old trees in the corner of the lot designated as a children's play area and asked Tyler, "Those swings we put up last weekend look pretty good, don't they? Good of you to volunteer at the town meeting."

Tyler shrugged. "I did nothing more than you, Maxwell, and Lucas did. Maxwell even donated the rope—all I did was—"

"Shimmy up the trees faster than I'd ever thought a grown man could," Lucas cut in, smiling.

"All right, enough chatter," Kathleen called. "How 'bout you big, strong men help us out with unloading this wagon?"

Everyone scrambled to follow instructions as the women assigned jobs. Soon Ginger was marshaling the older girls, loaded with foodstuffs, over to the potluck picnic tables. Amy and Isabel helped the little ones carry the lace collars over to the women's booth. The men busied themselves with setting up Tyler's cider booth and the mill's fabric area.

In just a few short hours, the lot bustled with activity, and the girls were trying to decide what to spend their treasure on. The church women's booth overflowed with lace collars, ribbons, and embroidered handkerchiefs. The men's booth burst with the stick horses, wooden hoops, and spinning tops the male parishioners made in their spare time. Along with the rope swings and wooden seesaws set up in the corner earlier, the toys would entertain the little ones for most of the day.

An area reserved for foodstuffs stood a little ways off. Since the potluck dinner was provided by the community, the townspeople were expected to purchase their evening supper. Thankfully, Maxwell and Carter had generously offered to buy this for the girls.

The general store had donated fruit, licorice, and gumdrops. The baker showcased all manner of breads and pastries—including cream puffs. Next to him, the owner of the dairy farm offered slices cut from a few large wheels of cheese. The fishermen offered a multitude of fish and lobster, and a grill stood ready for use.

A small platform had been raised in the corner of the open picnic area, waiting for the traditional raffle and Mayor Smythe's speech. The raffle prizes were nothing short of decadent: The ladies' sewing circle presented a lovely appliquéd maple-leaf quilt, and Vivian Steadman's generous contribution of a precious silver tea set would surely increase ticket sales. Not to be outdone, Mother Ross offered the pièce de résistance: a small box pianoforte.

None of the townspeople could possibly know the value Amy placed on the instrument. Amy had played that very pianoforte the night she met Jason. She would have loved to own the instrument as a keepsake of that night, and her fingers itched to make music. He'd told her he'd never enjoyed music so much. Only Mother Ross knew its significance, and she would rather see the piece raffled off to someone she didn't know than let her daughter-in-law enjoy it.

Looking at the pianoforte regretfully, Amy resolved not to let the memories she cherished stand in the way of making new ones.

Chapter 7

At one o'clock, after Parson Hull asked God's blessing, the potluck picnic began. Sandwiches, deviled eggs, bread and cheese, shepherd's pie, crab cakes, fried chicken, sauerkraut, and a variety of fresh produce and salads awaited the hungry townsfolk.

Everyone hustled around the picnic area, smoothing old blankets across the summer grass and gossiping about who sat with whom and who brought what. Several people eyed the large group in the northwest corner, speculating about the connection between Amy Ross and the new man in town.

"Don't mind the old biddies," Kathleen advised them with a smile.

Tyler agreed wholeheartedly, hesitant to examine the warm feeling that came from Amy's name being linked with his. "I don't understand the fuss. Why two neighbors can't sit with sixteen girls and three newly married couples without raising eyebrows is beyond me."

"And Davey," added Susannah, sending an adoring gaze to Isabel's younger brother. The fourteen-year-old girl had become quite attached to the young man who had arrived in town scant months ago.

"David," he corrected good-naturedly, probably resigned to the nickname Susannah persisted in using. Clearly, the attraction wasn't as one-sided as he let on.

Tyler, for his part, tried to ignore the icy stares "Mother Ross" aimed at Amy. He hadn't missed Amy's longing glance at the pianoforte earlier, either. With a little prompting, Isabel quietly revealed the history behind it.

He shook his head, hardly tasting the delectable crab cake he bit into. He knew as well as anyone how anger and blame over unresolved issues could leave a person bitter. Why the older woman felt so toward her daughter-in-law stayed a mystery to him, but her behavior was unconscionable.

He snuck a glance at Amy. The dappled sunlight weaving through the leaves played on the loosened curls around her face, giving her an almost angelic appearance. Her expressive gray eyes appeared almost violet as she laughed at something Ruthie said. Amy wore a light shade of something lavender-pink that flattered her coloring, and he had a sudden flash of her adorable face covered in the dye from her ribbons. He couldn't help grinning at the memory—he didn't know any other woman who could pull off a purple-pink face with half the dignity she'd managed.

His grin slipped when he remembered the raking-down Mother Ross gave her for that little lapse in decorum. It only happened because Gussie had slipped through the fence when he wasn't looking. If the girls didn't love the silly goose so much, he'd cook the bird for dinner for all the trouble she'd caused. Gussie had even tried to run down Amy again the day they'd juiced the apples. Of course, he certainly couldn't fault the fowl for bad taste. Who wouldn't want to be as close to Amy as possible?

Geese were good watchdogs, but their bad tempers and tendency to bring trouble put him in mind of. . .well, Mother Ross. What kind of woman would rather see something that would bring her daughter-in-law joy go to a stranger rather than release a grudge? Amy should have the pianoforte. If only there was a way he could buy a lot of tickets without raising questions about his financial situation. . . .

He looked up to see Kathleen and Isabel watching him. Apparently, he'd missed something.

"I'm sorry, I was paying more attention to my stomach than the conversation." He threw in his best smile for good measure. It didn't work. The two women shared a knowing glance before answering him.

"We just said that you seem somehow familiar. Are you absolutely positive you never passed through town before?"

For a moment he stared at their expectant faces in panic. His tall, broad frame bore similarities to Maxwell's, but he wasn't nearly as tan. Carter was thinner, and Lucas was a bit stockier, but their coloring was lighter than his. All three possessed brownish eyes; his were green. They boasted varying shades of brown hair compared to his black. The Steadman nose might mark him, but he'd broken it long ago and he'd thought the resulting bump would hide its shape. But apparently it wasn't enough to stop his cousins' new wives from recognizing the vague resemblance. The strong Steadman jaw, stubborn chin, and wavy hair probably gave him away. He saw the similarities right away, but he searched for them, so he hadn't expected others to notice just yet.

"I came a few weeks before I moved here, and you might have seen me then. Other than that, I seriously doubt such an. . . observant town would fail to notice if I passed through."

Maxwell clapped him on the shoulder. "If that's not the blessed truth, I don't know what is."

Congratulating himself on his narrow escape, Tyler's gratitude turned to Amy when she asked if they wanted dessert. Watching her lead some of the girls to the picnic tables once again, he found himself wondering whether he should tell her his secret. He didn't think she'd try to charm money from his pockets when she learned his identity, and he'd already decided to make amends for his misplaced suspicions. The idea had definite possibilities.

◆　◆　◆

After a day full of excitement and treats, everyone flocked once again to the picnic area with their supper to hear the mayor's speech and find out who won the raffle. Carter and Maxwell generously purchased supper for everyone, letting them choose whatever they wanted from the many foodstuffs available—so long as it wasn't candy or sweets.

Tyler had been rather busy. He'd found each girl and given her a nickel apiece to purchase two raffle tickets, to be under Amy's name, then bought a few more for good measure. Yep. Forty raffle tickets should do the trick. He couldn't wait to see the expression on Amy's pretty face when she won that little pianoforte. He'd also enjoy hearing her play it on Sundays, when he maintained a standing invitation to dinner. On Sunday afternoons while the womenfolk sewed, he read Bible parables to the girls and led a short time of worship.

For now, everyone politely pretended to listen to Mayor Smythe's annual, long-winded speech about Founder's Day. The townspeople bore the tradition good-naturedly, knowing that the raffle announcements and "a special surprise, courtesy of the Steadmans" awaited them.

Finally, raffle time came. Peg from the mill won the beautiful quilt, and Parson Hull's wife proudly carried away the silver tea set. A hush fell over the crowd, but Tyler barely noticed it. His gaze glued on Amy's wistful expression as the time for presenting the pianoforte arrived.

The Mayor Smythe dug deep into the third hatbox and dramatically flourished the winning ticket before proclaiming grandly, "Amy Ross."

Amid the shrieks and hugs from all the girls, who carefully protected their secret, Amy stayed seated, her eyes shining in stunned disbelief. She finally stood when the mayor repeated her name, and made her way to the makeshift platform, where he shook her hand. The mayor assured the crowd that no one deserved it more, and the pianoforte would be delivered to Kindred Hearts the very next day.

Tyler nearly burst with pride at the tears shining in Amy's eyes when she returned. He'd done that, and the wonderful feeling it brought surprised him. When she sat down, he reached out and squeezed her little hand, giving her a supportive nod to let her know he shared her happiness.

When the fireworks began in great, booming sparkles, Tyler barely paid attention. For some reason, his entire focus centered on the dainty hand that lay so sweetly in his.

◆　◆　◆

Amy still couldn't believe what a perfect day it had been—or how much of it had been Tyler Samuels's doing. How had she ever thought him to be disagreeable? From the moment he'd picked them up, giving the girls those coins, to his comforting clasp as they watched the fireworks, he'd demonstrated the gentle warmth and selflessness she'd noticed regularly for weeks.

Why, the only happy spot of the day that couldn't be attributed to him was winning the pianoforte. When Isabel scrawled "Amy" on a ticket, Amy warned herself not to be overly hopeful. The Lord certainly did work in mysterious ways.

She wondered whether Tyler's interest was confined to the welfare of the girls or if perhaps he returned her regard in some small measure. Amy tried to tamp down the requisite feelings of guilt that sprang up at the thought. His warm hand encircling hers surely provided proof that he did.

The removal of that comfortable clasp shook her out of her reverie. Cool autumn rain sprinkled the area. She quickly took charge of the situation, helping the girls gather their trinkets and blankets. They all headed for the wagons.

Amy was still smiling when she said her prayers after sending the girls to bed. In fact, the feeling lasted through the next morning, when she started down the stairs and ran into Jessica.

"Oh, I was just coming to get you," the girl cried. "It's Prudie—she's sick!"

Chapter 8

Hurrying to the remade study where Prudie roomed, Amy realized with a sinking heart that the precious little pickpocket, flushed and shivering under her blankets, was indeed ill. The ride home in the rain last night had taken its toll.

Amy crossed the room to the bed where Prudie lay in the grip of a fever. "Prudie, Sweetie, I'm here." She held her small, hot hand. "Soon you'll be right as rain." Her heart ached at the sweet smile Prudie managed before she gave way to a fit of coughing.

Amy took charge of the situation. "Jessica, I need you to go fetch Dr. Steadman right away and see if Ginger can come help with the young ones. Susannah, cool cloths would be welcome, and have Faith get some applesauce. Alys, please keep the other girls away from this room."

Susannah bustled in with the cold compresses, and after thanking her, Amy sent her back to the kitchen to fetch the teakettle. Inhaling the steam would help the child breathe more easily as they waited for the fever to break. She would do all she could—hopefully Dr. Lucas would be there soon.

◆ ◆ ◆

Tyler saw Jessica hurry out of the house without her bonnet. The morning was damp from the previous night's rain, so he called her name to stop her. When she turned, he saw her face and dread swept through him.

"What's wrong?"

"Prudie's ill, Mr. Samuels. She caught a chill from the storm last night, and I'm off to fetch Dr. Steadman."

He nodded. "You forgot your bonnet. It wouldn't do to have you get sick, too. Go back inside and help as best you can. I'll get the doctor."

"Ginger, too. Aunt Amy needs her to help with the younger girls."

He quickly agreed and set off, worried about the adorable rascal who'd practically killed him with her lemonade the first day he'd met his precious neighbors.

◆ ◆ ◆

When Tyler brought Ginger and Dr. Steadman back, Amy was holding a towel over Prudie's head, encouraging her to take deep breaths from the steaming teakettle.

Ginger immediately set about making the girls breakfast, but Tyler couldn't stop himself from hovering near the doorway with Amy to hear Lucas's pronouncement. After all, it was their fault. He'd promised himself he wouldn't let this happen to another orphan, but he'd been so distracted by Amy last night that he hadn't noticed the gathering clouds. Neither had she. A surge of male satisfaction at knowing he'd distracted her filled him, but he beat it down. Now wasn't the time.

He gazed at the little lump in the bed until the doctor came to the door and blocked his view.

"She has a chill," Lucas proclaimed. "Unless I miss my guess, the coughing has already improved." He looked at Amy and received an affirming nod. "So I'd like to alternate between the steam treatments and using cool cloths to help bring down the fever. She needs to be drinking a lot of fluids. It seems as though you have things well in hand here. She ought to be fine—and the other girls shouldn't be in any danger. I daresay companionship will help her forget her discomfort and help her recover even more quickly."

Amy relaxed a bit. "Thank you so much for coming, Dr. Steadman."

The kindly doctor smiled. "Glad to do it. But I thought we'd agreed on Lucas?" Smiling, he turned toward Tyler and gave him a nod. Heading for the door, Lucas added, "I'll have to go now, but I'm pretty sure Ginger will want to stay. I'll be by a bit later to check on Prudie."

Tyler turned to Amy. "Do you mind if I see her?"

"Since she's awake, that will be fine. But it's best if we don't tire her out too much. She quite dotes on you—maybe you could get her to eat some applesauce. . . ." Her voice trailed off. Although she obviously found some relief in the doctor's words, Tyler could see Amy still fretted. She should be concerned. This could never be allowed to happen again.

Seeing her questioning look, he quickly stepped into the sickroom. He stood over the bed. "How are you doing, Prudie?"

"I'm better, Mr. Sam," the child whispered. "Thank you so much for yesterday—it was the best day ever."

His heart twisted at her words. It should have been a wonderful memory, untainted by her illness.

"How about some of this great-looking applesauce, hmm? Maybe you could try a few bites? Hey, you could even slurp since you're sick. Slurping," he confided, "is absolutely the best way to have applesauce. Want to try it?" He brought the spoon to her mouth as she dutifully opened up.

Amy joined in. "Oh, come now. That is pitiful. You have to really get into it to make the sound impressive." Prudie's giggle lightened Tyler's mood considerably, and the improved slurp was met with enthusiastic approval from both adults. The game continued until the young patient took another steam treatment, then slipped into a light sleep.

The difference between Amy's concern for Prudie's well-being and Mistress Lowland's complete disregard for Emma's health struck Tyler forcibly. He'd been wrong about her, too easily casting her in the light of a cruel orphanage mistress to give himself a reason to stay. Now he had a completely different reason than he'd ever expected to remain in Eastead.

"Aunt Amy?" Evangeline stood in the doorway. "Ginger sent me to get everyone's clothes from yesterday so we could wash them."

Amy gave her an encouraging smile. "Certainly. Let me just grab Prudie's." She reached for the damp dress on a peg nearby, and as she handed it to Evangeline, something fell out onto the bedcovers.

Tyler didn't miss Amy's concerned glance his way as she ushered the child out of the room, then returned to Prudie's bedside herself. He picked up the golden timepiece—his pocket watch. *How odd. I never misplace this, but this is the second time Prudie found. . .*

It all fell into place. Prudie, talking to him by the pump. Amy's odd behavior as she'd returned the watch. Her hesitance over letting him reward Prudie for her "good deed." It hadn't been because she'd wanted to deny the child; she didn't want to encourage her because. . .

"She's a pickpocket?" He saw resignation on her face as Amy took a deep breath.

"It's really not her fault. Prudie learned to survive on her own before coming to the orphanage. She does her best to stop, but sometimes she slips and does it again. It takes time to break old habits." Her eyes pleaded with him for understanding.

"It's all right. Everyone has secrets." Tyler looked into her incredible eyes and came to his decision. "In fact, I have a few of my own."

Taking a deep breath, he plunged in. "My real name isn't Tyler Samuels—it's Tyler Steadman."

Ignoring Amy's gasp, he continued. If he stopped now, he'd never finish. "I'm the only son of Esau Steadman. His family cut him off when he married my mother, a woman whose social station didn't match his. They moved away rather than be separated, and they had me and a little girl, Emma. My parents died in a carriage accident when we were young. Word was sent to my uncle Ebenezer, but he turned his back on us. We were sent to an orphanage, where my sister died of malnourishment and disease." He stopped for a second, asking the Lord for the strength to continue.

"I was adopted soon after by a kind man, and I took his name. When he died, I set off on journeys, running from my past. Even though my adopted parents taught me the Lord's way, I still blamed my uncle and the orphanage headmistress for my sister's death. Much later I accepted what happened and realized I needed to forgive my uncle. That's why I came here."

Amy had reached out at some point during his speech and now stroked his hand comfortingly. "It's rare that someone forgives so much. I know how hard it is to lose someone. I lost my husband when I sent him out into a storm for the doctor. I still haven't forgiven myself, and I can't imagine how difficult it must be for you to forgive someone who took away your sister. You should be proud of the man you've become, not ashamed. You didn't need to hide who you are."

He took a deep breath, overwhelmed by her understanding yet determined to leave nothing out. "But there's more. When I arrived, my uncle was already dead. I prepared to leave—but then I passed by Kindred Hearts. When I saw all of the girls, I felt as though God had given me a new purpose. I moved in next door to keep an eye on you, to make sure you treated the girls fairly. I knew I would do anything in my power to protect them from the fate of my sister." He could feel her withdrawal.

"You thought I would abuse my girls?"

He rushed on before she could continue, aching to wipe the look of horror off her face. "Yes. I know now that I misjudged you. I've never seen anyone care for others the way you do—you're wonderful with them. That's why I'm telling you this now. I knew I would care for the girls, but I didn't expect to hold you in such esteem. You have made the past months the best in my life, and I don't want any more secrets between us. Can I hope that you will accept my apology and forgive me?"

He held her hand as a drowning man clung to a wooden board. He couldn't bear it if she refused. The tears in her eyes tore at his heart, and he prayed he could regain her trust.

◆ ◆ ◆

Amy couldn't believe it. What did he want her to say? What did he mean when he said he held her in esteem and didn't want any more secrets between them? Did this mean he saw them as a couple? The combination of Prudie's illness and his confession sent her head swimming. There was so much to think about.

She didn't blame him. It was admirable that he wanted to protect the girls. After all, wasn't that what she'd dedicated her life to? She could even see why he wouldn't want to be known as a Steadman until he got to know the cousins he'd never met. Still, where did that leave her—leave them? Precisely what was he saying about the future now that he knew the girls didn't need him to watch over them? What would he say if she told him she needed him? That last wild thought brought things into perspective. She most certainly wouldn't behave like a giddy schoolgirl.

She looked him straight in the eye. "There's really nothing to forgive. We all make mistakes about others, but at least you can admit when you're wrong."

"Thank you." He looked so relieved, she wanted to hug him.

"Where do we go from here?"

The question remained unanswered as Alys rushed into the room, startling them. "Oh, Auntie Amy, Mother Ross is here. She insists she must see you right away!"

Chapter 9

After excusing herself, Amy left the room to face her mother-in-law in the parlor. Since the parlor happened to share a wall with what used to be the study—and now served as the bedroom shared by Prudie and her room-mates—Tyler was privy to every word of Mother Ross's harangue. He could only be thankful Prudie still slept.

Dispensing with even the pretense of civility, Hortense Ross started in as soon as the door was shut.

"You wanton. What have you done? Only a shameless hussy would behave in such a manner with a man—in front of the whole town, no less! Everyone is talking about you two. Where did you get the money for those tickets? Payment for services rendered, perhaps?"

Her accusations shocked Tyler. Such profane allegations should never cross a lady's lips. Even as fury boiled in his breast, the harridan raged on.

"I held my tongue about the dresses, the fine china tea sets, porcelain dolls, tatted lace collars—I've even seen fine nightgowns hanging on the washline—but spending good money on a frivolous pianoforte for your own amusement? I will no longer sit by idle, watching you corrupt these girls the same way you ruined my son." Her voice broke, and she paused before continuing.

A sharp pang of guilt shot through Tyler as he realized his gift had sparked this diatribe. This was the second time his actions caused Amy trouble—first the wet ribbons, now the raffle.

"How can you dishonor Jason's memory this way? Wasn't it enough that you took him from me? That then you couldn't even bring my grandson into the world?"

Grandson? Amy had lost a husband and her child? Tyler's heart ached for her, and he began to understand the source of the older woman's bitterness, misplaced though it might be. He could even sympathize with the pain of her loss—until she went on.

"You are the downfall of everything you claim to care about—poisoning all you touch and sullying my family's name. Now you take up with this stranger, flaunting your sin in front of the whole town? No more! I refuse to house and feed such a je-zebel. You have one week to get your things together and leave. No, I'll not hear any of your vile lies. Nor do you need to concern yourself, if you ever really have, over the welfare of the orphans. I'll see to it that they're placed in homes where they'll learn the value of silence, hard work, and all the other virtues you lack. Don't let me see you again. It would be best if you left town altogether."

How could Amy sit quietly through this tirade? Tyler barely restrained himself from storming in there with a few choice words of his own. He'd seethed about how Mrs. Ross had denounced Amy, and her threats to use the children for slave labor only fanned the blaze. He'd never let it happen, and he knew his Amy would lay down her life for their girls. He only wished he could be in there so she knew how much he supported her. What was she thinking?

◆   ◆   ◆

Amy felt calmer than she had in a long while. She was used to Mother Ross's frequent vituperative attacks, which she'd come to dread. Not any longer. The big one had finally come, and the sense of freedom it gave her was incredible.

Mother Ross might be right that both Jason's death and the loss of their baby were her fault, but for once her mother-in-law was wrong about everything else. Since the axe hovering over her head for so long had fallen at last, Amy could finally tell her so.

If Maxwell and Carter—and now Tyler—didn't care so much for the girls, she might feel differently, agonizing over their welfare. God's providing hand could surely be found in that. Now she could humble herself to her friends and know the girls would be provided for. They'd never be subjected to the slavelike environment Mother Ross envisioned as fitting for the brave girls who had nothing but each other.

As Mother Ross prepared to storm out, Amy quickly blocked her path.

"You've more than spoken your piece. Now I'll speak mine. You didn't lose Jason. We lost him. I loved him, too."

Mother Ross opened her mouth to speak, but Amy rushed on, cutting off the woman's venomous words for the first time in years.

"As for my child, there isn't a day that goes by that I don't regret losing him, as well. I lost everything in one night, my husband, my babe, my hopes; all of which you throw in my face every time we see each other. Don't you know that I've held my tongue at every harsh word you've said because of my guilt? But that can't ease your sorrow or mine—and I can't bring them back."

Amy paused to blink back the tears that threatened to overcome her. Honestly, it was a marvel she hadn't started bawling long ago. When she saw the tears shining in her mother-in-law's eyes, she almost couldn't continue.

"Be that as it may, I've tried to make something of my life. These girls mean the world to me, and I won't let you hurt them to spite me. As for my relationship to Mr. Samuels, the girls and I are fortunate to have the support of such a wonderful, God-fearing man. He's shown nothing but compassion and generosity to the girls, and I'll be forever grateful to him for it. Nonetheless, that is as far as our relationship goes. We haven't crossed the boundary of friendship, and his conduct is impeccable. You won't cast aspersions on his character."

A sharp pang accompanied the words. How had she come to care so much for the man who'd just assured her his purpose in looking after the girls was over and he had no other reason to stay? Ignoring the pain for the time being, she continued.

"As for my so-called spendthrift ways, everything you've listed—the dolls, tea sets, dresses, and nightgowns—were gifts from the Steadmans. The lace for those collars came from an anonymous donor. The pianoforte was a simple matter—Isabel put my name on a ticket. You have no reason to cast me out. My behavior hasn't been the slightest bit improper, nor have I sullied our family name. You've wanted to do this for some time, and now you're convinced you have good reason so you can sleep at night. Don't bother to deny it. I'll be gone as soon as possible, but you won't get your hands on any of my girls. I'll see to that. Good day, Mother Ross."

Amy held the door open, feeling better than she had in years until her opponent made one last verbal thrust.

"Don't think your high-and-mighty words fooled me, Missy. I looked in the ticket box, and I know there were dozens of tickets with your name on them." With that, she swept through the doorway where Amy stood, dumbfounded.

◆   ◆   ◆

Tyler only stayed at the orphanage for as short a time as was seemly before beating a path to the elder Mrs. Ross's door. The time had come for the woman to hear a few home truths.

Amy's speech had been gut-wrenching. He ached for her loss and sense of guilt. He knew pride for the dignified way she'd stood up for herself. He loved how she'd championed him and protected the girls. Mostly, though, the hollow ache was due to her faint praise of his friendship. He'd left it up to her, but he'd never imagined she thought he only cared for the children. He hadn't spoken aloud the depth of his regard, but he'd thought she shared his feelings. How had he made such a mess of things?

His mental ramblings came to a halt when he reached the tidy brick house he searched for. Not a thing stood out of place—not even a stray leaf dared mar the premises of Hortense Ross's abode. He squared his shoulders and gave a quick prayer as he went to beard the lioness in her den.

That was the plan, anyway. Apparently, no one was home. About to walk to the church, Tyler heard sounds coming from behind the house. Following the noise, he found Mrs. Ross at the gazebo, massacring a hapless plant.

Tyler took a deep breath, knowing how much rode on what came next. He sent up another prayer, this time in hopes that the woman would be receptive to his words.

"Ma'am, I think we need to talk." *Well,* he assured himself as he received the full force of her formidable glare, *at least I got her attention.*

"I don't imagine that we do, Mr. Samuels. I usually don't speak with persons of uncertain reputation." She eyed him while ruthlessly snapping off another branch. The look she sent his way assured him she wished it were his head she was chopping instead of a bush.

Tamping down the spurt of anger she'd inspired, he concentrated on stopping her from entering her house. He could see no other way.

"The name's not Samuels, Ma'am. It's Steadman."

The look on her face was worth his left foot. Until the glare returned. "Don't lie to me, Boy. I know your name. Everyone does."

"No, only Amy and now you do. I'm the son of Esau Steadman." For once the biddy was silent. He decided that was encouraging and went on.

"You know his father cut him off when he married Mother. Both of my parents died years ago. When Ebenezer Steadman refused to acknowledge my sister and me, we ended up in an orphanage. My sister died there, but I got adopted soon after. Samuels is my foster name."

Surprisingly, he could see her softening. Her shoulders relaxed, and she stopped glaring as if she hoped she'd bore a hole straight through him.

"I'm sorry, Mr. Steadman. I know how horrible it is to lose someone you love." Her voice hardened once more as her scowl returned. "Ebenezer sacrificed your sister's life. Amy did the same to my son. What do you hope to gain by telling me this?"

Remembering how he'd reached her moments before, Tyler knew the woman was more receptive to his words than she wanted him to think. God's will would be done, and Tyler suspected it marched right along with his.

"Mrs. Ross, that's what I've come to talk with you about. I came to Eastead to forgive my uncle after years of hating him. I lost my chance to make things right because he'd already passed on. You still have the opportunity I missed." Seeing her open her mouth to interrupt, he continued.

"I know you blame Amy for your loss, and she holds herself responsible. But you've hurt her deeply over the past years with your actions. I realize you were overcome with pain, and that for a woman as concerned about doing the right thing as you are, you'll come to regret hasty words." She actually looked like she was considering his words. As the saying went, best to strike while the iron was hot.

"The Bible says, 'So that contrariwise ye ought rather to forgive and comfort, lest perhaps such a one should be swallowed up with overmuch sorrow.' You've added to Amy's sorrow, and now is the time to forgive her for what she never had control over. Then you can grieve together properly." He'd said all he could. He couldn't take it back now, even if he wanted to. She could throw him out of her yard or accept his message—it was between her and the Lord.

For the first time in his life, Tyler was happy to see a woman cry. He put his arms around the sobbing woman and waited. Finally it came, a broken whisper.

"I don't know if I can."

" 'I can do all things through Christ which strengthens me.' Shall we seek His help?"

Relief flooded his soul as they knelt in the gazebo together and prayed.

Chapter 10

Amy didn't know what to make of it all. First, Tyler told her about his past and claimed he wanted no secrets between them. In the next breath, he talked about how he didn't need to stay there anymore. Then, as soon as she'd returned from speaking with Mother Ross, he'd up and left with nothing but a hasty good-bye. At least Prudie was feeling better.

What I told Mother Ross must be right. He only cares about my girls, not me. The admission wrenched her heart, so she shifted focus to Mother Ross herself.

After her long-winded condemnation, Mother Ross has just returned to Kindred Hearts. Hadn't she said that she never wanted to see me again? Why has she come back?

Alys had just announced the older woman's return to the house and desire to speak with Amy. Confused thoughts raced through Amy's mind as she took her time reaching the parlor, where her uninvited guest awaited her. Considering that forewarned was forearmed, Amy prepared for battle as she entered the room.

And stopped short.

Mother Ross wasn't standing with rigid posture, wearing a glower that could melt ice as was usual. Instead, she sat on the red velvet settee, nervously fingering the gold filigree cross she wore about her neck.

What was going on? Recalling the image of a coiled snake that could attack with lightning speed, Amy proceeded with caution. "What can I do for you?" She couldn't quite keep the wariness out of her tone.

The older woman rose stiffly to stand before her. "Mr. Steadman came by to see me a little while ago, Amy." It was the first time her mother-in-law had used her nickname since Jason's death.

"Through much prayer and soul-searching, I've come to the conclusion that I've wronged you."

Amy could see what it cost Mother Ross to admit that. A million questions swirled through her brain, but she stayed silent to catch the rest.

"I don't know if I can ever forgive you for taking my son away, but I'm going to try. It was you who sent him for the doctor. . .but it wasn't your fault his horse spooked."

Tears filled both women's eyes.

"I'm sorry for how I've treated you the past five years, Amy. It wasn't Christian of me to try to make you as miserable as I felt. Can you forgive me for my cruel words?" Mother Ross lost the battle with her tears and began to cry at the same moment Amy did.

In that instant, Amy realized her mother-in-law spoke the truth. Jason's death wasn't her fault. Jason had willingly gone into the storm to fetch the doctor when she'd experienced complications with the pregnancy. She hadn't killed him. She'd blamed herself for so long when she didn't have to, and all she'd needed was for the one other person who understood her loss to tell her so. As understanding swept through her, Amy knew she'd forgive her mother-in-law all the horrible things she'd said in the past for the few kind words she'd just spoken.

Reaching out to envelop the older woman in a hug of shared pain and triumph, Amy stopped crying long enough to tell her so. The two women held each other and prayed together, thanking God for His healing gift. Mother Ross was the first to pull away.

"Thank you, Amy, for forgiving a stubborn old woman's bitterness. It's time for me to go. I know I have many amends to make, but I hope this is the first." She pressed a crumpled piece of paper into Amy's hand and left before Amy could say another word.

The tears she'd thought couldn't be left sprung to Amy's eyes when she realized what she held: the deed to her home.

◆　◆　◆

The next Sunday afternoon, everyone gathered in the parlor and dining room for their weekly sewing and Bible study. Amy's heart, which had been flying up to the rafters just the day before when Dr. Lucas pronounced Prudie "good as new," plummeted to the root cellar when she saw Tyler wasn't there. He'd become an integral part of their Sunday sessions, and she couldn't stop wondering if he'd already left town.

She remembered the conversation she'd had with Isabel and Kathleen just the day before. It had begun with her recitation of the astonishing events of the week and her somewhat gloomy conclusion that Tyler was probably just biding his time before he left.

To her surprise, her formerly supportive friends switched camps. "Piffle," stated Kathleen. "If he was just going to pack up and leave, he would have done it without baring his soul."

Isabel, the turncoat, chimed in, "He's a Steadman. Steadmans don't behave like that. We just knew there was something special about him, didn't we, Kathleen?" Encouraged by Kathleen's nod, she continued. "If you ask me, he's more reason to stay now than he ever did. Carter, Maxwell, and Lucas are crazy about him."

Amy couldn't stay silent at that sensitive remark. "Well, that's something encouraging. He'll stay for the men!"

Kathleen's reproachful look shamed her. "No. What it means is, now that he's found his roots, he'll be ready to start a family of his own."

"So when did he tell them?"

"Last Tuesday. He asked them all to meet him, and he explained everything. Carter wanted him to move in so they could get to know each other better, but he said he liked his house just fine. Claimed it had a better view." This last comment was accompanied by a knowing look.

"Do you think that could mean he really wants to stay?"

"For such an intelligent woman, you're being inordinately foolish," Kathleen retorted.

"Excuse me? I told you what he said."

Isabel shot a questioning look at Kathleen, who nodded slowly. They each grabbed one of Amy's hands.

"What's going on?"

Isabel smiled. "We have some good news for you."

"Proof positive." Kathleen actually made something akin to a bounce. "At the church bazaar, we saw Tyler giving the girls extra nickels. We didn't think of it at the time. . . ."

"But after you told us what Mother Ross said about the ticket box, we asked Evangeline about it. She confessed that Mr. Sam had given them all enough to buy two tickets apiece, with specific instructions to write your name on them!"

He did that for me? Amy just knew she was grinning from ear to ear as she and her friends agreed there was hope, after all. Amy sighed. But that had been yesterday, and there was no sign of Tyler today. By all rights, he should be at the head of the dining room table with his big Bible, reading another parable, as he had for months.

She couldn't bear to make small talk with her friends for another minute. Even they were beginning to look around expectantly.

When all three exchanged a heavy glance and simultaneously asked for some water, Amy was relieved. She rushed off toward the kitchen to collect her thoughts. Why had she gotten her hopes up? Everything had been going so well. She shook her head to clear it. It wouldn't do to sulk. She had better just march on out there and act like everything was dandy. But if everything was so fine, why was she still mulling over how empty the dining room looked without him?

◆　◆　◆

Tyler looked at the ring nestled in his hand doubtfully. Isabel, Kathleen, and Ginger had all approved of his plan and assured him it would go well. But was it big enough? Would the girls want him as their father? Would Amy want him to be her husband? There was only one way to find out.

Taking a deep breath, he poked his head through the door in time to see Amy leave the room and Kathleen give him a huge smile and exaggerated wink. Well, that was a relief. If all went as planned, he'd get the girls' support, then ambush Amy when she got back.

He stepped in, prepared to humiliate himself in pursuit of the most perfect ready-made family ever.

◆ ◆ ◆

Amy had just about convinced herself to trudge back to the parlor when her knees threatened to give way. Was that Tyler's voice, asking her girls if they would let him adopt them? It wasn't enough that he'd stolen her heart—would he leave her completely alone?

She knew he could provide for them better than she would ever be able to. His house alone told her that.

Pushing back tears until she'd stifled them, she commanded herself to move. When she reached the parlor, she thought her heart would break. Tyler was buried under her girls, all of whom were trying to hug him. Even Ginger, Kathleen, and Isabel were sitting on the sidelines, grinning like fools. Didn't they realize what this meant?

She stepped into the room, cleared her throat, and ignored the fluttering in her heart when he turned her way. He gently shook off his living coat of girls and walked toward her. Of course, he'd need her permission to take them away forever.

She could have fainted when he dropped to one knee and held up a diamond.

"Amy. . ."

Ooh, how she loved the sound of her name on his lips.

"When I came here, I'd planned everything. I knew I'd love these girls who've just agreed to become my family. The only thing I didn't expect was to fall in love with you. Would you complete my happiness by becoming my wife?"

There was no helping it. Amy Ross—soon to be Amy Samuels-Steadman—burst into tears as she flung herself at her new fiancé. Being in his arms was every bit as wonderful as she'd imagined, but she had to make sure it was real.

"Are you certain you really want this?"

"I've never been more positive in all my life. Amy, with you as my wife and these precious girls as our family, I'll be the most blessed man in all of Massachusetts. I love you." After the cheers subsided and they'd held each other for awhile, Tyler continued. "Is there anything else you need to know?"

"I love you, too. That's all I need." It was absolutely true. She'd never thought to have a husband again or to lose the guilt she'd carried for so long. As the Good Book said, "Your heavenly Father has plans for you, plans to prosper and not harm you. . . ." Indeed, He'd brought this wonderful man into her life to make her heart whole again, and it was more than she'd ever dreamed. Amy's joy would have been complete if Prudie hadn't chosen that moment to call her attention to one other tiny detail.

"Are we gonna move next door with Gussie 'cuz Mr. Sam's our new daddy?"

Amy suddenly found she needed one other thing. "Yes, we are, Honey. But," she gazed mischievously into Tyler's amazing green eyes, "you'll have to build a pen for that goose."

Epilogue

Tyler surveyed the scene around him with satisfaction. Now that they'd started taking in boys, there was even more activity to deal with. But he wouldn't trade it for the world.

They were having a family picnic, complete with all the Steadmans except Lucas and Ginger, who were at the University of Edinburgh in Scotland, doing research.

Isabel and Amy reclined on some old blankets in the shade while Kathleen chatted with Vivian. The children surrounded them, romping around with high spirits now that school had let out for the summer again.

Maxwell proudly displayed his new son, Baby Max, as Carter and Tyler compared notes on Isabel's and Amy's pregnancies.

"How do you deal with it?" Tyler appealed to Carter. "I just can't get her to sit down and rest. She just smiles and says there's too much to do to coddle her."

Carter nodded sympathetically. "Yes. Isabel was the same way with Michael. Told me to stop treating her like a porcelain figurine."

Maxwell tossed his two cents in the pot. "It'll change soon enough when they're about seven months along. Then they don't have a choice—getting up is too difficult."

"Whoa, there." Carter's hand shot out to catch Molly from toddling straight into Michael.

Tyler shook his head, grinning from ear to ear. "If you'd told me two years ago that I'd be standing here, talking with my cousins about our coming children, I'd have thought craziness ran in the family."

"Yeah, we sure are lucky, aren't we?" Tyler could always trust Carter to understand what he meant.

"How's business?" Tyler turned to Maxwell.

"Great. Those tips on cheap sugar cane made us a tidy profit. Thanks."

"The mill's accident rate is much lower since we widened the aisles."

"And the young lovebirds?" Maxwell indicated the corner where Davey and Susannah, now seventeen and sixteen, strolled arm-in-arm.

"Just great. The house was a wonderful engagement gift, Tyler." Carter clapped him on the back.

"So long as they wait a bit, first. To tell the truth, it wasn't my idea. Amy wanted Susannah to stay close to home when she married, and the house was just sitting empty since we moved here and took on the boys. . . ."

"Our women have hearts of gold." Carter's comment met with warm agreement as the men looked over fondly at their wives.

Tyler watched as Amy got up and began hustling some of the youngsters their way. It was naptime. As she neared him, he breathed a quick prayer. *Oh, Lord. Thank You for Your many blessings. I ask for nothing more than I already have, except a long while to enjoy it with my precious family.*

KELLY EILEEN HAKE

Kelly Eileen Hake received her first writing contract at the tender age of seventeen and arranged to wait three months until she was able to legally sign it. Since that first contract a decade ago, she's fulfilled twenty contracts ranging from short stories to novels. In her spare time, she's attained her BA in English literature and composition, earned her credential to teach English in secondary schools, and went on to complete her MA in writing popular fiction.

Writing for Barbour combines two of Kelly's great loves—history and reading. A CBA bestselling author and member of American Christian Fiction Writers, she's been privileged to earn numerous Heartsong Presents Reader's Choice Awards and is known for her witty, heartwarming historical romances.

Leap of Faith

by Pamela Griffin

Dedication

A heartfelt thanks to all my crit buds and especially to Mom, who helped teach me how to take a leap of faith—one I've chosen many times and have never regretted. Most of all, with loving gratitude to my Lord Jesus, the foundation for the faith by which I stand.

For therein is the righteousness of God revealed from faith to faith: as it is written, The just shall live by faith.
ROMANS 1:17

For by thee I have run through a troop: by my God have I leaped over a wall. As for God, his way is perfect; the word of the LORD is tried: he is a buckler to all them that trust in him.
2 SAMUEL 22: 30–31

Chapter 1

Missouri Ozarks, 1869

An eye-pleasing blend of cedar, pine, and hardwood trees just beginning to bud after a long winter blanketed the gently rolling hills that surrounded Amanda's valley home. Here and there, pink-blossomed redbuds mingled with white-blossomed dogwoods, providing splashes of color. The morning sun cut a golden swathe between two tall hickory trees, casting light into an area often in shadows, and highlighted the few workers building the church for Hickory Hollow.

Amanda watched one man in particular as he helped lift a heavy stone block to place it on another. Rays of sunlight outlined his muscles through his shirt as he toiled alongside the others.

"Amanda Hodges, you stop ogling that man," Ivy Randall stage-whispered to Amanda, loud enough so the other two girls in their company could hear. "Zeke wouldn't like it."

Amanda's eyes slid shut in exasperation. Sometimes the blue-eyed woman with the fair hair was her tormenter, sometimes her bosom friend. Today she'd proven to be a little of both. "Ivy, I told you, I'm not interested in your brother."

One of the workers called out to another, reclaiming Amanda's attention. She looked at the growing rock wall of what would be their new church building. The little timber schoolhouse was fast on its way to becoming unable to hold the growing congregation.

Heavy *chinks* of hammers striking iron stakes, boring holes into rocks that would support the roof's wooden beams, echoed throughout the otherwise peaceful valley. A chill wind had arisen minutes ago, but the change in weather wasn't fierce enough to send Amanda seeking shelter.

The Wilson boys—ten months apart but as alike as two pecan halves in a nutshell—busily worked, slapping and spreading mortar, then together lifting the next block of rock and setting it into place. Zeke Randall worked with them, though he didn't appear as busy as the others. Amanda's father also worked alongside the few townsmen who'd turned out to help. Though he was well into his forties, his body was strong, and he easily kept up with the younger men. Amanda's attention again settled on one dark-haired man in particular, and a wistful smile lifted her lips.

Matt Campbell was relatively new to their mountain valley town, but already he'd proven to be a help to any in need. When a strong set of shoulders was required, he was the first in line to offer his services. And what a nice, strong and broad set of shoulders he had. . . .

"Your mother's coming round the bend," Ivy said into Amanda's ear a little too loudly. "And I'll tell you again, it sure doesn't look proper for the preacher's daughter to eyeball all the workers."

"I'm not eyeballing all the workers," Amanda muttered between clenched teeth and lifted her fingers to the offended ear to rub it. Her statement was true. She had no interest in any of the men, with the exception of one.

She moved toward her mother. "Need some help, Ma?"

Huggably stout after bearing seven children, three of whom had died at birth, Clara Hodges gratefully handed a basket of freshly laundered linens to her daughter. "Do see to this, would you, Dear? I must run over to Sally John's and check on her and the baby. She wants your pa to come, but he's so busy I hate to bother him. Would you ask him for me later?" She swiped a damp lock of graying brown hair from her eyes. "And please start supper."

"I'll see right to it, Ma."

Being a preacher's wife and seeing to a host of needs, not to mention also acting as midwife in their town, her mother carried more than her fair share of duties to Amanda's way of thinking. Amanda walked past several of many hickories clustered in bunches throughout the area and quickly approached their three-room log cabin, with its cedar shakes for a roof and the gray stone chimney along one side. The other girls followed like a flock of cackling hens.

"I surely don't understand what you see in Mr. Campbell when you kin have Zeke Randall," Selena Mills stated. "Mr. Campbell wears his hair too long, his nose is bent—and why ever set your cap for a man who limps when you kin have someone with two strong legs?"

"A pair of shears would fix Matt Campbell's hair right nicely, though it does look smart when it's combed sleek and shiny and brushes his shoulders." Amanda dropped the basket onto the table and gave the redhead a sideways glance. "As to the other, there's a lot more to life than dancing, Selena. I think Matt's limp adds character. As does his not-quite-straight nose, his lean jaw, and that fine dark stubble on his face he always seems to have." She giggled. "He's quite a handsome fellow if you want my opinion."

"We're all well aware of your opinion, Amanda, but you best not let your pa hear you talk like that," Ivy put in. "And calling Mr. Campbell by his Christian name. . .Honestly! You sound almost brazen. Nothing at all like a preacher's daughter should be."

In truth, Amanda felt little like a preacher's daughter. She often spoke her mind and was anything but meek and humble, much to her parents' consternation. Yet she couldn't help the way she was—nor the way she wasn't.

Her hand stilled from laying folded dish towels on a high shelf, her gaze going dreamy as she looked toward the windowpane. "Tell me truthfully, girls, did you ever see such lovely blue-gray eyes as Matt has? They look like the sky after a storm's swept it clean, all sparkling and clear—but sort of misty, too."

"Land's sakes!" Mayflower Starnes replied in mock dismay, her brown eyes wide in her freckled face. "Now she's gone poetic on us. Ladies, we best leave afore she starts recitin' 'An Ode to Love.' "

"Humph." Amanda resumed her chore. "I'm not the romantic in this bunch, Mayflower. That would be you." Though lately Amanda had thought more about love and marriage, especially now that she was seventeen—and now that Matt Campbell was a resident of Hickory Hollow.

"Well," Ivy intoned, "all I have to say is your pa will never let a stranger court you. No one in the hollow knows anything about him. He talks about as much as a turtle, and his snap is likely as vicious. When he gets that brooding look, he almost scares me."

"Oh, fiddle-faddle," Amanda said. "At least he doesn't run off at the mouth like some folks I know."

"Meaning Zeke, I suppose?" Ivy asked in an affronted tone.

Amanda sighed. "It's not that I have anything against your brother, Ivy. I just don't care to have him as my beau."

"You're gonna wind up breaking his heart. I just know it. He's liked you since we were in school together."

Break Zeke's heart? Hardly. That is, if he had a heart to break. Amanda kept quiet, realizing nothing she said would matter. Many in the hollow had already paired her and Zeke as a couple.

Forgetting the three other women, she gazed out the window toward the rock wall a short distance away and watched the tall man who limped in the opposite direction.

◆　◆　◆

Matthew Campbell straightened to a stand, letting the mortar-covered spade drop to the ground. With his sleeve, he wiped the moisture from his brow, then put his hands to the back of his sweat-sodden shirt and tried to massage the kinks out. Damp weather often made his back and hip ache, though he was just twenty years old. Yet after what he'd been through these past few years, he felt like he'd lived a coon's age three times over.

To the west, above the thick forest of oaks and hickories, Matt noticed a swollen storm cloud creeping in their direction. The sun had disappeared more than an hour ago, leaving behind skies of pale gray. An irritated grunt escaped his throat, and he put his work-worn hand to the partially built wall of cold stone, still damp from the last downpour.

"We best get busy and try to finish up before the sky unleashes on us," he told the group of three men who crouched nearby for a breather.

A fair-haired man with a well-groomed mustache straightened, still holding the dipper from the barrel of collected rainwater. His pants, shirt, and vest were neatly pressed, and his lightly sunburned face wasn't one bit shiny from exertion. Probably because Zeke Randall did the least amount of work possible, though he gave the appearance of being busy at his task. Matt knew better. He'd been watching the dapper son of the lumber company owner all afternoon and noticed how he lollygagged behind the others. And why come dressed for a hard day's work all gussied up as if he were attending his own wedding?

A belligerent expression crossed Zeke's face. "I don't recall anyone dying and making you boss, Campbell." His voice was low but loud enough to issue a challenge.

Matt decided not to take the lure. He'd dealt with a lot worse than Zeke but wasn't interested in a fight. He'd encountered enough violence in one lifetime for ten men.

Bob and Pete Wilson rose from their hunched positions with goofy smiles, their dark gazes focused beyond Matt's shoulder. Matt turned to see what had caught their interest so.

Zeke's sister Ivy stood nearby, staring at both brothers and giggling. Yet it wasn't on Ivy that Matt focused his attention, but rather on the woman next to her—with thick hair the shade of rich coffee containing a dollop of cream. Slightly plump, her skin like pale pink roses after a frost, Amanda Hodges looked his way. Her eyes were as spring-a-green as the buds on the trees, able to rivet a man where he stood—and they did so to Matt now. He felt as if lightning had raced out of the approaching storm clouds and struck him dumb.

Matt swallowed hard when she continued to stare. Some might think petite Ivy with her angel-like features was the only beauty of Hickory Hollow, but Matt would disagree. Amanda's nose might be just a tad too tilted and her lips a mite wide, but her face and eyes shone with the vibrancy of her personality.

Zeke stepped forward. "Ivy, this is no place for you—nor you, Amanda. I'm quite busy with helping your pa. Run along home. We'll talk later." He moved to take hold of Amanda's elbow, but she jerked it from his reach the moment he touched her sleeve.

"I didn't come to talk to you, Zeke." Amanda turned her fascinating eyes away from Matt and to the north end of the church wall. "Pa! I need to speak with you if you have a minute."

A short, sinewy man with tufts of silver hair sprinkled among the dark strands turned from his task. "Trouble?" He pushed his hat farther back on his head and approached his daughter, the hammer still in his hand. His gaze swerved to Matt, then returned to Amanda. His lined brow clouded.

"No, Pa. Leastways I don't think so. Ma said that Sally John Adcock asked you to drop by—you know how nervous she's been about the new baby, it being her first and all."

"Amanda, if there's no emergency, then tell your mother I'll visit later," Pastor Hodges said, "after I get a good day's work in."

As if his words were a signal, the sky unleashed a smattering of raindrops on their heads. Ivy squealed and raised both hands above her piled-up braids. Seemingly bent on being stubborn, the drops abruptly turned into sheets of hard rain.

"Get on back to your homes," Pastor Hodges yelled above the loud sound of water spraying on stone. "We'll try again next Saturday." A deep bellow of thunder underscored his statement.

Matt anchored his hat more firmly on his head and stared through the veil of silver rain at what little progress they'd made. He knew Pastor Hodges was itching to get the church built, but it seemed one delay after another prevented them from doing so, and the fact that so few men turned out each Saturday didn't help matters one bit.

Before heading to his cabin farther up the mountain, he chanced a look in Amanda's direction and watched her hurry through the door of her home. Matt forced his gaze away. He had no business thinking about a preacher's daughter. Not after the shameful life he'd led before coming to Hickory Hollow.

Chapter 2

S miling, Amanda inhaled the spicy-sweet scent of warm cinnamon bread. She finished wrapping a second loaf with a towel and stuck it in her basket. If she hurried, she could beat the rain. These past two months their little mountain valley had gotten more than its fair share of that type of weather.

Her mother bustled into the kitchen. "Are you taking the bread to Gloramae?"

"Yes, Ma."

"Let her know I'll be by later. Her ankle seems to be mending, but oh, won't it be nice when young Dirk comes home from medical school and takes up a practice in the hollow? I'm still not certain that Gloramae's ankle isn't broken, with the way she squeals when she puts weight on it. If only we had a doctor to see to things here— that is, if the hill people will let go of their silly superstitions and accept a doc's help. Imagine Sally John putting a knife under the bed to cut the pain during childbirth! Whoever heard such nonsense? Hopefully, with Dirk being a native to the hills and not an outsider, they might listen to him."

Amanda agreed with her ma, then said a hasty good-bye and slipped outside before her tongue could get the better of her. She would wager a cupboard full of cinnamon bread that the miller's daughter was pretending the injury was much worse than it was so she could get out of doing housework in her widower father's home. She and Zeke would make a lovely pair. Amanda grinned at the thought.

A cool mist caressed her face while she strolled over the lush valley and alongside the narrow river. What used to be Rockford Jones's homestead sat nestled at the edge of the thick wood. The old prospector had traveled farther west years ago in his search of gold. Now the one-room log cabin belonged to another.

Amanda ran the edge of her teeth along her lips to bring out more color, nervously cleared her throat, and rapped on the door. After what seemed an eternity, she knocked again—harder this time. Disappointed when no one appeared, she stepped away. The door swung inward with a protesting creak, and with a smile she pivoted back around. The pleased expression froze on her face.

Matt weakly leaned against the doorjamb, jaw unshaven, blue-gray eyes bleary. From beneath the filthy blanket he clutched around his shoulders, she could see the faded red legs of his long underwear. "Miss Hodges," he rasped in surprise. "What brings you here?"

"Matt Campbell. You're ill!" she softly cried in dismay. "No wonder we didn't see you at the church meeting. Well, this will never do. It's a good thing I decided to bring you some cinnamon bread." She bustled past him—and gaped in horror.

Dirty tins and remnants of food cluttered a pine table that bowed in the middle. Mud caked the wooden floor, and the odors of sweat and vomit permeated the stale air. Her stomach lurched, but she set her basket down on the arthritic-looking table, determined to stay the course.

"Miss Hodges," Matt said from where he'd taken up residence on a chair that didn't look any better off than he was. "You shouldn't be here. Your ma and pa...they wouldn't like it. . . ." His words trailed off into raspy breathing.

Suspecting the worst, Amanda moved toward him and pushed up her sleeve. She placed her forearm against his forehead. "Why, you're burning up! How long have you been like this? Never mind. It's a good thing I came by when I did. You just sit right there 'til I can clean up some."

Before he could argue with her again, she pushed up her other sleeve, prepared to get to work, and moved to the tangled bedding. "Ma has so much to do today— every day, really—and probably won't have time to come now and take care of you. She's taught me well, so don't you worry."

When he didn't answer, she looked at him. His head was propped against the log wall as though he'd been unable to hold it up any longer. His eyes were closed, and a fine sheen of sweat beaded his face. Her heart skipped a fearful beat. Just how sick was he?

His bedding needed a thorough washing, but there wasn't much she could do about that since she saw only the one blanket. A set of ivory-handled revolvers in a gun belt on the floor caught her attention, making her wonder. Every man in the hollow owned a shotgun, but she'd never seen such fancy handguns as Matt had. She looked at them a moment longer, then set to work.

What she could do to clean things, she did, hurrying so she could get Matt back into bed. He didn't seem to notice when she nudged him awake, then helped him to the narrow cot. Supporting him with one arm, she slowly walked with him while he leaned heavily on her, his limp pronounced. He sank onto the straw mattress with a crisp rustle, wincing when he put his weight on his left hip.

Hurriedly, her face warming, Amanda covered him to the chin with the blanket, keeping her eyes averted from the tall form clothed in long underwear. She then laid a fire in the small fireplace and set about putting the room to rights. Once the dishes were washed and the room swept clean, she furrowed her brow. Matt needed something besides cinnamon bread, but she'd found nothing but an inch of wheat left in its sack, a modicum of sugar, and a jar of strawberry preserves.

She frowned. Just who would have brought him strawberry preserves?

Her gaze darted Matt's way again, and her miffed little frown changed to one of concern. Maybe she should drop off the other loaf of bread at Gloramae's right away, then seek out Ma. Matt really didn't look good.

Grabbing her basket, Amanda hurried through the cabin's open door, shutting it firmly behind her.

◆　◆　◆

"Is it the cholera?" Amanda whispered fearfully from the foot of Matt's bedside.

At the terror-inflicting words, Matt cracked one eyelid open. Mrs. Hodges stood next to her daughter and poured some foul-looking blackish brown liquid from a bottle into a tin cup. "Nothing so tragic, Dear. By the looks of things, he has a case of stomach complaints and stuffiness in his chest, such as Roscoe Fulton had two weeks past. Enough to make him miserable, but that's about it. A dose of this Hostetter's Celebrated Stomach Bitters, which I bought from that peddler last summer, ought to cure him well and good."

Matt weakly pondered the woman's reassurances to Amanda. He was sure he was dying and they were coddling his senses by not telling him so. Only a dying man could feel this awful.

Steps creaked on the boards, coming closer. A plump, cool hand slipped under his sweaty neck. "Open up, Mr. Campbell," Amanda's mother said in a no-nonsense tone. "I know you're awake. I saw you open your eye."

A foul stench drifted up to assault Matt as the lip of the cup was placed near his mouth. He'd heard somewhere that these potions contained a good deal of alcohol, and while he wasn't a drinking man any longer, he was sure that the brew must contain something even more foul. Like slime from the river bottom.

With what little strength he had left, he pulled his head back in retreat. Regardless, the woman tipped the container, scalding his mouth and tongue with a fiery, bitter brew. He coughed, choked—then gagged, reaching for the pot.

Once he weakly settled back onto the mattress, Amanda gave him a sympathetic stare. Not for the first time since she'd arrived at his cabin and found him in this condition, then brought back her ma, Matt wished she'd just go. It was bad enough for any woman to see him in such sad shape, fit for nothing, ready for the casket. Yet for that woman to be Amanda was about as bitter to swallow as the devil's brew forced down his gullet—and hard on a man's pride.

"You go on home, Amanda," Mrs. Hodges said as if reading Matt's thoughts. "I need to apply a mustard plaster to his chest. And be sure to put on your go-to-meeting dress. I invited Zeke Randall and his cousin for dinner tonight."

"Oh, Ma," Amanda protested, clearly disgruntled. "Zeke Randall? Why'd you have to go and invite him?"

"Amanda, to hear you talk! Zeke is a nice young man, and his cousin is only visiting this week. Don't you deem it right for the pastor's family to exhibit a little Christian charity during his stay in the hollow?"

"I suppose."

Matt forced both eyelids open. He was startled when he saw Amanda staring at him. A wistful look filled her eyes, and a becoming flush settled over her cheeks. He wondered what she was thinking.

It didn't sit well with him that Mrs. Hodges evidently considered Zeke Randall a fitting suitor for her daughter. But even if Matt weren't dying, he could do little about it. He certainly couldn't call on Amanda, even if he were hale and hearty.

Closing his eyes, he wondered if she would mourn his passing and put flowers on his grave.

◆　◆　◆

Amanda wandered home, in no hurry to dress for supper. Hearing someone humming a tune, she peered toward the swiftly flowing river.

Jeb Hunter sat under one of the willows alongside the water. Clutched between both his hands, which rested between propped-up knees, a long branch extended over the water, a string tied to one end. The thirteen year old reclined his back against the tree trunk, a piece of straw sticking from his mouth. His dirty bare feet tapped a rhythm on the damp, mossy ground.

"Jeb!" Amanda shouted, affecting a stern expression, though her spirit identified with the boy and she wished she could sit beside him. She hadn't been fishing since she was a girl in calf-length dresses and pigtails. "Shouldn't you be in school?"

When his name was called, Jeb dropped the pole and unbent his tall form, scrambling to his feet. Seeing it was only Amanda, he relaxed. A twisted grin stretched across his freckled face, revealing crooked teeth. Lazily, he scratched his stomach, which was covered with a thin undershirt, its sleeves pushed up to the elbows. The color of the material had probably once been white but now was a shade of indeterminate gray. A pair of suspenders held up his trousers, one brown pant leg sporting a hole in the knee.

"Well now, Miz Amanda. I reckon it'd be all right to miss teacher's jawin' jis' this once. The fish are bitin' somethin' fierce. Reckon it be 'cuzza all the rain we got last week? I caught me four already, and I ain't been here but an hour."

Unable to resist his contagious smile, Amanda smiled back. "Well, I guess this once is all right, Jeb. Class will be letting out soon. But just between us, I wouldn't refer to Mr. Pragmeyer's teaching as 'jawin'' again—especially to his face. I'm certain your ma will be happy to get the fish for supper."

Happy was an understatement, Amanda knew. Many families in the area, including the Hunters, were poor. Years ago, not long after her family moved to Hickory Hollow when Amanda was eleven, she had been dismayed to learn from a seven-year-old Jeb that the Hunter children had eaten nothing but sorghum, corn bread, and wild berries for three days. Wanting to help, Amanda rode up the mountain with her pa to take the Hunters some rabbit stew. They stopped their horses in front of the Hunter cabin, staying mounted, and her pa cautiously yelled out, "Hello! Any Hunters about?"—the universal greeting if you didn't want to get your head shot off.

Mr. Hunter came to the door, shotgun cradled in one arm, though he didn't aim it their way. Matter-of-factly, he refused the food, telling them, "Thank ya kindly, Preacher, but we Hunters don't hold to no charity." Amanda returned home that day with a full pot and an empty heart. The spicy stew hadn't tasted at all good that night, not with the image of the Hunter children's thin faces branding her memory. The Hunters weren't the only ones to refuse charity, Amanda soon discovered. Every well-meaning overture had been politely but firmly refused. Yet since Jeb's father had an accident last fall, he wasn't able to go hunting as much anymore.

A plan crystallized in her mind. Excited, Amanda said a hasty good-bye to Jeb and hurried home, hoping to talk to her pa.

◆　◆　◆

"That was a fine meal, Mrs. Hodges," Zeke said, pulling out the napkin tucked in his starched collar. "I do believe I've never tasted chicken quite so tender. When I went back East last summer, I visited a number of restaurants of high caliber, as my grandmother is quite wealthy," he pompously added. "You could easily open your own eating establishment and compete with the best of them."

"Why, thank you, Zeke." Amanda's mother gave him a flustered smile.

"I agree with everything my cousin said," Ned Randall added. "I haven't had a meal this fine since I left my ma's doorstep in Liberty."

"I'm so glad you both enjoyed it."

"Amanda, I understand you made the dessert." Zeke turned his probing gaze her way. "Peach cobbler always has been a favorite of mine."

"That's nice," Amanda dutifully responded. She turned to her mother. "Should we save the broth for Mr. Campbell? It would probably do him a world of good."

Everyone looked at her. Her pa and Ned appeared surprised, her ma exasperated, and Zeke seemed annoyed. Even her younger siblings—Rosalie, Edmund, and Charmaine—stared at her.

Flustered, Amanda rose from the table and began gathering dishes. "I'll just take these to the sideboard."

An uneasy silence elapsed. "We should be heading home," Zeke finally said. "Again, thank you for the meal, Mrs. Hodges."

"Do you really need to be hurrying off so soon?" Amanda's mother protested. "I'm sure Anson would enjoy a game of checkers with you while we women take care of the cleaning."

Zeke looked Amanda's way. Hurriedly, she focused her attention on scraping three-year-old Charmaine's discarded potato skins onto a plate.

"No," Zeke said a little gruffly. "We best be going."

"Amanda." Ma's voice sounded stern. "Rosalie can do that. Please see our guests to the door. And while you're at it, take the rest of the scraps to the hogs. I do believe everyone is finished. Yes?"

Pa set down his half-eaten honeyed biscuit and looked at his wife in bewilderment. Ma's blatant attempts to push Amanda into Zeke's company made Amanda clench her teeth, but she replied with a dutiful, "Yes, Ma."

"I hope to visit with your mother soon, Zeke," Ma said in a pleasant voice. "I miss news of what's happening back East."

"I'll tell her. I'm sure she'd enjoy a visit; she does enjoy talking to anyone who'll listen."

Amanda dumped the scraps into a pail by the stove, picked up the container, and stiffly moved to the door. Zeke and his cousin hurried to follow.

"Will you be attending Tom and Mayflower's wedding, Amanda?" Zeke didn't waste any time once they were outside and away from her family's hearing. His cousin trailed behind.

"I suppose," she said, never breaking stride as she moved toward the pen out back. Why was he asking her such a thing now? The wedding was weeks away, sometime after Tom completed work on the new cabin.

"It's about time we had a wedding in the hollow," Zeke said.

Amanda came to a stop at the pen. The hogs' grunts turned to ear-piercing squeals as the animals trotted toward them on stubby legs. Amanda upended the bucket over the fence. The scraps fell in lumps, some landing on a gray-and-white-splotched head, but the hog didn't seem to mind.

"You ought to think about getting married soon, too," he continued. "I mean, you are seventeen. And I'm nineteen."

Amanda blew out a little breath and faced him. "Honestly, Zeke. When the time comes for me to marry up, it'll come, I suppose. But I have too much going on to think about it now."

He frowned. "I hear you've been playing Good Samaritan today."

At the accusation in his tone, she narrowed her eyes and crossed her arms, the pail still dangling from one hand. "So?"

"So I'd stay away from Matt Campbell if I were you. He's bad news."

Amanda laughed shortly. "If being selfless, considerate of others, and always ready to lend a helping hand is 'bad,' then my pa's been preaching the wrong sermon of a Sunday morning."

Zeke scowled, evidently not finding her retort the least bit amusing, but then Amanda didn't expect he would. He'd been a trial ever since they were children. Now that he was following in the footsteps of his wealthy father, Zeke had become downright intolerable, thinking he owned everybody. Including Amanda.

She glanced at Ned, who stood several feet away, hands clasped behind him, evidently uneasy with the conversation since he intently focused on a nearby mountain and his face was flushed pink.

"Well, I'd best be getting inside. It was a pleasure to meet you, Mr. Randall. Good evening, Zeke." With a short nod, Amanda headed back to the cabin.

◆ ◆ ◆

Trying to ignore Ned Randall's outright stare, Matt took a seat on a pile of rocks and balanced his plate on his knee. Zeke's cousin had helped in building the church today. Each time Matt looked his direction, Ned had been staring openly at him, then quickly focused his attention elsewhere. Matt wasn't overly alarmed. Ned didn't seem shocked or suspicious. Only curious. He probably wondered how Matt had gotten his limp.

Matt took a swig of cool water and watched Amanda dish thick stew onto a tin plate she then handed to Mr. Wilbur, the last to be served in line. Amanda reminded Matt of a bright butterfly, though the dress she wore was a faded gray. A few women, including Ivy Randall, wore more colorful frocks, but Amanda outshone them all. Her face was rosy and animated, and her eyes sparkled with life.

"Good thing we were able to finish that wall today," Pastor Hodges said from behind.

Matt almost strangled on his water and hurriedly looked away from Amanda. "Yes, Sir." He noticed that Pastor Hodges was watching her. After a moment, he turned his gaze to Matt.

"My daughter had a good idea—getting the womenfolk of the workers to bring a food item, then putting it together in a pot to have us a community stew after the day's work was done. First time I've seen those Hunter children with smiles on their faces due to a full belly."

A grin lifting the corners of his mouth, Matt looked at the two youngest Hunters. Light-haired Audelia and Aubrey Hunter engaged in a game of leapfrog by the shallow stream that ran close to where the church was being built. Not old enough yet to write their numbers or letters, they were the most athletic of the Hunter brood.

"Amanda has a good heart, but she's still childlike in her thinking," her pa continued. "Because of that, her outgoing behavior is apt to get her in a muddle. A muddle that, if I can help it, I'm determined to see she doesn't wind up in."

At the subtle warning in Pastor Hodges's tone, Matt looked his way. Piercing gray-green eyes pinned Matt like a coon in a trap. Matt wished he weren't holding a plate in one hand and a cup in the other so he could tip his hat downward and escape the accusation written there. Did Amanda's father think anything improper had happened at the cabin earlier that week, during the three days Matt was ill?

"Sir, let me assure you, when your daughter took care of me without her ma's help that first day, nothing occurred for which either she or I should be ashamed— nor on any day thereafter."

"I know Amanda well enough to be assured of that. It's not that which concerns me. Amanda's strong in both body and spirit—but she's headstrong, as well, and too young to know what's good for her. A stranger new to town, seeming to be without background or history, might prove too strong a fascination for her idealistic young mind." He focused on the two children frolicking like march hares on the grass and took a drink from his cup. "Am I making myself clear, Mr. Campbell?"

"Yes, Sir. Perfectly clear." The pastor's words made Matt squirm inside, like a worm at the end of a hook, but he didn't move a muscle. This was the opening for Matt to tell something about himself and his family. To relieve the man's mind and prove to him that he was a wholesome character of moral upbringing, worthy of taking an interest in a preacher's daughter.

However, Matt couldn't say a word—though he wished with all he had in him that he did have the right to say those things. As he'd done on numerous occasions in the four months since he'd arrived in the hollow, he remained silent, the silence only serving to further condemn him.

Amanda came their way, a plate of pie in each hand. "I brought you dessert," she said, her green eyes sparkling with vivacity and trained on Matt. "The way it's disappearing, I wasn't sure there'd be any left. I hope you like strawberry pie, Mr. Campbell."

Matt roused a smile and took the offered plate. "Thank you, Ma'am. I do at that."

Her smile dimmed as she searched Matt's face, then looked at her father. "Pa?" She held out his pie. "Is anything wrong?"

"Of course not," her father said, somewhat curtly. He took the plate from her. "This meal was a superb idea, Amanda. We'll have to do this each Saturday. Hopefully the idea of free food will bring more volunteers to help build the church, as well as feed the needy."

Amanda's brow cleared. "I convinced Mrs. Hunter to take some stew home with her. She refused at first, but when I said it would probably just go to feed the hogs, and after all, she contributed an onion, so it was partly hers as well, she agreed to take some. Let's just hope Mr. Hunter is as agreeable." Her gaze turned Matt's way again. "It's nice to see you up and fit again, Mr. Campbell. I trust you're fully recovered?"

"Yes, Ma'am. Thanks to you and your ma."

"Amanda, Ivy is trying to get your attention," Pastor Hodges abruptly said.

Amanda stared at her pa strangely but looked over her shoulder. Ivy crazily motioned with one arm for Amanda to join her. Amanda blew out an exasperated breath and focused on Matt. "I best go see what she wants. I hope you enjoy the pie, Mr. Campbell. I picked the strawberries yesterday—the first of the season. Eating fruit fresh is so much better than using preserves from a jar—don't you agree?" Before moving away, she offered another sweet smile, warming Matt clear to his boot tips.

◆　◆　◆

"All right, Ivy. Tell me what couldn't wait during those few minutes I had to catch a breather." Amanda was annoyed. The solitary moment she'd finally found to exchange a few words with Matt had been interrupted.

Ivy frowned. "Zeke's looking for you."

"Is that all?" Amanda rolled her eyes heavenward. "With the way you were flapping your arm at me, I thought some emergency had cropped up." She turned to go, but Ivy touched her sleeve.

"He's upset. I think you should find out what's bothering him. He's over there." Ivy nodded toward the bank on the opposite side of the stream at a place where the water widened a few feet.

"Honestly!" Amanda released a frustrated breath when she saw Zeke near some dogwood trees. He stared in her direction. "Oh, alright. I'll go see what he wants."

Muttering to herself about spoiled little boys who never grew up and always had to have their way, Amanda lifted her skirts a few inches and stepped onto the smooth rocks of the shallow stream. Once she joined Zeke, he grabbed her elbow.

"What did Mr. Campbell say to you?" he insisted.

"That's none of your business." Amanda snatched her arm away. "And furthermore, you have no right to act like some sort of scalawag!"

163

His smile wasn't kind. "You're getting your name-calling mixed up, Amanda. It's Matthew Campbell who's the scalawag, not I."

"What are you talking about?" She gathered her brows.

"My cousin was outside the bank that got robbed in Liberty a few years back. Amid all the shooting, he got a close look at one of the outlaws as he fled—the man dropped his moneybag in front of where Ned was standing, and the kerchief slipped from his face when he bent to scoop it up. This afternoon he stared long and hard at Mr. Campbell for the first time. Ned said he'd swear on a Bible, in court, that Matthew Campbell—of whom you think so highly—is a member of the James Gang."

Chapter 3

For seconds after hearing Zeke's grim words, Amanda only stared. Then she laughed. "That's preposterous! Matthew Campbell is no more a member of Frank and Jesse James's Gang than I am a follower of the infamous Belle Starr! Can't you just see me toting a gun?" She giggled again.

Zeke frowned. "Laugh all you want, Amanda, but what do you really know about the man? He doesn't talk about himself to anyone and evades any questions people ask. Suppose he's here to stake out our town or something equally despicable? I've heard it said that the James Gang was spotted near here a couple of weeks back."

"Zeke, if he were a wanted man—and I'm not saying he is, mind you—we don't have a bank in this town to rob," Amanda countered, though a niggling doubt began to squirm into her mind. She took a few edgy steps from the dogwood, then faced him again. "Most of the hill folk pay in hogs and eggs and the like. All that aside, Pa's always said a man has a right to his privacy. And I should think that rule applies to Matt Campbell, too."

"Maybe we don't have a bank to rob, but Father has a safe full of valuables. In any case, outlaws don't just rob banks, Amanda. They rob stages and trains and towns—any place they can get their hands on gold or money." Zeke gritted his teeth. "But you've veered away from the discussion. We were talking about Matt Campbell—"

"No, *you* were talking about Matt Campbell. As far as I'm concerned, this discussion is closed." Turning her back on him, Amanda hurried across the rocks of the stream.

She was irritated with Zeke for his outrageous accusations, but even angrier with herself for the doubts that crept in concerning Matt. Why was he so quiet? Was he just shy? Amanda didn't think so. If he were hiding a secret—though surely it couldn't be as terrible as what Zeke suggested—then the first opportunity she could get Matt alone, she would try to find out just what that secret was. Privacy or not, she owed it to herself to discover the truth if she planned to marry the man someday.

◆　◆　◆

Matt strolled along the path, his footsteps making slurping sounds on the soggy earth. A pale sun shrouded by gauzy clouds shone through the branches of a tall maple as if not quite sure it wanted to make an appearance. The cloying aroma of nearby honeysuckle drew the bees, and Matt swatted his hat at one lone, winged insect that seemed more interested in his plaid shirt.

Or maybe it was the lingering sweet smell of soap coming from the material that drew the bug. Matt wasn't sure what Amanda put in the soap, but it wasn't plain lye. Actually, when he thought about it, his shirt smelled of her—like wild roses—and he could imagine her holding his large cotton shirt in her soft, small hands, folding it with great care, then laying it in the basket to deliver to him, as she'd done the day after the sickness left him. It had been a surprise when she'd arrived at his doorstep and had taken his spare clothing and bed linens to wash. He wondered what her ma had thought about that. Certainly Mrs. Hodges couldn't have been too happy with her daughter, though it was a kind gesture. Amanda had done all she could to make Matt feel welcome in the hollow. Matt supposed with Amanda being the preacher's daughter she'd been taught at her pappy's knee to be charitable to her fellow man.

Tinkling laughter sailed from beyond the bushes, startling Matt.

"Miz Amanda, iffen ya keep up yer gigglin', you'll scare away the fish," a protesting young male voice said from beyond some hawthorn bushes.

"Sorry, Jeb. But if you don't want me laughing, then you'd better stop giving those imitations of your teacher. I shouldn't be laughing in any case, encouraging such horrid behavior."

"Aw, I don' mean no dizespect, Miz Amanda; ya'll know that. Ma says I got me a gift for copyin' people's voices, though she don' know what good such a gift'll do me. So I needs ta find some way to use this here gift. Makin' people laugh's a good thing—don't you reckon?"

"Yes, that's true, Jeb. But you shouldn't use your gift at other people's expense. And poking fun at your teacher isn't a nice thing to do."

Curious, Matt moved off the path and through an opening in the bushes, making a loud rustle as he parted them. The surprise on Amanda's features must have equaled the surprise on Matt's face to see her sitting on the ground next to Jeb, a fishing pole in her hands. She awkwardly scrambled to a stand, dropping the stick. It fell halfway in the water. Jeb grabbed the pole before it could slide all the way in the river and held it out to her. Her face going rosy, she darted a look Matt's way.

"You won't tell?" she asked

"Tell what?" Matt replied.

She glanced at Jeb, as though uncertain, then focused on Matt again. "I need to speak with you in private." Before Matt knew what she was about, she approached, stopping less than a foot in front of him. Her wide eyes glistened like the leaves after a spring rain. "You won't tell anyone you saw me fishing?" she whispered.

"I won't if you'd rather I didn't," Matt answered, befuddled either by her strange words or her close presence. Which it was, he couldn't rightly say. But suddenly his brain refused to work right. "Uh. . .if you don't mind me asking, why should it be kept secret?"

She blew out an exasperated little breath. "It's the silliest thing, really. Ma doesn't consider it proper for a lady to go fishing. She and Pa grew up back East, where everyone is fussy about things like that, I reckon, though here in the hollow such notions seem odd." She tilted her head to one side. "You don't consider it improper, do you?"

He squirmed. "Well, now, Miss Hodges, I don't s'ppose my opinion matters one whit in light of your ma's wishes."

"Oh, won't you call me Amanda? We're not exactly strangers. And I'll call you Matt." She smiled, her teeth as creamy white as a hawthorn's blossoms in springtime. "Or would you prefer I call you Matthew? Matt is how I think of you, so it would be easier to call you Matt, but I surely understand if you'd rather I didn't. I despise it when people call me Mandy." Her words hinged on bold, but her eyes betrayed uncertainty, making her appear almost vulnerable.

"Matt's fine." He cleared the huskiness from his throat. "I'd best be going. I'm heading to town for some supplies."

"Wait. I'll join you. I should be getting home anyway." She looked toward the river. "Jeb, I'd consider it a favor if you'd take my fish to your ma. Rosalie breaks out in hives when she eats catfish, so Ma wouldn't take too kindly to my bringing them home for supper."

Jeb shook his head. "Thanks jis' the same. But I cain't take no charity. My pappy wouldn't like it."

"Oh, Jeb. Consider it thanks for the pointers you gave. Without your help, I wouldn't have caught those three little fish—it's been so long since I held a pole—so they're just as much yours as they are mine. Either that or throw them back. I simply can't take them." Amanda turned from the boy and moved through the bushes.

Matt waited to see what Jeb would do, then joined her.

"Did he take them?" she whispered.

"He tied them to his catch."

"Good! I know Mr. Hunter's leg has been paining him since that tree limb fell on him last fall, and he can't go hunting as often as he used to. It was a horrible accident, with the way he got caught in that storm. But that's no excuse to let his family go without, even if it means accepting a handout now and then."

"The folks in these hills are proud," Matt countered, thankful she'd taken a different tack in the conversation than where he thought it was heading. He didn't want to tell her how he'd gotten his limp.

Amanda sniffed. "Proud enough to let their children starve, I reckon. I get so weary of their stubbornness—and their superstitions. If Hickory Hollow is going to grow into the kind of town Pa and Mr. Randall are striving for, then a lot more people are going to have to learn to put aside their old ways and work together."

"I reckon so. But you're dealin' with a stiff-necked bunch."

"Don't I know it!" She sighed. "I suppose it'll take a leap of faith to save them."

"A leap of faith?"

"One of Pa's examples from his Sunday preaching. He said when something looks downright impossible, you need to believe beyond what you've done already.

You need to spiritually move out in faith and leap over your chasm of troubles, while holding fast to God's promises from the Holy Bible."

Matt rolled the words around in his head.

"At least Ma and I can feed the poor every Saturday, after you menfolk build on the church—those who'll come, that is." She looked at him, her eyes curious as though an idea had just occurred to her. "Are you from around here, Matt? You seem to know something about the hill people."

Uneasy, he looked ahead. "I come from the hills. In Tennessee."

"Oh?" She was quiet a moment. "Have you got any family?"

Matt hesitated. "A brother. Both my parents are dead."

"I'm sorry." Her gaze dropped to the ground. "And do you hear from your brother much?"

Matt stopped walking and looked full at her. "Why do you ask?"

She seemed startled by his abrupt question. "No reason. Just trying to make conversation."

Matt forced his tense shoulders to relax. She didn't know who he was, after all, or rather who he'd been. "My brother and I parted ways awhile back."

"Oh." Her reply came soft.

They continued walking. Matt felt a twinge of guilt for speaking so harshly and broke his usual silence to ask a question of his own. "What made your parents decide to leave the East and make their home in the Ozarks?"

"Pa felt led to come to the hollow and do his preaching here."

"Your pa is a good preacher."

"I think so, too." She smiled at him. "What about your pa? What kind of man was he?"

Relieved that they'd come to the clearing that led to the town's buildings, Matt raised two fingers and a thumb to touch the brim of his hat. "Well, I'll be tendin' to my business now. Have a nice day, Miss Amanda."

He walked on but could feel her intent gaze burn a hole through his back the entire way to the mercantile.

◆　◆　◆

The weather cooperated the next Saturday so that the men could work on the church without getting rained on. Yet what should have been a good turnout, due to fair weather, wasn't. Several men were down with the sickness Matt had grappled with weeks ago, and the total number of workers at the church was five: Matt, Bob and Pete Wilson, Pastor Hodges, and a slow old codger named Frank Whipple, who barely could lift a hammer—much less hoist a heavy stone block—and whose arthritic bones made him shuffle from corner to corner. Matt supposed the idea of free food had lured the old bachelor from his home. Yet Matt knew the preacher was grateful to any and all who volunteered their time, whether young or old.

Matt watched six-year-old Edmund who was "helping" by stirring mortar, then lifting the stick out of the pail and staring at it with extreme interest. With his finger, he poked at a gray glob hanging from the stick.

"Edmund Cornell Hodges." Amanda's soft, stern voice came from behind, startling both Matt and the child. "You'd best stay out of that goop before Ma sees you. You ruined your one good shirt last week—and that's your only spare."

Edmund frowned but dropped the stick back into the bucket. Warily, Matt faced Amanda. She smiled, holding out a tray with tin cups on it.

"It's cider—nice and cold. Ma always keeps a jug cooling in the stream. I thought—that is, Ma thought—you and the others might like some."

"Amanda," her father called from the other side of the church wall. "I sure could use some of that cider."

She offered an apologetic smile to Matt and handed him a cup. "Excuse me."

Matt relaxed once she'd moved away, and he swallowed the cool apple drink in several gulps. Since the day he'd caught her fishing, Amanda had come around a few times while he worked, often shelling out a barrage of questions involving Matt's history that Matt didn't feel he could answer. Worse, the more time he spent in her company, the more he experienced a keen desire to share some of his past with her. Not the kind of information that could get him strung up with a rope, but the regular, everyday sort of conversation that people engaged in all the time. Amanda was pleasant company, but to tell anyone even a little of his past could prove dangerous.

As he feared, when Amanda finished handing out the refreshment, she returned to his side, supposedly to keep an eye on Edmund. The boy squatted a few feet away from Matt and watched a big black bug crawl down a limestone block.

"It sure is fine weather to be outdoors." Hugging the empty wooden tray to her chest, Amanda inhaled deeply, as if by doing so she could drink down the sun's golden rays. Maybe that would explain why her face shone with such vitality. Sunshine dwelled inside her soul.

She turned laughing eyes his way, her grin laced with mischief. "Of course, on a day like today, I'd much rather be fishing."

Matt smiled. "The fish might not be biting this late in the afternoon."

"Oh, fiddle-faddle. Fish'll eat when they're hungry, just like people do, I expect." Her gaze briefly dropped to the ground as if she were weighing her words. "Matt, would you consider coming along? After supper, of course. I reckon you know of a lot better fishing spots than I do."

Matt wondered how she'd arrived at such a conclusion, since in the short time he'd been a resident of Hickory Hollow he'd only been fishing twice. "You sure you want to go this late in the day? The best time would be early morning."

"Wonderful!" she exclaimed brightly. "Then it's settled. We'll meet at dawn at your cabin day after tomorrow. We can't go tomorrow, of course, it being the Lord's Day and all. Oh, no—wait. Monday is washday, and I promised to help Ma with her visits to the sick this week, too. Thursday then."

Matt blinked, stupefied. Had he agreed to go with her? "Well, uh, I don't know—"

"Oh, don't back out on me now," she hastened to say. "Jeb's coming, too. It's for his family's sake I'm doing this. Whatever I catch, I'm going to make sure he takes home, like last time. Please, come with us." Her expression was guileless, entreating him, but her soft words made Matt's heart pound with strange foreboding.

"Say that again to my face!" The sudden shout erupted from one of the Wilson boys and stymied whatever reply Matt might've given. He turned to see Bob facing down his brother, his hands clenched, his face an angry beet red.

"Alright, I will." Pete's usually easygoing features appeared as if they'd been etched in stone. "I said, Miss Ivy's too smart to have anything to do with a slow-witted ox like you." Pete emphasized each word. "And I'll be the one dancin' with her at Tom and Mayflower's weddin'."

Bob growled and swung his fist, connecting with Pete's jaw. Pete jerked a few steps backward, then lunged at Bob, wrapping both arms around his waist and driving into him like a locomotive. Both men hit the ground, upsetting a bucket of mortar. Their heads came close to cracking against a huge stone block. Amanda gasped. The boys' ma cried out.

Matt pushed his empty glass into Amanda's hand and sped toward the dueling brothers. With a good deal of effort, he pulled Pete off Bob. Another man grabbed Bob. Pete tried to lunge at his brother again, but Matt caught his arm and brought it up hard behind his back. "Stop it! The both of you. You should be ashamed, upsettin' Preacher's doin's like this. No pretty gal is worth fighting over if it means splittin' up kinfolk." Matt growled the words low, but he spoke from the heart.

Once he and Buck had fought over a charming belle who liked to play brother against brother, like pawns on a chessboard, and had fluttered about, smiling at each in turn, feeding upon their jealous rivalries as a she-cat feeds upon its kill. That had been the start of the trouble between him and Buck.

Pete spat on the ground and wiped the back of his hand along his bloody mouth. His narrowed gaze was fixed on his brother the whole time, but he gave a short nod, and Matt dropped his hold. The other man followed suit and released Bob. The youth picked up his hat from the ground and made as if to go, but Matt wasn't finished.

"Now shake."

Both brothers looked at Matt in disbelief. Their jaws, covered in peach fuzz, set stubbornly, and they crossed their arms over their chests.

"I said, 'shake,'" Matt muttered, not giving an inch. "You've upset the women-folk with all your carrying-on, and you'd best make it right between you and ease their minds. Or have you forgotten we're trying to serve God and community by building a church here? You two ain't no Cain and Abel, that's for sure, so shake hands and be done with it."

At mention of the women, Pete's gaze went beyond Matt to his ma and a few other ladies staring in their direction. Ivy was absent, and Matt wondered if her presence would have prevented the brawl between the brothers.

His mouth thinning, Pete jerked his arm out toward his brother, clearly reluctant. Bob stared at the proffered hand a minute, then clasped it tight. Pete winced, but the two shook hands, and Matt retraced his steps to Amanda. Her eyes were strangely sad.

"Amanda," her pa called out. "You'd best be going about your business. We men need to do more work on the church before we have our supper."

"Yes, Pa." She gave Matt a lukewarm smile, then turned away, heading for the two women who stirred something in a huge black kettle over flaming logs.

Scratching the back of his neck in puzzlement, Matt watched her go. What had happened to cause such a rapid-fire switch in her emotions? A bleak thought struck.

Did Amanda care for one of the Wilson brothers, who both apparently preferred her friend Ivy? The brothers couldn't be more than sixteen, if that, but folks around these parts married young. Some as young as fifteen. And Amanda certainly was the right age to be a bride. She'd make some man a fine wife one day, Matt was sure. She possessed an inner strength and tenacity mixed with the right amount of gentleness to be a rock-solid support to the man she picked for her husband. And Matt was certain she'd have it no other way. She wouldn't let someone choose her mate. No sirree, not Amanda. She'd be the one doing the choosing. . .and suddenly Matt envied the unknown suitor.

At the sudden sharp and unwelcome twist his thoughts took, Matt set his mouth grimly and resumed work.

Chapter 4

Thin patches of white mist curled between the thickly wooded hills and the valley floor as Amanda, Matt, and Jeb tramped over the mountain in search of the perfect fishing hole. Or at least that was the original plan; with all the walking they'd done, Amanda was beginning to wonder if "the perfect fishing hole" was in another county!

The cooing song of mourning doves occasionally rippled through the damp air, which still held the bite of morning chill. Wildflowers in a rainbow of shades grew in abundance. The hardwood trees had traded their sprinklings of cheery spring buds for lush mantles of greenery that cloaked the surrounding mountainside.

Earlier, Amanda had sped through her chores. The moment her siblings headed for the little log schoolhouse and her ma had taken Charmaine with her to visit Zeke's mother, Amanda sped from the cabin. She'd been relieved and happy when Matt answered his door with a fishing pole propped on one shoulder. His eyes had seemed wary, but the smile he'd given her and Jeb was friendly enough.

Yet for the past two hours little conversation had flowed between them, and Amanda figured it probably was easier to get a mule to talk than it was Matt Campbell. She still fretted over his remark concerning women the other day, when he'd broken up the fight between the Wilson brothers. He'd said, "No pretty gal is worth splitting up kinfolk." And while she supposed that was true, Amanda couldn't help but feel his meaning went deeper and that Matt had little regard for women in the marrying sense.

Two long blasts from a steamboat whistle broke through the forest stillness. Amanda hurried to a clump of trees and moved a leafy bough aside. Through a willow's branches on the riverbank, she could just make out the majestic, three-storied side-wheeler a few hundred feet away, as it glided along the water, its massive wheels churning up white froth.

"Isn't that just the prettiest sight you ever did see?" Amanda murmured when she heard Matt come up beside her. "One day I'd like to ride on a riverboat so fine and see what life's like beyond the hollow."

"You might be disappointed," Matt said as though to himself.

She glanced his way. "In what? The world beyond or the riverboat?"

Her question startled him into looking at her, and a grin played with the corners of his mouth. "Both, probably. People's expectations are often too high."

"What about you, Matt? Have you seen the world?"

The smile disappeared, and he looked toward the river. "I've seen my share."

The reply wasn't satisfying, but at least he was talking. "And were you disappointed with what you saw?" When he didn't answer, she asked another question. "What about riverboats? Ever been on one?"

"Once."

"Oh—what's it like?" She could barely contain her excitement. "Are there riverboat gamblers with evil designs who prey on defenseless young women?"

He raised his eyebrows. "It sounds like you've been reading those dime novels."

Her face went hot. "Not me. Ivy. She told me all about riverboats."

Matt thought a moment. "I've met my share of gamblers, but you'll find those everywhere. Not just on riverboats."

"I suppose that's true." Amanda looked toward the steamboat that was disappearing from view. "Wishing for a trip upriver on one of those is pointless in any case. Ma would never allow it. She shares Ivy's opinion that riverboats are full of sinful men. Though if I were aboard one, I certainly wouldn't have anything to do with those sorts of people, so she needn't worry."

She let go of the branch, which rustled back into place. Turning, she was about to suggest they go, but was struck speechless by the hopeless longing in Matt's beautiful eyes as he stared at her.

"Matt?"

He seemed to snap out of whatever had him misty-eyed and moved away. "Jeb must've gone ahead. I don't see him."

"He's probably chasing another chipmunk," she said, hurrying to catch up. "He'll find us. Did I say something wrong?" She lifted her skirts and stepped over a lichen-covered boulder in her path. "Is that why you look so upset?" Suddenly she halted. "Oh, Matt. Your pa was a riverboat gambler, wasn't he? That's why you're upset. I shouldn't have spoken so."

He stopped walking and turned, his mouth open as though he would offer a hasty reply. Instead he hesitated, then closed it. "No. He wasn't a riverboat gambler."

"Your grandpappy then? No, that can't be right. Riverboats have only been around for the past fifty years or so, though come to think of it, I reckon it could have been your grandpappy—"

"Miss Amanda. . ." Before Matt could complete the thought, big, wet splats hit Amanda's head and cheek, and Matt blinked one eye as though something had gotten in it. They both turned surprised gazes to the sunny sky. A small rain cloud hovered overhead, as if intent on making itself known. A light shower began to sprinkle upon them.

"Oh, my," Amanda squealed, then laughed.

Matt grabbed her arm. "Come on—before it gets worse."

Together, they ran as fast as they could to a nearby towering oak, whose many leafy branches swept outward and upward, providing shelter to keep them dry. Watching the rain softly fall, Amanda remembered how Jeb's father was wounded when lightning struck a tree, much like this one, last year. She shivered, though there weren't any detectable rolls of thunder or flashes of light in the clouds.

"You're cold," Matt said and propped his fishing pole against the wide trunk. To Amanda's surprise, he looped his arm around her shoulders, drawing her close. Maybe if he were wearing a jacket, he would have put that around her shoulders instead, but Amanda couldn't help but feel grateful that the day was too warm for such outerwear. Being this close to him made her feel safe, content, and sped up her heart a few beats with an emotion still new to her. Was it love?

Feeling as if she were caught up in some wonderful dream, she tilted her head to look at him.

Matt gasped as though suddenly short of breath and dropped his arm from around her. "Don't look at me like that!"

"Like what?" Not understanding his swift change in mood and smarting from the sharpness in his tone, Amanda clutched her elbows. "Did I do something wrong?"

He briefly closed his eyes. "No. I don't reckon you did," he said at last. "You have no idea what I meant, do you?"

She shook her head.

He stared at her with an expression she couldn't define, as though he didn't want to look at her but couldn't keep from it. With wonder, she felt his rough fingertip stroke her jawbone to her chin, then watched his head lower. Cold rainwater dripped off the brim of his hat onto her scalp, but when his soft cool lips touched her brow, she forgot the minor discomfort. "Stay sweet, Amanda," he said, his voice husky.

Feeling suddenly hopeful and a little reckless, she lifted both hands to his rough-whiskered jaw and softly pressed her lips to his. He stiffened, and Amanda, now horrified by her boldness, began to draw away, but his strong arms suddenly wrapped around her waist. His kiss was more fervent than hers had been, and Amanda's heart soared. He must feel the same way about her that she did about him!

Within seconds, he pulled away, the bleak expression in his eyes puzzling her. Why should he look so sad when she felt so happy?

"I shouldn't have done that," he whispered. "You don't want to get hooked up with a man like me, Amanda."

Discouraged, she regarded him. "You're wrong, Matt. Why would you even think such a thing?"

He somberly shook his head and stared up at the sky as though he couldn't stand looking at her any longer. Steady splashes of water hit the leaves and ground, the only sounds heard. Amanda relived the last few minutes over in her mind while she stared at his sober profile. He obviously cared for her; otherwise he wouldn't have kissed her—would he? Why should he think he wasn't worthy of her? Unless. . . unless Zeke's hateful words about Matt being an outlaw were true. Yet the man Amanda had grown to know was far removed from her idea of an outlaw.

"It's beginning to clear," Matt said. "We should find Jeb."

The shower had ended as quickly as it began. Amanda followed Matt from beneath the shielding oak, feeling as if the small rain cloud had drifted into her heart and watered down her joy in the day. Matt's sudden interest in Jeb's whereabouts was odd, considering the boy often roamed the foothills alone and didn't answer to anyone but his pappy. In fact, the youth probably knew this mountain better than anyone in the hollow. Not too surprising, Jeb spotted them before they ran across him.

"Come see what I found!" he yelled from a nearby covering of pines. A flash of gray broke through the underbrush as he beckoned in a wide motion with his arm, and half of his moon face could be seen. Then both the face and the gray-sleeved arm disappeared, and a loud rustle followed as Jeb darted back through the forest.

Amanda and Matt left the well-beaten path and moved in the direction they'd last seen him. A new sense of excitement winged through Amanda, and she wondered what treasure Jeb must have found. Rarely had she seen him so enthused about anything.

The trees stood close, blocking her vision of what was ahead, and she didn't see the small clearing with the aqua-blue spring until she'd almost come upon it. Jeb excitedly pointed to a midsized bluff of jagged gray-and-tan rock, only one of many bluffs scattered throughout the area. Wild ferns and undergrowth grew tall against the coarse stone, almost shielding the black hole at the bottom.

"I ain't never seen this cave before," Jeb exclaimed excitedly. "You reckon it's linked to the one over yonder, acrost the mountain a ways—the one that has water comin' out the hole and runnin' into the stream?" As he talked, he moved toward the cave. "That one you cain't get in 'cuz it's too high. But this one should be easy enough, I reckon."

"Be careful, Jeb," Matt warned. "You don't know what might be waitin' inside. A grizzly. A copperhead. . ."

"I agree with Matt. Come away from there."

Amanda wasn't sure why, but she felt a niggling sense of danger, though she couldn't put her finger on what seemed wrong. As always, the forest was eerily quiet, except for the occasional rustles in the undergrowth or the distant shriek of a hawk or other bird. Yet today the thick wood seemed almost too quiet. Perhaps it was the presence of the cave that bothered her. Amanda never had liked caves, which were scattered throughout the mountains as thickly as fleas on a sheepdog.

Jeb paid them no heed and tromped on ahead. Amanda shared an exasperated look with Matt, then followed the boy, stepping over the smooth, gray rocks that lined the muddy ground at the front of the bluff. Up close, the cave's black entrance was taller than a man but not quite wide enough to stretch her arms out when she touched the sides. She put her hand to the coarse rock at shoulder level but moved no farther. Cool air drifted out, brushing against Amanda's face and stirring her damp tendrils. Shivering, she looked away from the gaping hole that led to who-knew-where.

An orange-and-black-spotted reptile, about six inches long with the tail, rapidly skittered along the face of the bluff, near her fingers. She squealed and jerked her hand away.

Jeb laughed. "Aw, it's jis' a salamander, Miz Amanda. It won't do you no harm."

"Thanks," she said drolly. "It only scared a year's life out of me, is all." She eyed the creature with disgust. It had halted its rapid pace and seemed to regard Amanda with black, beady eyes.

"We need to be heading back." Matt's voice came abruptly from behind, startling her. She looked his way. His gaze was caught up in the trees near the spring. His jaw was tense, his manner alert.

The hairs on the back of Amanda's neck prickled. "Matt, what's wrong?"

He looked at her. "Nothin'. We just need to head back." He took a firm hold of her elbow and turned her in the direction from which they'd come, as though afraid she might refuse. "Jeb, you, too."

Startled, Amanda darted a glance over her shoulder at Jeb, who shrugged, obviously as ignorant to what was bothering Matt as she was.

"But. . .aren't we going fishing?" Amanda sputtered.

Matt didn't answer but kept walking, pulling her along with him. For a man who limped, he certainly was keeping a fast pace. Amanda didn't have time to think about his odd behavior, struggling as she did to keep up with him.

◆　◆　◆

On the evening of Mayflower and Tom's wedding, Matt gathered his few belongings and left the cabin for what would be the last time. When he'd kissed Amanda yesterday in the rain, he had wished it could have been the first of many kisses. Because of that, he was doing the best thing for all concerned and leaving Hickory Hollow. For good.

It would be hard not to see her once more, not to look into those clear green eyes or hear her sweet voice. Yet Matt knew Amanda, and he knew his heart. With the strong way he felt about her, the love he now recognized he had for her, Matt figured it would take little persuading on her part to get him to stay. For her sake, he couldn't allow that to happen. She was different from the scheming women he'd known. Women like Maryanne, who with one word or look could rip a man's heart to shreds. Amanda was sweet. Headstrong, but sweet, and as innocent as a lamb.

Pushing all bittersweet memories of Amanda aside, Matt settled his hat more firmly on his head and closed the door. He had one last order of business to take care of before leaving the hollow. If the rumors he'd heard were true, then Buck was on this mountain. And sure as shooting, those squashed cigar stubs Matt had spotted near the cave entrance had been his brother's, as well as the empty whiskey bottle underneath the bushes. He knew he'd seen movement in the trees and didn't think it belonged to a moonshiner using the cave for a still. A moonshiner would have confronted Matt, Amanda, and Jeb with a shotgun before they'd so much as stepped into the clearing; whereas an outlaw might have hidden in the trees until it was safe to come out—unless he knew he'd been spotted. Then there would have been shooting. No, it wasn't any moonshiner spying on them. Which meant only one thing.

The gang must have found another hideout.

Matt rubbed his sore hip, his fingers brushing against the ivory-handled butt of the Colt .44 revolver in his holster. Scowling, he looked at a nearby bluff, remembering the day he'd been shot by one of the boys, though he didn't know which one had done it. The impact of the bullet in his leg and the fiery agony of splintering bone had knocked him off his horse. Once he hit the ground, he'd rolled and gone over a short bluff, much like that one, and been left for dead.

Wouldn't Buck and the others be surprised to see how alive he was?

Chapter 5

Haunting strains of a dulcimer mingled with the twanging of a banjo and the merry strings of a fiddle as the people danced and clapped and stamped their feet, locking arms from time to time in the rollicking mountain reel. Laughter and smiles abounded, but Amanda didn't feel one bit joyful. Not after the talk she'd just had with her pa.

Spotting Zeke, she curled her hands into fists at her sides and marched over to where he stood on the fringes, watching the merriment. He raised his brows when she stopped in front of him. "Care for a dance?"

"Don't you talk to me about dancing," Amanda fumed. "How dare your pa take the land for the church away from my pa! He promised it to him. Your pa had no right to go back on his word."

Zeke regarded her, a patronizing look on his face. "Now, Amanda, don't fret so. Nothing was signed. Father recently realized he'd made a mistake—a business error, if you will—in issuing the use of that land to your father. Your pa can build his church elsewhere on the mountain. Father told him that."

"Build elsewhere? The church is already halfway to being built, Zeke. Maybe nothing was signed on paper, but there's such a thing as a gentleman's agreement—yet your pa's obviously no gentleman!"

She whirled away, but Zeke caught her arm before she could take more than two steps. "Marry me, and I'll persuade Father to give us that land for a wedding present. Then you can give the deed to your pa. I'm sure I can get Father to agree. I know something about his affairs he wouldn't want Mother to know." He grinned slyly.

"You'd blackmail your own father?" Amanda asked incredulously. She sobered. "Zeke Randall, I wouldn't marry you if you were the last man to draw breath in all of Hickory Hollow." Zeke's face grew tight, and she jerked her arm from his hold. "You're just like your pa. You think you can order everyone around, and if that doesn't work, then you try and buy people or bully them to get what you want. Well I'm not a woman who can be bought—or bullied!"

"It's Matt Campbell, isn't it?" he sneered. "Ever since he came to the hollow, he's been nothing but trouble, messing in our affairs."

"*Our* affairs? Oh!" She stamped her foot, wishing it was his shoe she was stamping instead. She didn't believe the man's gall. "We don't have any 'affairs' between us—never did—and this has nothing to do with Matt. It has to do with something you obviously know nothing about. Integrity and honor and. . .and. . .well, just doing what's right!"

178

Noticing they were drawing unwanted attention from those dancing nearby, Amanda bustled away. Before she could reach the edge of the clearing, she met Ivy. Her eyes were troubled. "Amanda, I'm so sorry about what my father did. I had no idea. . . ."

Amanda's anger waned a bit. Ivy was the only Randall with any shred of decency; one reason the two of them had been friends since they were children. "I don't blame you." She darted a look up the mountain. "But if I don't get away from here, I'm sure to embarrass my parents. I need to calm down. If they should ask for me, tell them I'll be back shortly."

Ivy frowned. "You're going to see him, aren't you?"

"Just tell them!" Amanda stomped up the path. She had no doubt that the "him" to whom Ivy so disdainfully referred was Matt. Amanda didn't understand what Ivy had against him; he was so nice to everyone. Knowing that, Amanda wondered why he hadn't made an appearance at the wedding. He and Tom seemed to get along well.

As she neared his cabin, she relaxed. She wished to speak with Matt about this latest occurrence, even if he only gave his usual scant replies. Simply being in his presence made her feel better.

At the door, she knocked, waited, then knocked again. She frowned, remembering that spring morning when she'd found him ill. Wondering if she should peek inside, she suddenly noticed fresh boot prints in the mud. Many of the hill people were trappers and hunters and took to wearing knee-length moccasins, but Matt favored boots, so she assumed the prints were his. They led over a path that wound higher up the mountain.

She thought a moment, looking in the direction of the wedding celebration, though she couldn't see the clearing from this point. But she could hear faint strains of music floating over the air. It was doubtful her parents would look for her or be concerned; Ma left early to help deliver a baby, and Pa had gone home, discouraged by Mr. Randall's news. The cruel buzzard could have at least waited until after the party to break it to her pa.

Amanda looked up the mountain and decided to follow the tracks and find Matt. She was still too angry to rejoin the others.

The birdsong in the trees was noisier than usual, as if the feathered creatures were complaining about the exuberant music from the clearing. Amanda climbed higher, crossed a ridge, and took another path that ascended, leading around the mountain. The tracks moved along the same path Jeb had taken them on their quest for the perfect fishing hole they'd never found.

The prints veered off the path, deeper into the thick wood. Amanda hesitated, then followed, realizing Matt must have gone in the direction of the cave. Why? He didn't seem to have any interest in exploring it when they were there yesterday. Cautiously she walked over the damp, black soil, avoiding stepping on a stick that could snap and give away her presence, though why she felt she should be so secretive, she didn't know. Yet, just like that other day, something didn't feel right.

Before she reached the clearing, she heard the rise and fall of men's voices. Surprised, she moved closer so she could hear, pressed herself against a thick trunk to hide, then cautiously peeked around the bark.

About twenty yards away, Matt stood facing a young bearded man the same size as he in both height and form. His hair was almost as long as Matt's, and like Matt, he wore the same type of boots. A wide-brimmed felt hat was pulled over his forehead. A gun belt was strapped around the stranger's waist, and Amanda noticed that Matt also wore his guns.

"So, what did you come for then?" the man groused. "You gonna spout that same religion garbage to me?"

"No," Matt replied. "We had the same mother, and she taught us from the same Bible. You know the Gospel same as me, Buck. That's why I had to leave the gang. I couldn't abide the stealing and killing anymore."

Amanda gasped. What Zeke had said about Matt being an outlaw must be true!

The man named Buck grunted. "You were a fool to face 'em down and tell 'em you were turnin' over your share of the gold and givin' yourself up. If you'd gone through with it, you woulda been hanged."

"What's the difference?" Matt asked dryly. "A rope or a bullet—both bring about the same end. Death. Only whichever one of the others shot me when my back was turned didn't succeed in killing me."

Crossing his arms over his chest, Buck regarded Matt. "What makes you think it was one o' the others?"

"Who else? Oh, no." Matt's voice went hoarse. "Not you—my own brother?"

At Matt's distress, Amanda's heart wrenched.

Suddenly a large, dirty hand clapped over her mouth, and someone grabbed her around the waist from behind, pulling her hard against him. "Now, whatcha have to go and snoop 'round this neck o' the woods for?" a young man's voice rasped near her ear. "You should be home, like a good little girl, tendin' your chores and mindin' your own business."

Amanda tried to scream and struggled, kicking back with her heels toward her attacker's shins, though he stood with his feet planted apart so it was hard for her to make contact. Matt ran into view, a long-barreled revolver in his hand. His eyes widened when he saw her, but his gaze immediately veered to the man holding her, and he raised his gun to aim.

"Let her go, Jesse," Matt ordered. "It's me you want. Not her."

The ominous click of another gun's trigger being cocked sounded to their left. Amanda's eyes flicked that way. A slender man with a hawk nose and sandy hair and beard casually stood, his gun trained on Matt.

" 'What fools these mortals be,' " he said quietly, quoting Shakespeare. "Drop the gun, Matt, and kick it away. Buck might have missed your heart last time, but my aim is true, as you know."

Matt hesitated, then let the gun fall and did as ordered. The man holding Amanda released her with a little forward push and moved to pluck the weapon from the ground, then took a stand near the gunman. Like the other man, he trained Matt's gun upon them, motioning with the barrel for Amanda to move next to Matt. The second gunman's hair under the hat was darker, his features boyishly handsome, but the blue eyes that glittered in the smooth face were hard and unyielding. Both men wore long soldiers' overcoats and appeared to be in their early twenties.

"Well, Frank," the one who'd grabbed Amanda said, his tone almost cordial. "What do you reckon we ought to do with these two?"

The bearded gunman looked at Amanda and smiled, though the expression wasn't pleasant. "You know more about these things, Jesse. You decide."

Amanda gulped a shaky breath, faint with the knowledge that struck her. Frank. . .Jesse. . .

She was a prisoner of the James Gang.

◆ ◆ ◆

Hands and feet tied, Matt leaned his shoulder against the cave wall. Amanda was also tied, but her hands were bound in front of her, whereas Matt's were tied behind his back. The small fire Frank had started once it grew dark flickered eerily on the tan stone around them, making huge shadows. The flames produced little warmth for Amanda and Matt, who sat about fifteen feet inside the cave entrance. Still, the fire did give off light, which offered some comfort amid the high-pitched squeals of the bats. The black winged creatures flew from wall to wall, obviously upset to have their peace disturbed. Matt knew they were harmless and told Amanda so, but he noticed her dart an anxious glance at them from time to time and shiver when one swooped too close.

Jesse strode toward them, a bowl of something steaming in his hands. He hunkered down beside Amanda. "Squirrel stew," he said with a grin, watching her. "Best eat it while it's hot. Never let it be said that the James brothers let their prisoners starve. Especially when the prisoner is such a purty young thing."

Amanda scowled and turned her face away. From behind Jesse, Frank chuckled. " 'Frailty, thy name is woman,' " he mocked.

Jesse set the bowl down and stood. "We got a stubborn one here, all right."

He rejoined Frank and Hugh, another gang member who'd recently arrived. All three men stood at the entrance and conversed.

"An outlaw who quotes Shakespeare," Amanda muttered, her bitter gaze on Frank. "How amusing."

Surprise made Matt speak. "You know Shakespeare?"

"Ivy has a book of his plays and sonnets," she said, still not looking at him. She hadn't looked his way since they'd been forced into this cave at gunpoint, hours ago. Not that he could blame her.

Matt sighed. "You better eat. You need to keep up your strength."

"What about you? I notice they didn't bring you any."

Matt didn't say he was certain that the brothers had decided his fate. Where they planned to send him, he wouldn't need food, but at least Amanda would be safe. The James brothers had never harmed or killed a woman, not to his knowledge, and when Matt had mentioned that Amanda was a preacher's daughter, a look of grudging respect lit the brothers' eyes. Jesse and Frank's pa had been a preacher. But he'd left the ministry for the gold fields when Jesse was just a boy and had died there.

Perhaps his pa was the reason Jesse carried a Bible wherever he went, though the life-changing words obviously had never entered his heart.

"Go on and eat," Matt quietly encouraged.

Amanda awkwardly picked up the bowl with one hand, managing to bring it to her mouth. In the process she sloshed some liquid on her dress and scowled. The round neckline had gotten snagged on a low branch during their trek to this cave, though the tear was modest. But an angry red scratch could be seen on her collarbone. "It would've been nice if they could have untied me first," she mumbled between sips. "I can barely feel my hands anymore."

"Amanda, you don't know how sorry I am that you got involved," Matt said forcefully, keeping his voice low so the others couldn't hear. " I'd do anything I could to undo the past."

In the scant firelight, he saw her brow soften. "I know. I heard what you said to your brother before I got caught. I can't say as how I understand why you got involved with them in the first place, Matt, but I can tell you're not one of them anymore—and I surely don't blame you for what happened to me." She glanced at the stony ground. "It was my own stupidity that got me in this pickle. Like Ma says, I'm too willful for my own good."

"I reckon it'll take quite a leap of faith to get us out of this one, huh?" His words were light, meant to relieve some of the dread she must be feeling.

Surprise, then excited certainty swept across her face, filling him with awe. Most women would be in tears by now or cowering against the wall. But not Amanda. In the dim firelight, her eyes seemed to crackle, regaining their vibrancy.

"You're right," she exclaimed softly. "That's exactly what's needed. Thank you for reminding me." She closed her eyes, and the sweetest expression came across her features as her lips began to move and she murmured words Matt couldn't hear.

Uncomfortable, he shifted his gaze to the boot tips of his tied feet. He couldn't pray; not when he felt such bitterness. His original desire in finding Buck was to persuade him to leave the gang and give up this life, which was no life at all—always on the run, always hiding out. But all such notions fled after Buck's revelation. Buck hadn't come right out and said he was the one to shoot Matt, but he'd implied it. His own flesh and blood tried to kill him! How could Buck have done such a thing?

I forgave you all your sins; do likewise to others, My son.

Matt blinked hard at the soft urging that tugged at his spirit. No. . .he couldn't. Yet he had no choice. Not if he wanted to stay in God's favor. God forgave Matt for all the robbing and shooting during his wild days with the gang, when he'd been an uncertain, bitter youth of seventeen. . . .

Matt swallowed, his mind forming a wordless plea for strength to do what the Lord willed him to do.

◆　◆　◆

After Buck finished his stew, he brought a bowl over to Matt. "You need to eat, too," he said gruffly.

Wary, Matt regarded him. His stomach was coiled in knots, and he doubted he could get anything past them. Buck also seemed tense, his eyes not able to meet Matt's, but he didn't move away.

"Were you the one who shot me?" Matt asked quietly, needing to know.

Buck paused for a few nerve-rending seconds before answering, "Yes."

"Why?" Rolled into that one word was all the frustration, hurt, and bitterness Matt had felt since he suspected his brother had betrayed him.

"Hush up!" Buck darted a glance toward the front of the cave, where the others sat and conversed, then looked at Matt again. "I did it to save your skin, you fool," he growled quietly. "If one of them had shot you, you think you'd be sitting here now?"

Matt drew his brows together. "I don't understand."

"Jesse said you had to be stopped, and I volunteered. After I shot you, I rode back to where they waited and let 'em know. I figgered when you came to, you'd find yourself wounded—yes. But you'd be alive. How was I to know you'd roll over that bluff? But it turned out to be a good thing, 'cause Jesse wanted to see for sure you were dead. So I took the boys to the edge of the bluff where they could view your body. I guess they figgered no one could survive that fall."

"Did you think I was dead?"

"Naw, I knew you were breathing. I climbed down to check before I rejoined the others." At Matt's stunned expression, Buck added, "Who do you think sent that old hermit your way?"

"You?" Matt asked hoarsely, something making sense that never had before. Like how quickly the hermit had found him and stopped the bleeding. He swallowed over a tight throat. "You had no idea that hermit was a doc, did you?"

Surprise lit Buck's eyes. "Well, that explains how you survived."

"God took care of me, Buck. Even then."

The admission made Buck look away, and the strong need to try again and talk sense into his brother rose up in Matt.

"Buck, you're not like those two. So why keep riding with them? Give it up. If not for me or you, do it for Ma's memory. I know we had some bad blood between us on account of Maryanne—and I'm sorry about that—but you're all the kin I got left. And I don't want to see you danglin' from the end of a rope."

At mention of the cruel young belle who'd brought animosity between them years ago, Buck's mouth tightened. He set the bowl of stew down with a dull clunk and stood. Before moving away, he stared at Matt awhile longer, then moved to the fire to light a cheroot. Matt closed his eyes, leaned his head back against the cold rock wall, and took his own leap of faith.

◆　◆　◆

Shivering, Amanda watched the bats dart past eerie flickers of light and shadow on the strange formations of stone around her. From deep within the cave's bowels, she detected the hollow sound of trickling water and remembered Jeb's comment about this cave possibly being linked to one with a stream. With all the rain they'd gotten, what if there was a flood? She'd heard older residents of the hollow spin yarns about flash floods in caves. Grimacing, Amanda stared at a pile of brittle bones. Would she and Matt get out alive, or would these outlaws leave them behind until they shared the fate of whatever animal had huddled near the opposite wall long ago?

Minutes earlier, Jesse, clearly the leader of the gang, had given orders to both Hugh and Buck before looking Amanda's way. "Sorry we have to leave you tied up like this, Miss. But I'm sure you understand why we can't let you go. We'd prefer not to have your kinfolk come lookin' for us 'til we're a fair piece from here."

"You're not actually going to leave us in this place?" Amanda's eyes were huge. "Defenseless against any wild critters that might wander inside?"

"Considering the circumstances, there's little else to do." Frank grabbed a burlap sack and slung it over his shoulder. In the eerie semidarkness, his eyes glittered like black pebbles. "Remember, Miss Hodges, 'He's mad that trusts in the tameness of a wolf.'"

"Enough of the Shakespeare," Jesse muttered, grabbing his shotgun. "Let's get the horses and get on outta here." A short whispered conversation among the four outlaws at the mouth of the cavern followed before the James brothers exited the cave.

As Amanda watched, the man named Hugh spat on the ground, said something to Buck, then he, too, left the cave. Buck continued to look out the entrance, his tense stance betraying his nervousness. Suddenly he turned, whipped a hunting knife from his belt, and rushed toward Amanda and Matt.

Matt gasped, his eyes wide in horror. Amanda's blood ran cold. *Jesus, help us!* The cry winged through Amanda's soul.

Buck dropped to his knees once he reached them. The knife arced, the gleam from the fire bringing out yellow glints on the deadly blade, which came down with force toward Matt.

"No!" Amanda screeched.

"Hush up!" Buck threw her a disgusted glance. "Are you trying to get us all kilt?"

For the first time, Amanda saw the ropes around Matt's legs had been cut. Buck quickly did the same to the rope tying his brother's wrists, then faced her. Amanda barely had time to think before he'd sawed through her ropes. Uncomfortable heat tingled through her hands and feet as blood rushed back into them. She felt as if she were being pricked with dozens of pine needles.

"If you two have any sense at all," Buck muttered, "you'll sit like you was. I doubt Hugh'll look close enough to see what I done. When I give the word, you both run outta here like a bear was chasin' you for its evenin' meal."

Matt drew his hands back behind him and crossed his wrists, his eyes gleaming with something suspiciously close to tears. "Thanks, Buck."

Buck sheathed the knife, a smile on his whiskered face. "You don't think I'd let my little brother and his woman become a victim of what they'd planned, do ya? Maryanne's history; it ruffled my feathers is all. When I shot you that day, I was only tryin' to save yer hide."

"I realize that now," Matt said quietly.

Buck stood. "Stay alert, and wait for my signal."

"Buck?"

"What now?" Matt's brother turned and looked at him.

"About what we talked on earlier. Think on it some?"

Buck hesitated, then nodded.

Amanda watched him move to the fire, glad that Matt and his brother were obviously on good terms again, also glad Buck was on their side. God was working it all out, and she couldn't help but feel convicted regarding her lapse into fear earlier. Remembering what her pa preached about in the book of James concerning the double-minded man who would receive nothing from the Lord, she realized she couldn't pray for one thing, then believe another. If she was going to pray that the Lord would deliver them from evil as His Word said He would, then she'd better start speaking right words and believing them, too.

Amanda smiled at her fellow prisoner. "We're going to get out of here alive, Matt. God's taking care of us."

An awed expression came across his face, but he only nodded.

She wished she could slide over and put her hand in his, but that might not be the best thing to do, considering they had to pretend they were still tied up. It had felt good to hear her being referred to as Matt's woman, but even so, Amanda was curious about the girl Maryanne and what she'd been to Matt.

Hugh returned to the cave and glanced at the two sitting against the wall before he crouched in front of the fire. He and Buck shared little conversation. Hugh slowly ran both sides of his knife along a piece of whetstone, then tossed the stone aside and began to whittle on a stick. Buck wiped his whiskered jaw and stared into the sputtering flames, as though something were bothering him.

"Hugh! Buck!" Jesse's voice abruptly sounded outside the cavern, raspier than usual. "Get on out here, and make it fast!"

Both outlaws scrambled to a standing position and looked at each other. Hugh ran from the cave. Buck stared at Matt, his expression grim. Alarmed, Amanda shot her gaze to the cut ropes, loosely wrapped around her wrists and ankles for effect, then looked Matt's way.

His eyes somber with warning, he slowly shook his head.

Chapter 6

Buck gave Matt one last look before leaving the cave after Hugh. Matt understood what his brother didn't say. If Jesse saw their cut ropes, Buck was a dead man. Yet Matt's first concern was Amanda and getting her out of here. *God help us all,* he silently prayed as he hurried to stand.

After sitting on the cave floor for hours, his hip ached something fierce, but he forced himself to act. He helped Amanda up, then moved with her toward the entrance. Since Jesse had taken his gun, Matt grabbed the shotgun that Hugh had left and plucked up Hugh's knife for good measure, tucking it in his boot.

"If anything happens to me," he whispered to Amanda, "run and hide."

A loud rustle came from some nearby bushes. Matt turned his head in alarm and watched as a tall, shadowed form materialized and approached. Matt raised the shotgun. "You might as well just stop right there. I'm takin' Miss Hodges outta here, and ain't nobody gonna stop me."

"I ain't aimin' to stop ya, Mr. Campbell," a cheery young voice said. Jeb walked closer, into the firelight. "I come ta help."

"That was you who cried out for Hugh, wasn't it?" Amanda said from behind Matt in amazement. "I thought the voice sounded too raspy to be Jesse's, but it sure fooled them. Oh, Jeb, you're wonderful!" She moved forward and gave the embarrassed youth a hug, then straightened suddenly. "But where are they?"

Jeb held up a thick branch and grinned wickedly. "Them two got what was comin' to 'em, I reckon."

"Jeb!" Amanda gasped.

"Aw, no call to look like that, Miz Amanda. I didn' kill 'em. But they sure is gonna have some powerful headaches come mornin'."

"We better leave while we can," Matt said. "Though with how dark the mountain is, it'll be dangerous walkin'."

"No, it won't," Jeb shot back. "I got me a lantern. Left it over yonder." He pointed toward the pines. "I came back yestiday and been watchin''em ever since."

"Your ma must be worried something fierce," Amanda gently rebuked.

"No, Ma'am. I tole my pappy I was goin' a-huntin'." He grinned again. "And I reckon I did—caught me two skunks, leastways. Guess my gift for copyin' people's voices done some good, after all."

"It most certainly did," Amanda said with a smile.

Jeb looked beyond the spring. "I reckon they'll be out 'til we can git help. Too bad I couldn't ketch the others, but my stick weren't gonna hold up to no shotgun, an' they had horses, b'sides."

With Jeb carrying the lantern for a guiding light, Amanda walked beside Matt down the mountain. She wished there was a law official in the hollow, but no such person existed. No jail did, either. If trouble arose between the hill people, they battled it out among themselves. Or the tough men who worked for Zeke's father intervened.

As they walked, Amanda had time to think. "Who's Maryanne?" she asked casually.

Matt's head turned her way, and he seemed to hesitate. "She's a girl Buck and I both liked once. Like Buck said, she's history."

Amanda decided to be content with that. She really didn't want to know too much about any other woman associated with Matt, especially if she was no longer part of his life. Amanda was here with him now, and she intended it to stay that way.

After more than an hour's walking, they neared the clearing. Through the trees, the church's three rock walls glowed in the moonlight. More than a dozen torches flamed across the black night and appeared to be coming closer.

"Uh-oh," Jeb muttered. "Looks like there be trouble."

Curious, Amanda walked with Matt into the clearing. Spotting her father in the row of men moving their way, she halted. "Pa?"

"Amanda!" He hurried to her and clasped her shoulders. "Did he hurt you?"

"Grab that no-account and string him up with a rope," Zeke yelled. "We'll show him how we deal with his kind!"

Three men grabbed Matt by the arms. Matt's shotgun fell, but Jeb picked it up before anyone else could.

"No!" Amanda broke away from her father, moved a step Matt's way, then swung back around to face her pa. "Aren't you going to stop them?"

"Amanda," he said haltingly, as if he were in pain. He reached out to touch the torn flap of her dress.

"No—you don't understand." She shook her head, then again looked toward Matt. Zeke and the others were pushing him toward a sturdy oak with low-hanging branches. The search party had turned into an angry mob yelling for Matt's death.

"Pa—you gotta stop this!" Amanda cried. "Matt didn't do anything. You can't just stand there and let them kill an innocent man!"

Not waiting for his reply, she picked up her skirts and ran toward the group. "Wait!" she yelled. "He didn't do anything!"

The men paid her no heed, and she doubted they could hear her over all their shouting. In the eerie half ring of fire from the torches, she watched as someone threw the rope over a branch and pulled one end down. *Dear God, I know You promised to deliver us from evil, and I'm aiming to keep my mind on that promise. But how do I get them to listen?*

Her gaze darted to Jeb, who stood near the church about thirty feet from the others. She ran to him, grabbed the heavy shotgun from his arms, and cocked it.

Aiming the barrel toward the sky, she pulled the trigger. A shot exploded through the night. The stock slammed against her shoulder from the impact of the rifle going off, threatening to knock her off her feet, but she stood her ground. Unnatural silence filled the air as every man looked her way.

She lowered the gun, keeping hold of the slender barrel in one hand. "Now, if you'll just listen, I'll tell you what happened. Matt didn't hurt me. We've been held prisoner by the James Gang."

"The James Gang!" someone exclaimed. "What would they be doin' on our mountain?"

"I'll tell you what they're doing," Zeke spoke up. He pointed at Matt, who stood silent, his manner resigned. "He's one of them. He was sent to spy on our town."

"No," Amanda countered. "That's not true! Matt was a prisoner just like me. They tied us both up, but we got away."

"My cousin saw him rob the bank in Liberty," Zeke argued.

Several men began to murmur and eyed Matt. "That true?" asked a gruff-looking man with a long beard. "You one of Jesse's gang?"

"I was," he said quietly.

"That's all we need to know," one man called out. "Let's get this over with!"

Amanda watched in horror as the thick rope was looped around Matt's neck.

"Lynch the thievin' skunk!"

"Hang him good!"

"No!" Amanda lifted the heavy rifle and sent another wild shot into the air. This time she hit a branch, which fell to the ground with a rustle, almost hitting one of the men. He jumped and scurried a few feet away. Again she had their undivided attention.

"How can you talk about hanging a man who's done nothing but good for the hollow? Mr. Wilbur," she said, looking at a scrawny man, "Matt fixed your wagon wheel when it broke off and you were stranded on that cart path. And Mr. Conners," she said, directing her words at a grizzled-haired man, "he helped you get those boulders off your land so you could plant seed." She motioned with the gun to the walls behind her. "Matt's the only one of you who's given up every Saturday in helping build our church. Though if Zeke's pa takes the land, I don't know what we'll do."

"What?" Mr. Wilbur turned to Zeke. "What's she blabberin' about?"

Zeke looked uncomfortable. "Nothing we can't discuss later. The point is, what are we going to do about him?" He threw a malevolent look Matt's way. "Don't forget," he said, addressing the others, "it could have been one of your daughters or sisters out there tonight instead of Amanda."

"And I told you," Amanda shot back, "nothing happened."

Mr. Wilbur and Mr. Conners looked undecided, as did the other men.

"I say we let Matt speak," Pete Wilson piped up. "Let him tell us why he done what he done."

"Yeah," Bob Wilson added. "Why'd you go lookin' fer the James boys tonight, if you weren't up to no good to begin with?"

A hush settled over the area. Matt's somber gaze sought Amanda's, and it was as though he was speaking only to her. "What I did in riding with the gang was wrong, and I'm not saying it wasn't," he said slowly. "I'm not excusin' my behavior. But I need to tell you something so you might better understand.

"Durin' the War Between the States, my ma argued I was too young to join up with the Confederacy, saying she didn't want to lose two sons to the cause. At the time I would've given anything to fight. Then, the last year of the war, my parents died. I was almost seventeen. My brother, the only kin I had left, came home not long after. He'd met the James brothers when he served under Anderson's guerilla band and brought them with him. They talked about avengin' the South and fightin' against the persecution of the North, and I decided to ride with them. I was angry, bitter at God for taking away my parents, and bitter that the South had lost the war."

He shook his head. "Only the bank robbin' and train holdups didn't seem much like helping the South, and I didn't like the shootin' and killin' that came with it, either. My ma raised me on the Bible, and I didn't feel right about what we was doin'. One day I'd had enough. I told the gang I was leaving and taking back my share of the gold—that I was puttin' myself at the law's mercy. Only before I could get far, one of the gang shot me. That's how I got my limp."

Her heart full, Amanda loosely cradled the shotgun, stepping closer to the oak tree, her eyes never leaving Matt's.

"An old hermit, a doc, found me, cut the bullet out, and nursed me back to health. He'd been as bitter as me, havin' lost a daughter after the surgery he'd done on her didn't spare her life. But he was closer to God than to most people, and durin' those six-and-a-half months I stayed at his cabin, he pointed me back to the Lord."

"If that's true," Mr. Conners said, "how come you was with the gang tonight?"

"I wanted to talk some sense into my brother. I wanted him to leave the gang."

"Yes," Amanda agreed. "Everything Matt said is true. I followed him, without him knowing it, and heard it all. Then later, after Buck cut our ropes and Jeb knocked two of the outlaws out, Matt's only thought was for my safety."

"My Jeb knocked two outlaws out?" Mr. Hunter said from within the crowd, pride in his voice.

"Sure did, Pappy!" Jeb called out. "And they're still up there, I reckon."

"Well, what are we standin' here for?" Pete Wilson said. "If there's a gang to be caught, let's kitch 'em. I could use some reward money."

"We'll split it betwixt the all of us," one man said gruffly. "Fair's fair."

"Wait!" Zeke motioned to Matt. "What about him? He's an outlaw, too. You heard him admit it!"

Amanda's pa stepped forward into the ring of firelight. "From the way I hear him tell it and what I've seen of his character thus far, I believe this young man is truly repentant and has received just punishment for his mistakes. Earthly punishment, that is. God has already forgiven him for his crimes."

Amanda's heart leapt for joy, and she could have run over and kissed her pa then and there.

"I reckon that's good enough fer me," Mr. Conners said and turned to go.

"He's the preacher," Zeke argued. "Of course he's gonna say something like that!"

"My pa is an honorable man," Amanda defended him. "He wouldn't say something if it weren't so."

Mr. Conners scratched his jaw, then looked at Amanda's father. "Preacher, you willin' to stand by what you said and keep an eye on Matt here 'til we kin look into it?"

"I'm willing."

Mr. Conners nodded and joined Jeb at the foot of the path. The others followed.

"But. . .but," Zeke sputtered.

"Let it go, Zeke," Bob Wilson said and moved to join the rest of the men, leaving only Zeke and Matt underneath the tree.

Zeke glared at Matt, shifted his gaze to Amanda, and tossed the end of the rope he still gripped away from him. It swung madly in the air. "This isn't over, Campbell," he growled, then stormed off in the direction of his home.

Amanda's pa cleared his throat. "We best let your ma know everyone's all right."

Amanda glanced at him. "Give us a minute alone, Pa?"

He paused, looking between the two, then nodded and left.

Awkwardly holding the rifle, Amanda closed the distance until less than a foot stood between her and Matt. In the light of a torch someone had stuck in the ground, she could see a smile flicker on his lips as he held out his hand for the shotgun. Gladly, she relinquished the heavy weapon to him.

"You're amazing," he said quietly. "I have you to thank for my life."

"I only used a shotgun once before, but my aim wasn't good. I put a hole through Ma's sheet hanging out to dry instead of hitting the can." She felt giddy with the gentle look in his eyes and wasn't quite sure what she was saying.

Suddenly she frowned, noticing the rope still circling his neck. She stepped closer to lift the noose over his chin and forehead, then tossed the vile rope to the ground. Picking up his hat from where it had fallen, she brushed it off and set it on his head. Her gaze met his, and she smiled.

"Amanda. . ." His voice was hoarse. "I don't deserve a woman as fine as you."

"Nonsense," she murmured. "Besides Pa, you're the most honorable man I know. Any woman would consider it a privilege to grow old with you. In fact, now that there are no longer any secrets between us. . ." Her words trailed away as she shyly lifted her face to his. "There aren't, are there?"

Matt grinned. "No. You know everything there is to know about me now. . . except for how much I love you."

Amanda thrilled to his words. With his free hand, Matt drew her closer and dipped his head, tenderly covering her lips with his.

◆　◆　◆

Indian summer appeared to be visiting the mountain valley, though an earlier bout of cold weather had painted the hardwoods in bright hues of reds and yellows, amid the constant evergreen of pines. The day was warm and bright, perfect for the dedication of the new church.

Amanda stood beside Matt, hand in hand, as they stared up at the finished building of stone with the wooden double doors and gray roof. Narrow rectangular windows ran along the sides and at the front. A steeple perched on top, and Zeke's father had promised to donate a bell soon. Once the townsmen discovered Mr. Randall's decision to seize the land, they'd ridden on horseback one night, carrying torches, and gathered outside the lumberman's home, while Mr. Conners confronted him, saying, "We Conners don't take to a man who don't honor his word." Some of the hill people agreed, saying it less kindly, and Amanda had heard there'd even been threats.

The next morning a surly Mr. Randall approached Amanda's father with news that he'd reconsidered and the preacher could have the land. After that, more towns-people began to show up on Saturdays to help, as if the incident had jarred them into realizing that by working together, they could make a difference. The frequent rains ceased, and the church went up faster than Amanda would have believed possible.

"There for awhile I was wonderin' if your pa's dream would ever be realized," Matt said. "It feels good to see it happen."

Amanda smiled at him, so thankful for this man beside her. Next week, her own dream would be realized when she and Matt would become man and wife. It seemed fitting that theirs would be the first wedding to take place in the new church.

Remembering how she almost lost him the night the mob tried to hang him, she held his hand more tightly. Amanda had learned that once the posse arrived at the cave, they'd found no signs of the outlaws, but they did spot the two sets of cut ropes, proof that Matt was telling the truth. Then, two weeks ago, a stranger rode into town with a letter for Matt, one he was asked to deliver. The blank envelope contained a brief missive from Buck, stating that he'd left the gang and telling Matt not to worry about him any longer. A huge worry did seem to lift off Matt, making him smile more often, but both he and Amanda never ceased to pray for his brother.

"Amanda?"

Ivy's faint voice came from behind, and Amanda turned in surprise. Since Zeke had left town the morning after Matt had almost been lynched and hadn't been heard from since, Ivy and her family had treated Matt and Amanda with contempt, which stung deeply.

Ivy looked as perfectly put together as ever, with her light-colored ringlets bouncing beneath a fashionable hat that matched her blue dress. Yet her eyes were troubled. "You've heard I'm going back East this week, to be a companion to my grandmother?"

Amanda gave a short nod, and Matt gently squeezed her hand.

"I may not always understand you or your choices," Ivy said, flicking a brief look Matt's way. "But I'll always love you like a sister. And I don't want to leave with ill feelings between us."

"Oh, I don't want that, either!"

Teary-eyed, the women hugged. Ivy was the first to break away. She swiped a finger underneath her eye and solemnly stared at Matt. "I won't tell you to take care of her, because I know you will. And I won't tell you that you're getting the best girl in all the hollow, because I think you know that already." She lifted her chin. "But I will tell you this: If ever I hear that you've done anything to hurt her, I'll be back here and on you so fast it'll make your head swim!"

Matt grinned. "You're a loyal friend to Amanda, Miss Randall, and you're welcome in our home any time."

"Yes, well. . ." His words clearly flustered her, and she gave him a polite smile. "Thank you."

"Ivy!"

The stern bellow came from her father, and Ivy turned an anxious glance his way. She looked at Amanda again and clasped her hand. "I'll write. Good-bye."

Pensive, Amanda watched Ivy hurry to rejoin her parents, who stiffly stared at Amanda and Matt. Amanda knew Mr. and Mrs. Randall considered it an affront for her to refuse Zeke's offer of marriage and that they blamed her for their only son leaving the hollow without word to anyone. What leap of faith would it take to bridge the distance between families?

Matt gently tugged her hand, and she looked his way. "They're starting to gather," he said quietly. She nodded, and they joined the crowd of people at the corner of the building.

"Well, Matthew," the elderly Mrs. Conners said from behind them. "Now that ya'll be gettin' yerself a wife, I reckon there be no call for me to bring ya my strawberry per-serves."

Amanda whirled to face the gray-haired woman. "That was you?" She could feel Matt's curious look, but she smiled. "Oh, no, Mrs. Conners. Please, do! You make the sweetest preserves in all of Hickory Hollow. I could never make them so fine. Maybe you could show me how?"

The woman beamed and nodded, and Amanda faced the church again.

"What was that all about?" Matt whispered.

Her heart light, Amanda's smile only grew wider.

Amanda's pa took a place at the front, a twinkle in his eye that Amanda hadn't seen in a long time. "It gives me great pleasure to stand among you here today, to tell you that God does indeed fulfill His promises," he said once the buzz of voices died down. "When the Lord first showed me to build this church of stone, a lot of you questioned why we shouldn't make it from lumber instead."

A few men chuckled, and some nervously darted a look Mr. Randall's way. Grim-faced, he didn't move a muscle.

"In all honesty," her pa continued, "I never foresaw the many obstacles that would arise—the complications that would beset us—and it took a great leap of faith not to let circumstances overwhelm me." His voice filled with emotion, he looked at Matt. "I think it fitting that my soon-to-be son-in-law, who had such a hand in bringing this day about, should continue with the honors. Would you mind reading the dedication, Son?"

Matt paled, but he released Amanda's hand and moved forward, his limp more pronounced, proof he was nervous. Her father clapped Matt on the back, and Matt took off his hat, holding it against his heart as he faced the cornerstone.

"Despite all manner of hardship that rose against us," he slowly read aloud in a strong voice, "we, the people of Hickory Hollow, through the Lord's divine favor, have prevailed. From this day hence, may future generations who look upon this spot remember not the adversity that threatened to tear us apart; but rather let them recall the unity that bound us together, as one body, in building this House of God. On this eighth day of November, in the eighteen hundred and sixty-ninth year of our Lord, this church is hereby dedicated to God's glory, consecrated for His service, for all generations to come. So be it."

A cheer arose, and Amanda's eyes blurred with tears. Underneath the dedication were inscribed the names of all those men who helped build the church. Matt. Zeke. Her pa. The Wilson brothers. Mr. Whipple—all of them.

Her father held out his hand to her mother, who went to join her husband, and they led the townspeople up the steps and into the church for its first meeting. Matt rejoined Amanda, drawing her to his side. His eyes were gentle. "This is a happy day for Hickory Hollow."

"For all generations to come," she agreed with a contented sigh, slipping an arm around his waist. "For our sons and daughters. And for our grandsons and granddaughters. Because finally, we're a town built in unity."

Matt took her other hand and brought it to his lips, and Amanda looked at him with all the love in her heart. Then, together, they walked into their new church home.

PAMELA GRIFFIN

Pamela lives in Texas with her family. Her main goal in writing is to help and encourage those who know the Lord and plant a seed of hope in those who don't, through entertaining stories. She has over fifty titles published to date, in both novels and novellas, and loves to hear from her readers. You can contact her at words_of_honey@juno.com (Also, please note: The characterization of the James brothers for this story of fiction was created from both historical fact and legend.)

A Blessing for Beau

by Darlene Franklin

Pride goeth before destruction,
and an haughty spirit before a fall.
PROVERBS 16:18

Chapter 1

Ruth Fairfield rubbed her aching back. Cutting squares of sod used muscles she didn't need in the schoolroom. The people of Calico, Kansas, had gathered to build a home for the orphaned Pratt children. Now that their mother's brother had come to town, the three children and their uncle could spend the winter snug in their new soddy.

"What is such a pretty lady doing over in this corner, trying to break up the hard ground all by herself?"

Ruth held back a chuckle as she straightened. No one had ever mistaken her for a beauty. Pleasant, yes, and kind. But pretty? Even her mother reminded her that internal beauty mattered more than what could be seen on the outside.

She straightened up, up, up, taking in boot-clad feet and denim-covered legs, until she met brown eyes the same color as the dirt beneath her feet, sparkling like a fresh spring rain. A ten-gallon hat sat atop hair streaked with summer's gold, a little long. Everything about him screamed cowboy. Ruth herself was tall, taller than some men, but not this giant. Charlotte Pratt had spoken of her brother to Ruth, but she hadn't mentioned his jaw-dropping good looks. "Mr. Blanton?"

"As I live and breathe, but you can call me Beau." He swept his hat from his head. "And you are Ruth Fairfield."

"Please, call me Ruth. I feel like I already know you from what Charlotte told me."

"Uncle Beau!" Dru Pratt, a happy, gangly twelve-year-old who had taken the loss of her parents hard, threw herself at the cowboy. "This is my teacher, Miss Fairfield."

"We've already met." Beau's smile revealed even white teeth. "So how is my niece doing in class?"

Ruth relaxed a bit. Her students were her favorite topic of conversation. "She's doing very well, as are her brothers. I might even go so far as to say that Allan is my star pupil. I believe he would do well at the university."

"Don't know about that. He'll have work a lot closer to home." The cowboy's earlier cheer turned into a rumble of thunder.

When would Ruth learn to keep her mouth shut? Not everyone welcomed the idea of further education, nor could everyone afford it. Her gaze flicked to the spot where Allan Pratt worked side by side with Haydn Keller. To look at them, no one would guess at Haydn's college education. She peeled off the garden gloves she had worn to protect her hands. Teaching school didn't leave her with much time to tend to gardening.

Dru dashed away in pursuit of Grace Polson, the younger sister of Ruth's friend Gladys. The cowboy hoisted the squares of sod Ruth had cut to his shoulder as easily as he would a cornstalk. His eyes surveyed the horizon, as if envisioning the crops that would grow there someday. "Percy managed to choose a good spot for his homestead."

"Charlotte loved it here." She had loved Percy, too, in spite of his penchant for mishaps. "When she described their acreage, I could almost see waving wheat and rose trellises, fish caught in a favorite spot by the creek. We were all saddened when they died in that terrible fire." Ruth finished digging around the last square and tipped it so she could slip her hands underneath. A snake slithered onto her arm, and she flicked it off.

The cowboy laughed. "Let me get that." He staggered a bit under the weight of the third square. He nodded at the snake. "You and Charlotte sound like two peas in a pod. Most women I know would scream at the sight of that sand twister."

"We grow them tough out here." Ruth chuckled. "Although I almost screamed the first time one of my students gifted me with a garden snake. He was disappointed when I just took it outside and continued with class."

◆　◆　◆

Beau scratched his forehead with the brim of his hat, holding back a grin at the picture of the proper Ruth carrying a snake by its tail and calmly dropping it on the ground. The children newly left to his care loved their young teacher. Allan raved about her with all the ardor of a schoolboy crush, she had found a way to make Dru enjoy learning her multiplication tables, and even Guy admitted she was "nice enough"—high praise from a fourteen-year-old.

"I'd appreciate anything you can tell me about those three." He clapped the Stetson back on his head. "Charlotte saw them all with a mother's rose-colored glasses. As for Percy, best said that he was too busy to do much with them. I can tell they need a firm hand to guide them."

Ruth bit her lip. Although he appreciated a woman who could keep quiet, Ruth's silence didn't mean she didn't communicate her thoughts. Her open face betrayed her displeasure at his plain speech.

When she did speak, however, she addressed a different issue altogether. "You must have a lot to do to get started again here. And the children have settled in so well at the parsonage, we'd be happy to keep them awhile longer."

Another interfering do-gooder, like the ones who took him and Charlotte in when their parents died. He could have taken care of them on his own. He was as old as Allan was now and able to do a man's work. Watching his oldest nephew stagger under the weight of two squares of sod, Beau had doubts about how tough the boy was. But now that Beau was here to take a hand in his upbringing, he'd toughen up soon enough. He had to. Beau was determined to make his sister's dream come true: a homestead, proved up, ready to hand on to one of her children.

"That won't be necessary. The four of us will get along fine. We have plenty to do getting the soddy ready for winter and gathering as much food as we can. Don't worry, I'll get the younger ones to school when it starts next month."

A frown chased across Ruth's features. The liveliness of the emotions playing across her face made her downright pretty, softening the angles that would look harsh in an immobile face. He held out his free hand.

Her lips perked upward as she shook his hand. "You must know you don't have to worry about food. Everyone feels so bad about what happened. My mother organized the pound party going on in the wagon my father drove out here this morning. And here comes Sheriff Carter, bringing the rest of it."

Beau's antennae quivered at the words "pound party" and the even more ominous "rest of it." "Is that so?" He trotted to the place where people alternated squares of sod like fine bricks, placed the three he was holding on the ground, then paced quickly to the wagon. Food for dinner could be expected, but now he wondered if there was more. Flicking back the cover revealed flour, sugar, honey, cornmeal, canned fruits and vegetables, lard, dried apples—enough to last their family of four for the winter and beyond. Clucking alerted him to the presence of a rooster and five chickens in a crate. And more was coming?

Dust kicked up on the road subsided, showing a figure on horseback leading a cow. Did the people think he couldn't take care of his own? He walked to the spot where Ruth's father leaned over the sides of the wagon.

Pastor Fairfield looked up. "It's coming along well, Mr. Blanton." He clapped him on the back. "You'll be nice and snug in that place, come winter. Our folks have become experts at this sort of thing."

Beau wouldn't admit that he only learned how to build a soddy a few weeks ago, when he knew he'd be taking over the homestead. In his work as an itinerant cowboy, he'd always bunked at someone else's place. "So the children are getting the mud ready?" He looked over to where the children were working, just in time to see Guy fling a handful of gooey brown mess at Dru, who ran away, squealing. Those two needed to be brought under control.

The pastor smiled at the interplay, his grin echoing the same expression on his daughter's face. "Reminds me of the time Mrs. Fairfield made me mud pies back when we were children. Nothing like a good mud pie to cement a friendship." He chuckled, but then he returned his attention to the wagon. "You've discovered our little secret."

"Your daughter told me." Beau didn't like confronting a man of the cloth, but there were times. . . "I appreciate the thought, but we don't need your charity." He had to force that last word past his teeth. "You can return everything to the people who brought it, or put it in your church pantry, or whatever best use you can find for it."

The pastor rocked back on his heels. "I know you only accepted help with the soddy because you wanted to get settled as soon as possible. If it helps, I had nothing to do with this. The deacons asked their wives, and they put it all together. Truth is, this year's been pretty good to the folks of Calico, aside from the fire that killed Mr. and Mrs. Pratt. We can't think of another family as needful and deserving of help as yours." He spread his arms. "The Bible says it's more blessed to give than to receive, but my experience says both sides need God's grace. Sometimes it's harder to receive than to give."

Especially when you've learned gifts usually come with strings attached. "As I said, I can afford to buy the things we need."

"You might as well accept it. My wife will make me drive back out here if I bring it home."

A rustle of skirts alerted Beau to the presence of a woman, and he withheld his answer.

"You might as well accept it," Ruth repeated. "Papa won't let you refuse a gift." She hugged her father. "Mama says it's time for you to return thanks for our meal."

"Come along, son. We mustn't keep the women waiting."

Beau frowned at the grocery-laden wagon. Why did he have the feeling he and the lively Ruth Fairfield would cross swords over more than unwanted groceries?

He almost looked forward to it.

Chapter 2

When Ruth was a girl, the last few weeks before the start of school flew by. Now that she was grown, nothing had changed. Whereas in the past she enjoyed the last few days to play and spend time with friends, now she had to prepare for the next year's lessons.

With the addition of two new books for younger and older students, as well as several well-worn giveaways contributed by members of the community, the school library was off to a good start. She planned to make a soddy behind the schoolhouse to teach her students practical lessons on math and science. After she incorporated lessons on different building materials for homes, she'd add a timeline of American history. Building the new soddy for Beau Blanton and the Pratt children had given her the idea.

She couldn't get the Pratt children off her mind. Over the summer, Dru had a growth spurt, and she needed new dresses to accommodate her changing figure. Ruth was glad she had been there the first time the girl experienced her monthlies; she didn't know how the uncle would have dealt with such a thing. The very thought of it brought heat to her cheeks.

Ruth had finished another dress to give to Dru. She'd even brought it with her to church last Sunday. But she couldn't make herself approach the uncle who had wanted to reject Calico's gift. If he saw the need for new clothes, he'd probably hire Birdie, the local seamstress, to sew something.

She tucked the material she had bought for men's shirts—sturdy brown cotton, buttons, thread. She smiled at the buttons. These days Birdie had all the buttons she needed for her seamstress business. She hadn't wanted charity either. Given her friend's previous occupation, Ruth could understand her reluctance to trust others. Why Beau rejected it made less sense.

Charlotte had spoken in high terms about her brother, how kind and thoughtful and protective he was, but she hadn't mentioned his pride. Ruth could only pray that he would accept the clothes she had made for the children.

If God didn't intend for Ruth to help the Pratts, He would bring someone else into her life who could use the clothes. Drifters stopping by the parsonage for a warm bite of food and a place to sleep generally accepted whatever was offered. If that was what God intended for her mission project, she'd accept it.

But all year long, Ruth had waited for God to show her that one special person or family He meant for her to help. After God led Gladys to Haydn Keller, Annie to Lieutenant Arnold, and even Birdie to Ned Finnegan, and thrown in Kate Polson and Norman Keller for good measure—she had hoped that maybe, just maybe, God had someone special for her. No one was ever going to marry her for her good looks, but she hoped to share in some special man's vision of helping people in the community.

No, Ruth had resigned herself to official spinsterhood with a bevy of students for children, until Percy and Charlotte Pratt died in the fire and the Fairfields took in their children. She couldn't pinpoint the reason, but somehow the three young people had burrowed themselves deep in her heart.

Since Ruth was an only child, Allan, Guy, and Dru might come as close to nieces and nephews as she would ever have. She bundled up her sewing supplies and headed for Annie's house. Rejoice, and again rejoice! In everything give thanks, even if everything for her included less than she dreamed of.

Her route to Annie's house took her past Aunt Kate's diner. The door swung open, and Birdie came out, waving at her friend Michal Clanahan inside. God had taken care of that detail, providing employment for every lady who wanted to leave the saloon.

Birdie still wore the sunbonnet that protected her from unwanted stares as much as from the sun, but she no longer kept her eyes trained on the ground. When she spotted Ruth, a smile brightened her face. "Ruth! I'm glad you're here. We can walk together."

Birdie's sewing bag overflowed with a dark blue calico.

"Who is that one for? Has Owen lured another victim into his clutches?" Ruth asked. "Mama thinks it's just a matter of time before the town council votes Calico dry and runs him out of business completely."

"A true miracle." Birdie hugged the bag closer. "But no. I've started a quilt. I'd like to give one to each of my friends for their hope chests." She brought her free hand to her chest. "I've even thought about making one for myself. Who would ever have thought it? Birdie Landry, prime entertainment at the Betwixt 'n' Between. . .a merchant's wife." She giggled self-consciously, a carefree sound that brought joy to Ruth. "How about you?"

Ruth spared a brief thought for her own wedding quilt, tucked away in her hope chest for the past five years. "I'm working on clothes for the Pratt children. They lost everything in the fire, of course, and they've all grown over the past few months."

They walked at a leisurely pace, crossing in front of Finnegan's Mercantile. Ned waved at them through the window, and Birdie's face blossomed. As they made their way to Annie's house, Birdie floated as if she walked on air.

Rejoice with those who rejoice. "You're happy."

"Your father told me once about the difference between joy and happiness. When I read Paul's command to rejoice, I wondered what I had to be happy about."

Ruth nodded. "I've received that lecture before—after my heart was broken when my best friend moved away and I thought I would never have another friend."

The memory brought a smile to her face. "What silly things upset us when we're children."

Birdie turned thoughtful. "After my mother died, I didn't feel happy again for a long time. Your father explained that I could always rejoice because God's love would never ever leave me alone again. . .and then I met Ned. I'm glad God loves me, but I'm thankful that a good man loves me as well." She patted the bag dangling from Ruth's arm. "Are you interested in the Pratt children—or in their handsome uncle?"

"Birdie!" The word burst out of Ruth's mouth at the same time heat rushed into her cheeks. "My only business with Mr. Blanton concerns the children."

"Uh-huh." Birdie sounded doubtful.

At times like this, Ruth wished she hadn't committed to this sewing circle. Nine months ago, they were all unmarried, with a common passion for helping others. They bonded together in spite of the difference in their ages. Now that she was the only unattached woman in the group, she felt her spinsterhood more than ever. Especially when they kept insisting God had someone special in mind for her.

Beau Blanton. She mustn't let her imagination—her heart—get carried away because he was one of the rare unmarried men to show his face in Calico. She would treat him like any of the fathers—the married fathers—of her students. Any basis other than friendship would crumble beneath her feet. Even friendship might prove difficult as long as he resisted "charity." As much as she'd like to avoid the confrontation, she should talk with him about the clothes.

◆　◆　◆

"I can't go to school today." Dru remained in her nightdress while Guy was ready to leave for town in plenty of time for the first school bell.

"You have no cause to stay home. Allan and I will be busy all day. I don't want you staying here by yourself." Beau wiped a weary hand across his eyebrow. "I thought you liked school."

"I do." A single tear slipped down her cheek, and she shuffled her feet without looking at him. "Uncle Beau, I only have three dresses, and two of them don't fit."

Beau looked at her nightwear. The hem hit her leg halfway between her ankle and her knee. It fit a little more snugly than most nightclothes. He tried to remember what she wore yesterday. It seemed to fit her fine.

"What about the dress you wore yesterday?" A pretty soft blue calico with small pink flowers, from what he remembered.

"I wore it all last week. It's in the wash. I can't wear any of my other clothes." Her voice wobbled. "I'll wash it today with the rest of our clothes. I can go tomorrow."

Peeved, Beau considered demanding that she get dressed so he could see for himself. But he couldn't blame her. All the children's belongings had burned along with the house, and Dru had obviously outgrown what people had given her. He stretched his memory back. Come to think of it, Dru had worn the same dress every day since his arrival. He had been too busy to notice. His mouth worked around the impossibilities presented by the situation.

"Very well. You can wash the dress today and return to school tomorrow. And I'll see about getting you something else to wear." Beau had seen some ready-to-wear dresses for sale at Finnegan's Mercantile. Maybe one of them would fit, or someone—the seamstress? Dru herself?—could adjust it to fit. "Allan will draw the water for laundry before he comes out to help me." Next Monday Beau would have to figure out a different way to get the clothes washed. Dru couldn't run the household and go to school. To respect Charlotte's wishes, Dru had to stay in school.

What Beau would do instead, he didn't know. He turned the matter over in his mind throughout the day as he and Allan worked on plowing up the fields. Even if they couldn't get a crop for the fall, the plants would help enrich the soil for spring.

"Uncle Beau?" Allan ran up the row to where Beau worked.

Working with his nephew didn't leave Beau much time for meditating. Before he came to the homestead, he figured nothing could be harder than the long, hard days of riding herds. Who would have thought that taking care of three nearly grown children would demand so much more of him? Why didn't Allan know more about the land that was his heritage?

"I found these by the river. I think they're wild onions, but I'm not sure." Allan held the bulbs up to Beau.

The aroma tickled Beau's nostrils. He grunted. "Onions. They'll taste good in our potato soup tonight."

Allan grinned as if pleased with bringing in something useful. He glanced down the road to town. "Guy's home from school."

More dust than a single horse should kick up flew through the air along the tracks made by wagon wheels. As they drew near, he could see that Guy was not alone.

Why couldn't Miss Ruth Fairfield leave him alone?

Chapter 3

"Y ou did what?" Beau didn't touch the garments of folded cotton in the bag. "Miss Fairfield!" Dru waved from her spot by the open campfire where she was cooking supper. The mild weather made a number of everyday tasks easier while it lasted. Winter fell early and hard in this part of Kansas.

Ruth must have caught sight of the scowl on his face, because she answered with a scowl of her own. A scowl that showed itself in stormy gray eyes, creasing the lines at the edge of her eyelids, but didn't erase the pleasant expression on her face. "Professional smilers"—that's the way Beau's father had characterized pastors one time. Unbidden, a smile came to his face, and the teacher relaxed.

With a glance at Dru, Ruth lowered her voice. "Dru in particular is in need of new clothes. Since you haven't been around them for a while, you can't know how much she's sprouted up." She looked as if she had more to say, but she kept her mouth closed. "The boys, as well."

Beau chomped on a blade of grass before he said something he might regret later. Why hadn't Dru mentioned her need for new clothing before Ruth had decided to intervene?

Ruth leaned a little closer. "I was concerned when she didn't come to school today. Guy mumbled something about her dress."

Beau's mouth tightened at that. Hadn't Percy taught his children not to blab about family matters?

Ruth must have caught his expression. "Don't worry. He didn't talk out of turn. I wouldn't last long as a teacher if I couldn't worm the truth out of a reluctant witness." She held the bag by the tips of her fingers, ready to drop it into Beau's hands. "I started the dress while Dru was still living with us. Please accept it."

She lifted one finger from the bag, and Beau almost reached out to catch it. On the top, he spotted brown cotton. It looked very much like a man's shirt. Instead of accepting the bag, he removed the shirt and shook out its folds. "This isn't for Dru."

"No." Her expression remained calm, but fire burned in her eyes. "The boys also lost everything in the fire. Most of what they have to wear are hand-me-downs. I thought they would appreciate something that fits right." Now worry wormed its way into those expressive eyes. "I didn't have their exact measurements, so I hope these fit all right."

Beau brought the shirt up close, studying the workmanship. The shirt was quality, made of good, sturdy material, with fine stitching to match. He grunted in approval. These clothes could withstand the kind of stress two youths could put on them. He had a couple of shirts Allan and Guy could wear, but they were worn out and torn in a few places.

"I'll be back in a minute." Beau motioned for Dru to join them. "I bet Miss Fairfield will be happy to tell you whatever you missed today." He didn't look back as he ducked into the soddy.

◆　◆　◆

Ruth stared at Beau's departing back. He had dismissed her, but at least he had taken the bag of clothes with him. She wouldn't allow her disappointment over his attitude to interfere with what Dru needed. She headed in Dru's direction and began taking down Levis hanging on the line. "I can tell you've been busy today with the laundry."

"Someone had to." Dru had internalized a lot of her emotions since her parents died, acting like the little mother of her two brothers—not that they always appreciated her interference. Ruth had hoped that the arrival of an adult relative would allow Dru to once again become a twelve-year-old enjoying her girlhood, but it appeared that hadn't happened.

When Dru stirred something in the kettle over a campfire, Ruth knew her fears were well grounded. No wonder the girl had almost fallen asleep in class a couple of times already.

Ruth spied a flat iron heating in the campfire and the pile of clothing needing attention. On top sat Dru's blue dress, which she had hardly removed since she received it. "I'll finish this for you while you take care of the Levis." She made a mental note to find someone to help with household tasks if Beau would accept the help.

"Can you stay and eat with us?" Dru sounded wistful. "It's just beans with some salt pork."

Ruth made an on-the-spot decision. This early in September, she could join them for an early supper and get home before full dark. "I would love that, as long as I leave before evening falls."

Dru's step sped up at Ruth's words. She whisked up a batch of corn bread in the iron skillet. Last of all, she started coffee boiling.

The cow stuck her head over the fence and lowed softly. Ruth fed her a handful of grass and glanced at her udder. It was shudderingly full. She glanced around for a milk pail. Guy ran up. "Don't worry, I'll take care of her."

Allan followed at a slower pace. He leaned next to Ruth against the fence. Dark circles she hadn't seen before marred his face, and his shoulders slumped over. When he removed his gloves, Ruth could see the angry red on his blistered hands. He tried to hide a grimace, but she could read him as easily as her Bible.

"I've missed you in school." With only a year to go before he finished his public school education and hopefully headed to college, every day of school missed was a tragedy.

He shrugged, his silence saying volumes.

"I have a new book you might like." Although Allan especially liked mathematics—even at times exceeding Ruth's understanding of advanced geometry— he also won spelling contests and poetry recitation contests on a regular basis. He wouldn't stay away from school of his own accord. She was as sure of that as she was of anything.

She couldn't, she wouldn't, disrupt his uncle's authority with his new family. *Oh Lord, give me strength to hold my tongue.* "If you like, I can send it home with Guy tomorrow."

"Please." Much youthful angst and despair came through in that single word.

Ruth wished she could hug him to take the pain away, but she couldn't do that with the lad who was more man than boy. "I'm praying for all of you as you make this transition. But for now. . .I'll make sure you have books to read."

Ruth set up an ironing stand and finished the dress and one shirt before Beau came back outside. The bag hung limp from his hand. Good, he had accepted the clothing.

Supper passed pleasantly, and soon Ruth had started gathering dishes. Beau carried the last remaining platter to the sink. "I'd like to speak with you before you leave."

She nodded. "This won't take much longer. What is it about?"

He reached for his back pocket.

◆　　◆　　◆

Beau watched Dru and Ruth at work while he waited in the doorway. Dru looked livelier than she had since his arrival. Ruth had dived right into ironing. He grunted. Maybe taking on whatever task needed doing came naturally to a pastor's daughter. For Dru's sake, he was glad. All of them were working as hard as they could. Except maybe Allan. He was always a step behind. Beau had to work twice as hard to make up for his slack.

He needed to find a way to make life easier for Dru. Ruth might know of a woman willing to take on some of the household duties. Which would take more money. Beau's new responsibilities ate into what he had saved to sink into a ranch of his own someday. Finishing his contract for the current season and collecting his full pay was the reason he had arrived so long after the fire.

The fire was the latest, and most severe, time he had had to rescue Charlotte and her family. Percy was a good-hearted sort who worked hard, but first he ran his father's business into the ground. Next, the small printing press he started didn't succeed. Beau had made it his mission to make sure Allan was better prepared for life than his father had been.

Ruth looked his way, the enthusiasm she must bring to her class every day evident in her face. If he'd had a teacher like her, he might not have disliked school so much. Maybe that explained the silly look that appeared on Allan's face when he mentioned school. Perhaps he liked the teacher more than the learning.

Ruth said something to Dru that Beau couldn't hear. Putting her fingers to her mouth, Ruth whistled—a shrieking sound worthy of a boy catching his first snake—or a teacher aiming to gain control in the classroom. Guy raised his head, then Allan, and she waved her arms, inviting them to dinner. Beau glanced overhead. Good sunshine would last for at least another hour. Beau kept an eye on the horizon, gauging when Ruth must leave to reach town before dark. Guy milked the cows while Allan talked with Ruth.

Supper ended on the right note, with a final bite of corn bread and butter and a deep draw of cold water. By the time Beau's glass touched the table, Ruth was on her feet. She prepared dishwater while Dru shuffled their plates into a pile, added their forks and knives, and dropped them in the soapy water.

Beau moved into action before Ruth finished the last glass and rode off into the sunset. "I'd like to speak with you before you leave."

Her eyes brightened with curiosity, and she nodded. "This won't take much longer. What is it about?"

Beau wished he could stay and watch her work, but duty called. Last night's rainstorm had exposed a chink in the soddy walls, which he intended to fix before it grew bigger. "I'll be at the back of the soddy." His fingers brushed the seat of his Levis, against the comfortable bunch of his wallet.

Her eyes narrowed at the movement. Ruth's students might adore her, but any man interested in her would be subject to her strong opinions.

Why did the thought cause him worry?

Chapter 4

Beau didn't leave the ranch until Saturday, when he took the family into town. Allan disappeared in the direction of the diner, where Beau suspected he had his eye on a pretty young waitress. Dru hovered at her uncle's side, as if she didn't want to let him out of her sight. Guy had chosen to stay back at the ranch, offering to work on the fence. His willingness to undertake the task Allan hadn't finished impressed Beau.

First stop, the newspaper office. In the short time since his arrival, Beau had discovered the *Calico Chronicle* as a primary source for local happenings. One of Charlotte's last letters had mentioned the start of the paper and the romance blossoming between the editor and a local young girl as well as between the editor's once-reclusive grandfather and Miss Kate. Charlotte had used the outbreak of romance around town as an excuse to inquire after Beau's love life.

"That's the school." Dru pointed at the proverbial red schoolhouse that sat down the street from the newspaper office. The front door hung open, revealing a glimpse of Ruth at the blackboard, and he wondered at her working on her day off. Dru's expression said she'd love to say hello.

"Would you like to check on Miss Fairfield?"

"May I?" Dru pleaded, as she dropped her hold on his hand.

"Yes, but don't bother her too much." Dru disappeared so fast that he didn't know if she heard him. He almost wanted to call her back. He had parted with Ruth on a harsh note, his insistence that he pay her for the new clothes angering her.

Ruth came to the door at Dru's approach. Surprise mixed with genuine pleasure lit her face, and she embraced the girl. She waved at Beau, and he returned the gesture. At least she hadn't stayed angry with him. His steps trended in her direction until he remembered his purpose for coming to town today. In his new life as mother, father, and provider for three adolescent children, he found he had to make every minute count. If the sight of one pretty face distracted him from his goal, he had spent too much time with cattle.

Increasing his speed, Beau headed toward the newspaper, a small office crowded with a printing press and typesetting equipment. Peering through the window, he saw a man in the back sweeping the floor. A knock on the glass got his attention.

The lanky man with light brown hair opened the door. "Welcome to the *Calico Chronicle*. Mr. Blanton, is that it?"

Beau nodded. "Call me Beau. I want to place an ad in next week's paper."

"Come right this way." He gestured for Beau to enter the office and grabbed a yellow-lined pad of paper and a pencil. "The name's Haydn, by the way. How can I help you?"

"I have it right here." Beau unfolded the paper he had written out the night before. He wouldn't let Dru or Guy suffer the same fate he had, missing so much school he sometimes found it difficult to compose a letter. "Do you know of any woman who is looking for work as a cook or housekeeper?" The man sitting in front of him would know the pulse of the community better than anyone. "We need some help now that school's back in session."

Haydn made a note. "One of Birdie Landry's friends might be available. Or you could inquire over at the parsonage."

A trip to the parsonage would probably involve crossing paths with Ruth again. Dru would like that. For that matter, Beau would like that.

"If you find someone before next Thursday, let me know, and I'll yank the ad from the paper."

"How do I get in touch with Miss Landry? Does she live in town?"

"She lives at Aunt Kate's boardinghouse, but she'll be at the parsonage later today. The sewing circle is meeting there this afternoon."

"I'll head over there later." If he could get an answer before next week, it would solve a lot of his problems. He paid for the advertisement and headed for Finnegan's Mercantile.

Business was brisk at the store, so Beau browsed around the shelves. He noticed a sign advertising the services of a seamstress. Good, he'd found a solution to the clothing problem. Ruth wouldn't leave him alone until he took care of it.

The crowd thinned out, and Beau approached the pretty young woman at the counter. He handed her the shopping list he had written down. "I need these items. And are you the one I ask for seamstress services?"

"No." She flashed a shy smile in his direction. "Mr. Finnegan takes care of those orders."

"Shannon, did I hear my name?" A thin man, the perfect image of a shopkeeper with his glasses and pale skin, slipped behind the counter.

"Mr. Finnegan, this gentleman. . ." She looked at Beau.

"Beau Blanton."

"Mr. Blanton was asking about seamstress services. I told him you could help him."

"Miss Landry does beautiful work." Finnegan motioned him forward. "Did you see the ready-to-wear dresses on the table? If nothing there suits your needs, or if you're looking for men's trousers and shirts, I can arrange a meeting between you." He led Beau to the table. "What are you looking for?"

"A couple of dresses for my niece." Beau stared helplessly at the stacks. "But I don't know what will fit."

"My fiancée may be able to help you with that."

Perhaps she was a member of the sewing circle Mr. Keller had mentioned. "How old is your niece?" Ned asked. "Most of these clothes are for adult women."

"She's twelve. Not too tall." Beau indicated a height that didn't quite reach his shoulders. "She's in town with me today. Is it possible to meet with Miss Landry?"

"I believe she's hard at work this morning. She will be heading over to the parsonage this afternoon for the sewing circle."

"Will I be welcome at the meeting?"

"The Fairfields never turn anyone away. Tell Birdie I sent you, and she'll take extra good care of you."

The clerk, Shannon, prepared his sack. Beau raised his eyebrows at the price but dug in his pocket and counted out the money.

Finnegan pulled his ledger out and entered numbers. When Beau handed the money to Shannon, Finnegan interrupted. "There's no need to pay right now. You can settle the account later."

"I'd rather take care of it now." Beau counted out his money. He'd find a way to cut costs. Maybe Guy or Dru could find a job after school. God could provide for them in a dozen different ways.

Finnegan maintained a neutral expression on his face. "I mean no offense. Most of the farmers around here keep an account, including your brother-in-law. Just offering to make things easier for you, with all the difficulties your family has been through."

"You'll soon find out I'm not my brother-in-law. I won't take things I can't pay for." Beau knew he was being less than gracious. He carried the sack out to the waiting wagon. Time to round up Dru and eat before dropping by the parsonage.

Where he would face the biggest challenge of the day so far: paying Miss Landry for work Ruth was willing to do for free.

◆　◆　◆

"I'll see you on Monday." Ruth ached as she watched Dru walk away from the parsonage, where they had gone from the schoolhouse. Because of daily use her new dress already showed signs of wear. Unfortunately, Charlotte's brother wasn't like his sister. She wouldn't have let pride stand in the way of her children's needs.

Standing in the doorway, she watched Gladys approach with Haydn. At the corner, he turned in the direction of the newspaper office, and Gladys walked toward the parsonage. Ruth opened the door for her first guest.

"Haydn says Mr. Blanton came into the office today." Gladys's sewing bag bulged with the squares for her wedding quilt. She greeted Ruth's mother with a kiss. While Gladys kept up the chatter with Ruth's parents, Ruth's mind wandered. In spite of weekly church attendance and Dru and Guy's regular presence at school, she hadn't spoken to Beau Blanton since the debacle of her visit to the soddy.

The gall of the man, insisting on paying her for clothes she had given to him. He'd held it out to her. When he tried to drop the money into her hand, she brushed it away and it landed on the ground. "You're welcome," she had said before she backed away from the embarrassing moment.

She later learned he'd given the money to her father. Papa had bragged on

Beau's generosity and dropped the money into the box for missions. "He said he appreciated everything we'd done and to use the money wherever there was the most need."

Perhaps that was what God wanted after all. Even though she assumed God wanted her to help someone in Calico, maybe she was meant to help with overseas ministry, along with her mother and the other women of the larger group. Maybe she was getting too old for such girlish dreams.

She should accept her position as resident spinster of Calico, Kansas.

Chapter 5

Someone knocked at the door. Ruth's mother asked, "Ruth, will you get it, please?" She had her arms in dishwater up to her elbows.

A glance out the window revealed the guest: Beau Blanton. Dru and Allan accompanied him, and Ruth's heart lifted. If only Guy had come along. He needed tutoring in basic math skills, and she'd have squeezed in a few minutes before the sewing circle started. From what Dru said, all of them jumped into farm chores as soon as they arrived home and didn't stop until bedtime except for dinner and a chapter from the Bible.

Think happy thoughts. That would help Ruth keep a pleasant expression on her face, instead of imagining the impossible with Beau. Some might expect a pastor's daughter to want to marry another man of the cloth, but she didn't want that either. She couldn't keep the kinds of secrets her mother had to carry. As soon as her parents figured that out, they had done as much as possible to shield her from the more unsavory aspects of their ministry.

If the worst Beau Blanton had done was to value independence over offers of help and to fail to understand three young people, when he'd never had children himself, she had no reason, not to mention no right, to be upset with him.

After the scolding Ruth gave herself, she opened the door with a smile. "Gladys—Miss Polson—told us you might be stopping by. How can we help you?"

Beau removed his hat as soon as he entered the door, and Allan followed his example. Dru hung her cape on the coat tree. Beau shrugged. "I'm looking for someone willing to help us with the housework a few hours a day." He draped an arm around Dru's shoulders and hugged her. "Dru has been doing a yeoman's job, but it's too much for her, what with school and all."

At least he hadn't been blind to the dark circles under Dru's eyes. "Are you looking for live-in help?"

He frowned. "Perhaps. I'd offer room and board in exchange for a few hours' work, but. . .you've seen the soddy. It would be a tight fit. I know we're at a distance from town." His shoulders sagged. "Will that cause problems?"

"Not necessarily. I have some ideas, and my mother will probably know of more."

"Know what?" Mama came to the door, drying her hands on her apron. "Mr. Blanton, how lovely to see you again." The smile she offered their guest was wholehearted. "Since the sewing circle is meeting in the parlor, why don't you join me in the kitchen? If you need my husband, he'll be back eventually. He's over in the church praying over tomorrow's sermon."

Ruth said, "Dru will be visiting with us in the parlor, so you can visit privately. Allan—you may wish to peruse the study. Papa brought home some new books when he went to Topeka last week."

"Thanks." Allan disappeared down the hallway before his uncle could call him back, and Dru followed at a slower pace, entering the parlor to warm greetings.

Beau didn't move in the direction of the kitchen, his eyes fixed on the floor. He rubbed the brim of his hat. Without lifting his head, he asked, "Is Miss Landry here? Mr. Finnegan referred me to her."

Ruth could think of only one reason Ned would refer Beau to Birdie. She tensed, grateful he wasn't looking up and so couldn't spot the anger she couldn't keep from her face. She drew in a breath before she answered. "Yes, Birdie is here. Come join us when you finish your business with my mother." She escaped to the parlor before he looked up and caught her expression.

From her spot on the sofa, Dru was rolling skeins of yarn into balls. Ruth was glad the girl had a day off. She'd make a good teacher someday if God led her that way. If her uncle allowed her to finish the additional schooling she would need. And if she didn't fall in love and get married, like most young women. Charlotte had strongly supported the idea, but Beau didn't value the same things his sister had.

Birdie pushed her needle in and out of the hem of a black gored skirt. "Dru says Mr. Blanton wishes to speak to me." She peeked up from the fabric in her lap. "Is that all right with you?"

Dru's eyes widened in surprise and her mouth opened.

"I suppose any way they get the clothes they need is acceptable." Ruth's throat tightened as she forced the words out of her throat. "It seems all God wants from me is to help people who come to us for help, but I was already doing that." How she wanted a chance to do something significant. Be a missionary to China. Run an orphanage. Even just marry a good man. She loved teaching, but some days she wanted more from life. It seemed instead of her helping Beau, he was helping her by forcing her to examine her life.

Birdie narrowed her eyes. "Mr. Blanton's arrival in town is timely. Naomi is ready to join Michal and me if we have enough work, and Orpah is in need of work until Gladys is ready to leave the diner. If he is willing to have someone with our history working in his home, that is." She secured the needle in the fabric and patted Ruth's knee. "You do the Lord's work every day. The other day I read in the Bible that the soldiers who fight in the battle should share the spoils of war with those who stay with the supplies. God knows each and every thing you do day in and day out for the needy around us."

She started working the needle again. Dru had finished balling the yarn and started casting stitches onto a pair of knitting needles.

Annie giggled. "If you really want to sew for Mr. Blanton, you could sew the clothes and Birdie could pretend she made them."

That drew an answering giggle from Dru.

Ruth took a moment to picture a dress made in a cheerful yellow calico before shaking her head. "It's not the same. He will still insist on paying you—"

"And of course I'll give you the money."

"But that defeats my reason for doing this."

"I could talk to him. . ." Dru stuck her needle into the first stitch, but the movement was awkward. The stitches were probably too tight, the way most of her knitting started. "No," the women chorused.

"I'll find a way to speak with him," Ruth said. "Just promise me you'll be praying for me."

"Always." Gladys smiled. "You don't have to ask."

◆ ◆ ◆

"Are these women"—Beau couldn't bring himself to call them "ladies"—"the only ones looking for work?"

"They are the ones most in need of gainful employment. God has been doing a tremendous work among the women who lived in that unfortunate place. No one was more surprised than I was when Miss Landry came to us, about a year and a half ago now, hungry for God and desperate to leave that life. Because of her testimony, we've seen at least one woman leave each month. They are willing to work hard and are thankful for the opportunity."

"But Dru. . ." Beau couldn't believe he was even considering the possibility. "She'd be a bad influence on Dru. I'm sure of it."

"She'd be an excellent example of God's grace and His transforming power. I agree that she should maintain her home in town. You both want to avoid any appearance of evil."

"I will think about it." Although Beau already knew he would rather accept Ruth's help than hire a former soiled dove. The longer he lived in Calico, the more strange facts about the town he discovered. Ladies on a mission to make a difference. A hermit brought out of self-imposed solitude. Prostitutes leaving their employment and being accepted as part of the community. An entire fort outfitted by a single woman. Not to mention an interfering schoolteacher, although that might not be so strange. As a cowboy, he didn't have exposure to towns much beyond trail drives, and Dodge City was nothing like Calico. No wonder Charlotte liked living here.

Asking Miss Landry to make their clothes didn't feel as out of place as inviting a woman to help with housework. Their business could all be conducted through a third party, such as Ned Finnegan. Now there was a strange pairing. He shook his head. If God had found such a—colorful—wife for the bland shopkeeper, maybe He had someone in store for Beau. Someone as spontaneous as Beau was reserved, someone as giving as he was cautious. . .someone like. . .Ruth. *Don't even think like that.*

After Beau finished the plate of cookies Mrs. Fairfield had served him, he ventured down the hallway to the remaining rooms. From the parlor, he heard feminine voices and soft laughter. He hurried past, looking for Allan. A door stood open to the left, and he poked his head inside. Allan's fingers traced the lines of text before he turned the page. Since he appeared unaware of his uncle's arrival, Beau cleared this throat.

Allan dropped the book on the desk. "Are you ready to leave?"

"Almost." Beau surveyed the room. He couldn't imagine a single person needing so many books, when he only had one to his name, the Bible his mother had given him. "I wonder if Pastor Fairfield has read all these books." He approached a shelf, studying the titles stamped on the spines. Some of them didn't even seem to be in English.

"Yes." Allan didn't seem to find that unusual. "Most of them he's read several times. He gave me a new book to read every week when we stayed here this summer. Today he said he had a new book for me to take with me. And we could talk about it when I come to church." He pointed to the book on the desk. "You don't mind, do you?"

Beau stared. Why anyone would choose to read when he could be outside under God's heaven baffled him to start with. But the wistful look on Allan's face stumped him. "As long as you read in the evening, after the day's work is done."

"Great!" Allan sprang to his feet, clutching the book as if he might lose it if he loosened his hold.

"You have a few minutes. I have some business to discuss with Miss Landry." At the door to the parlor, Beau paused. Dru was laughing. *Laughing.* At the soddy, she always seemed so serious. He had treasured the quiet, but laughter was even better.

He rounded the corner, and the smile disappeared from Dru's face. "Is it time to go?"

"In a few minutes."

"Have a seat." Ruth gestured to a comfortable-looking chair next to a table with a Bible, a book Beau didn't recognize, and a pair of reading glasses. "Papa won't care."

Beau studied the women around the room, trying to guess which name went with which woman. Ruth was the epitome of a schoolteacher. He'd guess either the blond or the redhead was the former saloon girl, although the brunette was pretty enough. This group had turned the town upside down. Only Ruth had remained relatively uninvolved, from what he had heard. As part of the pastor's family, she did a lot for others all the time. As a teacher, she exercised more influence on the future of Calico than almost anyone in town.

Given the fire in Ruth's eyes when Beau asked Miss Landry to sew for him, he knew she wanted more. For some reason unknown to him, she felt God had something else for her to do.

Beau had always trusted his own judgment. Only now, when a spitfire of a teacher challenged his long-held opinions, did he question himself.

And he didn't like it.

Chapter 6

I'm sorry, but I'm unable to take on your project at this time." Birdie Landry smiled as she said the disappointing words. "If you can wait for two months, after Miss Kate marries Mr. Keller, I can work on it then."

Since Ned had said she might be able to help, Beau found the situation confusing. Miss Landry exchanged glances with Miss Polson, who was engaged to the young Haydn Keller, from what he understood. "But Ruth has offered to make whatever you need, *now*, and she won't ask money for it." Her brilliant smile made it impossible for Beau to refuse without appearing mean-spirited.

Pleasure lit Dru's face, giving her a moment of carefree happiness. Cautious pleasure chased surprise off Ruth's face. "You might even say I consider it my mission in life."

Her mission? Beau's ire rose at that description. He wasn't a grumpy hermit, nor did he frequent the saloon. He was a simple, hardworking man, taking care of his family the best way he knew how.

But he couldn't sew. "You won't accept money no matter how much I insist, will you?"

Ruth shook her head. Miss Landry chuckled. "I did the same to Ned. He kept looking for ways to help me, but I insisted I pay my own way. I didn't have the money to buy buttons, thread, and other sewing notions, so he had people drop buttons and other things in a button jar and fooled me into accepting the gift."

"In other words, you'd better accept the clothes before Ruth figures out a way around your objections." Gladys nodded her head emphatically. "She loves your niece and nephews. Let her do it for them if not for you."

"I give up!" Beau threw his hands in the air. "I accept whatever you have already made but no more. And actually, I have another area where I need your help."

❖ ❖ ❖

What? Mr. No-thank-you-I'll-do-it-myself was asking for help? Instead of the pleasant expression she wished she could freeze on her face, Ruth was sure her shock at his statement must shine from every pore.

Beau laughed, a deep, hearty, masculine, happier sound than she had ever heard from him. "You are the only schoolteacher I know of in Calico, and I believe Guy could benefit from your help as he starts his job."

His words distressed Ruth anew. First Beau pulled Allan, who loved school, and now Guy would also work? Allan had motivation to learn on his own, but Guy needed a teacher's guidance more. What was next? Would he ask Dru to stay home to take care of the house?

As the daughter of a man who had attended seminary and a mother who taught school before her marriage, education had always mattered to Ruth. "I'll be happy to help Guy in any way I can." She felt compelled to address the issue of school attendance. "But at school the other students are also a great help. They explain things in different ways to each other."

"He's not that fond of school." Beau's face twisted in puzzlement. "That's no reflection on you. I'm sure you are a good teacher. He's looking forward to working where he can make a difference."

In Ruth's opinion, school attendance should be required and not left to choice. Not everyone agreed, of course. Charlotte had always insisted her children attend school, even when Guy swore never to return after sitting in the corner with a dunce cap on his first day.

Ruth blinked at the memory. "Tell me about this job."

"The bank needs a clerk. I know Guy's not that good at arithmetic, but I was hoping you could help him improve his skills. Then maybe he could take over the books at the ranch as well."

Ruth coughed and covered her mouth to hide her dismay. Maybe if she explained, Beau would understand. From what Charlotte had said, he was a reasonable man. "I'd be happy to help Guy keep up with his schooling. Allan as well. Allan was one of my best students last year. Charlotte and Percy had high hopes for him. In fact, Allan could tutor Guy."

A glimmer of something—disappointment? Discouragement?—flittered across Beau's face. "Allan already has his hands full with the farm. He was moping about school so much that I promised him he could continue lessons with you if he didn't go around quoting poetry all day long."

Ruth's heart sank another inch. Schooling wasn't the only problem. Allan's heart wasn't in the farm. Maybe Beau needed more time to recognize that. If she could get a job for Allan at the newspaper, Haydn could discuss subjects like philosophy and the classics with him as well as the prospects for this year's crops.

Beau's face darkened, and Ruth bit her lip. *Forgive me, Lord, for wanting to interfere where it's none of my business.* "Of course I will do everything I can to help. For any interested students, we offer a reading club, music lessons, a class in the wifely arts. We're also looking for men to teach our boys useful skills. The children are welcome to attend any of those classes, and I would be happy to tutor Allan and Guy two days a week." Ruth caught herself. The way she was prattling on, Beau would think she was as bad as the older girls in her class, who turned into chattering magpies as soon as a handsome lad caught their eyes.

Beau rubbed his chin. "I might consider teaching a boys' class next year. Right now it's taking twenty-five hours out of every twenty-hour for Allan and me to try to get some kind of crop out of the ground before winter comes."

Of course. "How foolish of me to suggest he do anything other than farm."

Flames licked her face, a rare fit of anger building up in her.

"Ruth?" Mama called to her from the kitchen. "Would you come in here and give me a hand, please?"

"I'll be right back." When Ruth stepped into the kitchen, she didn't see any work to be done.

"Come over here by me." Mama stood by the window, looking out on the apple tree that provided shade in the summer, fruit in the fall, and preserves year round. "Sounds as though you need to go outside and look for any fruit that's ripened early. Unless you think you can bring yourself under control." She leveled a look at Ruth that could have sunk the Spanish Armada. "That poor man is our guest. He's just lost his only sister and found himself a father overnight. I know you don't like the way he's handling things, but don't you dare say a thing against him." Mama paused. "He's not doing any *harm* to those young folks, is he?"

"Not unless you call wasting a good mind harm, which I do." Ruth joined her mother at the window. "You're right; he's been gentle with them as far as I can tell. We just have different ideas about what's best."

"So did Barnabas and Paul about John Mark, and look what God did with that. Doubled the number of missionary teams. You just keep doing what God has called you to do. *Teach.* Sometimes it's in the classroom and sometimes it's by the side of the road." Mama broke a gingersnap in two and handed her half. "Maybe one day you may even find yourself teaching a certain farmer a thing or two about raising children."

Ruth almost choked on the cookie.

Mama hugged her. "Have you calmed down enough to go back in the room and be nice to Mr. Blanton?"

Ruth nodded. Shame followed on the heels of her earlier anger. Beau was standing, as if waiting for her return. Was it her imagination, or did a shadow of shame lie on his features as well?

"So can you tutor Guy and Allan on Mondays and Thursdays?" Beau repeated his earlier request.

"Of course." Ruth extended her hand to shake his. "It will be my pleasure. I love teaching."

His hand lingered on hers. "Once my life settles down, I'd like to teach the young men. I just can't do it right now."

"That would be wonderful if you want to. But not everyone is meant to be a teacher. Or a farmer."

After he dropped her hand and said good-bye, Ruth realized she hadn't thought about Allan once when she said not everyone was meant to be a farmer or a teacher.

She'd been too busy thinking about the tall, handsome farmer who was holding the teacher's hand.

Chapter 7

Guy stomped up the steps to the parsonage door. Allan followed right behind, shaking his head at his brother's behavior.

Not a good day. Today the boys might need more than Ruth's tutoring.

"I've got them a bite to eat. That might help," Mama whispered in Ruth's ear.

Ruth waved them inside. "Good evening, Guy, Allan." Ink and lead smudges darkened the knuckles of Guy's calloused hands. "Let's start in the kitchen. We can spread out our work there."

Guy slammed the textbook on the table. "It doesn't matter. I can't do arithmetic."

Ruth bit back her automatic response of "Of course you can." She had found that facts mattered little when a person's emotions were involved. "I know it doesn't come easy to you. I appreciate your hard work."

"Work." Guy made it sound like a curse. "The bank manager fired me today. I made too many mistakes in my figuring." He broke a gingersnap between his teeth with an angry crunch.

Allan held out the chair for Ruth, and she slid into it soundlessly. He quietly set his satchel on the floor. The silence lengthened as if the boys waited for Teacher to perform some kind of magic on Guy's situation.

"Oh Guy. I'm so sorry." Her brain stumbled for a response.

"And Uncle Beau, he's going to be mighty upset with me."

"From what I've seen, your uncle is a reasonable man." Ruth hoped one of the boys would speak up if they had a cause for concern.

"He would never hurt us." Allan must have sensed her worries. "But he does have high expectations of all of us. He keeps telling us how he's been a working cowboy since he was Guy's age." A slight shudder ran through Allan. Had his uncle been encouraging Guy to quit school and go to work?

She had waited long enough. She *had* to speak up.

"I'm coming home with you."

◆　◆　◆

"She's pretty nice." Dru spoke of the woman who had spent yesterday at the cabin tidying up and fixing a roast and vegetables they could eat over the next few days. Dru was kneading biscuit dough to eat with the leftover roast.

Beau grunted. He still was of two minds about hiring one of "Birdie's girls," as they seemed to be known. No one could deny the change in Birdie, but did that mean he should hire one of her friends to work in his home alongside his impressionable niece? Much better for her to be under the influence of someone like Ruth Fairfield, even if she did place too much value on school learning. Intelligent, kind, compassionate, someone who loved the Lord as much as her preacher father did.

Stop it. If Beau kept this up, he'd sound like he was describing the woman from Proverbs 31. While he admired many of Ruth's qualities, he didn't want to marry her or anyone else. He expected marriage to come before children, but God had changed the order in his case, and he didn't have time to court a lady properly.

Something rumbled outside, and Beau went to the door to check the sky. Even this late in the season, tornadoes were still possible. *Please, Lord, protect us from a bad storm while we still only have this dwelling of mud and sticks.*

Clouds scudded across the darkening sky, but no wind stirred the dead air. The rumble came from the ground, from horses' hooves and wagon wheels. The boys were back early.

The wagon came into view, a second horse in the harness and a third figure in the wagon—Ruth Fairfield. She held the reins, pushing the horses to a faster speed than usual. As they approached, she pulled on the reins and stopped their progress. Drawn almost against his will, Beau approached and offered her his arm. "Good evening, Ruth." Her name floated across his tongue like sweet honey. "Supper's warm on the stove. Come on in and eat with us."

Ruth took a seat on one of the rickety chairs inside the soddy. Allan took a seat on the single bed, and Guy sat beside him, his eyes trained on the floor. Allan tucked his book bag under the bed and fiddled with the strap, releasing it then cinching it again.

"Miss Fairfield!" Dru set down a plate of biscuits and flung her arms around her teacher. "I didn't know you were coming tonight. Let me get you some coffee."

"That would be nice, Dru." Ruth waited, her hands folded in her lap. She accepted the mug from Dru, who then served her brothers. Allan waved it away, but Guy gulped the coffee like an elixir.

As soon as Ruth sipped the drink, Guy spoke. "Uncle Beau, I lost my job at the bank."

Beau was flummoxed. He had never lost a job. The only people he had known to lose a job were either thieves or just plain lazy. Guy was neither of those things. Working his mouth, he came out with the words. "What happened?"

This time Guy looked at Ruth, who gave him a small, encouraging nod.

"I just couldn't do the numbers right. I've never been good with numbers. Ask Miss Fairfield."

She nodded regretfully. "Math has always been. . .difficult. . .for Guy. He's a fine young man but not suited to work at the bank."

Beau still didn't understand the problem. "That's why I asked you to tutor him at night, to catch him up on his figures."

Allan glanced at Ruth, who said, "That's not the answer. Guy can do arithmetic well enough for most things, but a banker needs a feel for numbers. Guy's interests lie in other areas."

Beau snorted. Guy's *interests*? Most of the time life didn't consist of a list of choices. A man figured out what he was supposed to do then went ahead and did it. That was it.

The two boys scooted closer together on the bed, and Dru joined them. This felt like a conspiracy.

Allan sat tall, his shoulders getting broad enough to equal Beau's own. "The thing is, I would love a job at the bank instead of working out here at the farm. You've seen me around here. I'm more likely to hit my thumb than a nail with the hammer. Sometimes I feel like I can barely tell the difference between a bull and a steer. But I'd do well at the bank, I know I would."

Guy looked up. "And I go to school 'cause Ma and Pa expected it, but my favorite times are in the fields." He dropped his gaze again.

Ruth drained her cup. "There is a simple solution. Let Allan and Guy switch places. I wish they could both continue in school full-time, but Allan doesn't need much before he's ready to apply for the university, if he has a mind to when the time is right. And Guy would relieve some of your anxiety about the farm."

"Do you have any tricks up your sleeve for Dru?"

The girl squirmed in her spot next to Guy.

"Unfortunately, no." Ruth turned a tender smile on Dru. "I think you are all coping admirably in very hard circumstances. My preferences, as you can imagine, would have all three in school full-time. But I believe my suggestions may help make the best of a difficult situation."

Anger stung Beau. He had managed to keep outsiders from intruding on his life since he struck out on his own. Ruth Fairfield was determined to give him advice whether he wanted it or not. Not that advice was always unwelcome—he had asked for advice more than once—but never from a stranger and certainly not from a woman. Even a woman as sensible and as pretty as this one was. "We can try it your way."

Dru giggled, and Guy seemed to grow two inches.

"For two weeks. If things aren't any better by then, I'll decide what needs to be changed."

Ruth nodded, smiling, as if ready to join him for another conference in a fortnight.

"On my own. I don't appreciate interference in my family's affairs, and I don't believe Charlotte or Percy did either."

Ruth's smile dimmed. "Of course, the bank president has to agree to Allan taking the job, but I'm sure he'll be happy to do so."

We'll see. Beau took the coffee Ruth poured for him. *We'll see.*

◆　◆　◆

A month later, Allan was happily settled at the bank, covering nearly as much in his biweekly tutoring as he had while attending school full-time. He could apply for university next fall—Haydn would love to write a reference for him—but Ruth knew Beau was opposed to that. He didn't have to say a word.

Guy was happier than he ever had been in class. His hours at the farm, doing work he loved, made him appreciate the breaks for classes. He would never make a bank clerk or a reporter, but he had a good grounding in reading, writing, and arithmetic, as well as American history and geography, and a natural knack for leadership that emerged as he found more confidence in his growing body.

The only Pratt child who still troubled Ruth was Dru. Beau was either blind to the physical changes in his niece or he hadn't found a solution that didn't offend his sensibilities.

Ruth brought up the problem with the sewing circle again. "I still feel like I should make some clothes, maybe even some unmentionables, for Dru. You should see her." At least the tears in her voice didn't drip down her cheeks.

"We see her on Sundays. Even the dress you made for her while she was living with you is getting small on her," Birdie said.

"I've been trying to think what I did when I was growing like that. I wore hand-me-downs from my sister and from Mama. But Dru. . ." Annie shrugged.

"Dru doesn't have any sisters, and all her mother's clothes burned in the fire. She doesn't have any family to give her things." Ruth fingered the sheet she was making for Birdie's growing group of girls. "You know I'm happy to make these, Birdie, but my mission is with the Pratts. I believe so now more than ever."

"Well, then," Birdie said in a matter-of-fact voice new to her, "you should just make her the clothes and let God take care of the rest of it."

"Thank you for reminding me." Ruth relaxed. "I'll do just that. I'll finish a dress for her this week. Maybe give it to her on Sunday. Mr. Blanton can't complain too much in God's house on the Lord's Day."

Ruth didn't have to wait for a trip to Finnegan's Mercantile to start. She had purchased the ideal calico weeks ago, the soft yellows and greens making her think of Dru as soon as she spotted it. She had even marked the pattern lines on the fabric, but then had stopped, not convinced that she should proceed with the project, waiting for clear direction.

That had happened after convincing Beau to let the boys switch positions and while watching Dru shoot up over the past four weeks. Now Ruth studied the pattern lines again. If she narrowed the seams and took out two darts in the front and back, it should fit. As for the hem, she had left it overlong until she could measure the correct length. Now that the girl had reached Ruth's height and passed it, Ruth made the hemline an inch and a half lower than those for her own dresses.

In fact, when Ruth finished making adjustments, she realized Dru's measurements came close to her own. The girl could wear Ruth's hand-me-downs, and she'd be happy to give her a few. Which would bother Beau more: hand-me-downs or specially made dresses?

Since either choice would test Beau's patience, Ruth decided to give Dru what would make a young girl the happiest. New fabric, a newer design, a few ribbons.

Taking her scissors, she cut the fabric. Soon her needle was flying through the fabric while the conversation turned in other directions.

Chapter 8

In fact, Ruth finished the dress right before the Thursday tutoring session. But she didn't want to create problems for the boys by sending the unwanted gift home with them, so she kept with her original plan of giving it to Beau on Sunday.

When Dru arrived at school on Friday, Ruth almost regretted her decision. The girl's dress dangled inches above her ankle and hugged her waist so tight that Ruth wondered how she could breathe. The pained expression on Dru's face and her general disinterest made Ruth suspect the girl had a worse than usual case of the monthlies.

When at last the class had a recess, Ruth kept Dru back. "Let me get you some willow-bark tea and you rest in here a spell. Unless you want to go outside?"

The misery with which Dru shook her head convinced Ruth she had the truth of it. Dru stumbled as she got to her feet then immediately sat back down. "Miss Fairchild."

That single mortified cry told Ruth what had happened. "Don't worry. I'll get one of the older girls to take over the class while I take you to the parsonage. We'll get you fixed up right away."

They headed out the door, Dru's coat hiding her embarrassment, and they arrived at the house within minutes.

Dru mumbled a few words that verified the nature of the problem, and Mama hugged her. "My dear child. I'll start some bathwater and salts for you. A good bath always helps me feel better when I'm hurting."

"I don't want to be a burden. . ." Dru started out in a good imitation of her uncle.

"Don't worry about that. This isn't the first time a girl's been caught unawares."

"I've got to get back to school." Ruth took the coat from the girl, her heart hurting for the motherless child. "But before I leave, there's something I want to give to you." She ran to her room and took the dress from its knob.

"But what am I going to wear?" Tears hovered behind Dru's words.

"We have some things," Mama assured her. "And it's early enough that I might be able to rinse this out and get it back to you before the end of the day."

Ruth set up the curtain around the bathtub in the back room so Papa would know to stay away.

Mama led Dru into the room and smiled. "And besides, I think you might have another choice."

224

Ruth held the dress up to Dru. "I made this with you in mind. And it seems that God's timing was perfect, that I would have this ready for you when you needed it the most."

Ruth didn't miss Dru's gasp of pleasure, nor the frown that followed it. "But Uncle Beau. . ."

Mama gently helped Dru slip out of her dress, clucking over her like a sympathetic hen. "The good book says to let tomorrow take care of itself. God has helped you today. We'll worry about tomorrow when it comes."

When Dru didn't come back to school that afternoon, Ruth hurried for home right after the final bell. Dru sat in the kitchen with Mama, looking a lot better than she had that morning. "I'm coming home with you. That way you can ride and not have to walk when you're already sore."

"Uncle Beau might not like that."

"Your uncle has never had to walk two miles when his insides hurt. Or at least not in the same way. And Mama is sending some food home with you so you can rest."

Some twelve-year-olds had to cook and keep house. Others had to deal with maturity and the challenges it presented all alone, without another woman in the home. Not many had to do both at once. Ruth's heart went out to her young student.

Dru didn't protest any further, allowing herself to be cosseted in blankets in the back of the wagon. Beau met them at the edge of the field where he and Guy were working. "You appear without warning, Ruth." He jumped the simple fence they had posted to keep deer and other grazing animals from the growing plants.

"Dru! What happened?"

◆　◆　◆

Beau had rarely spent such a sleepless night. After a few hours of forcing himself to stay still and not toss and turn, he went outside, pacing the perimeter of the cabin to keep an eye out for dangers he was more comfortable with than the ones he had encountered today.

He didn't know what to make of it all. Women's troubles, Ruth explained with little more than a slight blush. A new dress against his explicit refusal. Food from the parsonage. The Fairfields seemed determined to help him whether he wanted it or not.

But if the common lot of womenfolk was bad enough to send his niece away from school in the middle of the day, maybe he needed the help more than he knew.

For sure, Ruth Fairfield had plenty of gumption, but she exasperated him in equal measure. She'd plowed into his life like someone convinced she knew what was best, like the people who had tried to split him and Charlotte up after their parents died.

He'd seek out advice about Dru, although he couldn't imagine asking another female about it. There had to be books that taught about such things, some kind of medical manual. In fact, he might shut off all contact from Calico, aside from Allan's work. They'd stop the tutoring for sure, keep Dru home for a few days, until he could get their lives straightened out. Without the help of the interfering Miss Fairfield.

"Beau, what about asking Me for My help?" The Lord whispered to Beau as the night turned to day, but Beau turned a deaf ear. It seemed to him like God would be on the pastor's side.

Beau didn't share his plans with the family on Saturday. He allowed Dru to spend the day in bed and kept the boys away to accommodate her need for privacy. The problem was, he didn't have any of the resources a lot of homesteaders started out with, including a basic medical book. He'd had no need for such a volume in his travels, and he didn't know where to get one.

No one said anything about the change of schedule, although Allan had protested when they didn't go to church on Sunday. "Why, Uncle Beau? Dru is well enough to get up and about."

"It's okay to spend a day at home every now and then. We'll have our own worship service here, in the soddy." He pulled the Bible he'd kept in his saddlebag onto his lap. "I thought we could share some of our favorite verses or stories. You know, the Bible says wherever two or more are gathered in His name, He's there with them. That's us today."

Allan flicked a glance at Beau. "I might as well start. I've always loved Bible stories. David and Goliath and the ark are as exciting as anything I've ever read by Homer or Shakespeare. When I think of David going after the giant with only five small stones, I get more courage the next time I set out hunting." Beau had to answer Allan's small grin with one of his own. He had seen fewer young men less at ease behind a rifle barrel, although Allan could hit a target straight and sure. Percy had done one thing right. Shooting was even more necessary than reading for someone out on the western frontier, at least in Beau's mind.

Allan proceeded to tell the story with such imagination that Beau could almost smell the sweat, blood, and dust of the battlefield. After his start, everyone shared. Guy quoted John 3:16 and talked about the day he had asked Jesus to be his Savior. That reassured Beau's mind, especially when the others shared their testimonies as well.

"How about you, Uncle Beau?" Dru asked. "Are you a Christian?"

"Yes." Should he tell the long version or the short one? "I invited Jesus into my heart when I was just a little bit of a fella. I'm ashamed to say I drifted away." Mad at God for sending one of His "ministers" to split up their family. "But there's something about days on the open prairie, with only yourself and cattle for company, that turn a man's thoughts to God." More time than he had taken recently. He had to make spending time with God a priority, no matter how busy he was around the farm.

Dru shared a story next. "I like to read about Dorcas. She helped the widows and orphans in her church, and then she died and Peter raised her back to life. Miss Fairfield's friends are like that. I just hope one of them doesn't die, because we don't have any apostles around to bring anyone back to life."

Dorcas. Of all the stories in the Bible, of all the women in the Bible, why did

Dru have to go and mention Dorcas?

"Didn't you invite Me to this meeting?" the Holy Spirit prodded Beau.

Just because Dru mentioned Dorcas didn't mean they were candidates for charity. No sir. Beau decided to break the news now. "You might as well know that you won't be going back to school in Calico. You'll either study at home or go to school in Langtry."

"No. If I can't go to Calico, I don't want to go at all." Dru jumped up, whipped her cape and bonnet from the door peg, and ran out the door.

Chapter 9

Beau thought about chasing after his niece but decided against it. Maybe all Dru needed was time alone. She'd had a difficult week. But after she hadn't returned half an hour later, he went outside to check. Dru was nowhere in sight.

"Dru!" He called at the top of his voice. "Come on back! Dru!"

Mist gathered above the ground, rising to meet storm clouds gathering overhead. It looked like fog was forming, making visibility difficult. A harsh wind whipped across the open ground, and Beau shivered with the cold. Although early in the season, snow was always a possibility.

His worry deepened as he checked the animal shelters. Everything was empty. He needed his coat, hat, mittens, gloves—maybe some extra cover for Dru. That cape couldn't keep her very warm.

"You didn't find her, did you?" Inside the soddy, Allan had prepared to leave. He handed Beau a mug of coffee and sliced bread and ham wrapped in a towel, unspoken accusations burning in his eyes

"It shouldn't take that long," Beau said.

"You don't know our Dru." Allan clipped his words. "And it's fixing to snow out there."

Guy added a sweater to the saddlebag with more food, as well as a blanket. He had chosen well. The boy had grown, putting on height and weight and muscle during the weeks he had worked on the farm, approaching his brother in bulk. They were both growing into good, strong men.

They finished up the leftover eggs in the skillet and ate a can of cold beans in about two seconds flat before heading out the door. They searched the yard and outbuildings for a second time. It didn't take long. The small lean-to they had built for the animals until they could finish a barn only took a minute, even with poking among the hay bales.

Next they checked the wagon. Beau had heard about secret places in wagon beds, especially in tales he'd heard about the Underground Railroad, but this one was solid wood.

All that remained were the open fields and plains. Dru couldn't have run far, but where was she headed? Did she even have a specific destination in mind?

You don't know our Dru. Allan's accusation repeated itself in Beau's mind. No he didn't. How could he? He didn't know much about girls, not even his own sister.

He'd expected Dru to have returned by now, to have run out her anger. But she was still out there. He'd thought he knew boys better, but his nephews defied his understanding as well.

What was it David said in the Psalms? *O Lord, thou hast searched me and known me.* "Why don't you ask Me about the children? I am acquainted with all your ways. I'll lead you to Dru."

Beau halted his horse and looked up at the heavens, where the white ceiling was lowering close to the ground and cold air blew from the north. *Forgive me, Father, for thinking I know better. You made these young'uns. You understand them inside and out. You created women different from men, and I ask You to give me enough understanding of my niece so I can find her before she gets hurt.*

"C'mon, boys. It's time to extend our search." The boys mounted their horses. "Has Dru done this kind of thing before? Do you have any idea where she might go?"

Guy immediately shook his head, but Allan hesitated before nodding.

"What is it?"

The expression on Allan's face could have passed for a smile in other circumstances. "There were a couple of times Guy and Dru ran away and camped out by the river for a night. Ma had me keep an eye on them. Pretty much as soon as they ran out of food, they came on home."

"Oh yeah. I wasn't thinking about those times." Guy pulled the reins tight. "But those were in the summer. Not like. . .this."

"Take me to the spot by the river."

Five minutes later, they had reached the place. Beau could see how it would make a pleasant summer hideaway. Plenty of water, shade too, maybe good fishing. Next year he would check it out.

Although they dismounted the horses and searched the banks on both sides, they found no traces of recent disturbance. They rode up and down the river from that favorite spot. Once Guy spotted something that turned out to be the beginnings of a beaver dam. Another time Allan found the remnants of a fox den.

With the storm hovering, the sky dimmed fast. They continued their search, knowing Dru might be only a few feet away and they wouldn't see her. At one point, Allan came to Beau and shared a slice of bread and a slab of ham along with a swig of cold coffee from his canteen.

The sky grew gray, then black, the soddy little more than a smudge on the horizon. Beau decided to call a reluctant halt to the search and whistled for the boys to join him. "We'd best get on back."

Both Allan and Guy nodded their acceptance. "I'd say to come out again with torches, but. . ." Allan shrugged. "We wouldn't be able to see very far."

"We'll start at first light tomorrow." Beau would pray all night long for God's protection of Dru during the long hours.

Even taking a straight path to the soddy took longer than expected, and Beau realized how far they had searched. How far could a girl in ordinary shoes and a long dress travel on foot? He didn't know. His last hopes for a happy ending to the day were dashed when they arrived at an empty soddy, devoid of light or warmth. Dru had not returned.

After they finished chores, they built a small fire and collapsed onto the beds without seeking further refreshment. Against all expectations, Beau fell asleep quickly, his rest punctuated with snorts of wakefulness. Each time, his chest tightened, and he sensed his heart had been carrying on its own conversation with God even while his body rested. He woke early in the morning and rustled up some eggs and hardtack that brought the boys to wakefulness. After a quick breakfast, Beau discussed what to do. "We didn't check much west of the yard yesterday. I thought we'd start that way today."

Allan shuffled his feet. "I was wondering if she'd circle back to the road once she got away from here. She might have gone into town. One of us should head that way in case she's heading home. I can ask when I get to the bank."

Allan had proven himself a strong presence in this emergency. He might never make a good farmer, but he had courage and common sense. "Tell you what then. Guy, you finish up the chores here and wait for my return." Cows had to be milked and animals fed, no matter what. They decided to meet back at the soddy at lunchtime. "And if it starts to snow. . ."

"Don't worry. I know what to do." Guy interrupted before Beau could continue his lecture. Revelation upon revelation about his nephews was piling up on this day.

◆　◆　◆

Ruth woke early Monday with a heavy heart. Every weekend since Beau's arrival, she had run into him somewhere. A couple of times he had dropped by Aunt Kate's diner. He had shown up at the sewing circle more than once, and he'd been mentioned every week. That thought brought a blush to her cheeks. Then there was Finnegan's Mercantile, the parsonage, and even the school. His absence this past weekend troubled her more than it should.

She wasn't truly distressed until the family missed church. Was one of them sick? By Sunday, Dru's distress should have subsided. After attending each week as faithfully as the pastor did, their sudden absence created a void on the third pew on the left side of the church, their usual spot to sit. She checked it before the service started, glanced during the morning prayer—and caught the gaze of young Georgie Polson. Even though she didn't hear any opening or closing of the church doors, she kept hoping they had snuck in without her knowledge until at last Papa said the final amen and she made her way down the aisle.

The weather turned cold, hinting that the first freeze of the season would arrive before morning. But Beau didn't seem like the sort to let a little cold keep him from what he wanted to do. If anything, he'd plow his way through six feet of snow if he set his mind to it. Her concerns about the well-being of the family increased. All Sunday long she fought her conscience about making another unannounced visit to the soddy. Someone else should go, but she still felt like the "someone" meant to help the Pratts was her.

Monday morning dawned chilly, air whisking through the chinks around her window, and she dressed in underthings designed for cold weather. Hopefully the temperatures would rise as the sun came out. If the clouds covered the sky all day, sunshine wouldn't stretch the warmth very far.

Since the hour was early, she could go to the bank and speak with Allan before school started. But what if he wasn't there? She discussed the problem with Mama.

"I'm truly concerned something has happened. A soddy isn't the best place to pass a winter, and Beau doesn't have much experience. I'm afraid something's happened to one or all of them."

"I pray you'll find Allan at the bank and everything is fine."

Bless Mama, she didn't tell Ruth her concern was unjustified. "But if he's not there?"

Mama took a seat opposite Ruth and looked her straight in the eye. "What do you want to do?"

"I want to ride straight out to the farm and check. A man probably should come with me. Except I can't go to the farm and start school on time."

Mama waved that concern away. "I'll stay with the children. You've planned your lessons so well, they're easy for me to follow."

Ruth sped from the parsonage to the bank, arriving at the same time as Allan.

"Miss Fairfield!" He looked flustered, and dark circles ringed his eyes, confirming her fears.

"What's happened?" Ruth stepped away from the entrance of the bank. A few children crossed the street in front of them on their way to school, and Ruth waved.

"It's Dru. She's run away. We haven't seen her since Sunday morning."

The first flat snowflake floated between them, landing on Ruth's coat like a strand of wool from an unraveling sweater.

Chapter 10

Ruth glanced back at the bank. "You need to get to work."

Allan shook his head. "I'm going to ask them if I can take the day off and look for Dru. I know Uncle Beau is going to ask people to help search."

After his departure, Ruth glanced up and down the streets, looking for someone to come with her. Not seeing anyone, she decided she could make the trip on her own. She shouldn't have any problems if she left in time to get back before the snow made travel difficult. Backtracking to the parsonage, she saddled her horse and headed west down the rapidly disappearing road.

She kept her speed slow, in case she caught sight of Dru or the road grew slick underfoot. Each plop of the horse's hooves thudded in her heart. Dru, dear, sweet, Dru, who had trusted her like an older sister, had run away. In her heart, Ruth knew the way she had pushed Beau had something to do with it. Before she said one word to Beau about his niece, she'd better ask his forgiveness for interfering and for how that had led to today's events.

The flakes grew closer together and smaller, the kind of snow that could end in great drifts. A coated and hatted figure emerged from the whitening horizon—Beau.

He saluted her with his hat. They both picked up speed and met, about a yard's distance between them. Ruth said, "Allan told me about Dru. Oh Beau, I feel like this is all my fault. If I hadn't interfered"—a lump formed in her throat—"this might not have happened."

◆　◆　◆

Allan must not have told Ruth the whole story. The fault belonged entirely to Beau.

"I'm the one who needs to ask your forgiveness. If I hadn't been so determined to do things my own way, this wouldn't have happened." Beau swallowed. "I put my pride ahead of my family's needs. I want to talk more about that with you later. But you haven't seen Dru?"

"No." The wind blew a strand of Ruth's dark hair away from her face, a whirlwind of white snow and dark circles of hair. "I want to help."

She would. Regardless of how little help a woman would be searching through a snowstorm, she'd think herself equal to the task. "But what about school?"

"Mama took over for the day. Although if the weather keeps up, she might send the students home soon. The one we have to worry about is Dru." Ruth paused. "I expect she found shelter somewhere. She's too smart to let herself get caught out in this." One bright red mitten embraced the gray horizon. "But we need help. We should—" She paused, her face flaring a pretty red like her mittens. "That is, if you agree with me."

He gestured for her to continue.

"I'm sure my sewing circle friends would be willing to help. And their beaus." Her voice stumbled at the wordplay between his name and the common usage of the word.

His heart surged with warmth in spite of the swirling snow. Could Beau be someone's beau? Could he be Ruth's beau? *Another time.* "That sounds wise. We could cover more territory that way."

He, Guy, and most of all, Dru needed help. Beau had already decided to drop his pride and accept the help a circle of good Christian people wanted to give him. "I'm supposed to meet up with Guy at the soddy at noon. Let's gather everyone and cover the town before we head back out this way."

As they rode back into town, the wind blew from every direction, pushing them first one way then the other. The horses plodded steadily along. Beau's stomach suggested the hour had reached midmorning, but he couldn't tell by the sky.

"We'll reach Finnegan's Mercantile first," Ruth called against the wind. "Mr. Finnegan can circulate word for people to keep a look out."

His family at the center of the town's gossip mill. *Your will, Lord.* Beau swallowed past his pride.

Ned hovered at the door to his store, Birdie at his heels, locking the door behind them. "You almost missed me." He unlocked the door. "What can I do for you?"

"We don't need to buy anything," Ruth started to explain.

"Come in out of the weather." Ned held the door open, and Beau waited for the ladies before ducking his head under Ned's arm.

"My niece, Dru, is missing. She ran away." Beau stated the cold, hard facts, not caring what they might think. Pride was running away from him as rapidly as the snow accumulated.

"We'd like your help in looking for her." Ruth took off her mittens and rubbed her hands in front of the small fire Ned had left burning in the store. "We're going to ask everyone in the sewing circle to help get the word out. Can you get in touch with Annie while we go for Gladys and Haydn? Tell everyone we'll meet at Aunt Kate's diner in half an hour."

Thirty minutes later, they met in front of the diner. The doors remained open, Aunt Kate serving hot cocoa to anyone bold enough to brave the weather.

"I wonder what's keeping Haydn." Gladys rubbed a spot in the window. "He promised he'd come right away. We don't want to wait much longer."

In addition to the sewing circle, several other members of the Calico community joined them in the diner. Half of them, Beau couldn't put a name to their faces. Without his saying a word, the men organized search teams while the women decided which homes to set up as relay stations, places to return for warmth and refreshment. A few of the women, Ruth among them, wanted to hunt along with the men, and no one denied them.

Beau cleared his throat, and the room quieted. "I promised Guy I'd be back by noon. I'll head on out with whoever is coming with me."

"I am." Ruth's gray eyes met his.

Another man joined their party. They'd barely reached the town square when Pastor Fairfield clanged the church doors behind him, head lowered into the wind.

"Wait. Let's see what he has to say." Ruth nudged her horse forward toward the bent figure.

Pastor Fairfield lifted his head, hand clamped on a broad-brimmed black hat, and joy sprang on his face at the sight of Beau and the others accompanying them. "Good news, brother!"

Chapter 11

S it still, teacher!" Dru giggled. "That's what you always tell us, and you're worse than the first graders."

Ruth smiled at the two of them in the mirror. After Papa had greeted them with the news that Dru had spent the night before safe and sound inside the room at the church, they had reached quick decisions. Beau headed for the soddy to catch Guy and hunker down before the storm let loose its full fury. Everyone agreed that neither Dru nor Ruth should face the weather without good reason. Once again Dru was a guest of the Calico parsonage.

The snow continued unabated for the rest of Monday into Tuesday. As usual, Aunt Kate and Mama and Papa took in those schoolchildren who lived too far away to reach home safely. Ruth had always enjoyed these times; they were part of the reason she had decided to become a teacher. After this most recent experience, she allowed herself to admit that perhaps they helped reveal a desire for a family of her own. A family with children of her own to love, special ones like Dru. . .and Allan. . .and even Guy. With someone like. . .Beau.

His name aroused a raging fire of emotions in her. She must have mistaken the spark she'd seen in his eyes when they went looking for Dru. Silly woman, to mistake feelings stirred by the disappearance of his niece for romantic longings of a lonely soul. He hadn't even returned to town to take his niece home, although Allan had come by on his first day back at work to let them know the three menfolk had survived the storm.

"Now you've got that dreamy look in your eye." Dru ran the brush through Ruth's hair another time. "Do you want to keep it down around your shoulders? Or I could braid it and put it in a bun." Dru ran her fingers through the long strands. "Although that would be a pity. It's too pretty to hide. Or I could pile it on top of your head like a crown. . . ."

Ruth studied her image in the mirror. Not so long ago, she had worried about how to fix her hair. A simple bow holding her dark locks at the nape of her neck once brought her pleasure. Now she went with the most practical style for teaching, away from her face. During the summer, she kept her hair off her neck and let it down again when the weather turned cold.

But Dru was so eager, Ruth agreed to the experiment. "Whatever you like, as long as you don't cut it."

"I would never do that. It's too pretty."

Dru made a pretty picture herself. Now that Beau and Ruth had achieved peace between them, Ruth had finished another dress for Dru. This one was a soft green wool, one that would look lovely with her coloring, with white lace at the collar and cuffs, and a gored skirt in the back, flared just enough to look fashionable. Earlier today Dru had put the dress on for the first time, and Ruth had pinned her hair up in a simple bun. A little too grown up, too dressy for a weekday, but girls liked to dream.

Dru put a finger to her lips and turned Ruth around so she could study her face. "If you don't mind. . .I'd like to fix it the same way you fixed mine."

Happiness flooded Ruth's chest as if the girl had just said she wanted to become a teacher. "That's sounds wonderful."

Dru kept Ruth facing her while she led the girl through the steps. "That's perfect!" With a flourish, Dru held up the hand mirror for Ruth to see her reflection.

Ruth gasped. She hadn't looked so pretty, so young, so vulnerable since she began teaching five years ago. She touched the smoothed edges of brow and skin and cheek and hair. "You're a wonder, Dru Pratt."

The girl giggled again. "I'll remind you that you said that the next time I get into trouble at school." She tugged at Ruth's arm. "C'mon, stand up. I want to see us side by side."

Their hair was different colors. So were their eyes. But something—the joy in their eyes? The laughter on their lips? The shine of their hair?—made them look as alike as sisters.

"I wish you were my sister. Or my mother, since my ma died." The young lady slipped into a child again as she flung her arms around Ruth's neck.

"I am your sister in Christ. And you can always come to me with questions you don't feel comfortable asking your uncle." Ruth wondered whether she was wise to make such an open-ended invitation. If—*when*—Beau married, Dru should go to his wife with her questions.

"Everything would be perfect if you would just marry Uncle Beau. Then I could have you all to myself."

Ruth turned away before Dru could see the telltale heat streaking across her cheeks. "He has caught the attention of several ladies of the church. It won't be too long before you have an aunt you can go to with your questions."

Dru's mouth drooped. "I want you for my aunt."

"What you want and what God and your uncle Beau want may be different things. I'm where God has placed me, teaching the Calico School. I don't expect marriage to be part of my future." She reached for her hair, ready to ruin the fancy hairstyle. With a look at Dru, she dropped her hand and sighed.

◆　◆　◆

Beau waited in the parlor for Mrs. Fairfield to call Dru. He leaned forward, not meaning to eavesdrop but unable to close his ears and unwilling to move where he couldn't hear.

I don't expect marriage to be part of my future.

The words hit his soul like a death knell. Dru appeared in the doorway and squealed, and Beau hastened to paste a smile back on his lips. She must have seen his unhappy frown, however. "Uncle Beau, are you mad at me?"

She wore a pretty green gown that showed a lovely young woman, one who was growing into the image of her mother. Beau blinked at the tears the memories of his own dear sister brought to his eyes. "Mad at you? Yes, and worried and relieved and. . ." He drew in his breath. "Mostly, I'm mad at myself that you felt you had to run away rather than stay with me."

Dru looked at the floor. "I acted like a child. All you wanted me to do was to get my schooling someplace else. You weren't sending me off to someplace like the Betwixt 'n' Between, like the fathers of some of Birdie's girls did."

Of course Dru had heard some of the stories, as much as Beau wished he could shield her. "I was treating you like you were still seven years old and didn't have any ideas of your own. Expecting you to run the house and then not respecting your opinion about what was best for our family. . .that wasn't very smart of me."

"Maybe." She dragged her gaze to look at him. "So we're all right, then?"

"More than all right." He opened his arms, and she flew into them. He hugged her to his side, feeling once again the sizzle of joy he had felt each time he had reunited with Charlotte. He took a few steps with her. "Come outside with me." When he whispered in her ear, she followed with wide eyes the snow-packed path leading from parsonage to church. Once he found a secluded spot, he shared his plan with his niece; he had already talked it over with Allan and Guy. When a fit of girlish laughter collapsed her, he led her into the church. "Why don't you wait in here? I'll come for you soon."

"Of course. And Uncle Beau?"

"Yes?"

"Don't hurry back."

◆　◆　◆

Ruth caught sight of Beau and Dru hovering behind the back wall of the church. Young couples who thought that was a good place for privacy didn't know that the parsonage bedrooms looked over their hideout. Most of it was innocent enough, although once or twice Papa had to step in.

Whatever Beau wanted to discuss with his niece was none of Ruth's business. She shut the curtains against the sight and rustled through her closet instead. Over the months she had filled a box with things she had made for the Pratts. The bed quilt wasn't quite finished, so it lay on top where she could grab it and work on it during odd moments. She had shirts and pants for the boys and a skirt and blouse for Dru. Annie had added socks. After she finished reviewing the contents, Dru and Beau still hadn't come back inside. She twitched the side of the curtain; they had disappeared from view. Frowning, she pressed her head against the glass but didn't see either one of them. He hadn't taken his niece home without saying good-bye, had he?

"Ruth." Mama knocked on the door. "Mr. Blanton would like to see you in the parlor."

Ruth's heart leaped at those words in a way that didn't reflect well on her continued peace of mind. "Coming, Mama."

Beau stood at the entrance to the parlor. Something about the way he held his hat in his hands, hope shining from his eyes, made her glad for the extra pains she and Dru had taken with her appearance today. "You're looking mighty fine today, Ruth."

Heat rose in her cheeks as she entered the room. He rushed to the back of the chair closest to the fire and held it for her. "Let me take that for you." He took the basket of shirts and household goods from her with a glance. "Let me guess. Your needle's been busy again."

"Yes." Ruth studied his face, nervous that he might reject her gift. She held her breath.

"Good." He smiled.

"So you're not mad?"

"How can I be mad at you for blessing me even when I was too stubborn to accept help when we needed it?" He set the basket beside him, on top of his coat, where he could easily pick it up when he left. "Mad? I should be offering my gratitude as well as asking for your forgiveness."

"Given. And I should ask for yours as well."

"We've already discussed all that." He didn't speak again for the space of a few seconds. "That's what I want to talk to you about. You've already forgiven me for being a stubborn fool. But I was wondering if you could do more than forgive me." His eyes searched hers. "If you could, perhaps, even. . .love me? Love me enough to marry me, to raise three children and any others the good Lord sees fit to give us?"

Mama poked her head around the corner. "Your father has already said yes." With a wink, she disappeared again.

Ruth blinked, certain Beau could read the answer in her eyes. . .her mouth. . .even in the way her ears reddened. "Yes yes yes!"

She couldn't wait to tell the Calico Sewing Circle that their mission was complete. Matchmaking and all.

DARLENE FRANKLIN

Bestselling author Darlene Franklin's greatest claim to fame is that she writes full-time from a nursing home. She lives in Oklahoma, near her son and his family, and continues her interests in playing the piano and singing, books, good fellowship, and reality TV in addition to writing. She is an active member of Oklahoma City Christian Fiction Writers, American Christian Fiction Writers, and the Christian Authors Network. She has written over fifty books and more than 250 devotionals. Her historical fiction ranges from the Revolutionary War to World War II, from Texas to Vermont. You can find Darlene online at www.darlenefranklinwrites.com

American Pie

by Debby Mayne

Dedication

Thanks to Mark and Shari Turner for their dedication to the ministry of Oakbrook Community Church.

Chapter 1

Southern Mississippi, 1890

"Mm-mm, somethin' smells mighty fine, Miss Sophie."

Sophia turned around and looked her mother's housekeeper, Dora, in the eye and smiled. "It better smell good. I've been workin' on it all morning. It's apple pie. Mama's recipe."

Dora stepped closer, clicking her tongue. "Apple pie. My goodness, Child. You gonna spoil that man and make him think he done died and gone to heaven."

"I wouldn't go that far, but I sure hope it tastes as good as it smells."

"Looks good too," Dora said. "But you didn't have to go to all that trouble for Mr. Jacobson. He's so sweet on you, you coulda made a mud pie, and he woulda bid his right arm on it."

"Maybe so," Sophia agreed, "but Mama wouldn't approve. She insisted I use this recipe." With a soft chuckle, she added, "You know how Mama is."

Dora shot Sophia a quick side-glance and shook her head.

"Think he might pop the question soon?" Dora asked as she stuck her finger into the mixing bowl, then pulled it out to taste it. "Mm-mm. That's some fine cookin'."

Sophia inhaled deeply, then slowly let out her breath. "Who knows," she said. "Men can be so thick-headed sometimes."

"Don't I know it." Dora shook her head as she chuckled and headed toward the kitchen door. "Just try not to trip when you're carryin' that thing across the church yard."

"I'll try not to," Sophia replied.

As soon as Dora left the kitchen, Sophia backed up and sank into one of the half dozen kitchen chairs that surrounded the large pine table. The last thing she wanted was to become William Jacobson's wife, but it appeared that they were meant to be together. Ever since they were children, their parents had been planning this wedding, hoping to bring the two families together. Mama had told her she'd never meet a finer man than William, which was probably true. But whenever Sophia was around him, she felt shackled, like she couldn't be herself. He was so quiet, she often thought of him as moody. However, he was a Christian man, and that was the single most important feature she must look for in a husband.

As far as Sophia was concerned, arranged marriages should be banned. While her parents said she didn't have to marry William, she knew they'd be deeply disappointed if she didn't. That is, if he ever got around to asking her.

Sophia was beginning to think he dreaded the thought of it as much as she did.

If that's the case, she thought, *then it better not happen. No sense in two people being disappointed.*

"Sophia, better hurry up. The auction starts in an hour, and it's a good half-hour ride."

"Comin', Mama," Sophia said as she stood up. Better get there on time or the whole congregation would wonder what had gotten into her.

Sophia held the pie in her lap as her mother chattered nonstop all the way to the church. "Don't think for one minute you're the only girl there with a delicious pie, Sophia," she said. "You have to smile at William and let him know you're interested."

"I know, Mama."

"And you can't leave it up to him to do all the talkin' once he wins you in the auction."

"Once he wins my pie, Mama," Sophia corrected her.

"That's right. You have to let him know you like him without seeming too eager."

Sophia swallowed hard. Based on how it had started, this was going to be a very long day.

As they rode the rest of the way to the church, Sophia's mind wandered while her mother's incessant chatter droned on and on. Every year, each of the single, available women from the church baked a pie that was to be auctioned off at the Fourth of July celebration. Men—or suitors, to be exact—bid on whatever pie their favorite girl brought, as people standing around watching chuckled and made appropriate comments, encouraging them to start thinking about the rest of their lives. And some did. The Church on the Hill had a very high number of proposals on July Fourth, and weddings generally followed soon after. Most couples didn't want to wait too long once they'd decided they wanted to spend the rest of their lives together.

Sophia liked William Jacobson enough to consider him a very good friend. In fact, he was the person she chose to sit next to at potluck dinners and during fellowship gatherings—any place where she needed to keep quiet. But marriage? William's solemn manner and brooding disposition would surely depress her if she had to face him every day for the rest of her life.

"Okay, Sophia, hop down and get on over there. Looks like the rest of the girls have found their spots."

She glanced over at the long row of tables that had been set out on the church lawn. Young women—some her age but most a year or two younger—were standing behind their creations, chattering and giggling to each other. This all seemed so silly to Sophia.

"Hey, Sophia," her best friend, Gina, called. "Over here."

At least there was one person who understood her. "Coming," she called as she glanced around to see if Mama was looking, then hiked her dress and ran, precariously carrying the pie in one hand.

"Look at all the men," Gina said. "Looks like they're all hungry too."

"Men are always hungry," Sophia said with a snort. "But I guess this is for a good cause."

"That's right; don't forget about the cause."

Gina and Sophia had already agreed that if this auction didn't bring in a huge amount of money for the orphanage the church helped support, they'd never in a million years agree to be part of it.

"Is Richard here yet?" Sophia asked.

"I don't think so. He's almost always late for everything. That's why I told the pastor I wanted to go last. Richard would just die if someone else bid on my pie and he wasn't even around to outbid him."

"At least you know you love him," Sophia reminded her.

"You poor dear," Gina offered sympathetically. "I know you like William, but you should never have to marry him if he's not the man you love with all your heart."

"I just wonder if such a man exists. Maybe I should just do what Mama and Daddy want me to do and get on with life."

"You always do what they want you to do. I would have given a few people a piece of my mind by now, if I were in your shoes."

Gina probably would, too. She often accused Sophia of trying too hard to make everyone around her happy when she was suffering greatly. Sophia just didn't like to disappoint those she loved, so she'd always gone along with whatever her parents wanted. Why should she stop now?

Reverend Breckenridge tipped his hat as he walked by the end of the long row of tables. "Mornin', ladies."

"G'mornin', Reverend," Gina said. "Looks like we have quite a turnout on this lovely day."

"It's mighty hot already," he said with a chuckle. "I hope everyone stays long enough to bid on all these pies."

"I'm sure they will." Gina had picked up a church fan and begun waving it at her face.

The minute Reverend Breckenridge turned his back and walked away, Sophia laughed. "I don't know how you do it, Gina, but you can talk to anyone about anything."

Gina grinned back at her. "Not really. I just don't have a fear of anyone here, but put me in front of a group of schoolteachers and my tongue freezes."

Sophia remembered when they were young girls, talking about what they wanted to be when they grew up, her best friend said she wanted to be a schoolteacher. "They get to boss everyone around all the time, and everyone thinks they're smart."

"That's hardly a reason to become one," Sophia had argued.

"It's good enough for me."

But Gina hadn't become a schoolteacher, and Sophia hadn't been married right out of school like she'd thought. Both of them still lived at home with their parents, helping their mothers run their households and trying to figure out what the Lord had in store for them.

"Maybe we'll never figure it out," Gina had said the week before the auction. "Look," she now whispered, her voice tinged with excitement. "That man over there. I've never seen him before."

Sophia glanced over in the direction Gina was nodding. "I think I might have seen him in church last Sunday. Isn't he one of the new men on the lumberyard?"

"Oh, that's right. Andy Sawyer said they hired some more men to supervise on the yard. He's probably one of them."

"He sure is handsome," Sophia noticed.

Gina leaned back and gave Sophia one of her practiced schoolteacher looks. "Now don't go gettin' any ideas about this man, or you might cause William to faint dead away."

Sophia waved her hand from the wrist. "Don't be silly. William couldn't care less if I think some other man's handsome."

"Maybe so, but there's rumor going around that William's looking at building a house on the back of his family's property," Gina said in her all-knowing way. "And you know what that means." She gently placed her hand on Sophia's arm. "Brace yourself for the proposal."

With a long sigh, Sophia wiped her forehead with her handkerchief. "I don't know anything about it."

Gina turned her attention to the woman who'd come up on the other side of her and set her pie on the table. While they discussed recipes, Sophia fought back the urge to take her pie and run as far away as she could. This whole pie auction was wrong for her. All her life, other people had decided what she should do and where she should be. She'd gone along with whatever they wanted because she didn't want to upset her mama and daddy.

William was a very sweet man, but she never felt anything when he'd kissed her—either time. Both kisses had been short and sweet, but nothing had happened. No sparks. No music in her heart. No racing pulse. Nothing. Surely the Lord would want her to feel something.

Sophia didn't expect too much from life, but she wanted a husband who could give her something to look forward to each day when he came home from work. She knew that if she loved her husband as much as her mama loved her daddy, she'd want to cook and decorate, doing all the things to make her home a comfortable place for the man who headed her household. With William, she'd wonder what sadness he would bring home.

Although William was sweet, he was sad all the time. He rarely smiled, but Sophia understood why. His family had relied so heavily on him since he'd been big enough to help out in his father's store, he'd never been allowed the opportunity to be a happy-go-lucky child.

"He's responsible," Mama had said when she started talking to Sophia about her future. "You want a responsible husband."

Yes, that's exactly what she wanted, but not William. All she wanted from William was friendship, but that didn't appear to be what she'd get.

Sophia knew, long before the pie auction started, that William would most likely be the only man bidding on her pie. He'd get the opportunity to have lunch with her, and they'd slice the pie for dessert. He'd take the rest of it home, and everyone would say what a wonderful wife she'd make because she could cook. It was all so predictable. Why couldn't Sophia have the freedom to fall in love with someone of her choosing? And why couldn't she have more excitement and fun in her life?

She shut her eyes for a short prayer before the ceremony began. *Lord, I'm here to serve You, and I want to do Your will. Please give me peace and joy as I do Your work. Amen.*

When she opened her eyes, Sophia saw that the reverend had gone up to the podium that had been set up on the small wooden stage. His voice was strong, so he didn't need the megaphone he'd pulled out. But he used it anyway.

"Before we start the auction for these delicious pies, I'd like to hear from some of you what this Fourth of July celebration means to you."

At first, no one volunteered, so Reverend Breckenridge called on one of the elderly men in the front row to speak first. The gray-bearded man hobbled up to the podium with his cane, then looked around at the crowd and grinned. "We are all here to give thanks to the Lord for placing us in this fine country where we are free to worship Him without fear." He opened his mouth like he had something else to say, then he held his hands up, shaking his head. "That's all. Amen."

A few people laughed out loud, but most hid smiles behind their hands as they tried to be polite. He might have had few words to say, but Sophia felt like they were words filled with truth.

"Amen," she whispered as he walked back to his wife, who was smiling with pride at her husband.

Several more men stood and talked about how the Fourth of July would always be significant because of freedom and liberty. They each related their own experiences, telling how they'd been able to choose their paths in life. "Without freedom, I'd never have the acres of farmland and my beautiful bride," another elderly gentleman said. His wife of nearly fifty years blushed and reached for him as he joined her. They'd been married the longest of any couple there. Sophia saw the love and tenderness they shared, and she wondered if she'd ever have a relationship like that with a man.

Then, to everyone's surprise, the new man Sophia had noticed earlier stepped up to the podium. Everyone hushed as he looked around at all the staring eyes.

Suddenly, his voice boomed through the megaphone. " 'For all have sinned, and come short of the glory of God; being justified freely by His grace through the redemption that is in Christ Jesus,' Romans 3:23-24." He cleared his throat before he continued. "The only freedom we have, folks, is through Him, our Lord Jesus Christ, and I for one give thanks to Him every day for what He did for me. No country, no free land, no government can take away my relationship with my Lord. He will always be with me. Amen."

After that powerful speech, no one dared come forth to add their thoughts of freedom. He'd said it all.

Sophia felt an odd tingling sensation in her stomach, almost like butterflies were fluttering their wings against her ribs. She watched the man as he made his way back to where he'd been standing, less than twenty feet from her end of the pie table. She wasn't sure of his name, but she intended to find out.

William appeared from out of nowhere. "Hi, Sophia. Your pie looks mighty good."

Her lips were still dry from the effects of the stranger. She turned to William and forced a smile. "Why thank you, William."

He looked down at his feet, then back toward her, although not directly at her. That had always annoyed Sophia, the fact that he rarely met her gaze. Her mother had said that was because he was shy, which sounded silly to Sophia. But Mama was probably right as usual.

"I'll see you in a little while," William said as he backed away from Sophia. "Your pie will be one of the last to be auctioned." Then he was gone. He didn't even have the good graces to say good-bye.

When Reverend Breckenridge moved back to his position behind the podium, speculation ran through the congregation. He said a prayer, reiterating what the stranger had already said. Then he said, "Let the auction begin."

The first was a cherry pie baked by Lucy Morris. Two men bid for the pie, but from the very beginning there was no doubt who'd win. Her brother's best friend had already expressed his intentions, and Lucy was thrilled to walk away from the pie table arm-in-arm with him.

Sophia felt the tension build in her chest as the pies and single ladies disappeared with their bidders. When it was her turn, she had to force herself to smile and not run away. Mama and Daddy would be furious with her if she didn't go through with this. She shut her eyes and begged the Lord to not have William propose on this day.

William placed the first offer, which was a very paltry amount. Sophia was embarrassed, but she knew William didn't have very much money. She started to pick up her pie and head over to him when another bid came in, this one doubling William's offer.

Everyone in the crowd turned and stared as the bidder stepped forward. It was the stranger who'd shushed everyone with his comments on freedom! Sophia felt her face grow hot as the bidding war began.

William had already bid dangerously high for his salary. Sophia felt sorry for him and found herself calculating how she'd offer to reimburse him for that stranger's stupidity. Didn't he know this wasn't done?

Finally, when the stranger bid a sum that had people gasping, William faded back into the crowd.

"Sold!" the reverend called out. "Miss Mayhew, you may take your pie over to the payment table and join Mr. Ellis for a picnic lunch. Enjoy your pie. I'm sure it's worth every penny."

Sophia's knees grew weak as she did as she was told. Every eye was focused on her, making her feel like crawling into a hole. But she had to keep walking toward the man who'd bid on her pie, past William, past Mama and Daddy, past all the leering people who knew this was significant. What would she do now?

Chapter 2

That pie looks scrumptious," the stranger Reverend Breckenridge had called Mr. Ellis said. "I can hardly wait to cut into it."

"Who are you?" Sophia asked since he didn't appear anxious to introduce himself.

He grinned. "I'm Hank Ellis. I thought you might know my name. Sorry for my rudeness."

Sophia felt ashamed of herself for being so abrupt. "I'm sorry too," she said. "I'm Sophia Mayhew."

"Yes, I know. In fact I've known who you were for quite some time now."

"You have?" she asked, her voice a much higher pitch than normal. She lifted her free hand to cover her mouth as she cleared her throat. "How?"

"I've been watching you for several weeks, and I asked some of the other church members."

Sophia studied his face for a few seconds. "You've been going to church here for several weeks?"

"Yes," he replied with a deep, hearty chuckle. "I'm afraid I'm one of those people who likes to sit on the back pew. But I do listen to everything the reverend says, and I read my Bible every day." He lifted his right hand. "I promise."

She laughed with him. "You don't have to go that far. I believe you."

Hank took the pie in one hand and offered his other arm for her to take. "Shall we?"

"Yes," she said as she glanced nervously over her shoulder at all the people behind them. Just as she'd thought, everyone was still staring at them. Well, let them stare. Maybe they'd learn something.

"How's that oak tree over there?" he asked. "I see someone has put a settee beneath it, just for us."

Sophia's heart fluttered as she looked at Hank Ellis's profile. He was a handsome man, and he smiled a lot. She liked that.

"I hope you don't mind if we eat right away," he said. "I'm starving."

Sophia didn't want to admit that when she took his arm, her appetite had vanished. Her stomach was filled with those butterflies. With a shrug, she replied, "I ate a big breakfast this morning, right before we came here. But go ahead and get something for yourself."

"I'll be right back," he said as he backed away from her, leaving her sitting beneath the oak tree with her pie. "Don't go anywhere."

She lifted her hand and waved her fingers, smiling. "I'll be right here when you get back."

Hank almost ran smack dab into the reverend before he turned around and caught himself. Sophia watched him apologize, walk briskly toward the picnic table filled with food brought by the married women, then appear once again with his plate piled high. He didn't waste any time coming back to her.

"I thought you might want a little nourishment, so I brought enough for both of us." He tilted his head forward and looked at her teasingly from beneath hooded eyes. "That is, if you don't mind sharing a plate."

Sophia had never been asked to share a plate with a man before, and this sounded quite adventurous. "I don't mind at all," she replied.

Although she wasn't the least bit hungry, Sophia picked at the items she could lift with her fingers. This was more fun than she'd ever had with a man before. In fact, other than William, this was the only man she'd ever been alone with.

"I hope you aren't too upset about me bidding on you so unexpectedly," Hank said between bites. "I was afraid I might lose you to that other gentleman who seemed determined to win your pie."

Sophia nibbled on a slice of bread she'd lifted from his plate. "William is an old friend of the family."

"Is that all? I sort of got the impression there might be more to it."

"Well, maybe, but not for me."

"So you're saying you're a single woman with no attachments?" he asked.

With a slight hesitation, Sophia nodded. Her face felt flaming hot. She'd never been so bold in her life, but he'd asked a question, and it would be rude not to answer it. She wanted to get to know Hank Ellis.

Hank leaned over and brushed a stray hair from Sophia's cheek, then lifted her chin with his fingertips, turning her toward him. "No need to feel embarrassed, Sophia. I only wanted to make sure I'm not interfering in something you already have going with another man."

"You're not," Sophia managed to say, her voice softer than she could ever remember it being.

He smiled, lifted his arms to the sky, and said, "Hallelujah!"

Sophia had never seen William express himself so openly or with so much enthusiasm, making the difference between the two men so great there was no comparison.

"Want to know what I find so appealing about you, Sophia— besides the beautiful honey-blond hair and those large brown eyes of yours?"

She looked at him and waited. No words came to mind. Even if they had, her voice had gotten lost somewhere in her astonishment.

"You wear your heart on your sleeve and your thoughts in your eyes."

Leaning forward, Sophia scrunched up her forehead and managed a weak, "What do you mean by that?"

He belted out another hearty laugh, something she could easily get used to. "I can tell you care deeply for others, and you have a strong emotional side to your being."

"Doesn't everyone?"

"Oh, no," he replied. "If they did, this world would be a much better place. As for your eyes, I can look into them and see to the depths of your soul."

"Then maybe I should shut them."

Hank reached for her cheek and touched it softly before pulling back. "Your skin is like peaches and cream, so soft and touchable."

Sophia wanted him to keep on telling her more of what he liked about her, but she didn't dare ask. "Thank you, Mr. Ellis."

"You must call me Hank if we're going to continue seeing one another."

She smiled back at him. "Hank."

"That's right. Now, my dear Sophia, let's cut into this delicious-looking pie and enjoy the fruits of your labor."

With every bite, Hank Ellis smiled and offered his gratitude for her culinary skills. He told her more than once how much he enjoyed fresh apple pie and said he'd love to see what else she could do in the kitchen.

Sophia knew that others were staring, but she didn't care. All that mattered to her was how she felt with this man—the only one who'd ever made her feel so exciting, so beautiful, so vibrant and alive. All the Williams in the world couldn't measure up to Hank Ellis.

◆ ◆ ◆

Hank knew that Sophia was holding something back, but he wasn't about to press her for more details. He already felt as though he'd expected too much from her. In fact, he was surprised at how open and willing she'd been to talk with him.

He also felt the scorching heat from the stares of that man called William. It was painfully obvious that the man held a torch for this woman. No wonder. She was a raving beauty, and she was sweet. The fact that she could bake was a bonus that delighted him to no end.

Hank could imagine himself falling in love with Sophia Mayhew, Lord willing. But he knew he needed to tread lightly, or he'd risk dividing loyalties within the church. He'd seen it happen before over matters of much less consequence than this. One of his earliest memories had been of a man turning his back on the church after his daughter had been inadvertently overlooked during a church pageant. That one simple oversight had caused people to take sides, and the church temporarily lost half its flock. The pews were bare for several weeks until the pastor managed to soothe the hurt feelings. After seeing the hurt caused by that situation, Hank wasn't about to knowingly cause similar strife in another church.

As he and Sophia ate their pie, he asked her questions about her family. She was somewhat guarded, but he could tell she was interested in him by the way she looked at him. Her direct eye contact showed an openness and a willingness to share.

When she turned her back to check on her family, he looked up and mouthed, "Thank You, Lord."

"Well," she said as she abruptly stood up. "I hate to eat and run, but I really must go. It's getting late, and my parents are starting to give me anxious looks."

Hank tilted his head back and laughed. "I understand, Sophia. When may I see you again?"

Her face turned bright crimson once again, and he felt his heart melt with joy over seeing such honest emotion. She wasn't guarded in the least, which he appreciated. This would be a woman he could share his heart with and not have to worry that she'd trample it.

"I'm not sure," she said after hesitating briefly.

"Sophia, I'm sorry for being so direct if it makes you uncomfortable," he said as he stood beside her. "But I have a good feeling about us, and I'd like to pursue a relationship to see if we might have something in common."

"Oh, that's quite all right," she said in haste. "I just don't know how long it'll take me to. . ." Her voice trailed off as she glanced behind her once again. With concern etched on her face, she looked back at him. "I really need to go now."

Hank decided not to push too hard, or he feared he'd lose her altogether. So he nodded. "Then be on your way. I look forward to seeing you in church on Sunday."

"Good-bye," she said as she hurried away, leaving him standing alone beneath the oak tree.

Hank would rather have walked her over to her parents, but he wasn't sure that would be the wise thing to do under these circumstances. It was clear that they were concerned about their daughter. Besides, he needed to learn what their relationship was with that William fellow who kept casting jealous glances his way.

Once Hank was certain Sophia and her parents were gone, he strolled over to Reverend Breckenridge and placed his hand on the man's shoulder. "May I have a word with you, Reverend?"

"Why, certainly," the reverend replied. "I'll be right there. Give me just a minute with these folks."

Hank politely stepped back and waited, his hands in his pockets as he watched the rest of the people who remained behind, lingering over their desserts and having good, old-fashioned fellowship. This was a sight Hank had been looking for all his adult life. His church back in Alabama had grown so large that most members of the congregation didn't say more than a few polite words to each other. Since moving to Mississippi, Hank had tried to find a way to do the Lord's work when he wasn't at the lumberyard. The Church on the Hill seemed to be the perfect place for him to establish his spiritual roots. This was more of a church family, one he could grow with and be nourished in the Word with.

Finally, when Reverend Breckenridge came to him, some of Hank's urgency had faded. He had all the time in the world to win Sophia's heart. But he knew he needed to have some background information on William.

"It's nice having you join us, Mr. Ellis," Reverend Breckenridge said.

"It's nice to be here. I've really enjoyed the celebration."

"I see you've met Sophia Mayhew." The reverend had gotten right to the point, which was something Hank admired. No beating around the bush.

"Yes, she's a delightful girl."

"That she is," Reverend Breckenridge agreed. "I've always enjoyed the Mayhews. Very loyal to the church, that family."

"Have they been coming to church here long?" Hank asked. He wanted to know how long Sophia had been a Christian, and this was the best way he could think of to ask.

Nodding, the reverend replied, "Since a couple of years before Sophia was born. Her father's family lived on a farm about fifty miles from here. When her parents married, they saved their money and bought a place on the river."

"Are they farmers?" Hank asked.

"Yes, they grow sugarcane and corn."

"We have something in common, then," Hank said with pleasure. "My family farms cotton and corn back in Alabama."

Reverend Breckenridge thrust his hands into his pockets and rocked back on his heels as he studied Hank. "Are you looking for something to have in common with Sophia, Boy?"

So, the reverend was smart as well as blessed spiritually. With a friendly laugh, Hank nodded. "I suppose I am. And to hear that my quest is being rewarded in such a way is music to my ears."

"Sophia is a very sweet girl who is always willing to serve the Lord through good works. She reads her Bible, and she seems to have a fair understanding of the Gospel."

"More good news," Hank said. "I don't know how much more perfect that girl can get."

"Oh, she's not perfect by any means," Reverend Breckenridge said.

Hank frowned. He didn't want to hear anything bad about the woman he planned to court, especially from the pastor of her church.

"Granted, this isn't exactly a flaw, but it's something you need to watch out for."

"And what is this we're talking about?" Hank asked.

"Her family is quite close to the Jacobson family, one of the oldest and most established families in these parts."

"Jacobson?" Hank asked. "Do I need to know these people?"

"Trust me, Boy, if you don't know them already, you will soon. William Jacobson is the young man who kept an eye on you and Sophia."

Hank nodded. "Ah, now I understand."

"Most people have assumed for years that William and Sophia would court for a few years and become engaged. To my knowledge it hasn't happened yet. To be honest with you, I'm a little surprised."

"Surprised?" Hank asked as his heart ached. He didn't realize it was this serious between the woman he was terribly infatuated with and that man with the dirty looks.

"So far, I don't believe William has proposed, and from the way Sophia was talking to you, I'm not sure she'd accept if he did propose."

"So you think I might have a chance?" Hank asked.

Reverend Breckenridge placed his hand gently on Hank's shoulder as Hank had noticed him do to others with whom he spoke. "Yes, it appears that you do have a chance, but be advised to be very careful in how you go about wooing this young lady."

"Oh, I will," Hank said gladly. "I'll be very careful. But I want you to be the first to know that I don't give up easily once I set my mind to something."

The reverend chuckled. "I can see that in you."

Hank chatted with Reverend Breckenridge about upcoming church events for the next several minutes, but his mind wasn't on their discussion. All he could think about was how he could court Sophia without causing a stir within the church.

Chapter 3

How did Mr. Jacobson like your pie?" Dora asked as Sophia entered the kitchen.

"Mr. Jacobson didn't taste my pie."

Sticking her fist on her hip, Dora leaned forward. "What do you mean, he didn't taste your pie? You did go to the pie auction at the church, didn't you?"

"Yes, of course I did, but Mr. Jacobson wasn't able to outbid the other man." Sophia had to bite the insides of her cheeks to keep from smiling. The joy in her heart made her want to jump and shout, but she refrained.

Dora lifted one eyebrow as a smile twitched the corners of her lips. "So, you seein' another man now?"

"Yes," Sophia said before she thought. Then she corrected herself. "No, I'm not seeing another man. It's just that—"

She cut herself off in midsentence, not sure what it was between her and Hank Ellis. Although she found him terribly attractive and fun to be with, she wasn't sure that the reason he bid on her pie was because he didn't know about William's claim to her.

Sophia felt her chest tighten. Ever since she'd been old enough to consider marriage, her parents—and everyone else in the community for that matter—had pushed her toward William. And as much as she cared for William Jacobson, that feeling she always dreamed of when being with the man God had intended for her wasn't there. Her heart never once skipped a beat, and she didn't have a burning desire to see him again when they were apart. In fact, she dreaded the next time he'd call on her. The only time she enjoyed being with him was in church, and that was because she was expected to remain silent.

"Tell me, Child, who is this man?" Dora asked, still staring at her.

Sophia swallowed hard and shook her head. "He's from Alabama."

"Oh, I see. Alabama. I got people there."

"His name's Hank Ellis," Sophia went on.

Dora's smile widened. "You like this man, don't you, Miss Sophie?"

Once again, Sophia's face felt hot. She couldn't help but smile back at Dora. "He's very nice."

"Is he handsome?"

"Oh, yes," Sophia replied. Then she began to tell Dora how Hank looked, and without missing a beat, she went on and on about her conversation with him. By the time she came to a stopping point, she was out of breath.

"How's Mr. Jacobson feel about all this?" Dora asked.

"I don't think he much likes it."

"I s'pect not." Dora chuckled. "Hurts a man like Mr. Jacobson to see somethin' like what you done."

"What'd I do?" Sophia asked, suddenly confused. She couldn't remember doing anything to hurt William.

"You was havin' fun with that new man."

"Yes, but—"

Dora shook her head and clicked her tongue. "No man wants his lady to laugh at another man's jokes."

"Oh, I see." Actually, Sophia didn't see, but she knew William's ego was pretty powerful. And those stares he gave her and Hank were pretty telling of his feelings.

"Don't worry about it, Miss Sophie," Dora said. "He'll get over it. Just make sure you don't burn any bridges. If you start courtin' this new man, Mr. Jacobson's not likely to want you back."

Dora turned to face the wood-burning oven, which she opened. "Mm, mm, that sweet 'tater pie sure do smell good."

"Yes, it does," Sophia agreed, her mind already off and wandering again.

Sophia left the kitchen with its spicy nutmeg and cinnamon scents lingering in her hair. She needed to go upstairs to her room to think. Although she knew how she felt when she was around Hank Ellis, it was only the first time they'd been together. Maybe that feeling she had was one of newness and discovery. Perhaps it would fade over time, and she'd have the same feelings for Hank that she had for William.

"I need to talk to you, Sophia," her mother said from behind the wall in the parlor.

"Not now, Mama. I have a lot to do this evenin'. Maybe after dinner."

"No, Sophia, now." Mama's voice sounded firm, so Sophia stopped in her tracks. She blew out a sigh. "Okay, Mama, but I'm tired, and I need to get my clothes ready for tomorrow."

Noting her mother's tone, Sophia sat on the edge of the sofa, while her mother sat across from her in the rocker. *This should be quite a lecture,* Sophia thought, bracing herself for what was sure to come.

"Who was that young man who bought your pie?" Mama said, getting right to the point.

"Hank Ellis," Sophia replied. She bit her lip to keep from sounding too eager about Hank. Surely, Mama wouldn't approve of him for the simple fact that he wasn't William.

"Where does he come from?"

"Alabama. His family farms cotton and corn."

Mama paused for a few seconds before continuing her interrogation. "Is he a Christian?"

"I assume so, Mama. He goes to church, and he reads his Bible."

"Plenty of people go to church, yet we don't know what's in their hearts," Mama said. "We must be careful of those who have unsavory motives."

"Unsavory motives?" Sophia repeated. "What do you mean by that, Mama?"

Another long silence. "Be very careful of this man, Sophia. And don't ever forget that William loves you and most likely wants to marry you."

"But what if I don't want to marry him?" Sophia asked her mother for the first time.

"Sophia! How can you say that after spending only an afternoon with this stranger? You and William have known each other practically all your lives. He's kind and gentle, and he comes from a very good family. We know nothing of this Ellis family." She paused to look at Sophia with tenderness. "What you're feeling now is a fascination with someone you don't know."

"You're right, Mama," Sophia said as she sank back on the sofa, knowing it was futile to argue.

"William should be here in about an hour," Mama continued. "Go on upstairs and freshen up. I expect you to be on your best behavior in his presence, and there will be absolutely no talk of this Hank Ellis."

"Yes, Mama."

Sophia stood and did as she was told. She knew her mother wanted what was right for her. Besides, she was probably right. William had been steadfast and true for years. Hank was exciting simply because he was new.

Oh, but how she wished William didn't have to come for dinner—not after such a perfect afternoon. Sophia wished she had at least the remainder of the day to dwell on hers and Hank's conversation. She'd enjoyed every moment of banter, with more laughter than she'd shared with anyone in her life. Talking with Hank lifted her heart and made her want to sing. Now she had to get herself ready to spend time with William, which meant preparing for the song in her heart to dissolve.

As she was putting the final touches on her hair, Sophia heard a commotion downstairs. She stopped and leaned toward the door so she could hear better. The voice that floated up wasn't that of William, but of Hank. A smile instantly crept onto her lips, and her heart began to pound.

She took off running down the stairs, still trying to fasten the clip in the back of her hair. Hank was standing at the foot of the stairs, looking up and grinning right back at her.

"You left this," he said, holding out the pie tin. "I wanted to return it."

"My, that was fast," Sophia said. "You could have kept it until you finished the pie."

He looked down at his feet sheepishly. "I already finished it, Sophia."

She tilted her head back and laughed, with her mother looking on in dismay. "Sophia, I'll have to insist you take your guest into the parlor. We're expecting our invited company to arrive any minute now."

Sophia had never heard her mother take on such a tone. It was one of open hostility and anger. When she glanced at Hank, she saw he'd noticed it too.

"No, Ma'am," he said to her mother, tipping his head in a friendly gesture. "I only wanted to drop off the pie tin. I must be getting back to the boardinghouse. Tomorrow starts awfully early at the lumberyard."

Sophia's mother's eyebrows were raised as she nodded. "Thank you, Mr. Ellis. We certainly appreciate your consideration." She sounded very formal and much too polite.

Just as Hank turned to leave, Sophia took a chance and ran after him. "Wait," she said. "I'll walk you to your horse."

"That won't be necessary, Sophia," he replied with a glance toward her mother. "I shall see you in church on Sunday."

Sophia shrank back and nodded. "Okay, then. Good-bye, Hank."

Once Hank was outside, he put on his hat and waved in one fluid motion. "It's been a pleasure meeting you, Ma'am," he said to her mother.

"Nice to have met you too, Mr. Ellis. We'll most likely be seeing more of you." She lifted her chin as she added, "In church, of course."

Although it was a minor omission, Sophia noticed her mother didn't offer the usual, "Do come back." Instead, she'd given him the cold shoulder in her own polite way.

Long after her mother went inside, Sophia remained on the front porch, watching the cloud of dust kicked up by Hank's horse as it galloped away. She felt as though she must do something to see him again. But what? She didn't want to deceive Mama and Daddy. They loved her and only wanted what was best for her.

Several minutes later, she heard the shuffle of her mother standing at the door. "I suggest you stop pining for something you know nothing about and concentrate on making all this up to William."

"Make what up to William, Mama?" she asked.

"He was none too happy about all that carryin' on you and Mr. Ellis did in the church yard this afternoon."

"We weren't carryin' on. We were just talking," Sophia objected.

"I heard you laughing all the way across the yard, Sophia. How do you think that makes William feel?"

Sophia hung her head. She had no idea how that had made William feel, but she knew how Hank made her feel. But Mama was right about not knowing Hank well enough to get all worked up over him. Perhaps he was lonely and wanted feminine companionship, and she'd been the girl he'd picked because he wasn't aware of William. Now that he knew, he might not be so eager to court her, in spite of what he'd said.

Once Hank was completely out of sight, Sophia went inside. She headed straight for the kitchen, where she found Dora pulling biscuits out of the oven.

"Need some help, Dora?" she asked.

"If you can hand me that jar of butter over there, I'd be most grateful," Dora said stiffly. Sophia knew something was up with her.

"What's the matter, Dora?" Sophia asked.

"Nothin'." She banged the tray of biscuits onto the trivets on the counter before turning to face Sophia. "Your mama just gave me a tongue-lashin'."

"She what?"

"You heard me. She tol' me to mind my own business about Mr. Jacobson."

Sophia leaned back and studied the woman standing before her. Dora had become her best friend, since she'd practically raised her.

"What'd she say, Dora?" Sophia asked.

"It don't matter now, Sophie. All I know's I can't tell you to follow your heart. Your mama reminded me how much Mr. Jacobson appreciates my biscuits and fried chicken."

In spite of her frustration, Sophia laughed. Mama sure did know how to get her point across without having to come right out and be direct.

"Let's get the dining room set up before Mr. Jacobson arrives. He's likely to be starvin' since he didn't eat at the church."

"There was plenty of food," Sophia said. "If he didn't eat, it's his own fault, and it serves him right if he's hungry."

"That's what I told your mama, but she just gave me one of her looks."

Sophia knew that look. In fact, she'd seen it a few minutes ago when Hank came.

By the time William arrived, Sophia and Dora had set the table and all the food was on platters, ready to be served. There was enough food to feed twice the number of people who were there.

"Looks mighty tasty, Miz Mayhew," William said. "Tell Dora how much I appreciate her goin' to all this trouble."

"I'm right here, Mr. Jacobson," Dora said from the kitchen door. "I hope you enjoy it."

Sophia settled back in her chair and nibbled on small bites of the food she'd put on her plate. She couldn't remember a time when conversation had been so strained.

What bothered her the most was that all this bother was over William being outbid by Hank. Sophia knew she should be flattered, and she was to some degree, but she wished she didn't have to feel as if every single move she made was being watched. If it weren't for some unspoken agreement between her and William, Sophia was certain no one would be making such a fuss.

It was Sophia's father who brought up the subject of the lumberyard. Sophia's mama shot him that look, but he wasn't paying a bit of attention.

"Did you know that nice young supervisor at the lumberyard is regularly attending our church?" he asked.

"Why yes, I was aware of that," William said. "In fact, he's the man who bid on Sophia's pie."

"Oh," her father said, his fork inches from his mouth. He put his fork down, coughed into his napkin, then shook his head. "I didn't realize that was the man."

Sophia's mother tried her best to change the subject and bring on a more palatable discussion, but the damage had been done, and William was back to his moping self. Sophia wondered if he knew how unattractive he was when he frowned.

After dessert, which had been barely touched, William folded his napkin and placed it beside his plate. "I really must run now. Papa is expecting me to help him set lines in the pond tomorrow. We have to clean out the adult bream so the fingerlings can get food."

"If you have extra, we sure do love fried bream, Son," Sophia's daddy said. "I'll be glad to swap you some corn in exchange for a mess of fish."

"I'll tell Papa," William said with his usual somber expression. "No doubt he'll send me over with some."

Everyone stood up and walked William to the door. Sophia's father tried to chat with him, but William wasn't in the mood for small talk. That was just fine, since Sophia wasn't in the mood to be around William with him acting this way.

Once they were back inside the house, Sophia's mother turned and looked at her. She shook her head, then headed upstairs. Daddy, on the other hand, wanted to talk.

"So how do you like that new fella?"

"I beg your pardon, Daddy?" Sophia asked. Her father had always been more open and direct than her mother, but this still caught her off guard.

"That man from the lumberyard. The one who outbid William for your pie. What is he like?"

Sophia started to relax but then caught herself. She knew how her parents felt about William. "He's very nice, Daddy."

Her father nodded and rubbed his neck. "I'm glad, Sweetheart, but don't forget your relationship with William. There's talk that he's getting close to proposing."

Letting out another of her sighs that were coming with greater frequency, Sophia forced a smile. "So I've heard."

All night, Sophia lay in bed, pondering her dilemma. William was the man she'd been informally promised to, but Hank was the man who made her heart flutter. She kept going over what everyone wanted to remind her of. William was always there, and he was reliable. Hank was someone she knew very little about. It wasn't hard to figure out why everyone was so concerned. People knew William and loved him. Hank was the new man in the community who might one day up and take a notion to leave.

Sophia got very little rest that night, but she managed to awaken at the crack of dawn. She hurried and put on her clothes so she could meet Dora in the kitchen to help with breakfast, one of her favorite events of the day.

"Miss Sophie, you won't believe what everyone's sayin'," Dora said as she handed Sophia the pan for eggs.

"What, Dora?"

"That new man, Mr. Ellis, has plans for you."

"Plans for me?" Sophia said, her voice squeaking with excitement. "What kind of plans?"

"Well," Dora began as she thrust out a hip and shoved her fist on it. She looked away as she thought, then turned back to Sophia. "He told the reverend that he planned to give Mr. Jacobson a little competition."

In spite of how Sophia knew her parents would take this news, she grinned. It felt mighty good to have Hank willing to take such a big risk, just because he wanted to be with her.

"How did he respond?" Sophia asked. "Do you know?"

Dora shrugged. "From the way my daughter made it sound, he didn't seem to mind."

Cleo, Dora's daughter, was Reverend Breckenridge's housekeeper, so she often had the inside story of whatever was going on at the church. Most times, Dora didn't discuss matters her daughter told her, but Sophia guessed the older woman had made an exception this time because she knew the topic was important to Sophia.

"I wish everyone else had the same feelings," Sophia said.

"Only thing the reverend is worried about is how everyone else in the church will take this."

"Everyone else?" Sophia said. "Why would everyone else have a reaction?"

"You know how people are, Sophie. They make it their business to mind yours."

"But this is the church, Dora." Sophia carried a platter of biscuits to the rough-hewn pine table and sat down.

"People's people," Dora said with a shrug. "Don't matter whether they're Christians or not, they still talk."

As Sophia nibbled on a biscuit, she knew that Dora spoke the truth. Not only did she have to worry about upsetting her parents and William, she had the entire congregation to be concerned about. They all loved William, and most of them would stand behind him, no matter what.

"What should I do, Dora?" Sophia asked. "I like William. I truly do."

"But do you love him?" Dora asked.

"I'm not sure, but I don't think so." She sniffled. "Mama says I'll learn to love him over time."

Dora clucked. "Miss Sophie, it ain't none of my business, but I do know your face lights up whenever you mention Mr. Ellis's name."

"He's so fun and filled with joy," Sophia moaned. "Why couldn't William be more like that?"

"Some folks is just serious. Nothing you can do about that."

"I know, but I don't want to be serious all the time. God has blessed us with the ability to experience laughter, and I want to do it as much as possible."

"Then do what's on your heart, Miss Sophie," Dora advised. "Just be prepared to face everyone who don't agree with what you think you want."

Chapter 4

Sophia leaned back and thought about Dora's words: "Do what's on your heart." Those were powerful words, and Sophia wasn't sure if she could follow that advice. William's feelings were at stake, and she wasn't about to hurt the man her parents favored. Doing something so outrageous would surely upset more than a few people.

As she thought about the situation, she realized there was William, Mama, Daddy, William's parents. Then there was the woman who always grinned when she spotted William and Sophia standing next to each other. Besides that, many people from the church had let it be known they wanted an invitation to the wedding when it happened, not if.

"Miss Sophie," Dora said, startling Sophia from her thoughts. "You come help me stir these grits while I pick the bacon out of the pan."

Sophia was thankful for the interruption, since her thoughts had begun to depress her. She was terribly confused about what was the right thing to do. Would a good, Christ-loving woman so much as entertain thoughts of taking up with a virtual stranger when the man she'd known all her life was standing, watching?

"Don't you worry no more, Miss Sophie," Dora said as she took the wooden spoon out of Sophia's hand. "Let the good Lord do things in His own time; that's what I always say. And I dare say that's good advice."

"Yes," Sophia agreed. "I dare say it too. I'll pray about it and let Him take over."

A shuffling sound at the kitchen door got Sophia's attention. It was Mama.

"Mornin', Miz Mayhew," Dora said as she nudged Sophia out of the way. "Mistah Mayhew on his way?"

"Why yes, Dora, he's coming down directly. C'mon, Sophia, join me in the dining room to wait for your daddy."

"Okay, Mama." Sophia followed her mama into the dining room. Silence fell between them for a long moment.

Sophia's mother pulled out her chair but remained standing behind it, waiting for her husband to join them for a blessing before the family sat down to eat. She glanced at Dora as she came through the doors with a couple of platters balanced on her arms and shook her head. "Dora, I overheard you telling Sophia to let the good Lord do things in His own time. You weren't referring to something personal, now were you?"

Dora glanced at Sophia, then back at her employer. "Yes, Ma'am, it was very personal."

Sophia let out a long breath. She never would have expected Dora to lie for her, and thank the Lord she hadn't. It truly was a personal matter—one she didn't feel like discussing with Mama. Not yet, anyway.

When Sophia's daddy came to the table, his eyes gleamed with excitement. "What's goin' on, Daddy?" Sophia asked. "You look like a squirmin' snake on a hot summer day."

Grinning from ear to ear, he reached out and patted Sophia on the shoulder. "Our daughter sure is intuitive, Maggie. I do have some good news."

"Good news?" Sophia's mother asked, lifting one eyebrow inquisitively.

"Very good news, in fact. We have thirty men from the church coming over to finish working on the barn on Saturday." He turned to Dora as she came through the door to the dining room. "You hear that, Dora? We'll need plenty of food to feed an army of hungry men on Saturday."

Dora glanced at Sophia before turning to him and nodding. "Yes, Suh, I'll make sure there's plenty."

"And tell your folks they're welcome to join us," he added. "Every man should come to work, and the women can join us for a feast."

"I'll tell 'em, Mistah Mayhew. I'm sure they'll all want to be here."

Sophia's daddy turned back to her and her mama. "I want to make sure all the men have plenty to eat. If you speak to any of the women folk, let them know they're welcome to come."

"I have a social with some of the ladies tomorrow afternoon," Sophia's mama said. "Why don't you come along, Sophia? You're getting to the age when you'll need to know what's going on in our group."

In other words, Sophia thought, *marrying age.*

Sophia couldn't think of anything more boring than her mama's social club, but she nodded. "Okay, Mama, but I don't like sewing, so don't expect me to bring any."

Her mama tilted her head back and laughed. "Did we raise a tomboy, Edward?"

"I certainly hope not," Daddy replied.

"Whatever I am, I certainly won't be one who makes my own clothes."

"At least you're a good cook." Sophia's daddy shoveled a forkful of food into his mouth, then wiped his chin with his napkin as he stood up. "Gotta run, Sugah," he said as he leaned over and kissed her mama. "Try and stay out of trouble, Sophia."

"Yes, Daddy."

Why her daddy ever said that, she'd never know. Sophia never got into trouble. She had always been the most compliant child she'd ever known, but her parents were the kindest and most loving, so she figured they got what they deserved—a good, obedient daughter.

"You might want to bring some of those blueberry muffins Dora taught you to make, Sophia," her mama said, interrupting Sophia's thoughts. "I'm sure the other ladies would appreciate that."

"I'll bake them first thing after breakfast in the morning," Sophia said. "That way they'll be fresh and warm."

"Mm-mm. I can just taste them now." Her mama closed her eyes and grinned with her mouth closed, looking like she'd had a taste of heaven.

As soon as her mama left the dining room, Sophia lingered behind to help Dora clean up after breakfast. She wasn't about to leave with this big of a mess. Besides, she felt like talking to the wise elderly woman who knew practically everything going on in the community.

"I heard you tell your mama you'd go with her to her social tomorrow, Miss Sophie."

Dora hadn't wasted a single moment before speaking out and letting herself be heard. That's another thing Sophia loved about her.

"Yes, I'm going. Any idea what I should talk about?"

"Oh, Honey, I'm sure they'll give you plenty to talk about with all the questions they're sure to ask. You'll wish you could just curl up in a corner and be quiet before the morning's over."

Sophia let out a sigh. "You're probably right, Dora. How should I answer their questions?" She knew she didn't have to mention that all the questions were likely to be about William.

Dora stopped, put down the dish she'd picked up, stuck her fist on her hip, and bit her bottom lip as she thought. Then she turned to Sophia. "Just answer them honestly. Don't tell too much, and be sure to watch out for trick questions."

"Trick questions?"

"Those women are smart, and I'm sure they've been listenin' to all the talk that's been goin' on since Mr. Ellis bid on your apple pie. They'll find a way to set you up, Miss Sophie, so you better watch yourself."

"Oh," Sophia said as she gathered up the silverware. "Keep my answers short and don't tell them anything they don't ask, right, Dora?"

"That's right, Miss Sophie. You might even think of a question or two to ask them." Grinning she added, "Most folks love to yap about themselves. That'll get their mind off your business."

"Good idea."

After they cleared away the breakfast dishes, Sophia headed back to her room. The kitchen was hot, and she needed to freshen up before she went into town. Her mother had left her some money to pick up a few things at the general merchandise store. They were almost out of flour, and she needed some for the muffins in the morning.

The horse and buggy were ready for her when she went out on the front lawn. Other than the fact that Sophia didn't love the man her parents wanted her to marry, she felt that she was a very fortunate woman to have all the blessings God had given her. She never went without anything she needed, and her parents made certain she had most of what she wanted. If only she could figure out a way to prevent William from proposing, Sophia knew she'd be the happiest woman on earth.

She was halfway to town when she spotted the single horse and rider in the distance. Slowing down, she crinkled her forehead. Not many people came this way at this time of day. She wondered who in the world it could be.

The moment she was able to make out the form of the rider, Sophia felt excitement spread from her mind to her heart. It was Hank. He was coming to visit her. Nothing could have flattered her more.

Then she realized she was being silly. Hank could have been going to any number of places, including the farm on the other side of the Mayhews'. And even if he were going to her place, perhaps it was to see Daddy.

"Whoa," he said as he brought his horse to a standstill beside Sophia's buggy. Tipping his hat, he nodded. "Sophia, it's so nice to see you out and about."

"Good to see you, too, Hank."

"I'm glad you feel that way, Sophia, because I was coming to visit you."

Sophia was so flustered she couldn't speak. His quick, frank comment had caught her completely by surprise. "I, uh, I have to go into town for a few things. Would you care to join me?"

"That's an excellent idea. I'll just ride alongside, and we can chat when we get there."

Her hands shook as she held onto the reins. It took everything Sophia had to control her horse, but she knew she must not get too worked up over a simple social call from this very handsome gentleman who just happened to overbid on her pie. That thought caused a positively giddy feeling to wash over her.

When they arrived in town, Hank took care of her horse while she gathered her purse and parasol from the buggy. When she had gathered all her belongings, he offered his arm. Reluctantly, she took it.

"Oh, my," Mrs. Crandall from the church said as she passed them on the street. Sophia heard her whisper to her husband, "Did you see the Mayhew girl with that strange man? She's been promised to the Jacobson boy. I wonder if her folks know."

"Better keep that to yourself, Viola," her husband said. "You have no idea what's going on with those people."

Sophia tensed. Although they were whispering, it was painfully obvious to her that they wanted her to hear.

"I suppose I better keep some distance between us," Hank finally said as he gently pulled her arm from his. "I wouldn't want to be the talk of the town when I've barely warmed my room at the boardinghouse."

"That's most likely a good idea," Sophia agreed.

Hank walked with her as she shopped, and he carried her purchases to the buggy. Afterward, he turned to her and softly said, "I told you, Sophia, that I think we would be wonderful together, if I can ever get past your protective father." He offered a contrite grin. "Not that I don't respect your father."

Shaking her head in understanding, Sophia said, "You'll have to excuse Daddy. He's not used to all the goings-on with gentlemen callers and my pies being auctioned at church."

Leaning back and belting out a deep belly laugh, Hank replied, "I can certainly understand. If I had a daughter as beautiful and talented as you, I'd keep her under lock and key."

"He hasn't exactly done that," Sophia said softly.

"No, but he only lets you out of his sight when you're with William Jacobson."

"But—"

Hank reached out and gently touched his finger to her lips. "You mustn't feel that you have to explain, Sophia. I understand—at least I think I do. What I have to do is overcome that one big obstacle, William."

"Yes," Sophia said, her head held down, "I'm afraid so."

"Don't fear anything, my dear. If you and I are meant to be, then the Lord will pave my way. I have the utmost confidence in His ability to bring two searching hearts together."

"Yes, I believe you're probably right."

"Just tell me one thing, Sophia."

She turned and looked him in the eye, something she realized was a mistake the moment she saw the depth and intensity of their blueness. Her heart raced. "What's that, Hank?"

"Do you love William?"

"No, don't be silly. Although I am very fond of him, I only want to be his friend. You must believe that."

"Oh, I do. And since you have convinced me of your intentions toward him, I want you to know I plan to pursue you with all my abilities."

Sophia felt the heat as it crept up her neck and onto her face. "That's very sweet of you, Hank."

He laughed. "Sweet isn't the word I'd use, but I'll take it from you right now. Be warned that I can be very persistent."

They'd reached her buggy and paused to continue talking while people passed by, pretending not to stare. For once, Sophia wished she didn't know so many people.

Hank reached out and touched her chin, gently guiding it so she was looking him in the eye. "Don't worry about what everyone thinks, Sophia."

"I can't help it," she admitted. "Most of them have known me all my life."

"They know William, too, right?"

She nodded. The look on his face was one of understanding and kindness, not anger as she might have expected from someone else.

"You said you aren't engaged to William. Does this still hold true?"

"Oh yes, that's absolutely the truth."

"Then don't worry. You haven't promised your hand in marriage to another man, so you're free to be with me. We're doing nothing wrong, Sophia, so let yourself have fun."

In her head she knew he was right, and her heart was with Hank. But that didn't stop the guilt of letting her parents down as well as disappointing all the wonderful people from the church.

"I'll be working with everyone from the church on Saturday, so you'll see me then," he said.

"Saturday?"

"Your father's barn, remember?"

"Oh, that's right. My father told us about it at breakfast this morning. William will be there, too."

"Yes, I know, Sophia," he said as he continued smiling at her. "And I promise I won't cause a scene, even if I feel like it."

Sophia frowned at him. "Causing a scene wouldn't be a very good idea at all, Hank." She remembered the scene he'd caused at the church Fourth of July celebration when he'd bid such an exorbitant amount on her pie. Even though he hadn't intended to upset people, she knew that he had. Hopefully, that wouldn't happen on Saturday. But she didn't dare say anything about it.

"See you on Saturday?" he asked.

Sophia nodded but didn't say a word as she got into her buggy with Hank's help.

"Have a safe ride home," he told her as she pulled away.

"You, too, Hank," she whispered so softly she doubted he'd heard her.

All the way home, Sophia played over in her mind how it felt to be with Hank. It seemed so right, yet she knew how her family felt about William. Why did being with a man have to be so complicated?

Carrying the provisions into her house, Sophia was deep in thought about how she'd handle being around both William and Hank at the same time. She almost slammed into her mother, who was walking out the door right when she stepped up and across the threshold.

"Sophia, I'm shocked at your behavior this morning," Mama said without so much as a greeting.

"My behavior?" Sophia asked. She was confused. What had she done?

"Mrs. Crandall stopped by to let me know she'd seen you in town. Why didn't you tell me you were meeting Mr. Ellis? Do you have something to hide?"

Sophia's hand flew to her mouth as she found herself speechless. She knew Mrs. Crandall would talk, but she had no idea it would happen this quickly.

From the look on her mama's face, Sophia knew she had some explaining to do. She wasn't sure if what actually happened would be sufficient to satisfy her mother, based on the angry glare in her eyes.

Chapter 5

Sophia knew better than to lie. Not only would she not be able to sleep at night, she knew the Lord would accept nothing but the truth from her lips.

"Yes, Mama," she said as she hung her head. "I did see Hank Ellis."

"Why didn't you tell me you were meeting him?" Mama asked, her face registering pain and disappointment.

"It wasn't planned. He just happened to be riding out to see us, and we met on the road. Then he escorted me to town."

Silence fell over Sophia and her mama. If this was any indication of how things would be if she continued to see Hank, Sophia wondered if it was worth it. But when his face appeared in her mind, she knew it was well worth whatever it took because of the joy he brought her.

When her mama finally spoke, it wasn't with anger as Sophia had feared. It was with a weariness that was almost as bad.

"I only hope William doesn't catch wind of this. He will be so hurt if he finds out you've been meeting that stranger, Mr. Ellis, behind his back."

"He's not a stranger, Mama," Sophia reminded her.

"Maybe not a total stranger, but we don't know anything about him or his family."

Sophia had never defied her mother, but she felt the urge to stand up for the man her heart longed to see again. "I do know he's a Christian."

"How do you know?" her mama asked.

"He told me."

"Plenty of people walk around talking about their faith, Sophia. But we know William and that his faith is true. We've watched him grow up in the church, and we see him in action. His faith in the Lord is very real, day in and day out."

"Yes, I realize that, but I don't love William."

"Love will come in time." Sophia watched her mama's face change shape as she remembered something, most likely her courtship with Sophia's daddy.

Although no one had ever told Sophia, she suspected her parents' relationship had begun much the same as hers and William's. Their parents had known each other all their lives, and when her mama and daddy were teenagers, they'd attended the same church functions together. Based on how her mama reacted to Sophia's voiced concern about the lack of spark she felt toward William, she figured her parents had "grown to love each other" just as her mother had said would happen between her and William.

For years, that had been enough for Sophia. At least, it was enough until she'd met Hank. But now that she'd experienced that excitement and joy that she knew was possible between a man and a woman, she didn't want to settle for less.

"Run on to your room, Sophia," her mama finally said after they'd both pondered the circumstances of the day. "You need to think about what you're doing, and I'll speak to your daddy."

"Okay, Mama," Sophia said as she turned and did as she was told. She welcomed the opportunity to be alone with her thoughts, which would no doubt be about Hank.

Over the course of the next couple of days, several visitors stopped by the house to report on what they'd seen in town—Sophia and Hank talking intimately beside her buggy. Sophia was amazed at how people could speak of something they knew nothing about.

Dora had been right about the social. The ladies were very smart, and they knew just the right questions to ask, nearly throwing Sophia into a dither as she tried to avoid discussing how she felt whenever she was around Hank. Fortunately, she'd managed to turn things around once she remembered Dora's advice to start asking questions of the ladies. They absolutely loved talking about themselves. She knew this would only work for so long before they were on to her scheme.

Sophia wished Daddy would say something to clear the air, but he didn't. He remained silent, but he often looked at her with a curious expression, one that Sophia had never seen on his face before. She wondered what was on his mind.

Meals were strained, but nothing was mentioned of her encounter with Hank. If her parents would say something, Sophia could at least explain what had happened to both of them at one time. She thought of simply blurting out the story, but she decided it would be best if one of her parents brought up the subject. And they didn't until Saturday morning.

Sophia was startled when her daddy walked into the kitchen as she and Dora prepared breakfast for the crew that was due to arrive soon to help work on the barn. "Good mornin', Daddy," she said over her shoulder as she rolled out another sheet of biscuit dough.

"Hey, Sugah," he said as he bent over and kissed her cheek. "May I have a word with you before the men and their families start arriving?"

"Sure, Daddy, have a seat. I'll be right there."

Dora nudged her out of the way as she gave her a knowing look. "Go on, Miss Sophie. Talk to your daddy. I'll finish up here."

As Sophia sat down across from her daddy, she had a sinking feeling she was about to hear something she wouldn't like. "Yes, Daddy, what did you want to discuss this morning?"

"You and William," he replied. "And Mr. Ellis."

From the tone of his voice and how differently he'd addressed the two suitors, Sophia knew exactly how her daddy felt about both of them. She sighed.

"I understand you've been taking up with that new young man," he began. "I'm not so sure that's such a good idea."

Sophia sat and listened, wishing she could argue and tell her daddy how she felt, but she suspected he wouldn't pay much attention.

"As you know, everyone is expecting William to propose to you soon, and I'd hate for you to ruin the opportunity to take such a well-suited husband for yourself."

Now she had to say something. "But Daddy, I'm not so sure I want to marry William."

"Don't say such a thing, Sophia. William Jacobson is a fine young man, and he'd make an excellent husband for you. He knows how to run his family farm, and he loves the Lord."

"Yes, I know, but I don't feel. . .well, I don't have those feelings for him." There. She'd said it.

"Those feelings," her daddy began, "can get you into an awful lot of trouble, Sophia. People have been talking, and no one knows anything about this Mr. Ellis except that he's from Alabama and he works in the lumberyard."

"Daddy, he's a Christian man who makes me laugh." Sophia wasn't able to put all her other thoughts and feelings into words, so she knew her argument sounded mighty weak.

"Making you laugh is the last thing a husband needs to concern himself with, Sophia. You must look at the overall man. A good husband is someone who will provide well for you, uplift you spiritually, and be a good daddy to your children."

"Yes, I know, Daddy."

"Apparently you don't know as well as you think you do. I want you to stop this nonsense and concentrate on you and William."

His tone was strong and filled with conviction. Sophia bit back the words that threatened to pour from her lips. She didn't dare say the things that came to mind, so she remained silent.

"The men and their families are starting to arrive," her mama said from the kitchen door.

Sophia was startled by her mama's voice. She quickly stood up, straightened her apron, and resumed her position beside Dora as her daddy left the kitchen out the back door to greet his workers.

"Oh, Dora, what am I to do?" Sophia cried as soon as they were alone in the kitchen. "Daddy doesn't seem to understand about my feelings toward William and Hank."

"Yes, Miss Sophie, I heard every word. Don't do a thing. The Lord will take care of everything in His own time. Be the sweet young woman you always are, and I'll pray for you."

Sophia reached out and covered Dora's hand with her own. "Thanks, Dora. I love you."

Dora reached up and rubbed her nose with the back of her wrist as she sniffled. "I love you too, Miss Sophie. Now run along and carry some of them trays out to the workers. They need to eat something before they get started on the barn."

Sophia did as she was told, but she didn't like having to face her daddy and possibly William. Fortunately that problem was avoided because Mama was waiting by the table set up for the food.

"I trust you'll behave yourself, Sophia?" Mama said as she took the food from Sophia.

"Of course, Mama," she replied without looking her mama in the eye. It wasn't that she planned to misbehave; rather she wasn't about to be rude to Hank if he should strike up a conversation with her.

The sound of horses came up the dusty road, capturing both women's attention. It was Reverend Breckenridge and Hank Ellis. They'd come together, bringing a smile to Sophia's lips.

"Well, I'm not believin' this," Mama muttered. She fidgeted with her apron before turning back to Sophia. "Run on inside and get some preserves."

With a much lighter step, Sophia headed back to the kitchen, not wasting a single second. She grabbed a basket from the pantry, then pulled down half a dozen jars of preserves she'd put up weeks ago.

"They all here yet?" Dora hollered from behind.

"No, Dora, but they're gettin' here."

Sophia hurried back out with the preserves just in time to greet the reverend and Hank as they came to the table. She smiled at the older gentleman before turning to Hank.

"Hello, Mr. Ellis," she said in as formal of a tone as she could manage for the sake of her mother who was staring holes through her back.

He tipped his hat. "Sophia," he said softly, a mischievous smile teasing his lips. Then he turned to her mama. "Miz Mayhew, it's a mighty nice mornin' to work on a barn. I'm happy your husband invited me."

Sophia's mother appeared not to know what to say. She glanced back and forth between the reverend and Hank, as she shifted from one foot to the other.

Reverend Breckenridge slapped Hank on the back and pulled him forward by the arm. "Grab a plate, Hank, and pile it high with biscuits. Sophia is handy in the kitchen. She learned from the best. Did I ever tell you about their housekeeper, Dora?"

"No, Sir, I don't believe you did," Hank replied, still smiling.

Sophia could tell her mama didn't want Hank lingering around her any longer than necessary, but she was too polite to say anything in front of the reverend. Hank was a genius to have thought of enlisting Reverend Breckenridge for a traveling partner.

Reverend Breckenridge motioned for everyone to bow their heads for the blessing. When he finished, he grabbed a biscuit, chomped down on it, and said, "Mmmm, this is mighty fine cookin'. Biscuit melts in your mouth." He turned to Sophia and nodded. "You outdid yourself this time, Sophia."

"Aw, Reverend, biscuits are the easiest things in the world to make."

"I'm sure to someone as competent as you in the kitchen, they are," Hank said, "but if I were to attempt anything like this, we'd wind up with charcoal for breakfast."

Even Sophia's mama smiled at this comment. Hank had already begun working his charm on her, to Sophia's delight.

"We best get to work, Reverend," Hank said after devouring a half dozen biscuits and a couple of slices of cured ham. "I aim to work until this job is finished."

"That's my boy," the reverend said as he and Hank walked toward the barn, where several men had already begun working.

"Mama, would you like for me to bring you something?" Sophia asked.

Her mama was still staring after the men. She slowly turned back to Sophia and shook her head. "No, Sophia, I don't think so, not right now. Maybe later."

Sophia grabbed the opportunity to run back inside to tell Dora about what had just transpired. Dora listened with obvious delight, her eyes glistening and her lips turning up at the corners.

When Sophia finished, Dora looked up and said, "Praise the Lord. He's already working on your mama's heart. Now let's see how your young man gets on with your daddy."

"Daddy's much more difficult, I'm afraid," Sophia said. "He doesn't take to charm quite like Mama and me."

"Child, the Lord don't need no charm to do His work. All He needs is your trust."

Sophia sighed. "Yes, you're right, Dora. I have to have faith that I'll be free to love whomever I want."

"Remember what those men at the church Fourth of July celebration said before the pie auction?" Dora said.

"Yes," Sophia replied. "One man in particular. Hank's speech was particularly moving."

"Why yes, it was. But they were all good because they spoke of freedom and how we can make choices in this great country."

Sophia noticed the mist in Dora's eyes. Dora's parents and grandparents had been slaves during the Civil War. Until their freedom, they'd had to worship behind closed doors and in the small field shack they'd used as a makeshift chapel. Now, they could worship openly in the church that had been built specifically for the freed slaves. However, they had to work hard to share the Gospel, since many other former slaves had never heard the Word. Those who knew the Lord worked tirelessly, sharing their faith with others after putting in long days at jobs, often working for their former masters. This was a significant test of their faith, and Dora's people had passed with flying colors. Sophia envied the strength she saw in Dora and Hank.

Her own faith had been with her since birth. She'd never doubted the Lord's sovereignty, but she'd never had any reason to worry either. Dora, on the other hand, was a woman whose faith had brought her through all sorts of adversity.

Now Sophia found herself wondering about Hank's faith. Had he always been a Christian with parents who brought him to church faithfully and served the Lord with open hearts? Or had he come to faith later in life? Something about him was different, but she couldn't put her finger on it. She'd have to pay closer attention when he spoke and perhaps ask him if the opportunity presented itself.

Sophia continued cooking alongside Dora in the kitchen throughout the morning, cleaning up from breakfast and then starting the noon meal. All those men would be starving after working all day on that barn. From the looks of things, they'd be done before sundown, which would make her daddy awfully happy.

Ever since Reverend Breckenridge had come to pastor the Church on the Hill, people had started coming together to help each other in a way they hadn't in the past. Before he'd arrived, people offered their hands to each other, but it was never as organized as it was now.

Reverend Breckenridge had brought the men together, insisting they form what he called an "army of servants" who would do anything they needed to help one another. To everyone's amazement, this didn't require more work. The congregation grew closer, and the activities gave them the opportunity to strengthen their faith through fellowship and working toward a common goal.

As the sun moved to the top of the sky, the men began to come out of the barn, mostly for water. It was hot, and they were thirsty. Sophia was right there with pitchers of water and plenty of cups.

William came out of the barn wearing his usual somber expression. He walked directly over to Sophia and said, "I'll be in church early tomorrow morning."

"That's nice, William," Sophia replied without looking him in the eye. She knew he wanted her to say she'd get there early, too, if that pleased him, but she didn't.

However, her daddy was right behind William. "I think it would be a mighty fine idea if we got there early, too, Sophia."

"Whatever you say, Daddy."

Sophia turned to get more food, but her daddy reached out and grabbed her by the arm. "Why don't you and William have lunch together under the tree over there?" He pointed to the large oak tree on the edge of the lawn, away from the rest of the people.

William nodded, picked up his plate, and headed over in that direction. Sophia didn't have a chance to argue. He was gone before she could say anything.

"Let William know you're interested in him," her mama hissed from behind. "He's beginning to worry that you don't care about him. I can see it in his eyes."

"It's not that I don't care, Mama—"

"Go on before he thinks something's happened." Her mama nearly pushed her over, she shoved her so hard.

Chapter 6

Sophia," William said as she approached where he was standing. "How have you been?"

"Just fine, William," she replied politely. "And you?"

"Can't complain. We have most of the work done on the barn. Just a few finishing touches and we'll have it in tip-top shape." No smile, just his low voice. Sophia glanced around, looking for Hank, then she turned back to William.

"That's good. You always were very handy."

Sophia was running out of things to say, and she hadn't been standing there for more than a minute or two. She couldn't help thinking that would never happen with Hank. They'd always have something to say, no matter how long they were together.

William shrugged as he squatted down on the ground. "Care to join me?"

"Uh, sure, William," she replied. "Let me go grab a blanket and a plate, and I'll be right back."

Sophia ran to the house, pulled a small blanket from the top shelf in the hall closet, then headed out the back door. She heard Dora's voice behind her.

"Be careful not to get Mr. Jacobson's hopes up, Miss Sophie. Let him down real easy."

She snickered. It wasn't William's hopes she was worried about. Her own were probably much higher than they should be considering how little she actually knew of Hank.

But she knew enough to feel positively giddy whenever he was nearby—something she'd never experienced before. The mere sight of his face brought a smile to her lips and her heart. Sophia craved being with him, but she knew it wasn't a good idea today. She needed to have her meal with William, if for no other reason but to make Mama and Daddy happy.

Doing her best not to look over at the working men as they crouched down beneath the shade trees in the yard, for fear she'd find herself exchanging a glance with Hank, Sophia put a spoonful from each bowl on her plate and crossed over to where William was still sitting.

"Sorry it took so long," she said. "I had to go inside for the blanket."

He shrugged. "That's quite all right. I didn't notice."

That was another problem, she realized. He barely noticed her.

She knew she needed to attempt to strike up a conversation, since William wasn't likely to. "Have you thought about joining the choir at church?"

"No," he replied. "Have you?"

Sophia tilted her head back and laughed. "Apparently you haven't heard me sing lately. I'm afraid the angels would cry if I joined the choir."

William didn't join her in laughter. He just turned to her and stared, his face solemn.

Didn't he ever smile? she wondered. *Was he always this serious?* She knew the answer to that, and it made her own cheerful mood drop.

It seemed to take forever to eat her meal, but she finally finished a respectable amount. "Well, I must run and see if Dora could use a hand in the kitchen."

William nodded. "I'll be seeing you around, Sophia."

Sophia grabbed her plate and forced herself to walk at an even pace back to the house. It wasn't an easy task since she felt like lifting her skirt and running.

"How is William?" Dora asked.

Sophia leaned her head forward and glared at Dora from beneath hooded eyes. They both broke into giggles.

"Shame on me," Sophia finally said when she caught her breath. "I can't help it, Dora. He's so quiet, and I don't have any idea what to say to him. He must think I'm a foolish girl."

"You are not a foolish girl," Dora told her firmly. "Just a spirited young woman who wants a little fun in her life."

"Well, maybe so, but I'm afraid I need to tame my spirit a little in order to keep peace around here."

Dora shook her head and clucked her tongue. Sophia knew she did this when she was thinking something she knew was better left unsaid.

Footsteps from behind startled her. She spun around and found herself facing Hank.

"Just wanted to pop in and thank the cooks. Y'all did a mighty fine job with that chicken."

"Miss Sophie did most of the work," Dora said, grinning at him. "She baked some pies, too. I'll send her out directly when they're cooled. Y'all can take a little break in about an hour."

"I can hardly wait," Hank said. "Sophia, would you do me the honor of joining me for dessert?"

Sophia felt cornered. She wanted nothing more than to join Hank, but she knew she'd have the wrath of most of the congregation on her, so she felt compelled to turn him down.

"I'm sorry, Hank, but I—"

Hank didn't let her finish. "That's quite all right, Sophia. I understand. You mustn't upset William. And I wouldn't want you to. After all, he's been knowing your family for years."

Sophia stared at Hank. He grinned back at her, but she wasn't able to manage even a half smile.

He nodded. "See you around, Sophia. And Dora, you keep on doin' what you've been doing. The food is the best I think I've ever had." Then he was gone.

Sophia wasn't able to say a word after that. In fact, she was not sure why, but she went from a feeling of pure joy at seeing Hank's smiling face to wanting to cry in a matter of seconds.

The moment he was out of the kitchen, Dora turned to Sophia and clucked some more. When she finally spoke, she said, "Don't let that one get away, Miss Sophie. He's got that bounce in his step just like you. That man will make someone a fine husband."

Sophia had thought the exact same thing. Until now, she wasn't certain she should go against her parents' wishes to marry William. But there were a couple of reasons she had to do something. First of all, William hadn't even proposed to her yet. And secondly, she didn't want to go through life with a glum husband who barely noticed her.

"Oh, Dora," Sophia said as she tossed her dish towel on the table and sank down in the chair. "What should I do?"

"Talk to the reverend. He'll know."

"You don't think he'll understand what I'm going through."

"Surely he will," Dora replied. "He's a wise man who knows the human heart. He might even talk to your daddy if he thinks it'll help."

"Perhaps I'll talk to him, if I can't figure out what else to do."

Dora cackled. "You don't like turning things over to someone else, do you, Miss Sophie?"

"What exactly do you mean by that, Dora?" Sophia glared at the housekeeper.

"Your hands are tied, there ain't nothin' you can do, but you still won't trust that everything will be just fine."

Sophia grunted. "The Lord gave me a mind to work things out, and I plan to do that."

"Then what you gonna do, Miss Sophie?"

"I, uh, I'm not sure yet, Dora. I'll let you know when I figure it out."

Dora turned away, still cackling.

◆　◆　◆

Hank knew he needed to join the other men back in the barn before they began wondering where he'd wandered off to. But he felt drawn to the house where he knew Sophia was toiling with her mother's servant. Being with her seemed more important than anything else he could think of.

He could tell she was having a terrible time of dealing with her feelings for William. He saw in her eyes that she didn't love the man, and there was some doubt as to William's intentions toward her. Their parents had already decided Sophia's and William's fate, regardless of the younger people's feelings. Such a pity, too, Hank thought, but there was nothing he could do about it.

Sadness filled his heart, something that rarely happened to Hank since he'd discovered the Lord. He'd gone to church most of his life, but until he allowed the

Word to actually sink in, he never knew true joy. Since then, he'd started each day with a newness and overwhelming gladness that couldn't be stifled.

Reverend Breckenridge was waiting for him by the barn opening. "Been to see Sophia?" he asked.

Hank nodded. He wasn't sure what else he should say. The reverend already knew his feelings.

"You do understand this thing with William goes way back, right, Hank?"

"Of course I do, Reverend," Hank snapped. When he realized how harsh he'd sounded, he took a step back. "I'm sorry. I shouldn't have been so abrupt. It's just that—"

Reverend Breckenridge grinned, slapping Hank on the shoulder. "You're falling in love with another man's girl."

"Certainly appears that way."

"Then fight for her," Reverend Breckenridge said.

"Fight for her?" Surely, Hank hadn't heard right. He narrowed his eyes, looked the reverend in the eye, and said, "Could you please repeat that?"

Reverend Breckenridge opened his mouth to speak, but he quickly snapped it shut as he nodded toward the barn door. Hank turned around just in time to see Sophia enter the barn.

"Hank?" she said as she walked toward him, squinting.

"Yes, this is me, Sophia," Hank said. It took every ounce of willpower not to run to her and pull her into his arms. She looked so vulnerable walking slowly toward him. And oh, so beautiful.

"Good," she said, picking up her step and moving rapidly toward him. "I wanted to talk with you about something."

"Would you like to go outside?" he asked.

All hammers had stopped banging on the barn, and it was clear that every single man in the barn was listening to their conversation. That worried Hank.

"No, that's not necessary," she said.

"Okay, then what would you like to discuss?"

She smiled, her face glowing. He could tell she was nervous, but she was determined to say whatever it was she'd come to say.

"Us," she replied.

"Sophia, we'd better go outside," Hank said, taking her by the arm. "We don't need an audience."

She didn't resist. Instead, she literally leaned a little toward him, which made his heart race. He wished he could gently place his arm around her shoulders, but he doubted her father would approve.

Once they were outside, Sophia turned to him and said, "Hank, I don't know if I'm speaking out of my own foolishness, but I feel like you and I should get to know one another better."

"No, Sophia, it's not foolishness. I feel the same way. However, I don't want to do anything that will upset your family."

Reverend Breckenridge's advice came to mind. He'd fight, but not with recklessness. Instead, he'd woo Sophia Mayhew and earn the right to be with her. And he'd win her parents over in the process, no matter what he had to do. Hank knew they were good, God-fearing people who only wanted what was best for their daughter. And he knew he'd be the best man to make her happy.

"I don't really care anymore, Hank. All I know is that whenever I'm around you I'm happy and I feel free. It feels good to feel so free."

"Feeling free is good," Hank agreed. "But we need to keep our wits about us, or we won't feel so free."

He glanced up and saw that some of the men had followed them outside the barn and were staring. The few women who'd accompanied their husbands had also looked up from their needlework to see what was going on.

"Let us take this thing slow and steady, Sophia. I want to court you in the correct way and not ruffle too many feathers."

Sophia slouched back. "Yes, you're right, Hank. I don't want to upset anyone either."

"But we'll work together on this, Sophia."

One of the women had stood up and walked over to them. She tilted her head forward and scowled at Sophia. "I'll have a talk with your mama about your behavior, young lady. It's not becoming for a young woman to act in such an impudent manner."

Sophia started to argue, but Hank shook his head. He tipped his hat to the woman and smiled. "I really need to finish my work inside the barn, Sophia. I hope your mama is feeling better." Then he turned and went inside the barn.

"Is your mama not feeling well, Sophia?" he heard the woman ask.

Hank started to turn back around to take care of what he'd started, since he felt ashamed for leaving Sophia to pick up where he left off. But he spotted Dora standing by the kitchen door, waving him on. Dora was a good woman. He'd have to remember to thank her some day.

He let out the breath he'd been holding and picked up his hammer. The men had resumed their work, but he felt the tension all around him. No one except Reverend Breckenridge would look him in the eye. The reverend grinned and nodded but didn't say a word.

Chapter 7

Sophia was left speechless. She had no idea what to say to the woman.

Suddenly, Dora stuck her head out the kitchen door and hollered, "Miss Sophie, come quick. I need your help."

"I better run," she told the woman, then took off like a streak of lightning.

Relieved by Dora needing her, Sophia silently prayed that there wasn't a disaster in the kitchen. She was breathless when she got to the kitchen door.

"Yes, Dora, what do you need?"

"These pies are about ready to go out there. I reckon they've cooled enough to cut."

Sophia started to reprimand Dora for a false alarm, but then she realized what had happened. She smiled instead and gave Dora a hug. "Thanks for saving me from that awful woman, Dora."

"You better get used to people doing that, Miss Sophie. William's mighty popular around here, and people don't take kindly to another man coming in and taking what they think should belong to one of their people."

"I don't belong to anyone," Sophia reminded her. "Didn't you listen to yourself when you were giving me that talk about freedom?"

"I didn't say you shouldn't be free to love any man you want to. I just said you better get used to people acting like that woman."

"Oh," Sophia said.

She knew Dora was right. Not only would she have to face people's questioning, she had her parents to deal with as well. And they would be the most difficult of all, considering how they'd been planning hers and William's wedding for years.

The pies were all still warm to touch, but the aroma of fresh baked apples, peaches, and pecans wafted up to tease her nostrils. Pecan pie was Sophia's favorite, but she didn't want to eat something that was intended for the men who'd come to help Daddy. She left the utensils beside the pies on the table, then went back inside.

When she turned to look out the window, the men had swarmed around the tables, each claiming one flavor of pie, then moving on to snatch a sliver of another. Her gaze rested on the good-looking Hank Ellis. He managed to keep his mood high, even though it was painfully obvious that most of the others around him were giving him the cold shoulder. At least Reverend Breckenridge was being friendly.

Maybe Dora was right. Reverend Breckenridge would understand, and he'd have the wisdom to know what to do in this sticky situation. She'd have to go to the church and chat with him sometime next week.

By nightfall, all the volunteers had gone home, leaving Sophia to face Mama and Daddy alone. Not even Dora stayed behind. She had her own family to take care of.

"Sophia," Daddy said as he leaned back in his chair, his feet up on the tiny footstool with the needlepoint tapestry top Mama had made for him. "We need to talk. Sit down."

She crossed the room and did as she was told, choosing the straight-back wooden chair over the soft, stuffed sofa. "Yes, Daddy?"

"What's all that carryin' on with the new man all about?" He stopped and glared at Sophia.

"I wasn't carryin' on, Daddy. I was just talking to him."

"Talking to him is the same thing. Do you want people to talk, Sophia?"

She shrugged. At the moment, she didn't really care if people talked or what they did, for that matter. She was tired of feeling so constrained. There were times she felt as though she were in prison. But she didn't dare say that, or Daddy wouldn't let her out of his sight for days, maybe even weeks.

"Let them talk, Daddy," she said with a shaky voice.

"That's not a good attitude. We have a church family, and they are concerned about your welfare. I want you to come to your senses and pay more attention to William."

"I do pay attention to William, Daddy," she blurted out as she stood up. Pacing the floor, she continued, "It's William who acts like I don't exist."

"William loves you, Sophia."

"He certainly doesn't act like it."

Mama came into the room and stopped as she looked at her husband questioningly. "Have a seat. We were discussing her carryin' on with Mr. Ellis."

"I hope you told her to stop that nonsense."

"I certainly did," he replied. Then he turned back to Sophia. "From now on, you're to pay attention only to William Jacobson whenever you feel the need to flirt with a man."

She held her hands up in despair. "I wasn't flirting, Daddy. Don't you understand? William ignores me, Hank is nice to me, and everyone else in the church is mad at me. I can't win for losing."

"Don't take that tone with me, Sophia," Daddy growled at her. "Go to your room this instant. We'll see you in the morning for church."

Sophia stormed from the room, wishing someone would at least listen to her. But that was too much to hope for since they already had her future planned for her.

So much for freedom. In Sophia Mayhew's world, freedom didn't exist unless everyone in the church approved.

She found sleep in the wee hours of the morning. But when the sun rose, her eyes popped wide open. Dread washed over her as she remembered her daddy's words the night before. Without any enthusiasm, Sophia got up and dressed for church. She was in the midst of positioning her hat when Mama knocked at the door, then opened it.

"Good, you're almost ready," she said.

"Of course," Sophia said without looking her mama in the eye. "Why would you think otherwise?"

"Don't be sassy, Sophia. It doesn't become you. Now finish getting ready and come downstairs for breakfast. Your daddy wants to get there early."

Sophia knew why he wanted to get to church early. It was so she could spend some time with William before the services started.

No one in the family uttered more than a few words all the way to the Church on the Hill. Reverend Breckenridge stood outside greeting the early arrivals.

"Good mornin', Mayhew family," he bellowed. "So nice of you to get here at this time. I love it when my flock is eager to hear my sermon."

"Mornin', Reverend," Sophia's daddy said. "Have you seen the Jacobsons?"

Reverend Breckenridge's smile dropped, but only for a moment. He glanced over at Sophia, then turned to her daddy, nodding. "Why yes, they arrived early, too. I believe they're in the basement with the choir."

Sophia reluctantly started to follow her parents, but Reverend Breckenridge reached out and took her by the arm. "I'd like to have a few words with you if your folks don't mind."

Sophia's daddy turned and gave a curt nod. "Of course we don't mind, Reverend. Send her on down when you're done with her."

As soon as Sophia's parents were out of sight, the reverend gently placed his arm around Sophia's shoulder and pulled her to the side of the building. "Are you feeling well, Sophia?"

"I'm fine and dandy, Reverend," she said.

"No, you're not. I'm not blind. In fact, what I see is a woman who wants to be with one man, while the world expects otherwise."

"You noticed?" she said.

"Of course I noticed. In fact, everyone has noticed."

Her heart fell as she hung her head. "Yes, they have, haven't they."

"But don't you pay a bit of attention to all the gossip mongers. They don't have any idea what's in your heart."

She snapped her head up and looked him squarely in the eye. "Do you really think I should ignore them?"

"If you want happiness and love, you most likely will have to ignore plenty of people."

"But what about William? Mama and Daddy don't want me to make him angry. All I seem to do to William is upset him." She looked down again.

Reverend Breckenridge reached out and tilted her chin up so she was facing him. "Are you sure about that?"

Sophia held her hands out to her sides as she tried to explain. "He hardly even talks to me, and when he does, it's in short sentences that don't mean anything. I don't think I've even seen him smile more than once or twice since we were children."

The reverend belted out a belly laugh. "Darlin', you and William are still children to me. And your folks. But seriously, Sophia, you need to follow your heart. The Lord brought Hank Ellis to our neck of the woods for a reason, you know."

"Do you know?" Sophia asked. "Why the Lord brought Hank to us, that is?"

Reverend Breckenridge shrugged. "For all I know the only reason he's here is to work at the lumberyard. But perhaps the Lord brought him here for you."

"I never really thought about it that way," Sophia said as the feeling in her heart lifted. "But I still don't know what to do about William."

"Sophia, William is a grown man. He can take care of himself."

"I know, but Mama and Daddy—"

"Sshh. Let me handle them. I have a feeling they'll come around sooner or later."

"Sooner, I hope," Sophia said. "But later, I fear."

The reverend belted out another hearty chuckle that echoed between the church building and the trees. "We shall see. Let's pray about it."

He held both of her hands as he asked the Lord for guidance in this matter of the heart. Then he prayed that they'd do His will. When it was over and they'd both said "Amen," Sophia reached out and hugged her pastor.

"Have I ever told you how much I appreciate you, Reverend?"

His lips quivered into a smile. "That makes everything I've said worthwhile, Sophia. I'll continue to pray for you. Oh, and don't forget to meet your parents in the church basement. I'm sure they're waitin' for you now."

"Of course," Sophia said. "I'll go right down there."

When she got to the bottom of the steps, William was waiting for her. "Your mama said you were talkin' to the reverend. Can we go outside for a few minutes, Sophia?"

"Uh, sure," she said as she glanced around to see who all was in the basement. The choir members stood in the positions they'd take in the tiny loft behind the pulpit. Her mama and daddy were both watching as she turned back to William.

"Let's go," she finally said. She hadn't seen Hank, which was good.

Once outside, William asked her to walk over to the small courtyard where they held celebrations such as the Fourth of July pie auction. He led her to a bench that was nestled in the midst of several tall pines.

"What did you want to discuss, William?" she asked.

"How long have we known each other, Sophia?"

She was startled by his question. "That's silly. We've known each other for a very long time. Almost all our lives."

"That's right. And we both are very fond of each other."

"Yes, William," she replied. "We always have been."

Sophia sat and stared at William in horror as he stood up, glanced around, then got down on one knee. He took her hand in his and stared at it for a minute before he broke into a coughing fit. *What is going on?* she wondered. Her chest suddenly felt like it would cave in.

"William, what are you doing? You'll get your good Sunday trousers dirty if you don't get up."

"Sophia," he said slowly, not looking her directly in the eye. "Will you be my wife?"

Chapter 8

S ophia was so startled by his question, she was speechless. When she opened her mouth to speak, no words came out.

"Sophia, did you hear me?" he asked, no emotion showing whatsoever.

"I believe I heard you ask me to be your wife." She felt like jumping up and running away screaming, but she didn't dare.

"That's right," he said, "I did."

Sophia stood up and turned to William, who still didn't seem to want to look at her. Pointing to the bench, she said, "Sit, William. I have a question for you."

"What?" he asked as he complied.

If it was this easy to get him to obey, Sophia thought, perhaps she should consider accepting his proposal. But no, that's not what she wanted, and she now knew he didn't want it either. William didn't love her. That much was obvious.

"Why are you asking me to be your wife, William?" she asked in a tone that reminded her of their schoolteacher back when they were children.

"Because I want to marry you?" he said questioningly.

"Do you really?"

"Of course I do, Sophia. Why else would I ask you?" He averted his gaze.

"Look at me, William," she demanded. "Look me in the eye and tell me you want to marry me. To spend the rest of your life with me. To have children with me. To always be there through thick and thin with me."

He looked at her, then turned away. "I can't," he finally said.

"Just as I thought. Neither of us wants to marry the other, but we're acting like this on account of our parents, who want the best for both of us." Suddenly a thought occurred to her. "Are you in love with someone else, William?"

His face turned the brightest shade of red Sophia had ever seen. "Maybe, but I'm not sure how she feels about me."

"William!" Sophia said with more excitement than she'd felt since first meeting Hank. "This is grand! We have to tell our folks."

"No, I think that's a bad idea. They want you and me to marry each other, not someone else." The sadness in his voice made Sophia want to reach out and hug him. But she didn't dare. He would most likely get the wrong idea.

"We have to do something."

"Look, Sophia, I don't think there's anything we can do. They have their minds made up."

Sophia straightened and stamped her foot. "That's just too bad. We have to let them know we should be free to love whoever we feel like loving."

"Whomever," he corrected.

"Okay, whomever. C'mon, William. We'll tell them now."

Chapter 9

The first person they saw when they walked through the back door of the church was Hank, to Sophia's dismay. He stopped, took a step back, and surveyed them both, glancing back and forth between them as if assessing the situation.

"Mornin', Hank," Sophia said. She tugged on William's arm and pulled him away. "C'mon, William."

For the first time since she'd met him, Hank remained speechless. She feared he had the wrong idea, but there would be time for correcting that later. For now, she had to straighten out a few very important details of hers and William's lives.

Her mama and daddy were still in the basement waiting for her. When they saw her holding onto William's arm, both of them beamed with happiness.

"So you finally came to your senses," Daddy said. "I couldn't be happier."

"Yes, Daddy, we did come to our senses. William and I have something to tell you as soon as we get his parents down here." Turning to William, she said, "Any idea where they might be?"

William pointed to the corner of the room where several women were setting up refreshments. "My mother is with those women. She'll know where my father is."

Sophia let go of his arm and crossed the room to the refreshment ladies. As soon as she got Mrs. Jacobson, she sent William off to find his father.

"Looks like our children have finally gotten together," her daddy said to William's mother, who was beaming.

Sophia wondered if any of them would still be smiling once they heard what she and William had to say. She stood in one spot, tapping her foot with her arms crossed over her chest. Her thoughts wandered while she waited. If William hadn't been so shy about voicing his feelings to his parents, none of this would have to happen. But because he was timid and quiet, she had to be the forceful one, taking the lead to let everyone know she and William both wanted freedom in their choices.

To Sophia's surprise, both Reverend Breckenridge and Hank were with William and his father when he returned. Hank looked like he didn't want to be there, but the reverend had a knowing smile plastered on his face. Sophia had a sneaking suspicion that he'd had a hand in this whole thing.

"You have something you'd like to tell us?" William's father asked. "Some good news, I hope?"

William turned to Sophia as if looking to her to start. She opened her mouth but was quieted when he spoke up.

"Father," he began, then cleared his throat. "Mother, Mr. and Mrs. Mayhew, Sophia and I decided we wish to remain friends. However, we don't feel that we're suited for each other in marriage."

"What?" Sophia's mama cried.

"Son," William's father said as he took a step toward William. "Perhaps we need to discuss this, man to man, without anyone else present."

"I know this came as quite a shock to you," Sophia hastily intervened, "but William and I have already discussed it at length. He proposed marriage to me, I suspect to be polite and do the honorable thing, but I knew his heart wasn't in it. We were both relieved when I turned him down."

The two sets of parents looked confused.

"Remember when men stood up on July Fourth and talked about the freedom we have in this country?" Sophia asked. "William and I want the same freedom. We want to choose our life partners without interference from our wonderful, loving, well-meaning parents."

"But Sophia," Mama said in a squeaky voice, "we wanted to make certain you had a Christian husband."

"I want that, too," Sophia agreed, "but there are other Christian men besides William."

Reverend Breckenridge stepped forward and bellowed, "Congratulations, Mr. and Mrs. Jacobson and Mr. and Mrs. Mayhew, your children have finally grown up. This is a glorious day!"

All eyes turned to him. He nodded toward Hank.

"I suppose I don't need to let you know that I, for one, am very relieved," Hank said. After a nervous moment of silence, everyone chuckled.

Sophia turned to William. "Is there anything you'd like to tell us, William?"

His face turned red again, but he shook his head. "Not at the moment."

Hank reached for Sophia's hand and lifted it. "I have something to share," he said.

Reverend Breckenridge nodded. "Go ahead, Lad."

"From this moment on, I wish to pursue this woman in a courtship that I pray is happy, fun, and without too many distractions." He turned to Sophia's parents. "And I'd like your blessing."

"Go ahead and give it to him," Reverend Breckenridge said to them. "He's a persistent young man, so you might as well save yourselves some trouble."

They both finally nodded but continued their stunned silence. William's parents also appeared to be in shock.

The two families, as well as Hank, sat together in church and listened to the sermon with interest. Reverend Breckenridge spoke of both the seriousness and the joys of relationships between men and women, pausing to let the meaning of his words sink in. Sophia felt as though he was speaking directly to her, so she listened with rapt attention.

After the service was over, the congregation stood up, shook hands, then headed for the door. This particular Sunday, no picnic was scheduled. Some people went down to the church basement for quick refreshments before departing, while others left the church.

Sophia had no idea what was in store for her, but at least she now had the freedom she'd wanted since becoming an adult. Her parents had accepted the news, but they still didn't have much to say about what had transpired. She suspected they had quite a bit to think about and discuss between themselves before she heard their feelings on the subject.

As they stood outside the church, saying their good-byes, her daddy surprised her and turned to Hank. "Young man, if you're not doing anything later on this afternoon, we'd be honored if you'd stop by so we could get to know you."

A look of joyful surprise crossed Hank's face as he nodded and said, "Yes, Sir. What time should I be there?"

Everyone laughed at his eagerness. Sophia's heart was so filled with happiness she thought it might burst.

◆　◆　◆

Two months later, Hank and Sophia sat in the tree swing on the front lawn of her family farm. He lifted her hand to his lips and gently kissed the back of it.

"Sophia, I don't have to tell you how I feel about you. It must be pretty obvious by the way I act."

"Yes, Hank, it's pretty obvious." She giggled, covering her mouth with her white-gloved hand. Hank beamed from the inside out to see her so happy. "But I would like to hear it just the same."

"All right then," he said as he stood up and looked her in the eye before getting down on one knee. Her face registered a combination of the surprise and pleasure he felt every time he was with her. "Miss Sophia Mayhew, I love you with all my heart. I would go to the ends of the earth to make you happy. My sole wish is to look into your eyes and see the same love I have for you reflected in them."

"Oh, Hank, I do love you," she said breathlessly.

"Good," he said as he covered her hand with both of his. "At least you won't think me the complete idiot for what I'm about to ask."

"Yes, Hank?" she said with childlike impatience.

He touched his forehead to her hand, then looked back into her eyes. "Sophia, I pray that this is not too soon to ask you to marry me, to love me forever, and to share our faith in our Lord as husband and wife."

Sophia threw her arms around Hank's neck and pulled him back into the swing. "I thought you'd never ask."

"Then please loosen your grip. You wouldn't want to strangle your future husband," he said as he resumed his position in the swing beside Sophia.

They both burst into laughter.

"When did you want to have the wedding?" she asked. Before he had a chance to reply, she went on. "We need to let your parents know so they can be here. Is there anyone else?"

Hank raised both hands to the sky. "I want to let the world know, and they're all invited, every last person and creature God has created!"

"Then we might want to have the wedding outside," Sophia said with a chuckle. "All God's creatures won't fit in that little Church on the Hill."

"We can have it anywhere, any time your heart desires," Hank said, "as long as you promise to love me to the end."

"I have an idea," Sophia said. "Why don't we have it on the church lawn where we first met, and we can plan it for the Fourth of July, right after the pie auction."

"Excellent idea," he replied, "with one exception."

She cast a look at him with the prettiest frown he'd ever seen. "An exception?"

"Yes," he replied. "We shall have it before the pie auction. I don't know if I can wait any longer."

Hank's heart swelled with more joy than any one man deserved as Sophia hugged him once again. He looked up and quietly said, "Thank You, Lord."

Still holding onto Hank, Sophia added, "Amen."

DEBBY MAYNE

Debby Mayne has published more than 50 books and novellas, 400 print short stories and articles, more than 1,000 web articles, and a bunch of devotions for women. She has been managing editor of a national health magazine, product information fashion writer for HSN, product writer for Zulily, creative writing instructor for the Long Ridge Writers Group, and etiquette expert for About.com. Most of her stories feature strong, southern women who overcome all sorts of obstacles.

Victorious

by Kathleen Y'Barbo

Dedication

To the prayer warriors,
without whom this book would have never been finished.

Wait on the LORD, and he shall save thee.
PROVERBS 20:22

Chapter 1

January 1891

As he warbled the last line of "Rock of Ages" and then took his seat, Gus Drummond tried in vain to ignore the swaying blue feather on the pretty Pinkerton's Sunday hat. Doubtless he'd see the feather, and the fair-haired Pinkerton beneath it, at close range come the end of Sunday service, for he'd avoided her all week.

With some swift detective work on his part, he'd managed to slip out of the hardware store when she wasn't looking, and he'd avoided her at the hotel by consuming his meals in his room. He'd even taken to walking rather than chance a meeting with the woman at the livery.

How like the Lord to show His sense of humor by placing her across the aisle from him at church this morning.

Ever since she'd come to his office last Tuesday morning asking for the train robbery case to be reopened, he'd seen right through the ruse. Obviously, she was sweet on the banker and buying time in Windmere Falls by creating a situation to be investigated where there was none. It was common knowledge she had orders to board the first train back to Chicago once Moment Alexander and Brady Miller's march down the aisle was over.

He'd listened, sort of, to the female Pinkerton's ideas and given her the only answer he had. The case was closed, and she'd best tell Will Bowen good-bye, then pack her lace and linens and catch the first train back to Chicago. Or, preferably, give up the ridiculous pursuit of a man's career and head back to England, where, no doubt, some duke or prince pined away for her.

When that woman bit into a topic, however, she seemed to chew it until nothing was left. In this case, her topic was the identity of the Ghost, and she didn't care that the man who'd confessed to being the fellow in the flour sack mask now sat behind bars awaiting the hangman's noose.

No, she dismissed that little piece of evidence with a wave of her gloved hand and informed him she intended to get to the bottom of the investigation with or without his help. Typical hardheaded female.

Still, the memory of high color staining her face as Miss Vicky stormed out of his office caused Gus to smile. One thing about this Pinkerton, she took her job seriously. If only she didn't expect him to take *her* seriously.

And as much as he hated to admit it, she *was* right about the fact that the rest of the loot, a good half of the take, hadn't been accounted for. To Gus's mind, however, the gold had been spent long ago on high living and low women, but he had no proof. It unsettled him a bit that the little Englishwoman thought better of his conclusion and intended to prove him wrong. If she hadn't stated that fact in front of the sheriff, he'd be long gone, sitting in his place in Denver spending the winter in his own warm bed and planning that cabin he would build come spring.

His gaze dropped from the feather to the fancy hat and finally to the bothersome woman beneath. As pretty as a new pony, Miss Vicky had chosen an outfit of chestnut brown trimmed in lace dyed to match her eyes.

A sane man would have looked away when those eyes met his across the aisle, but every bit of his sanity had fled when the Pinkertons in petticoats came to town. With a polite nod, he ignored Miss Vicky's frown and transferred his attention to the bowler-hatted dandy on her left. Irritation rose and stuck in his gut.

Whatever possessed the woman to take a shine to the citified banker? Looks, money, and social standing most likely, but could Bowen make camp in the Llano Estacado or track a renegade desperado? With his lily-white skin and soft hands, he'd be sunburned and lost before he hit the edge of town. No, that wasn't right, Gus amended. Will Bowen would pay one of his flunkies to do the work for him while he sat in his office and counted coins.

Gus stifled a snort of amusement and shifted positions, forcing his mind back to the task at hand. He'd learned if he kept his knee pressed against the pew in front of him, the splinters caused just enough affliction to keep him awake until the reverend finished his business and turned the crowd out to meet the afternoon.

Somehow, though, his thoughts kept leaving the trail and heading off in the direction of the blue feather. Before he knew it, the closing hymn had been pounded out on the dilapidated organ and that feather dangled just under his nose.

"Mr. Drummond?" The Pinkerton peered up at him from beneath the brim of her hat. "May I have a word with you, please?"

Brady Miller and Moment Alexander filed past, and Gus nodded in their direction. He owed them more than a passing greeting, but the Pinkerton woman had his spleen in such an uproar that he'd hardly provide tolerable conversation for these nice folks. He'd have to make amends outside if the opportunity presented itself—that is, if he could rid himself of Miss Vicky and still manage to be civil.

The object of his irritation yanked at the sleeve of his coat. "Excuse me, please," she said, "but we've a bit of *business* to discuss."

Once again, he ignored her to watch the faithful trod outside only to see more trouble headed his way. Right behind the newly engaged Pinkerton couple, Mabel Hawkins, passable organ player and all around busybody, glared at the little circle in which he stood.

Gus stifled a groan. Doubtless she'd stir up some sort of trouble come Monday morning, most likely setting him in the midst of some sordid love triangle with the English-woman and her banker friend. He pictured her narrow eyes and thin lips as she repeated the story, embellishing it a bit more each time until it reached epic proportions over the Monday washday special of beans and rice at the hotel.

To his mind, Miss Mabel read too many dime novels, and the last time the pastor approached him with concern after hearing one of her tales about him, he'd told the man so. If only the life of a Pinkerton were half as exciting as the one Miss Mabel claimed he had.

"*Mr.* Drummond."

There was that feather again, this time so close it nearly tickled his nose. He stared at it a second, then braved a glance into the face of its owner. Once again, bright red stained Miss Vicky's cheeks despite the relatively cool temperature of the morning. Once again, she looked like one of heaven's most elegant angels, lost among the mortals and ready to fly home without warning.

Thoughts of Miss Mabel evaporated.

Her soft pink lips puckered with hostility just like his mother's used to when he'd stuck his finger in the pudding before the meal had been properly served. Quite the character, his Scottish-born mother, as was the lady Pinkerton. Those pink lips began to move.

"A *word* please, kind sir."

Gus broke into a smile that would have made Mama proud as he curled his fists and fought the urge to pluck the blue feather right off her brown hat. "Why, of course."

"Thank you," she said on a soft breath as her features relaxed and her beauty increased.

"And that word," he said before he could change his mind and tell her all she wanted to know and more, "is no."

Gus looked past her, open mouth and all, to the slick-haired banker who stood waiting like a calf on a tether. Several possible responses to Bowen's bland greeting occurred to him, none of which were acceptable beneath the roof of God's house.

Squelching the need to say them anyway, Gus tipped his Stetson and pressed past the well-matched pair to follow a grinning Miss Mabel outside. If he couldn't win, he'd walk away.

◆ ◆ ◆

He walked away.

Victoria gathered her irritation and her reticule and turned to follow the impossibly stubborn lawman outside. She'd allowed him to believe he had escaped her too many times this week, reasoning that if she gave him the privacy he desired, he'd have time to do some serious thinking on the topic at hand.

Obviously this had not been the case.

"Shall we, Miss Barrett-Ames?" Mr. Bowen's arm linked with hers, punctuating the request with a slightly possessive tug to bring her sharply to his side. "After all, the temperature is unseasonably mild and the day is still young, as are we."

Victoria turned her attention away from the broad back of the retreating Pinkerton to the handsome banker. An impertinent response lay on the tip of her tongue, but she swallowed it along with most of her anger.

After all, William Bowen was the closest thing to a gentleman Windmere Falls had to offer, and she did enjoy his company. What harm was there in being cordial in return?

Still, she wriggled out of his grasp and busied her fingers with the ribbons on her bonnet. Above all, she was a Pinkerton woman, and until she'd heard otherwise, she must conduct herself as if she were on assignment at all times. What good would it do to allow a bit of fancy to sway her when she had a case to complete?

And, no matter what Gus Drummond and the other three ladies believed, this case was far from closed. She could only pray that word would not get back to headquarters before she had her proof. At least she had until Moment's wedding next month.

"Miss Barrett-Ames, did you hear me?"

The banker's perfectly formed features were stricken with worry, and his full lips closed over a line of perfectly white teeth to offer a frown. Victoria moved instantly to repair the damage her inattention had caused.

"Of course," she said, as she lightly placed her hand over his, "although I must insist you call me Victoria."

The banker smiled as if she'd given him the most exquisite of gifts. "Only if you will address me as Will." Without waiting for an answer, he lifted her fingers to his lips, then abruptly grasped her elbow, leading her down the aisle toward the sunlit street. "Now, I've taken the liberty of having Cook prepare a repast for two, and I thought we might saddle the horses. There's the loveliest little spot where we can build a fire and enjoy our meal up past. . ."

His words disappeared as Victoria's thoughts intruded. While the Sabbath was not a day to spend in pursuit of the Ghost, it could be a day to leisurely seek a clue or two.

Perhaps Will, with his vast knowledge of the Windmere Falls citizens and their respective financial situations, might have some insight into possible suspects. Dare she mention to him that the ringleader of the gang might still be at large? She pondered this as he led her down the steps of the church toward his buggy.

". . .and I know how your countrymen love scones with their tea, so I felt obliged to have Cook. . ."

Victoria's concentration slipped once more when the sunlight hit her eyes. Blinking to retain her vision, she halted her steps. Oblivious, the banker continued speaking as he strode toward his buggy.

Gus Drummond stood with Moment and Mr. Miller, pretending deep conversation when she knew he'd been watching her as she emerged from the church. Their gazes met, and as her eyes found their focus, he had the audacity to wink.

"Quite the impertinent one, that Pinkerton fellow. I declare, it seems as though he's got something besides law work up his sleeve."

She turned to see Mabel Hawkins standing to her left, just out of Mr. Drummond's line of sight. "Indeed," Victoria said with a conspiratorial nod. "He certainly does."

Miss Hawkins's smile broadened. "So you agree that there's something funny about Mr. Drummond then?"

"Something funny?" Victoria studied the woman and the idea all at once. He *had* seemed strange each time she'd sought him out to discuss the train robbery case, and he *had* acted less than professional in his responses. Actually, his response had been no response at all.

Her Pinkerton's mind set to putting the clues together. There was a substantial sum of money missing, the case was due to be closed without finding that money, and Gus Drummond was most vocal in his opposition to continue searching for it.

An idea most bizarre and yet not totally far-fetched began to form. Out of the corner of her eye, she saw Moment climb into Mr. Miller's wagon. Perhaps she should share her suspicions with her dear friend. Then Moment smiled, and Mr. Miller wrapped an arm around her waist. Crime fighting with her friend would have to wait, Victoria decided.

She whirled around to face the most informed female in Windmere Falls. "Tell me everything you know about Mr. Drummond."

Chapter 2

Victoria took careful note of Gus Drummond's face as she stepped away from the crowd to speak to Miss Hawkins. To borrow a phrase from the man himself, he looked like he had swallowed a bug. She smiled. He was irritating on a good day, but he certainly had an unusual way with the English language.

"And so when I heard we had us a Pinkerton in our midst, I figured he would be rounding up those bad fellers in no time." Miss Hawkins leaned toward her. "Well, I say he coulda caught those robbers if he'd a wanted to."

"What are you saying, Miss Hawkins?"

"Well, when that Pinkerton feller first come to town, he kindly kept to himself, 'cept when he paid a call to the sheriff. All of a sudden, he was at the church every time the doors were open, and he and the reverend was thick as thieves." She paused. "Now we all know what come of the reverend's boy and his no-account friend."

"Yes, but I don't see how that—"

Miss Hawkins put her hand on Victoria's arm and drew her closer. "A man don't just give up his ways and go to church lessen one of two things has happened. Either he's found the Lord or he don't want somebody else to find him out." She gave Victoria a conspiratorial wink. "I reckon our Mr. Drummond fits into one of those two categories."

"I believe we all do." Victoria took a deep breath and tried to remember why she had credited Mabel Hawkins with owning any information that might help in the case. Instead of finding an answer, she found Mr. Drummond staring at them, and she waved. His response was to turn his back and focus his concentration on the reverend.

Of all the nerve. If she hadn't been raised a lady, she would go over there and—

"Victoria, dear, we really should be going."

She tore her gaze away from the uncivilized Pinkerton to see Will Bowen walking toward her. He looked so handsome in his well-cut suit and bowler hat, and his manners were impeccable. The fact that he never missed a church service and owned one of the finest stables of thoroughbreds she'd ever seen also did much to endear him to her heart. Why on earth did she let Gus Drummond affect her when she had a wonderful friend in Will waiting for her?

"Of course," she said. "Perhaps we can talk again soon, Miss Hawkins."

"I'd like that," the woman said as she looked past Victoria to Will. "Maybe we'll talk about something more interesting than that double-minded Pinkerton."

"Double-minded?" Victoria peered up into Will's hand-some face. "Would you give me just a moment with Miss Hawkins, please? I promise I'll tarry no longer than necessary."

Will smiled, a glorious smile that lit his entire face. "Of course," he said. "I only ask that I have your full attention for the remainder of the afternoon. For that, I would wait indefinitely."

"Will, you are a dear, and you have my promise I shall dote on your every word."

"Then I shall hold you to your promise, and I shall await you with great anticipation. I suppose I can bide my time by contemplating the pastor's words. The day is certainly fit for thinking on the Lord." He leaned toward Miss Hawkins and took her hand. With great flourish, he kissed it and then repeated the process with Victoria, tarrying a bit longer and making eye contact as he released her fingers. "As always, Miss Hawkins, it has been a pleasure. Victoria, I am patient but I am human, so don't keep me long."

She watched him stroll toward the buggy. How very blessed she was to have a true gentleman interested in her. Dare she allow the feelings budding within to find the light of day? Perhaps with Will she might finally find a man who—

"Miss Barrett-Ames, I do declare you're plumb smitten with that banker fellow."

Victoria turned her attention back to Miss Hawkins, fully aware the woman had read her expression and guessed the direction of her thoughts. As a Pinkerton, she'd just committed a serious breach of protocol.

"He's a wonderful man," she said in as neutral a tone as she could muster.

"He is that."

Victoria regained her focus on the investigation. "Forgive me for changing the subject, Miss Hawkins, but I believe you mentioned you were concerned that our Pinkerton man might be double-minded."

Miss Hawkins nodded. "All I'm saying is I believe a Pinkerton's gonna get his man if he wants to. Talk around here's that he brought in some help to get those boys caught, but I ain't seen no sight of any other Pinks around here. Ain't nobody new come down since you and Miss Moment and the other two ladies showed up. Now I might have seen some things in my day, but I don't believe I'll live to believe that you four ladies are the backup for that big old Scotsman over there."

Victoria giggled and then forced a serious expression. "It does seem a bit far-fetched, doesn't it?"

"It does indeed," she answered. "And that's why I'm saying I think that Pinkerton man's got something up his sleeve." Again, she leaned toward Victoria. "You can't tell me the boys who admitted to the robberies had the time or the brains to get rid of all that money."

Victoria adjusted her hat and shook her head. "Well, it does seem to stretch the imagination a bit."

Finally she'd found someone who agreed with her assessment of the situation. If only it were someone a bit more respected than the town gossip. Still, the facts were the facts. An astonishing amount of money was missing, presumed by law enforcement to have been spent. All those responsible for the crime were said to be behind bars, and the case was declared closed.

Mr. Fletcher's last letter had insisted Victoria only remain in Windmere Falls long enough to attend Moment's wedding. By the end of February, she would be on a train to Chicago, the sole person who believed justice had not been done in this situation.

The worst part of it was that Moment, her best friend in the world, doubted her theory. If only she could find some proof.

"And so I told the reverend that if I had the proof, I'd go straight to the sheriff, but no, he says to me—"

"Excuse me, Miss Hawkins. Did you say the reverend has proof of your theory?"

She shook her head and rested her hands on her hips. "Lands no, Honey. I know you're not from around here, but don't you English ladies know a body can only talk about one subject until a more interesting one comes along? Now what I was saying was that I saw Alice Duncan yesterday and she told me—"

"Forgive me, Miss Hawkins, but I really must go. I'm afraid Mr. Bowen will give up and leave, and I'll miss a wonderful afternoon. Do come and see me at the mercantile, won't you?"

With that she made her escape, heading for the buggy where Will waited. He stepped out to help her settle comfortably on the seat. Before climbing in and taking the reins, he tucked what looked to be an authentic sable spread over her lap.

"To keep you warm." He smiled. "I'd like you to accept it as a small token of my affection."

Victoria ran a hand over the lush fur and recognized it as Russian sable, a favorite of her grandmother, the duchess. Back in England she owned several coats of this quality, but here in the American West she'd seen nothing of the kind. Even in Chicago, furs of this caliber were a rarity.

Her Pinkerton training sounded a warning. How would a banker living in tiny Windmere Falls manage to acquire such a beautiful fur? Dare she consider Will Bowen might be capable of acting as the mastermind behind the string of robberies?

"Really, that wasn't necessary. I'm afraid I could never accept a gift of such value. It wouldn't be proper," she said as she cast a wary eye upon her companion.

"I disagree." He offered a wink, snapped the reins, and urged the mare into a trot. "Actually, I had an ulterior motive."

"Oh?" Victoria waved to Moment and Mr. Miller, then pointedly ignored Mr. Drummond, who continued to ignore her. She gathered a handful of the luxurious spread and buried her fingers in the fur. It did feel heavenly. "And what might that be?"

"Well, I don't think it would be too presumptuous of me to assume that you are used to the finer things in life."

Victoria froze. *How could he know that?* She had been careful not to draw any undue attention to herself or to act in any way that might cause the citizens of Windmere Falls to think she was anything other than a shop girl.

"You look surprised." His smile melted most of her fears. "Forgive me. I suppose I should explain myself."

"Yes, please do," she said as evenly as possible.

He shrugged. "You see, I've known for quite awhile who you really are."

If Will Bowen knew her to be a Pinkerton, she'd just acquired either an ally or an enemy. Slipping one hand beneath the throw, she reached into her reticule and wrapped her fingers around the pistol she'd thus far only used in target practice back in Chicago.

"I'm making you nervous." He rolled his shoulders and sat up straighter on the seat. "Perhaps I should start at the beginning."

Victoria nodded.

"I don't know if you realize this, but I'm not actually from Windmere Falls."

"I guessed as much."

"I grew up back East. New York, actually. My father was a furrier by trade." He cast a sideways glance at her. "He did quite well for himself. He insisted I seek the education he had not received. In time, I went off to university at Oxford."

Oxford. Her father and brother's alma mater. "I see," she said, hoping against hope the connection ended there.

"And I took a liking to polo."

Victoria swallowed hard. Polo had been a favorite sport of both Papa and Charles. During his time at Oxford, Charles had captained a team two years in a row. What were the odds, though? Still, if he knew anything about her past, she had to consider he might know about her present situation as well.

"Of course." Her gaze drifted past him to check for other travelers on this road. Unfortunately, they were alone.

Will pulled the buggy to a sudden stop and turned to face her. "I can't tell if you're following me, Victoria."

"Please just state what you mean," she said as she tightened her grip on the pistol.

"I rode with your brother, Victoria." He grasped her free hand in his and stared at the robin's egg blue glove before lifting it to his lips. "I know who you are."

◆　◆　◆

Gus Drummond's gaze scanned the horizon searching for the fancy buggy that held the banker and his date. He tried not to think that his suspicions might be correct, but any investigator worth his Pinkerton badge could tell that Victoria Barrett-Ames was just biding her time until the banker asked her to open a joint account.

To think that she might actually try to involve him in her plan to lure the banker into matrimonial bliss really galled him. Why didn't she just tell the fellows up in Chicago the truth and keep him and his office out of it? Just because her friends had all snagged themselves husbands didn't mean Miss Vicky had to do the same.

After all, the robberies were solved and the money was spent. What more was there to talk about?

Gus stalked back to the hotel with a little more attitude than a man fresh from church ought to have. By the time he reached his room, he felt good and convicted. The next time he saw Victoria Barrett-Ames, he wouldn't let her trample on his joy. No, sir, the one Pinkerton who failed to catch a crook wouldn't catch him acting anything but nice.

Chapter 3

Victoria held fast to the pistol hidden beneath her skirts and contemplated her options. She must determine exactly how much Will Bowen knew about her life after coming to America.

As if he'd guessed her thoughts, he tightened his grip on the reins and swung his gaze back to meet hers. "Your secret is safe with me, Victoria."

She toyed with using the direct approach, questioning Will as she had learned to do with a potential suspect, then decided against the hard approach. It never seemed to work for her in practice anyway, and she'd never tried it on anyone except her instructor. He laughed every time, causing her to do the same.

Pasting on a casual look, she released her grip on the pistol and allowed it to slide back into its place inside her reticule. "Will, I have no idea which of my many secrets you've guessed. Please do enlighten me."

With a flick of his wrists, he set the buggy back into motion. "I wrote to your brother to tell him I had chanced upon his sister in the Colorado wilderness." He let the statement linger between them a moment before commenting further. "I'm sure you understand I had your best interests at heart."

"Indeed." Victoria held her feelings in check, but just barely. If Father and Charles were to discover the job she'd described to them as a secretarial position had turned into actual crime fighting, one or both of them would be on the next ship headed west. "Dare I ask what my brother's response might have been?"

"His first response was the same as mine." Will gave her a sideways glance. "He expressed surprise at our finding each other in a country of this size. Of course, while he attributed it to luck, I admit I must ascribe this to the mysterious workings of the Lord. Perhaps He intended me to protect you while offering some civilized companionship."

She relaxed a bit more. Yes, perhaps the Lord had placed her in Windmere Falls for this very reason, although the thought of a Pinkerton in need of protection from a civilian did cause her to smile.

"You have a beautiful smile, Victoria."

"Thank you." She rested her hand on the thick sable blanket and pondered her next words carefully. "Did my brother happen to mention anything else about me that you'd like to share?"

Again, he slid a glance her way. "Is there anything in particular you're concerned about? I assure you I have been completely circumspect in my correspondence with your brother. Above all, we are both gentlemen, and you are Charles's sister."

He looked completely flustered, a reaction that both charmed and pleased Victoria. Perhaps the banker did have an interest in more than a friendship. Would that be so bad?

"Did he mention anything about my being employed?"

Will shrugged. "He told me you'd been doing secretarial work in Chicago. He expressed surprise at your change of location."

"Secretarial work, yes, that's right." Again, she paused to size up the situation. While she felt an instant trust for Will, something kept her from revealing her true mission in Windmere Falls. Perhaps it was her Pinkerton training, or maybe it was the fact that once she admitted she was a Pinkerton, she would then have to admit she was the only one in their group to fail in her mission to catch the person or persons responsible for all the robberies.

A notion occurred to her, and she filed it away to discuss with Moment at the first opportunity. With Will's connections in banking circles, perhaps he could be of some help in locating the missing funds.

She would have to do a cursory check of his background, just a basic report to assure her of his credentials. Once that was accomplished, perhaps she and Will would become the crime-fighting team she'd hoped she and Moment would be.

Or perhaps she and Will would more closely resemble the soon-to-be-formed team of Moment and Brady Miller. The thought made her blush. It also intrigued her immensely.

◆　◆　◆

Monday morning just after first light, Gus joined the sheriff at a table near the front window of the restaurant and ordered the breakfast special. "You're up early, Luke. Anything going on I should know about?"

The sheriff nodded. "Well, I don't know if it concerns you, but last night we had us some suspicious activity at the saloon, the livery, and the telegraph office."

"Is that right?"

"Just some fooling with the locks and such. Nothing stolen outside of some horseshoe nails and such. Probably kids up to no good." He shifted positions and speared a piece of sausage with his fork. "You looking to head back to Denver soon, Gus?"

"Looks like we ought to have all the loose ends wrapped up by the end of the month, but you never know." He tucked his napkin into his shirt collar and sipped at the worst coffee this side of the Mississippi. "No matter what, I aim to sleep in my own bed come the spring thaw."

Sheriff Luke Masters laid down his fork and shoved the sugar bowl toward him. "Three, four big spoonfuls of this and you won't even taste the bitterness—much."

Gus nodded and lifted the bowl to pour a healthy amount of sugar into his cup. "Why'd I let you throw the only good cook in town into the jailhouse? If I didn't know better, I'd think you trumped up those charges just to get a better cup of coffee over there."

The sheriff grinned. "Who could predict he'd have warrants that would get him sent to Denver? Guess we'll never eat good in this town again." He paused to shovel the last bit of runny eggs onto a corner of his toast. "You said you were tying up the loose ends in that train robbery case?"

"That's right," Gus said as a plate of eggs, sausage, and toast was set before him. "Looks like we caught the lot of them. Now all I've got to do is file the paperwork and wait for the judge."

"You sure you got 'em all?" Sheriff Masters asked.

Gus choked down his bite of breakfast and gave the sheriff a look intended to show he'd heard just about enough of what he was about to hear.

"I see." The sheriff jerked his napkin from around his neck and tossed it on the table along with payment for his meal. "I hear tell not everybody's sure all those men were caught." He paused. "You sure don't look like you're too worried about it."

Gus stifled his rising anger and let his fork drop. "What're you getting at, Luke?"

"Nothing," he said. "Except I have to wonder how a collection of fellows who don't seem to be the smartest group of men managed to pull off all those robberies *and* find time to spend all the loot." He pushed back his hat to scratch his head. "Just don't quite seem possible, although I'd have to take the word of a Pinkerton man over the opinion of a lowly sheriff, wouldn't I?"

"I reckon you would, Luke," Gus said slowly, "but I wonder if there's something else you're wanting to say."

The sheriff stared at him for a minute and then stood. "I believe I've about said all I need to."

"I believe you have," Gus responded as he returned to his breakfast.

Before the seat beside him had time to get cold, the prissy Pinkerton Victoria Barrett-Ames had settled herself into it. Today she wore green, a frilly frock with ruffles at the neck and a hat that looked even more absurd than yesterday's feathered fiasco.

"Good morning, Mr. Drummond," she said.

Rather than speak, he nodded. Let her think he was too busy eating to talk.

"I've a favor to ask."

"A favor?" He grumbled under his breath at the woman's ability to draw words out of him despite his intention of silence.

She folded her hands on the table and offered him a smile. "Just a small one."

"Then call me Gus if you're going to ask me a favor." The smile edged up a notch, and Gus's heart sank. This Pinkerton was as pretty as sunrise on a spring morning. Whatever she asked, he'd probably do it. "But I'm not re-opening the case and that's final."

"While that remains to be seen, Mr. Drummond, that's not the favor I wish to ask." Her smile broadened.

Gus let his fork drop again with a satisfying clatter and steepled his hands before meeting her gaze. What in the world was this woman up to?

"Miss Vicky, I'd agree to just about anything right now if it meant I could finish my breakfast in peace and quiet."

"Now don't say anything you don't mean."

Her tone was playful, but the look on her face told another story. He decided to proceed carefully. "Is this business or pleasure?"

She cupped her hand against her chin and leaned toward him. "Business," she whispered.

He pushed away from the table and stood. As pesky as this Pinkerton in petticoats had become, he might as well get this showdown over with sooner rather than later. He would have to let the kid down gently, maybe give her a little encouragement that there were a lot of things a pretty lady could do with herself before he told her the plain facts. Not everyone was cut out to be a Pinkerton.

Discretion being the better part of valor, he decided to take the woman and the discussion elsewhere. No sense letting the whole town see the Englishwoman in tears.

He groaned. One thing he couldn't abide was a tearful woman. Every last one of his six sisters could reduce him to a babbling fool with their feminine tears. For that reason, he'd fled Scotland and vowed to remain a single man.

Women were just plain trouble—and the worst of the lot sat next to him. The first sign of tears from those eyes and it would all be over.

Maybe he should stay right there in full view. He looked past the lady Pinkerton to see Mabel Hawkins bearing down on them, winding her way through the Monday morning crowd like a wet hen heading for cover.

What a conundrum. Should he take his chances with Miss Mabel or risk Miss Vicky's tears? Both choices sounded about as appealing as slow dancing with a porcupine.

When Miss Mabel waved, his decision was made.

"Why don't you and I take a stroll?" Gus practically lifted the female Pinkerton out of her chair and onto her feet. As gently as he could manage, he linked arms with her and set her to walking toward the nearest exit. "It's a beautiful morning, and this place is a bit crowded for my liking."

The Pinkerton stumbled, and Gus caught her, steadying her arm as she set her silly hat to rights.

"But your breakfast, you haven't finished," she said. "Oh, look, there's Miss Hawkins."

The overly chatty organist called out a greeting, and Gus answered with a polite but firm hello and good-bye all in one breath. Stepping aside to allow a couple of hungry cowhands to enter the restaurant, he prayed while he counted the seconds until Miss Mabel had them in her grasp.

His prayers were answered when he saw through the front window that she had found someone else to visit with this morning.

"Thank You, Lord," he whispered before ushering Miss Vicky across the street toward the livery and a quiet spot where they could speak privately.

He'd have to remember that little blessing in his prayers tonight. If only the

Lord would allow him one more blessing, that of being free from the tangle of the last of the Pinkertons in petticoats. Unfortunately, when he cast a glance beneath that silly green hat to the source of his irritation, he realized he just might miss her.

Their casual banter often ended up in heated debate, and he'd learned the lady could match wits with the best of them in conversation. A man who didn't know better might even think a sharp mind lay beneath that fancy hairstyle and foolish hat.

He shook off the silliness and led her to the side of the livery, where he pointed to a bench half-hidden from the road. Gus took up a position against the wall of the livery and lightly rested his fingers on his revolver. From the street, the casual observer would not see the lady but would have a clear view of him.

Miss Vicky arranged her flouncy skirts and settled her purse onto her lap. A light breeze danced around them, skittering across her feather and sending it into motion. As he had yesterday at church, Gus turned his attention to the feather rather than the lady beneath it.

"I'd like to state my request and be on my way. Moment will be wondering where I am."

"So whatever this business favor is, your friend isn't in on it then?"

For purely investigative purposes, he studied her face. It didn't take a Pinkerton to tell that this woman had something to hide. But then, didn't they all?

Something slammed against the side of the barn, and Gus went for his pistol. Miss Vicky jumped to her feet, producing a gun from her lacy purse.

"What?" she whispered. "Surely I'm not the first Pinkerton you've seen with a pistol."

Another thump inches away from the side door prevented him from answering. Gus touched a finger to her lips and pointed toward the door. With care, he reached for the latch and pushed. The door swung in on silent hinges and he peered inside.

Nothing but horses and straw in sight.

Out of the corner of his eye, he saw something dart across the shadows and disappear into an empty stall at the end of the stable. He gestured for her to stand still and then crept toward the stall.

To her credit, Miss Vicky kept her silence and stayed rooted to the spot. At least she could take orders from a superior officer. Perhaps their conversation on her career change, if it happened today, would be a short one.

Gus moved slowly, sticking to the shadowy side of the space until he reached the stall door. It stood half-open, hiding whomever or whatever might be standing behind it. He reached for his pistol and placed his palm on the door. Something shuffled in the straw, and he looked over his shoulder to see if Miss Vicky had moved.

Good. She hadn't.

Another shuffling sound, this one seemingly coming from behind the door where he stood, told him he and the lady were not alone in the stable. He raised his pistol and took another step forward.

The mare in the stall nearest the door whinnied, and Gus jumped, collecting his wits just in time to keep from firing his pistol. He whirled around to see Miss Vicky petting the animal and frowned.

Then he felt the cold steel against the back of his neck.

"Drop the gun and turn around real slow, Pink," the deep voice said.

Gus's gaze darted to Miss Vicky, who stood scratching the mare's ears like she hadn't a care in the world. What a time for him to be without a real Pinkerton as backup. Just wait until he told the guys back in Chicago how their petticoated Pinkerton performed under pressure.

If he lived that long.

Chapter 4

Victoria heard the gruff voice and knew it couldn't belong to Mr. Drummond. Hiding her pistol in the folds of her skirt, she turned to get a better view of the big Scotsman. Cloaked in shadows, he appeared to raise his hands in a gesture that resembled surrender.

Her senses on alert, she nudged past the mare. Mr. Drummond's revolver glinted silver as it hit the ground and skittered toward the center of the aisle. She moved a bit closer, catching his attention when she reached a spot only a few feet way.

The Pinkerton's expression, visible despite the dim light, warned her to stop. She ignored him to creep into a position where she could see the situation more clearly.

Behind him were two men, a nervous-looking fellow with a pistol and an over-sized man with a rifle. The barrel of the rifle rested against the back of Mr. Drummond's neck, and a white sack dangled from his hand.

A white sack.

Her detective's mind began to race. Could one of these men be the Ghost? Had the money been hidden in the livery all this time?

There was only one way to know for sure.

The reality of the situation assaulted her. Unlike the practices she and the other ladies had performed in Chicago, this was a real crime in progress. No instructor would appear to order the scene stopped. The criminals were real and so were the bullets in her gun—the gun she had prayed she would never have to use.

Focus on the task at hand, Victoria. Remember your training. Don't ponder the possibilities; just aim and pray.

Blood pounded at Victoria's temples as she debated which of the men to aim for. If she hit the one with the sack, she might be credited with catching the elusive Ghost, but she might risk allowing Mr. Drummond to be shot in the process. If she took aim against the other man, the fellow holding the money might get away.

"Fetch that lawman's gun," the man with the rifle said. "We ain't got all day."

Lord, what do I do? I can't possibly shoot anyone.

As the man reached for Mr. Drummond's gun, Victoria took a deep breath and raised her pistol. With Drummond's gun in hand, the nervous fellow darted toward the stable door. Victoria dove into the nearest stall and landed in a pile of hay and horse manure.

"Say good-bye, Pink," she heard the man say.

Before she realized what she'd done, Victoria jumped to her feet and released two shots from her pistol. The first hit the man with the rifle just below the knee, sending him sprawling to the floor. The second merely winged the nervous fellow on the arm, but the subsequent blood caused him to faint.

Covered in straw and horse dung, she handed Mr. Drummond his revolver and stored hers in her reticule, then reached for the bag. The contents shifted, lifting Victoria's hopes that at least part of the money would be returned. She turned the bag up and prepared to watch gold pour out. Instead, out came horseshoe nails, horseshoes, and various pieces of tack.

"Mr. Drummond, I heard a couple of shots. What happened?"

Victoria stood to see the sheriff barge into the livery through the side door. Drummond stepped between her and the lawman and gave her a warning glance. As the ranking officer on the case—and the only one not under cover—it fell to him to handle any contact with the law. Quickly she let the bag fall from her fingers.

He clapped the sheriff on the back and pointed him toward the stable, where the two thugs sat in the corner. "Miss Vicky and I were just having ourselves a private conversation when these two gentlemen decided to pull their weapons, Luke. I believe they just might be the two fellows you went looking for this morning."

The sheriff peered into the stable. "Good work, Pinkerton," he said. "Looks like you caught the fellows who've been plaguing the livery."

The nervous one moaned and clutched at his arm while the other remained motionless and pale. Neither seemed permanently injured. God must have directed the shots because Victoria certainly could claim no part other than pulling the trigger—and she had no real memory of doing that.

"Nice shooting, Gus," the sheriff said. "A couple of inches either way and these fellers would be sitting in a pine box instead of a jail cell come this afternoon."

A couple of inches. Pine box.

The bile rose in Victoria's throat.

"Why don't you see the little lady home and then stop by to fill out the paperwork?" He tipped his hat to Victoria. "You all right, little lady?"

Victoria tried her best to affect a helpless female stance, enabled in part by the unsettled state of her stomach. "I'm fine, thanks to this big strong Pinkerton."

"Very funny," Mr. Drummond said under his breath as he led her out of the livery.

"Indeed."

"If you hadn't been petting horses, I might not have given up my gun so easily." He cast a sideways glance in her direction. "I figured I could take one before the other one got a shot off. I was just afraid that shot might hit you instead of me."

"Thank you."

He tipped his hat but said nothing further.

Matching his long strides with difficulty, Victoria met his gaze. The big Scotsman wore a bit less of his usual formidability, but then a close encounter with a bullet would do that to a person.

A bullet.

Victoria's knees threatened to buckle. She'd not just shot one man, but two. Considering she had never even fired the thing at a living target before today, she'd done a fair job. Neither man had been seriously hurt, and the criminals had been captured before either did serious harm.

Oh, but what if she had missed? What if her incompetence and lack of formal Pinkerton training had caused a fellow agent to be hurt—or worse?

She squared her shoulders and pushed away the awful thought. Until now her image of a Pinkerton centered on saving lives, not taking them. She'd even entertained the notion that God was proud of her career choice. Now that He had seen her wound not one but two of His creatures, dare she believe He still held that opinion?

Perhaps the gentlemen in Chicago were right. Perhaps a lady didn't possess the temperament necessary for proper crime fighting.

No, Moment, Sydney, and Ruth certainly proved that wrong. And what of the famous Kate Warne, the lady Pinkerton who saved President Lincoln from an attempt on his life just prior to his inauguration? Without Kate's successful foiling of the assassination plot, Abraham Lincoln would never have become president.

Stories of Kate Warne and others like her had fueled Victoria's desire to become a Pinkerton. Dare she now give up on her dreams merely because she'd been forced to use the weapon she disdained?

Mr. Drummond nudged her side with his elbow. "A penny for your thoughts, Miss Vicky."

Why did the ruffian insist on calling her by that dreadful name? Worse, how could she tell someone as insensitive as he of her concerns? Another person might offer words of comfort or advice, but what would Gus Drummond have to offer?

Most likely a sarcastic comment or a derisive laugh at her expense. Better to keep silent rather than share her thoughts with her fellow Pinkerton.

A chill wind danced past and caused her to shiver. Looking up at the sky, she saw the portent of rain, possibly even snow. Would spring ever come?

She pretended an interest in the items for sale at R & S Fashions across the street. The beautiful frock and matching hat in the window reminded her of the sorry state of her current ensemble, and she stifled a groan.

"I'll say it again. A penny for your thoughts."

"I'll keep my thoughts to myself for now, if you please."

"Suit yourself." He chuckled. "Not that you need my permission to do that."

They walked along in silence for a moment until Mr. Drummond stopped abruptly at the stairs behind the mercantile and turned to face her. She took a step back to gain a bit of distance and peered up into a blinding ray of sunlight. Blinking, she shaded her eyes and waited for him to come into focus once more.

"This isn't easy to admit." He wrapped a big hand around the stair rail leading up to Victoria and Moment's second-floor rooms. "I owe you a debt of thanks."

His honesty took her by surprise. So did her heart's reaction to the look on his face. Where she had once seen disdain, there now appeared to be a genuine respect.

Or was it merely an illusion caused by the blinding light of the morning sun?

Victoria stepped into the shade covering the first riser of the stairs. Her position brought her nearly eye level with his chin, a definite advantage over her usual height deficit. If only she could conquer her fears as easily.

She dared another look at him. Whatever she'd seen—or imagined she'd seen—was gone, replaced by the old Gus Drummond's usual countenance.

Perhaps someday she would discover what lay behind the gruff lawman's ill-tempered disposition. Right now it was all she could do to stand in his presence. For that matter, standing at all was becoming quite the ordeal.

Why did she have to shoot those men? Couldn't God have thought of a better plan?

"You might want to sit down until your knees stop knocking."

His smile mocked her as he reached for her elbow, but her knees thanked her as she relieved them of their responsibility and settled on the step. Before she could protest, Mr. Drummond landed on the riser beside her, crowding her against the rough wooden rail.

"The first time's the worst," he said. "Not that it gets any easier."

Victoria scooted as far as possible from the Pinkerton and wrapped her arms around her knees. "I don't know what you're talking about."

"Shooting someone. It's hard but it's part of the job." He reached for her hand. "I don't believe God gives the responsibility to anyone who would take it lightly."

Rather than respond, she stared at the hand enveloping hers. A scar ran across three knuckles, and a light dusting of cinnamon-colored freckles could barely be seen. These were the hands of a capable lawman. Hers, by comparison, looked frail and inadequate.

Like her.

"That was some fine shooting though," he continued. "Neither will forget they met up with a Pinkerton anytime soon. What you're feeling now, it'll pass."

Victoria sighed. "Indeed."

Mr. Drummond squeezed her hand and then released it. An awkward silence fell between them as she realized she missed the warmth of his touch.

"You say that a lot. 'Indeed.'"

His affectation of her native inflection made her laugh. When their gazes met, she averted her eyes and studied her fingers. "Do I?"

"I'm of a mind to ask you a question."

"Ask away."

"What leads a woman who doesn't like shooting to be a Pinkerton?"

What indeed? If she attempted to answer the question properly, they'd be here all winter.

"One might argue a case of foolishness was to blame, but I prefer to think the Lord had something to do with it," she said instead.

"What sort of foolishness?"

She shook her head. "The sort that a man wouldn't understand."

"You might be surprised what a man will understand." His gaze softened. "I do have six sisters. Why don't you give me a try?"

Where was the gruff lawman who'd made it his business to irritate her? She tried to picture him living in a house filled with sisters and failed.

Silence once again reigned between them as Victoria looked away. Mr. Drummond's shoulders moved, brushing hers, and his fingers once again wrapped around her cold hands. When she looked back toward him, he had leaned so near that their noses nearly touched.

For a long moment, neither moved. The absurd thought that her nemesis might actually kiss her popped into Victoria's head.

Strange, but the idea held some appeal. Actually, it held great appeal. She puckered her lips and waited. He seemed to be doing the same.

Victoria closed her eyes.

An instant later, the whistle of the morning train from Denver sent her skittering to her side of the stairs. Her face hot with shame, Victoria snatched her hands from his grasp and buried them in the folds of her skirt.

To his credit, Gus Drummond looked as flustered as she did. "I believe all this started when you interrupted my breakfast," he said. "Something about some business you wanted to discuss with me."

Victoria cleared her throat and attempted to speak. "Yes," she finally managed, "actually I have a favor to ask."

"Considering I owe you my life, I suppose I can take on a favor from a fellow Pinkerton." He paused and looked as uncomfortable as she felt. "As long as you're not asking me to reopen the train robbery case."

"No, I'm not asking you to reopen the case, at least not yet."

He lumbered to his feet and turned to face her. "Oh no, you don't. We've had this discussion one too many times. The Ghost has been caught, the money was spent, and that's the end of that."

Victoria leaned back on her elbows to look up into his face. "Casting aside the flaws in your theory, namely that the gentleman who confessed to being the Ghost is a known liar and braggart and the fact that no evidence to prove the money has been spent exists, I will let you have your opinion for now." She held up a hand to stop his protest. "I am merely asking you to use your connections to do a background check on someone."

"Who?"

"Will Bowen."

"For what purpose?" He scowled and crossed his arms over his chest. "As if I didn't know."

"As I told you in the restaurant, this is strictly Pinkerton business." She adjusted the feather on her hat and made him wait a moment more before stating her reasons. "I have reason to believe Mr. Bowen's expertise could be of some use on a case I am investigating."

"I'll bet."

Victoria rose and turned to head for the solace of the apartment she shared with Moment. How dare the ruffian question her motives?

Certainly she *did* enjoy Will Bowen's company, and he *was* a refreshing change from the usual caliber of man to be found in the American West, present company included. Still, did he honestly think her unable to separate Pinkerton business from affairs of the heart?

Somehow Mr. Drummond reached the top of the stairs before her and blocked the door. "How about you and I talk turkey, Miss Vicky?"

Victoria held tight to the rail and stared up at her adversary. What had she been thinking when she considered actually kissing the man?

"What an interesting way you have with the Queen's English, Mr. Drummond. Would you please elaborate? I'm afraid I am unfamiliar with the term 'talk turkey.'" She pasted on a smile. "In Britain our turkeys are quite silent."

He took a step toward her and she stood her ground. She was, after all, a Pinkerton.

"Forget the Queen's English," he said. "You're asking me to use my sources to check out your gentleman friend. I fail to see how that can be called business." He paused. "Looks like it would come more under the heading of pleasure than business. But what do I know about the situation? Could be you and old Will are thinking of becoming the next crime-fighting couple."

Victoria let the accusation hang between them before taking a deep breath and asking God for a bit more patience. "I have reason to believe that Mr. Bowen could be instrumental in determining what happened to the missing money. All I need is the assurance that he is who he claims to be so that I can feel safe in revealing my identity as a Pinkerton to him."

"I knew it!" He slammed his fist against the rail, and Victoria felt the wooden structure jump beneath her feet. "I told you that case is closed. Forget it! I will not play matchmaker between a citified banker and a lady Pinkerton who wants to hang up her pistol and take on a husband."

With that, he stormed past her, shaking the stairs with every step. Victoria waited until he reached the ground to speak. While she longed to bite back with a harsh rebuttal of his ridiculous claim, she decided to present a composed facade. Only she would know what raged just beneath the surface of her smile.

"Oh, Mr. Drummond," she said in her sweetest voice. "I believe you've forgotten something."

He froze. "What?"

"You seem to have forgotten that you pledged to owe me a favor for saving your life." She watched with pleasure as he pivoted on his heel to face her. "I'm collecting that favor."

"And to think I almost kissed that man," she whispered as she watched him storm away.

Chapter 5

T o think I almost kissed that woman."

Gus rounded the corner, nearly knocking a farmer off the sidewalk. As he helped the man collect his bags, he let his mind wander to the pretty Pinkerton.

One thought of Miss Vicky and he got mad all over again. What was it about that lady that got his goat every time he tried to have a civil conversation with her? Worse, what was it about her that drew him like a moth to a flame?

Even covered in straw and horse manure, she looked prettier than any woman he'd ever met up with. The truth be known, he'd been as nervous as a long-tailed cat in a room full of rocking chairs ever since the first time he caught sight of her.

He'd gone to the Lord with his troubles, but the Man Upstairs seemed to be taking great delight in his predicament. He'd even mentioned in a letter home that a particular Englishwoman had been plaguing him. His dear Scottish mother's response: "Marry her then."

Marry her? The thought of spending the rest of his born days in proximity to the feisty female set his liver on edge. Since Victoria Barrett-Ames had arrived in Windmere Falls, he'd not had a moment's peace.

Gus tipped his hat to the farmer and continued toward the telegraph office. The worst of it all was that he ended up doing exactly what he'd decided he wouldn't do—meddling into a lead that might reopen a closed case.

No, she couldn't really want information on the banker for the reasons she claimed. The pretty Pinkerton had her fancy feathered cap set for the Bowen fellow, and there was nothing he could do about it.

Not that he would want to stop her. They were quite a pair, the both of them, and he wished them all the happiness in the world. The sooner he got this over with, the better. He did owe the woman a debt, and Gus Drummond always paid his debts.

He reached for the latch on the telegraph office's door, still grumbling inwardly at his predicament. In his haste, he nearly ran down Will Bowen coming out of the telegraph office. He stood back to let the banker pass and muttered a greeting. To his surprise, Bowen shook his hand and greeted him like an old friend.

"Pressing business, Mr. Drummond?"

"Matter of life and death." He took note of the folded paper in the banker's vest pocket, out of place with the perfection of his fancy suit and shiny shoes.

Bowen pushed the paper deeper into his pocket and clapped a hand on Gus's shoulder. "Ah, well, I won't keep you then, my friend. Take care."

While Gus had made casual acquaintance with the fellow, he hadn't seen fit to spend much time with him. About the only good thing he could say in regard to Will Bowen was that he had backed a posse of men when the worst of the robberies were taking place. At the time, he figured it had to do with Bowen's concerns that some of his money might get stolen in one of the robberies. Now he wondered if maybe he really was a good guy.

Miss Vicky sure seemed to think so.

"Oh, Mr. Drummond?"

Gus turned to see that Will had followed him back into the telegraph office. "Yes?"

The banker smiled. "I understand you and Miss Barrett-Ames were involved in a bit of excitement at the livery stable this morning."

News travels fast. "That's right," Gus said.

"I'd like to thank you for protecting Victoria. She's such a fragile creature and very precious to me." He paused and leaned close. "Actually, I'm of a mind to make her my wife someday soon, so you can see what a dear cost it would have been had she been injured or worse. I wonder if there is anything I could offer you as a reward for your valor."

Gus nearly slugged him. Instead, he turned him down flat and headed for the telegrapher before he could change his mind. Reward money held no interest for him, but landing his fist on the city boy's nose sure did.

So much for giving his penchant for irritation to God. But then it seemed his live sacrifices climbed off the altar regularly—another thing to work on.

Guess You and I will be talking about that later, Lord.

That evening what he and the Lord ended up discussing was another subject entirely, or maybe it was a related one. Ever since he sat on those cold steps with the prissy Englishwoman, he'd denied one thing—the feeling that the Lord had put them together for a reason.

Trouble was, he hadn't been able to decide whether that reason was crime fighting or courting. He decided to do neither until God spoke a bit plainer.

◆　◆　◆

Late Saturday afternoon, Victoria surveyed the magnificent sweep of snow-covered mountains from her perch atop Paint, her favorite of all Will's horses. "The day is absolutely gorgeous."

Will rode to a stop beside her and smiled. "I'm glad you like it. I ordered it just for you."

They'd ridden a few times before, but never had Victoria been so nervous about being alone with Will. She attributed her uneasiness to the anticipation of waiting for confirmation from Mr. Drummond, but she knew a part of it was that she really liked spending time with the banker.

Their common backgrounds and shared love of horses gave them plenty to talk about, but today her side of the conversation had been limited to the occasional comment about the weather and the price of yard goods at the mercantile. Mostly Victoria felt content to enjoy the ride and the company in silence. Thankfully he seemed to agree.

"Race you to the river." He spurred his horse into a gallop and headed for the valley and the ribbon of blue green in the distance.

Victoria followed, trailing Will until the very last when she managed to pull ahead. At the river, he climbed off his horse and helped Victoria to the ground, lingering to hold her hand a moment longer than necessary.

"I'd like to speak to you regarding a matter of some importance, Victoria."

"Oh?" Her gaze met his. He looked much too serious for such a lovely day. Had he discovered her secret?

"I've made no secret of my feelings for you," he said. "But I'm not certain you understand the depth of my affection for you."

Victoria swallowed hard and tried to think of a diversion. As much as she cared for Will Bowen, a Pinkerton couldn't allow herself to fall in love while working on a case. It just wasn't done.

True enough, Ruth, Sydney, and Moment had found love while crime fighting, but this was different. Her friends had all managed to actually solve the crimes they investigated. She alone remained as the Pinkerton who had not earned her title.

"Will, really, must we talk about such things?"

The banker lifted her hand to his lips. "I had hoped you shared my feelings. Did I speak too soon, Victoria?"

She took a deep breath and let it out slowly. "Perhaps."

"I see." He released her fingers and turned to reach for Paint's reins. "Then we should agree to discuss this at a later date. Shall we return these horses to the stable?"

"Of course."

She knew she'd hurt him, and the knowledge stung. If only she hadn't pledged her allegiance to fight crime for the Pinkerton Agency. That vow precluded any others she might want to make.

Then there was the pesky matter of Gus Drummond.

For some strange reason, memories of her near miss with kissing him on the back stairs of the mercantile had stayed with her far longer than she deemed appropriate. Strange, considering she thought the Scotsman irritating at best.

◆　◆　◆

Gus thought on the situation until his thinker got tired and he had to quit. In short order, Miss Vicky had crawled under his skin but good, and the Lord seemed to take great delight in pointing that out regularly.

Just yesterday he had been a man with a purpose—namely to take up the cause of justice as a Pinkerton and to settle someday in a nice quiet place, devoid of chattering females, to spend the last of his days before Jesus called him home. And then came Miss Vicky. Overnight his plan and his peace shattered.

Actually, if he were to admit the truth, the prissy Pinkerton hadn't achieved the feat quite so fast. No, somewhere between her arrival and this morning she'd become. . . what?

He shoved back from the clutter on his makeshift desk and stood to pace the tiny hotel room he'd called home for far too long. That's it—he must have cabin fever.

Leaning against the sill of the big window that faced the mountains, Gus let his mind roam free. While his body stood in Windmere Falls, his thoughts headed for Denver and the little patch of heaven just west of town where the mountains met the flat plain. He saw the patch of ground he'd staked out for clearing last time he'd visited, and he imagined the little cabin he would build beside the brook that babbled slow in the winter and ran fast in the spring.

He made two more loops around the room and then reached for his gun belt. Rather than pace like a caged tiger, he decided to do his thinking in a larger and more convenient place—God's great outdoors.

Loping toward the rocky outcrop that was his favorite thinking spot, he gave thanks for the beauty of the day but soon found himself thinking of the beauty of Victoria Barrett-Ames instead. "She just ruins everything," he muttered as he reached the rocky point and dismounted.

"Who?" a voice said out of nowhere.

Gus went for his gun and nearly blew the feather off Miss Vicky's bright red hat. Where in the world did the woman buy her clothes? Surely no one in Windmere Falls could supply the outfits she wore.

And yet there she sat, curled up just as comfortable as you please in his thinking spot—his very own place of solitude. In her lap was a small sketchbook, in her hand, a pencil. He squinted to see that she'd drawn a passable sketch of the valley and the river beyond.

"Did I frighten you?" She closed the book and stuck the pencil behind her ear.

Gus holstered his pistol and forced his breathing to slow to normal. "Miss Vicky, you frighten me on a regular basis."

She looked pleased. Funny, how he liked that look on her.

"Would you care to join me?" She patted the spot beside her. "It's such a lovely view. I've been coming here quite often since I discovered it."

Rather than comment on how long *he* had enjoyed this view, he settled beside her and stretched his legs out in front of him. The sun bore down almost warm, but the clouds off in the distance warned of impending snow.

"I didn't know you could draw."

He lifted the sketchbook out of her lap and opened it before she could protest. Unlike the sketch of the valley, which was still in its beginning stages, the other drawings in the book were fully formed and excellent in quality. He flipped past a picture of a crumbling castle, a scene that put him in mind of the cliffs at Dover, and a detailed drawing of the Statue of Liberty.

"Give me that." She took a halfhearted swipe at the book and missed.

"These are really good," Gus said. "I didn't know you were a Pinkerton and an artist."

Something between pleased and perturbed decorated her face. "There are many things you don't know about me, Mr. Drummond."

"Is that a fact?" He grinned. "Tell me something I don't know about you, and I might consider giving your book back."

She screwed her lips into a pout that nearly caused him to hand the book—and his heart—over immediately. Thankfully, she looked away.

"All right. I love horses." She looked at him expectantly.

"Nope, I figured that one out a long time ago. Try again."

"I'm hopelessly in love with eye-catching dresses and matching hats."

Again Gus shook his head. "You're going to have to do better than that, Miss Vicky."

"My grandmother called me that."

Something in the way she spoke the words melted his heart. "Oh?"

"Yes" came out soft as a whisper. "I miss her terribly. She taught me to ride and to paint. Drawing came about as a necessity when I found I preferred to sketch rather than work in oils."

"Nope, that's real sweet but not exactly what I was looking for." He weighed the open book in his hand. "For something this special, I'm going to need a real juicy secret."

"Is this how you interrogate all your suspects?"

"Just the hard cases."

The lady Pinkerton giggled. "Very well then. If you must know, my grandmother had a deep dark secret that I've never told another soul."

"Let's hear it." He pointed his finger at her. "And it better be good."

"Oh, it is." She leaned closer, and he could smell the soft scent of vanilla. "Before Grammy married Grandpa, she longed for a bit of adventure, so she left home and hearth and followed her dream."

He feigned boredom with an exaggerated yawn. "And?"

"And she joined the circus. As an aerialist, no less."

"You're joking."

"I assure you I'm quite serious." She gave him a direct look. "Now, I've shared my deep dark family secret. Please give the book back."

Gus shook his head and opened the book to the place where he'd stopped before. "I was expecting something a bit more adventurous. I mean, an aerialist isn't quite a lion tamer or a bearded—"

He turned the page and froze. Staring back at him from the white sheet of paper was a precise likeness of himself. From his crooked nose to the scar just beneath his right eye, she'd captured him in exacting detail. He allowed his gaze to drift from the art to the artist. Finally he allowed her to snatch the book back.

And then he kissed her.

Chapter 6

Threading his fingers together to form a pillow for his head, Gus Drummond shifted away from Victoria and leaned back against the rocky outcrop. "Now *that* was a kiss," he said with a satisfied sigh.

"Indeed."

Victoria clutched the sketchbook to her chest and measured her breathing, all the while listening to her pulse galloping. Yes, that *was* indeed quite a kiss. It was a kiss that made her long for many more kisses, a kiss that could spark a lifetime of more kisses. A kiss that had far exceeded her wildest dream of what the perfect kiss would be.

It seemed as if the Lord had given her a little taste of heaven on earth and called it a kiss. And yet the whole situation was most unsuitable.

Mr. Drummond was a fellow Pinkerton and a man who could irritate her with great ease. They had absolutely nothing in common, and merely being in the same room generally caused one or both of them trouble. He was everything she did not seek in a lifetime partner and was a Scotsman to boot. What would her father, the loyal Englishman, say?

And what of her heavenly Father? Surely He did not mean for her to be yoked to a man like Gus Drummond.

Even if the Lord did bring him to mind regularly when she prayed for guidance regarding her future, the thought of actually having feelings for the man seemed preposterous. No, she must put a stop to this at once.

And yet, when she thought of that kiss. . .

Out of the corner of her eye, she saw that the object of her thoughts had tipped his hat low over his brow and closed his eyes. She braved a closer look and frowned. Could the brute be taking a nap?

How dare he kiss her soundly and then fall into a doze while she fretted? Victoria's ire began to rise. Did he think so little of their kiss that he could fall into a stupor upon its completion?

Well, she certainly did not have to stand for this sort of treatment. She crept off the rock and headed for her horse as quietly as possible. If the cad wanted to kiss and snore, he could do it without an audience.

"Farewell, Sleeping Beauty," she said under her breath as she headed for her horse.

◆ ◆ ◆

Gus peeked at the retreating form of the pretty Pinkerton, cursing himself for a fool. He shouldn't have kissed her. And yet the power of that one kiss shook him to his boots.

He wanted to tell her so, wanted to stop her and convince her to marry up with him on the spot like his mother and the Lord had suggested months ago, but something inside him froze. So rather than make today the best day of his life, he let Miss Vicky ride away without saying a word.

Someday he would make it up to her; someday he would gather the courage to tell her just what she'd come to mean to him. Someday, if God gave him another chance, he'd be ready and he'd do right by her.

Right now he had enough trouble just sitting still and listening to the Lord shame him for a fool.

◆ ◆ ◆

"You're just mad because Gus Drummond kissed you and then fell asleep. It doesn't help that he hasn't been around to court you properly for the last two days." Moment shook her head. "I'm sure he will make amends when he returns from Denver. Why don't you wait until then to do something you might be sorry for later?"

"You're my dearest friend, Moment, but I wish I hadn't told you a word of what happened between that irritating man and me."

The bell sounded as the door opened. Moment gave Victoria one last look of incredulity before calling out a greeting to the pastor's wife. While Moment went to wait on Mrs. Griffin, Victoria began to sort through the facts of the train robberies yet again, putting any personal thoughts of Gus Drummond as far out of reach as she could manage.

As the door closed behind Mrs. Griffin, Victoria reached the same conclusion as before. In her estimation, a large amount of stolen money was hidden and waiting for someone to find it.

When she shared her opinion with Moment a few minutes later, she met with the same resistance she'd encountered before. Given the fact that Moment was up to her sunbonnet in wedding plans, Victoria set about handling the situation alone.

If only she didn't have to wait for Mr. Drummond's results before she firmed up her plans. Prudence told her to delay, but a nagging suspicion that the more time that passed, the less likely the loot would be found forced her to a quick decision. She must take Will into her confidence.

"Moment, dear, would you mind terribly if I ran a quick errand?"

"Of course," she called.

Lord, if this is the wrong thing to do, please stop me.

A few minutes later, she'd donned her coat and slipped past the tellers in the bank to deposit herself in the chair across the wide desk from Will Bowen. Before proper greetings could be exchanged, a clerk appeared at the door and beckoned to Will, leaving Victoria alone in the office.

The wood-paneled space reminded her of her father's study. Her gaze flitted across the desk, carved of walnut and adorned with two neat stacks of papers and an ornate silver inkwell in the shape of a horse's head.

In a straight line to one side of the inkwell, three matching silver pens glittered in the afternoon sun. Directly behind the massive chair, a pair of polo mallets hung above a painting of a string of ponies.

Victoria smiled. How could a man who loved horses as much as Will Bowen possibly be deemed untrustworthy?

"Please forgive me, Victoria." He swept past her to take his seat at the desk and offer a warm smile. "To what do I owe the pleasure of your company today?"

As usual, his grooming was impeccable, his manners divine. She couldn't help but contrast him with the pesky Pinkerton. "Actually, I would like to discuss a matter of some importance."

"It wouldn't have anything to do with what you *didn't* want to discuss a few days ago, would it?" He gave her a hopeful look. "If so, I would declare it an answer to prayer."

Her heart sank. Someday soon she would have to confront the problem of Will's feelings toward her. Until the Lord told her otherwise, she could merely be his friend.

"I'm sorry, Will," she said slowly, "but, no, it wouldn't."

His smile faded a notch and then broadened once more. "Of course."

Victoria shifted in her chair and went over the words one last time before determining to speak them aloud. "You see, when last we spoke regarding my work at the mercantile, I was not at liberty to tell you that—"

"There you are!" Gus Drummond strode into the office like he owned the place and snatched Victoria up by the elbow. "I'm sorry, Bowen, but I'm going to have to borrow your companion for a moment. I'm sure you won't mind. Pinkerton business, you see."

"I'm afraid I'm going to have to protest, Mr. Drummond."

He whirled around to stare down at Victoria. "It's *Pinkerton* business, Ma'am, and right important."

Will rose and placed his palms on the desk. His gaze went from Victoria to Drummond and then back to Victoria. "Perhaps you should go with him, my dear. I'm sure he merely wants information." He turned his attention to Mr. Drummond. "Am I correct?"

"You are correct," he said. "I'm merely after information. So if you'll excuse us, Bowen." He gave Victoria's elbow a firm tug. "Shall we, *my dear?*"

With that he led her out of the office and onto the sidewalk, ignoring her silent protests to the contrary. He covered the distance between the bank and the mercantile in record time, leaving Victoria to scurry to keep up.

"Morning, Miss Alexander," he called as he barged through the mercantile's front doors.

Moment called a greeting as she appeared from the back storeroom. "Is this your errand?" she asked, sizing up first Victoria and then Mr. Drummond with a smile. "Welcome back, Mr. Drummond."

"No, this is *not* my errand."

"It's grand to be back, Miss Alexander. Now would you excuse us?" he asked. "Your friend and I need to have a little talk."

"I just made a fresh pot of coffee." Moment smiled. "Help yourself."

He released his grip on Victoria and cast a glance at Moment over his shoulder. "If you weren't getting hitched to Brady Miller, I'd marry up with you myself. You make the best coffee this man's ever tasted."

Her friend practically blushed pink at Mr. Drummond's statement. Yes, Moment's coffee was excellent, but really. The best he'd ever tasted? Worth marrying over? Well, that was taking it to the extreme.

Honestly, how difficult could it be to make a cup of coffee? Perhaps she should learn.

Victoria shed her coat and trailed the Pinkerton up the stairs and into the kitchen of the tiny living space she shared with Moment. His presence in the room seemed to shrink it to minuscule proportions. She thought of the last time they'd been together in such close proximity, and heat rose in her neck.

She certainly would not be kissing him this time. That would absolutely *not* happen. Besides, he couldn't possibly be interested in a woman whose coffee-making skills were nonexistent and whose kiss left him in need of a nap.

Why do I care?

Because you love him.

Victoria quickly discarded the ridiculous thought and pressed past the Pinkerton to lift two china teacups off the shelf. While he poured the coffee, she set out sugar and milk. Finally, they settled across from each other at the little table.

"What do you think you're doing?" he asked as he dumped spoonfuls of sugar into his cup. "Did you tell him you're a Pink?"

His stare bore hard on her, making her want to spill the contents of her soul in answer to any question he might ask. The effect was disconcerting, to say the least. No wonder he was considered such a good lawman.

Victoria stirred a bit of milk into her coffee and took a sip. It scalded her tongue, and she bit back a cry as she settled the cup onto the saucer with a shaky hand.

"Not yet," she said when she recovered, "but I was about to."

Drummond slammed his fist on the table, and the cups rattled in their saucers. "Have you lost your mind? Do you know what it means to give away your identity as a Pinkerton?"

"Everything all right up there?" Moment called from downstairs.

"Everything's fine," they said in unison.

"Yes, I know what it means," Victoria said slowly. "It means I'm taking Will Bowen into my confidence, but I have a good reason."

He snorted. "I'll bet."

She ignored the ruffian's indelicate behavior. "I believe he has information that would make this a worthwhile risk."

"You do?" Again the sarcasm was evident.

"Yes." She toyed with her spoon and then glanced up at him. "What better person to help find a large amount of missing money than a banker, especially a banker with connections in Denver and New York?"

Mr. Drummond seemed to consider her words for a moment. Perhaps the man did not possess the extreme amount of stubbornness she believed. While he looked away, deep in thought, she studied him.

What was it about being near to Gus Drummond that befuddled her so? Why hadn't she noticed the width of his shoulders, the self-assured bearing, and the sparkle in his eyes before?

And then there was the way he spoke of the Lord as if He were a dear friend. How reassuring it would be to be loved and cared for by someone so capable, so close to the Lord. Yes, this gruff lawman did hold a certain appeal.

What am I thinking? This is insanity. No, this is love.

Without warning, he swung his gaze back in her direction and caught her staring. The collision rattled her, and she nearly dropped her cup. Thankfully, he seemed completely ignorant as to the direction of her thoughts.

"Let's say I do agree the money's still out there somewhere." He held his hand up. "Just for argument's sake, that is."

"All right."

"Then I'd have to say you might be on to something." When she opened her mouth to agree, he held his hand up once more. "However, that doesn't tell me *why* you think this Bowen fellow is so trustworthy."

"Because. . ."

She struggled to find the right answer. Mentioning his near-proposal was certainly out of the question, as was his connection to her brother. Until she could sort out her tangle of feelings for him, the less Gus Drummond knew about her, the better.

"I see." He pushed back from the table, eyes narrowed. "So there's no particular reason you want to tell me about?"

She averted her gaze. "None that I would like to share at the moment."

"You two in love?"

The question startled her. "Why do you ask?"

"Because in my line of work, I only know two reasons why a woman would trust a man with something that could mean her life. One of them is if he's a blood relative, and the other's if she's in love with him." He paused. "You're not kin to the banker, are you?"

She shook her head.

"That's what I was afraid of."

Moment's light step on the stairs kept Victoria from commenting. It did not, however, keep her from thinking.

"Did I miss anything important?" Moment asked as she stepped into the kitchen.

"No," they said in unison.

Mr. Drummond glared at Victoria and then offered Moment a much kinder look. "Your friend here is about to give away her identity to a civilian."

The look on Moment's face cast away any hopes of support Victoria might have had. "You can't be serious, Victoria."

"Oh, she's serious, all right." He rose from his chair. "Serious about pretending to catch a crook while she's busy catching a banker."

The comment stung, but Victoria could find no retort. She looked to Moment for help and found none forthcoming. Rather, her friend seemed to pity her, or at least the expression on her face conveyed that feeling.

Mr. Drummond paused to collect a piece of folded paper from his pocket and toss it toward her. It landed on the table inches from her teacup. The paper unfolded slightly to reveal a telegram.

"You'll be glad to know your banker checks out clean as a whistle. I hope the two of you will be very happy together."

"Honestly, you sound as if I'm looking to marry the man."

Out of the corner of her eye, she saw Moment suppress a smile as she turned to make a discreet exit. Drummond, however, stood his ground and seemed less than amused.

"Well, aren't you?"

To continue this conversation from a seated position put her at a disadvantage. Standing, she realized she still possessed a disadvantage, and it had nothing to do with height.

She knew without a doubt that she loved this impossible, irritating scoundrel, and yet he bore her nothing but ill temper. She couldn't make coffee, couldn't solve a crime to save her life, and her kisses sent him into a deep slumber. To make matters worse, she would be returning to Chicago forthwith while he would reside in Denver.

With so many factors weighing against them, why would the Lord possibly want her to have feelings for Gus Drummond? And yet the knowledge that He did had enveloped her prayers even before their ill-fated kiss. She'd merely been too stubborn to acknowledge the fact.

She and God would be discussing this promptly. But first she must rid herself of the Pinkerton's presence.

"Thank you for the information, Mr. Drummond." She settled back down in her chair and pretended to busy herself by stirring her coffee. "I'll be sure to keep you informed as to the status of my investigation."

"You do that, Miss Vicky," he said as he stormed out. "Just don't expect me to come to the wedding."

"Who said you were invited?" she called.

"I didn't want to come anyway," came the answer from the bottom of the stairs. A moment later, the front door bell jingled, and he was gone.

Moment reappeared in the doorway, her smile broad. "It doesn't take a Pinkerton agent to see that Gus Drummond's in love with you."

"Do you think so?"

Her best friend nodded. "I know so."

Victoria allowed the spoon to fall from her fingers. "Moment," she said as she regarded her friend helplessly, "how did you know Brady was the one?"

Chapter 7

Long after Gus had gone and Moment had returned to her bookkeeping duties downstairs, Victoria sat at the table staring at the folded papers. Her conversation with Moment gave her the unfortunate reassurance that she was indeed in love with Gus Drummond. Worse, she realized her prayers led her to believe God blessed the union and planned for them to be together.

What she didn't know was how He intended to bring His plans to completion. According to Moment, Victoria's only recourse was to wait and see what He would do. No amount of action on her part, Moment had urged, would bring about God's perfect plan for Victoria's life.

The thought filled her with dread, disgust, and excitement all at the same time. She'd determined to make her own way in the world, and now this.

"Lord, can't You at least tell me what I can do while I wait? Surely there is something worthwhile I can accomplish here in Windmere Falls."

Quietness filled her spirit as the answer settled around her like the softly falling snow outside. *Do nothing.*

Frustrated, she walked to the basin and rinsed the cups, taking care not to chip the delicate china as she dried each one and put it away. She thought of Mr. Drummond's big fingers wrapped around the fragile cup and smiled.

The Scotsman was nothing like what she'd expected God to give her in a man. But how like God to do the unexpected and have it turn out so much better than she could imagine.

Now if he could just get to work on Gus Drummond in a timely manner.

Outside, the snow had begun to fall in earnest, and a few inches of powder decorated the sill. The occasional snowflake bounced against the glass and slid to its doom in the gathering pile below.

The sky held nothing but gray, and if not for the snow, she could have been standing in her ancestral home in England looking out at the January sky over London. By nightfall, a blanket of white would cover all of Windmere Falls.

Despite the warmth of the little kitchen, Victoria shuddered. Would spring ever come?

An idea took form. God told her she must wait on Him, but He didn't tell her she must wait alone. The least she could do was continue with her plan to find the last undiscovered link in the train robbery case—that of the missing money—while the Lord took care of more important matters.

Surely He wouldn't mind if she took that small responsibility on herself. After all, He *was* terribly busy changing Gus Drummond into a fitting husband for her and could hardly be bothered with a few last details of a crime that seemed so easy to solve.

And He *had* given her the ability to solve crimes. Wouldn't it be a disgrace not to act on that ability? She tucked the telegram into her reticule and reached for her coat, secure in the knowledge that her endeavors were for the glory of the Lord and the cause of justice.

This time when she walked to the bank, she made certain no one detected her presence. Rather than enter by the front doors, she slipped in the unlocked employee entrance at the back. Announcing herself with a note delivered by a skeptical but willing teller, she awaited Will Bowen at a prearranged spot adjacent to the church.

While she bided her time, well hidden from the prying eyes of Gus Drummond or anyone else who might happen by, she prayed for God to bless her plan. With His help, she would have the answer to the riddle of the Ghost and his hidden treasure before week's end. With that feat accomplished, Victoria could wait and see how God would do His part.

She flicked an errant snowflake from the sleeve of her coat and frowned. Now if Will would just arrive before she froze to death.

"Victoria, I came as soon as I could."

She looked up to see Will approaching and held a finger to her lips. He nodded and crossed the distance between them in silence.

Before she spoke, she guided him out of sight of the street and into the small stable at the rear of the church. The earthy scents of the little barn contrasted sharply with those outside, but it was warm and private.

Besides, her purpose for being here would be short-lived. In the future they could arrange for a more suitable meeting place, one that included fewer aromas and more security.

A mule protested loudly as the stable door swung shut on creaking hinges. Will seemed positively appalled at the place where his polished shoes now stood. Ever the gentleman, she thought. He said nothing of his plight but rather focused his attention on Victoria.

"I'll be brief, Will," she said as she cast about for the words. "This is a matter of the utmost importance. Before I begin, I must have your word as a gentleman that you will reveal nothing of what I tell you."

Confusion marred his handsome features, but a smile touched his lips. "Of course, Victoria, but I must say this situation is highly irregular."

"I understand your confusion. Let me explain. I am not who you think me to be." She shook her head. "Actually, I am who you think I am, but I'm also more than a mere shop girl."

"I know that, my dear. You are much more than a mere shop girl. You're a woman of exquisite tastes and breeding. Do you think I would allow you into my heart. . . ," he paused to broaden his smile, ". . .and into my stable if I thought otherwise? Why, my stable hands thought I'd lost my mind when I told them Miss Victoria Barrett-Ames was to be given complete access to all the horses at her very whim."

"I do appreciate what you've said, Will, and allowing me the enjoyment of your horses has meant more than you'll ever know."

He took a step forward and reached for her fingers. "Not nearly the enjoyment I've received in knowing I've met someone who shares my enthusiasm."

"Yes, well, I don't think I'm making myself clear."

Victoria snatched her hand away. There could be no misunderstanding her purpose in what she would tell Will. From now on, their relationship would be strictly business, and it would be her job to make him understand this.

But first she had to make him understand who she was and why she now lived temporarily in Windmere Falls, Colorado.

"What I mean to say, Will, is that I am acting the part of a shop girl in order to fulfill my current assignment. You see, back in Chicago, I do not officially hold a secretarial position. I felt free in telling my family this because that constituted the bulk of my work for the past three years, and thus it is not a lie." She paused. "Besides, I knew Father and Charles would fetch me home if they knew the whole truth."

Will sagged against the wall and blinked hard. "What are you saying, Victoria? Are you involved in something illegal? If so, you have my complete assurance I will assist you in extricating yourself from the situation. You are very dear to me, and I couldn't bear to think of you in some kind of danger."

"No, Will, but thank you. Actually, quite the opposite is true."

"Oh?"

She locked gazes with him. "I am a Pinkerton agent. I was sent over from the Chicago office in response to a call for help from Gus Drummond." His blank stare gave her hope, so she pressed on. "I would like to enlist your help in ascertaining whether certain large deposits have been made in Colorado banks over recent months."

"Really?"

"Yes. It is my belief that the money from the train robberies is hidden rather than lost, and the man who calls himself the Ghost is still at large."

His chuckle surprised her—then it infuriated her. When it continued well beyond the point of propriety, she stormed toward the door.

Will called to her, and she ignored him. His laughter was soon joined by the braying of the mule whose home they had invaded.

Blast after blast of cold air slammed against her face and stung her eyes as she strode toward the street. Anger bit against her heels with every step, followed by remorse. Tears threatened. Why had she gone outside God's directive to wait on Him?

At least Will hadn't believed her when she stated she was a Pinkerton. The situation could be worse.

"So you did it. You told him."

Victoria whirled around to see Gus Drummond leaning against the side of the church. Gathering the remnants of her pride, she gave the lawman a wide berth and turned toward the mercantile. The last thing she needed right now was to hear the cocky Pinkerton's indictment of her impetuous behavior. She already felt enough remorse for the both of them.

The sound of boots pounding against wooden sidewalks echoed behind her. When she picked up her pace, he matched it. As the mercantile came into view, she practically raced through the heavy snowfall toward the glow of the upstairs lights.

At the last moment, he stepped in front of her and blocked her way. With the snow coming down in near-blizzard proportions, the streets were deserted. She and Gus Drummond were the only two fools still about on this bleak January afternoon.

"Go away," she said as she attempted and failed to move past him.

His eyes flashed anger. "What did Bowen say?"

Drawing herself up to her full height, she regarded him impassively. "If it makes you feel better, he didn't believe me." With that, she left him standing ankle deep in snow on the sidewalk.

◆　◆　◆

The weather kept Victoria and the other citizens of Windmere Falls indoors for four days and effectively halted all commerce. Even the trains ceased their arrivals until the safety of the bridges in the outlying areas could be determined.

During that time, Victoria busied herself with two things, prayer and helping Moment to sew her wedding dress. Often she did both at once.

Knotting thread and stitching lace seemed to go together quite nicely with prayer, at least once she got past her inadequacies in the sewing department. Moment had patience in teaching her how to sew, just as God had patience in teaching her how to wait.

How thankful she felt that Ruth and Sydney had been chosen to work as seamstresses on this assignment rather than she and Moment. While she had no doubt her dear friend could hem and repair with the best of them, she knew no one would be fooled if she attempted to pass herself off as a professional in this area.

At the end of the fourth day, she'd nearly perfected her sewing technique. The waiting, however, would be much more difficult to master, for she ached to do something—anything.

However, when the sun shone bright on the morning of the fifth day, melting the snow so rapidly that it ran in rivers down the streets, Victoria almost felt disappointment. Life began to pick up its pace, and the next morning little was left to show of the snows save the mess it made of the unpaved streets.

Will visited the mercantile twice, but both times Victoria fled to her room. When she saw him picking his way across the street toward her for the third time that day, she knew she could avoid him no longer. Rather than race upstairs, she stood at the window and raised her hand in greeting. He returned the gesture and added a smile.

"You look lovely, Victoria," he said when he'd removed enough mud from his shoes to step inside. Taking her hand, he touched it to his lips. "Actually, I thought you might be avoiding me."

She looked away, toying with the ivory ribbons on a plum-colored bonnet. "I suppose I have," she admitted. "I felt a bit uncomfortable, as you can imagine."

"Understandable, considering the uncouth manner in which I behaved." He leaned against the doorframe and regarded her openly. "Honestly, I had no idea you would say what you said. Will you forgive me for my beastly behavior?"

"Of course."

Victoria tried and failed to read the emotions crossing his face. Dare she think he might believe she worked for the Pinkertons? And if he did, what did he think of the fact?

Will pulled a gold watch from his vest pocket and checked the time. "I'm afraid I must go, my dear. I've a train to catch."

He nodded toward the stairs. Victoria turned to see that Moment had joined them.

"Wonderful to see you again, Miss Alexander," he said. "I come bearing bad news regarding your wedding."

Moment looked alarmed. "Oh?"

"Pressing business in New York will keep me away from Windmere Falls for a few weeks."

He swung his gaze to Victoria. "It's my father. He's finally decided to retire, and he demands I come at once to assist with the arrangements."

"I see," Victoria said.

"We will miss you terribly," Moment added. "Even if you are an awful cad."

"Would you like me better if I brought you and Brady something wonderful from New York?"

Moment laughed and waved away the question as she busied herself at the cash register.

Will kissed Victoria's hand one last time and made his exit. Relief flooding her, Victoria sank onto the nearest stool and expelled a sigh while Moment merely smiled and headed back upstairs.

At least she would not have to keep up the game of hiding from Will Bowen. Now if Gus Drummond would stop hiding from her.

Chapter 8

The Pinkerton continued to make his presence scarce, even as January slipped into February. Victoria watched him ease into the back pew at church on Sunday, then noticed he'd already disappeared by the time she made her way out the doors afterward.

He no longer took his meals in the restaurant nor strolled the streets of Windmere Falls. Only the fact that his horse still remained stabled at the livery kept Victoria hopeful that Gus Drummond did indeed still reside there.

The morning before Moment's wedding, she awoke with a strange yearning in her bones. Stretching to climb out of her narrow bed served to make her want to fall right back in and pull the covers over her head. Contemplating which frock and hat to don made her wish she had the option of putting on her riding clothes instead.

Part of the trouble, she knew, was the impending nuptials. While she felt nothing but happiness for Moment and Brady, she did admit to a bit of jealousy that her best friend had found a partner for life so easily. She still believed the Lord had something in store for her and Mr. Drummond, but without the big Scotsman's cooperation, how would He ever manage to accomplish it?

Then there was the matter of the missing robbery money. She'd prayed and pondered and still couldn't account for the theory that the money was not out there somewhere waiting to be found. Jackson Griffin's claims of being the Ghost also fell flat. To believe the man's confession would be to discount the fact he would have had to be in two places at once.

How could he pull off the robberies and hide the money, all the time going unseen by the others in the gang? In addition, he could produce neither the white duster coat nor the flour sack mask to back up his claim.

It made no sense. At times she wondered if perhaps her initial instinct that Mr Drummond might be involved might actually be true. After all, he was the loudest critic of her theory.

And what of Gus Drummond? Since her time in Windmere Falls would end in a few days, had she misunderstood the Lord's leading? Perhaps she was destined to return to her Pinkerton duties in Chicago rather than contemplate a life with the Scotsman.

With these concerns weighing heavily on her, Victoria decided to seek solace in the one place where she knew she could find it—astride a horse. She ventured downstairs to clear her plans with Moment and found her friend deep in conversation with Brady Miller.

Nose to nose over the plans for an addition to Mr. Miller's cabin, neither looked up as Victoria made her way across the mercantile to peer out the front window. "Lovely day, isn't it?" she called, noting with glee that the couple jumped at the sound of her voice.

"Well, good morning, Miss Victoria," Mr. Miller said. "Pleasure to see you today."

Victoria turned and smiled. Love was indeed a wonderful thing to behold, unless the Lord was making you wait on your turn at it.

"Oh, Mr. Miller, you're not looking at anyone but Moment these days," she said.

He looped arms with Moment and offered her a chaste peck on the cheek. "She's right," he said.

Moment patted her fiancé's hand and then turned to face Victoria. "You look a bit pensive this morning, Victoria. Something wrong?"

She shrugged. "We're not busy. Do you think I might take the morning and go for a ride? I promise to return in time for lunch, and then the afternoon is yours."

Ten minutes later, she released the latch on the gate at the edge of Will's property and began the short walk to the stables. The air felt crisp, with just enough bite to require a light wrap. Victoria snuggled against the soft knitted shawl, one of the few relics of her English past. Even on this sunny Colorado afternoon, the scent of England still awaited in the folds of soft wool around her shoulders.

The ground wore the first tentative shoots of what would be grass and flowers by March. Trees still bore their bare branches, but closer inspection revealed tiny buds of green awaiting the spring.

The beauty of the landscape was tempered only by the question of whether Victoria would be there to see it upon full bloom. Only the Lord knew the answer, and today she decided she would leave the knowledge with Him.

To ride and forget that question and all the others was her goal. What a privilege to have the finest equine stock in Colorado from which to choose.

Victoria released the latch on the stable door and stepped inside. The earthy scent of hay and well-groomed horses wrapped her in familiar comfort as she waited for her eyes to adjust to the dimmer light.

At the far end of the stables a half-door filtered sunlight across two dozen magnificent thoroughbreds. Rather than call for help from one of the stable hands, she strolled toward the tack room. Generous to a fault, Will had secured all the items necessary for a lady to ride.

Today, however, Victoria decided to be bold. Bypassing the sidesaddle she generally chose, she headed for the one Will preferred. Heavier than she expected, the saddle slipped out of her grasp and plunged to the stable floor, knocking down a barrel and a stack of blankets as it fell.

She tried and failed to right the barrel and ended up dragging the saddle mere inches before tiring. Out of the corner of her eye, she saw a figure pass by the small, high window.

"Perhaps I shouldn't attempt this myself," she said as she stepped over the saddle and headed toward the window. If she climbed on the side of the trunk that sat beneath it, she could look out the window and beckon to whomever stood outside.

A patch of white nearly hidden by the overturned barrel caught her attention, and she stopped to reach for it. Rather than the cloth she expected, a bleached feed sack emerged—a feed sack with eye holes cut into it.

The Ghost's mask.

Her pulse began to gallop as the importance of her discovery dawned. A rattling noise alerted her to the opening of the stable doors.

Rather than be caught inside the stable without backup, Victoria elected to seek an exit and return to fight another day—or at least with another Pinkerton in tow. To that end, she climbed atop the trunk and pressed against the tiny window. It refused to budge.

The horses stirred. Someone definitely had walked into the barn, but whom? Will wasn't due back for another week, possibly longer. Could it be that the Ghost had used Will's absence as an opportunity to hide the evidence?

Perhaps the vile creature even intended to set Will up.

Hay crunched outside the tack room door, and Victoria discarded her theories in favor of finding a place to hide. The barrel might have worked had it not been upended by her own incompetence.

The only place left was the trunk. She raised the lid and prepared to climb inside, only to find it full of tack, saddle blankets, and a single white duster coat.

"Victoria?"

She whirled around to greet Will, losing her footing when her riding boots tangled with one of the saddle's stirrups. Plunging forward, she reached for Will and caught his hands. The mask fell, but thankfully she did not.

"Oh, Will, I'm so glad you're here," she said when he caught her elbow and righted her. "You're not going to believe what I found."

"Good work, Pinkerton."

"You believe me."

"I always did." His fingers tightened around her elbow as he led her away from the tack room and into the stable. "Perhaps you and I should take this evidence to the sheriff."

"Good idea. We'll need to stop and let Mr. Drummond know." She began to contemplate just how she would bear the news to the stubborn Pinkerton. Several different scenarios began to take form, none of which she intended to carry out.

No, better to take the evidence to the sheriff than send word to Drummond that it rested there. Any further investigation could be done by Drummond and whomever the agency sent to take her place.

Funny how she felt a certain peace in knowing she'd been right, and yet she would not be staying around to finish the job. Suddenly there was no great urge to *do something*. It was as if God had chosen this very inopportune moment to work His miracle on her. Dare she hope He had worked a miracle on Mr. Drummond too?

Without warning, Will took a sharp turn to whirl her around and face him. "This is as far as you go, my dear. I'd hoped it wouldn't come to this, but you're just too persistent."

"What are you talking about?"

"The Ghost." His tone was mocking, cold, and the expression on his face matched it. "How clever of you to deduce it was me."

"But I—"

"No matter. The funds will never be found. After all, what safer place for money of any kind than in a bank?"

"A bank?" She shook her head. "You mean you had the train robbery money in your bank all along?"

He laughed as he thrust her against the wall and then pushed her into an empty stable. She fell backward, landing with a thud in a thin layer of hay. Her head cracked against the hard-packed dirt beneath the hay. The room began to spin.

The last thing she saw before the room went black was Will Bowen standing over her with a gun. The last thing she heard was the sound of the gun as it fired.

"Victoria."

The voice teased at her ears and pulled at a memory. A fog thicker than any she'd seen in London settled around her and weighed her down.

"Victoria. It's all right. Bowen's never going to hurt you again. After the doc patches him up, the sheriff's got a warm bed for him down at the jail. We've already got men at the bank auditing the vault. By next week, the banker'll be sleeping at the penitentiary."

Again the voice, gruff yet tender, pleading but firm. This time she knew it to be Gus Drummond's. She tried to answer, searched in vain to formulate a response. She felt herself being lifted off the ground, possibly being cradled in someone's arms.

Was this how the Lord carried one home? If so, it felt fine.

"Victoria, wake up."

She tried to open her eyes. Failing that, she began to pray.

I'm waiting on You, Lord.

"Sleeping Beauty, if you don't wake up, I'm never going to get the chance, and the Lord's going to be right irritated with me."

Then came the kiss.

Slowly, Victoria's vision returned and the image of Gus Drummond swam before her. "No more irritated than I, Gus Drummond."

He cradled her to his chest and held her there. "I'm a fool and I know it. I hid from you all this time because I was a plain coward. I didn't know how to tell you I love you."

Even though her head throbbed, she managed to focus long enough to capture his gaze. "Are you telling me that now, Mr. Drummond?"

"I am, and call me Gus." He smiled at her. "I'm not afraid to add that I want to marry up with you. Will you take this Pinkerton to be your wedded husband, Miss Vicky?"

Chapter 9

Will you take these Pinkertons to be your wedded husbands?"

Moment and Victoria responded with an "I do." A short while later, they walked down the aisle with their Pinkerton husbands to the strains of Mabel Hawkins playing the wedding march. Outside on the lawn, the guests gathered to offer their congratulations to the two newlywed couples.

Gus tore himself away from his new bride long enough to take Moment and Brady aside. "I'm right thankful you didn't mind sharing your day with us, Mr. and Mrs. Miller."

"Pleased to accommodate the last-minute arrangements," Brady said.

Gus cast a glance over his shoulder at his bride, who was engrossed in conversation with the pastor's wife. "I feel real bad I didn't believe her about the missing money. I'm a Pink. I should have seen something was wrong."

Moment touched Gus's hand. "None of us believed her. Who would have thought Victoria would be the one to solve the most complicated of all the crimes?"

The object of their conversation strolled toward them, the feather from her blue wedding hat dancing in the soft breeze. "What am I missing?" she asked as she linked arms with her husband.

Ruth and Sydney and their husbands joined the circle of friends.

"Not a thing as far as I can see," Gus answered. "And I intend to make sure I don't miss anything either. Now how about you and me say our good-byes and head for the honeymoon? I've got another mystery for you to solve."

"Oh, really? And what might that be?"

"How many kisses we can share in this lifetime." He scooped her into his arms and winked. "Here's the first clue."

And then he kissed her.

KATHLEEN Y'BARBO

Bestselling author Kathleen Y'Barbo is a Romantic Times Book of the Year winner as well as a multiple Carol Award and RITA nominee of more than sixty novels with almost two million copies in print in the US and abroad. A tenth-generation Texan, she has been nominated for a Career Achievement Award as well a Reader's Choice Award and Book of the Year by *Romantic Times* magazine.

Kathleen is a paralegal, a proud military wife, and an expatriate Texan cheering on her beloved Texas Aggies from north of the Red River. Connect with her through social media atwww.kathleenybarbo.com.

Language of Love

by Janet Lee Barton

Dedication

To my Lord and Savior for showing me the way,
to my family for all the precious memories we share,
and to "The Aunts."
I love you all.

Chapter 1

Breaux Bridge, Early December 1918

After days of travel, and wondering if he'd ever get home, Nicolas LeBlanc finally stepped off the train that brought him back to his beloved Breaux Bridge. One arm still in a sling, he took a deep breath and, with his good arm, picked up his duffel bag. He slung it over his good shoulder and headed for home.

There was a crispness to the air that could only be felt in the late fall and early winter in this part of Louisiana, and he knew his mother would be feeling the chill of the morning. But, after being in Europe for the past year and experiencing a different kind of cold, he felt quite comfortable.

Hungry for the sight of home, he couldn't get enough of the scenery as he walked away from the railway station. Just past dawn, the mist rising up from Bayou Teche spread up over the bank, while tall live oaks, dripping moss from their branches, grew beside the bayou. Bald cypress trees that had lost their leaves for the winter rose out of the water, and here and there grew magnolia trees, their glossy green leaves wet with dew. He could almost smell the sweet, huge white blossoms that would bloom, come spring.

Although he'd let his family know he was coming home, he hadn't told them what train he'd be taking. No need to worry *Maman* if the train wasn't on time. She'd been through enough, worrying about him overseas and suffering through the death of his papa from the influenza that had swept the country this past year.

Nicolas sighed deeply as he neared the cemetery. His heart felt as if it were in a vise, being squeezed tighter and tighter at the thought that his dear papa had died while he was gone. His father had been a good man, loving his family, and teaching them to love God, to have strong faith. But now, as Nicolas walked toward the LeBlanc family plots, he acknowledged that, unlike Papa, he'd been questioning God more than he'd been praying.

He'd seen so much. Lost so much. When he'd been wounded, his best friend had taken his place in the foxhole and lost his life that same night. Nicolas had been sent to a hospital in England, and it was there that he'd received the letter telling him about the death of his father. Even here in this place, beside his father's grave, he couldn't seem to find the words to pray, and the sorrow of it all had his throat so full of unshed tears he could barely breathe.

The crackle of leaves sounded behind him, and with the instinct of a soldier, he quickly whirled around. Nicolas let out a relieved sigh as his brother-in-law came walking out of the mist.

"Nicolas! It's about time you returned. I've been meeting the train for a week. You would pick the one morning I was late getting there!"

"Adam! It's good to see you." Nicolas patted his brother-in-law on the back with his free hand while the other man enveloped him in a bear hug. "How did you know I was here?"

Adam took Nicolas's bag and headed for the 1916 Model T parked outside the cemetery while Nicolas followed close behind. "The stationmaster told me you'd headed home. As I hadn't met you on the road, it didn't take much to realize where you were."

"Maman? How is she doing?" Nicolas asked as he settled himself in the passenger seat, while Adam started the car.

"She'll be better once she sees you." Adam shook his head. "I won't lie to you. Maman has aged this past year. She misses your papa. It's helped having Suzette around to help with the children."

"Suzette? Who is this person?"

"You don't remember my little sister?"

Nicolas vaguely recalled a young blond girl at the wedding of Adam and his sister, Felicia. But she was several years younger than Adam. "Oui. I do—"

"Well, she's grown-up now. . .and she's a new teacher here. Your parents were kind enough to offer her a place to live. You didn't know?"

"No. Oh, I think there was mention of a new teacher, but I didn't know she was living with Papa and Maman." He wondered why no one had written him about it.

◆　◆　◆

Suzette hurriedly washed the last of the breakfast dishes as the children prepared for school. She brought the coffeepot over to the table. Lucia LeBlanc was not her mother, but she'd opened her home to Suzette and made her feel one of her own. She loved the older woman, and it hurt her to see her so sad. Would Nicolas never get home? "Would you like more coffee before we leave for school, Maman LeBlanc?"

"Yes, thank you, dear. Is there anything particular you'd like for supper?"

"Anything you decide on is fine with me." Suzette prayed that Lucia would get her appetite back soon. . .she'd lost too much weight. "The children love your gumbo."

Lucia nodded and smiled. "They do. And should Nicolas return today, he'll be very happy. It's one of his favorites."

Suzette hoped that this Nicolas, whom she only vaguely remembered from her brother's wedding but had heard so very much about since moving here, would indeed return today. His mother needed him, and the children needed him. She glanced at the clock and called to the children, *"Dépêchez vois autre!"*

"We're hurrying," Amy, the fourteen-year-old, and the oldest still at home, answered as she rushed into the room and kissed her mother. "Have a good day, Maman."

Lucia's other children—twelve-year-old Julien, ten-year-old Jacques, and seven-year-old Rose—followed behind, each kissing her on the cheek before heading out the door.

Lucia followed them outside and leaned against the porch railing, to see them off to school. "Amy, make sure Rose stays up with you. And the rest of you, behave yourself for Suzette, you hear?"

"We will, Maman!" Amy called back as the children waved to their mother and headed down the path.

Down the road a bit, Suzette and the children drew close to the house of her brother Adam and his wife, Lucia's daughter, Felicia. Felicia came outside to greet them, a cup of coffee in her hand. "How is Maman this morning?"

"Hoping your brother makes it home today."

"Oui. Adam has been gone longer than usual. I am hoping he brings Nicolas back with him."

"I'll pray he does," Suzette assured her as the group continued on.

"Thank you. I'll walk over to Maman's to be there either way."

"That's a good idea!" Suzette called as she waved and hurried to catch up with her students.

◆　◆　◆

"What is that?" Nicolas asked as a new building came into sight when they rounded a bend in the road.

"That's the new schoolhouse," Adam said. "The one your brothers and sisters attend and the one Suzette teaches at."

Nicolas nodded. "It's good that it's so close."

"Yes. It's very modern on the inside. You'll have to take a look one day."

"How did your sister become a teacher out here, so far from New Orleans?"

"Oh, I'd been telling her how badly we needed good teachers here and how hard it was to find one willing to live away from the cities. I've also been telling her, for several years now, how beautiful it is here on the bayou. She came to visit and decided to stay."

Nicolas wanted to ask how she came to live in his home, with his mother and siblings, but he didn't have to as Adam continued.

"As teachers are hard to come by down here and the community can't afford to pay much, your maman and papa offered her a place to live. We've all been glad she was there, especially after your papa died. She's been good company for Maman and the children."

And now she will either have to move back to the cabin—or I will. "I'm sure Maman has been glad of the company. It was hard for her?"

"Oui. It's been very hard. I think the only thing that may pull her out of it is seeing you, *beau-frère*. Your papa was very ill. So many were sick. . . ."

"I wish I'd been here."

"You were doing what you had to do. You were one of the first from Breaux Bridge to be drafted. . . . Papa was very proud of you. It was. . .bad over there?"

Nicolas sighed deeply. "It was bad."

"I am glad you are home. Your arm will heal. Things will be better after a while."

Would they? Nicolas knew they would never be the same. Could they ever be better? "I thank you for working both your farm and ours, Adam."

"No thanks are needed, you know that. Your papa and I shared the work when he was well, and you would have done the same. And everyone helps out at harvest so we can all get it done. But I'm glad you are back to take your place at the head of your family." He turned to grin at Nicolas. "Your sister and I are starting our own."

New life! Nicolas could honestly be happy about that! "Now that is some good news to hear, mon ami! That is good news for sure!"

They rounded another bend, and Nicolas caught his breath at the sight of home. It looked the same as when he'd left—the long porch along the front of the house, the chinaberry tree in the front yard, and the garden out back. He could make out the roof of the cabin down closer to the bayou. Home.

"You go on in and see Maman. I'll bring your bag," Adam said.

Nicolas needed no encouragement as his mother opened the screened door to see who'd driven up in her yard. The look on her face was enough to send Nicolas hurrying out of the car and up the steps to envelop her in a hug. She did indeed look older, sadder, and very tired.

"My son, oh, my son! You are finally home!" Her arms wrapped around him.

"I am, Maman!" Nicolas couldn't keep his own tears from forming as his mother began to cry. He bent and kissed the wetness of her soft cheek. "I'm so sorry I wasn't here for you—"

"You are here now. And your papa was so proud of you. . . ." She nodded. "He was proud. So was I, my son. But I'm glad you are home."

"So am I, Maman." More than he'd even realized he would be.

"I knew God would take care of you. He wouldn't give me more than I could bear. It was a hard time over there?"

Nicolas couldn't speak for a moment. Instead, he rocked his mother back and forth, his chin resting on the top of her head, until he found his voice again. "It was. But it's over now. And I'm home to stay."

"And we're all so glad of that, brother! We've missed you!"

Nicolas turned to see his sister Felicia slowly climbing the steps with Adam. Obviously, she was indeed expecting a baby. He grinned at her. "I'm to be an uncle, am I?" He turned to wrap his arms around her, being careful not to hug too hard.

"You are. . .after the first of the year—but it can't be too soon for me!" She rested her head on his shoulder, and Nicolas could tell she was stifling a sob. "It's good to have you home."

Nicolas nodded as he held her. "It's good to be home. . . . I just wish—"

"Maman," Adam interrupted, "Nicolas was on the early train. I think he must be hungry. . .do you have any breakfast left for him?"

"No leftovers for my son. I will make him anything he wants," Lucia said, leading the way into the house. "And tonight for supper we'll be having the gumbo for

Nicolas's homecoming. You both must join us!"

"As if we don't take most meals together, anyway, Maman," Felicia said. "Oh, Nicolas, just wait until you meet Suzette!"

"Oh yes, Nicolas…Suzette has your room. You won't mind taking over the cabin as your own, will you?"

"Of course not, Maman." The cabin had been the original home of the LeBlanc family, until this larger home had been built. Several of the male members had lived there through the years. Now it seemed it was his turn. "I'll get settled after breakfast."

The rest of the morning was spent trying to catch up on all that had been going on in his absence and answering the many questions they had about the war and all the places he'd seen. After breakfast, Adam walked with him down to the cabin to settle in, while Felicia helped his mother clean up.

He was surprised to find the cabin so clean and inviting. There were curtains on the windows and fresh linens on the bed, now covered with a homemade quilt. All he really had to do was unpack his duffel bag and buy the few groceries he'd want to have on hand. "Maman must have been cleaning for weeks to get this in shape for me."

"Actually, Suzette cleaned it up. She lived here up until your papa died. Then we all decided that Maman could use the company, and so she moved in the big house. It's worked out well. And we've been expecting you for several weeks. I'm sure she's tried to keep it clean."

Nicolas was having a difficult time picturing Adam's sister as an adult, but the more he heard about her, the more anxious he was to meet this woman who'd been such a help in his absence. "I'll have to thank her for all she's done."

"She's come to love Maman and the children. And she's grateful for a place to live. Felicia and I offered, but our home is still very small, and with the baby coming, Suzette felt more comfortable accepting your parents' offer of a place to live. Now she feels that at least she's giving back something by being there for Maman."

"Still, I will thank her." Nicolas was getting more curious about this sister of Adam's with each passing moment. . . . She sounded too good to be true.

Nicolas spent the rest of the day with Adam driving him around both farms so that he could see how things were doing. It was nearing suppertime when they returned home, and Nicolas looked forward to a supper of the gumbo he'd dreamed about while he was away.

◆　　◆　　◆

Suzette and the children came home to a different Lucia. The look on her face, one of sadness mixed with joy, was one Suzette knew she would remember forever. Nicolas had indeed returned, and Lucia and Felicia were busy making a celebration meal. Suzette said a silent prayer of thankfulness as she donned an apron and lent her two hands to the task.

The children helped with setting the table and filling glasses with water, practicing their English as had become the custom ever since Suzette had come to live with them. In their excitement, their words seemed to tumble over each other as they waited for Nicolas and Adam to return.

Suzette found herself looking out the open window in anticipation of meeting this son and brother that she'd heard so much about. She'd never say a word to any of them, but he sounded a bit too good to be true.

Chapter 2

The smells wafting out of the house as he and Adam walked up to the porch had Nicolas's mouth watering in expectation. He couldn't wait to see his siblings and share a meal with them, speaking once more in the familiar language of his ancestors rather than the English he'd adopted during the war.

He walked into the house and was quickly overtaken by the hugs and laughter from his siblings. . .they all seemed to have grown at least a foot in his absence. He hugged each one before turning to find Adam pulling a petite young woman forward.

"Nicolas, this is my sister—"

"Suzette. I'm pleased to meet you—again. I've heard much about you today, but Adam did not tell me I would not recognize you," Nicolas said, taking her small hand in his.

"Ah, my brother has been talking, has he?" Suzette smiled up at him.

"A little." Nicolas was surprised at the way his heart seemed to skip a beat as he looked down into her blue eyes. He could see no resemblance at all to the awkward adolescent he remembered. Adam's sister had grown into a beauty. An enchanting one at that, he thought, as he watched her blush when he held her hand for a moment too long.

She gently slipped her fingers out of his grasp and took her seat at the table. The ongoing chatter hadn't stopped, but it wasn't until Nicolas took his place at the table that he realized they weren't speaking in Cajun. They were all speaking English—and being corrected by the vision sitting across the table from him.

"What is this? When did this family start speaking the English at home?" he asked.

"Since Suzette moved here and became our teacher. It's a game we play that she thought would help us to learn faster," Amy said.

Nicolas was a little confused. What had changed since he'd been gone? "Why do they need to be in a hurry? The language spoken here in bayou country is Cajun."

"Yes. But it won't be many years before *only* English is spoken at school," Suzette said.

"Then they can speak it at school—at home they will speak the Cajun."

"But if they speak English more at home, the easier it will be—"

"Not in this house. They can learn at school." The conversation was over as far as he was concerned. She was the teacher. She could teach them at school. He watched as Suzette took a deep breath and exhaled.

"Nicolas, they are talking about passing a law." Suzette looked at him from across the table. When his gaze met hers, she continued. "And when they do, *all* subjects will be taught in English. I just want to make the transition easier on the children."

"Non!" It appeared he'd been right in his assessment. She *was* too good to be true! Beautiful, yes—enchanting, without a doubt. But she also appeared to be stubborn and argumentative!

"Nicolas." Lucia quietly got his attention.

"Yes, Maman?"

"It was your papa who agreed for us to help the children learn. It was what he wanted. I ask you to honor his wishes."

Nicolas sighed. Had he fought a war, been wounded, come home to the death of his father, only to lose his right to speak his own language in his home?

"You may speak the Cajun at the table," his mother continued. "The children can speak the English. It will be a game and help them also. Please, Nicolas?"

Nicolas looked into his mother's eyes. He sighed deeply, knowing he couldn't say no to her. At least *he* could speak his own language at his supper table—but it appeared that he wasn't going to be able to listen to it there. He nodded and gave in to his mother. "All right, Maman."

◆　◆　◆

Suzette did the dishes and cleaned up the kitchen, so that the family could spend Nicolas's first evening at home together. As she washed and dried the dishes, she could hear the murmur of voices coming from the living room. She couldn't be happier for the LeBlanc family—that their Nicolas was finally home.

It must be a bittersweet homecoming, knowing his papa had passed away while he was in Europe. Tears stung the back of Suzette's eyelids just thinking of the joy mixed with sorrow he must be feeling. And because of that she would overlook his irritability over speaking English in his home. She certainly didn't want to bring him more pain, but it was imperative that the young ones learned to speak English well.

Hopefully, she would be able to make him understand the importance of it soon. As it was, she was just thankful that Maman LeBlanc had calmed him down and gotten him to agree to both languages being spoken at home. Still, he must have been longing to hear his Cajun spoken after being gone so long. What horrors he must have seen. . . .

Suzette shook her head. She didn't want to even think about those. She smiled as she heard a burst of laughter coming from the front room. It was good to hear. Maybe now that Nicolas was back, there would be more of it. He looked little like she remembered at her brother's wedding. Although more handsome to her, he also looked older, but she was sure that was from all he'd experienced overseas and the deep sorrow he felt over his papa's death.

She sighed deeply as she dried the last dish and put it away. Turning, she found

Nicolas standing in the kitchen doorway, watching her. Suzette caught her breath and held a hand to her rapidly beating heart.

"*Sa me fait de la pain*—I mean. . .I'm sorry. I did not mean to startle you," he said. "I was just wondering if there was any *café* left?"

She let out the breath she'd been holding. "There is. I'll get you a cup."

"Non. I can get it. You've worked long enough tonight. Thank you for helping Maman."

Suzette waved his thank-you away with her hand and took a cup from the cabinet. "It is the least I can do for your mother. She is a wonderful woman."

Nicolas grinned at her. "Ah. Something we can agree on."

She poured the coffee and asked, "Café au lait?"

"Non." Refusing the addition of milk, he took the cup from her. "Thank you."

She smiled and answered in his Cajun, "*Il y a pas de quoi.* I feel bad about taking your room. I will be glad to move out to the cabin, Nicolas—"

"Non. It is fine. I have my things there already, and you are fine here."

"But I don't mind."

He nodded. "I can see that. But it will be better for me to sleep out there. I sometimes have nightmares, and I don't want to frighten the children."

Suzette's heart melted at his admission and his concern for his siblings. She nodded. "All right. But should you change your mind—"

"I will let you know." He took a sip of his coffee. "Maman has sent the young ones to bed. I'm going to join her on the front porch. Would you like to join us?"

Suzette poured the last cup of coffee and added a large dollop of milk and sugar to it. "Thank you, but I think I'll turn in. Besides, your Maman has missed you terribly. It will do her good to have you to herself for a while." She picked up the cup of café au lait and turned to face Nicolas. "I'll take this out to her for you. She likes a cup of café au lait before she turns in."

"Thank you for reminding me. If you put it on a tray, I can take it to her."

Obviously, he wanted no pity for his wounded arm. Suzette put the cup on a small tray, and he added his own to it before taking it from her.

"Thank you. Good night, then."

"Good night, Nicolas. Tell Maman LeBlanc I'll see her in the morning, please."

◆　◆　◆

Nicolas kicked the screen door open and held his foot in place when it closed, easing it out slowly so as not to slam the door loudly and wake the children. He handed his mother the tray Suzette had fixed for them before joining Maman in the swing his papa had hung there when Nicolas was only a child.

"Suzette was retiring for the night." Nicolas took his cup from the tray. "She said to tell you she'd see you in the morning."

His mother nodded as she took her cup of coffee and set the tray on a side table. She took a sip. "She has been such a blessing to this family. I don't know what I would have done without her to help with the children after your papa passed away."

"I'm so sorry I wasn't here, Maman."

"You were where you were needed most, my son. I understood that. Your papa did, too."

Nicolas was glad it was dark out so that his mother couldn't see the sudden tears that formed in his eyes. "I know. I am glad to be home."

And he was. But things seemed so different now. So much had changed since he'd been gone. . .or maybe it was that he had changed. Right now Nicolas wasn't sure which it was.

"Suzette offered to move back out to the cabin, but I told her no."

His mother pulled her shawl closer around her. "It will take some time to get used to being back home, I think," she said, as if she could read his mind. "Your papa said you would probably prefer to be out in the cabin for a while when you came home. So it is a good thing that Suzette had already moved out."

They swung in silence for a while, enjoying the night sounds from the Bayou Teche. It was music to Nicolas's heart. He wondered if Suzette liked the sounds and then wondered why he was thinking of her. She'd been very sweet tonight when he'd lost his temper about speaking the English at the dinner table. And it was obvious that his family liked her. "Is she a good teacher?"

"Suzette? Oui. She is very good. The children love her. She is only trying to help them, Nicolas. Before long it will be against the law to speak French or our Cajun on the school grounds. There has been talk of it everywhere. She is only trying to make it easier for them."

"Maman, I agreed to your terms. But I don't have to like them."

"Non. You do not have to like them. But I thank you for agreeing." She drained her cup and put it back on the tray before getting to her feet. "I am so glad you are home, Nicolas. I'll have breakfast ready for you in the morning. I hope you sleep well."

He stood and bent down to kiss her on the cheek. "I am glad, too, Maman. I'll see you in the morning. Good night."

"Good night." She took his cup from him and added it to the tray before going inside.

Nicolas stretched. It was getting late, and he had much to do tomorrow. He headed down to the cabin along the bayou's edge. The cabin had its own small porch facing the water, and he looked out on the moonlit bayou. Home. He was finally home.

But his heart hurt from both joy and sadness, for it wasn't the homecoming he'd envisioned. Nicolas fought the tears that gathered behind his eyes and shook his head. He'd missed so much in the time he'd been so far away. His papa was gone and there was no bringing him back. His precious maman had aged in her sorrow. His siblings had grown by leaps and bounds, and he barely recognized them now. Amy had turned into a blossoming *memselle*, while Julien was on the verge of becoming a *jeune homme*. Only Jacques seemed similar to the child he'd been when Nicolas left. He wished he could say the same about Rose, but he couldn't. She'd lost her babyish ways and was in school now. Nicolas shook his head.

Changes. . .there were so very many to get used to. One of the biggest was the petite schoolteacher ensconced in his room in the big house. . .that somehow no longer seemed so large or familiar to him. . .and the news she brought that his beloved language was in danger of being outlawed.

His heart ached with all the changes around him, and yet deep down there was a joy that he was finally back with his family. He let the night sounds wrap around him—the water lapping gently at the bank, the quiet broken by the loud slap of a beaver tail on the bayou, or the hoot owls calling out across the way. The familiar sounds gave him some comfort in knowing that some things *did* stay the same. He only wished everything had.

◆　◆　◆

Suzette was still awake when Maman LeBlanc came back inside. She heard her steps on each of the stairs and heard her check in on the girls in their room and the boys in theirs before she went to her own.

Tired as she was, Suzette hadn't been able to drift off to sleep. She couldn't get Nicolas out of her mind. When she'd turned to find him in the kitchen entryway, there was an expression in his dark eyes that had her pulse racing and her heartbeat loud to her ears.

But the look in his eyes had changed as he glanced around the kitchen, and it had her wanting to tell him everything would be all right, and she didn't even know what was wrong.

He'd just looked so. . .*uncomfortable* was the only word that came to mind. As if he didn't quite feel at home yet. At the same time there was a hint of the joy he must feel at being home. She sent up a prayer that he would adjust to being back home quickly and that he would soon feel more joy than sadness.

Chapter 3

The nightmares he'd experienced in the last few months did not give Nicolas a break on his first night at home, and he was awake long before daybreak. But he wrapped himself in a blanket and went out to the porch to watch the morning mist rise and then disappear over the bayou, leaving behind a beautifully clear blue sky. How he'd longed for the sight of dawn here in Breaux Bridge. He tried to soak it all in—the beauty, the sounds, and even the smells he grew up with—before realizing that if he wanted to join the children for breakfast, he needed to hurry. Dressing quickly, he headed to the main house, and his stomach rumbled with hunger as the smell of pork sausage, eggs, and grits wafted out to greet him.

When he entered the kitchen, the happiness on his mother's face as she greeted him was something he knew he'd never forget. He thought she even looked a little younger this morning.

"Good morning, Nicolas!"

He crossed the room to give her soft cheek a kiss. "Good morning, Maman."

"Did you sleep well? Sit, I will have your breakfast before you in a moment."

He didn't want to tell her he'd been awakened by the nightmare of war. "I woke to the sounds of the bayou. I missed them while I was gone. Where are the children?"

"They've already eaten and are now getting ready for school. Julien wanted to go wake you for breakfast, but I thought you might need your sleep after the long trip home."

"I should have come over earlier. I forgot about the children going to school."

"There will be plenty of time to have breakfast with them. It will take you awhile to get used to the change in time, I would imagine."

"Yes, I guess that's what it is." Tomorrow he wouldn't dawdle. He'd hoped to have breakfast with the whole family this first morning, but instead Suzette was trying to hurry them along and from what he could see, she was doing a good job of it. In only minutes they'd each kissed Maman and him, also, before heading out the door.

"Good morning, Nicolas," Suzette said with a smile.

"Miss Suzette, hurry, hurry," Rose said with a giggle.

"And good-bye!" Suzette told him with a chuckle as Rose pulled her along and out the door.

Before he could take a sip of the coffee his mother set before him, Rose had run back in and climbed up into his lap. She planted a big kiss on his cheek and said, in his beloved Cajun, "I love you, Nicolas! I'm glad you are home."

"I'm glad too, Rosy. Have a good day." His heart swelled with love for the child as he followed her to the door and saw that Suzette was waiting for Rose as the others had run on ahead. Rose skipped to meet her, and something about the way the young schoolteacher smiled and bent her head to hear what Rose was saying to her touched Nicolas. It was as if Suzette had nothing else to do but listen to what the child was saying.

His mother touched him on the shoulder. "Your breakfast is ready, son. Come eat."

Nicolas turned back to the table. "I'd better hurry, I see Adam coming down the road."

"Non. No need to hurry. Your sister gets sick at the smell of breakfast cooking. I'm sure he'll be glad to join you."

His mother was right. Adam was more than happy to take time for breakfast before they set out to check on the small herd of cattle that provided both families with much of the meat they ate.

◆　◆　◆

Suzette was a little taken back by how eager she was to arrive at the LeBlanc home that afternoon. She told herself it was because the children were so excited about Nicolas's return that some of their enthusiasm had rubbed off on her. But she knew it was more than that: She wanted to know how his day went and see if some of the sorrow had left his eyes.

It had been difficult to concentrate on the lessons she taught that day, as she couldn't get thoughts of Nicolas out of her mind. She'd been trying to avoid thinking of him, but it wasn't working. She wondered how he would react to the English lessons at the dinner table tonight. Would he find out that she'd been speaking English so long that her French was a little rusty? And that she was much more familiar with the Creole French spoken in New Orleans than with his Cajun French—the French that had come from the Acadians. She could actually use his help in understanding what the children said at times, but how to tell him that without sounding as if she only wanted them to speak English for her sake?

It truly was only a matter of time before speaking French of any kind in the classrooms and even on the school grounds would be a thing of the past. She didn't like it any more than he seemed to. Her ancestors had spoken French, too. But in New Orleans, it was more common to hear English than here in bayou country. And she'd learned very quickly that the Cajuns clung tightly to their traditions. Giving in to the new rules would be hard on every family she knew in Breaux Bridge. She wanted to make it as easy on them as she could.

She loved this part of Louisiana. Her brother had been telling her for years how much she would like it, but it hadn't been until this past summer when she came for a visit that she decided she wanted to stay. Her decision probably had as much to do with the LeBlanc family as with life along the bayou. She'd fallen in love with them all, and she'd immediately felt at home there. No wonder her brother had never gone back to New Orleans for more than a few days at a time.

Now as the LeBlanc home came into sight and the children ran ahead, Suzette wondered if Nicolas was there or out getting familiar with the land and the bayou again. When he came out onto the porch, a cup of coffee in his hand, and waved, she was surprised by the way her heartbeat skittered in her chest. She waved back and watched as he greeted first one child and then the next.

But once they'd all gone to greet their mother, Nicolas stayed outside, watching her approach. What was it about this man that made her pulse race at just the sight of him?

"Good afternoon, Suzette. How was your day? The children all behaved themselves?"

She couldn't tell Nicolas that her day had been filled with thoughts of him, so she answered the latter question only. "Good afternoon, Nicolas. The children all behaved very well today. How did your day pass?"

"It was a good day. Adam and I took stock of what needs to be done this winter before spring planting gets underway. Several fences need repairing, and we want to enlarge the barns on both our properties. Your brother is a hard worker and because of it, we are well supplied from the fall harvest. My sister did well in her choice of a husband."

"My brother made a good choice, as well, seeing what a wonderful wife he has in Felicia." Suzette climbed the steps to the porch. As she came abreast of Nicolas, he seemed even taller than the day before. "Together, they make each other stronger, and I think they are going to be wonderful parents."

"Oui. I'm looking forward to being an uncle, and it will be good for Maman to have a baby around again."

"It will be good for us all. I'd better go help your maman with supper."

"The girls will help. You've been working all day."

"Yes. But I love being in the kitchen with your maman. I've learned much from helping her."

"Ah." Nicolas smiled and nodded. "She is a wonderful cook. If you want to help, I'm sure they would be glad for an extra pair of hands."

Suzette opened the screen door, but Nicolas stopped her from going inside by his touch on her shoulder.

"Wait."

She turned to him.

"Maman has told me how much having you here has meant to her. I thank you for being here for her, especially after Papa died."

"You are welcome. I would not have wanted to be anywhere else." She hurried inside before the tears in the corners of her eyes spilled over.

◆　◆　◆

Nicolas went to check the livestock and met up with Adam and Felicia on the way back to the house. When they entered the house, they found it full of the delicious smells that seemed to always come out of his maman's kitchen—and the sweet sounds of women talking and laughing as they got supper ready. Felicia hurried to join in, and he and Adam just grinned and shook their heads. How those women managed to keep up with what each other was saying was beyond them, but they did.

He and Adam played *faire la statue* with the younger children, moving about the living room freely until the leader said stop. Then each one froze in position, and the leader picked the funniest posed person to be the next leader. Soon the laughter in the living room drowned out the giggling in the kitchen.

It was music to Nicolas's heart. They were sounds he'd longed to hear for so long, and he was sure his papa would be glad that the family could finally laugh once more.

By the time the whole group was seated at the table, Nicolas's stomach was rumbling with hunger. The meal of roast pork, potatoes, and gravy, along with his maman's homemade bread, satisfied him in more ways than one.

It was only as the children began to speak the English with Suzette that his mood was dampened. But he'd made an agreement with his mother, and he meant to keep it, no matter how he longed to hear only the Cajun spoken in his home.

But as he listened, Nicolas had to admit that Suzette had a way of making learning the language a game.

She pointed to the platter of roast, and Rose rushed to say, *"Daube de cochon!"*

"Pork roast," Suzette prompted.

Rose grinned and repeated, "Pork roast."

Then Rose pointed to the fresh loaf of bread, *"Pain."*

"Bread," Suzette said. Then she pointed to the bowl of gravy.

Jacques jumped up. *"Sauce rouge!"*

Suzette grinned and said, "Gravy."

"Gravy," Jacques agreed.

And on it went until nearly everything on the table had been named. Even Maman, Felicia, and Adam joined in the game.

When Maman got up and brought back a chocolate *gateau*, everyone except him yelled, "Chocolate cake!"

Obviously they'd learned a prior lesson very well. Nicolas hadn't participated in the game, but he couldn't keep from joining in the laughter.

Chapter 4

With each day that passed, Nicolas began to feel a little more at home. He still half-expected to see his papa each morning when he entered the main house, and he wasn't sure his heart would ever stop aching for that sight. But his mother's smile helped ease the pain, and he was glad to see that the corners of her mouth seemed to turn up a little bit more each day.

It wasn't until the end of the next week that he was reminded that Christmas was nearly upon them. No one had mentioned it, and it was only when he overheard the children talking about their upcoming school break as they came home from school on Friday that he realized he needed to talk to Maman about it.

He waited until after the children had been put to bed before bringing up the subject, knowing now that his mother and Suzette usually had a cup of café au lait together before retiring for the night.

He joined them in the kitchen and asked for a cup for himself. As they sat around the small kitchen table that was also used as a worktable, he took a sip of the fragrant liquid and thought about how to bring up the subject. Perhaps the easiest way would be through Suzette.

He looked over at her. "The children are on break next week?"

"Yes. They are out for Christmas and New Year's."

"Christmas! It is so soon?" Maman asked, on the verge of tears. "I knew it was coming, but I put it out of my mind. I can't imagine it without Papa."

"It's all right, Maman. I'd almost forgotten, too."

"It is understandable," Suzette tried to assure them.

"But the children—" Maman began to cry. "We must try for their sake."

Nicolas and Suzette were both up and at her side. Nicolas gave her a hug and kissed her on the top of the head. Suzette refilled her cup of coffee and patted her on the back.

"Don't cry, Maman. The children do not need to know we nearly forgot."

"And it is not too late to prepare for Christmas. I will help and so will Felicia."

"But your parents are expecting you home for Christmas."

Suzette shook her head vigorously. "Non. I told them in a letter that I wanted to stay here. They mentioned that they might come to stay with Adam and Felicia, but I don't think they've told them yet."

"Oh, I am glad you will be here, Suzette." Maman sniffed and blew her nose with the handkerchief she pulled from her pocket. "And Papa would want us to do our best to carry on without him." She fought more tears. "It will be hard, but the children have been through so much sorrow already. I don't want them thinking they can't get excited about Christmas."

"You are right, Maman. It is what Papa would want. Adam and I will go look for a tree to put up tomorrow."

"And we can have the children help decorate it. They can help make candy and cookies, too."

"Maman, if you think of what you would like to get each one, I can take you into Breaux Bridge and buy the presents for them."

"Oh, I don't know if I can go without Papa, Nicolas. Not this year. Maybe Suzette can go with you?" She looked expectantly from one to the other.

Nicolas wasn't sure how he felt about spending a day in town with Suzette, but he couldn't say no to his mother. "Of course, Suzette can help me, if she doesn't mind."

"I'll be glad to go help Nicolas, if that's what you want, Maman LeBlanc."

"Thank you both. That puts my mind at ease."

That settled it. Nicolas couldn't tell how Suzette felt about the shopping trip, but it seemed neither of them was willing to upset his mother by telling her no. "I'm glad. Just make up a list, and we'll take care of the rest, Maman."

Nicolas drained his cup and stood. "I'll see you in the morning."

"Good night, dear," Maman said as he kissed her forehead. "I am so very glad you are home."

"I'm glad to be here, Maman. Good night to you both."

Suzette smiled at him as she gathered the cups and took them to the sink. "Sleep well, Nicolas."

He went out the back door and headed for the cottage, glad that he'd talked to the two women and relieved that Suzette would be staying for Christmas. With Papa gone, they would need all the help they could get to make it through the holidays.

As Nicolas walked down the path to the cabin, he suddenly stopped in his tracks. He was actually looking forward to spending a day with Suzette. He frowned. He wasn't sure this eager anticipation to their outing was a good thing. She was lovely and sweet, and he'd be lying if he said he wasn't attracted to her, but she was part of the system that was trying to do away with his beloved Cajun and he couldn't let himself forget that fact.

He couldn't seem to quit thinking about her—that she cared about his family was totally obvious, but it was just as clear that she didn't seem to understand the way of life in this part of the country. Not yet.

◆　◆　◆

Suzette washed up the cups and cleaned the kitchen while Maman LeBlanc started on her Christmas list. She found herself looking forward to the shopping trip with Nicolas in spite of herself. The last thing she needed was to fall for a man who resented her for wanting to teach English. He just didn't seem to understand that it wasn't that she wanted his language to be extinct anymore than she wanted the Creole French she'd grown up speaking to be a thing of the past. But neither of them could ignore the changes that were occurring in this part of the country. . .no matter how much they might want to.

The state of Louisiana was leaning heavily in the direction of wanting all of its citizens to speak and learn the same language. Laws were going to be passed. It was inevitable. And all Suzette wanted was to make the transition easier on her students. One day maybe Nicolas would understand what she was trying to do, but she had a feeling that he didn't even want to try right now. And she could understand. He had more than enough to adjust to, just by becoming the head of his family now, responsible for his mother and his siblings, and trying to help them all through this time of year when his own heart must be breaking.

That was one reason she'd told her parents that she was staying here for the Christmas break. After all the LeBlanc family had done for her, she couldn't bear the thought of leaving them to get through this first Christmas without Papa LeBlanc.

Maman LeBlanc broke into her thoughts, "Suzette, are you sure it is all right with your maman and papa for you to stay with us over your break?"

"I'm sure." At least she prayed they were all right with it. Suzette was hoping her parents would come to see Adam and Felicia and spend the holiday with them all. They might then finally begin to understand what it was about these people that had a hold on her heart. Their love of family and spending time together was one of the things she loved most about them. "If they don't come for Christmas, I'm sure they will come when the baby is born. I think they are excited about becoming grandparents."

"Oui, I'm sure they are. I can't wait to hold that baby in my arms. I just can't believe my Felicia is old enough to be a parent. Time passes much too quickly."

◆　◆　◆

Julien and Jacques were thrilled the next afternoon when Nicolas and Adam let the two boys go with them to find a Christmas tree. There was a stand of young pines on the property, and Adam was sure they would find one that would work.

The girls were equally happy to be included in the candy making. Felicia had come to help, and Suzette thoroughly enjoyed the day. It was fun to watch Maman LeBlanc try to find out what the girls wanted for Christmas. They really asked for very little—and Suzette had a feeling they were trying to make things as easy on their mother as they could. By the time the men were back with a tree for both homes, there was a fresh batch of pralines cooling on the kitchen table and several trays of cookies in the oven. Maman LeBlanc had put on a pot of bean soup, and after supper the children begged to put up the tree early instead of waiting until Christmas Eve.

"Please, Maman. Can we put it up tonight?" Rose asked.

"Yes, please, Maman," Amy added. "We almost had Papa talked into putting it up early last year. Please let us."

"Oh yes, please do, Maman," Jacques begged.

"You are right, Amy. Papa was for it. I was the one who said no. So. . .yes! We will put it up early as Papa nearly agreed to last year. Nicolas, would you bring the decorations down from the attic, please?"

"Of course, Maman," Nicolas quickly agreed.

Suzette had a feeling he thought it would be easier to start a new tradition of putting the tree up a few days early than to continue with the old. She thought so, too. He and Adam brought the boxes down to the living room, and Suzette and Felicia carefully unwrapped each ornament. Then they handed them out to the children to put on the tree while Maman made hot chocolate and brought in a plate of the cookies they'd baked earlier.

Suzette's heart went out to them all as they each seemed to try to hide the sorrow they felt that Papa LeBlanc wasn't there. She had a feeling that tears would be shed when they turned out the lights that night, but for the moment they all seemed to want to make the evening easier on their mother. She tried to help by playing the language game, pointing first to the tree.

Jacques shouted, *"Arbre de Noël!"*

"Christmas tree!" Nicolas answered back. The mood in the room lightened as he joined in the game, and Suzette's heart expanded with joy to see Maman join in the laugher that ensued.

◆ ◆ ◆

Nicolas brought his papa's 1916 Ford around to the front of the house to pick up his family for church the next morning. Rose sat on Maman's lap, up front with him, and Amy and Suzette sat in the back. Adam and Felicia had already picked up Julien and Jacques.

Nicolas's first instinct had been to miss church, but he knew his mother wouldn't allow it, so he'd dressed in his one and only suit, which thankfully still fit, and done what he knew was expected of him.

The whole time he'd been overseas, even after he'd been wounded and his buddy killed, he'd felt close to the Lord. But ever since the day he received word about his papa, Nicolas had been filled with more questions than answers, and he'd found it increasingly hard to pray, hard to take everything to Him. At home now, he questioned why his language might soon be extinct. It seemed all he had for the Lord were questions of *why*.

Still, he was a little surprised by how good it felt be back in church with his family again. To sit on the same pew they'd sat on for years. . .and to be sitting beside Suzette. He needed to thank her for helping make last night much easier than he thought it would be. Her silly language game had helped more than he liked to admit, and the least he could do was thank her for being there for them all.

Maybe now it was time to pray, to thank the Lord for getting him back home safely and for keeping the rest of his family safe, for bringing Suzette into his family's lives to help them when he couldn't. And for him to accept God's will. Nicolas bowed his head and silently did just that.

Chapter 5

With Christmas falling on Wednesday, Nicolas and Suzette had little time to spare in getting to town to shop. He was glad that Monday was sunny and not too cool. They had made plans to go into Breaux Bridge right after breakfast, and he was glad to see Suzette ready and waiting for him when he pulled the Ford around.

Maman waved them off with a smile on her face, and for that Nicolas was extremely grateful. He knew everything was an effort for her with Papa gone, and he loved her all the more for trying to carry on so gallantly without him.

"Ready?" He turned to Suzette as she took her seat beside him.

"I am. I have your mother's list with me. I hope we will be able to find everything."

"I hope so, too. We'll do the best we can. So, what is it we are looking for?"

Suzette pulled the list from her coat pocket. "Let's see. For Amy, she would like us to find a scarf and gloves to match in red or purple. It seems Rose has hinted for a new baby doll and Jacques would like a toy boat. Julien would like a new slingshot. I don't think those will be too hard to find, do you?"

"I don't think so," Nicolas swerved the automobile to avoid a rut in the road, and that sent Suzette sliding across the seat and into his arm that was still in a sling. It didn't hurt, but he was surprised by the electric charge that shot up his arm. He'd been trying to do the exercises the doctor had given him before he was discharged and sent home, but this was the first time he'd felt anything from his fingertips to his shoulder. Perhaps he'd get full use of it soon.

"I'm sorry," he apologized as she tried to right herself. "These roads have gotten worse since I've been gone. Are you all right?"

"I'm fine. But are *you* all right? Did I hurt your arm?"

"No, you didn't. It's fine."

"Good." Suzette straightened the knitted cap she had on and continued with their conversation as if nothing had happened. "She also has a few things down for us to try to find for Adam and Felicia. I hope we haven't waited so long that the stores are sold out of what we need to find."

"There are several different stores in town that we can try. Breaux Bridge has grown even since I've been gone." He did hope they could find it all. The only problem he could see was that his mother had asked him to pick up a gift for Suzette also, and he didn't know for sure how he was going to get that done. If he couldn't manage it today, he'd just have to run back into town tomorrow.

"I do like Breaux Bridge," Suzette said as they entered the town. "It's such a pretty town, sitting here on both sides of Bayou Teche with the bridge connecting it. It's not so big that you don't know anyone, and yet it is large enough to find what you need."

"Well, we hope so," Nicolas said as he parked the car. "Let's go to the Main Street Mercantile. It's really more of a department store than it used to be, and it should have most of what is on Maman's list."

"All right, if we can't find it all there, Maman LeBlanc said there was a ladies store we could try."

"A ladies store?" Horrified with the idea of going into a store for women, Nicolas must have looked as appalled as he felt because Suzette giggled.

"I'll go in, Nicolas. You won't have to. But Maman seemed to think the others might be sold out of scarves and gloves."

His sigh of relief brought another chuckle from her. "I'm relieved to hear that, Suzette. But let's see what we can find in the department stores first."

The Main Street Mercantile did indeed have most of what they were looking for. They found Rose's doll right away. It had brown hair and blue eyes that opened and closed, and they both agreed that Rose was sure to love it. They also found a red and blue toy boat for Jacques and the slingshot Julien was hoping for. But Amy's present was another matter. Both department stores in town had sold out of the items they were looking for.

"Don't worry, Nicolas. I'll run over to Goodwin's and look. I'm sure they will have scarves and gloves to match."

"Are you sure you don't mind?"

"I'm sure. I can meet you back here—"

"No. Let's meet at the Acadian Café for lunch. Then we can see where we are in our shopping. I want to find something for Maman." He thought for a moment. He'd been through a world war—surely he could manage a ladies shop. "But perhaps I should just come with you and see what I can find there for her. Do you think they would have a cape for Maman? I'd like to find her a nice one."

"I'm sure they will. I've seen one in the display window in the past. But I'll be glad to look for you and let you know if they have any I think she'd like when we meet for lunch."

"No. I'll come with you." He might get an idea of what Suzette liked if he went along. And he'd much rather go in with her to look for Maman's gift now than to go by himself later.

Actually, he rather enjoyed accompanying Suzette to Goodwin's. And once inside, there was nothing terribly frightening about being in the store. The displays were tastefully laid out and since it was two days before Christmas, he found he wasn't the only man in the store.

The salesclerk showed them several styles of capes, and he chose a black silk-lined wool one for his mother. It was simple but elegant, and he hoped she would like it. The store had a nice selection of scarves and gloves, and they picked out a royal purple set for Amy. They both left Goodwin's happy that they'd found most of what was on Maman's list. But Nicolas still didn't know what to get the children from him.

"Actually, Amy likes to read. She loved reading the *Anne of Green Gables* series. The newest book in that series was written last year. It's *Anne's House of Dreams*. I think maybe she'd like a copy of her own. Maybe we could visit the bookstore?"

"That is a wonderful idea, Suzette. Thank you."

"You're welcome. I think Rose might like some paper dolls to play with. Maybe we can find those there, too."

"Oh, I think she would like that. Let's go get something to eat, and then we can finish up our shopping." He had a feeling he would be happy with his purchases for the children if he just listened to Suzette. He'd been gone a long time, and she seemed to know their likes and dislikes much better than he did now.

◆　◆　◆

They'd met up with several friends and extended family of the LeBlanc's as they'd gone around town, and it was obvious that Nicolas was well respected by them all. Now, sitting in the café across from him as they were served steaming bowls of red beans and rice, Suzette wondered how she could ever have thought him gruff.

This shopping trip showed just how much he cared about his family. Her respect for him soared as he'd entered the dress shop with her. There was no way her papa would have entered that shop, yet Nicolas had put away his natural reluctance to go in so that he could get his mother a wonderful present. The salesclerk had almost ignored the fact that Suzette was with Nicolas in her eagerness to help him. But she couldn't blame the young woman. Nicolas was a handsome man, and Suzette had to admit that she was quite pleased to be escorted by him.

"I'm still not real sure about what to get the boys," Nicolas said before blowing on the spoon of beans and rice to cool it down.

"Maybe we'll spot something while we are looking for the girls," she suggested.

As they talked about where to go next and what to get the boys, she felt encouraged to bring up a subject she wasn't sure he would welcome. But he *was* the head of the LeBlanc household now, and she needed his help.

"Nicolas, I must to speak to you about the children's English lessons." She could tell from the way his left eyebrow raised that she was right. He didn't welcome the subject.

"Yes? What about them?"

Well, at least he was willing to listen to what she had to say.

"I've noticed that until the night we put the tree up, you hadn't joined in our word games. You haven't been speaking your Cajun at the table, either." In fact he usually didn't speak at all when they were playing the game.

"I thought the idea was to speak the English only," he said gruffly.

"No. The idea is to teach them the differences in the two."

"You seem to be doing a very good job of that."

Suzette sighed. He wasn't making this easy on her. "I'm sure you've noticed that I don't always get things right."

His tone softened a bit. "I have noticed that sometimes you don't quite seem to recognize the Cajun word, but I thought you were doing it wrong for the children's sake."

She smiled and shook her head. "Non. It is that sometimes the Creole French I grew up speaking and the Cajun spoken here are a little different. It's not too bad with my students, but when their parents. . .or even when you and your Maman and Felicia get to talking so fast, I can't always keep up."

"Oh, I didn't realize—"

"I could use your help, Nicolas." There. She'd said it.

"Mine? In what way?"

Suzette hesitated only a minute. "To help me translate sometimes when I don't quite understand what is being said."

Nicolas bent his head to the side and sighed before saying, "I will think about it."

That was more than she'd hoped for. In that moment, Suzette knew she was beginning to care for Nicolas LeBlanc. "Merci."

"*Pas de quoi.*" He smiled at her.

Oh yes, she cared. Deeply.

◆　◆　◆

Nicolas wasn't sure just how Suzette had gotten him to agree to even *think* about interpreting the Cajun she didn't quite understand yet. Maybe it was the sweet expression in her eyes when she smiled at him, but he had a feeling it had something to do with the fact that she'd trusted him enough to admit she needed help.

After they left the café and went to the bookstore, they found exactly what they were wanting for the girls, and Suzette even found a couple of books that she thought the boys would like. Then they went back to the department stores to find the things Maman had asked them to pick up for Adam and Felicia.

They split up after that, saying they had a few things to pick up on their own, but Nicolas had a feeling they were both doing his mother's shopping for each other.

He'd been able to ask the salesclerk at Goodwin's to add a blue scarf and gloves that his mother had requested for Suzette to his purchases without Suzette knowing what he was doing, and he went to pick those up first. Then he went to do his own shopping. He picked up several boxes of chocolates and a few things for stocking stuffers, but he didn't know what to get the woman who'd helped his maman so very much.

By the time they got home that evening, Nicolas realized he'd enjoyed the day with Suzette more than he'd enjoyed anything since he'd been home, and he hated to see it come to an end.

Maman had a pot of jambalaya simmering when they entered the kitchen, and the girls had the table set already. Nicolas and Suzette quickly hid their purchases until they could get them wrapped, and then they joined the others for supper. The children knew they'd been shopping for Christmas, and their excitement was contagious. By the end of the evening he was sure that he wasn't the only adult thankful to have children around this first Christmas without Papa.

Chapter 6

The next day was filled with delicious smells, whispered secrets, and visits by family and friends. A telegram early that morning brought good news for the family. Maman's sisters were coming from Lafayette for Christmas.

Nicolas drove into Breaux Bridge to pick them up, and he'd never been happier to see his aunts. *Tante* Julia and Tante Louise were both older than his mother and widowed, so he knew their attentions to his maman would be especially tender and go a long way in helping her get through the next few days without Papa.

"My, how handsome you've become, Nicolas," Tante Julia said on the way back home. "I'm sure you have the young ladies lined up for your attentions."

Nicolas laughed. "Tante Julia, I haven't been home long enough to even pay attention to the ladies." That wasn't entirely true. He hadn't been able to get one in particular out of his mind.

"Well, it is about time you do. You aren't getting any younger, you know," Tante Louise said bluntly.

"Oh, Louise, you talk as if he is an old man! He has time. And now that he's back home, I'm sure it won't take him long to find the right one."

That started an in-depth conversation about what kind of woman they thought would make him a good wife.

"Of course she should be a good Christian woman," Tante Julia said, matter-of-factly.

"Well, of course! There is no question about that," Tante Louise agreed. "And after that, she should love your family."

"That just goes without saying, Louise," Julia said with a shake of her head. "Nicolas would not consider anyone who did not fit in with the family."

Nicolas rushed to assure them both, "No, I wou—"

"Of course you wouldn't pick someone who didn't like your family," Tante Julia interrupted. "And she must be able to cook, of course."

"Oh, Julia, of course he will pick a woman who can cook. No self-respecting Cajun would choose a woman who couldn't cook!"

"Well, you'd be surprised, Louise! A pretty face can sometimes sway a man."

"A woman can be nice looking and be all of the things Nicolas would want in a wife."

Tante Louise sighed with what sounded to Nicolas as exasperation. "Well, of course she can be, Julia! I didn't mean that he shouldn't marry a pretty girl—just that she shouldn't be *only* pretty!"

"Oh! Well why didn't you say so in the first place?" Tante Julia asked.

By the time Nicolas pulled the automobile up at home, he was extremely thankful that the trip from the train station was a fairly short one. He wasn't sure how much longer he could listen to their suggestions for the perfect wife.

He carried in the aunts' bags while they were pulled into his mother's welcoming arms. Talking over one another as they had in the car, he couldn't help but smile. His mother had their full attention now, and he was a little relieved that she would be on the receiving end of their coddling, and their concentration would be on her and not on what kind of wife he should choose—should he ever get to that point in his life.

He interrupted their welcome only to ask where he needed to put their cases.

"They go up in your old room, Nicolas," Suzette said from behind him.

He turned to find her smiling sweetly at him. "But what about you? Where will you be sleeping?"

"I've already moved my things into Amy's room, and Rose is going to sleep with Maman," Suzette said.

"Oh." He nodded. The arrangement made sense to him. "All right, I'll take them upstairs, then."

His appreciation for Suzette soared that she'd happily given up her room to the aunts and moved in with Amy for the duration of their stay. She didn't seem the least bit put out about it, either.

"I'll help," Suzette said, taking one of the smaller cases and following him up the stairs. As they made their way up the stairs, then down the hallway, Suzette said in a low voice, "I came up because I wanted to tell you that Maman and I got all of the presents wrapped this morning. I hope it was all right that I wrapped what you bought, too. You might just want to put tags on them."

"Thank you, Suzette! I was wondering when I was going to get around to doing that." He'd given the presents for Suzette to Maman the day before, so he wasn't worried that she saw anything bought for her. "Where are they?"

"They are in Maman's room. I'll go get them." She put the small case on the dresser in the room she'd been staying in and then ran across the hall to his mother's room.

Nicolas set the cases on the bed that used to be his and looked around. It had a feminine feel to it now and smelled lightly sweet, like Suzette. It didn't seem like his old room at all and, feeling as if he was invading her space, he hurried out of the room and met her in the hall.

She handed him an armful of prettily wrapped packages. "I've put the names in pencil on the bottom of each one. All you need to do is sign the tags and tie them to the bows."

"Thank you, Suzette. These are lovely and much better wrapped than if I had done them."

"You are welcome." She handed him several blank tags.

"Are you sure you don't mind giving up your room for the aunts?"

"Of course I'm sure. It's the least I could do. After all, you gave it up for me, didn't you?"

Somehow, he didn't think he'd done it as graciously as she had.

◆　◆　◆

Suzette fell in love with the aunts. They talked constantly, argued a lot, but under it all, she could see that they both had hearts of gold. What they wanted most was to ease some of their sister's pain.

So they kept Maman LeBlanc busy talking, cooking, and laughing all afternoon and into the evening. The house filled to the brim with family and friends who stopped by. Suzette and Felicia helped cook, but it seemed their main job was to keep the dishes washed up for the next meal. But there was so much cooking, baking, and tasting going on, one didn't know when one meal stopped and another began.

At one time there must have been five different conversations going on, and even though Suzette had a hard time keeping up with it all, she loved being in the middle of it.

It wasn't until after the last visitor left, the latest dirty pot washed and put away, that the aunts turned their attention to Suzette.

"So, you are the new schoolteacher in town?" Tante Louise asked.

"Yes, ma'am, I am."

"And do you like teaching school?" Tante Julia quizzed.

"I love it."

"But you would like to marry one day?"

Suzette could feel herself blush. "Of course I would, one day."

"Our sister says you have been a blessing to her and the family," Louise said. "Thank you for being here for her."

"She is a blessing to me—they all are."

"Hmm," Louise said, nudging Julia.

"Ah. You like this family?" Julia took a sip from her coffee cup.

"I love this family, Tante Julia. I think they are the primary reason I decided to move here."

"Ah. And do you cook?"

"I love to cook. I've learned much from Maman LeBlanc."

"Hmm," was all Julia said before Nicolas and Adam entered the kitchen.

"I think the children are asleep," Nicolas said. "Is it time for us to put the presents under the tree and fill the stockings?"

"It's time," Tante Louise said before anyone else had a chance to reply.

◆　◆　◆

Christmas Eve was the first night in months that Nicolas didn't waken from a nightmare. He'd dreamed, but all he could remember was that his aunts were in it, his tante Julia smiling and saying, "We told you so." And Suzette seemed to be wandering in and out of it—why he didn't know—but it was a wonderful change from the horrors of war he'd been fighting for months.

He looked out over the bayou and found himself thanking the Lord.

"Dear Lord, I know I haven't been talking to You much lately. I still have so many questions about why Papa died, and my friend David. . .and so many changes that are occurring here at home. But I know that You have blessed my family and You have given me a respite in the nightmares that have plagued me. I thank You for both those things and ask that my nightmares continue to stay away. Please help me to help Maman and the children through this day without Papa. And thank you for sending the aunts. . .and Suzette to help us all. In Jesus' name I pray, amen."

As Nicolas saw a light in the kitchen window, he dressed, gathered the presents he'd wrapped in the cabin, and hurried over to the main house. Dawn was just breaking, and Christmas day promised to be bright and beautiful.

The children were still sleeping, but Maman and the aunts were in the kitchen, along with Suzette, making a breakfast of *beignets* and sausages to tide them all over until the big meal they would have midafternoon. Nicolas couldn't wait to taste the fried puffed pastry, dusted with sugar and cinnamon.

"Maman, please, may I have one now?" he asked with a grin. "I haven't tasted a beignet since I left home."

"Oh, the poor boy," Tante Julia said. "Lucia, give him that beignet you are taking out of the oil."

Tante Louise handed his mother a saucer. "Here, put it on this," she said. "Suzette, get him a cup of café to go with it. Add a dollop of milk to it."

"Non, Tante Louise. No milk this morning."

"No café au lait?"

"No, ma'am. I got used to drinking it without milk overseas. It was hard to come by. The coffee wasn't great either, come to think of it. But it served its purpose and kept me awake many a night when I needed it to."

"*Tsk-tsk,*" Louise said. "I'm so glad that war is over."

"We all are," Maman said, giving Nicolas a hug.

The smell of cooking must have wakened the children because Nicolas barely got his beignet down before they heard the clamor of feet on the staircase. The women hurried to meet them in the living room, Louise with a platter of beignets and Maman with a plate piled high with sausages. Julia made sure the adults' coffee cups were full, and Suzette followed behind with glasses of milk for the children.

Presents and stockings were distributed, and paper was torn as packages were unwrapped. The children seemed thrilled with their gifts, and Maman seemed to really like her cape. Suzette was quite pleased with the scarf and gloves Maman had him pick up for her. She thanked him for the box of chocolates he'd bought for her. But the biggest smile he saw was when she pulled out the note he'd written and stuffed into her stocking. He'd merely written, "Yes, I will translate for you."

"Thank you, Nicolas!"

"Just let me know when."

As his mother and aunts were curious to know what Suzette was thanking him for and all started asking questions at once, Suzette laughed and said, "Now! Please!"

Nicolas chuckled and began translating the things she was having a hard time keeping up with and the words she didn't quite get. He actually found it quite fun to be able to interpret for her. He had a feeling that, although she'd picked him up a tie from Maman and added a store-bought box of the pralines he had a weakness for as her own present to him, Suzette's real gift to him was to allow him to teach her something.

Chapter 7

Christmas day went by easier than Nicolas had expected, and he gave much of the credit for that to Suzette and the aunts. Not to mention that it seemed every friend and relative they knew stopped in at some point during the day and evening, keeping them all busy.

Extended family members he hadn't seen since he'd been home came by. Friends of Felicia and Adam stopped by. Families who lived nearby came over. Many came just because it was Christmas and it was their habit to do so. It was a good thing there were extra hands in the kitchen because it seemed food flowed out from it all the day long.

It was a day filled with precious memories of Christmases past when Papa was with them, and there were both tears and laughter. All in all, it was a good day, but emotionally tiring for his whole family because one of them was missing. He was sure that no one was happier to have the day over with than his mother was.

Wanting to make sure Maman was all right, Nicolas stayed until everyone had gone home and the children were in their beds. His mother and aunts were relaxing around the kitchen table while Suzette made them all a cup of café au lait.

"You want a cup without milk, Nicolas?" Suzette asked.

"Non. I don't think I have room for one more thing. You all outdid yourselves this year. The meal was delicious."

"I don't think I could have done it this year without Julia and Louise and Suzette. I thank you all so much," Maman said.

"It's always better if you have lots of hands preparing. I'm glad we came," Tante Louise said.

"So am I," Nicolas added.

"Did Felicia seem more tired than usual to you, today?" Suzette asked.

"I think she was just missing her papa," Tante Julia said.

"My Felicia is running out of energy, I think," Maman said. "I know she misses her papa, but it is also getting close to her time."

"Do you think Felicia may have the baby early?" Tante Louise asked.

"Wouldn't she be more energetic if she was about to have the baby? I always had a burst of energy when it was time," Tante Julia said.

"I guess it's just a feeling I have," Maman said. "I think it might come early."

"We just may have to stay until that baby is born, Louise," Tante Julia said.

"You'll stay? Really?" Maman seemed to perk up at their words.

"Might as well. With our children visiting their in-laws over the holidays, we have nothing we need to attend to right away," Tante Louise said.

"Oh, I am so glad. So glad you are going to stay with us," Maman said.

And so was Nicolas. His aunts' visit had been good for his mother, and they seemed to help her in a way he couldn't. Somehow he felt it might be easier for her to talk about her sorrow with them.

At any rate, Nicolas decided his maman didn't need him tonight, and he didn't need to hear all this talk about having babies. He pushed away from the counter he'd been leaning against. "I'm going to let you all decide when Felicia's baby will be here. Me, I'm going to bed." He kissed his mother and then his aunts on the cheek. "I'll see you all tomorrow."

He left the women to their talk and went out to the cabin. He'd come to like it quite well, although it was really only large enough for two people. He couldn't help but wonder about his ancestors who'd first lived here, who'd raised their families here long before the main house was built. They had to have been strong in all kinds of ways to have settled here and carved out a place for generations to call home.

The cabin had been built back in the 1700s and had been in his family ever since. It had held up well and been taken care of through the generations, and it was only now that he was living in it that Nicolas had given much thought to the men and women who'd called it home.

Ever since he'd been back home and living in the cabin, it had become a place to reflect upon all manner of things for him. Tonight it was a place to reflect on the day and the people who meant so much to him. When he'd left to fight in the war, he thought it would be an adventure to see other parts of the world. But what he'd found was that he longed for home and this corner of the world every minute of the day. Now he never wanted to leave it again. His aunts were right in that when it came time to marry, he needed to choose a woman who would love his family and their way of life.

As she did more often than not when he was in the cabin alone, Suzette came to mind, and he let his thoughts rest there. She was everything his aunts said he needed. She loved the Lord; she loved his family. That had been obvious to him from the moment they'd met. And she was a wonderful cook. Not to mention that she was lovely.

She was caring and kind to everyone she met, and Nicolas could no longer deny that he cared for her more and more with each passing day. But she did not understand the Cajun way of life, and he wasn't sure she ever would. If she did, she would be trying to preserve their language instead of trying to help do away with it.

◆　◆　◆

Once the aunts heard that Felicia had indeed had a burst of energy the day after Christmas and cleaned her house from top to bottom, they agreed with Maman that Felicia's time was near. And because Maman was worried about

Felicia being by herself while Adam went for the doctor, she went to stay with the couple so that Felicia would not be alone, leaving the aunts and Suzette in charge at home. Amy and Julien were to take turns running to Adam and Felicia's every hour to bring back news. So as not to be left out, Jacques and Rose accompanied them.

But the waiting wasn't easy, and the aunts and Suzette decided to clean the house to ease their nerves. Nicolas wished he could find something to do to ease his. He went out to check on the livestock, stopped by to see how Felicia was doing, and found that she and Maman were in high spirits as she was indeed in labor. Adam, however, seemed to be feeling the strain of waiting, as Maman told him it wasn't yet time to go for the doctor. Knowing that he didn't dare pull Adam away at this time, Nicolas decided he was better off helping the tantes and Suzette than pacing the floor with Adam.

It wasn't long before his tantes decided that Nicolas's cabin needed a thorough cleaning, too.

"Non. It is fine," he said.

"I don't think it can be very dirty," Suzette said. "Maman LeBlanc and I cleaned it before Nicolas came home."

"Still, he's been here awhile. We will clean for him," Tante Louise said.

"We won't bother anything," Tante Julia said.

"There truly isn't much there to bother. . .or to clean." Nicolas looked in Suzette's direction, hoping she would help convince them that his cabin did not need their attention.

"I think they just need more to do," she said in their defense. "We're all very nervous, waiting for news."

In the end, Nicolas led the aunts to his cabin and let them at it. He moved the furniture—the bed, table, and two chairs—so that they could clean under it. They scrubbed the iron stove in the corner, and then their attention was given to the small loft above the kitchen.

"What is up there, Nicolas?" Tante Louise asked.

"I don't know."

"You've never looked?"

He shrugged "Non. I had no reason to. I think it's just things that have been left here through the years."

"Well, it probably needs a good cleaning up there."

"Maybe, but you two are not climbing up there. I'll go take a look."

"We aren't so old we can't climb a ladder, Nicolas," Tante Julia said.

"No, but if you fell and broke a bone, Maman would never let me hear the last of it. I don't want her angry with me for letting you climb an old ladder. Besides, once Felicia has the baby, you'll be needed even more."

"You're right," Tante Louise said. "Lucia would not be happy if we fell. But you should see if it needs cleaning up there."

"I'll go take a look." He took a lantern up with him but was surprised by how neat things were up there. "Maman and Suzette must have cleaned here, too!" he called back down. "Everything looks orderly. There are some boxes and an old trunk or two."

"Don't you want to see what is in them?" Tante Julia asked.

He was curious. Maybe it was because he'd been thinking about his ancestors lately, but he did wonder if there was anything up here that would tell him more about them. Besides, Nicolas had a feeling that it would do no good to argue with the two women when they were so determined to keep their hands and minds busy. He just wished Felicia would have the baby so they could give their attentions to her.

Lifting the lantern over the trunks, he saw several books and what looked like a Bible in one. He pushed the lantern to the edge of the loft and looked in another. There were all kinds of old paraphernalia that he would like to go through some day, but Nicolas didn't want to hoist everything down right now. In the boxes were some old clothes.

"Here, Tante Louise, would you take the lantern? There's only this trunk I'd like to bring down right now."

After getting rid of the lamp, he slowly eased the trunk down the rungs of the ladder and put it on the small eating table. "I think this may have some personal family items. Let's see what's here."

"Ah, Nicolas, look. . .a family Bible from long ago," Tante Julia said, pulling the worn leather-bound book out of the trunk. "It's dated in the early 1800s. And what are these? It looks like they're handwritten journals."

Nicolas picked up one of the books and found that it was indeed a journal of some kind. And it was handwritten in his beloved language. He pulled out another, but before he could take a closer look at it, Suzette burst into the cabin.

"Amy and Julien say the baby is on the way! Adam has gone to get the doctor."

◆　◆　◆

Nicolas took the bundle that was his nephew from Suzette. He was small but solid. "Ah, he is a handsome one, isn't he?"

"He is. I see some of your papa in him," Tante Julia said.

"And Adam, too, of course," Suzette added.

"Oui," Tante Louise said. "He does look like his papa."

Nicolas didn't know who he looked like, and it didn't matter. His nephew had a place in his heart already, his tiny finger wrapped around Nicolas's thumb.

"He's adorable," Suzette said, looking over Nicolas's shoulder at the baby.

Just then André Devereux scrunched up his little face and let out a tiny wail. Nicolas jiggled him as he had Rose when she was tiny, but the baby cried only louder. "I think he might be hungry."

"No. He's just been fed," Tante Julia said.

The baby began to exercise his vocal cords in earnest. "Well, something is bothering him. Does he need to be changed?"

"I changed him right before I brought him out," Tante Louise assured him.

"Let me see him." Suzette reached for André. She cuddled him close and began to hum a tune. Soon the crying had stopped, and he was fast asleep in her arms.

"He was just tired of all the commotion, I think," she said.

Nicolas couldn't help but notice how beautiful she looked gazing down at his nephew. She seemed meant to have a baby in her arms, and he'd never seen her look lovelier.

Chapter 8

The next week sped by with everyone's attentions on the new baby in the family. Friends and family flowed between both households, with Nicolas's aunts and Suzette providing the meals for all.

On Sunday, it was announced in the small congregation they attended that André Devereux had arrived. Over the next few days there were even more visits to see the baby and bring gifts. Nicolas was a little surprised that Adam and Suzette's parents couldn't see their way clear to come see their new grandbaby, but he didn't want to upset either one by mentioning it.

That didn't stop the tantes from doing so, however. The day after the baby was born, they were in the kitchen putting together a meal when Tante Louise asked, "Your maman and papa aren't coming to see baby André, Suzette?"

After one look at Suzette's face and seeing that she was upset about it, Nicolas wanted to shush his tante. After all, it really wasn't their business, but he kept silent as he was curious to hear the answer as well.

Suzette shrugged and shook her head. "Non. I went into town with Adam when he telephoned them to let them know little André was here. They just said they couldn't come right now." Her voice filled with tears. "I think he is very disappointed. I wish they could have seen his expression when they said they would come later."

"I'm sure they will pay a visit soon," Tante Julia tried to assure her.

"I hope so. They don't know what they're missing. They're sending a layette from New Orleans, as if that—" Suzette broke off the sentence and sighed deeply. It was clear that she didn't want to talk ill of her parents even though she was not happy with them.

Tante Julia hurried to give her a hug. "They will come, and they will fall in love. Then you won't be able to keep them away."

"Maybe," Suzette said. But she didn't sound as if she believed it. She busied herself with kneading the bread she was making.

Nicolas couldn't help but see the look his aunts exchanged with each other. He could almost hear the silent *tsk-tsk* that surely passed between them. They didn't ask any more questions about the Devereuxes and instead seemed to go out of their way to let Suzette know they didn't blame her for her unfeeling parents.

Nicolas didn't know what to say to her, but he began to see why she was so taken with his family. . .and at the same time how she didn't quite understand the Cajun way of life.

◆ ◆ ◆

Nicolas did enjoy seeing his aunts interact with his mother, with Suzette, and the rest of the family. They had strong opinions and weren't afraid to voice them. By New Year's Eve, it was apparent that his aunts had taken quite a liking to Suzette, and they were quite vocal in suggesting that he would do well to court her. At every turn they let him know what they thought. Thankfully, they did not say so in her hearing.

"Nicolas, Suzette is so good to your maman," Tante Julia said one morning after Suzette had gone to help at Felicia's. "She couldn't be better to her if she were her very own mother."

"Yes, she's good to us all."

"She loves our family," Tante Louise added her opinion. "And, poor dear, I can see why. At least we show her we care. I wonder what kind of parents the Devereuxes are. That they haven't even come to see their first grandchild is unthinkable to me!"

"I know," Tante Julia agreed with her sister. "I do not know how they can stay away. Why, we have to practically make your maman come home."

"I know." Nicolas didn't feel he had to give long responses to his aunts' comments. He knew them well enough by now to know that they didn't expect—or want—anything more than his agreement with them.

"Well, I must wonder if they realize what wonderful children they have in Suzette and Adam. I am so glad Felicia married Adam, and it will be a lucky man who wins Suzette's heart," Tante Louise said.

"A lucky man, indeed," Tante Julia added.

Nicolas silently agreed—but was very relieved when Amy and Julien came in just then to ask him to take them all to see the baby. It put an end to the conversation for the moment. He didn't want to hear any more about some lucky man winning Suzette's heart.

◆ ◆ ◆

Suzette was going to miss the aunts. They had been so kind and loving to her since they'd been there. And their visit had helped Maman LeBlanc get through Christmas. Now, maybe the new baby in the family would help ease some more of her sorrow.

"We're leaving tomorrow, dear," Tante Julia said the day after New Year's. "You'll be back teaching school next week. Lucia will be spending most of her days with Felicia, even though she is doing very well. We know our sister is going to be all right with all the love and care she receives from you and Nicolas and the others."

"She will hate to see you two go, though. I know she has loved having you here."

"We'll be back. Hopefully soon," Tante Louise said. "But we can't thank you enough for helping Lucia through such a hard time. We are all blessed you are here."

At hearing those words, Suzette blinked quickly to keep her forming tears at bay. She hugged the older women. "I am going to miss you both."

And she would miss them. She loved hearing the loving banter between the two women. To some it seemed as if they argued all the time, but she'd seen them look at each other with a teasing glint in their eyes and realized it was just the way they related to each other.

They'd both hinted that she and Nicolas would make a good couple, but Suzette had tried to ignore their subtle suggestions. It wasn't that she didn't like him, for she did. The longer she knew Nicolas, the more she realized she was falling in love with him. But she had no idea how he felt about her, and in fact thought that maybe, with the way he felt about her teaching English, she was probably the last woman he'd let himself become attracted to. But at night, in her dreams, there was no ignoring that she would like nothing more than to become a real member of the LeBlanc family, by way of becoming Nicolas's wife.

◆　◆　◆

Nicolas hated to see his aunts leave. He'd enjoyed their visit more each day and had grown to enjoy their verbal sparring. But it was time to take them to the train station, and he loaded their cases into the car while they said their good-byes to Maman, Suzette, and the children.

The sisters were close, and their tears flowed freely as they left, waving at his maman and the others until he drove the automobile around the bend in the road. Then there was much sniffing and dabbing at their eyes before his tante Julia addressed him. "Nicolas dear, Louise and I can't go back home without speaking to you straight."

"What is wrong, Tantes?"

"We are afraid you are a blind man, and we cannot leave without making sure that you are aware that you have the right woman for you sitting right here beneath your very nose," Tante Louise said bluntly.

"You are speaking of Suzette?"

"You know we are," Louise said. "She loves the Lord with all her heart, and she loves your family, Nicolas."

"Yes, she does." And his family loved her.

"She is a wonderful cook."

"She is that." And she was getting better each and every day.

"She is the *right* woman for you."

"Non. She does not understand the Cajun way of life."

"How can you say that, Nicolas?" Tante Julia asked. "Suzette loves it here in Breaux Bridge. She loves the life we Cajuns live. The closeness—everything!"

"If she loved it so much, and understood, she would not be trying to take away our language!"

"Nicolas, she is not trying to take it away. She is only trying to make things easier on the children," Tante Louise insisted.

"You could try to explain to her what is important to you, Nicolas," Tante Julia implored him.

Nicolas only shook his head. It saddened him that they did not understand, either.

"You need to open your eyes and your heart—not to mention your ears, dear Nicolas. You will find your heart's desire, if you only do," Tante Julia urged.

Chapter 9

The house felt lonesome after the aunts left, and Suzette was glad school was back in session. But when she was called into the principal's office that first day back, she was apprehensive about why he wanted to see her.

"Miss Devereux, please. . .take a seat," Mr. Fortier said, motioning to the chair across from his desk.

Suzette sat down and folded her hands in her lap, trying not to show how nervous she felt as she waited to hear why she'd been called to his office.

He looked over his glasses at her and smiled. "Relax, Miss Devereux. You are not a student in trouble."

Suzette released a big sigh and said, "Now I know what my students must feel like when I send them to see you."

They both chuckled before the principal informed her of why he wanted to talk to her.

"Actually, the school board asked me to present a proposal to you. As you are well aware, the state is planning to take away our right to speak French of any kind at schools. It may be a year or so from now, but there is more than a distinct possibility that it *is* going to happen."

"Yes, I am aware. I've been trying to prepare my students for that eventuality."

"That has come to our attention. The children are enjoying the word games you play with them, and it has greatly strengthened their use of English. What the school board is proposing to do is to start an adult evening class where those parents who wish to help their children can learn to speak English, too."

"Oh, that's wonderful. . .but do you think there will be many who will actually want to attend? I know some in the community are upset at the prospect of losing the right to speak their own language at school."

"Yes, well, so am I. But these people love their children and want what is best for them. Most do want them to speak English even though they want them to be able to keep Cajun as their first language. I feel the same way. But we must be prepared for the future and make the transition as easy on our students as we can."

"I agree."

"I know you do. That's why we want *you* to teach the class."

"Oh. I—I don't know if I am good enough. . . ."

"Miss Devereux, you are the most qualified teacher we have for this."

"But for the parents—I am afraid I am not familiar enough with the Cajun dialect to—"

"Knowing you come from New Orleans and are more familiar with the Creole French, we have thought of that. You may have an assistant. It can be anyone in the area whom you feel comfortable enough to work with, who can translate for you and help the parents at the same time."

"That would be a great help."

"Just consider it and think about whom you might ask to be your assistant. I know you can do this and make it fun for the parents at the same time. With having to work around the planting seasons and again at harvest time for some of the families, we'd like to start this at the beginning of next month or even sooner, if possible. Please think about it, and let us know as soon as you make up your mind." Mr. Fortier stood, letting her know that the meeting was over.

"I–it sounds like a wonderful opportunity. I will let you know soon," Suzette agreed. "Thank you and the school board for your confidence in me, Mr. Fortier."

She left the office and went back to her classroom feeling elated. This was something she would really like to do. It would make things easier on the children and their parents in the long run. But there was only one person who came to mind as an assistant, and Suzette didn't hold out much hope that he would agree.

◆　◆　◆

They hadn't played the language game in several weeks, and she was almost afraid to start it again. But it might be the only way to find out if she even dare let Nicolas know about the school board's proposal.

But apprehensive as she might be about beginning the game again, the family wasn't. Felicia and Adam came to the main house for supper for the first time with the baby, and that gave them an opportunity to start the game again. In fact it was Maman who started it. She pointed to André and said, *"Enfant."*

"Baby!" Rose shouted. Then she pointed to the tiny thumb in his mouth.

Jacques yelled, *"Pouce!"*

To which Suzette corrected, "Thumb."

She then pointed to his nose and said, *"Nez."*

"Nose," Felicia said, turning baby André to her and kissing him on the tip of his tiny nose. "It is a beautiful one, isn't it?"

The baby gurgled and kicked, and from then on the game was forgotten as they all oohed and ahhed over every move and sound he made.

Suzette tried to discern what Nicolas thought of taking up the game again, but he was unreadable tonight. She found his eyes on her more than once, but he'd only smile or look to someone else for the moment, and she couldn't tell what he was thinking. She would just have to gather her courage and ask him for his help. The worst he could do would be to say no.

Before approaching Nicolas, she waited until Felicia and Adam took the baby home, and Maman went up to get her younger ones in bed.

"Would you like a cup of café before you leave, Nicolas? I'd like to talk to you about something."

"Oh? Oui, pour me a cup and tell me what you sound so serious about."

She sat a cup down in front of him and joined him at the table. "I was called into the principal's office today."

"Oh? For what reason?"

"The school board would like to start an adult class for parents."

Nicolas leaned back in his chair and raised an eyebrow. "What kind of class?"

Suzette took a deep breath before letting the words rush out of her mouth. "They want to start an English class for them so that it will make it easier for them to help their children to learn, and they want me to teach it." She watched as Nicolas sat up straighter in his chair, and she could tell he didn't like what he was hearing. But there was no point in stopping now. She hurried to finish. "They also said I could have someone to assist me. Will you help me, Nicolas?"

He pushed his coffee cup to one side and rested his forearms on the table. "Let me understand. You want me to help you teach your adult students English by teaching you Cajun?"

"Well, yes and no. I do need your help with the Cajun. But I want you to help me teach the parents, by translating for us—them and me—when we don't understand each other, or when we talk too fast."

Nicolas pushed his chair away from the table and stood. "Suzette, you are trying to get whole families to quit speaking the Cajun even at home, now? You really are trying to do away with my language!"

"Nicolas, you must know that is not what I want. It isn't that I want anyone to stop speaking Cajun. I just want it to be easier on the whole family when the children can't speak it at school any longer."

"And you are positive that is going to happen?"

"From what the school board and the newspapers are saying, yes, I think it is."

"But it hasn't happened yet."

"No. It hasn't."

"Maybe I should run for office and try to stop it."

Suzette smiled at him. "You could do that. The state could use men like you to help run it."

"Do you have any idea how much I looked forward to hearing Cajun all the time I was away, Suzette?"

Her heart went out to him. "I'm sure you did. It must have been very difficult to be away from everything familiar."

"I had no idea how hard it would be not to be able to speak my natural language. But I do realize it was a good thing I'd been taught the English. Otherwise I wouldn't have been able to communicate at all. I have no problem with the children learning the English. I just don't want them having to give up their own language to do it. And if we teach the parents. . .one day our language will disappear."

"Nicolas, it doesn't have to be that way."

But he didn't seem to hear her as he paced the floor. "Did I fight for this country only to come home to help my people lose their freedom to speak the language they love? Non! I will not help you!"

Suzette was speechless as she watched Nicolas charge out the back door. When the screen door banged behind him, she flinched and began to cry. How could he be so unyielding and stubborn? Anyone but him could see that she only wanted to help. Her dreams of a future with him seemed to shatter with each tear she shed. Maybe it was time she went back to New Orleans.

Chapter 10

Nicolas slammed out the back door and headed for his cabin. His chest burned with frustration. How could Suzette think he would help do away with his language! His aunts were wrong. She did not understand at all, and he didn't think she ever would.

He entered the cabin and flung himself on the bed, angry that she'd even thought he might be willing to help. And yet, as he remembered the look on Suzette's face as he told her no, his heart twisted in his chest at the thought that his words had hurt her. That he loved her was no longer a question within him. He knew that he did, but she was not the woman for him. She could not be if she did not know what it meant to be Cajun. And without that knowledge, they could never have a good marriage. He was foolish to have listened to his aunts and to begin to think they might be right. They were wrong, and it deeply pained him that Suzette did not understand the ways of his people—his ancestors.

Nicolas sat up on the bed and lit the lantern. He picked up one of the journals stacked up on the table, left there from the day he and his aunts had cleaned. Opening it, he found it was written by Capucine, the wife of Michel LeBlanc who built the cabin and was the first of his ancestors to settle here. The next journal was written by Josée LeBlanc, married to Capucine's and Michel's grandson, Edouard. One after another he read the journals, long into the night. By the time he was finished, Nicolas had much to think about.

Through each and every journal there seemed to be a deep longing for his relations to be a part of this country, to belong. Many of his ancestors had strived to learn the English and to teach their children to speak it. They spoke their beloved Cajun language, to be sure, and wanted to preserve it, just as he did. But they wanted to be able to speak and understand *both* equally. One of his great-great-grandmothers had even taught the neighbors to speak the English from this very cabin. How had he not known that?

Maybe it was because he never bothered to find out. Maman had said it was Papa's wish that they help the children learn. He wanted to support Suzette's efforts to make things easier on them. And tonight it'd been obvious that Felicia and Adam wanted their baby to know both.

Was it possible that Suzette knew the hearts of his family better than he did? All he'd been thinking about since he'd been home was how unfair life was. . .especially to him. Yes, he'd endured much in the last year, losing his papa and his best friend, and being wounded. But others had lost even more. And even if they had loved ones, their relationships weren't always what they could be. Look at how Adam and Suzette's parents treated them. They didn't even seem to care that they had a new grandson—nor did they seem to want to know anything about the family their daughter was living with.

And yet, Suzette and Adam were loving and kind people. Suzette had helped his maman and siblings when he couldn't be here to do so. She'd only been kind to him, in spite of the rudeness he'd shown her at times. He'd be lucky if she even spoke to him again after tonight.

He'd been blaming God for his losses while she'd been holding his loved ones up in prayer and showing Christian love to them. All he'd been doing was feeling sorry for himself. God had been there for him all along. He'd brought him home safe, and his arm was healing and getting stronger each day. He'd brought a woman into his life who was right for him, just as the aunts had told him. And now he might have lost her because of his own stubbornness.

If he'd ruined things with Suzette, he wondered if his heart would ever heal. If not, there would be no blaming God for that. Nicolas knew full well that he'd have no one to blame for that heartache but himself.

◆ ◆ ◆

After tossing and turning for the rest of the night, Nicolas was a little late getting to the main house the next morning. Suzette and the children had already left.

"Suzette promised the children that if they hurried, they would stop by and see if baby André was awake. That's all it took for them to rush out the door," Maman said.

Nicolas poured himself a cup of coffee and sat down at the table. "I think maybe she didn't want to see me this morning." If he thought his mother would be sympathetic to him, he was wrong.

"I heard you storm out of here last night, son. I was not proud of you—especially when I came into the kitchen to find Suzette crying and talking about going back to New Orleans."

Nicolas's heart plummeted in his chest. For a moment the pain that she might leave took his voice away, and he shook his head. "She cannot leave, Maman! I was wrong. She is good for this family and the community needs her right now."

"It's about time you figured that out, Nicolas. But I'm not the one you need to tell it to. You are going to lose her if you don't do it soon. She was talking about turning in her resignation last night."

Nicolas was on his feet in a flash. "I'll try to catch up with her at Felicia's. If they aren't there, I'll go on to the school."

His mother waved him out the door. "Go. Hurry!"

Nicolas rushed out the door and took off in a run. He could only pray that he hadn't waited too long. *Dear Lord, please let me convince Suzette to stay and do the work You've called her to do. Please let me prove to her that I love her and believe in what she is trying to do. And please forgive me for blaming You for my sorrows. Please help me to be the man You would have me be. In Jesus' name I pray. Amen.*

Suzette and the children weren't at his sister's. And no one was on the school grounds when he got there. He didn't know which room was Suzette's, but he'd come this far and he wasn't turning back now.

He entered the school building and headed toward the principal's office. Thankfully, there was a receptionist there. "Could you tell me where Miss Suzette Devereux's room is?"

"You are the parent of one of her students?"

"No. I am the brother of several of her students. I am Nicolas LeBlanc."

The name must have been familiar to her because she nodded and smiled. "Mr. LeBlanc, her room is number 7, right down the hall to your left."

"Thank you." With that, Nicolas was on his way. Adam was right. The school was modern, much more modern than the one he and Felicia had attended. The wood floors gleamed, and the corridor was so quiet you could hear the tick of the large clock at the end of the hall.

Suzette's classroom door was shut, but light shone through the frosted-glass window in the door. He knocked.

When Suzette opened the door to see him, soft color flooded her cheeks, and for a moment, Nicolas thought she was going to tell him to go away.

"Nicolas! What is wrong? Maman? Felicia—"

"Nothing is wrong with them. I just need to talk to you."

"But school is in session, I can't—"

"It's school business I need to discuss with you."

"Oh?" She looked back into the classroom. "Children, please study your spelling words. There will be a quiz when I return. I'll be just outside the door, so behave yourselves."

There was a bench just outside her room, and she led Nicolas over to it. "What school business do you wish to talk about?"

Nicolas wasn't going to waste time. "I wanted to know if the position of your assistant is still open?"

"My—I'm not even sure I'm going to need an assistant. I may be going back to New Orleans soon."

"Non! Suzette, you cannot do that. This community needs you, and I'm sorry I did not see how much until now. You must take the position. I've been wrong. I've seen the world and know times are changing. I realize that the children will be better off knowing and speaking both languages—and being able to make the choice on which one to use the most. I realize now that you've been trying to help in the best way."

"What brought about this change of heart, Nicolas?"

"Last night I read some journals that were left in the cabin and found that you knew the heart of my people better than I did. I would like to become your assistant, and help you teach the parents, if you can forgive me for my words last night."

The corners of Suzette's mouth turned into the most beautiful smile Nicolas had ever seen. "Oh Nicolas, of course I forgive you! I'm so happy you're willing to help me!"

"There is one more condition. . . ."

"Oh? I'm not sure—"

"I love you, Suzette. I'll be the happiest man on earth if you'll agree to be my wife and help me to teach our children *both* languages. Will you marry me?"

His heart almost stopped as he waited for her answer. But Suzette didn't make him wait long.

"Oh, Nicolas, Je t'aime! And oui, I will marry you."

Nicolas pulled her into his arms and bent his head. Their lips met and clung as they sealed their promise to each other in the language of love.

JANET LEE BARTON

Bestselling author Janet Lee Barton is a Romantic Times Book of the Year winner as well as a multiple Carol Award nominee. She and her husband live in Oklahoma and have recently downsized to a condo, which they love. When Janet isn't writing or reading, she loves to cook for family, work in her small garden, travel and sew. You can visit Janet at: www.janetleebarton.com

A Shelter from the Storm

by Marjorie Vawter

Dedication

To my paternal grandparents, the real Nelson and Mildred, from whom I borrowed their first names, portions of their characters, and one small part of their love story. I miss you, and I look forward to the day when we will be reunited in our precious Lord's presence.

Special thanks to Rebecca Germany and Joyce Hart and
my own hero, Roger, for believing in me and
encouraging me in my writing journey.

For thou hast been. . .a refuge from the storm,
a shadow from the heat.
ISAIAH 25:4

Chapter 1

Hill Country, Texas
December 15, 1918

Mildred Zimmermann looked out the railcar window, vainly searching for a speck of light to indicate home was within reach. Nothing. They had to be getting close. She glanced at her military-issue wristwatch and sighed. Ten thirty. Too late for any of her family to meet her.

But Harold might be there. Surely he was home from the war now.

"Fredericksburg, next stop," the conductor called out as he entered the railroad car.

He shut the door behind him, closing off the cool draft before walking up the aisle toward her. He stopped to speak to a man Mildred had noticed as soon as she entered the car in San Antonio—absolutely the most handsome man Mildred had ever laid eyes on. Not that she was looking. But after serving nearly two years in field hospitals in Belgium and France, she could safely say she'd seen her share of men, good-looking and otherwise.

The train slowed, and steam from the locomotive billowed past her window. Finally home. Excitement tickled her stomach as she reached down to grab her pack—all her worldly goods in one small bag. She hadn't needed much outside of her navy nurse's uniform, but it would be nice to wear something different for a change.

"Excuse me, miss."

A man's rich baritone startled her out of her musings. She looked up into steely blue eyes that contrasted sharply with his dark brown hair. Her handsome fellow traveler. Heat rose from the pit of her stomach, and she prayed it would stop before it reached the top of her high-necked blouse.

Swallowing hard to dispel the rock stuck in her throat, she mentally shook herself for her reaction to this stranger. "Yes?"

"The conductor said you might know if there is somewhere to stay the night, a hotel or boardinghouse? I didn't expect to get in so late."

"You must be new to Fredericksburg not to know that this train never keeps its published schedule." Mildred smiled. "But surely someone is expecting you."

"Dr. Bachman, yes. I am his new assistant."

"Dr. Bachman needs an assistant?" Neither her parents nor her doctor uncle had mentioned it.

The train lurched and slowed as the whistle blew its warning, and the stranger grabbed at the back of the seat to steady himself. Only then did she see his cane. "Oh my." She scooted closer to the window. "How rude of me to make you stand. Please, sit down."

Relief shone in his smile as he sank into the seat next to her. "Thank you. I'm still getting used to this." He raised the cane in the air.

"What happened?" She winced. "I'm sorry. I have no right to ask. Just my nurse's training."

With more heat radiating from her cheeks, she looked out the window as the train bumped to a stop. A handful of people stood on the platform, but not her parents.

"Oh look." She nudged her companion. "There's Dr. Bachman. You won't need the hotel after all."

"Yes." The man's voice was hesitant. "Are you here to give Dr. Bachman a hand with nursing?"

Mildred lifted her eyebrows. "Why on earth would you think that? As soon as I can get out of this uniform, my nursing career is over."

"Oh, well. . .I thought that in light of. . ."

His hesitation made her stomach clench in unease, and she looked more closely at the elderly doctor on the platform. Now she saw his tired—no, exhausted—stance. Exhaustion etched his wrinkles deeper than she remembered in the beloved face. After seeing so many fatigued military doctors, she hadn't expected to see her uncle in the same state.

Turning back to her companion, she struggled to keep the alarm out of her voice. "Who are you?"

"Dr. Nelson Winters." He stood and held a hand out to help her rise.

But she ignored it. Tightening her grip on her bag, she stood without his assistance. And immediately noticed he was a head taller than she. She'd long ago gotten used to the fact that she was taller than many men. Even Harold, at five foot eleven, looked her straight in the eye.

A blush rose up her neck at Dr. Winter's close scrutiny, and she lowered her gaze and made her way past him, taking care not to knock into his cane.

"Spanish influenza," he said as she started down the aisle to the car door.

She looked at him over her shoulder. "Excuse me?"

"Have you heard of it?"

"Yes, of course. We had several cases at the last field hospital where I worked. But surely that's just in Europe." She stopped and turned toward him, catching his solemn demeanor. "Oh no. . ."

He nodded. "It's here in the States. And here in Fredericksburg." Shrugging, he added, "That's why I'm here and why I thought you. . ."

Mildred forced her feet to move her toward the door and down the steps, wondering at the tingle in her elbow as Dr. Winters steadied her from behind.

"Mildred, *liebchen*. Welcome home." Uncle's gravelly voice greeted her when she stepped onto the station platform, and he wrapped her in a warm hug. "I see you've already met Dr. Winters. I hope he's brought you up-to-date with our current problem."

Clutching her uncle's sleeve, Mildred nodded and looked over his shoulder at the others milling around. "But Uncle Will, Mama and Papa—are they all right?"

"Uncle? Dr. Bachman is your uncle?"

Mildred barely spared a glance for Dr. Winters. "And Harold?"

Her uncle wrapped his arm around her shoulder and pulled her close. "Harold. . .I don't know. We've not seen him. Everyone is fine at the farm, liebchen." A chuckle rumbled in his throat. "Did you not tell Dr. Winters our relationship?"

Mildred shook her head. "There wasn't time. We just. . ."

Uncle hugged her closer and spoke to Dr. Winters, who looked a bit confused. "This is the great-niece I spoke to you about. Mildred Zimmermann."

"Ah."

The syllable held a wealth of meaning that Mildred couldn't fathom. What had her uncle said to the man?

"Pleased to meet you at last, Miss Zimmermann."

Heat rose in her cheeks, making them tingle in the cool night air. "I seem to be always apologizing to you, Dr. Winters. Forgive me for not telling you of our relationship when you first mentioned my uncle."

"No need to apologize. I could hardly expect you to enlighten me at first acquaintance." He turned to her uncle. "I will get my other bags from the baggage car. Where should I have them taken?"

"There's one bed left at my place. It is yours until we can make further arrangements."

As Dr. Winters walked away, Uncle Will said, "Your parents want you to stay at the Sunday house until they can get into town. Do you have more bags? We should have told Dr. Winters to get them with his."

"No." She looked at the bag she'd dropped at her feet. "This is all I have. I'll be fine." She looked around the thinning crowd. "You haven't heard anything from Harold?"

"When did you last hear from him?"

Uncle Will's eyes reflected his weariness, and Mildred hated to add to his burden. Harold should have been here to meet her.

"He telegraphed a week or so after Armistice Day. Said he was headed home already; he would meet me here." Uncle Will didn't need to know the rest of the message. *Plans have changed. Letter to follow.* Only it hadn't. Mildred swallowed hard.

"*Ach ja.*" Her uncle reached into his coat pocket and drew out a telegram. "This arrived for you today. Maybe it has the answer you seek."

Taking the distinctive Western Union yellow envelope, she ripped it open with shaking fingers.

MISS ZIMMERMANN. YOU ARE LISTED AS CAPTAIN HAROLD BADER'S NEXT OF KIN WITH THE UNITED STATES WAR OFFICE. WE REGRET TO INFORM YOU THAT CAPTAIN BADER DIED NOVEMBER 20. CAUSE OF DEATH—SPANISH INFLUENZA. HIS BELONGINGS WILL FOLLOW.

Her nerveless fingers released the telegram. As it floated to the platform, the words echoed in her head: *Harold. Dead. Spanish influenza.*

Welcome home, Mildred.

Chapter 2

Nelson sat on the edge of the bed and reached for his cane. The pale light edging around the window shade told him morning had finally arrived.

And none too soon. When Dr. Bachman showed him to the small room last night, Nelson had gratefully eased his aching leg under the quilts on the comfortable bed. But instead of the sleep his body so desperately craved, his mind remained alert, his thoughts so jumbled even he couldn't keep them straight.

Nelson sighed and rose, balancing on the cane until his bad leg would agree to carry him across the room to the washstand. The cold water on his face startled his muddled thoughts and focused them sharply on one picture. Mildred's face.

She had to be the Millie Harold talked about so much, though she was much prettier in person than in Harold's blurred print.

His heart winced at the thought of Harold. Dr. Bachman had told him of his friend's death last night, after they had seen a very distracted Mildred to her family's Sunday house.

Sunday house. That was one oddity Harold had never mentioned in all his talk about Fredericksburg. He'd have to ask why these people called the small houses by that name. Maybe it would ease his guilty conscience whenever he thought of Harold.

Grimacing at his reflection, Nelson ran a comb through his thick hair. Then, as he finished tying the knot in his tie, a sharp knock on the door startled him. His leg gave way as he turned toward the sound, and he grabbed at the side of the wardrobe to keep himself from collapsing on the floor.

"Dr. Winters?" The elderly doctor's voice sounded strained. "Are you awake?"

"Yes." Nelson gripped his cane. "Come in, sir. And call me Nelson, please."

Dr. Bachman eased the door open but didn't come in. "Didn't you sleep at all, son?"

Nelson shifted his weight and indicated the unmade bed. "Not much." His mouth tightened. "But not because of the bed, sir. Just the leg talking to me."

Dr. Bachman nodded. "I hate to disturb you so early, but we have a problem."

Nelson followed his superior to the kitchen where Dr. Bachman motioned him to a seat at the table.

"Coffee?"

"Please." Nelson sniffed the air. The coffee smelled rich and strong, just the way he liked it.

"Cream? Sugar?"

"No, sir. Thank you. Just black."

Dr. Bachman nodded his approval as he poured coffee into two large mugs and brought them to the table. Then he lowered himself into a chair across from Nelson.

After a cautious sip, Dr. Bachman asked, "Are you ready to get to work?"

Nelson nodded his assent. Anything to keep his mind occupied and away from the distraction Mildred posed.

"I had planned to ease you into the workload, but this blasted influenza isn't slowing its attack on the people of this town." The older doctor's fingers played with the handle on his coffee cup. "We had five more patients come in last night."

"Where did you put them all?" Nelson knew from the quick tour Dr. Bachman had given him last night that there weren't that many beds in the tiny clinic attached to his home.

Dr. Bachman shrugged. "That's the problem. The men are on pallets in my exam room. The one woman is on the settee in the parlor. And the *kinder*, the children, are on the floor there, too."

"Not ideal, but what else is there?" Nelson couldn't help wondering why this town only had a small clinic. From what Harold and Dr. Bachman had told him, quite a large rural community relied on Dr. Bachman's medical care. There used to be a larger hospital, but it had been abandoned in favor of a smaller clinic. The old hospital building now housed a mercantile.

Dr. Bachman took a large sip of coffee then speared Nelson with his dark chocolate gaze. "We ask Mildred if we can use the Sunday house." He paused, contemplating his next words. "And we need her nursing skills."

"But—" Nelson heard Mildred's words from last night echoing through his head.

"I know." Dr. Bachman nodded sharply. "She's done nursing. But there's no way around it. We need her." Another nod. "And that's where you come in, my boy."

"Me?" Nelson's eyebrows rose.

"*Ja.* You persuade her to be a nurse a little longer, so she can care for patients at the Sunday house."

"Why me?"

Dr. Bachman's eyes twinkled with mischief. "Because you are young, good-looking, and persuasive."

What a joke! He'd virtually run away from Arlington to get out from under his father's insistence he join the family practice. Nothing he said, persuasive or otherwise, changed his father's thinking. And now this man wanted him to use his nonexistent power of persuasion on Mildred?

Dr. Bachman nodded again, confirming his words, and stood. "Right after we eat some breakfast, you go and persuade her, ja?"

Nein. But one look at the man's face convinced him not to express it. The matter was already settled. "Ja."

◆   ◆   ◆

After a small but substantial breakfast of pumpernickel and ham, and a quick round to see the patients with Dr. Bachman, Nelson found himself standing outside the tiny house they had escorted Mildred to the night before.

In the light of day, he compared the Zimmermann Sunday house with those close by. This one had a lean-to added onto the back, making it larger than most. Still, Nelson wasn't sure it would be big enough to house more than a few patients. And how would they keep everything sanitary? Field hospitals were bad enough, and these houses looked pretty basic without the modern amenities of indoor plumbing.

He edged to the side of the house and located an outhouse on the back of the property. He grimaced. This didn't look too promising. However, he'd committed to recruiting both Mildred and her family's Sunday house. Dillydallying out here on the walk wouldn't get the job done.

Taking a calming breath, Nelson climbed the two steps to the small porch and knocked on the door.

"Come in," Mildred's soft alto called out.

Come in? She didn't even know who was outside. Surely she locked the door. Nelson hesitated then put his hand to the handle just as it turned.

He snatched his hand back as though it were on fire and gazed at Mildred's beautiful face.

"Good morning, Dr. Winters."

"Uh. . ." All words rushed from his mind.

Pink rose in Mildred's cheeks, and he realized he was staring. *Say something, you idiot.* But still, words wouldn't come.

"Didn't you hear me say to come in?" Mildred motioned him into the room. But his feet had grown roots and anchored him to the porch.

"Uh, no, I mean, yes. . ."

Her smile stretched wider, deepening a dimple on her right cheek.

Nelson closed his eyes. What was he thinking? He was here on business, not pleasure. He would do well to remember Helena. Romance, love, wife, family—all were out of his reach now. Helena and the constant ache in his leg had taken care of that.

Nelson cleared his throat and opened his eyes. "Your uncle sent me to talk to you."

Mildred held the door wider. "Okay, but could we do it inside? It's chilly out there. Besides, you can sit down in here."

All his mother's teaching on propriety and what society expected of a gentleman did not include what to do in a small town set in the hill country of Texas. But he hesitated only a moment longer. She was right. He'd be more comfortable sitting, out of the chilly air.

He followed her in the door and eased it shut behind him. Habit had him looking for a lock on the door to click in place. . .but his fingers searched in vain.

Mildred laughed, a pleasing sound. "Where are you from? A big city is my guess."

What did that have to do with no locks on doors? "Arlington, Virginia. Right outside Washington, DC."

"Well, city boy, we don't lock doors around here." She shrugged and motioned to a small settee for him to sit. "There's no need. We all know each other."

But they didn't know him. He eased himself down on the settee, loosening his coat as he sat. The room was furnished with beautiful wood pieces—a pie safe near the wood cookstove, a lovely mantelpiece surrounding a small fireplace, the settee, a wood rocker.

A door near the cookstove had to lead to the lean-to he'd seen outside.

Mildred's amused voice broke into his perusal of the small living area. "Does the room pass muster, Dr. Winters?" Her eyes twinkled as provocatively as her uncle's had earlier.

He quirked his lips into a smile of appreciation. "Yes. It's lovely. The furniture is very unique. That rocking chair, especially. It's similar to the one in my room at the doctor's."

"It should be." She laughed. "My father built all the furniture. It's what he does."

"But I thought your parents were farmers."

Mildred shook her head. "My father is the oldest son, so when his father died, he inherited the farm. But he was already an established carpenter and furniture maker. They needed a bigger home, so they moved out to the farm where Father now has his workshop. My uncle George, Father's brother, farms the land."

"So, why is this called a Sunday house?"

"When the town's founders came to Fredericksburg from the old country, they settled outside of town. But they didn't want to miss church services, so they built these small houses for the weekends. They would come into town to get supplies on Saturday and then stay overnight, go to church on Sunday, and return to their ranches and farms Sunday afternoon." She shrugged. "At first they all looked alike— one room with a sleeping loft for the kinder. The stairs are outside so as not to take up room inside. Eventually most of them had rooms added on and indoor plumbing installed. Gas lighting replaced kerosene lamps, and now electric lighting is starting to replace the gas."

Nelson's mind grasped onto one of the improvements. "Indoor plumbing? You have it here?"

"Yes, of course." She motioned toward the back of the house. "Father built the lean-to for his first workshop, but today it's a bedroom with a small bathroom partitioned out of it." She stood. "Do you want to see it?"

"Uh, sure." He knew his mother would be cringing at all the "improprieties," but she wasn't here, and this was a different world.

They stepped into a cozy room with a bed, wardrobe, and nightstand. To the right, a door led into a small bathroom containing a sink, a claw-foot tub, and a toilet. All sparkling clean.

Dr. Bachman's idea made more sense now. All he had to do was propose it.

Mildred stood to the side of the bathroom door watching him. He carefully pivoted and led the way back into the main room. "Very nice. Your uncle was talking about the Sunday house this morning."

Mildred reached for a coffee cup on the shelf above the stove. "Really? Why?" She motioned him to a chair at the table then picked up the coffeepot off the back of the stove. "Would you like some coffee?"

"Yes, please. Just black is fine." He settled into the chair and wondered how to ease into his task.

"So what did Uncle Will have to say about the house?" Mildred gave him the coffee then sat next to him, cradling her own cup.

"He would like to use it as an overflow clinic."

"Why?" Mildred's piercing gaze drove the words from his mind again. "What's happened?"

"Five more influenza patients came to the clinic last night. And more arrived just as I was leaving to talk to you. There simply isn't more room."

Her mouth tightened as she took in the implications of his words. "Is it really that bad?" At his nod, she asked, "Who would care for them?"

Nelson swallowed hard. This was the tricky part. "You."

"Oh no." Mildred set her cup down hard and started to rise.

Nelson put his hand over hers, and she sank back into her chair. "I know what you said last night, but I don't think either of us knew the extent of the influenza here."

She hadn't removed her hand from under his, and he allowed his thumb to caress the soft skin. She still wore her nursing uniform—judging from the size of her small pack, she probably had no other clothes with her. He didn't say anything more, letting her process her uncle's plan while he memorized her features. As if he needed to, judging by the picture in his mind all night and into this morning. He knew he shouldn't even entertain the thoughts being in her presence inspired, but he was unable to check them.

Finally, her chocolate-brown gaze met his and then flicked around the room before settling on him again. "Okay. But we'll have to rearrange this room. Henry can help us."

A flash of jealousy caught his heart. "Henry?"

"My brother. I called out to the farm this morning. He's driving the Model T in to get me." She flashed a small smile, so quick he almost missed it. "At least that was the plan."

Her gaze dropped to their clasped hands. She gently removed her hand, reached for their cups, and stood. "How many do you think we can care for here?"

Chapter 3

Mildred stretched to a full standing position and reached to touch the low ceiling of the Sunday house. Her back ached from bending over the patients in her care. She glanced around the small front room at the beds lined along the right and left walls—five on each side—with a narrow aisle between the feet leading from the kitchen to the front door. A sense of satisfaction rose within her, and she allowed herself to bask in it for a moment.

For the last three days, she'd been busy with the twenty-four-hour care her patients needed, snatching small naps when nothing else demanded her attention. Uncle Will and Nelson—um, Dr. Winters—needed more help, but the demand of the influenza epidemic extended across the country. Even with the doctors and nurses returning from the war, there still weren't enough people to fight this home-front battle.

Mildred eased the front door open and stepped onto the porch, pulling down the mask covering her nose and mouth. Drawing in deep breaths of fresh air, she sank into one of two rocking chairs and absently stroked the silky-smooth wood arms. Her father made these chairs for her mother shortly after they were married. Back when his woodworking barely had enough income to support a wife and three young orphaned cousins. God honored Papa's commitment to fulfilling the purpose He'd intended for him, and now the business continued to thrive, in spite of war and economic hardship.

A flood of grief for *what could have been* washed through Mildred's thoughts, and she laid her head against the high back of the chair, closing her eyes. Harold was dead. It was hard to believe she'd never see him again. She'd planned to return to the farm until her wedding and then settle into married life. But Uncle Will's plea for help couldn't be ignored. So she'd only seen her parents and siblings a brief few minutes on Sunday when they stopped by the Sunday house after church.

Tears seeped out from under her eyelids and slid down her cheeks.

"Are you okay, Millie?"

Mildred startled and opened her eyes. "Clarice!" Her best friend and cousin perched on the bottom step to the porch. "Uncle George told me you were in San Antone."

Clarice hopped up the stairs and held her arms out for a hug. Mildred rose and returned the embrace then held her petite cousin away from her to gaze at her sweet face.

Clarice was her opposite in almost every way: short to Mildred's tall; fair-haired to her own chestnut bob; vivacious and outgoing to her quiet shyness. Mildred couldn't imagine life without Clarice in it.

Pulling her into another hug, Clarice asked again, "Are you okay?"

Mildred released her friend and sank back into the rocker, indicating the other for Clarice to sit. Fingering the strings to her mask dangling around her neck, she said, "Harold's dead, Clarice."

"Oh honey, I know. Mama told me."

Clarice reached over and covered Mildred's hand with her own, bringing to mind Nelson's touch a few days before. Harold's touch never ignited a fire deep within her like Nelson's did, and try as she might, she couldn't erase that sensation from her mind.

"I am sorry." Clarice gave a final squeeze and let go. "I know you're missing him."

Mildred nodded.

Clarice sat quietly for a moment, but in true Clarice-like fashion, she couldn't stay silent for long. "So who's taking care of the patients while you're out here?"

"No one. Everyone is resting, and Nelson is over at the clinic with Uncle W—"

"Nelson?" Clarice's eyes lit up even more. "Is he the new doctor Mama mentioned?" She leaned forward and lowered her voice. "Is he as handsome as Evie says he is?"

Mildred squashed the unexpected stab of jealousy at hearing Clarice's younger sister's description of Dr. Winters. Accurate, though. It was her first thought of him a week ago. "Evie's right on that count." She smiled.

"So, what's he like otherwise?" Clarice practically bounced in her chair.

Mildred laughed. "Why should you care? What would Thomas say?"

Clarice shrugged. "Just because I'm getting married in twelve days—but who's counting?—isn't a reason not to scope out a good man for my best friend."

Mildred's humor evaporated.

Clarice slapped her forehead then reached over and covered Mildred's hand with her own. "I know you're grieving, but Millie. . ."

Mildred sighed and squeezed Clarice's hand. "Go ahead. Spit it out."

"Well, it's just that you and Harold were really good friends, and I know you planned to marry him after the war, but"—Clarice scrunched her pretty little nose—"you know."

Mildred shook her head. "No, I don't know. Not until you tell me, silly."

Clarice took a deep breath. "Okay. You and Harold never had the spark between you. . .you know, like Thomas and me. I mean, I simply melt every time he holds my hand or kisses me. You and Harold were always so. . .um, businesslike when you were together. Not really in love." She let go of Mildred's hand. "Oh, I don't know. I'm afraid I'm not being very clear."

Mildred pulled her lips into a wry smile. "Only too clear, dear cousin."

"I probably said too much." Clarice grimaced. "I'm sorry."

"Don't be. You've said nothing more than what I've already thought." She was sorry Harold was dead. She'd even shed tears. But no matter how she tried, she couldn't conjure up the grief she imagined she should have for the man she expected to marry. Only regret at her own actions. If only she hadn't written that last letter. . .

"Okay then." Clarice's eyes danced again. "What's Dr. Winters like?"

Mildred turned her gaze down the street—toward downtown where Nelson was—as though conjuring him up in her mind. Not that she had to. She shook her head in disgust. What was wrong with her? She couldn't be in love with a man she just met. Even if she had spent more time with him in the last week than would normally be considered proper. Their patients were usually their only chaperones.

Their patients. How long had she been out here? She looked at her watch. "Oh goodness. I only meant to come out here for a quick breath of air." She stood. "I've got to check on the patients and get a meal started."

Clarice stood with her. "I actually came to help you for a bit, and here we sit. . . talking." She pulled a mask from her skirt pocket, looped the strings behind her ears, and tied it into place. "Tell me what you need me to do."

Relief surged through her at her cousin's request. For the first time, Mildred noticed Clarice was dressed in a serviceable gray skirt and white shirtwaist. Almost as severe as her own nurse's garb.

"Are you sure you want to risk it with such a short time before your wedding?"

Clarice fluttered her hands at Mildred's question. "Pooh! I've been helping Dr. Bachman off and on all fall. I'm fine. So quit arguing and tell me what to do."

Mildred shrugged and led the way inside. She knew better than to try to stop Clarice when she had a mind to do something. "First, let's get you an apron to protect your clothes." She headed toward the cabinet next to the stove. Clarice shut the door quietly behind her then followed. Mildred pulled a fresh apron off the middle shelf and handed it to Clarice.

"Where do you wash?" Clarice tied the apron and held her hands up like a doctor preparing for surgery.

Mildred smiled and pointed to the sink on the other side of the stove. "We have running water there, but the water isn't always hot enough. So use some from the kettle on the stove." She lifted a jar from the ledge above the sink. "And Nel—um, Dr. Winters wants us to use the carbolic acid solution to sterilize our hands. Like this."

Setting the jar on the edge of the sink, Mildred turned the spigot for the hot water, lathered her hands with lye soap, and rinsed them in the bowl Clarice filled with hot water from the kettle. Then she poured a little of the solution into her palm and worked it over her hands and up her forearms before rinsing them again.

Clarice nodded her understanding and went through the process as Mildred dried her hands on a clean towel. Coughs and wheezes and the occasional moan punctuated the silence, and her heart stirred once again, thankful for the ability the Lord had given her to ease pain and suffering.

"Is it time for medications?" Clarice's low voice cut into her thoughts, and Mildred turned toward the table. The plain wood kitchen table had been transformed into a laboratory worthy of the finest training hospitals in the East. She smiled, seeing Nelson bent over the petri dishes and medicine components far into the night.

"Nel—Dr. Winters believes in newer methods of treating the influenza." She reached for a green bottle that contained a smelly goo and held it up for Clarice to see. "This Vicks VapoRub helps ease the tightness in their chests from the cough, though Dr. Winters says it does little else."

She motioned Clarice to follow her, and they stopped by the closest bed to the kitchen. "You know Johnny Zuckerman, right?" She waited for Clarice's nod, watching Johnny's gaze dart back and forth between the two of them. "Is it okay for Miss Clarice to help you, Johnny?"

He grinned slightly and nodded a yes. Then coughed.

"Cover your mouth when you cough, please." Even to her own ears, the words sounded rote—spoken without thinking. But Johnny flashed an apology with his eyes as he raised his hand to his mouth.

Mildred handed the jar to Clarice then pulled the sheet and blanket covering Johnny down to his waist. Under his nightshirt, she had placed a padding of cloth on his chest. When she lifted it, the sharp scent of wintergreen wafted to her nose.

"Everyone has a compress like this on their chests." Mildred looked around the room. "You can add another layer of the Vapo Rub and replace the compress."

Clarice nodded.

"Women and children are on this side." Mildred waved toward the other four beds stretching away from Johnny's bed. Then she nodded to the beds across the small aisle, which ran down the middle of the room. "Men are over there."

Not all the beds had occupants. Some had improved enough to go home. Those beds lay bare of sheets or blankets. After administering aspirin to each patient, she and Clarice would make the beds ready for new patients. Unfortunately they never stood empty for long, and sadly the epidemic didn't look like it was letting go of its grip on Fredericksburg anytime soon.

Sighing, Mildred turned to the table to prepare the next round of medications.

Chapter 4

Nelson rubbed his eyes and then stretched his arms above his head. Silence reigned in the Sunday house as the patients eased into sleep, some deep and healing, others uneasy, still struggling to breathe. He really should take a quick walk around the house to stretch his aching leg. Absently he rubbed the scarring around his wound, wondering if he could talk Mildred into joining him.

He glanced toward the closed door into the lean-to where she had disappeared a few minutes before. Earlier that day, she attended her cousin's wedding, serving as maid of honor, and she'd returned even more subdued than usual. Was she thinking of Harold and their plans for a future? Plans that died with Harold. Plans he had helped destroy.

Sighing, Nelson turned back to the petri dishes and his handwritten notes lying on the table before him. Speculating on Mildred's broken dreams wouldn't get the report to the Public Health Service.

Much as he would like to pursue Mildred, comfort her, hold her in his arms, she would no doubt reject him.

As Helena had done.

Not for the first time he wondered why he had never caught on to her shallow character. Images of Helena as he'd last seen her refused to be squashed. Nelson squeezed his eyes shut, allowing the scene to play again in his mind.

That bright fall day in October, when the doctors told him he'd never walk unassisted or without pain, was the day he lost Helena. Though if he were honest with himself, Helena had been pulling away ever since the navy sent him home for further treatment at the military hospital in DC.

Though she still wore the extravagant ring she'd insisted on when their betrothal was announced before the war, she barely found time for him. Then her grandmother's death in Rochester, New York, took her away for a while. Finally, Nelson received word that Helena and her family had returned and they were receiving visitors. But when Nelson dutifully presented himself, she acted as though he were the last person she wanted to see. And even Nelson's ardor, much as he hated to admit it, had waned.

He'd expressed his regrets over her grandmother's death, but she shrugged it off. *"It's for the best. Grandmama was old."*

Hard. Cold. Bullets of ice pelting his mind. The woman shooting them was not the Helena he knew.

Though she sat in a wing chair to one side of her sitting room fireplace, she didn't offer for him to sit. Only his mother's strict social training kept him upright. "You still have that stupid cane. Isn't it about time you throw it away?" The scorn dripping from her words sizzled into his heart.

"I can't."

Her eyebrows rose into sharp peaks. "Can't? Or won't?" She stood and paced the area between her chair and the door. "I never knew you to back down in the face of a challenge."

"And I'm not backing down now." Nelson placed his hand on the back of the chair Helena vacated, willing her to sit again. "The muscles are too badly damaged. I'll never be able to walk without a limp. . .or the cane."

That brought her to a standstill right in front of him. She eyed him warily. "Is this a play on my sympathy? Because if it is, I warn you, I'll not put up with it."

He reached for her hand, but instead she jerked the cane from his other hand and threw it across the room. It crashed into an expensive vase, splintering the vessel, before coming to land in the debris.

Involuntarily he took a step or two across the room to retrieve it. And his leg buckled under him, sending him to the floor.

Helena laughed—a high, shrill sound with a touch of hysteria in it. But her words drove themselves into his heart with as much force as the bullet that shattered his leg.

"Surely you don't expect me to marry you now!"

He couldn't answer as he struggled to a sitting position.

Neither did she wait for him to respond. She went on speaking in that bone-piercing pitch. "Look at you! You can't even stand without that horrible cane." A sneer twisted her lips as she yanked the ring from her finger and threw it at him. "I could never love a man who is less than perfect. No matter how rich he is."

It hit him square on the forehead, and he could feel the blood trickle down his nose. He put his hand to the small cut and winced, then picked the monstrosity off the floor.

She turned away. "I'm not willing to be shut up with an invalid the rest of my life."

Helena slammed the door on her way out, leaving him to drag himself across the room to his cane. Using the table the vase recently occupied, he pushed himself to a standing position. Once he stabilized, he concentrated on getting out of the room and the house where he was no longer welcome, leaving his dreams in the rubble of the vase.

A soft hand touched his shoulder, pulling him out of his memories, and he looked up into Mildred's face. A question he hadn't heard puckered her forehead.

He blinked. "I'm sorry. Did you say something?"

"I asked if you were okay." Removing her hand, she sat down in the chair next to his. "You looked like you were a million miles away. . .and not in a good place either."

The compassion in her voice soothed his troubled mind, and he smiled. "Neither so far away or as bad as I once thought." Though the sting of Helena's rejection still pricked, it wasn't the heart-stabbing wrench he remembered. Much of that had to do with Mildred's gentle acceptance of his deformity. "I thought you'd gone to bed. You seemed rather tired after the wedding."

Mildred's lips turned up, but the smile didn't go all the way to her eyes. "I was, but more because it wasn't the double wedding Clarice and I had always planned—her and Thomas, me and Harold." She sighed and looked over at the beds lining the walls. "I'd rather be out here than alone with my thoughts." Pulling the sheaf of papers to her, she went on, "Do you need me to help record your notes?"

His heart warmed. Her melodic voice was low, quiet, so as not to disturb any of the sleepers. She was always thinking of others.

"But it's late." She stared into the dim room. Then she pulled her chocolate gaze back to him. "You look like you could use some sleep."

He massaged his forehead and temples and rolled his shoulders. "It's just a headache." Brought on by reliving his memories, no doubt. "I really need to finish this report before going to bed."

She reached for the pen lying beside the microscope. "You dictate. I'll write. Then you're going to bed." Her voice was firm, her gaze penetrating.

Heat rose to his cheeks under her scrutiny. Would she interpret it as fever? A cough tickled the back of his throat, and he reached for his coffee cup.

Her eyebrows rose. "We can't have you getting sick, too."

Chapter 5

Mildred looked down at Nelson lying in one of the patient beds. She might have avoided the nightmare of the last three days if she'd insisted he go to bed when he admitted to the headache. With his stethoscope extending from his ears, Uncle Will sat beside Nelson on the bed, listening to his heart and lungs.

Finally he pulled back. "It sounds like you're on the mend, my boy." He patted the younger man's shoulder then stood.

Mildred let out a sigh of relief. "Thank God."

Nelson touched her hand. "Yes. Thank Him."

Tears burned her eyes, and she turned to the stove to hide them. What was wrong with her? Except for a few tears, she still hadn't cried over Harold, but she couldn't keep the tears away as she nursed Nelson. She wiped her hands on the towel she'd soaked in the carbolic acid solution, and thought about Nelson's rapid descent into the illness that had killed so many.

While they had worked on Nelson's report for the Public Health Service, he reached for another petri dish to examine under the microscope and brushed her arm. He protested when she pulled a thermometer from the jar of alcohol and forced it between his teeth.

His fever raged at 104. She promptly put him in the closest available bed. . .on the women's side. No matter. They had rigged curtains to surround each bed for privacy. So she kept his pulled, except for the side that faced the kitchen.

Not many patients remained in the Sunday house, so she was free to focus most of her attention on Nelson. Thankful for the telephone her father had installed two years before, she used it to call Uncle Will. He'd come immediately and together they fought Nelson's copious nosebleeds and racking cough.

Now that the initial danger had passed, she would classify that day—the day she'd planned to marry Harold alongside Clarice and Thomas—at the top of her worst-times list. It confirmed what she'd suspected ever since arriving home—God didn't hear her prayers anymore. He'd allowed Harold to die, robbing her of her dreams of being a wife.

"Look at Nelson, My child."

The almost audible voice startled her. Had Uncle Will spoken to her? She turned from the stove where she stirred the savory chicken noodle soup she'd started earlier. But Uncle Will sat on Johnny's bed, laughing at something the boy said.

Nelson lay propped against a mound of pillows, his eyes closed. Though still pale and a little blue around his lips, he was definitely on the mend. A testimony of his own treatment methods, yes. But an answer to her prayers? Nelson's falling ill on her almost-wedding day rankled. No, she wasn't ready to accept that God heard her prayers.

Mildred turned back to the soup, gave it one more stir, and reached for the bowls. "Lunchtime." She spoke over her shoulder, catching her uncle's eye.

He stood, squeezed Johnny's shoulder, and stopped by Nelson's bed. "Well, my boy, God is good to spare your life. Now eat. We need you working."

Nelson quirked his lips and nodded but didn't speak.

Uncle Will came up behind her and placed a gentle hand on her shoulder. "Do you need help, my dear?"

Mildred shook her head. "No, Clarice will be here any minute to help me get lunch out." She nodded at the table. "Sit down. I'll get you a bowl of soup before you leave."

"How long. . .have I been. . .sick?" Nelson's voice, though low naturally, rasped from coughing.

"This is the fourth day." An eternity. After serving Uncle Will, Mildred set a bowl of the steaming broth on the stand next to Nelson's bed then went to the table to retrieve a chair. She would feed him. Clarice could take care of the rest.

Nelson swallowed. "Didn't. . .realize. . ." His words trailed off in a paroxysm of coughing.

Mildred frowned. "Don't try to talk. I won't be able to get any food into you at this rate."

Uncle Will laughed. "Better listen to her, Nelson. A woman needs to fill her man's stomach. It's the way to the heart, you know."

"Uncle Will!" Fire burned her cheeks.

Still chuckling, the old rogue raised his hand in farewell as he walked down the aisle between beds to the front door. He stopped to let Clarice in before he closed the door behind him.

Mildred set the bowl back on the stand and marveled that nothing spilled. The way her hands shook. . . Of course it was only a reaction to seeing Clarice back from her wedding trip, not a result of her uncle's words. Her man, indeed!

Clarice's gasp scattered her thoughts and she jerked to a stand, whirling to face her cousin.

"Nelson?" Clarice's gaze took in Nelson, the curtain shielding him from the other patients, and the soup bowl on the stand. "What happened?"

"He—"

"Influenza." Nelson shrugged and attempted a weak smile. "Didn't know"—he coughed—"you were back from. . ."

Mildred handed him a clean rag to spit into and pressed his shoulders back down on the pillow then gave her cousin a hug. "How was the trip?"

"Wonderful." The words came out on a sigh, and her face radiated her joy.

Mildred looped her arm through Clarice's, pulling her fully into the kitchen area. "I'll be back in a minute, Nelson." She looked his way but couldn't bring herself to look him in the eye. Her cheeks still burned. Maybe she should take care of the other patients and let Clarice feed him his lunch.

Clarice freed her arm, shrugged off her fashionable outer wrap, and hung it on a hook near the lean-to door then turned to the sink. "As soon as I wash up, I'll get lunch out to the others. Doesn't look like there are as many here."

Mildred shook her head. "There aren't. Most everyone has gone home to convalesce." In fact, only two out of the dozens of patients she'd cared for under Nelson's tutelage died. He said the disease had advanced too far in them to be affected by any kind of treatment.

"So go, before his soup gets cold." Clarice made shooing motions before grabbing a bowl and filling it with Mildred's soup.

"But—"

Mildred slid a glance over to Nelson, and her eyes collided with his. A hint of amusement in the depths of his steely blue eyes rekindled the fire in her belly. She turned away and lowered her voice. "I was going to let you feed Nelson. I can take care of the others."

"Now why would you do that?" Clarice, making no attempt to hide her astonishment, paused ladling soup into the bowls. "I'm fully capable—"

Flustered, Mildred stammered, "I—didn't mean to—" She stopped. Why was everyone pushing her toward Nelson?

Shoulders slumping, she turned back to Nelson's bed and the soup bowl waiting on the stand.

"Is my presence upsetting you?"

She met his gaze briefly before allowing it to skitter away.

"I—no—uh, yes—" Brilliant. That should make him feel better. She swallowed and tried again. "Sorry. No."

He studied her face. "No, what?"

"No, your presence doesn't upset me. In fact, I'm"—she stopped, not sure how to describe her feelings now that he was on the mend—"relieved you're getting better."

Nelson said nothing, but his intense gaze probing deep into her soul did nothing to settle her shaking hand. What was wrong with her? None of her other patients made her quiver with pleasure deep within her, setting every nerve ending in her body tingling.

Mildred took another shaky breath, willed her hands to stop shaking, and without another word spooned some soup into Nelson's mouth.

Chapter 6

When Nelson woke, Mildred sat next to his bed, crocheting. Or knitting. He could never tell the difference. Taking advantage of her absorption in her work, he studied her. An occupation he found quite enjoyable.

Her calm spirit wrapped around his, enveloping him with peace. Not passive. Her mind was too quick and intelligent. Over the last couple of months, through the worst of the influenza epidemic, he'd thanked the Lord many times for giving him a nurse who rarely allowed impatience or a ruffled spirit to show to the people in her care. Even when he knew she was exhausted, she calmly pursued her duties, never rushing.

A shadow passed over Mildred's face as she started a new row. What troubled her thoughts, he couldn't imagine. She was much what he'd expected from Harold's descriptions and the portions of her letters he'd read aloud to those who would listen. What Harold hadn't mentioned was her sharp mind, her understated sense of humor, and her ability to laugh at herself.

Except when it came to his "new-fangled" methods of treating the disease. He smiled at the memory. When he first told her what medicines he wanted dispensed, how much, and how often, she'd dug in her heels, certain all her patients would die under his care. Until the evening he'd forgotten to put away his notes on the research he'd been doing for the Public Health Service.

Shortly after they set up the Sunday house for patients, Nelson moved into the upstairs loft, accessible only by the steep staircase attached to the outside wall. One evening a few days later, Nelson had come downstairs to check on the patients and to get the notes he'd left on the kitchen table. When he walked into the main room, he found Mildred reading the pages. Her concentration was so complete, he checked on his patients before disturbing her.

"What do you think?"

Startled brown eyes stared up at him. "Oh, I'm so sorry." She dropped the papers onto the tabletop and rose.

Amusement tickled the corners of his mouth. "For what? Reading my reports?"

Her cheeks sported a lovely shade of pink, leaving him breathless. "I didn't mean to snoop."

"I wouldn't have left them out if it were something I wanted to keep private." He

pulled out the chair across from her and sat. "Sit with me a moment. Please."

She hesitated. "But the patients. . ."

"Are fine." His eyebrows rose, challenging her to comply with his request. "I want to hear your opinion."

"Oh." She sank into the chair and met his gaze. "On your research?"

"Yes." He resisted the urge to squirm under her intense scrutiny, as if he were a blob in a petri plate under the microscope.

"In my experience, doctors aren't interested in their nurses' opinions. They want blind obedience." Then the edges of her mouth quirked up and her eyes sparkled. "Except Uncle Will."

When she paused, he held his breath.

"And now you."

The rush of pleasure at being put into the same category as her beloved uncle swamped his mind, blocking any coherent thought.

"After reading your notes everything makes sense. I mean"—she waved a hand at the patients—"you've introduced some interesting methods of treating the influenza. Some things I've never heard of or considered." She stopped and chuckled. "And I've been the silly hen who thinks the sky is falling if we try something new when the old ways aren't working."

He laughed out loud at her analogy. "Go on."

"Well, your methods are born out of your research. I understand why you insisted we follow your somewhat unorthodox treatments. And why they're working—" She broke off, looking dazed.

He couldn't wipe the huge grin off his face. She got it. What would it be like to share his life with a woman like her? One who truly shared in his work?

The next day he moved all his research downstairs and set up his lab on the kitchen table. And she proved to be an able assistant with that as well. He'd never had a better research partner.

Now, Nelson could keep his mouth shut no longer. "A penny for your thoughts?" He kept his voice low for the other sleeping patients, but the words still rasped his sore throat.

Mildred startled, dropping the yarn and hook into her lap. "Oh." The pink rose in her cheeks, making her even more beautiful in his eyes. He shut his eyes against the thought. When had he gotten so sappy about a woman? Never before. Certainly not with Helena, though maybe he should have.

"How long have you been awake?" Mildred's low voice broke into those unproductive thoughts. "Do you want something to drink?"

"Hot tea? Or coffee?" He hoped the hot liquid would clear some of the raspiness in the back of his throat. He reached out a hand when she started to rise, stopping her. "Tea, I think. If the water is hot."

She glanced at the stove a few feet from his bed. "The coffee is hot and somewhat fresh. Uncle Will was here a bit ago. I made some fresh for him. And the water is hot. Just need to steep the tea, add some honey."

He smiled, delighting in her nervous babble.

Mildred caught his smile and looked away. "I'm babbling." She stood and laid her work on the chair. Hopefully that meant she planned to sit with him a little longer. "I'm sorry. I'll get your tea."

While the tea steeped, Mildred checked on the other patients. When she came back around his curtain, he asked, "How many are here?"

She carefully poured him a cup of tea she'd sweetened with honey and put it on the table beside him. "Besides you, three. Mrs. Klus, Pastor Gloeckner, and Johnny." While she spoke she fluffed the pillows behind him and helped him sit up against them. Then she handed him the teacup. "Johnny and Pastor Gloeckner should be well enough to finish convalescing at home."

"And Mrs. Klus?" She was more at ease talking about her patients. "How is she? Didn't she come in the day I got sick?"

Mildred picked up the yarn and hook and sat back down. "Yes. She'll be here a couple more days." She refused to make eye contact with him, busying herself with her handwork.

His time was also limited. It wouldn't be right for him to stay at the Sunday house, even in the loft, if there were no patients. Truthfully, he'd be better off in his own room at Dr. Bachman's, away from Mildred's distracting presence.

He snorted. Who was he fooling? She had invaded his thoughts from the moment he met her. Time to change the subject. "So what about that penny for your thoughts?"

Mildred shot a quick glance at him and back to her knitting. Or crocheting. But she didn't reply.

"At least tell me what you're doing. Knitting? Crochet?"

She quirked a smile. "You have a mother and a sister, and you don't know the difference?" The bantering tone matched his own.

"Nope. They only do embroidery."

"Well, at least you know that much." She held up the scarf she was making and showed him the hook. "Crocheting uses a hook. Usually just one." She set them in her lap and rooted in a cloth bag at her feet. She pulled out two long sticks and waved them in his face. "Knitting uses two needles."

"Those are needles?" He studied the two pointed shafts of wood. "Doesn't look like any kind of needle I've ever seen. Where's the eye?"

She laughed, low and melodic. The sound sent shivers of delight to the pit of his stomach. "No eyes. They aren't sewing needles."

"They aren't suturing needles either. Can you imagine sewing up a cut with a needle like that?"

"Knitting uses the sticks to make loops and draw the yarn through them." She reached into the bag again and pulled out another piece of yarn work.

He really didn't care which was which. He only wanted to keep her talking. To keep her near him. Forever.

Mildred held up the yarn patch for his inspection. "This is knitting." She reached for the other, lacier, much larger piece. "This is crocheting."

"So I can tell the difference by how lacy a piece is?"

"Not really." She flashed him a cheeky grin. "Knitting can be lacy, too." She looked down at the smaller piece. "But I'm not very good at knitting, so I usually choose the denser patterns for that. And crocheting can be dense, too, depending on the stitch I choose to use." She looked back at him.

"In other words, it depends on whether you're using a hook"—he pointed to hers—"or n–needles." He stumbled a bit over the word. Still didn't look like any needle he'd ever seen.

Mildred nodded approval, put the knitting away, and picked up the crocheting.

Nelson wasn't fooled. She still hadn't revealed her thoughts in answer to his first question. Determined to get it out of her one way or another, he looked forward to the verbal sparring match. What better time than now to probe into Mildred's thoughts?

But she beat him to it. "Who's Helena?"

He stared. "How do you know about Helena?"

"You had a pretty high fever that first night, and. . ."

Great. "I was delirious, obviously." But since he entertained thoughts of Mildred as his wife, it was much better to learn now whether she would reject him for the same reason. "She was my fiancée."

She met his gaze, studying him. "Was?"

He nodded. "She consented to become my wife after the war. But when I came home wounded. . ." He grimaced. "Then I learned I would always be somewhat crippled, would always have to use the cane to walk. When she found out. . ." He swallowed hard.

"She rejected you because of your war wound?" Mildred's voice rose. She stared at him, wide-eyed. "Why, it's a badge of honor in itself."

His heart warmed. He decided to exorcise Helena, once and for all, from his thoughts. "The actual medal appealed to her more."

"You received a medal? Which one?" Mildred laid down her crocheting and focused all her attention on him.

"The Silver Star."

Her eyes narrowed. "What kind of woman wouldn't want to marry a man of honor, recognized for valor by his country?" She spoke so softly, he leaned forward to hear her. "And recognized by God for his faithfulness."

Shame threatened to smother blossoming hope, and he rubbed his wound. "But I failed God. . .lost my faith."

She gazed at him steadily. "No faith? Then who has prayed with every patient he's seen the last two months? Who prays before eating a meal? Who speaks of Christ to his patients—and to me—and tells of His compassion and love for those who were sick and hungry and. . .lame?" Her voice broke and she swallowed. Her lips set in a thin line, yet respect and loyalty shone in her chocolate eyes, wrapping him in their sweet goodness.

How he loved her—her passion, her loyalty, her commitment to duty and serving others. "But—" Dread boiled in his gut, and he drew in a shaky breath. She had to know the worst about him. "I killed my best friend, your fiancé."

Chapter 7

"Harold?" Mildred couldn't believe she'd heard Nelson right. "My Harold?"

Pain radiated from his blue eyes before he hooded them. His fingers plucked at the blanket covering his lap. "Yes." The word came out in a whisper.

"But he died of the Spanish influenza." Mildred couldn't grasp what Nelson meant. He was already home, convalescing from his wounded leg, well before Harold died. "I—I don't understand." Her voice faded to an almost inaudible whisper, and her fingers choked the yarn ball in her lap.

Still, he heard her. But he hesitated. Then he motioned her closer. She dragged the chair forward a few inches, until her knees dug into the bedside table leg.

"Sit here instead." Nelson patted the bed beside him.

Her heart rate sped up. That close? But she pushed her chair out of the way and sat beside him on the bed. She realized then that she still had a death grip on the yarn, so she reached for the bag and emptied her hands.

Immediately she regretted her action. What was she to do with her hands now? She clasped them together and stared at them, not wanting to make eye contact with Nelson. She needed to hear what he said, not distracted by the way his penetrating stare seemed to read her like a book.

She risked a glance and saw that Nelson's eyes were closed again, his lips moving in a silent prayer. Bowing her own head, she breathed her own petition, fully expecting no answer in return. *Oh Father, help.*

"Listen to him, My child."

Mildred's eyes popped open. That voice again. Was it only that morning she'd heard it the first time?

Was that You, Lord?

Nelson's hand covered her clenched fists, drawing her eyes to meet his own. She didn't try to remove her hands from his comforting grasp. It calmed her spirit, warming her from the icy pit in the depths of her stomach all the way to her heart.

"Do you really want to hear this?" Nelson's gaze intensified as he sought his answer in her eyes.

Mildred's nod was more of a jerk. "Yes. Tell me."

"Did Harold ever tell you of the Meuse-Argonne Offensive in September?"

Mildred nodded. "He was sure he would have died if it hadn't been for his best friend. . ." Nels. That was the name he'd written. "Nels? You?"

◆　◆　◆

Nelson closed his eyes against the pain of hearing Harold's nickname for him. "Yes." He let loose a low, bitter laugh and gripped her fists a little tighter.

Mildred loosened one fist, turned her hand palm up, and twined her fingers through his. Surely she felt the electric shock that bolted through his heart. When he dared to look at her again, memories clouded her vision. She said, "Harold always shortened names."

"Millie?"

Her laugh sounded almost as bitter as his had. "Or Mills." She winced. "I hated that one, and he knew it. For some reason it amused him to see how many ways he could shorten a name."

"Especially when the owner of the name protested."

"But Harold was alive after that battle. I mean, he wrote me afterward."

Nelson shuddered. It wasn't a memory he wanted to dwell on, even if his leg served as a constant reminder of his sin. "His unit was ordered to flank the front line of attack, and to stand ready to charge when the command was given. But their commanding officer was shot and unconscious."

Mildred's fingers tightened around his. Oh, how he would love to raise her hand to his lips. But now was not the time to romance her.

"I was part of the attending medical unit, and when we got the message about the lieutenant, I was sent in to get him out. I had combat training, as well as battle-field medical training." He swallowed. "I worked my way to the front lines without too much trouble. I was armed, of course."

Staring at the wall opposite him, Nelson could recall in vivid detail the horror of that mission. "When I found them, the lieutenant was dead. The rest of the unit had gone to earth in some nearby foxholes—dug by the Germans. But Harold spotted me checking on the lieutenant, and he ordered his unit to retreat." Tears streamed down his face. "I shouted, 'No,' but they didn't hear me. The Jerries opened fire and mowed down the lot of them."

Mildred gasped. "But Harold?"

"I tackled him, sending him back into the foxhole. And took his bullet." He motioned to his leg.

"But how is that killing him?"

"Not then." Nelson felt his chest tightening. Lung spasms. He needed to finish his story before the cough returned.

"We waited for dark. Harold took off his uniform jacket and pressed it against the wound, slowing down the blood flow. If he hadn't, I probably would have died from blood loss." He sighed. "That would have been best in the end."

"How can you say that?" Mildred demanded. "You saved his life."

"In order to take it away from him in the end." More tears trickled down his face, but he didn't try to remove them. "Harold was second-in-command. His orders were to continue the charge if his commanding officer went down. When we got back, I had to report his giving the order to retreat that killed his unit and wounded me." He swallowed hard. "His failure to follow through resulted in the loss of many lives and nearly cost us the battle. He was facing a court-martial."

Mildred's eyes widened and he looked away. He didn't want to see the condemnation he knew he deserved in her eyes.

"That's still not killing him." Her grip on his numb fingers relaxed a little, and they tingled as the blood flow increased.

"I didn't realize his cowardice would result in his going AWOL."

She gasped. "AWOL?"

He nodded. "One more death sentence if he was caught." What was he trying to do? Alienate her completely? He expected her any moment to snatch her hand away from his.

But she didn't.

He could feel her eyes on him, but he refused to meet her gaze. He had to finish this. Then he could sink back into the rising fever and encroaching pneumonia.

"I never saw him again. Didn't know what happened to him until Dr. Bachman told me about your telegram."

Mildred shifted on the bed and brought her other hand up to cup his whiskery cheek. "Those were his choices, Nelson. Not yours. You only did what was your duty."

Nelson shook his head fretfully. How could she be so compassionate when he killed her husband-to-be? She would never be his. She would never—

He heard her gasp of alarm and felt her snatch her hand out of his grip before he sank back into the blessed darkness. *Please, God, take me home.*

Chapter 8

Clarice squeezed Mildred's hand as Uncle Will leaned over Nelson, once again listening to his heart and lungs. The toll of the last twenty-four hours caught up to her, and she clung tightly to Clarice's grasp. Nelson's relapse after telling his story shook her more than the news of Harold's death.

She hadn't had time to examine why. Nelson's fever, which had hovered around 104 all the previous night and that morning, finally broke around midafternoon. She hadn't even thought to get a message to Uncle Will, until he stopped in that morning to check on the patients.

He'd been the one to get Clarice to come care for Mrs. Klus, after he sent Johnny Zuckerman and dear Pastor Gloekner home. The pastor had prayed over Nelson before he left. And then Uncle Will had helped her nurse Nelson. Even though Nelson's temp had come down, he hadn't regained consciousness.

Was God going to take him, too? Despite his confession last evening, she didn't want to let him go. Not with the guilt he carried over Harold's death. Guilt she knew was misplaced. He had relapsed before she could tell him about her last letter to Harold. The guilt was all hers, not Nelson's, and she longed to tell him.

Uncle Will straightened. "He'll do."

Relief surged through her, weakening her knees.

"Careful, honey." Clarice patted her hand.

Mildred caught the meaningful look Clarice and Uncle Will exchanged, and the starch returned to her legs. As she pulled away from Clarice, Uncle Will turned back to Nelson.

Clarice grasped her wrist and tugged her toward the front door. But Mildred refused to budge. "Is there something I can do for him, Uncle Will?"

The fatigue lines in his face gentled when he looked up at her. "Take a break."

"But—"

"Doctor's orders, liebchen." He waved his arms toward the door. "The best thing you can do for your young man is get some fresh air and rest, or you will be the next to join your patients."

When Clarice tugged again, Mildred followed. But it felt as though she moved through quicksand. Outside, the sun shone brightly in a cloudless sky. Mildred sank down into a rocking chair and took in a deep breath.

Clarice took the other rocker. "What an absolutely gorgeous day!" She tipped her head against the back of the chair and took a deep breath.

"Just what the doctor ordered?" Mildred couldn't resist the opportunity to tease her cousin.

Clarice grinned. "You heard what he said. Besides, we haven't had a chance to chat since before the wedding." She winked. "And you obviously have some talking to do, girlie."

"I do?" Mildred knew better than to act as though she didn't understand Clarice, but her relief brought out her ornery streak. "How was the wedding trip?"

Clarice twisted her features in mock despair. "Don't think you're getting away with that approach."

Mildred's lips turned up at the corners in spite of herself, and she laid her head back and closed her eyes. The sun was bright and the air crisp. Perfect for someone who had stayed inside too long. She closed her eyes. "Well?"

Clarice exhaled loudly. "It was *wunderbar*."

"That good, huh?" Mildred opened one eye and scrutinized her cousin. She only used German to express the highest form of approval.

Clarice's face glowed with contentment and happiness. Mildred's heart twisted and she closed her eye. But the pain she'd expected from the loss of her dreams didn't come.

"Better than good." Clarice giggled. "You'll understand when you have your turn."

Mildred's eyes shot open. "My turn at what?" A wedding trip? "In case it escaped your notice, Harold and my dreams of marriage and wedding trips and children are finished. Kaput."

Clarice arched her eyebrows. "Somehow I don't think the man in the bed in there would say so."

The heat rose in Mildred's cheeks.

"And neither do you really believe it." Clarice laid a deliciously cool hand over Mildred's fiery cheek. "Honey, ignore it all you want. It doesn't change the truth. I only pray you wake up and recognize it before you push it—and him—away."

Clarice broke the connection and Mildred stared into the distance. Surely Clarice was mistaken. Not about her feelings. She'd known for a few days that she'd fallen for Nelson Winters—hard. But he could never love her back. Not with Helena's name still on his lips. Besides, whatever Clarice said to the contrary, she'd loved Harold.

"I'm not saying you didn't love Harold."

Mildred switched her gaze to her cousin who had the uncanny knack of reading her mind. "I did. I mean, I still do."

"Really? Then tell me, who comes to mind when you think of marriage? Even more, who were you thinking of at my wedding? The day you were to have married Harold?"

Mildred, unable to tear her gaze away from Clarice's knowing eye, desperately wanted to say Harold. But it would be a lie. So she pressed her lips together and said nothing.

"Uh-huh. Just what I thought."

Mildred rolled her eyes and sat back.

"Don't roll your eyes at me, girlie." Clarice smirked. "You never loved Harold more than a brother. You fancied yourself in love with him, and you would have married him, too. You believed it was your duty because that's what everyone expected. But you would have been miserable." She put her hand on Mildred's. "Honey, you have to know. . ."

"Know what?" Mildred forced herself to look Clarice in the eye.

"I prayed every day you were away that the Lord would open your eyes before you married Harold."

"So you prayed him dead?" Clarice's prayers felt like betrayal. Bitterness rose in her like bile, burning her throat.

"Of course not!" Clarice sat up straight. "What are you talking about?"

"You prayed for God to remove Harold from my life. And he died. How can you say you didn't pray him dead? What about me? What about my dreams?" The words spewed from her mouth and flowed over her like hot lava. Yet she found it impossible to stop the eruption.

"I loved Harold. More than a brother. I would have made him a good wife. Yet you prayed him dead." Hot tears flowed over her cheeks. "I thought you loved me."

Clarice stood next to Mildred's chair. She laid a hand on her shoulder, but Mildred shrugged it off, knowing how Clarice would respond. Without a word or a backward glance, Clarice went down the steps, onto the sidewalk. Back to her precious Thomas.

Leaving Mildred to smolder. Why couldn't she keep her mouth shut? Her own words had robbed her of all she held dear.

The door to the Sunday house opened behind her, and Mildred stood to go inside. But Uncle Will blocked the door.

"Liebchen." He stretched his arms toward her. She walked into them and burst into tears against his broad shoulder. His arms wrapped around her, he stood like the rock she needed as she allowed the remorse to drain from her heart.

Remorse for her words to Clarice. Remorse for her last letter to Harold. Remorse for the love she might have had with Nelson but now lay in ruins before it got a chance to build.

All because of words. Her words.

Chapter 9

Mildred woke to silence. Blessed silence. The lean-to's door stood ajar, open to the empty main room.

Uncle Will had sent Mrs. Klus home the day after Mildred's outburst, and then he moved Nelson back to the clinic and his room there. Although Nelson protested having to go the two blocks in a wheelchair, Uncle Will's stubbornness had overruled. Mildred smiled at the memory.

Uncle Will, sensing her discomfort at having to face her patients after her awful explosion, sent her to bed and called for another volunteer to do night duty at the Sunday house. The number of flu patients had decreased to just a handful at the clinic, and Mildred was no longer needed.

She rose from bed, washed her face in the sink in her miniscule bathroom, and dressed. Today her brother Henry was coming to help dismantle the beds and cots and take down the curtains they'd placed between the beds. She would have the Sunday house back in order before the end of the day.

Then what? She could move out to the farm with her family again. But her spirit was restless. They didn't need her either. Maybe she would stay in the Sunday house and work somewhere.

She knew Uncle Will would be glad to have her continue nursing for him. But now it would be too awkward having to work alongside Nelson.

As she went about preparing a small breakfast of oatmeal and toast, her cheeks burned when she remembered realizing Nelson was awake. She'd caught his gaze for just a moment but long enough to see the compassion in his eyes. Along with the pain.

Her oatmeal ready, Mildred sat at the table, said a quick prayer of thanks, and ate. Or attempted to. Like everything else she'd tried to eat the last couple of days, it tasted like the sawdust that carpeted her father's workroom. She choked down a few bites before pushing the bowl away. Even the toast slathered with her mama's delicious plum jelly was tasteless.

Mildred dumped her uneaten cereal and toast into the slop bucket by the stove and set the dishes on the counter by the sink. She'd wash them up later.

Right now, she needed to get to Clarice's before her courage failed her. It wouldn't be the first time in their longtime friendship that she'd had to apologize. She also knew from experience that Clarice would wait her out. Mildred would have to go to her.

423

She looked at the time on her watch. Her late start guaranteed she'd find Clarice at home.

Only she wasn't. No one answered the door when Mildred knocked on Clarice's door fifteen minutes later. She walked around the house, thinking Clarice might be hanging clothes. But no one stirred.

Surely Clarice was shopping and would return soon. Mildred found a bench on the flagstone area and sat. She breathed deeply the balmy air, her back resting against the house.

Spring was just around the corner, but already Mildred could smell jonquils and the agarita bushes by Clarice's porch bore tiny white and pink petals. It wouldn't be long before her favorite bluebonnets were in bloom. Now that her nursing time was over, she could spend time in the wildflower field her mother had planted so many years ago. There might be a few early bluebonnets already peeking through the grass.

Glancing at the time, Mildred stood, looking both ways along the block. Henry would be at the house soon.

Deciding to take the longer route back to her house, Mildred strolled toward downtown. Maybe she would run into Clarice coming back from shopping.

Mildred greeted several townspeople shopping downtown but still saw no sign of Clarice. She walked by the clinic and thought about stopping to visit with Uncle Will a few moments. But knowing Nelson would be there, too, kept her feet moving.

What a mess her words had created.

As she rounded the corner to her own street, she saw the Model T parked in front of the house and Henry sitting on the porch.

Someone was with him, but she couldn't see whom, since he sat back in the shadows. Her heart raced. Something about him made her think of Nelson. . .again. Truth be told, he was rarely far from her thoughts. But she couldn't imagine any reason he would seek out her company now.

Still, she couldn't stop her heart bursting into song when she turned onto her house's front walk. It was Nelson, watching her approach.

Henry didn't bother with the stairs but bounded up to her and planted a loud smooch on her cheek before she could fend him off. His exuberant approach to life, so different from her own, always brought a smile to her face.

"What are you doing out here, lazy boy?" Looping her arm through his, she forced him to walk her sedately onto the porch.

"Lazy?" He guffawed. "Where have you been? We were waiting for you to supervise the work."

"We?" Mildred smiled a welcome to Nelson. "Surely you're not well enough to—to—" She waved her hand indicating the work. Mercy goodness. Why did words always fail her around this man? Or turn her into a babbling fool?

"Oh but I am." His intense blue eyes twinkled, and he made a small bow toward her. "Just awaiting your command."

Fire burst in her cheeks and, flustered, she turned to open the door. "You don't need me to get started. Why didn't you go on in?"

Henry pushed past her and entered the house first. "I just got here. Dr. Winters, uh, Nelson was already here."

"Why?" Mildred looked over her shoulder at Nelson, who motioned her to enter before him.

"I came to see you." His voice was soft and low, for her hearing only, and her unruly heart leaped into her throat.

"Me?" It came out as a squeak. "Why would you do that?" She fumbled with the button on her cardigan, and her neck tingled when he put his hand up, ready to help her remove it.

She turned to take the sweater from him, and his gaze trapped her again. Something she couldn't read lurked in the depths.

He cleared his throat. "We hadn't seen you at the clinic the last few days. So I came to see if you were well."

"A house call from my doctor then?" Pushing away her disappointment, she turned away and laid her wrap over the arms of a nearby wingchair.

"No. Not a house call." He paused then laid his hand on her arm, turning her toward him. "Liebchen." The endearment was almost inaudible. "Look at me."

Henry, the beds, the temporary clinic—all vanished from her mind when she met his gaze. "I came to see *you*. To see if you would take a walk with me this afternoon."

She couldn't speak, so she nodded. He wanted to see her. To walk with him. To spend time with him. Her heart burst into a symphony of praise. He didn't abhor her.

"So where were you, sis?" Henry's voice broke into the silent conversation flowing between her and Nelson. She turned toward her brother.

"What?" She swallowed. "Oh. I went to see Clarice, but she wasn't home."

"You shoulda waited for me. She's helping Aunt Leisel. Uncle George has the Spanish influenza."

Dismay clenched her stomach. "Oh no! Is it bad?"

"Naw. He's on the mend now." Henry pulled the mattress off the bed nearest the door. "But Clarice went to help her mom with the younger kids." Another mattress hit the floor.

Mildred's stomach slowly relaxed. "Maybe I should go out to check on them." She glanced at Nelson, who nodded. "How are you transporting these things, Henry? It all goes back to the clinic."

"Yes. That's why I brought the wagon instead of the Model T."

How had she missed the wagon? She stooped to look out the low window. "That's not Papa's automobile?"

"That's your Uncle Will's." Nelson spoke behind her.

"Uncle Will has a Model T?"

"Oh yeah." Henry piled another mattress with the others by the still-open door.

"I believe he said he got it shortly after you left for the war." Nelson sounded amused. "Says he thought it would make the house calls outside of town easier."

Henry paused in pulling a bed apart. "Only he can't figure out how to fix it when something goes wrong." He laughed.

Mildred smiled. Sounded like Uncle Will. Uncomfortable with modern conveniences. "But you can, I assume?" She looked at Nelson.

"Yes." He shrugged and bent to help Henry with the bed deconstruction.

Was there anything the man couldn't do? "Do you want all your lab things to go with the beds?" The paraphernalia still littered her kitchen table, though she'd pushed it together to make a space for her meals. "And the medicines in the cabinet?"

Her father had built a cabinet into the main room wall next to the fireplace. It had served well as the medicine closet the last three months.

Nelson straightened and stretched his back. He grimaced. "Let's move the medicine back to the clinic. But would it be okay to store the lab stuff here for a while longer?"

"Of course." Mildred looked at the growing stack of bed parts. "We need to start getting some of this out of here, don't you think?"

Henry started for the door. "I'll bring the wagon and horses around." He slammed the back door shut behind him.

Of course. She'd forgotten about the old watering trough at the barn on the back edge of the lot.

Mildred grabbed her cardigan from the chair then headed into the lean-to. She had an empty box stored under the bed she could use for the medicine bottles.

When she came back into the main room, Nelson had shifted some of the mattresses onto the porch. Mildred could see the wagon backed up to the porch and Henry pulling a mattress into the wagon bed. That should keep them busy for a while.

She turned to the cabinet, placing the box on a low table nearby, and started removing the bottles and other medicine-related items. The one part of nursing she really enjoyed was preparing the medicines. It fascinated her how different chemicals and herbs worked together to treat various illnesses and ailments.

Before she'd gone to Europe, she had started a study on the various medicinal qualities of herbs and other plants. She knew many doctors had no use for "medicine women," preferring to rely on new discoveries. But she believed there was a use for both. Maybe she could take up that study again, now that she was no longer needed for nursing.

As she packed the last of the jars into the box, she looked around the room now stripped of hospital beds and nightstands. They would have to get the other furniture in from the barn where they were stored.

She carried the box to the door, intending to give it to Nelson to put in the Model T, and found the furniture crammed onto her porch and front lawn.

"Do you want everything back where we had it before?" Henry paused next to a large buffet.

"That will be fine." Mildred moved out of the way and let the men move the furniture back into place. She would get the doilies and dresser scarves out later, when she was alone.

Once they were done, Henry jumped into the wagon seat and took up the reins. "I'll meet you over at the clinic, Nelson."

"Be there shortly." He waved Henry off then turned to Mildred. "Henry says the jonquils are already blooming in the wildflower field your mother planted."

"Oh good. I thought I smelled some over at Clarice's." Maybe tomorrow she would ask Uncle Will for the use of the car, go see Clarice and her aunt and uncle, and stop by the field.

"Would you like to take a drive this afternoon instead of a walk?" Nelson stood in front of her, clutching his hat. "I'd love to see your favorite place."

A sudden shyness descended between them, almost as tangible as a curtain. Mildred took a deep breath and tried to dispel the awkwardness. "I'd like that." She smiled. "Very much."

Chapter 10

Nelson watched Mildred out of the corner of his eye, managing to keep one eye on the road. More like a cow path. He hoped no other vehicle—wagon or automobile—met them. There was no place to go, except into the ditch that ran on either side of the road. And he didn't want that, especially not at ten miles per hour, the fastest he dared to go.

They didn't speak. The rumble of the motor overpowered all sounds. But as the distance from town increased, Mildred's facial features relaxed until a small, contented smile rested on her lips. Peace rolled off her, bathing him in its blessed calm. He loved discovering there were depths to her that delighted him, though he wasn't sure why it should.

Helena hated the country. As soon as the thought wriggled through his mind, he squashed it. Why did he continue to compare the two women when there was no comparison? He knew he was well rid of Helena, but she crawled into his thoughts at inopportune moments.

Banishing Helena from his mind, he intended to enjoy this day with Mildred. Sweet, quiet, calm Mildred. Even the fiery explosion he overheard last week didn't scare him away. Her feisty spirit brought a grin to his face.

When she told Henry this morning that she'd gone to see Clarice, he'd rejoiced that she was trying to make amends with her best friend. He knew the ties between them were strong and that Mildred's love for her family ran deeper than most.

Intent on his thoughts, he startled when Mildred's hand rested on his arm for a brief moment. She pointed ahead. A wagon pulled by two huge draft horses rounded the curve in front of them. He braked until the speedometer showed three miles per hour.

But he still didn't see a way out. Casting in his mind for a turnout he might have missed, he realized he'd been so preoccupied with his thoughts that he hadn't taken in much of the countryside.

Mildred touched his arm again and pointed to a grassy area to the side of the road a few yards ahead. He nodded to show his understanding and directed the steering lever in that direction. But as the automobile pulled out of the ruts, the right front tire blew, jerking the lever out of his hand and sending the vehicle back into the rut.

The car ground to a halt a few feet short of the turnout. The farmer with the wagon stopped his horses, and for a moment the two men stared at each other.

"Papa!" Mildred fumbled with the door handle.

Nelson reached across her and opened the door. Mildred leaped onto the grassy verge and ran toward the wagon.

The older man, his tanned, leathery face wreathed in smiles, jumped down to meet her. He caught his daughter up and twirled her around as if she were a young child.

Nelson slid awkwardly across the seat and exited the passenger door. His usual method of jumping in and out of the automobile over the stationary driver's door was impossible now with his leg. Grasping the cane from behind the seat, Nelson balanced himself before trying to navigate over the uneven ground. He maneuvered to the front of the car and choked the engine.

"Papa." Mildred's sweet voice sounded clear in the sudden quiet. "Come meet Nels—uh, Dr. Winters." She grabbed the older man's hands and pulled him toward Nelson.

Hank Zimmermann stood an inch or two taller than Mildred and had the upper body musculature of a man who wasn't afraid of hard work. The hand that rested on Mildred's shoulder was scarred, and the grip of welcome on Nelson's outstretched hand was strong yet gentle.

"Pleased to meet you, sir."

"And I, you." The older man studied Nelson for a moment or two then nodded. "Young Henry speaks nothing but good of you. As does my wife's uncle Will."

"They are kind." Nelson basked in the secondhand praise and wondered anew at the ready acceptance that characterized all the members of Mildred's family. It was as if they didn't see the cane, his limp.

"Papa, would Clyde and Sam be able to pull the Model T to the turnout?"

Mr. Zimmermann turned toward his wagon. "Sure they can." He reached the horses. "What about it, boys? Ready to take on Uncle Will's automobile?"

The horse closest to Mr. Zimmermann whickered and nuzzled his shoulder as the older man undid the traces. Once they were loosed from the wagon, he led them forward, turned them around, and backed them to the automobile. Nelson eased himself across the passenger seat and positioned himself behind the wheel, pulling the gear lever out of gear.

After harnessing the horses to the front axle of the Model T, Mr. Zimmermann took the reins and gave his horses the command to pull. In short order, and with very little strain that Nelson could detect on the part of the horses, the car came to a stop on the grassy verge, out of the way of the wagon.

Nelson crawled back out of the car. While Mr. Zimmermann and Mildred loosed the horses, Nelson examined the ruined tire and thanked the Lord he'd thought to put a few spares in the trunk.

Well, it wouldn't take long to fix and they would soon be on their way.

Nelson pulled out a spare tire and tried to roll it toward the front of the car. But he hadn't counted on his gimpy leg and the cane. The task proved much more difficult than he'd remembered.

"Here, let me help." Mildred's strong, capable fingers wrapped around the thin rubber tube and carried it to the front of the car.

Nelson's shoulders slumped. Helena was right. He was useless with his injury. A burden on everyone around him. A large, work-worn hand landed on his shoulder, and Nelson looked into the bold-featured face of Mildred's father.

"Son, God never intended for anyone to go it alone. In fact, you have it better than most of us."

Nelson quirked an eyebrow. "How so?"

"You have a tangible reminder to depend on God and the people with whom He surrounds us." He nodded toward Mildred, who had equipped herself with the necessary tools and was very capably changing the tire. "The sooner you allow her to help you, the better off you'll be. She doesn't easily take no for an answer." He grinned. "Just like her mother."

"I heard you, Papa." Mildred winked at her father. Then she grabbed the tools and restored them to the trunk.

With a final slap on Nelson's shoulder and a quick hug for his daughter, Mr. Zimmermann climbed into the wagon seat and took up the reins. "Better get to the river and load up the wood I cut last week." The horses started forward. "Bring the good doctor to supper, sweetie, since you're out this way. It will be a treat for your mama."

Mildred smiled up at him. "I was planning to." She raised her hand in farewell and watched until the team disappeared over the next swell in the road.

Nelson stood beside the open car door, waiting. But Mildred turned away from him and waded out into the fragrant and colorful sea of grass and flowers edging the road.

"Come on, Nelson. I want to show you something."

He shut the automobile door. "What about the wildflowers?"

She grinned and waved her arm across the field. "Right here."

She waited for him to come alongside her, then looped her arm through his and guided him along a narrow footpath he'd not seen from the road.

His heart sang as Mildred pressed in closer and gave him the support he needed to negotiate the rough path with his injured leg. He inhaled the fragrance of the flowers and her hair as her head brushed his shoulder. Not for the first time he wished she could care for him as he did for her. He'd fallen fast and hard.

Mildred stopped to point at a gazebo perched on a foundation of rock in the center of the field. "Here. This is my favorite part."

She moved quickly away from him, and his eyes followed her movements as she stepped from one clump of flowers to the next. She reached down to stroke the petals, breathing deeply of the rich aroma.

When she reached the gazebo in the center, she paused on the bottom step and looked back at him, grinning. "What are you waiting for? We can sit in here."

He moved toward her, leaning heavily on the cane. Then he felt her hand on his arm as it slid down to grasp his free hand. Her father was right. Mildred made a very good partner. With her, he felt whole again.

She led him up the steps and sat next to him on the bench that lined the outside latticework of the building. Absently rubbing his leg, he took in his surroundings.

The wide wood planks of the floor matched the latticework of the low walls. Overhead, perched on long spindles stretching toward the sky, a cedar-shingled roof protected them from the sun. The craftsmanship was superb. "Your father built this?"

"Yes. He built it for his and Mama's wedding. I often dreamed of it during the war." Mildred's voice was hushed, reverent. She made a jerking motion with her free hand. "It's so peaceful. A piece of heaven on earth." Her laugh matched her voice, and she looked at their linked hands. "Sounds kind of silly put that way."

"Not at all." Nelson wished he'd had a place like this to take his mind away from the horrors of war. "A shelter. A refuge from the storm."

Mildred met his eyes, her own shining. "Exactly."

"Your mother planted the seeds?" Nelson was intrigued. "What kind of flowers are these? The blue ones—I've never seen them before."

"Those are Texas bluebonnets. Wait another couple of weeks and the whole field will be blanketed with them. Then there's the Indian paintbrush. Jonquils. Primroses." She pointed to different plants as she said their names. "Mama and her students planted them. She was the town's teacher and planned a day outing near the end of school. Papa drove them out here in wagons. They brought a picnic lunch and the seeds. But before Papa could get back to pick them up, a storm overtook them. By the time Papa found Mama, she was unconscious from a fall. Papa says she scared him so bad that when she finally woke in the clinic, he proposed."

Nelson scanned the sky for storm clouds and laughed at himself. Had he hoped for similar circumstances? He looked down at Mildred's hand, still encased in his. Sure, Mildred patiently assisted him, instinctively understanding when he needed support and when he could manage on his own. But even if she loved him, it would quickly wear thin, and she would soon tire of caring for a cripple.

Galloping hoofbeats pulled Nelson from his troubled thoughts. Mildred jerked her hand out of his and stood at the top of the steps, the better to see the road. He laid his hand on her shoulder as he came up behind her, and she raised hers to cover his.

As the rider came into view, he glanced their way and checked the horse's forward motion. "Millie!" He got the horse under control and trotted the animal through the field, careless of the flowers he trampled.

"Ernie! What's wr—"

"Oh Millie." The boy gulped back a sob. "First Mama...then Henry...sick..."

The color drained from Mildred's face. But she stiffened her back and pitched herself at the horse's bridle.

"Off." Her voice was sharp with command.

"But—"

"No!" She barely waited for Ernest to jump down before flying onto the horse's back. "Come with Nelson."

Chapter 11

Mildred sank into the rocker next to Mama's bed and listened to her labored breathing. How quickly the day had disintegrated into horror. Both Mama and Henry struck down with the Spanish influenza.

Her worst nightmare come true.

She'd allowed herself to think her family was safe, now that the epidemic had slowed in town. Allowed herself to take a day off. Allowed herself to hope Nelson would take a hint from the story she'd told of her parents in that lovely, romantic wildflower field.

She let out a soft snort. As if Nelson would even consider her as a suitable mate. But still she'd hoped. Foolish woman.

Leaning her head back against the rocker, she closed her eyes, letting her thoughts run over the events of the afternoon. After Ernest's interruption of the idyllic afternoon, she arrived at the farm mere minutes before Nelson and her youngest brother. Nelson helped her get Mama and Henry into their beds. Her box with all the medicines was still in the jump seat of the Model T, so she'd wasted no time in getting the proper medications started. A few petri dishes she'd slipped into the box now contained sputum so Nelson could try to isolate a bacteria.

Mildred's heart clenched. The onset was so sudden. But Nelson seemed to think if they made it through the night, they would be out of danger. It would be a long night.

He'd gone back to town to return Uncle Will's automobile. She hoped he'd be back in the morning. Papa and Ernest finally agreed to settle in the front room—Papa on the sofa, Ernest on a pallet on the floor. Much better than having them both pacing between the sickrooms. Her younger sister, Klara, tended to Henry, sponging his hot skin, trying to get his fever to break.

Mildred pushed herself off the rocker and laid a hand on her mother's forehead. Still much too warm. She reached for the washcloth in the basin on the bedside table and started the sponging routine once again.

What would she do without her mother? She wished she could send for Clarice, but she was busy nursing her own family. Besides, Mildred still hadn't apologized.

Please, God, spare Mama. And Henry. Please. But she didn't hold out much hope.

Harold died after her letter containing harsh words for his lack of attention, for the furloughs he'd taken—with other women. She closed her eyes against the pain of that betrayal. It had taken the surprise out of Nelson's revelation of Harold's cowardice. Why had Harold even bothered to telegraph her about coming home and his change of plans?

Then she'd spoken harsh words to Clarice last week, and now her precious mama and brother were near death's door. A verse from her childhood floated into her mind. *"If I regard iniquity in my heart, the Lord will not hear me."* It was her punishment for not controlling her tongue.

"But God isn't like that." Nelson's words from a late-night discussion over the petri dishes on her kitchen table drifted back to her. *"He doesn't exact vengeance on His children. He extends love, grace, and mercy."*

A longing to know this God of whom Nelson spoke—so different from the judgmental, wrathful God she knew—welled up and threatened to drown her in the impossibility of it. Her parents had taught her of the God Nelson talked about, but the war and its aftermath caused her to doubt the truth as they all saw it.

"No man is expected to bear difficulty alone. God allows these things to cause us to depend on Him." Her father's voice from that afternoon was so clear, she glanced at the door, half expecting to see him standing there.

Had she misunderstood God? Had she somehow missed Him in the horrors of the war? *Who are You, God?*

Mama moved restlessly then coughed, a deep, tight sound that told Mildred the influenza was digging its ugly claws into her mother's lungs. She redoubled her efforts to lower the excessively high temperature, wondering if Henry was responding better for Klara. She would need to check on them soon.

◆ ◆ ◆

Nelson stepped into the kitchen and met Dr. Bachman. "Ah, you have returned." The doctor's gaze sharpened. "What is wrong?"

Nelson eased down into a chair, and Dr. Bachman placed a plate of scrambled eggs, toast, and bacon on the table. The aroma caused his stomach to rumble, and for the first time realized they had not gotten their promised supper.

"Mrs. Zimmermann and Henry both contracted the Spanish flu." He raised a quick thank-You to the Lord for the food then shoveled the first bite into his mouth.

"Amelia?" Dr. Bachman sat heavily across from him. "When?"

"This afternoon." He knew the older doctor wanted a full report, but his stomach was more insistent at the moment.

As if understanding, Dr. Bachman waited until Nelson pushed away his empty plate. "Did you come back for medicine?"

Nelson shook his head. "Mildred put the medicine from the Sunday house in the car this morning. I didn't unload it before taking her for a drive. So she has all she needs." He took a long swallow of the coffee Dr. Bachman poured for him. "Mildred will call later to report on their condition."

The doctor nodded then reached to the desk behind him and grabbed a distinctive Western Union telegram envelope. "This came this afternoon." His voice sounded tired, resigned. "I hope it isn't bad news."

But it would be, of course. Nelson ripped the envelope open and pulled out the message.

COME HOME. NEED YOU. SPANISH INFLUENZA RAMPANT. HELENA ILL. CHARLES.

Nelson squeezed his eyes shut, wishing he didn't have to obey his brother's summons. But it was no use. Duty called.

"What is it, son?" Dr. Bachman's compassion reached into his heart, soothing his troubled thoughts.

"I'm needed at home. The influenza is still raging there." Nelson's fists clenched. Oh, how he wanted to stay.

"I see." Dr. Bachman rose. "When will you leave?"

Nelson stood, too, and met the kind doctor's eyes. "On the first train going East in the morning." At the doctor's nod, he turned toward his room. "I need to pack."

◆　◆　◆

A light knock on her parents' bedroom door roused Mildred from her doze. Fear clutched her heart, and she reached out to touch her mother's hand. Warm, but not hot. Then she heard the breathy rasp in her mother's throat, and she relaxed.

The knock sounded again. "Yes, come in." Her father wouldn't knock. Had Nelson come back? Her heart raced and she stood to greet him.

But the words died before she spoke as the expected tall outline morphed into one much shorter. And feminine.

"Clarice!" Mildred kept her voice low, not wanting to agitate her mother. "What—"

"I heard about Aunt Amelia and came as soon as I could."

"But your father?"

"Is fine. Recovering."

"Then why—I mean, after my—" Mildred shut her eyes. Why couldn't she apologize without stumbling over her words? They were fluent enough other times.

Clarice wrapped her arms around Mildred's waist and squeezed tight. "You need me. I came. You would have done the same for me."

Only she hadn't. She'd allowed Henry to convince her everything was fine.

"What about Thomas?"

Clarice released her and stepped back. "He told me to come." She pushed her light shawl off her shoulders, tossed it onto a small table under the window, and headed for the washbasin. "What do you need me to do? Who's caring for Henry?"

"Klara. I'm sure she'd welcome your help." Mildred watched her in a daze. "How did you find out? Nelson?"

"Nelson? No. Haven't seen him. I thought he'd be here."

Mildred handed Clarice a clean towel. "He returned Uncle Will's automobile. But he said he'd be back in the morning."

"That's fine then." Clarice laid the towel beside the washbasin. "Where's Henry?"

"Upstairs." Mildred started to follow Clarice out of the room, but Clarice put up her hand.

"No. Stay with your mama." She quirked a little grin. "I know what to do."

Mildred responded with a smile of her own. "I know." She leaned down for another quick hug. "Thanks, Clarice." God must be listening after all.

Returning to her mother's bedside, Mildred picked up the stethoscope—the one Nelson left—and listened intently to Mama's lungs. Were they a little clearer than when she listened last? Or was it wishful thinking? She rested the back of her hand against her mother's forehead and cheeks. But they remained cool. The fever had broken.

The bedroom door opened again, but Mildred didn't turn.

"How is she, liebchen?"

"Uncle Will?" She looked behind him for Nelson, but the doorway remained empty. "Mama's past the worst of it, I think."

"And Henry?" Her uncle placed his bag on the bed near her mother's feet.

"Klara was still sponging him down the last time I checked. Clarice is with him now."

"Then I will check him first." Her uncle turned to leave.

"Uncle Will. Wait." Mildred peered hopefully over her uncle's shoulder. "Where is Nelson? Didn't he come with you?"

Uncle's Will's shoulders slumped. "He's on the train going home." He held out a paper. "This came for him last evening."

Mildred moved closer to the gas lamp next to the door as Uncle Will slipped out of the room. As she read, two words seared her mind: *Helena ill*.

Chapter 12

Mildred crossed the road, skirted the turnout, and stopped a few feet into the wildflower field. Bluebonnets vied with primroses and Indian paintbrush as they crowded the dance floor of green foliage and grasses. Everywhere she looked the flowers bent their fragrant petals in the gentle April breeze in a graceful country-dance of bowing and scraping.

She closed her eyes and took in deep drafts of the fragrant air. Mama would have loved to come with her, but Mildred needed to be alone. Besides, Mama hadn't fully recovered from her near brush with death. Which was why Mildred was still on the farm. Caring for her father and younger siblings kept her busy from first light until well past sunset.

Today Ernie and Klara were on a school outing until after supper. Henry was busy with Papa in the furniture workshop. So Mildred took advantage of the break in routine and walked to the field.

She reached into her skirt pocket and pulled out the ragged yellow paper with the message that had called Nelson home. Four long weeks ago. Then, she thought he was beginning to care for her.

But one telegram bearing Helena's name took him away. And she hadn't heard from him once. Mildred's heart clenched against the familiar ache, and she buried the paper out of sight again. When she got back home, she would put it in the burn barrel. Not that it mattered. The contents were etched into her memory.

Mildred picked her way along the narrow path, wading through the bluebonnets that spread their petals in a purply blue canopy. She stopped several times, reaching down to pinch off dead flowers, making room for more to grow in their stead.

Since that awful night at her mother's bedside, Mildred was learning to take delight in the many ways God showered her with His mercy and grace. He had heard her desperate prayer when all she could do was lean on Him. First Clarice came, without being asked, and then Uncle Will came to aid her.

The Lord even allowed Nelson to stay long enough to see that his patients were stable before going to get Uncle Will. Then Papa and Uncle Will were the towers of strength she needed when she learned Nelson was gone.

But why hadn't he written? Not even to Uncle Will. She could understand Nelson not wanting to write to her. After all, he went back to his Helena. They were probably engaged again and planning their fancy June wedding. But he could have let Uncle Will know what his plans were. She hadn't thought he could be so rude, so uncaring. That wasn't the man she thought she knew. And loved.

Mildred climbed the stairs of the gazebo and gazed toward the river. *Father, why can't I let Nelson go? What purpose does it serve for me to keep dwelling on him? Please, please take my love for him away.* Her decision to follow the God of love Nelson believed in brought her more peace than she'd thought possible. And she reveled in the intimacy of prayer. Still, she didn't understand why He hadn't answered this particular prayer.

A flash of red in the trees near the river caught her attention. Low, just above the blue carpet that continued past the edge of the wooded area. Curious, she left the gazebo and made her way toward the river.

Like a homing pigeon, she tracked her way through the flowers until she saw the object. A man's tie?

She reached to free the fabric from the low branch that had snagged it. Not just any man's tie. She recognized the small blue pattern.

"Nelson?" They'd gotten no farther than the gazebo the last time he was here. Besides, he wasn't wearing his red tie that day.

Crushing the fabric in her fist, Mildred allowed her gaze to dart across the field again. No one there. She turned back to peer into the undergrowth in the trees leading down to the water's edge.

"Father God, what's going on?" This was Nelson's tie. She had no doubt. But what was it doing here?

Shrugging, she turned away from the river and smacked into a man's hard, broad chest. A man who grunted at the impact and wrapped his arms around her, keeping her pinned to him.

Too stunned to fight off the liberties the man was taking, Mildred inhaled the spicy tang of Nelson's cologne. *Wait.*

She twisted and gazed up into his face. The familiar blue gaze radiated joy and love, and Nelson held her as though he would never let her go.

She closed her eyes, sure that when she opened them he would vanish. Instead she felt the rumble of laughter roll from his chest.

"Nelson?" She jerked from the comfort of his arms. "How—how—despicable—" How dare he laugh at her? He went running back to his Helena. He shouldn't have been holding her in the first place.

"Despicable?" Another shout of laughter echoed through the trees.

Mildred pulled her gaze away from his mouth, along with the thoughts of what it would be like to be kissed with those lips. Ugh! Now who was despicable?

Tears started to her eyes, but she furiously blinked them back. "Why are you here? So you can gloat over your good fortune?"

Confusion clouded the joy still radiating from his eyes. "What?"

She ripped the paper from her pocket and shook it in his face. "Your precious Helena." Her voice made the woman's name sound dirty and twisted, like the crumpled paper in her hand.

Nelson gently grabbed her fist and released the paper. Keeping her hand captured in his, he smoothed out the telegram. A line appeared between his eyes. "Where did you get this?"

◆　◆　◆

"You left it behind in your hurry to get to your ladylove." Her words pelted him like stones, but they didn't carry the bitterness he'd expected. Or deserved.

He honestly couldn't remember what he'd done with the telegram. But he never expected to find it Mildred's possession. Why she'd kept it. . .

His lips trembled with suppressed mirth. How predictable, yet so contradictory, she was. And he loved every aspect of her complicated being.

He knew he'd have his work cut out for him in order to win her back. She had every right to be angry. He'd wanted to see her last night as soon as he arrived, but Uncle Will advised against it. Not until the older man had prepared Mildred for the shock. But Nelson couldn't resist spending more time in the wildflower field, recalling the short time they'd spent together there before their worlds fell apart.

Then, little Ernest's news derailed the words of love he'd worked up the courage to speak. So when she strolled into the field this afternoon, he praised God for smoothing the way before him. He wasn't about to waste any more time.

He crumpled the ragged paper and tossed it toward the river. She followed the yellow ball with her eyes until it plopped into the water and disappeared.

He wrapped his arm around her waist. "The cat got your tongue?"

Her lips firmed into a thin line. He pulled her tight against his side and tilted her head toward him. "Mildred, sweetheart, look at me. Please."

Relief flowed through him when she finally raised her gaze to his. Questions, reproach, and something else warred in her eyes. Love? For him?

"I didn't go home because of Helena. How could I when my heart was here?"

"Then why?"

"My brother never, ever asked for my help before. Although his wife, Charlotte, was instrumental in getting navy nurses into the field hospitals in Europe, he never approved of my going to war. Even as a medic."

Nelson tucked Mildred's head under his chin, and she nestled against him, but she didn't relax.

"In fact, it was because of him I decided to accept your uncle's invitation to join him here. I had no plans to return to Virginia for any length of time." He paused. "And I still don't. Fredericksburg is my home."

"But why didn't you write?" The anguish in her tone wrenched his heart.

"I did. Long, long letters every night, describing my days, my nights, working and longing for you. I even wrote to Dr. Bachman telling him when I planned to return."

She pulled back and pinned him with her gaze. "But we. . ."

He sighed. "Two evenings ago, I discovered them in my mother's desk."

"What?" Disbelief and indignation poured out from her. "Your mother took your letters out of the mail?"

"Yes." Once again he felt the sharp pang of disbelief. His own mother. "Almost every day I asked if any mail had come for me." He shook his head. "Every day the answer was the same. I could understand why you might not want to answer"—he ignored her protest—"but hearing nothing from your uncle bothered me. He'd always been so prompt to reply before."

"So how did you find out?" She snuggled back against him again.

"When I said I was going to check with the post office about the missing mail, Mother finally admitted her interference." Until then, he had no idea that she sided with his brother about Nelson's going to war. Plus she nagged him unmercifully about repairing his relationship with Helena. It would be a long time before he could trust her. If ever.

"Anyway, you can read the letters later. I decided to special-deliver them. But before that, I have something to ask you."

"Hmmm?"

"Can you ever forgive me for killing Harold?"

Mildred jerked away from him. "What? Are you on that again?"

He tottered at her sudden movement and reached for her. But she stepped away and handed him the cane he'd placed against the twisted mesquite next to the path.

"Nelson, you're not the only one who had harsh words with Harold. I found out"—she whirled away from him as her voice cracked. "He—he said, promised, he would spend his last furlough with me."

Nelson touched her shoulder, but she shrugged him off. She wiped tears from her face with the back of her hand. "He spent his leave with. . ." She gulped in a breath and finally turned back to him. "With another girl." Her mouth twisted into a wry smile. "I'm sure you can imagine that last letter I wrote."

He could, but it made him smile, not shudder. "Maybe he didn't get it before he fell ill."

She gave a short laugh. "I hoped that, too, until I got all of his personal items. The letter was there, opened and well read. He even made notes for his reply." She groaned. "He was going to tell me about you. Said we'd make a good match if you ever got your head on straight about Helena."

Amazement sizzled up his spine and seized his brain. Words failed him.

"Come." Mildred motioned him to follow her. "You need to sit."

No, he didn't. His plans didn't call for sitting, but he followed her to the gazebo. When she sat, she patted the seat beside her. Instead, he leaned his cane against the bench and knelt in front of her.

Her eyes widened when he gathered her hands into his.

"Mildred, when we were here before, certain events—God's timing—prevented me from speaking my love for you. I didn't go home because of Helena. I couldn't when I loved you. In fact, I never saw her." His bad leg protested and he shifted his weight. "After this last month, I knew that I never want to be separated from you again. You complete me as no other thing or person ever has. Please say you care about me. . .at least enough to consider marrying me."

She slipped off the bench and knelt in front of him. "Yes, yes, yes!" She pulled her hands from his and wrapped her arms around his neck. "I love you, Nelson. More than I can say." Her eyes radiated the truth of her words.

His eyes drifted down to her lips that begged to be kissed.

He needed no second invitation as he wrapped his arms around her and sealed their love with a kiss that exceeded his expectations.

MARJORIE VAWTER

Marjorie is a professional freelance editor who proofreads and edits for CBA publishers, edits for individual clients, and writes. An avid reader, she also judges for several prestigious awards in the inspirational marketplace, and she serves as conference director's assistant for the Colorado and Greater Philadelphia Christian Writers Conferences. She has published several articles and numerous devotionals, many of them in Barbour publications. Mom to two adult children and a daughter-in-love, Marjorie lives with her husband, Roger, and cat, Sinatra, in Colorado. You may visit her at www.marjorievawter.com.

JOIN US ONLINE!

Christian Fiction for Women

Christian Fiction for Women is your online home for the latest in Christian fiction.

Check us out online for:

- Giveaways
- Recipes
- Info about Upcoming Releases
- Book Trailers
- News and More!

Find Christian Fiction for Women at Your Favorite Social Media Site:

 Search "Christian Fiction for Women"

 @fictionforwomen